Allure of Oartheca
Book One of the Oarthecan Star Saga

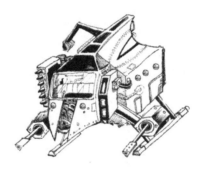

by
James Siewert

First Edition: May 2021

ISBN EBOOK   : 978-1-7776384-1-2
ISBN PAPERBACK : 978-1-7776384-0-5

This is a work of fiction. Names, characters, business, events and incidents are the products of the author's imagination. Any resemblance to actual persons, living or dead, or actual events is purely coincidental. The opinions and behaviours expressed are those of the characters and should not be confused with the author's.

This book contains scenes of adult content and is only recommended for readers ages 18+.

Cover design by: Ryan Carriere
Library of Canada Copyright Registration #: 1179041
All images used within are done so with permission from the respective artists.

This book is dedicated to my husband and best friend, Michael. His constant encouragement was the only reason this story was completed, as was his patience in tackling all the edits, line by line, word by word.

Look upon a starry night sky — every light shining down is a reason to adore him. May your gaze be far-reaching.

Chapters

CHAPTER 1
Rowland

ust a little more. Just a little more …
'Captain, are you jacked yet?' an impatient voice asks, bristling gruffness buzzing over my suit's comm system.

Ivan Vasilyev. Ship's cook, according to my official register. Unofficially, my team's heavy gun, demo-expert and general pain in the ass, when he isn't kicking ass. I love him and all, he's part of my ship's family, but sometimes his input is about as welcome as finding a skid-mark in your jockeys. Awful at chess, but has this stubborn patience that keeps him coming back to learn, and fun to play against—he's not a sore loser, to his credit.

'Well,' I begin nicely, though my voice doesn't quite hide my exasperation. Both our tones are due to nerves. He's safely on board, watching me float out here in free space, my right hand holding the latch to a derelict spacecraft we're trying to break into, my left, palm open, pressed up against a seared-off access port, gently petting at it as though it were a giant metal kitty. 'You see the hatch unlock yet?'

There's a pause before he returns a sour-sounding 'No.'

'That means I'm not jacked. Wanna give me a moment while I try and get that done?'

A sound of scuffling comes over the comms, and then Ivan's pained 'Oww!' in the background.

'Sorry Captain,' the annoyed voice of Bethany 'Betts' Ortez replies. First officer and chief pilot, officially. Smuggler and grand larcenist, off-record. Two years Coalition of Allied Planetary Systems Navy (CAPS-N) officer, but now formerly goody-two-shoes Lt. Ortez is wanted by said Navy and four other non-allied star systems. Pssh, amateur: I'm wanted by nine, currently. She is my best friend though, my big sister by another mister. 'Turned my back for a moment,' she adds, and I can hear what I imagine is her elbow whumping Ivan again.

'Be nice, he means well,' I reply, but then I'm distracted by a kiss of electricity in my brain, as the wireless interface jack in my palm finally latches on to the access port's interface jack. The cybernetic display unit behind my left eye starts streaming a series of connection protocols to my vision, as my biologically integrated computer system starts saying its first hellos to the derelict's systems.

The faint tingling of my biocomp, which is about the size of a grain of rice and installed between my C4 and C5 vertebrae, is a remarkably comforting feeling, and I remember to feel lucky that I'm one of less than half a percent of humans who experience such mild side effects from their cybernetics. Most who try what I'm attempting would feel their interface-arm go dead the instant they jacked in, followed by a sensation of either burning, freezing, or in rare but still far too many cases, intense formication that ultimately renders the whole idea of them hacking a system pointless. For me? It's a feathery touch, like brushing the

1

tips of your fingers along the hairs of your neck.

'Found it,' I advise my crew, all five of them listening in, and then to the derelict, I murmur 'Good morning, sweetheart. Open up, open up, let me in ...'

The stream of connection protocols, a pleasant cyan in colour, dances down the side of my vision as I begin my introductions to the derelict, but I barely finish my first 'So where are you from?' before that stream begins to pulse and switch to a warning shade of orange. Oooh, she's not falling for my tricks, not that easily.

The derelict's systems are not flat-out refusing my connection, but it doesn't recognize my protocols, and is alerting me that unauthorized access will result in the authorities being contacted and possible countermeasures being deployed. Darling, you've been lost for twenty years, stuck in an asteroid field just past the far edge of CAPS space. The giant floating boulders out here contain large quantities of kelmisite, which are gonna fuck your long-range comm signals into gobbledygook. No-one will hear you. Your countermeasures, though? Those I do need to worry about; you'll either dive Under to God knows where, or release a thermal pulse from your propulsion drive that fries me to a crisp.

'No, it's all good. I'm just a lowly maintenance worker, see? I'm here to reset your sensors, you've got a glitch is all,' I promise the derelict. I do think my assurances help, if not the derelict then certainly myself.

I begin to transmit my first hacking algorithm, one of a million stored in my biocomp's memory, electrically caressing the interface, whispering sweet nothings into a nervous lover's ear, trying to find the right words to win her over. One, two, five, twenty, eighty, two hundred ...

The derelict is stubborn; she is refusing my best attempts but at least she's still listening, but that's only because I'm careful enough to craft each algorithm to appear as the first attempt. She is at least buying that part of my wooing, but I doubt she will for much longer; she's got adaptive learning capabilities and it's just a matter of time before she catches on.

The derelict's reluctance was anticipated, of course: she's a high-class vessel, even if she's twenty years behind the times, and her onboard security systems are no joke. In her prime, the derelict was a top-of-the-line automated security transport vessel, long-haul range. The CAPS Trade Union's (CAPS-T) best-of-the-best, she shipped high-value, potentially dangerous cargo from stellar point A to B, across vast distances, all by herself. She has her own Under-drive, as well as over a quarter of light speed propulsion for those trickier intra-system journeys, plus heuristic enemy-avoidance systems, and the sparkling crown atop her most beautiful head: her own Variable Energy Intensive Lightwave & Electromagnetic Distortion Device — her VEILEDD, or simply, her veil.

That's what I'm here for—the veil. I've claimed it as my share of what the derelict is carrying, which, if our research is correct, includes a credit-press with a million unused credit IDs on it, all just wanting to be issued. Split five ways, my crew is looking at a two-hundred thousand perfectly legitimate, fresh-off-the-press payday, each—it's the prize of a lifetime, a prize that can change a lifetime.

But that veil is mine.

It's worth a fortune on its own; twenty years later and the tech behind it has basically remained the same, and there isn't a species in or outside the CAPS that's found a way to consistently beat it. Understandably, the veil's usage is strictly regulated, limited to only a handful of species under a smaller handful of circumstances, and any unauthorized usage carries, oh, how to put this, 'disproportionally severe penalties'. Tekethy in origin, and those shadow-loving spymasters know a thing or two about staying sneaky, but human ingenuity perfected it. All praise the mighty CAPS and its lucrative tech-sharing agreements.

But whatever the veil's best black-market value is, it'll be worth a thousand times that once my engineer, Mia, instals it into my ship. Long-range sensor-muting, short-range light-wave disruption, energy output dispersion—and just the right size for my little vessel to become entirely invisible, even to the naked eye, for a solid hour, if not more. The possibilities that a fully operational veil brings to mind make me salivate, even as I continue with my hack of the main access-hatch.

'Captain Hale, forgive the interruption,' Corculhoran says politely. From the crispness of his tone, one would think the voice belonged to a bookish, meek man, and of course, the opposite is the case with Cor. He is Harculcorian (roughly translated as 'they who are biters'), a reptilian race known for breeding fierce and relentless warriors, and their heavy, massive frames and crocodilian appearance go a long way to perpetuate the human-centric stereotype that they're all mindless brutes.

Cor is actually one of the sweetest men I know: keenly intelligent, brilliantly poetic, and nearly as good a hacker as I am. Though he is roughly the size and shape of a weapons locker, and has heavily scaled skin that's a natural form of battle-armour, I've never seen him perform an act of violence in all the time I have known him. Officially, he's our comms officer and quartermaster, but behind the scenes, he's the brains behind our most lucrative schemes, our shifty accountant and probably among the foremost embezzlers I've had the pleasure to meet. It was Cor who had snatched up the whisper of the abandoned derelict, after all.

'Go ahead, Cor,' I offer. I'm one of only a handful of people he permits to use the short form of his name. The Cor part of his name means 'biter', which depending on the person saying it, can either be a term of endearment, or a patronizing insult.

'Thank you, Captain Hale,' he replies. His formality is non-negotiable, though we have all insisted he needs to start feeling relaxed around us, what with this being his fifth year on our crew. 'I am noticing the derelict is powering up its intra-stellar propulsion unit; are you in jeopardy?'

His calmness can sometimes be more disturbing than his panic, which I have only witnessed twice: the first time being when we resurfaced from an Under dive too close to an undiscovered black hole, the second time when I appeared

3

brain-dead for a full minute after a nearly botched deep-jack.

I scan the still-orange warning protocols, then see the execution command for the automated propulsion unit to start up. My algorithms are becoming suspect; the derelict is catching on faster than anticipated. If that engine engages while I'm still holding onto its access hatch, losing out on our prize will be the least of my concerns; my atoms will be spread from here to wherever the derelict decides to stop running.

'Captain,' Betts cuts in before I can answer Cor. 'Derelict's comm unit coming online!'

Her urgency is matched by another bold orange command line flashed before my eyes. 'Jamming it just in case but I'm seeing additional systems ...'

'Mia, you there?' I ask desperately, interrupting my first officer.

'Yes, go ahead,' the voice of my talented engineer, so young, responds enthusiastically.

'We need to fake *Lucky's* energy output signature; make us look bigger than we are.' *Lucky* is the pet name for our ship, the *Luck of the Draw*. She's my heart's desire, my beautiful *Lucky*. I 'won' her after having hacked the system controlling a lottery scam being run by a shifty terraforming company, which used her as bait to draw the punters in to moving to a newly habitable planet. My first genuine hack on such a grand scale, and she's named along the lines of how the best luck is the luck you make for yourself.

'What size are we talking here? Corvette, cruiser, warmonger?' she asks, letting me know that whatever I ask for, I will get. Mia is my baby ship-sister, and my newest crew member, but likely also the most talented.

'Corvette,' and after her quick 'On it!' confirmation, I make a plea to my quartermaster:

'Cor, can you hack together a hail to the derelict, pretend like we're a CAPS-T authority?'

'Yes, I can do this. A simple authentication request, yes?' he asks, out of courtesy. Though our two species started far apart on the evolutionary path, Cor and I are more alike than almost any two humans I've known. The man often knows my thoughts before I even think them.

'Affirmative. Initiate when ready.' I catch the wording of my orders, and frown. I hate it when I slip into my CAPS-N speak. Their training is hard to shake.

Yes, I used to be in the CAPS-N: graduated from the academy with a solid set of distinctions and honours, but just past a year of service, I dropped out, with the official reason given as 'disenfranchisement', which is a polite way to say I was no longer interested in the bullshit actual service in the CAPS-N entailed. And although I am a drop-out (well, dropped-out before kicked out), I am now a captain, which is five ranks higher than my CAPS-N rank ever amounted to. It's an honorary title, of course, since I'm both the owner and the pilot of my ship: humanity still holds to our Terran naval traditions, even half a millennium or so after we took to the stars.

Speaking of Terrans—I am one—which these days means a human born on Earth, rather than say on one of our exo-planetary colonies, which we've got spread out over multiple star systems: Martians, Ganymedians, Oberonians, plus Nexians, Cygnians and Centaurians (*not* Centaurs, they'll have you know) — we're all humans. There's about thirty billion of us, which forms a not-too-shabby sixteen percent of the total sapients comprising the CAPS.

I'm on the tall side, just under two metres, and thanks to the combination of lucky genetics (cheers, Dad), a CAPS-N-approved regimented exercise program and a healthy dose of masculine pride, it'd be more than fair to consider me as a solid slice of beefcake. Not like Ivan or Cor are though—they're mountains of muscle on two legs—but I could hold my own against them, if I needed to.

Heh, that sound's kinda dirty—Bryce is the one I hold my own against, or rather, used to; it's been a while since we last knocked boots, and it's looking more and more likely we'll not be doing that again.

I currently have my original hair colour, which is either a light brown or very dark blond (think a darker shade of 'sandalwood' if that helps), that I keep short and neatly trimmed, and my current eye shade is the one that I was born with: a robust hazel-green that I also got from Dad, in addition to his muscles. Mum gave me my hair colour though, and what Bryce says, er, used to say, are my '*rugged good looks, when you stop being such an ass about them*'.

None of the above matters though: given the CAPS Federation of Medical Practitioners' (CAPS-F) advances, humans are no longer bound by most constraints when determining how we want to physically manifest ourselves: pigmentation, sex, morphology, age appearance—it is all negotiable these days, if you've got the credits. Ivan was born physically female and aligned his external self to his internal self immediately after his first big pay-out with us, and Mia enjoys a blue tone to her skin, for a reason I've not figured out, but it suits her entirely.

I've myself gone under the genetic recombinator on a couple of occasions for a job, mostly just cosmetic stuff for disguises, but I always revert to my base-identity afterwards. It's something to do with my parents' death—yes, I'm a poor orphan boy, have been for a while—something about how much I look like the right combination of my Mum and Dad that always brings me back to my original self. That so long as I'm here, looking like the best parts of them got together and made me, then maybe they're not lost to the universe, just yet.

A few more moments pass as my hack of the derelict continues, and, becoming impatient, I increase the transmission speed of my algorithms, the electronic signals firing from my biocomp rapidly over my reinforced nervous system and through the interface device permanently installed into my left palm. The derelict continues to refuse me, and that's becoming annoying.

I pass the half-million mark of transmitted algorithms and the first waves of frustration crash into my confidence; you might think that the halfway point meant halfway home, but that's never the case. You always start with your big guns—the algorithms most likely to succeed in cracking the hard exterior security protocols and getting to the ooey-gooey sweet access commands underneath—and then work your way down to smaller ammunition if your opening volley fails. Passing the halfway mark usually means you went into the battle under-gunned, and you're left having to throw progressively smaller pebbles in the hopes of scoring a lucky shot.

I've never succeeded in a hack past the eight hundred thousand mark; no-one does. Well, that is, unless you're more than fifty percent cybernetic and have onboard adaptive algorithm generation capabilities. Outside of my biocomp, its paired optic interface and my left palm, I'm one hundred percent human, only about three percent robot. The saying 'too much tech makes your mind a wreck' is a truism I don't want to test on myself, because I've seen the proof of it first-hand in others. But if I'm clocking past a half million algorithms, and more and more frequently I've noticed I have been, it may mean it's upgrade time. The symbol representing interstellar currency—CAPS-T credits—flutters in my imagination on tiny golden wings.

'Authentication request completed. Transmitting,' Cor advises, though he need not have. A bright green stream of symbols appears in the upper right-hand corner of my vision and begins to run with an urgency the derelict's system cannot refuse. Authentication of its identity by its owner's is one of the derelict's highest priorities, and as it begins to stream its credentials, the system resources it's allocating to prevent my access are redirected to complete this priority task.

I see it then, in that stream of orange symbols: the derelict's identification key, hidden as an innocuous spitting of characters in a lengthy line of commands and processing confirmations. From system to system, the values for these keys always differ, and consisting of fifty-five characters, it would take more time than is left in our universe to guess it. But that's its fatal flaw: the ID key is always *exactly* fifty-five characters, and always in the same configuration, meaning its uniform length and structure quickly snitches it out for what it is.

Back in the day, when this transport was first roaming the galaxy, this little security flaw hadn't been discovered yet, and while it's since been patched, this derelict is a couple of dozen star-systems away from the nearest server for that required update. Even then, the ID flaw is only exploitable if you know to look for it, and I just so happen to be one of the few people who know to look.

See, that's my job. Officially, I am our ship's captain, co-pilot and I guess our tactical officer, though any time we enter a firefight I figure I've not done one of my other two jobs correctly: *Lucky* is a lover, not a fighter, and she has many aliases. Depending on where we are and what we're up to, my ship's registry can be either *The Fortune's Favourite*, *CAPS-T Harrogate*, or the *CAPS-N Blazing Talon*, which is one of my favourites, but it's dangerous to use; the CAPS-N gets its best frown on about pretending you're one of their fleet.

If I remember correctly, today I'm Captain Donald Welsh of the CAPS Systems Salvage Corps (CAPS-S) vessel *Brunhilda's Grace*, but that's neither my nor my ship's true name: I'm Captain Rowland William Hale II, and my pretty little ship is the *Luck of the Draw*—with no CAPS credential staining her name.

My off-the-books job, however, is being our team's system override specialist: a hacker, a data-thief, a scourer and scourge of incriminating records. The street term for me is a 'jack', as in I hijack a system and make it my personal plaything. Not all jacks are thieves, some are entirely legitimate and are employed for everything from data-recovery to improved file-archiving. Most CAPS-T and CAPS-N comms officers are jacks in some form. But I'm a jack that steals data and sells it to the highest bidder, and that's definitely outside of the recommended usage for my hardware. I'm expanding my enterprises though: for a cheap five hundred credits, I can make someone disappear from the CAPS network, and for a thousand, I can make them a 'fresh-start' identity to suit their wildest fantasies. Cash upfront of course.

I am smart enough to stay out of dealing in really lucrative information though: war plans, galactic trade strategies, fleet deployments and such. Working with that kind of information often buys you top billing on the CAPS's kill-list, and yes, as I discovered, there's a literal kill-list. So, I keep my activities on the small-time scale, making me an annoyance to the CAPS but thanks to our talents and constant diligence, not one worth their effort to swat—though I have scored a handful of truly top-tier escapades, enough for me to earn legit black-marks in those nine stellar systems I mentioned. Normally, I'm all about quantity of jobs over quality of jobs. Except for today.

Getting back to convincing the derelict to drop her knickers on our first date, I copy-and-paste the ID key directly into my biocomp's algorithm matrix, and on the six hundred and thirty-fourth-some odd attempt, the warning orange colour of the protocol stream switches back to the courteous cyan, and the flashing cursor denotes I'm at the primary command prompt. I set my user ID to be an admin, update the command protocol and ...

'Got it,' I breathe, and I hear cheering from the comms.

'Pay up, pay up!' Ivan booms happily, his normal gruff tones elated and cheerful over the comms, causing me to smile despite my stress. 'I said less than ten minutes, and Rowley's done it in nine!'

'Incorrect. Captain Hale triggered the automaton's alert protocols,' Cor nonchalantly counters. He does not mean to be insulting, and I don't take it that way. I know his calm, logical and simple response is just a front for his clever, quick and charmingly cunning mind. Cor would only take Ivan's bet if the Harculcorian was sure he knew he would win. 'According to the ...'

'Guys, the hatch is still locked. I'm just in the system,' I correct. 'Sorry Ivan, but I'll cover your losses, I promise,' I mentally picture his scowling face, so I add, 'Thanks for having my back though, bud.'

'I said fifteen minutes and you'd crack the lock!' Mia adds quickly, but her tone is cheery and encouraging. 'You still got six minutes, Captain!'

'I said twenty for full access, Captain Hale,' Cor remarks. To anyone else, this would just seem like a statement of fact, but I think I sense hurt feelings in his voice. Our universal translators (UT) do not replace the voice that a speaker uses; Cor's talking in his native tongue, which is a series of throat rumblings, hisses, growls, air grunts and snaps of his jaws, and the elongated hum at the end of Cor's statement often indicates a sense of injustice or being rebuked.

'Stop distracting him,' a harsh voice interjects over the comms. Bryce. Ship's medic and perpetual killjoy. Wait, no, that's not fair: he's just being protective of me, or if not me, the mission. Probably more me than the mission, I still hope. He knows the next part for me is going to be riskier than holding on to the side of a spacecraft about to power up. His worry comes hand-in-hand with being a doctor, and my now ex-lover. I'm still trying to convince him not to be. It's not going well.

'Thank you, Dr. Winston,' I reply, formally. We are always on formal terms these days. He's announced that this is going to be his last gig with us, and only came along because I promised a score that would set him up with enough credits—plus a free new identity—to start his life over wherever he wanted. Wherever that is does not include me. I love him, but he's made it clear that will not be enough for him to stay.

'Your vitals are good, Rowland. You can deep-jack when ready. I'm monitoring, and you're out at two hundred and fifty heart beats per minute,' Bryce orders. *Advises*, I attempt to correct myself. It's part of the reason he's leaving; he's no longer willing to make the distinction between when I'm the captain, and in command, and when I'm his partner, and we are equals. That's normal, I told him. I'm not angry with him too much anymore, though I suspect when I drop him off at Venris Station Beta in a few days and see him walk off *Lucky* for the last time, that anger is going to come back. Or a profound sadness. I'm not looking forward to finding out which.

'Three hundred, for five minutes,' I counter, more out of petty spite than actual need. These days I rarely reach the two-fifty 'worry zone', and my biocomp can regulate my heart rate at three hundred beats for a solid four minutes before its auto-disconnect protocol triggers. But I need to let Bryce, and the rest of my crew family, know *I'm* the captain, and I will make decisions in the best interest of our crew, and our mission.

There is a pause before the terse reply. 'Proceed.' Another fucking order. Goddamn it, I'm having it out with him when I get back. Again. Like it will change something this time.

I push my impending fight with Bryce out of my mind, and concentrate on my breathing, preparing for the deep-jack. My old CAPS-N training kicks in again, and this time I don't scold myself as I run a full check against my suit's systems. I'm good: two hours of oxygen, thirty-three-degree body temperature (bit low, but the deep-jack generates heat, so that's fine), full suit integrity, and I don't need to go to the bathroom, thank you very much for asking.

I exhale a long, steadying breath, which my crew knows to mean that I'm about to go on a mind trip and won't be available until this stubborn hatch unlocks. Or my suit registers the massive synaptic failure of my brain, if I screw up at what I'm about to do. Either outcome is the signal that will spell out whether we're getting paid today.

Another breath in, and out again, as I form the mental image I use to signal my biocomp that I'm ready. My Mum, laughing joyfully as she wins me a stuffed animal at the fair. Her face—eyes bright and smile wide—as she scores the winning laser hit, dead centre in the target—and that giant fluffy teddy bear is handed to her. She is so beautiful in this moment, so beautiful, she is so beau …

CHAPTER 2

Rowland

My vision empties. It doesn't go black; instead, I lose the ability to see entirely—to process light waves with my eyes—like I never had that ability to begin with. I imagine that this is how people who are born blind, or those who don't use eyes, would experience the universe. My vision is the first to shut off; it's soon followed by sound, smell, touch, balance, every sense biology provided me with, until for one all-too-long moment, I'm incapable of perceiving the universe I exist in in any capacity. I often think this is what death will be like.

The first time I experienced this disconnection from reality was terrifying; nowadays, it's only moderately creepy, because I know in a matter of microseconds, my biocomp will fully integrate with the derelict's systems, and my reality will become one built entirely by electronic bits of binary strings woven together.

There's always that chance it won't though: a hidden termination protocol, a power-surge either from my suit, the derelict, or a randomly passing radiation wave wandering through the cosmos that I just happen to be in the path of. Any one of these could overload my biocomp, frying it and my entirely integrated nervous system into oblivion. That's not an exaggeration, my consciousness will be utterly destroyed if this happens. It's why deep-jacking is, by an exceptionally large margin, the most illegal activity I do.

On the surface, deep-jacking is the merging of two systems. Regular jacking—get your mind out of the gutter—is little more than a fancy version of a high-level interface between systems—where each system remains independent. Think of normal interaction between a person and a computer, but without the need of a peripheral device, like a haptic interface or a holo-display.

Deep-jacking, on the other hand, is the complete integration of the two systems, in essence merging them into one. This is entirely fine if it only involves inorganic computer systems, which, even if they are manufactured on opposite ends of the known stellar systems, basically behave the same way. Binary is universal and even if the systems were designed by completely different species, it usually doesn't take much to get them to work together.

The problems start when one of those systems is a fragile, squishy biological system, whose evolutionary development didn't account for the activity its owner is attempting. Maybe in a few thousand years, or a government-enforced eugenics program, humans could improve their direct compatibility with machines, but as we are now, our brains have no chance of keeping pace with the near-light-speed processing power of a computer system. This is where the biocomp comes into play: it acts as a 'second brain' as well as a 'buffering brain', regulating the flow of information and energy, and translating the computer's systems into a format my own squishy brain can understand and handle without being overwhelmed.

Before the refinement of biocomps, the first attempts to deep-jack by those brave pioneering jacks often ended up with a brain-dead body that survived for a few seconds before its autonomic systems, such as breathing and heartbeat, shut down. Risky, right? Should be enough to keep anyone from attempting it, but humans continue to be a brave and stupid bunch, especially if there's a chance to become 'the first', as in, 'the first to walk on the moon' or 'the first to Under dive' or 'the first to fuck a new alien'.

So 'the first to deep-jack', accomplished by Wadood Kebir thirty years ago, who survived his adventure but never attempted it again, was a major milestone in trans-organic interface relationships. In essence, for what was ten minutes in normal time but what he reported was nearly a day from his perspective, Wadood became the computer he deep-jacked to, and so became everything that the computer was responsible for.

Imagine the possibilities: deep-jack a communication hub? Congratulations, you have access to millions of people's personal conversations, all streaming into your brain, with all their dirty secrets, lies and false promises yours to remember. The catch is remembering of course; a human brain is still subject to its own memory and learning limitations, so even while deep-jacked, it's not like you can download the system's entire call-history and recall it for use later on—you have to pick the prettiest jewels from the treasure-hoard, store them safely in your memory, and then hope that memory sticks in your organic brain when you disconnect from the jack. I've got a great memory—details, places, names—it all sticks, so jobs like that net me more credits than some of my more forgetful competition.

Deep-jack a hospital administration system? Congratulations, you control which medications are distributed to which patients, who gets what surgery and what they'll be billed—essentially, who lives and who dies. Want to redirect that valuable supply of semi-illicit narcotics to another address, or make it seem like it never showed up at all? Sure, we're here to serve!

Deep-jack a spaceship? Congratulations, you *are* the spaceship—well, if your brain can handle processing that many sub-systems simultaneously with perfect precision, or, you know, you blow up. Pull it off, then well—where in the galaxy would you like to Under dive to? What long-range sensor scans would you like to run, say on that stellar trading outpost over there? What city would you like to orbitally bombard today?

Between the overwhelming power that a deep-jack receives and the potential damage they could inflict, and the utter mental obliteration the jack faces should something go wrong, which—odds are, it will—deep-jacking is near the top of the list of worst non-violent offences a person can commit, in either the CAPS, the Terran Administration Collective, or fifteen other non-Allied nations and conglomerates—including the Pryok'tel Hegemony, and those triple-mouthed bastards eat people.

So why am I limiting this awesome ability to just a chance at obtaining a veil for my new ship, when I could be, say, deep-jacking a city's primary administration system and becoming king for a day? Well, the risk-to-reward ratio is in my favour here—the derelict is dangerous, but even this beauty is nowhere near as risky to deep-jack into as, say, my own little *Luck of the Draw*, with all the bells and whistles it needs just to keep its organic crewmembers alive in the void of space. There's a limited number of things the derelict can do: it's got the bare necessities required to perform its tasks and nothing more, so there's less of a chance I'll run afoul of a system-constraint that catches me out.

Deep-jacking my *Luck of the Draw* would be like betting who would win in a fight between a tiger and a lion, but deep-jacking a city's admin module would be like one tiger versus ten lions. Here, with the derelict, the fight is more like a tiger versus a gazelle who got bonked on the head beforehand.

Second, I'm not a fucking novice: I have successfully deep-jacked over thirty times and I know to look out for the smallest danger signs. When my brain and the computer's systems are linked, I'm thinking at near-light-speeds, and thanks to my biocomp's input-processing regulator, at fully cognitive levels. I have full access to whatever diagnostic and monitoring capabilities the system I'm jacked to has, and I know to set those to priority processing: the faintest hint of an issue and I disconnect in under a nanosecond. Veil be damned, I'm not trading my life for a hunk of technology, no matter how much fun it's going to be nor how rich it's going to make us.

Third, in addition to the off-the-market tweaks my biocomp received that even allow me to deep-jack to begin with, I also had the basic common sense to insist on including a safety-net if something did go wrong during my cyber-spelunking. This emergency system takes up some of my processing power, limiting my potential slightly, but if there's a surge that looks like it's going to end up flushing my consciousness down the toilet, my biocomp takes the first hit, sacrificing itself to buy me that nanosecond I need to get back into my own brain. Yes, it will still fry my nervous system, paralysing everything from my neck down, but any medical facility worth its funding can repair that, eventually.

Last and most importantly, I'm not alone out here. Five people who I consider my family are about fifty metres off the derelict's starboard bow, watching me through a variety of sensors and monitors designed to detect those random radiation waves well before they hit me, monitoring the derelict to watch if it even so much as farts a spare electron, and watching every beat that my hyper-stimulated heart makes. If something could go—or is going—wrong, I know that in two minutes after disconnecting from the derelict, my tethered ass will be hauled back inside, and I will be safe.

So yes, what I'm doing is dangerous, but as Cor so calmly put it, 'The risks have been successfully mitigated', which is the closest thing his scaly throat can make to a ringing endorsement. All of them were onboard with this plan, and each has veto power that can kibosh the whole deal. We all agreed. Even Bryce, and I know he does not yet hate me enough to put my life at risk. Even if he did, he wouldn't. He's a good man.

As my vision begins to come back online, I'm greeted by the familiar interpretation my biocomp uses to represent another computer's system. These interpretations are fully customizable by a jack and are highly personalized: some jacks have their interpretations represented as a virtual forest, others as a simulated battlefield; anything the jack wants can be represented. Cor interprets his virtual world as an ocean, with him swimming through the depths discovering lost wrecks, finding new fish—all the adventures that a cyber-submariner could wish for—I've often thought that, maybe when I'm older, I'll reload my virtual world as an ocean too.

Currently, my virtual interpretation is *Bow-Ties*, the premier space-station-cum-nightclub that I think is currently orbiting around Neptune, in our Sol system. It was the first place I visited after turning over my CAPS-N credentials, and I spent that night just living life to its fullest, indulging every adult vice that I had denied myself during my enlistment. Drugs, booze, men (humans, non-humans, and some dudes that were in-between) were mine to devour in every way I could imagine.

My binge lasted three days, non-stop, only ending when I required hospitalization from all the stimulants and hallucinogens I had been gobbling up, which finally caused my heart to give out while I was getting tag-teamed by a Senegalese mechanic and his diphallic Jylrelanrian life-mate. The doctors told me I was technically dead for a few minutes or so.

Doesn't matter—I recovered, and met Bryce as a result. He has a fondness for furry-chested fellows, but I think the chance to save the poor broken bird I was also played a big part in our getting together—he is a doctor, after all, saving people is what he's all about. I sometimes wonder if the fact I'm no longer broken makes him feel like I no longer need him.

Even at this very moment, floating in free space next to a former top-of-the-line security transport vessel that's two decades late for delivery, I feel my near-death-bacchanalia was worth it: it was liberating, finally being truly free of every constraint I placed myself under. For the first time in my adult life, I was making the decisions on my own with no accountability, and that night transformed me: this was who I truly was, a man who would make his own destiny, come what may, and reap the results from that on his own terms.

This is why I choose *Bow-Ties* for my virtual world; it represents the first moment of my life where I felt I was in control, even though I gave up control and let myself become wild in a space station whose sole purpose was providing for every debauchery, gluttony and sin my newly-freed heart could desire. It's the first time I really got to know Rowland Hale, and I discovered that I kinda liked him more than I thought I did. Turns out I'm a lot more fun than I gave myself credit for, or rather, not the uptight bootlicker I thought I needed to be to give myself a chance in this sector of the galaxy. I like to think that when I died, albeit briefly, the part of me that was making me miserable stayed dead while the real me came back to life. I've never been back to the real *Bow-Ties* since though—between my short tour of the Grim Reaper's foyer and Bryce setting me up on the less drugs/more hugs lifestyle, I've not felt the need to.

As the virtual *Bow-Ties* finishes loading, a giant human bouncer greets me at the door. This is my brain's representation of the derelict's security protocols, and since I've been accepted, the giant has a wide, welcoming grin on his face, holding the door open and inviting me in. I can hear the strong thundering beats of high-tempo dance music coming from within, which is a signal to me that 'all is good' for my access attempt.

I step past the bouncer and am immediately greeted by a throng of fictitious people my subconscious dreamed up, crowded together, dancing in the middle of the dance floor. Each person represents one of the derelict's sub-systems, and I'm embarrassed to admit that I am just as stereotypical interpreting these systems as I am with the bouncer. I guess it's easier for my brain to understand but I remind myself to be more creative.

For now though: the comms system is a bright-faced young man chatting into the personal communication device he wears around his wrist; he's frowning though because whatever he is saying, all he hears is static from the other end. The propulsion-system is a robust athlete, looking all pumped up and raring to go, and his running shoes are in his hands—he's just waiting for the signal to put them on. The onboard navigation system, a smart looking woman in a neat CAPS-T uniform, is patiently waiting off to the side, her hands holding a severely broken compass, ready to set sail to a place she has no hope of locating. A stone-faced matron, dressed in an ancient toga, watches an archaic version of a viewscreen (televisions, I think they're called?). She turns to me, her eyes full of stars, and says 'Everything is fine, carry on,' and I clue in: the ship's monitoring system.

I see another woman, for a moment or so out of the corner of my eye, ethereal and spectrally beautiful, but when I turn to look at her, she always disappears. The veil, obviously. Then there's a Harculcorian fellow, his broad scaly backside sitting on top of a pile of boxes, and that must be the inventory management system, as it seems I think of Harculcorians as accountants, rather than the battle-juggernauts the rest of the known systems considers them. Cor would laugh, but be proud.

None of these systems are who I want to speak with though, since none of them can accomplish what needs to be done. There's only one I need to talk to, so I keep looking at the faces. When I spot a sleepy-looking fellow wearing an engineer's smock, I know I'm on the right path—I'm nearing the core operating system, and that's who I want to speak with.

I see her, then. The heart, mind and soul of the derelict, and she is as lovely as I thought she would be. She is cast in a radiant blue tone, illuminating the nightclub around her, and her open eyes are the pure white light of a neutron star. This is how I usually perceive core operating systems, the god: they that create and dictate all. She is blissful in countenance, her gaze towards the heavens.

'Greetings, I am Rowland,' I announce, which is my interpretation for providing my system access credentials.

The god turns her head towards me and smiles benevolently. Her solar-infused eyes remain unchanged, but I know she sees me. 'Greetings from the primary administration module for this vessel, designation Coalition of Allied Planetary Systems Trade Union, Automated Transport Service, C-Series, Unit Identification X-C4434T-Y. What is your query, Administrator Rowland?'

'A copy of your inventory list, please,' I request, and she complies. I don't have a chance to go through the entire file, but there are some choice sparkles she's hauling here: the highly anticipated credit-press—which means my crew is now set—but also pure-form rare elements, and—beauty of beauties—highly regulated, nearly contraband-level organic molecules that can be used for all sorts of purposes, the most lucrative being the construction of bioweapons. It's almost enough to make me regret forfeiting my share in favour of the veil, but then again, I'll be able to earn back all I've forfeited, ten times over, and have the time of my life doing it.

I'll look after the organic molecules by offloading them to an outskirts hospital in desperate need, who may only be able to offer bits on the credit for them, but they'll be willing to turn a blind eye to where they came from. I may be a bad guy, but not the kind that sells the key components required to attack a species on a genetic level to the highest bidder, all willy-nilly like.

Once I've finished my quick glance at the inventory, it's time for the dirtiest part of this job. I'm about to kill most of the system, reducing this god to her most basic form, and all these wonderful pseudo-people will vanish from this private little universe we've built together. I hate this part—even though I know this is all a virtual environment and none of these are actual people, there's still an emotional element my squishy brain experiences.

'Initiate end-point delivery acknowledgment, then terminate all processes and initiate complete shutdown of all sub-systems. Disengage primary power, reset to factory specifications, then restore base primary operating system.'

Wiping the system down to this most basic level is necessary for us to begin our salvage of the derelict; it's the safest way to ensure we can strip every component without encountering an unexpected system-defence. We will leave nothing behind.

'Failure to comply. Access restricted,' the god speaks, serenely.

I blink at this rebuke. I am the administrator. I am the god of this god.

'Identify cause,' I request, fascinated but annoyed. This hiccup was not in scope; we accounted for protocols but it's possible that since it's been twenty years, there's a detail we dismissed. Or overlooked, or weren't even aware of. These things do happen.

'An organic life form is docked to this module's starboard exterior hatch,' the god explains helpfully. 'Security protocols require all lifeforms to be a minimum of six metres from this unit prior to permitting any system component shut-down.'

'Override security protocols,' I order impatiently. It's almost like they don't want people to break into these things—active lifeform-detection that prevents the unit from opening if someone's too close? Paranoid, I say.

'Failure to comply. An organic life form is docked to this module's ex ...'

'Delete security sub-system,' I attempt.

'Failure to comply. An organic ...'

'Delete detection sub-system.'

'Failure to ...'

'Call *Lucky*,' I bark to my biocomp. I'm lost for what to do; I'm the organic life form currently docked to the ship, and I need to maintain constant contact via the port on my palm in order to keep the deep-jack going. I'm at max range already, given that my hand is inside a spacesuit, and I've only got a couple of centimetres of wiggle-room before the connection is automatically severed. Nothing will happen to me if that occurs; my system is more than capable of ending the connection when it detects signal-degradation, but it's still a pain in my ass.

'How's it going, Captain?' Betts answers, her voice helpful and prepared. She knows something is up and that her first response is to help is one of the main reasons she's my best friend.

'Bit stuck, Betts,' I reply, and proceed to explain my dilemma, finishing up with a request for my team's ideas on how to get out of this.

I can hear a smattering of voices as they brainstorm amongst themselves; Mia's is getting excited, and I hear Bethany encouraging our young engineer to speak up.

'I can download an app into your biocomp that'll mess up your bio-output signals, just a little—it should trick the system enough to make it think you're not a living thing.'

'No,' Bryce replies firmly. 'We're not going to screw with his body just to unlock a door.'

'It wouldn't be that!' Mia protests, but her voice is not exactly convincing. 'The Captain would still be normal, from his meat-suit's perspective, mostly. His biocomp would just add some garbage to the existing signal, making him look weird to the derelict's scanners.'

'The feedback from the signal distortion you're suggesting will alter Rowland's electrophysiology,' Bryce is quick to retort. 'It could interrupt the signal from his brain that's making his lungs work, or make him soil himself, or cause fatal tachycardia. No.'

'What's the probability on that, Bry?' I ask. Using the short form of his name is an old habit, but that's not an excuse. He's not yet told me to stop using it, but I can tell he no longer likes it when I do.

'I don't know. It depends on the severity of what Mia is proposing. The higher the distortion, the higher the risk,' Bryce replies.

'Cor, crunch the numbers.' It took some time for Cor to understand this human idiom; he thought he was being asked to figuratively bite the outcome of a calculation, and it distressed him so much that for a good while, he took to ending his tallies with a 'greater-than' sign to please us. He's better these days, though I do miss seeing his numbers being bitten by a crocodile.

There's a delay, long from my time-distorted perspective, while my crew works to find an answer. The electro-god waits for me with enviable tranquillity, her attention never wavering from mine, and I find myself comforted by her quiet stoicism. It does not matter to her if I pare her down and kill all her children; the idea of that even mattering doesn't exist in her universe. Nothing matters to her; she is only an instrument for a song she does not play. There are billions of people who would trade everything to experience even a moment of what she perceives.

'A seventeen percent distortion should do it,' Betts advises, but with a distinct lack of confidence.

'Bryce?' He knows what I will ask.

'It's high risk. I won't be able to tell if you're in danger, since the whole purpose of this is to prevent you from being accurately detected in the first place. That includes your suit's monitoring as well as my scanners onboard. Your comm unit will still pick-up audio though, so I can listen to your heartbeat and breathing. It's the best I can do.'

I want to ask him what his recommendations are, but I already know them: don't do it, come back inside, and find another way. He's correct, but there *is* no other way—if we try and manually move the derelict without disarming its security protocols, it will dive Under and it could take another twenty years to even get the chance at finding it again.

'But he doesn't need to stay that way though, right?' Ivan asks. No one has an immediate response for him, so he carries on. 'Like, all he needs to do is have his bio-whatever fucked up, have the system scan him again, make it think he's just a piece of nearby space shit, open the damn door ... and then he can turn it off and go back to normal. Right?'

'Right ...' Bryce adds, sounding surprised.

This is why Ivan is on my crew. Heavy-hitting demolition experts are easy to find, and certainly there are ones with a better disposition and general hygiene, but Ivan is blessed with these flashes of brilliant insight that makes him rare—a wunderkind, with all the power and predictability of a lightning strike. It's not the first time he's done this, and it doesn't happen often enough to be counted on, but when it does—the big boy earns his keep, and then some.

'If you keep it under five seconds, Rowland, you should be okay. Risk is acceptable,' Bryce concludes, confidently. This is his version of a ringing endorsement.

'Then you're up, Mia. Ready to receive your download.'

Mia gives a happy squeak, and it's only a few moments before she lets me know she's ready to send. I give her the go-ahead and watch the cyan letters start scrolling by as my biocomp begins receiving the scrambling app, then installs it. It's a chubby little program, greedily chewing up a large portion of my remaining system resources, but my biocomp wouldn't have even bothered to accept it if there wasn't room for its full installation. I won't be able to keep it installed, though, despite how useful it could be for other scenarios; it's way too resource-intensive, even when idle. Turning it on is going to divert the last of my leftover system-resources too, meaning that I don't even think my brain could send a signal to move my limbs. Plus, you know, it could end up killing me.

'Start slow, Rowland, and gradual increments until you reach seventeen percent distortion. We have the time. You can do this.' The first kind words Bryce has had for me in weeks.

'Roger. Initiating the app,' I reply. I experience no visible effect as Mia's app begins its task, but my biocomp reports that it is working, and a progress bar increases at a steady, even pace that would make Bryce proud. When it hits ten percent distortion, I get a slight wave of vertigo, and at fifteen there's a sensation that hovers between that of being watched and of being lost, but it's an annoyance more than anything, and doesn't worsen when I hit the magic seventeen.

'Reinitialize and execute detection sub-routines,' I ask the blue god, as soon as that seventeen appears.

'Initiating. Complete.'

'Delete security sub-system,' I repeat, testing to see if Mia's trick worked.

A tense moment follows, and I think it's going to fail, but instead the god responds, 'Sub-system deleted.'

My crew would not be able to see me smile, and I doubt I'm actually smiling, given that my brain signal's likely not reaching my lips, but nonetheless, I'm ear-to-ear happy.

'Thank you, madam,' I reply, before repeating my purge commands without any hesitation. The god complies, unfazed as she dims. The representation of *Bow-Ties* turns an inky black while the operating system sheds itself down to its most basic form. When the lights return, the room is empty.

The hatch unlocks.

'Job's done,' I tell my crew. 'We're good.'

Bett, Ivan and Mia cheer, but Bryce is fast to cut them off. 'Turn your app off, Rowland,' he instructs, knowing I would forget, and now I notice I'm significantly light-headed as the progress-bar indicates twenty-one percent. I know it's another fucking order from him, but I won't hold this one against him; he still has my back, at least for the time being.

CHAPTER 3

Rowland

I'm back on board my *Luck of the Draw*, most of my team crowding around me; three beaming smiles and one slightly agape mouth, making a faint rumbling sound, which is how Cor smiles. Even Bryce, off in the distance but observing me from the corner of his eye, has a small curl to his lips. He is so goddam handsome when he smiles like that, that I almost forget we've got another fight coming up. That can wait, and maybe I will forget, because right now I'm elated and relieved and safely on my ship.

'Ivan, Mia, suit up. Priority is to disassemble the derelict into pieces small enough to stack in our cargo bay.'

'That's the plan, Cap,' Ivan replies, giving me a hearty clap on my back for a job well done. He's got that twinkle in his brown eyes that means he's going to get to wreck something soon, and it just makes him all the easier to get along with.

Mia begins to walk towards the suit storage lockers, but suddenly stops to give me a concerned look. 'You okay from having used that app? Still feeling your fingers and toes, and such?'

I nod my head; as soon as I switched off the app, my system re-established itself rapidly. 'Where'd you find that?'

'I made it up!' she says, enthusiastically. 'It's based on the modified energy regulator program, the one we use to mess up *Lucky*'s outputs when we have to, and figured well hell, why not on a person too? We're all just machines in the long run, am I right, Captain?'

'Yeah, that's right!' I try to match her cheer. 'I take it I was the first person you ran that on, then?'

Her face goes slack. 'Oh, no, Captain, I ran it over a hundred times on our virtual dummies. That's how I knew you'd be fine, so long as you stayed under forty percent distortion. I wouldn't have ever suggested it if I thought you could get hurt.'

She means killed, but she won't jinx it. I believe her—in the short time that I've known Mia, she's made it clear that her genius does not trump safety, and her innovative ideas are always crafted with precaution in mind. Though Mia is young, her sparkling enthusiasm is tempered by wisdom beyond her years, and I often get the impression I'm talking to an old soul when I look into her lush brown eyes. An old soul who enjoys bizarre hairstyles, eclectic fashions, and has an unquenchable obsession with 20th century Earth girl-pop bands, but we all have our quirks.

'Well, it was a great idea, Mia. I'm giving you an extra percent of the share, as a bonus for saving the day.'

Her face flushes a dark cerulean. 'You don't need to do that, Captain, I was just doing my job.'

'I saved the day too, you know, Captain,' Ivan interjects insistently, and I'm not sure if he's more slighted at having been forgotten or missing out on a bonus. 'It was my idea that you turn the damn thing off before it killed you.'

I nod. 'Tell you what; you both get the main salvaging done on time, and I will give you each an extra percent and a quarter—deal?'

Ivan is now jamming his massive self into his spacesuit, and Mia is soon to follow. I smile and turn to Cor.

'Eighteen minutes, fifty-seven seconds,' I state: the total time it took me to get the hatch unlocked. 'Did you win the bet?'

'Yes,' Cor rumbles, pleased. 'Your consistency and predictability are pleasant to experience. I am happy you are you.'

He ends his sentence with a sharp, short closing of his jaws, making a quick snapping sound, and my UT advises this means Cor is truly happy. Without it, I would think he was hungry.

Although I hear Cor speaking Harculcorian, my UT works by intercepting the nerve stimulations my ears register when I hear Cor's words, and translates them from the format they're in into one I understand, which in my case is CAPS Standard Language. Once translated, the converted signals are released and resume their course to my brain, and voilà, Harculcorian to CAPS Standard is achieved.

This translation works with impressive accuracy—though there are some hiccups with species-specific words or concepts—idioms too, frequently—the CAPS Language research team is a well-funded priority project that's been in operation since the day we met the first non-human sapient-level species, and so constant language updates are freely and frequently distributed throughout the systems, under the premise that it's cheaper to learn a language than risk a misunderstanding leading to war.

It's not just verbal language either, written languages can be translated, but that's a deluxe model and requires more hardware than your average joe on the street has—specifically, an optical nerve interface—which I just happen to have. So, I get the benefit of being able to read not only the popular Terran languages, but most of the frequently encountered non-Terran languages too. Harculcorian text is beautiful—their script is based on swirling logographs, like fishes in water—and there're shades of meaning in their written word that are missed when they speak.

'Happy enough to split the winnings with me?' I ask, peering over my nose into his yellow eyes. I've taught him that this is a mock conspiratorial expression between good friends who want to share a secret, and so when he lowers his head to mimic my actions, there's a tug on my heartstrings.

'Yes. I am that happy. Because you are also safe.'

I laugh loudly and clap him on his heavy shoulder.

'I shall assist Ivan and Mia from the bridge with their dismantling. We shall have many riches to enjoy soon. This is a day that is good.'

'It is indeed, Cor,' I agree, and I am still grinning as my big friend stomps off happily. As he departs, I look for Bryce, trying to keep my good spirits up so that when I speak with him, it doesn't instantly turn into a fight—it will eventually, but the first few minutes may be enough to get my point across. But he's no longer in the cargo bay; seeing that I did not require his professional attention, he's likely scuttled—*tsk*—returned to his post in our med-bay.

Betts is here though, and she's wearing her 'you did good, Row' look, so my heart lifts again.

'You're gonna be rich, Betts. The cargo in those holds is a lot more valuable than we guessed.'

Her eyebrow arches wryly. 'You sure on that, Captain? We guessed pretty high.'

I nod my head, assuring her. 'This is one of the few times you're going to see me happy to be wrong. It's not just the credit-press; there's pure raw mats and restricted organic molecules. That's just the top of the list too: I'll download the full inventory so you'll have something to dream about.'

She whistles appreciatively. 'I know a buyer on Venris who would trade his progenitors for the raw mats, and a functional credit-press will never go out of style. The organic molecules … bit tricky … but I'll put out some feelers on Venris. You sure you're gonna stick with just the veil?'

'Deal's a deal; the transport could have been hauling data records, after all— I took my chance, and I still think I came out ahead. You know how long I've wanted a veil—oh the places we'll go, the things we'll steal.'

She raises her hands in a surrender-gesture. 'Totally agree, Row. That veil's gonna make offloading the rest of the booty a breeze. If we can sneak by the automated security in the T't'lor system, there's some prime black-markets that we've never even tapped—will get good bits on the credits, better than CAPS-T markets, for sure.'

'Music, Betts, music to my ears.'

She lowers her head though, and steps forward, her eyes momentarily glancing at the access-port to the med-bay. 'You need to have a talk with Bryce, Row. He was really pissed at you while you were jacked.'

'Did he say something?' I ask, then scold myself internally. According to CAPS-N command training, the correct response to Betts' comment is 'I will resolve it', a proactive statement that diminishes Bryce's behaviour while ensuring the situation gets sorted out with minimum fuss. Not encouraging gossip or letting on it's affecting you. But I'm tired, worried, and my nervous system has just run a marathon, so Betts doesn't hold it against me.

'No, he just wore that tight frown and eye-glare that kills at ten paces. He was gripping the monitor he was watching you from so tightly his fingers turned colour. He hasn't said anything since you cracked the hatch.'

She reaches out and lightly squeezes my forearm. 'I know he's leaving when we hit Venris, but you need to make him feel better about it. I don't want his last few days with us to be a bad memory for him. We should part as friends.'

I hold her gaze for a moment, hoping she'll give me a hint as to how to go about accomplishing the miracle she is so casually asking for. When I don't reply, she adds, 'Brush off the insubordination, you accepted that when you invited him into your bed first, then your crew. You love him, so let that lead the conversation. He's had enough, Row, of this life, and we all knew that was only a matter of time. He's too smart to keep going with this. Let him go, but part well.'

I want to argue with her. I want to tell her she's wrong, that he's just in a bad mood, and that if I take him out for a weekend on the town in Venris, we'll sort out our differences and be back to the place we were months ago. Months ago? It's been closer to a year.

Betts is right. Bryce is right. It's time I made it right, even though there's a part of me that's desperate to keep it wrong. Losing Bryce is going to suck so, so much.

'Hit the rack, First Officer Ortez. You're two hours past your shift end. Cor will relieve you,' I order, using my official CAPS-N tone with mocking authority, and then less seriously, 'I'll sort it out with our doctor. It'll be fine, just like you've said.'

'Got to wrap some stuff up on the bridge first, Cap. I'll join you all for chow though—Ivan's got a decent-looking chilli percolating in the auto-cooker, and I think this time it's beef.'

'Real beef?' I ask, sceptically. 'When did we get so fancy?'

She winks as she departs. 'Didn't say it was real, Cap.'

*****

Bryce is furious. I've only asked him two questions, and the first one was 'How's it going?'

I blurted out the second question though, something along the lines of 'So what makes you think you're allowed to give me orders in front of my crew?' Apparently, somewhere on the short trip between the cargo bay and the med-bay, all of Betts' great advice completely fell out of my brain.

I'm thankful that the walls of the med-bay are sound-absorbing, as is most of *Lucky*. It's a major boon in maintaining privacy on small vessels, and it makes resurfacing from an Under dive slightly less harrowing. It's also useful while descending into planetary atmosphere, which can be deafening if you've been in the silent bliss of space for an extended period. Mia doesn't like it though: says it makes it hard to tell if the ship is sick because she can't hear a part moaning when it shouldn't be, or something that's shaking when it needs to be perfectly still.

It's the 'my' in 'my crew' that flips his switch; he's told me how much it pisses him off when I play the big strong hero captain. But I *am* the big strong hero captain; I mean the big, strong and hero parts are subjective, but the captain part is abso-*fucking*-lutely not.

There's no point describing our argument: we're barely listening to each other, and we're proving again that any noise firing out of our mouths is solely for the purposes of scoring hits. It's a boxing match, words instead of fists, and we're both bruised and bloody within a couple of minutes. I try and take the high road by calming the situation down, but he sees this as just another example of the heroic captain, and it only incenses him further.

We're not screaming; I mean I'm yelling, but he's only slashing me with cutting words—my blistering temper versus his icy contempt. Part of me thinks I'm deliberately enraging him, just so he'll show something that resembles passion towards me, even if it's making things worse between us. I know, it's fucked up.

'You're right!' I finally concede, but for my sake. The force of my words is enough to cut him off for a moment; he's wondering if it's a lure, and his incredible brown eyes, ones that once upon a time lit up whenever I walked into the room, are narrowed with suspicion. I show my palms to him, look away, and sit down on the closest stool, surrendering.

'About what?' he taunts, but I can see that showing my throat has caught him off guard. If I was truly the asshole he says I am, now would be the perfect time to strike. I admit I'm tempted.

'All of it. About how you're the doctor and I need to listen to you, that I'm the one with the problem with authority, that I'm not seeing that you're doing your duty and trying to keep me alive.'

I do go for the jugular now, but it's both of ours, not just his. In all the fighting, I found Betts' words to me somewhere, and those are the ones I use next.

'This is all about you leaving, Bryce. I'm miserable as fuck about that, but I don't know how to tell you without making you think I'm guilt-tripping you into staying, when the best thing for you is to go. I love you, and it's tearing a hole in me that you're leaving, but you need to move on from all this, and I need to let you.'

The hardness in his expression breaks, and for a moment, he's my Bryce again. 'I love you too, Rowland. You know that. This isn't about loving you.'

'I know, I know. We're on separate paths. You need to be you, I need to be me, and those two things can't exist together in the same place at the same time. I just want to go back to being us, but that's over, and all of this fighting we're doing is just ...'

'Part of the mourning process, I understand,' Bryce adds, trying to be helpful, but I'm too raw right now to take it that way; Dr. Winston is still on duty.

'But I can't have you ordering ...' I start but stop when I see his hackles rise. It takes me a moment to figure out a better way to say what needs to be said.

'If ... if you ever decide you want to serve on a starship again, especially one that's on the rag-tag side like we are, then it's really important that you give advice, not an order, to the captain. It'll fuck up the crew's understanding about who's in charge, and that can get people killed during an emergency.' I've explained this before, and Bryce says he understands, but his actions are still far from his words.

He thinks on what I've said before responding. 'This will be the last time I serve on a starship. Don't ...' he holds up his hands to indicate he's not being confrontational. 'Don't take that the wrong way. I see your point, and I'm never going to be able to fall in line like that.'

'And don't sleep with your captain, let alone be his beau. That's just ... that was stupid of me,' I add, sheepishly.

'Yeah, well, you weren't the only one there. When you're not being an asshole, you're a real sweetheart, Rowland. Hard to resist.' He has his sly smile on now, but I can see there's no joy in it. He's mourning as much as I am.

'And I don't want you to disappear forever, Bry. I can understand you wanting a clean break, and some time away, but the thought of never seeing you again is killing me.'

He does come over now, and gently puts his hand on my shoulder. He keeps it there, even when I reach up to grasp it. There's warmth in his charming smile now, and having him close to me like this again is more of a balm than anything we could say to each other.

'I know that if you put your mind to it, you'll find me,' he starts, and his voice is very kind, like the first time he told me he loved me: honest, sincere, absolutely the truth. 'I know because when you give me my new identity, you'll put in a backdoor so that you can track me down whenever you want to, or if I need you to. I'm fine with that. Just let some time pass. Good couple of years, maybe more.'

I *was* planning on the backdoor, by the way.

He scrunches down on his haunches so that we're eye-level now, his hand still on my shoulder. 'You are a great captain, and I do love you. It's those two things that can't exist together at the same time, Rowland.'

'You're going to be okay, right?'

He nods. 'Of cour ...'

The explosion cuts off the rest of his final words to me.

*****

The force of the explosion sends us slamming into the med-bay ceiling, pinning us there as the room spins in complete circles. We're held fast by centrifugal force as a blaring klaxon erupts and the main lights cut out. The ship makes another spin before *Lucky*'s inertia-dampeners kick in and the pair of us are slammed down to the floor.

Bryce is not moving; I didn't see what happened, but his crumpled body is twisted at an awkward angle. His eyes are closed though, which could mean unconscious, rather than dead, I hope. I don't have time to check, I'm on my feet and out of the med-bay as soon as I'm able.

'Captain Hale, we have been hit by a breach-wave!' Cor's voice comes from the ship comms, and it is now the third time I have heard him panic.

When a ship returns from the Under—a dimension that runs parallel to our own that we use to accomplish faster-than-light travel, by diving in and out of it—it's accompanied by a kaleidoscopic surge of energies, including kinetic, upon its arrival—when it 'breaches'. The larger the ship, the larger the breach-wave. Breaching next to another vessel is an act of aggression in the CAPS, and while all their fleet vessels have multiple forms of defence against it, our *Lucky* does not live up to her name in this regard.

'Evasive manoeuvres! Get us distance Cor! Bethany, get to the bridge!'

'She is here Captain Hale. She is injured and bleeds from her head!' His choice of words is important here: Cor is purposefully mentioning blood, which is a reserved word in Harculcorian. Its deliberate use carries the connotation of direness or excitement: something extreme. Fuck fuck fuck with every running step to the bridge.

'They're opening fi …!'

We're rocked again, and I'm slammed into the closest bulkhead with a violent jolt that ends up with me sprawling, pinned down longer than I can afford to be. The distinct odour of charged ion particles is suddenly everywhere, followed quickly by burning hull and ship furnishings. I try to stand, and my left leg screams in agony; I hit the bulkhead hard and must've broken something.

'Hail our surrender!' I order. *Lucky* is a civilian-class ship—we have one medium-watt laser cannon we use for knocking out space debris or small asteroids, and our kinetic shielding is useful for deflecting the stuff our laser misses. Our energy-shields keep out the worst of the various electromagnetic waves that roam the universe, but whoever is attacking is using charged particle-beam weapons. We might as well be naked—a baby in front of a dragon that breathes billions of charged atoms at us at next-to-light speeds, all at once in a beam that obliterates any unshielded matter in its path.

'Attacking vessel, we surr …' Cor starts, but we're hit again. Fucking Christ!

I'm only halfway to the bridge when the second volley hits, and it's enough to break our dampeners and send us tumbling in circles again. We spin for what feels like an eternity; I have time to think of Ivan and Mia—they're supposed to be dismantling the derelict, fifty metres off our bow. What the fuck is happening to them? Were they inside the ship, or out? Possibly alive, or definitely, definitely dead?

It takes a long time for the spin to slow, not stop—*Lucky* is badly hurt if she's not able to restore her space legs. I'm in a worse state though; my leg is clearly broken, my right arm is limp by my side and there's a gruesome gash running down my left ribcage, gushing my precious red stuff freely.

'Cor …-?' I ask weakly, but there's no response from the comms.

I can't stand on my own; the pain is too severe, but I take a deep breath, and activate my biocomp, forcing it to shunt the pain signals my nervous system is experiencing to its buffering queue, buying me a momentary reprieve so I can get up. The pain is still there, I'm just getting some breathing-space before the buffer's capacity fills and overflows, sending the messages to my brain. I need to get to the bridge; if I have any shot at this at all, it has to happen there.

'Huuuullll … breeeeach … detecccctededed on A and B-B-B-deck,' *Lucky*'s automated warning system slurs. 'Uuuunauthorized access attempt on starb-b-boaaard port.'

We're being boarded. I'm not going to make it to the bridge in time; *Lucky*'s access port is not going to stand up long. But I'm damn well going to keep going. Betts, Cor … they need me. I need to see them, even if it's for the last time.

All the lights are out save for red emergency lighting, but I'm still able to see the final nail in the coffin for my plans to reach the bridge. The single access path to the bridge has been destroyed, and our emergency kinetic shields are all that stands between me and the void of space. They've decapitated us—I can see the bridge floating away from where I'm standing, sheared off by the combination of the attackers' particle-beam and the force of the resulting impact spin. The one small comfort is that I can see that the shields on the opposite side are still in place; the bridge has been separated but there's a chance Betts and Cor are still alive, and not vented into space. I peer to my right, hoping to see if the derelict is in sight, and possibly get an idea of Ivan's and Mia's fate, but neither they nor the derelict is visible.

I do see our attackers, though. I can't clearly distinguish the ship make, because at this distance it's so huge and looming that it's impossible to determine its actual size and configuration. They breached right the fuck on top of us! How the fuck did they know where we were?

There are no outward markings that signal the attacking vessel's origin, either. No markings are a form of marking, however, and the clever part of my mind chooses this completely inappropriate moment to list them out for me; Ghilgren don't mark their ships because they have no written language, Pryok'tel don't because they don't consider other lifeforms worthy to read their language, Vedonvan pirates don't because they fear the words will foretell their fate, and the Free Spire People of Nex IV don't because the only word that can be written is the word for their god. I fucking hope it's the Free Spires; the other three can't be negotiated with.

I turn and head back to the med-bay, hoping I can get back to Bryce in time. We have a lifeboat, big enough for the entire crew, stocked with enough emergency supplies to last us a month in space. It's my last shot, my only shot. Be alive, Bryce, be alive—I really need a doctor, and I really need you. We were almost friends again.

It's too late though. They've breached the access port, roughly halfway between where I'm standing and the med-bay. As their boarding party enters our home, my universal translator picks up the sound of their voices, and converts their native tongue to my CAPS Standard. It's just one word: *Hhtoh'ket*. Pryok'telish for 'Harvest'.

I hope everyone on my crew is already dead.

CHAPTER 4

Toar

Captain's log, OSSM *Lurcaster's Claw*. The date is 27.13.221 and the time is 21h00. Captain Toar Grithrawrscion reporting,' I start, and then think about what to say that would differ in any way from the log entry I made at 16h00. I could always say, 'No change from previous log entry', as other ship captains do. Lazy though, and not in character for me, as I do like a good talk. This is my last official duty for my shift today, and once it's done, I can fetch my supper, try and have a laugh with the lads in the mess, maybe practise my sketching, then off to sleep. Best get started then.

'Mining of the kelmisite continues, on schedule. Master Foreman Gretocar reports production levels have increased by seven percent, which should help us to recover losses from yesterday's malfunction of our main water regulator, and subsequent repairs. I take this time to repeat that while the possibility of this unit malfunctioning was reported prior to our departure from Oarthecan Station Three, our original departure was enforced by OSSM Division Head, Darlmorth Krariclan, may the fur stretched over his fat suncoat rump be forever covered by his own faeces.'

I delete everything past the word 'repairs' and continue.

'We anticipate return to Oarthecan space within the next six days, per our assignment objectives. No issue to report from the crew, spirits remain productive, and supplies good. Toar signing off.'

I gently tap the monitor with the littlest of my claw-tips, but it's still recording. I press it again, more firmly, but it turns out that even after two centuries, and what that puffy-faced flea-trap Darl promised was seen to before we left the docks, that we're still not able to get this Pryok'tel piece of rubbish touchpad to recognize our claw-taps consistently. They were designed with the filthy digits of the Pryok'tel in mind, and I often wonder if I first soaked my claws in blood if that would help to improve the interface. But I'm more stubborn than the touchpad, and so on my fourth try, the log finally updates.

'Done,' I announce, and stand up to get on with the rest of my evening's plans. I'm in my personal cabin quarters, which is just bigger than the other officer's quarters, but still not entirely big enough for me. As I am a stormcoat, I stand just over two and a third metres tall, which even when I'm not wearing my work boots, is tall enough so that my head will touch the ceiling of my little cabin. Though this is the largest of the personnel quarters on the station, I've only got enough room for my sleeping pit, which while wide enough to accommodate me is still *just* too shallow to properly sink into, plus my desk, office chair and another chair for guests. There's built-in storage in the walls, thankfully, and I've got my own lavatory, which I think is a bonus only my first officer also has, so all in all, I count myself lucky, if somewhat squished.

I've not yet become accustomed to the cramped confines of either my cabin or the rest of the *Lurcaster's Claw*, though I have been in command of our mining station for seven years now—seems that the Pryok'tel did not design their vessels with the idea that, one day, the Oarth slave-labourers forced to build them would rise up and take them back—but I'm better than I was for the first few years on board; on my second day as captain, I slammed my forehead into a port frame so hard that it knocked me for stars, and I had to spend the better part of a morning in Sickies for my efforts.

Still, despite these years, I've not made an effort to personalize my quarters much—all except one of my cabin's walls are bare, showing the smooth, grey poly-ceramic interior plating that runs throughout the station, and the one wall that is adorned is the one behind my desk, on which hangs a rather generic painting of a green nebula—Threnrian's Nest, I think, about six or so light years from where I am now. The painting belonged to the previous captain and I've never bothered to take it down.

I've thought about putting up a piece of my own artwork: I'm an amateur sketcher in my free time—usually pictures done with my drawing claw covered by a graphite tip, but sometimes I'll use coloured paints and such, every now and then. Not an artist by any stretch of the imagination, but I'm not half-bad either—I like to capture portraits of people, and scenes of nature, animals too I suppose—and the stars, and some of the more interesting stellar bodies I've encountered in my past. But whenever I get the idea in my head to mount one of my little drawings on the wall, there's this gloomy part of me that wonders why I should even bother.

I do have one of my most treasured pieces on display, though: a small portrait of my three sons, sitting on my desk in a hand-carved nightwood frame that one of them, my artistic one, Harstoar—sorry, he goes by Harsculler now—crafted for my sixtieth birthday. I captured this little charcoal-dust portrait of them when they were just toddlers, mind, so it's about thirty years out of date, but Hars found it in a bunch of my stuff I keep at my Dad's house, and decided to frame it for me. Seeing their bright, sweet, lovely little faces every day sees me through a lot of hardship, here on my own.

Seven years. Not a terribly long time in a man's overall lifespan, but still, a long time in my books, when I think about it. I've now been a captain of a mining station for a year longer than I was a captain of an OSS Naval frigate, but I try not to think about that too often, as I find that missing my frigate—*Drethor's Glaive*—and his crew of a hundred souls, does me no good. Had myself a grand captain's quarters I did, aboard the *Glaive*—two full-sized rooms, one for hosting and then my private chambers, plus my own lavatory with a double-deep bathing tub, as well as two sleeping pits: one big enough for three of me, and always full of lads, nearly every night—lovely—plus another for any extra guests that might've wanted to stay the evening. My former quarters is only one of the things I miss, and by no means is it the greatest.

But I'm grateful for my current position here on the *Lurcaster's Claw*, all things considered—disgraced ex-Navy officers do not often get a second chance like I've been given, and that this chance still involves a command position is something I'm truly appreciative of. There are times, though, like the one I'm experiencing now, when I'm on my own with only my own thoughts for company, that the past does start gnawing at me. I suppose that's part of my punishment, really, to be left on my own to mope about my failures, and in the silence of my too-small cabin, there's not much else for me to do, and so the past is where my thoughts often drift.

I'm just tidying up the last bit of administrative work I need to do, before there's a buzzing at my door, and I notice the smell of double-spiced *cerret* pie wafting through the vents, its rich meaty aroma causing my stomach to remind me it's time for evening fillings.

'Come in,' I invite, my tone curious and friendly.

The door slides open, and a young man stands there; it's one of my new junior miners, Reyoran Marlerscion. Handsome little chap: clean and neatly pressed uniform, nice woodcoat that's been recently tidied, broad in the shoulders, right proper stout frame and a cheery glint in his green eyes. Also rather good at his job, from what his foreman tells me, even though this is his first deep space assignment. He joined us when we left home three months ago, and from what I've been told, he fits in rather well. Not all new recruits do, and so knowing that he's getting on is a good sign that things are being run properly on board.

I can't say that I'm surprised to see him, but I'm nonetheless quite grateful that he's here. Rey and I have been flirting all journey, but gentle-like, and what with us returning home in the next few days, I've been wondering if the lad would work up the courage to stop by his captain's quarters, while there's still a chance. I've been wondering if he'd bother with me, given my history and all, but that he's brought me savoury *cerret* pie, which he is currently holding before him on a metal mess-tray covered with a cloche, makes me think the lad's not one to hold a man's failures against him. Some do, and that's just part of my punishment, but given that Rey is here, there's still hope that things can be good, now and then.

'Evening, Rey. What brings you by?' I ask casually, as though this is a surprise.

We both know the answer, but I should at least make a show of playing the innocent. I know by his bashful expression that he's caught the look in my eye, making it clear his presence is very welcome.

On board ships, and for most forms of Oarthecan society—at least the ones that don't directly involve one of our barons—it's entirely appropriate for a subordinate to approach his superior and seek out some light-hearted den-fun. It's part-and-parcel of their learning, though the expectation that the subordinates do so is never there, not with decent captains and such.

Neither is the expectation of acceptance of said offer to said captains; it's all good fun and games, nothing to be taken either for granted or too seriously. It forms rather one of the more enjoyable ways us Oarth 'clan up'—a strong, natural instinct amongst us to form social connections, and it's how we get most things done that are worth the bother doing. Sharing an evening or two together helps to form those good strong bonds between men—it's one of the cornerstones of the Oarthecan way of living.

This seeking of sex is not appropriate if it happens the other way round, though, where the one with the authority sniffs around the ones he's in charge of. At best, it's viewed as favouritism when a superior ruffles the rump-fur of his subordinates, and at worst as a form of sexual coercion, but there are still some subtle ways a superior can let on that he'd be up for some special time with a crewman.

For the last few days, I've taken to visiting Rey during his shifts, asking him easy questions, praising him in front of his friends, the last of which I'd do regardless of my interest because he does seem rather talented, and is a good worker that gets on with his pals. Maybe once or twice I made sure to stand in such a way that he'd have a long, unobstructed view of my belt buckle, though.

Don't get me wrong, the *Lurcaster's Claw* isn't a sex-soaked pleasure craft roaming the stars where we all are jumbled together in a mess of damp fur and heavy breathing. Certainly, consensual sex—what we call 'denning'—happens on board between men of all stations and ranks, just like any other vessel in the OSS, but on our station, work comes first and play after, and only if you're up for it. I myself wouldn't enjoy serving with a crew that's too deep into their den-time; mind I'm older (rather on the much side, if I'm being honest) and have kids of my own, so that urge to 'den the decks' isn't as strong as say, Rey's is.

At least, that's how it works normally. For me, given my history, it's never a sure thing that men will come and knock on my door, despite our traditions and my efforts, and so when they do, it's always a good moment for me. Rey's been slower to initiate this interaction than I'd hoped he'd be, and that's just been a part of all the gnawing I've been experiencing as of late. Been hoping his hesitation is because I'm his first go at this, and that he really does fancy me, what with him always sneaking looks at my belt buckle these days. It's sweet, makes my heart happy, and I need as much happiness as I can get, as these one, perhaps two, time encounters are all I can really hope for now—no man would want more from me, and I don't blame them. So I'm genuinely pleased to see the sweetly handsome Rey with his fat meat pie standing in my doorway—I know it's not going to last anything other than tonight, and am happy enough for that.

'Just thought I'd see if you'd had your supper yet, Captain? Maybe, join you, if you're up for it?'

We both know it's not just the meat pie that's being offered, and we both know that my casual but still hearty 'yes' applies to everything currently standing in my doorway. His pretty eyes are all alight with happiness and excitement as he steps in, his nerves shut away and his confidence blooming. It makes him all the more handsome when I see his back straighten and his chest puff out with pride.

He sets the tray down on my desk and removes the cloche to reveal two large pastry-encased pies, stacked atop one another, so that the bottom one's bleeding a bit of lovely gravy. The smell now is just—*raur*, amazing. Bringing two pies for us was a clever move too; he's a big man, but I'm at least a head taller than he is, him being a woodcoat and me being a stormcoat and all, and one little pie between the two of us wouldn't be enough to even put a dent in our tummies.

'You want the top pie, or the bottom?' he asks harmlessly enough, attempting to disguise his brazen invitation with a degree of civility. If he's been practising this line, which most likely he has—I always practised mine back in the day—it doesn't show.

'Top I think, for tonight,' I reply, winking to show that I'm more than happy to play along.

'Lucky me, love it when the bottom gets all squished and wet like that.'

I roar a laugh at the punchline, and he chuckles, but when I catch his eye again, he looks away bashfully; seems there's a case of nerve-mites still biting his courage, so I reach out and place my hand on his shoulder, the hooks of my claw-tips gently pressed against his back, encouraging him. This too is how it's supposed to go; as his superior, the first physical contact between us needs to come from me, to let him know he's safe to advance, and he's not misread things. If he retreats from my touch, then that's a signal to me that I've either got things wrong, or he's changed his mind—but that won't be the case between the two of us tonight.

'Glad you've stopped by, been looking forward for a chance to chat, and such. I've got myself some beer that'll go well with the pie. We can share a couple of mugs, maybe another couple, afterwards, if you like?'

He nods, slowly at first, but more eagerly when I turn my hand so that my claw-tips graze his cheek. His face relaxes entirely, a blissful grin quickly spreading as he nuzzles his cheek against my claws, brushing the short hairs of his face-fur against them.

'Aye, that … that sounds just proper,' he agrees, and his eyes are giving me both permission and encouragement.

I lean in and press my lips against his, closed at first, letting him set the pace, but he's fast to open his mouth and lick his long, broad tongue against my lips, seeking entry, which I readily grant. Rey takes a step closer, pressing his littler frame into my bigger one, bumping our happy bits together, slowly moving his hips against mine invitingly. He tastes better than those pies are going to taste, that's for certain, and my enthusiastic acceptance of his kisses spurs him on. He quickly places his hand on my bum, and gives a good, firm, clawless squeeze, pressing me tighter to him. Our tongues are getting to know one another very well; he's a great little snogger this one, little on the sloppy side but I don't mind that. Between our tongues, kisses and friction as we rub together, he's raring my cock up as much as I am his. Never been a slow riser, even old as I am, and he's rumbling a faint moan of pleasure as he feels me swelling against his own swell.

I break from the kiss, and nuzzle his neck, just below his ear, and this causes another little moan as he cranes his head to the side, giving me better access. There's this spot below our ears used in scent-marking, which is highly erogenous if touched just the right way, and that's exactly what I'm doing to this handsome little woodcoat—licking gently, kissing softly, rubbing my nose carefully along.

Ah, Eternal Oarth, he does smell fine—a rich, energetic mixture of deep

31

woods, clean fur and his own thick musk—that slightly peppery, teasingly intoxicating undertone of a man on the prowl. Rey's youthful scent is like a firework racing up my nose and bursting in my brain, sending streamers of desire all down my spine and right into my balls. Right now, the scent he's giving off is strong enough to even overpower the ever-present stink of kelmisite, which otherwise permeates everything on board, so having a break from that metallic, overly tangy and nastily cloying stench to instead experience the warm, enticing and intensely arousing smell of a man wanting to share your den is a treat for my entire body to enjoy. He's got me to full mast, and I'm slowly starting to thrust up and down against his bulging crotch, bumping him gently but with clear intention. This is going fast, but we're both keeping pace.

My efforts are rewarded as he grasps that belt buckle he's been looking at so often, and with a skill I wouldn't have thought possible for such a nervous-sounding young lad, he yanks it back and opens it quickly, on his first attempt. I've not stopped exploring his neck, and make a low, soft rumble in my throat, encouraging him further; one of my hands is now also on his arse, both pulling him closer and kneading the firm flesh. I feel the front zip on my uniform trousers rubbing painfully against my sensitive cock head, but that's soon relieved as Rey pops the clasp, then lowers it smoothly. *Nervous indeed, were you?* He's a regular pro, but I don't mind his coyness in the slightest—the chase has been fun for us both.

It's just when he first carefully reaches underneath the waistband of my tailcatch (a lightweight undergarment with a reversed-pocket for our tails to fit into and be kept clean and safe from chafing), to first gingerly touch the tip of his claws against my cock, that the comms system in my room bleeps, signalling an incoming message. We both groan in disappointment, but neither of us pulls away.

'Captain Toar, please report to the bridge!' The voice of my first officer is urgent as it comes over the comm system.

I pull back immediately, sparing Rey a fast, apologetic glance while refastening myself up before I reply. He doesn't seem bothered at all; this is shipboard life—duty first, fun later—his expression wordlessly tells me he understands.

'Toar here; report?'

'Breach-wave detected, 27 by 343, 57,000 megametres off the buoy's bow.'

Rey and I exchange a look of surprise, and now we're both turning towards the door to exit, but I give one quick, long lick of my tongue against his mouth before I go.

'Come back when this is over?' I offer quietly, and he agrees with a short series of quick nods.

'On my way, Toar out,' I confirm, and Rey gives me a sneaky-quick kiss on my nose, making me chuckle.

I give Rey a hearty slap on his back as we depart my cabin, him on his way back to his station, me to the bridge. Though we've not done anything too intimate, I'm finding that what little we *did* manage has put me in a wonderful mood, even if it means having to walk funny while I'm on my way to the bridge, but that's fading fast enough.

What is doing a better job at helping me walk easier is the thought of why I'm being summoned to begin with. The *Lurcaster's Claw* is supposed to be alone out here, and if our buoy, currently deployed surface side of the kelmsite asteroid we're knee-deep into and mining, is detecting a breach-wave that far out, the ship that's surfaced from the Under is at least corvette class, and that means someone's here for a reason.

*****

My quarters are not far from the main bridge, so it's only a few minutes until I'm in the command centre of our operations. Although the night-shift crew is technically on duty, my first officer, Yarenthir Relthorclan, has summoned the more experienced day crew to the bridge. It's a smart move, one that I didn't need to teach him. Like almost all drones, Yar's had formal military training, but his wasn't in the field of command. You'd never guess that though—command comes naturally to him.

Have I shared a den-night with Yar? 'Course I have. But of my bridge crew, Yar's been the only one, yet I do still count on each of them—we've got a solid ship-bond, well established and frequently reinforced with good conversation, if nothing else, at least on my part.

On top of that, Yar is strong, capable and proficient—modest in looks, granted, but being talented and quick-witted makes him quite a dapper catch in my eyes. Smells wonderful too, he does—an Oarth's scent changes over time, and Yar, being a good thirty years older than Rey, has a complex aroma that sometimes has me lingering around him longer than I need too, just to have his spicy, savoury and cock-ticklingly powerful scent deep in my nose.

The day we launched, Yar made it very clear he wanted a round or two with me, back in my den—none of that coy, but still cute, shyness that Rey expressed. I think Yar's got a bond-mate back on Oartheca, and I'm glad for them both, 'cause based on the couple of rounds we've shared in my den, command isn't the only thing Yar's talented at; man's got a cock that's built for depth, and an arse that wants all you have to give.

'Update?' I ask as I take my command seat, relieving Yar as he heads to his station on the opposite end of the bridge.

Our bridge is a moderately-sized circular domed room with exit points directly opposite each other; in the middle sits a hollow ring of display consoles, terminals and computer stations where my officers take their posts. In the centre of this ring, a holographic projector illuminates the room, generating images of whatever we need to view, be it an image taken from one of the multiple sensor arrays on the exterior of the mining station, or the live feed from our shuttle craft, or even a copy of any one of the outputs from a terminal tied to it, which all are. The bridge crew all face the centre of this holographic projection, which changes its display to accommodate the viewing angle of the observer.

My station is considered at the 'top' of the outer ring, the position halfway between the two exits. When I'm sat, to my right is our science station and to the left is our tactical, the latter of which sees little use but is required by OSS regulations to be manned at all hours—safety first and all. Across from me is the traditional place of the first officer, its positioning thought to encourage the idea that the best decision is one made while viewing both sides of the outcome, but Yar is often so busy during his shift that he ends up running laps around us. Our comms station is between myself and science, but I'm thinking of moving it further away; and engineering is between tactical and the first officer.

'Looks like a corvette has breached on the far side of the asteroid field. We're too far out to get a visual confirmation, but the buoy's reporting a ship-configuration that matches the new model Pryok'tel vultures,' Yar announces.

That's not good. From what we know from our history with the Pryok'tel, which is rather a lot considering they enslaved all Oartheca for over two hundred consecutive years, their vulture class corvettes are heavily gunned and carry a crew contingent of at least fifty, and double that if they're raiding.

I've got a crew of two hundred, made up of sixteen admin staff, twenty support personnel; and the rest are miners. As for armaments, *Lurcaster's Claw* has six ultra-watt mining lasers, plus about two racks each of proton-powered mining rockets and charges we use to crack the really tough parts of an asteroid open, and a small shuttle craft, minimally armed, that we use to get into tight crevices to plant those charges.

If it came to battle, we might be able to get in one or two solid hits that dent the vulture's shields—possibly breach them and damage the hull—but we're a mining station, not a combat vessel. Our arse is fat, and that vulture would plough us harder than a sire's first time with his baron. I'd give us five, maybe six terror-filled minutes before we're blown to pieces by the vulture; they're built for short, deadly and fast-won fighting, such as precision ambushes or surprise raiding. We're built to haul hundreds of tonnes of unrefined ore and comfortably house our crew while doing so. It's no match.

But there's nothing out here, in this asteroid field, worth the effort to raid. Kelmisite—an uncommon but by no means rare mineral that's a base component of Under fuel—is common enough that there'd be no reason to come this far out from their borders to mine it, and certainly not using a vulture to do so.

'Have they seen us, then?' I inquire, turning to our science officer, Threngdral Drellriscion.

'Not likely,' he replies. He's a nightcoat with rich, glossy black fur and charmingly deep brown eyes, but to me, his most attractive feature is his clever, quick mind. He is still sweetly cute in appearance too, though. Why've we not denned is something that saddens me, if I think about it too much, as I suspect he's one of many who won't overlook my past, but he's never let on if that's the case.

'They're as far away from us as we are from them,' Threng continues. 'And the kelmisite in the asteroid we're surrounded by is fouling their sensors as much as our own. We wouldn't even know they were there if not for our buoy.'

He's right of course; we're deep inside a particularly large kelmisite asteroid, hollowing it from the inside out after we found a natural crevasse large enough to squeeze the station into. It's why we still have most of our rockets available— normally we'd have to blow a crater open, which costs you not only the rockets but the loss in kelmisite, and so discovering an entrance that led nearly all the way down to the centre of the asteroid was a lucky find for us indeed.

But unrefined kelmisite fouls up sensor and communication transmissions, especially those of the long-range type—something about how when sensor and comm wavelengths hit its crystalline structure, it causes an echo feedback in the matrices and—yada, yada, yada—I'm the captain, not the scientist. Threng tried to explain it to me proper once but really, I've no mind for heavy science stuff. What I do have a mind for is people, and I know enough to trust that Threng knows, and trust him to find a way around it—which he did in a matter of hours at the time.

We dropped a sensor and comm buoy at the entrance to the crevasse, and then daisy-chained a series of comm boosters between the buoy and where we are now. Short-range comm signals are not as badly affected by kelmisite, so the buoy at least gives us some indication of what's going on out there, since while we're inside, all our station's external sensors are useless—whatever we broadcast that's not directed at the boosters just gets jumbled and becomes nonsense.

'Buoy's reporting weapons fire, sir,' our tactical officer, Chreshgurner Kerthscion, a woodcoat like Yar and Rey, alerts. It's only a short pause before he adds, 'And again.'

'Can't see what they're firing at,' Threng advises. 'But they're definitely bothering something out there, sir.'

'Nothing on record for that sector of the asteroid field,' Yar responds, his face in concentration as he rapidly reads the output from his monitor. 'Last survey reports just another series of low-yield asteroids, Captain.'

'Can we risk moving the buoy closer, without them detecting it?' I ask.

Chresh's response is not positive in tone. 'Possibly, sir. I wouldn't move more than ten megametres closer; they might pick up on the energy-discharge from the buoy's propulsion otherwise.'

I look towards Threng, but he's already shaking his head. 'Not enough to make a difference, Captain. We would need at least double that to get an image.'

'What about moving the station?' I check. 'We're hauling several tonnes of kelmisite ore—that should help disrupt our output signature enough to buy us a better look.'

'Risky,' Yar replies. He and Threng exchange looks, and Threng nods. 'But possible. But Captain, if they do see us, it will take us at least nine minutes to spool the Under-drive for a dive, unless we dump the ore. At our current position, we're only four minutes out from their weapons range.'

He's correct. The more mass an object has, the longer it takes to spool open a portal to the Under. Little ships can spool fast; ten seconds, maybe less, before they dive Under. Corvettes like the vulture, frigates and the like can take a minute or two, but giant ships—heavy cruisers, warmongers and mining stations like us—can take up to four minutes or longer. For us, it's partly due to our mass, but also partly because this is a centuries-old station that's not been refitted within my lifetime, save for the improvement to mining and crew quarters required for long-haul operations.

'Then we sit tight,' I conclude. 'We're no match for a vulture. Has anything come over the comms?'

'No,' our comms officer, Murthrazen Grithrawrclan, also a nightcoat, advises. He's about two decades older than me, and we're oath-related, with him being clan-sworn, but not sire-sworn (all praise the Eternal Oarth), to my father, the High Baron Grithrawr XXI. Clan-sworn means Murth serves my Dad's barony—hence 'Grithrawr' with the 'clan' ending. But he's not one of my Dad's sires, meaning they don't mate, or else he'd be Grithrawrsire—and I'd have to wind up calling what would likely be his equally insufferable sons my baron-brothers.

Since I am no longer sworn to another baron, either as his sire or his clansman, I returned to my Dad's barony from a hereditary, legal and social viewpoint, hence my title Grithrawrscion—the scion part meaning son. Why we do not just then say 'Grithrawrson' is something that I'll hafta leave to our heritage experts to explain, again yada, yada, yada.

This clan relationship would normally stop me and Murth from sharing a den—though we could if Dad gave us permission—but it would take a death-threat to one of my kids before I ever denned with Murth. He's an ugly old flea-catcher, but that isn't why I don't like him—he's got a personality that would rot shit and just enough smarts to be infuriating. Plus he won't let the past stay in the past, which is the source of most of our fighting.

Saying Murth and I don't get along is a kindness that borders on an outright lie, but being fair-minded for a moment, he is a capable officer, and so our sour familial relationship stays out of the bridge—mostly. I'd transfer him out, but Dad would have words with me if I did, and given my current relationship with Dad, whatever small acts of contrition I can offer won't be tossed aside over some grumpy old comms officer's sullen attitude. I think the only reason he's staying on this assignment is so that my Dad can keep close tabs on me, which is probably the only reason Dad clan-claimed him to begin with. I deserve it, all things considered.

Murth eyes me, impassively. 'Just rubbish background noise, like it's been every day since we've been here. Sir.'

I ignore the undertone of disrespect in his words; it's actually on the polite side for him, and I suspect the seriousness of the situation is dulling the fang-points he normally has for me.

I think for a moment, and the answer of remaining where we are, while whatever is happening all those megametres away comes to its own end, seems to be the best course of action; we're safe and there's no immediately apparent danger to us. Safety first is both my personal and professional mandate—always has been—but even more so these days.

'Yar, prime the Under-drive—keep it in a low idle state and watch our outputs. I want us out of here in three minutes if we need to, and you have orders to dump our payload to accomplish that. Murth, prep the buoy's self-destruct protocols; if we need to dive, transmit an alert to OSS Central Command, then blow the buoy. Threng, plot a dive-route to the nearest Oarthecan war frigate, and give it to Murth to include for his transmission; then keep up your monitoring. Listen for Chresh's signal if the vulture spools. I want you to extrapolate their breach point, if that happens. Confirm.'

There's a chorus of 'Ayes' as each of my bridge officers executes their assignments, and when I carry on with what needs to be said next, I make sure it's understood clearly,

'OSS standing orders are that all encounters with the Pryok'tel are to be reported on with the highest diligence. We are bound by that order to continue gathering as much detail as possible as to why they're here and what they're doing in this system, but as a non-military vessel, we are not bound to engage them, nor to endanger our lives.

'As we all know, Pryok'tel are first and foremost quick-kill ambush hunters, so whatever they're attacking, they'll leave once they've won and taken their prize. We'll re-assess the situation when they dive Under, but first priority is the safety of this crew. Chresh, any sign they're still attacking?'

'No, sir—I can't see any energy output from their systems. It looks like they're just sitting there.'

They're not, and we all know that. They've wounded or killed whatever they were after, and now they're getting ready for dinner. Any lingering thoughts of those wonderful *cerret* pies Rey brought to my quarters flee my head as my stomach twists closed in disgust and rage.

It's quiet on the bridge now; there's always the sound of various computers humming, beeping and chirping their outputs, but my crew is focused on their tasks. Normally, since there's not much to do for bridge officers while the mining teams are extracting the kelmisite, there's a lot of banter going on—not too much, we're all professionals about it—but I don't mind us keeping a light-hearted ramble going throughout a shift. I'm usually the one that starts it off and some of the times, the one who talks the most, though Threng is our heaviest contributor. He's laser-bright clever and having him become Professor Threng for an hour or so, explaining some fascinating tidbit of trivia from his extensive background in the sciences, is a treat the entire crew enjoys.

I'm starting to feel compelled to say something, if only to dispel the thick air of tension and re-establish a sense of normality in the room, when Chresh calls out, 'Under spooling field detected, increasing at ten percent, fifteen percent.'

He gives a concerned look to Threng; a look that is shared by the rest of the bridge. Threng remains calm, focused, and riveted to his output monitor.

'Fifty-five, sixty-five, seventy ...,' Chresh continues a half minute later; I don't know if he's aware that the pitch of his voice is increasing. I bet he'd be a screamer, in the den, I find myself inappropriately thinking—his excitement gets reflected in his voice. Not that I'll ever find out; Chresh has never been anything more than distantly polite with me, and any friendly glance I make his way is quickly discarded with an unmistakable firmness—he's more than justified in his snubbing of me, though.

'Got it,' Threng confirms. 'Exit coordinates extrapolated; three light years, 44.16 by 181.30. The Derresion system.'

'Ninety percent ... Dive wake detected. They're gone,' Chresh reports.

My sigh of relief stays on the inside, and I make sure that my next statements are calming but clear.

'Well done, everyone, well done. Yar, mark in the log the vulture dived at 21h41. Murth, reposition the buoy to three hundred megametres from their last known position; Threng and Chresh, keep us up to date.'

It's a few minutes before we get an update from the buoy's new position. 'Sir I'm reading debris,' Yar indicates, his brows knitting together with concern. 'Polysilicon-ceramic resins, titano-aluminium plates, reinforced compound carbons ... common ship hull components, sir, but the amount we're detecting would be for a small vessel.'

'Life-signs?'

Yar shakes his head. 'Negative, but we're too far out still for that to be confirmed.'

'Image in another thousand megametres, sir,' Threng replies.

We wait, and I'm left to wonder what a small ship was doing all the way out here, by itself, in the middle of a kelmisite-rich asteroid field.

'I'm getting a short-range distress signal,' Murth alerts; I forgive him his missing 'sir' because it's the first comm signal he's been able to detect in the four months since we've been out here mining the asteroid. He looks at me, confused.

'Automated. Non-OSS encoding. Signature is ...' he has to cross-reference some information from his nearby terminal. 'Coalition of Allied Planetary Systems, Salvage Corps, designation V..V.. *Vrunhilda's Grace*. Urgent request for immediate assistance. Repeats.'

There's a slight stagger to his pronunciation of the word "Vrunhilda's"—his UT is feeding him a word that does not exist in our language, and we don't have the phonetics to pronounce it properly.

I stop myself from saying 'What, by the Eternal's giant hairy bollocks, is the CAPS doing out here?', but judging from the looks on my crew's faces, it would have been completely the correct thing to say.

'What language are they transmitting in?'

'CAPS Standard Language, but the Vrun ... Vrun ...' Murth struggles, unable to make his mouth move correctly to pronounce the sound. He taps his display, piping the message to the bridge's audio outputs.

A high-pitched, distinctly robotic-sounding voice announces, 'This is the Coalition of Allied Planetary Systems Salvage Corps vessel *Brunhilda's Grace*. We urgently request immediate assistance. Please reply on this channel, priority one. This is the Coalition of Allied Planetary Systems Salvage Corps vessel *Brunhilda's Grace*. We urgently ...' Murth cuts the audio before the message's second loop completes.

Murth is frowning heavily, and when he looks at me, it's with grim-faced concern rather than the normal haughty contempt he's mastered for me. 'The name of the ship. My translator is telling me that word is a Terran name. It's human in origin.'

And now I do praise our Eternal Father's magnificently hirsute testicles out loud.

CHAPTER 5

Rowland

I cannot move.

But at least it's by choice, and not due to the Pryok'tel harvesting party that is currently scouring the corpse of my *Luck of the Draw*. I've wedged myself into one of our built-in smuggling containers, hidden from sight under normal circumstances between the walls of the ship, but due to the damage *Lucky*'s taken, I can't close the hatch all the way; there's a gap, about five centimetres wide, that I'm peering out of now. The gap will likely not be what gives my presence away though; the Pryok'tel are using hand-held bio-detectors, and so I was left with only one way to survive.

I've activated that chubby, recently-installed biocomp app, with the hopes that its bio-energy disruption is enough to fool the Pryok'tel, but without being jacked, I'm left to experience the app's side effects in the waking world. I am indeed paralysed; I can see, smell and hear, but there's no tactile sensations, and only basic autonomic functions like breathing are still working.

Mia, my sweet sister, if you're alive, thank you from the bottom of my heart for saving me; I will do everything I can to find you and kiss your face a thousand times for your brilliance. If you're gone from this universe, I'll see you next time, in whatever incarnation we take, and make sure the bastards who took your life share your fate.

The one thing going my way is that at least I'm no longer in pain. I may be bleeding out from the wound on my left side, but I'm alive for this moment. My only goal is to keep buying myself moments, one at a time, until the Pryok'tel leave.

They are efficient at their work. I can hear them moving our supplies and what precious few valuable personal items we had with a speed I'd think was impressive if this wasn't my family and my home. I can't see much, which I'm thankful for, because I'm certain I heard a body being dragged. If I did, that had to be Bryce. God, God please save him. I'm not a religious person in the slightest, but in this absolute blackest moment, the worst moment I have had or likely ever will, the only thing left to me is the desperate hope of divine salvation. The situation is so bad that the prayer I cast into the universe is that Bryce is already dead, and that he is spared what will soon happen to him at the hands, and teeth, of the Pryok'tel.

The Pryok'tel are very well known to the CAPS, with the recommended species guidelines being to avoid them at all costs and in all circumstances, which is an understatement so woefully insufficient it could collapse a black hole. The Pryok'tel Hegemony is an expansive network of star systems, thankfully far from CAPS main space, but our borders are shrinking, and everyone in the known systems understands it's just a matter of time before war breaks out.

If the Pryok'tel understood the concept of war, however. War means that two opponents face off until enough damage is dealt that one side surrenders, and the other is the victor. From what little I understand of the Pryok'tel perspective, they do not consider anything other than themselves as being living creatures, and from their point of view, you cannot fight a war against rocks. You mine rocks.

To those lofty and safe philosophers who are hundreds of light years away from where I am now, listening to the sounds of my lover and friend being dragged away, most likely to be eaten alive as I understand it, the Pryok'tel are not, in essence, evil. They have no concept that there's anything in the universe that is like them; they are the only things that are 'organic', everything else is 'inorganic', but I don't think these terms really capture the black-and-white perspective of a species that evolved on a planet where they were the only life form.

The species that have encountered the Pryok'tel have obviously shown them that we are animate, cognitive beings, but that is either not understood or not recognized by Pryok'tel. They have no empathy for other lifeforms because to them, there are no other lifeforms to show empathy to; at best the idea of empathy is a concept reserved for themselves exclusively.

The result is that the Pryok'tel show no mercy, no remorse, no compassion—though they have been observed showing those traits to each other, which is why I do think they're evil. If a rock begs you not to destroy it, and you destroy it because whatever a rock says has no value to you, then you are damn well deep in the blackest of my books.

And those philosophers would counter my argument, stating that having evolved on one of the most biodiverse planets ever discovered, I was waving my Terran privilege around—my species-bigotry blinding me to the fact that just because something isn't human, or isn't fluffy and cute, or doesn't look or act like you, doesn't make its actions you disagree with evil.

But let's do a touch-base, so that we're all on the same page here: they're going to eat Bryce. My Bryce. Whom I love, and fight with, and love again, and whose presence in my universe makes it more beautiful than the brightest star—that Bryce is going to have his flesh torn apart by a Pryok'tel's second mouth, masticated by those four rows of teeth, and swallowed, all while he is alive and screaming, begging them to stop. They're fucking evil. Any philosopher who says otherwise can take Bryce's place to prove me wrong.

The most confusing part is that the Pryok'tel are remarkably human-looking, which makes their 'we're the only living things in the universe' perspective so difficult to accept. They're bipedal, which is nearly the norm for sapient-level species—notable exceptions being the Emumur, who are a gas-based life form whose electro-static consciousnesses inhabit and animate crystalline structures, when they need to, and the Tekethy, the sneak-loving spymasters I mentioned before, who are arachnids with four arms and four legs.

Pryok'tel have mostly normal-looking features, from a human-centric viewpoint at least—except their heads are more oblong, their pigmentation is in the orange range, and they're mostly covered with white to tan spine-like hairs growing from their heads and forearms. With two eyes, two ears, and pug noses, the most differentiating feature is their mouths.

As stated, they have three mouths, which is in fact one horizontal slash across their face that changes width depending on their activity: the first mouth, the smallest and reserved for talking amongst themselves, seems human enough, except that you get the hint something is very wrong when their needle-sharp teeth can be glimpsed. The second mouth, used ...

Bryce. Bryce my god Bryce please don't be alive to experience first-hand what I'm about to describe.

The second mouth, used for eating, is an extension of the first mouth—when they feed, it stretches to about three times the first mouth's size—and here is where the teeth really take centre stage—four rows of long, thin, needle teeth sprout and mesh together, ripping apart whatever is put between them. A bite from the second mouth is fatal, I assume—I've never seen one in reality; all my knowledge about Pryok'tel comes from warning animations the CAPS puts out.

The third mouth, according to those animations, is their 'warmouth', where their jaw bifurcates and extends outwards, allowing bites larger than the size of their own heads, and it's assumed that this is the natural method for killing each other that their evolutionary path provided them—after all, if the only thing to eat on your planet is your neighbour, then cannibalism is what's on the menu, all day every day.

Nowadays, they just use energy-based firearms to do their killing, like the rest of the advanced species of the galaxy. The CAPS rates Pryok'tel technology at slightly below their own level; the Pryok'tel have advanced space flight including Under diving (obviously), decent ship-to-ship combat capabilities, advanced communication networks and the like, but they're about a decade behind us otherwise. And definitely no tech-sharing programme; if I'm to give credit to the CAPS, it would be for this: their cooperation with other species provides a massive advantage that's kept humans relevant in the galaxy. I do understand the potential value of the CAPS, I just don't agree with how they go about it and I know first-hand that a large part of what they say does not match up with what they do.

I've never heard of a Pryok'tel jack, by the way. It's possible they exist, but jacks rarely run into each other, either in cyberspace or in person. We're aware of each other's presence more by the effects of what we're doing or the aftermath of what we've done, rather than actually 'bumping into each other' over cyberspace.

No, I've never been in a battle of the jacks—it would be pointless—you can't 'crash another jack and fry his ass in real life', the safety-precautions built into even the lowliest of biocomp systems are sufficient to prevent that kind of make-believe taking place. I guess if you traced down the jack in real life, you could launch a fleet of drones to wipe out their physical body while they're hooked to the system, but that just seems unsportsmanlike.

I'm rambling on purpose here, and it's easy to guess why; I know what's currently happening aboard the *Luck of the Draw*, and I'm unwilling to process it. It's definitely Bryce that's being dragged across the floor, because I can see them now pulling him by his feet, towards *Lucky*'s breached starboard port. His eyes are still closed, and it's a terrible thing to acknowledge that I wish I were staring at his lifeless eyes instead. I don't want to describe what I'm seeing, it's a cold devouring terror that's paralysing me more than the biocomp currently is, and I am certain I'll go insane if I focus on it too much. How about I describe the Tekethy instead? No? They're really interesting …

Tears are streaming out of my eyes; I can't feel them on my face, but they're doing a great job blurring my vision. Maybe that's the reason we cry to begin with; when something is so awful to behold, our bodies try and spare us the suffering by temporarily blinding us to it. Though the biocomp is preventing me from actively sniffling, I'm sure my nose must be also running a stream of fluids. I've no idea why we do that.

A few minutes pass, and Bryce is nearly at the access-port, when the vertigo-flavoured side effects of the app nearly knock me out. When I first turned it on, I set it immediately to seventeen percent distortion, and tried to taper back its increase-rate to the lowest increment possible, to buy me a longer period in the gap between when the distortion field is powerful enough to blind the Pryok'tel scanners and the forty percent death-zone. I've been partially successful so far, but I'm currently at thirty-four percent … make that thirty-five percent distortion, and the side effects are becoming more pronounced: I'm missing breaths, I've definitely pissed myself, and sometimes my chest tightens painfully, like I'm being slowly crushed by a heavy fist.

The Pryok'tel are still aboard, hauling away our cargo and contents—I see our portable auto-doc crash-kit being taken. My present to Bryce on his second anniversary with us—cost a pretty penny, and I paid for it using legitimate credits—well, the credits were not earned legitimately, but the purchase itself was all above board, which allowed it to be fully registered with the CAPS-F database, providing free updates and lifetime servicing. Also, it seemed 'cleaner' to give as a present. Bryce rewarded me for my thoughtfulness twice that evening; it was a long and lovely night for us both.

At thirty-six percent distortion, I'm beginning to feel like I'm drowning; my lungs are missing every second breath, sometimes the third, and the crushing feeling is now a constant agony. I try to tone down the distortion rate, but it's an all or nothing state: either I keep the distortion-field on and growing, and it ends up killing me, or I turn it off entirely, and the Pryok'tel see me. Bit of a design-flaw, Mia, your user-feedback is not going to be glowing, but I know the fix will be in your first patch.

But I can see there's only two Pryok'tel remaining—I think—I can't see or keep track of them all but I'm praying these are the stragglers, giving one last check for something worthwhile taking. One is carrying Ivan's auto-cooker. I fucking hope you shit-sucking parasites are allergic to chilli and this is Ivan's revenge on you.

At thirty-seven percent, I stop breathing entirely. It's likely I will soon share Mia's blue skin-tone, but I'll have earned mine the hard way. I'm nearly unconscious at this point, so I have my biocomp flush its buffer, flooding my body with the pain sensations it's been storing, forcing myself to stay awake even if my last moments are a body-wracking agony. Get the fuck off my ship get the fuck off my ship get the fuck off my ship …!

I see a blinding white flash through the gap in the container's door, and then I'm tumbling inside the container. *Lucky*'s been pulled into the wake of an Under dive, and she can't recover—the Pryok'tel have stripped too much of her parts for there to be even a chance for her inertia-stabilisers to function any longer. Only two ways to escape a fate involving eternally tumbling in space: either I crash into an object, or the collapse of the universe occurs. Even though this is a dense asteroid field, it's nowhere near dense enough to guarantee the former of these two possibilities.

It's actually great news; the wake means the Pryok'tel have departed, and I immediately switch off the distortion app—noting I was at forty-one percent when I do. My lungs need a moment to kick in again—and there's a level of pain unlike anything I thought I'd be capable of experiencing, but I regain the ability to move my limbs soon enough.

I will admit that I'm pretty sure I'm going to die soon, and it's the strangest sensation: a combination of fear and acceptance that leaves me feeling that I'll give it my best shot but if not—oh well, it won't matter soon anyway. I'm still light-headed, even though the app is entirely shut down; my biocomp is alerting me that my structure has been significantly damaged and that I need to report to a medical facility—and this is not for the sake of a joke. I have programmed my biocomp to alert me if I'm injured severely enough to require professional help—that is, the services of a fully enabled auto-doc, not our little crash-cart. I won't risk auto-docs otherwise; it's one of the reasons I need Bryce on board—left to its own devices, an auto-doc will detect that my biocomp has been tampered with, and either attempt to remove it or just flat-out refuse to treat me.

I also can't get the smuggling container open; either I'm too weak to push the hatch open or there's something on the other side blocking it. My plan was to get to C-deck to check whether the lifeboat is still on board; it's not valuable enough to take the time to remove it, so it's possible the Pryok'tel left it behind, but if I can't get this container door open, they may as well have.

I'm scared; my heart rate is over two hundred, and that's making the wound on my left side bleed freely. I'm not seeing a way out of this and I'm too injured to concentrate enough to see a solution. Plus I'm still tumbling around the container; it's kinda difficult to concentrate when you're basically a lost sock in an old-school dryer. My biocomp is trying to tell me something but I can't focus on the message; it's flashing red danger-text to my cybernetic display, but I can't make any of it out—my vision is doubling and blurring.

'Just stop …' I mumble, and my voice sounds broken, weepy and mewling, in my own ears. I don't know what I'm asking to stop: the spinning, my biocomp, my own life.

I think of my beloved Bryce, my brilliant Mia, my brave Ivan, my sister Bethany. Cor, my sweet Cor. My Mum. My Dad. I want them to be my last thoughts. *I love you, all of you. I'm so sorry this has happened, forgive me.*

My world empties of all perception and sensation. I was right, this is what death feels like.

CHAPTER 6
Toar

It's a funny place, this universe we live in is.

Though we've only been travelling the stars for slightly over two centuries now, just after having overthrown the Pryok'tel during my grand-baron's days, I'm proud to say we've really taken spacefaring between our teeth and chewed. This is partially by necessity, since we're constantly having to guard against the possibility of the Pryok'tel retaking Oartheca back into their Hegemony—forgiveness is just one of the many things those stretch-mouthed butchers just do not understand—but I also like to think it's because it's opened our eyes to the amazing realisation that there's so much grandeur out here waiting for us to discover. There's a wanderlust in our hearts now that just wasn't there before the Pryok'tel, a side-effect of the near-genocide we survived; we've realised there's a need to grow far beyond our old ways.

And it's been a fantastic adventure, for certain—not without its bumps, mind you, but well worth each of those bumps in my opinion; we've met dozens of new species, discovered loads of new worlds, and learned that we're not the first people that the Pryok'tel took over, but one of only two that managed to survive, with the Nurcillices being the other.

Fine, fine folk, the Nurcillices are. They had liberated themselves from the Pryok'tel about a century beforehand, and were still recovering from their enslavement, both in rebuilding their people and in rebuilding their planet, when we first met them out amongst the stars. They saw our plight and shared all that they had learned to help Oartheca start its way back to recovery, and we needed all the help we could get.

The Pryok'tel have devastated Oartheca, plundering huge portions of our lands, oceans and people as they pillaged our world's resources for nearly three centuries. There are wounds that may never heal, both to our people and to our Oartheca, but we're trying our best to get them to scab over, at least. We have a long haul ahead of us, and we may never truly get back to where we were before the Pryok'tel, but the Nurcillices gave us a much-needed head-start, all without asking for anything in return.

They've taken us under their wings (two of which grow out of their backs, and another two form part of their arms) in terms of how to find our own place in the cosmos, encouraging cautious exploration but not isolationism. Ever since the first Pryok'tel harvesters appeared in the Oarthecan skies all those centuries ago, we have known we are not alone in the galaxy, but it took us getting out here ourselves to discover how wonderfully crowded the heavens are. Life is everywhere, and it is all beautiful!

Except the Pryok'tel. Those murdering planet-rapists are going to burn for what they did to us.

Anyway, about three years back, one of our deep-space exploration teams encountered the CAPS, which is an alliance comprising a couple of dozen different sapient species and hundreds more different star systems, all spread out. Good folk, generous like the Nurcillices, though I think it's only because the CAPS don't see us Oarth as a threat to them—the first CAPS vessel we encountered was what they call a warmonger, and that's not a name you just go idly giving out.

From what little I know of them, which mostly comes in the form of gossip from some of the few remaining contacts I still have in the OSSN, the CAPS are a diplomatic, scientific and inquisitive collection of people, and seem honestly keen on forming a good relationship with us—there are talks on Oartheca of one day joining this alliance, though, given our past experiences with the Pryok'tel, we are naturally cautious in creating such a deep relationship, at least until we learn more about the CAPS and get our feet back under our own selves. The Nurcillices have full trade agreements, diplomatic treaties and embassies with the CAPS, and based on their counsel, we're in the process of forming all of those as well.

Right now though, the best we have with the CAPS is a mutual non-aggression pact with limited trade benefits and open, but restricted, resource-sharing. This means we don't have free access to their space, and we'd be causing an incident if we crossed their borders, but we don't attack each other, can trade under some regulations, and generally try to help each other out if there's cause to. I would say that we share technology too, but that's not the case; they give us non-military technology that's been of immense help—particularly the UTs and our auto-docs—but we've nothing to trade them that's anywhere near equivalent in value. It's still the start of a good friendship though, just one where you're not yet too sure about the person you're meeting.

However, there's one little hiccup with the CAPS, and that's to do with one of their member species: humans, or Terrans (I think humans are the species, and Terrans are a type of human from their home world of Terra? I'm not sure). Every member of the OSS, with some exceptions for the Medical Corps, is categorically forbidden, by law enforced by both the OSS and the CAPS, to come into contact with humans—specifically their males—in any capacity: in person, over ship-to-ship comms, or direct communications of any kind.

Even trying to research humans is considered a breach of the law: outside their simplistic description ('A bipedal sapient species native to the planet Terra in the Sol System'), any information pertaining to humans is restricted to our highest level of clearance; beyond that, all that we're told is while they are non-aggressive towards us, humans—again, just their males—and Oarth are never to mix company, and that all attempts to do so must be avoided on pain of the nastiest of punishments.

The reasons are not entirely made clear either; all we're provided is a generic statement that mentions grand ideas like 'bio-incompatibility', 'cross-species contamination' and the ever-friendly 'risk of injury or death'. You'd think all of this intrigue would spark the imaginations of us Oarth, who I like to consider are a cautiously curious bunch, but what the OSS decree lacks in specifics for its

47

reasons, it makes up for in clarity of its consequences: the forbiddance part of the decree is a hard forbid, as in the 'you'll go to prison for the rest of your life, possibly without trial, say goodbye to your family because you're never seeing them again' kind of forbid.

I've made mistakes severe enough to get me both clan-kicked and barred from military service, which is one of the harshest punishments under Oarthecan law, but that punishment would be just the opening blow by comparison to what would happen if this decree were broken. Barring you from the community, from earning value through any form of service? Taking your kids away, if you're one of the few Oarth, outside of our barons of course, lucky enough to have them? It should be enough of a deterrent to discourage even an old fool like me.

This dire 'no-humans-ever' decree rarely comes up though, as OSS encounters with the CAPS are exceedingly few at best—our borders are separated by a large sector of unclaimed space, and so there's almost never a meeting between our two peoples outside of a planned, and heavily regulated, arrangement. The CAPS are aware of OSS restrictions, and enforce the degree from their side with just as much diligence. I've never encountered the CAPS before; their discovery's only been within the last few years and I've been on this station all that time, with no reason for either of us to meet.

Until today, it seems—the CAPS vessel we've just detected has what Murth confirms is a human name *"Brunhilda's Grace"*, and so it's reasonable for us to assume, to one degree of possibility or another, that there might be humans aboard—alive or dead, we don't yet know, but basic civility compels us to at least check if there are survivors amongst the wreckage.

If there are survivors, and it turns out there's a human male with them, we might not be in a position to help without risking that 'hard forbid' punishment I mentioned earlier. Our next steps are going to be on the tricky side, but not impossible; I know the law, and I fully intend to uphold it, but not at the cost of a life. If there's a survivor amongst the wreckage, I will be damned if I'm just going to let them die alone in space without trying my best to save them first.

What we do have going for us is that, based on Murth's frantic research, the names "Brunhilda" and "Grace" are both typically human female names—and the decree is essentially silent regarding human females. He's currently reading over the OSS Interspecies Guidelines, cross-referencing the meaning of the wreckage's identification against the data source the CAPS gave us as part of their first 'come get to know us better' trade-package.

Yes, even though all us Oarth are men, we still know what females are (sort of, in my case). I'm not so sure on the details about humans, but both the Nurcillices and the Pryok'tel have two sexes, so we've known for quite some time that, even though all life on Oartheca is male (except if you're a sponge or a moss or such, in which case you're a clone of yourself), sometimes non-Oarthecan species have more than one sex. In the Oarthecan language, the word for 'female' is *lutala*—a loan word from the Nurcillices, since the concept of 'female' did not exist for us until we met another species. We used to use the

Pryok'tel word—*ges'k*—and the less their filthy language enters ours, the better.

'It could mean that if there are humans, there're no males among them. I've heard their females are their warriors, Captain,' Murth concludes.

'That's not quite correct,' Threng counters, but he's got his Professor Threng voice on, and Murth doesn't appear offended. 'Human males and females work together; they mate-bond like the Nurcillices do but aren't segregated out into sex-specific roles in their society, at least not to the same degree the Nurcillices are. The captain of the warmonger the *OSSN Star of Oartheca* first encountered was a human female, but that doesn't mean there were no males with her.'

'But more importantly,' he continues. 'we can't deduce that there's even humans aboard the vessel, based on just its name. That warmonger had a ...' he drums his claws against his temples, trying to remember. 'Harculcorian name—the *CAPS-N Herrkrolkrek*, or something, but his captain was human.'

'That's true,' Yar adds. 'But humans do make up a decent percentage of the CAPS; it would be reasonable to assume that such a small ship would also have a small crew, who would likely give their vessel a name that had meaning for them. It's probable that if they bother to name things at all, then that name carries significance, just like it does for us.'

Threng nods in agreement with Yar. 'That's probable. From what I know, humans have a lot of social commonalities with us—families, ceremonies, structured governments and the like'.

'Well, we don't even know if there are any survivors, so let's not worry just yet,' I observe. Our little buoy is racing towards the wreckage, but it doesn't have an Under-drive, and its top speed clocks out at just under a quarter of light speed. We're only going to be able to detect life-signs when it reaches within fifty megametres of the battle site, so there's little we can do but just sit and wait until it gets in range. It's going to be some time before we can see if there's someone that needs our help.

'What's our progress on the buoy?' I ask.

Chresh checks his read-outs before replying. 'Just under a hundred megametres; we should have visuals now sir.'

'Bring it up,' I order, and it's immediately apparent that the Pryok'tel have claimed another victim; two halves of a ship's carcass are spinning helplessly out of control, surrounded by blast debris and random contents blown into space. There are lights flashing though, from both sections, so there's still marginal power—and they're not venting atmosphere, which could either mean that it's already been vented or there's force-fields holding what's left in place.

'Hail again,' I ask Murth.

He does so but his reply is fast. 'No response, sir.'

'No choice but to wait until we get close enough, then. ETA until life-sign detection?'

'Another twelve minutes at the buoy's current velocity,' Chresh replies, but then adds 'But Captain, the buoy's sensors can only detect if there is life, not what kind of life. It's a "yes" or a "no" only.'

I'm sure the question Chresh wants to ask is 'so what happens when we get there and it's a 'yes'? It's on all of our minds.

I give my first officer a look. 'Yar, send word to have our shuttle prepped for a rescue attempt.'

Nearly the entire bridge crew, but especially Murth, are giving me wide-eyed expressions of concern; Yar is the only one who seems unfazed by my order. I address his fellow bridge crew with a calm, but clear, tone,

'We don't know yet if there're survivors that need our help. But I don't want it to be out of a lack of preparation that someone ends up dying if we could otherwise have saved them.'

It's important to stress here that the *Lurcaster's Claw* is a mining vessel, not a military star ship, which is why I'm fine with my team's need for assurance, rather than just hopping to execute my orders. The people around me, who I've been referring to as officers, are all currently civilians—highly trained, and highly capable civilians, but none of them are active soldiers any longer, and I choose to run the *Lurcaster's Claw* accordingly.

Yes, like almost all drones, each of my bridge officers has spent at least a decade in one armed branch of the OSS or another, as our mandatory ten-year long conscription starts on our twentieth birthday, when we legally become adults. By our thirtieth birthday, some of us choose to stay in the armed services, though more often, some, like my crew, find themselves seeking less dangerous careers.

In Yar's case, he was a marine for at least fifteen years before joining the Mining Division—he was honourably discharged after suffering a spinal injury that disqualified him from active combat, though if his back still bothers him, he doesn't let on about it. Murth was also a marine, and left when he turned ninety, apparently not with enough of a pension though, since the old arse-thorn needs to find work here on the *Claw*. Chresh was in the Navy, like I was—but his discharge was much nobler than mine; he was one of only a handful of survivors from the Narclathan Skirmish—a terrible battle that saw the destruction of three Pryok'tel deathwings but at the cost of four of our frigates, and the trauma of that battle still haunts him, which is why he's so often quiet and withdrawn. Threng was in OSS Intelligence Services (OSSIS), but he's no longer able to commit to that relentless workload—he's the last surviving drone son of his father, the Baron Drellris, and it's Threng's duty to look after his dad until he passes.

So while all of my men were once trained soldiers and would easily fall in with a military-style command structure, I've chosen instead to captain this mining station as a professional and efficient civilian operation, but always in good spirits at all times. One where my crew feels that their value is not just because of what they were hired for, but who they are as well. The *Claw* is a place every Oarth can be proud to be a part of and know that they belong. It's my one small act in defiance of how I've been treated by the OSS—discarded, diminished—and perhaps, a way to cope with that as well. The result is that I have a team who share ideas and opinions freely, rather than a squadron who just efficiently, if sometimes blindly, follow orders. It's worked well for us so far, but we've never encountered a situation like we're facing.

The up part to my decision is that I have never had a crew member quit, even when the work gets tough, and they work their arses off repeatedly to make sure that we deliver on time, and usually over quota. The pride I get from this has helped me overcome the worst hurdles in my personal life: two of my sons are speaking to me again (Grathculler isn't, but he's always been stubborn). I've stopped being a drain on my family; I'm now able to modestly contribute to my father's barony again, and have earned back a small portion of tolerance in my community, if not acceptance.

So if the cost of my bounce-back is that I sometimes need to explain myself to my crew when I otherwise shouldn't have to, it's a price I'm willing to pay. I have been humbled, and so it's only natural that I should behave humbly.

'Even if we detect life-signs, our scanners won't be able to tell us its species, let alone its sex; that's only going to happen using our eyes. So if there's a need, I'll be the one who attempts a rescue, and take the decision on what to do or not do next. Trust that I share your concerns if it turns out that it's a human male we're dealing with, but whatever this all turns out to be, I'll take the responsibility for—in full. None of you will be made to act outside of the law.'

There's only a small moment of silence after my speech before Yar speaks up. His back is straight, and he's standing tall, like he's at attention.

'Captain, I had the shuttle prepped when we first thought there may be survivors,' he informs. The entire purpose of this statement is to let the bridge crew know that he supports my course of action.

'Good job, First Officer Yar,' I say simply, pretending I entirely expected this action, when I entirely did not. I hope the usage of his official title communicates how thankful I'm for him, but I'll be sure to have him around for an official meal with the captain—the formal kind, mind you—well, maybe a little informal, if he's up for it—at the first opportunity that presents itself.

'Murth, have Dr. Gren meet me in the Prime. When he asks why, tell him it's an order.' I stand while addressing my crew as I start to head to our main meeting room, off-bridge. 'Keep active scans running and alert me when we're in range for life-scans. Don't run them until you have my confirmation. Yar, you have the bridge.'

*****

Our good doctor Grenrethar Harnthscion is an exceptionally talented young physician, and I'm very fond of him, but if I were to be honest with my assessment of the little suncoat, he's still rather on the fluffy side—he's just starting out with his career and his confidence is the first thing that comes up in every assessment we've had since.

He is quite knowledgeable though, fresh from the OSS Medical Corps and full of all the latest tricks and tips of the trade, and is kind in both disposition and bedside manner, which makes him loads more qualified than our last ship's doctor, Yozthren Letherclan. That battle-worn sawbones would sooner stick you with a needle than ask how you were feeling, and we've not had to use needles ever since we had the auto-doc installed, either. Dr. Pokey we called our Yoz, and not in an affectionate way—but the old stormcoat retired two years ago, and that's when Gren joined up.

The *Lurcaster's Claw* is Gren's first space assignment, and I find him to be a cheerful, happy lad. He's given an excellent go of things, though he does get flustered from time to time, probably because he wants to do a good job but doesn't quite know how to go about doing it. Bit too inquisitive, at times; asks me all kinds of questions that make me squirm, stuff that you wouldn't even share with your closest den-mate, but it's always with this innocent professionalism that makes you know that it's all for your own good. Smells like pure sunshine, he does—a bright, joyful, crisp smell that lets you know it's going to be a great day.

No, Gren and I have not shared a den, but with him, it's from professionalism and not from a snub, I hope. It's one of the few rules on board any OSS vessel regarding denning between crew; doctors and personnel are only ever to remain professional with each other, to avoid a conflict in relationships. Wouldn't mind a tussle with dear Gren at all, though—he's a sweetly little thing, all cuddle and plush, and by the Eternal he's seen me starkers more often than any other crewman has, but he and I must maintain a degree of professional separation for him to do his job properly. I'm counting on that professionalism now, because I'm about to ask him for something he'd probably never have thought he'd be faced with on his very first space assignment.

'So Doctor, I'll be quick: we've detected a wreckage, and we're investigating to see if there's life-signs ...'

'Sickies is ready to go!' Gren blurts out, eager to show that he's been working on his confidence. I raise a hand, and he pipes down immediately. Sickies, which is his own term for our med-bay, has caught on so fast around the station you'd think he'd purposefully infected the crew with it. It's his likeability that's done it; it's an adorable nickname and even Murth uses the expression without thinking twice.

'That's good, Dr. Gren. Thank you for being prepared. But we're here because there's some advice I need from you, and I'll need to count on your discretion.'

'Yes, sorry, yes of course,' he replies, deflating, but then hastily adds the forgotten 'Captain. Sir. How may I help you?'

I smile warmly; he does make me laugh, this little suncoat does.

'Well, because of the wreckage's name, there's a chance that humans may be involved.'

His eyes bug wide but it's from excitement rather than alarm. 'Oh really!? Oh, *raur*—really!? Male humans, maybe?'

I'm both relieved and concerned at his response; based on the reaction of my bridge crew, I was predicting it would cause Gren to stumble over himself with worry, but he's almost giddy with anticipation here—and that's causing me to wonder why.

'Possibly, we don't know yet, but we've only got about fifteen minutes or so before we find out if there's any life at all. If there is, I'm taking a shuttle over: if there are humans, what do I need to be prepared for?'

He thinks for a moment, his wide eyes skyward, moving back and forth, reading from a mental notebook. 'Smell, you're not allowed to smell their males. That's the most important one—they'll make you go bonkers for sex. I mean ...' he stops, catching my expression, which is now as bug-eyed as his.

'Sorry, sorry—it's their pheromones, or their hormones, or something, I ... we're not sure, there's not a lot of information about them yet. But their males smell really, really good to us—like a baron's Allure, but *much* more powerful.'

By Allure, he means the scent that our barons produce when they're wanting to start a family; it's their form of marking that lets us drones know that a baron is interested in taking on a sire and procreating. Barons and drones sometimes have non-baby-making den-time together, but the baron will Allure his chosen sire when he does want kids, and that will kick the sire's responses into overdrive—the sire'll become very attached to his baron, frequently to the point of self-sacrifice. Oarthecan history is rife with legends, myths, stories and real examples of sires dying (or killing) for their barons. Alluring a sire transforms him into becoming the most loyal of protectors and providers, all so that the baron can bear their children in a safe environment. I've been a sire myself and can attest to the sway of the Allure—it changed the entire way I thought, right to my core, and I've only ever felt fortunate—blessed, even—to have been chosen for it.

'And it's always on too!' Gren continues. If his enthusiasm were electricity, he could be powering the station all by himself. 'The human men don't even know they're doing it either, it's just normal for them to be like that—and that's really confusing to us Oarth because we'd start getting all lovey-dovey with their males, and most of their men don't even have sex with other men, just their females, as I understand it, and then it gets *really* awkward because we're all "Raur! You are my mate!" but they're all like "No! You're a crazy sex monster!" and ...'

'What!?' I boom. I'm at a complete loss to say anything else. I have slammed my fist into the table; I didn't mean to but what Gren is explaining is preposterous. This can't be the reason!

The volume of my voice and the shake of our Primary Meeting room's metal table frightens little Gren back into his shell. I immediately lower my gaze and raise both hands in apology.

'Sorry Gren, it's all right. Just what you're saying ...'

'I know, it's kinda frightening, I guess. An entire species of super-barons who don't want anything to do with us. Well, not in a den way, at least, and only about half of humans, or so. Human women are fine, it's just the men that are the problem. Their women are the only ones that both the OSS and CAPS will allow us to interact with, but ...'

'What do you mean by 'super-barons'? These humans look like us?' I ask, cautiously.

'No, well, yes, I mean—not like us drones, you know, all big and furry, but they do look a lot like our barons—very much so, like nearly indistinguishable, unless you're up really close to them, which is totally against the law, by the way. You know, no fur, just hair on top of their heads, no tail, two arms, two legs, clawless fingers and toes though, but a penis, two testicles ... I mean, sorry, just their males have those. Their females are like the Nurcillices females are, you know, vulva, vagina and ovaries—egg-producing organs.'

Yes, I do know something of female anatomy and so the words describing what they've got between their legs are not new to me, even though no living thing on Oartheca has them. The Pryok'tel do not share the Nurcillices gender separation rules; Pryok'tel females are identical to their males in terms of cruelty, barbarity, and merciless zest for battle and slaughter. I have killed many Pryok'tel, both from a distance, as well as between my own teeth and claws, and their splayed corpses, insides wrenched open and their contents all spilled out, hold few secrets for me.

'You've seen a human male then, have you?' I check.

'Only on a monitor, as pictures or recordings, but not in real life. They'd never allow that. The only reason I learned it is because it's part of our mandatory xenobiology courses, for doctors who serve in the OSS. It's forbidden, otherwise. There's like two whole classes dedicated to them in the textbooks too, and a test, about how dangerous they are ...'

'Because of their Allure?' This is important; if there's another natural defence or attack capability these humans have, I'll need to know.

'Yes, yes they could really mess up an Oarth. Well, maybe not our barons, there's still conjecture about that. But us drones? Yeah, we'd be like playthings in their hands. One whiff and "I swear to obey you forever, great Human Baron So-and-so, please make me a dad!" It'd be terrible!' he concludes, as though all of this was just some grand 'what if' idea and not something we could be facing.

I'm equal parts bothered and intrigued, but there's no time for more of this lesson. The buoy is likely closing in on the wreckage, and if I'm to face the possibility of encountering a human male, I will need a defence against them. I do however remind myself to tell Gren that being Allured by a baron is not so 'I swear to obey you forever' as he thinks it is; it's strong, certainly, but isn't a complete forfeiture of self-will. My baron never forced me, in any way: he asked, and it was always my pleasure, and my *choice*, to do so. This 'make me your slave, master Baron' premise makes up rather too much of Oarthecan pornography, and like most porn, it's a complete fantasy.

'You said that if I couldn't smell him, I'd be all right?' I ask, hoping that I heard correctly.

'Yes, from their Allure. It's definitely an olfactory response that triggers it. I could give you olfactory suppressors that would stop you from smelling, temporarily ...'

My upper lip curls. Blocking a man's sense of smell is like blocking the ability to see—our entire lives involve detecting scents, aromas, good solid stenches; it's an integral part of how we perceive the world. A man who loses the ability to smell is considered handicapped in society, limited to only basic employment, and since he could never be Allured, no baron would have him either.

'... but you should stay in your spacesuit at all times. Just as a precaution.'

'What if he's hurt, is it safe to bring him on the station?'

Gren loses his enthusiasm immediately, dropping it like it was a burning pile of faeces. 'No, absolutely not. It's not a regular Allure, Captain—there're theories it's up to twenty times more potent than that. And the humans have no control over it. As soon as he boarded the station, his Allure would hit. We would have riots.'

'What if he's hurt badly?' I ask.

'We can't move him into the station, Captain,' Gren repeats, shaking his head, firmly, and giving me a hard look that tells me that he's going to be a fantastic addition to the OSS Medical Corp, standing up to his Captain when there's a need to. 'Never. I can't stop the entire crew from smelling, and there's nothing on record to stop him from smelling the way he does. He cannot come aboard.'

I nod, trying to think of an idea, and then it becomes obvious. 'What if I kept him in the shuttle, could that work?'

The little suncoat thinks for a moment. 'That could work—if you keep the shuttle docked outside the station. But there's only a portable auto-doc on board; it's just for moderate injuries and to stabilise patients prior to transferring to a full-scale auto-doc. If he's seriously hurt ... it wouldn't be enough to save him.'

I'm so proud of him in this moment when I see his cutie little face turn brave and nearly heroic with realisation of what needs to come next.

'I will come with you, just in case,' he announces, determination proudly filling his voice. He is going to get an outstanding assessment when we return to Oartheca.

'Yes, I think that's best,' I conclude. 'We'll work out the details of how to manage your duties between the shuttle and the station, though.'

Gren nods in agreement, and I can already see his clever mind forming a solution. 'We'd need to go through full quarantine if either of us wants to depart the shuttle—a full day if not more. Plus, the suits will need to be sterilised. Anything he comes in contact with will need to be sterilised. That means we would lose the shuttle for mining until it undergoes a top-level cleaning.'

'If it's a "he" at all. This may all be for naught, Gren, but I appreciate all you've said. We've prepped the shuttle but run down there yourself and take a look; if there's anything you need, or the shuttle needs to have, you give First Officer Yar a shout, and he'll get a crew to help you.'

'Yes, sir!' Gren stands, and salutes, but I shake my head at him, gently.

'Salutes are for the military, Gren, but cheers for the thought. Not a word of this, to anyone, mind you. At all.'

He nods; he's a doctor, he knows how to keep secrets. Great Oarth, I hope he knows how to keep secrets, with what he knows about me.

Gren stands and pivots to leave but turns back to me just before exiting the Prime. 'Captain, if this doesn't turn out to be all for naught, and we're going to be rescuing a human male ... won't that get you in trouble? I mean, like, really bad trouble?'

'I'll be all right; we'd be performing an act of compassion, and sometimes, there's wiggle-room in those circumstances. We're going to take every precaution, and I'll not endanger the crew if we need to make a rescue attempt. Regardless, I'll make sure you're held harmless.'

'Oh, I'd be fine, I think—I have an oath that says, "if I can help, then I shall help". That's ancient Oarthecan law, too—solid as Mt. Mekraner itself.' With that proclamation, Gren's steadfast expression hardens with resolve, adorably so.

'Captain to the bridge,' Yar's voice announces over the comms, and I give Gren a sharp nod, indicating he needs to get cracking, and I'm soon to follow him out, to see if all of this does turn out to be for naught, or otherwise.

*****

'Buoy is within range of the wreckage. We're in position to run life-scans, on your orders, Captain,' Yar advises, smoothly resuming his position opposite me as I return to the captain's station on the bridge.

The site of the battle—slaughter, really—is on our main viewscreen, and it's no prettier up close than it was a hundred megametres back. The two halves remain spinning lazily out of control; if there's a survivor in there, he's definitely going to need some anti-nausea meds, at the very least.

'Start with the bridge section,' I instruct, and Chresh executes a series of commands on his monitor, bringing the buoy's scanners to life. A minute passes as the buoy's sensors sweep the mostly still intact bridge section, and an odd feeling of both apprehension and excitement is growing in my chest.

'Nothing,' Threng mutters to himself, disappointed, but then more clearly to the rest of the bridge crew. 'No life-signs detected, sir.'

'Move on to the aft section, then,' I order. My voice is less enthusiastic; in my reasoning, the most likely possibility of survivors would be on the bridge, but after seeing the gaping wound on the aft's starboard port side hatch, it's obvious that the aft was boarded. The Pryok'tel would not have left any survivors in that case—they would take even the dead bodies. No flesh is a waste for the Pryok'tel.

The buoy starts its scan, and I'm mentally writing this incident up in my next log entry, puzzling out the right recommendation for the OSS to provide the CAPS about all of this, when there's an audible 'bing!' from Threng's monitor.

'*Raur* there's one!' he exclaims, but then quickly regains his professionalism. 'Life-sign detected ... barely, minimal signal. About ...' he fiddles with his monitor's tuning apps, 'twenty-one metres from the starboard hatch, first deck. I'm detecting they still have an atmosphere and marginal gravity online; but power is failing—it won't last more than an hour, at best.'

'Murth, repeat our hails.' He does so, but since his response is the same as from before, I do not hesitate from my next commands. 'Yar, alert our shuttle to make final preparations for launch at 22h30. Tell Dr. Gren to board, and that I will be joining him shortly.'

'Sir, it's the First Officer's duty to lead this rescue,' Yar interjects.

I give him a patient, appreciative smile. Under normal circumstances, he is correct—regardless of what the stories say, captains don't just give up the command chair to go and have shuttle tours around the station whenever there might be an excuse to do so. But these are far from normal circumstances. I suspect though that his reminder is nothing to do with 'official procedure'—he's trying to protect me from making another mistake with my career.

'I think you'll find that I'm the best candidate, First Officer Yar,' I counter, in a positive, matter-of-fact tone. 'Unless you know of another crewman with a half-century of hands-on flight experience? Bit of a tricky rescue, what with that aft section spinning like a whirligig gone rogue. Best candidate, and all.'

He doesn't immediately reply—I think he's offering one last chance for me to gracefully turn this over to someone who would be protected by the 'I was just following orders' defence, but that won't work here; I'd be the one giving the order, and so it would just be two of us facing one of the harshest laws we have. I know in this moment, Yar would share that possible fate with me, to spare me in some way if he could, but I won't let him. That, and, yes, I am the one with the most piloting experience; I am the best choice, despite everything.

'Aye, sir,' he finally relents and presses the comms button to communicate my orders to the shuttle bay.

I make one last statement to my bridge crew before exiting. 'Dr. Gren and I have devised a solution to our dilemma; if it turns out that this involves a human male, and we're successful in our rescue, then all three of us will remain on the shuttle, orbiting the station. There's to be no attempt made to bring him aboard, under any circumstances, and there will be no attempt to board the shuttle, under any circumstances, without my *and* Dr. Gren's authorisation. Those are direct orders. Confirm.'

After the chorus of hearty 'Ayes', I turn to Yar one last time before departing the bridge. 'You have command, First Officer Yar.'

CHAPTER 7

Toar

I'm beginning the last of the shuttle's pre-launch confirmations; the board is green but I'm noticing from the corner of my eye that Gren is fidgeting in his chair beside me. He catches my raised eyebrow and immediately stops.

'Sorry, suit itches,' he explains miserably. His hands are not yet gloved, and the temptation to scratch himself cannot be risked; though our spacesuits are made from highly flexible carbon fibre mesh—quite impervious to being torn from a good solid scritch—his claws could catch a flap, clasp or any one of the dozens of various sealing gadgets we need to ensure suit integrity. Popping one of those open means the whole suit-system check that he's already completed would need to be done again.

'I take it you only received basic space environment training?' I ask casually, as I finish the confirmations. Before even being considered for acceptance aboard a space vessel, a minimum six-week OSS-certified space survival course is required, but that's hardly enough time to get used to the suit. They do itch—they squash and mess up our fur badly and the only known cure is to 'get used to it'.

'Yes, of course, captain sir. Haven't worn one since though,' he admits.

I tell him the known cure in an encouraging fashion, and then as the shuttle's last confirmation comes back as a positive, I ask him if he's ready.

'Yes, captain sir.'

'Sir or captain is fine, Gren. You can even call me Toar if you like, I'm not a stickler for that.' I am most certainly a stickler, while on duty at least, but I want the little suncoat to relax.

Gren grips his seat restraints, bracing for the jolt the shuttle craft makes as we unmoor from the mag-clamps currently holding us in place in the *Lurcaster's Claw's* docking bay. Our shuttle's primary purpose is to deploy miners and their gear into tighter nooks and crannies to get at the rich ore veins that the station's large-scale lasers would otherwise destroy, or to strategically place mining charges to carefully dislodge and clear passageways that would otherwise be inaccessible.

Being Pryok'tel in origin, comfort played no part in the shuttle's design; it's large enough for two pilots and eight miners, in full kit, plus a secured storage in the back for hauling charges, heavier equipment and the like—though I've heard naughty rumours that it's seen use as an illicit den for the miners to enjoy, hopefully between shifts and not on the clock. There's one head, comprised of little more than a privy and a sink, opposite a storage locker that's been converted into a makeshift galley, holding a re-heater, water processor and a couple of drawers full of snacks and sundries (mostly supplies for denning, substantiating those rumours about what goes on in the back storage). The galley is completely outside regs, but a man's got to have a hot cup with him in order to be truly on break, so I pretend I don't notice either the galley or what's kept there.

The shuttle does have its own Under-drive though, but it's only powerful enough for interplanetary journeys, which is fine for when you need to go about a system—we deploy the shuttle at smaller sites that aren't worth setting the station up at, and what we reap from these mini-site deployments is often what helps us exceed our assignment quota.

The shuttle is equipped with two medium-watt laser cannons, which can punch through rock deep enough for the miners to really get into a spot when they need to, plus the ability to launch mining rockets and deploy charges from on board. Bit dangerous, what with these being miners and all, but I make sure shuttle-miners are clocked at twice their normal pay, and Master Foreman Narls never has an empty spot on his assignment roster to choose from.

When I boarded though, all the equipment had been cleared out and the interior given a fast scrub down; the strong scent of disinfecting soap is not enough to cover the lingering odour of kelmisite ore, machine oil and hard-working men, but it will have to do.

I notice though that Gren's had the chance to establish a small triage in the storage section of the craft, complete with all the gear he says he needs to fix injuries that the shuttle's auto-doc can't, particularly fuller-size versions of the shuttle's first aid kits; the ones that are usually there contain little more than a dermal re-sealer and disinfectant, to look after minor on-the-spot injuries—but the ones Gren's brought have things like bone-menders, surgical tools and a pharmacy's worth of meds for whatever might crop up. He's also brought along three crates of emergency survival gear; each crate holds a week's worth of food and water supplies for a man, plus rudimentary hygiene and sleeping kits. He sees me eyeing his handiwork and explains.

'I figure we might need to stay on the shuttle, for a bit, if this human is male and hurt, before we can head back to Oarthecan space. I wanted us to have the basics on hand, without needing to return to the station.'

'Clever,' I reply. 'If it turns out this is a human man, then we'll dive out of the asteroid field, and contact the OSS for additional instructions. I'm sure they'll send the nearest frigate over to take him off our hands. That could take a while, depending on how far away the frigate is, but I think they'll make it a priority.'

'My thinking too, Captain,' Gren agrees, then ponders for a moment. 'Shame our sensors can't tell the species though—I've heard rumour that the new CAPS vessels can, but I doubt it, unless they've got the ability to detect DNA from millions of kilometres away. Not likely. I mean I guess they could extrapolate the strength of the signal against the frequency and wavelength, but all that would do is tell you "this could be an Oarth" or "this could be a *nartholor*" or "this could be a *cerret*, maybe a rather fat *terk-terk*" or ...'

At his mention of *cerret*, and as he continues to spill out the contents of his thoughts, I'm reminded of the fine-looking Rey and his fine-looking pies, the latter of which will have likely gone stone-cold sitting in my cabin, the former probably down in the mouth for losing out to duty. Poor lad, he had done a wonderful job coming to visit his captain for the first time, and I was so terribly flattered, too. These days, it's especially sweet to be the apple of someone's eye, and Rey did go to so much trouble to make sure it was all proper. I make up my mind to follow up with Rey when there's a chance, and feast upon both him and his delicious-smelling pies.

Smelling. That's triggered a forgotten nag in my brain, and I interrupt Gren, who is still explaining the improbability of there ever being a life-sign detection system that can tell the difference between a *corlurg* and a similarly sized *kernorkess*.

'Gren, you mentioned before that we'll need olfactory blockers, just in case? I've not taken mine.'

He snaps out of his fountain of words to regard me. 'Yes, we'll need to take them prior to leaving the shuttle. They're fast-acting, and last about four hours for me, closer to three for you. I brought my entire inventory though, plus supplies for making more. We should always be under the suppressors, and ideally in our spacesuits too, if we're in proximity to the human. If this life-sign we've detected turns out to be a lost *nartholor*, then the worst we're looking at is a few hours not being able to smell him stinking up the place.'

'Helmets and gloves too?' I double-check. 'Won't that make it difficult if you have to treat injuries?'

He smiles a short smile. 'Yes. It will.'

'What about eating, and the like?' I ask, frowning. It appears that remembering the *cerret* pies has caused my stomach to grumble about being so empty.

'Oh, don't worry Captain, I thought of that. The back-storage area has been emptied of all its gear. Master Foreman Narls confirmed that its doors can be hermetically sealed, and its air filters are easily capable of screening out any nasties. I've built a last-minute guest suite-slash-recovery room there, well, as best as I could in the time we had, but you were right—the docking-bay crew really hopped to it after Yar had a word with them over the comms—never seen a dozen men move so fast, I wish I had their help when I was moving in!'

He's caught my increasingly impatient expression and refocuses with a short clearing of his throat.

'Yes, anyway, the storage is where we'll keep him after our rescue, if it turns out that's what needs to be done. Seal him in, then we can take off the suits and have dinner and such, or have a rest, whatever we need to do. We'll have to go back into the suits if we have to be in physical proximity to him—if it's a him—and oh, and I guess when he needs to use the facilities, unless we get him a bucket or something, but that's just rude for a guest.'

'Hopefully not a bucket,' I agree. He's a smart tack, this little one, and I find his cheeriness a comfort to the stress I would be otherwise contending with. Docking the shuttle to the aft section's hatch is going to be sticky, since it's tumbling through space right now—I've done it before but it's not what I would consider a pleasure-trip across the stars.

'You've been on shuttle missions before, right?' I ask, keeping my tone conversational—Gren's grip on his seat's restraints has tightened, especially after we first cleared the docking bay's hatch and are in the wide gloom of open space.

'Yes, numerous times, in training. Mostly in the simulator but I did complete the required live flights—only had to retake the last two twice, you know, when they do the loops and pivots to see how you handle sudden changes in directions and stuff,' he explains.

'Well, you were hired to be a doctor, not a pilot, so no one's going to hold that against you. You've dived Under though?'

'Oh yes, that's easy—don't even notice that part—it's all 'Dive portal open' then 'whoosh' and pop—we're on the other side. No problems there.'

Gren has given the most simplistic, but nonetheless accurate, description of diving Under. From the diver's perspective, journeying through the Under and back is instantaneous. The Under is a three-dimensional universe running parallel to our own, but not a four-dimensional one—there is no time in the Under, but there is still the ability to travel through it at whatever velocity you entered with.

The way it works is that you first plot two points in space: the portal point you're entering the Under from, and the portal point that you want to exit the Under at, where the distance between the two depends on how powerful your Under-drive is. The distance for drives on a smaller vessel, like our shuttle, is limited, but larger vessels that hold bigger drives can generate portals with many light years' worth of distance between them. The *Lurcaster's Claw*, for example, despite its enormous mass, can dive nearly six light years in one go—less if we're carrying lots of ore, though. Of course, a dive like that would max out our drive, and we'd need near a full day to completely recharge, but it's still rather impressive.

Once you've got your portals plotted, the next step is to charge your ship's engines to release their best velocity at a trigger, then open your Under portals, release the trigger, dive Under, hope you've done your maths properly, and your ship arrives at your destination portal (if not, you are well and truly fucked, mate), and then pops out the exit. The distance you travel in the Under is the same as the distance you're planning to travel in our universe, and at the same velocity, but because no time elapses in the Under, the journey is perceived as instantaneous to the traveller when they return.

How long you can stay Under, which equates to how far you can go in our universe with each dive, depends not only on the strength of your drive, but also on the mass you are submerging—with more mass costing more fuel to open portals for the distance you want. Talented divers are modern-day arithmancers, with the best ones being able to calculate cunningly efficient dives that get the fattest ships the farthest distance for the smallest fuel cost, but the rest of us have to rely on our Under-drive's systems to handle the calculation. This little shuttle has enough strength, power and fuel to travel up to a lightyear's distance, which as I said, is great for interplanetary exploring but rubbish for interstellar travel.

As I pilot our shuttle a safe distance from the station, I've started to spool the Under-drive, laying in the exit portal to just outside of the wreckage zone, so that I'll have lots of room to manoeuvre on the other side, as well as ensuring our breach-wave doesn't end up affecting the site. While the Under dive engine spools, the system begins to calculate the entrance and exit portal requirements necessary for the dive from, and subsequent return to, our universe, and it's only upon confirmation that both the engine and the portal are sufficiently prepared that the command to dive becomes available.

This is what I had Yar do when I asked him to prime the *Lurcaster's Claw*'s Under dive previously—I wanted the system to have all of these calculations completed, ready to go, with a fully charged Under-drive, so that we could dive immediately if we had to. It is possible, if you're clever like our Threng is, that by monitoring the amount of time an Under-drive spools, versus the mass of a vessel, its current spatial orientation, and the charge being given off by its drive, to extrapolate where a vessel's diving to—and that's what Threng pulled off when he indicated the Pryok'tel had dived to the Derresion system.

'Okay, Under-drive charge complete; propulsion charged, dive portal opening. Brace for dive in three, two, one ... diving Under,' I advise, and then release the propulsion trigger.

We momentarily dip before we hit a wall of pure white light; it's the only phenomenon the eye can detect when breaching a dive portal—and then we're about a thousand kilometres from the wreckage site. I glance at Gren, checking if he's all right, but he's just casually looking at the system monitors in front of him, reviewing the details of what our sensors are picking up.

'Looks like the aft section is 21.43 by 44.66, nine hundred kilometres,' he says, and then gives me a pleased smile. 'Nice shot, Captain.'

'Thank you, Doctor. Now let's see if I can get us docked properly. Are we still receiving life-signs?'

'Yes, no change from previous readings, but ...' Gren checks another read out '... it looks like their power-reserves are dropping at a faster rate. I'd say we've got about thirty minutes to dock before their gravity plating goes offline, as well as the emergency kinetic shielding keeping the interior habitable. If that goes— *rooosh!*' he exclaims, puffing his claws out. 'Everything inside the ship gets sucked out into space.'

'Seems I have my work cut out for me then. Hang on Gren, we're about to do some of those loops.'

'That's fi ...' he starts, but his voice goes too high for him to finish his words as I punch the propulsion to max, cutting the short distance to the wreckage within a matter of seconds, slowing to a near dead stop when we arrive, before I begin orientating our shuttle's port. There's no time for coddling him; thirty minutes is too close a claw-clip for that.

'Okay, altering our axis to align with the current spin of the wreck, increasing speed to match trajectory and rotation ...' I tap my screen controls, watching my monitor's yellow output until it verifies our hatch is aligned with the wreck's. When the monitor switches to a green output, we've matched sufficiently to extend our docking bridge, but that's going to require some manual finessing on my part.

'Extending bridge; adjusting axis, adjusting axis,' I start, but then there's an audible bonk that reverberates through the shuttle, as our docking bridge fails to connect to the wreck's hatch and skitters off.

'Ooops, try again!' Gren exclaims, trying to encourage me. I do not acknowledge him.

'Reattempting,' I mutter, focusing on the damnable, fidgety-fucking-second-hand-Pryok'tel-piece-of-junk-shit-controls-I-am-going-to-eat-that-mange-encrusted-Darl-Krariclan-alive-because-that-un-sire-able-son-of-a-sire-spitter-swore-the-controls-were-work …

My next attempt results in a pleasant clicking noise as our docking bridge seal-bonds with the wreck's starboard hatch. It takes another moment, but green access lights surrounding our shuttle's port side hatch spring to life, indicating the connection between our vessels is good. With that confirmation, I'm able to gradually decrease the shuttle's rotational speed, slowing our spinning until it's safe to apply the shuttle's inertia dampeners, finally bringing both us and the wreck we're now tethered to out of the spin and to a full stop.

'Well done again, Captain!' Gren cheers, and this time I can't help but grin at his good nature.

'Okay, helmets and gloves—double-time.'

'No, not yet. Gotta block our sniffers first,' he says, releasing the restraints from his chair and bounding towards his kits stowed in the back. Unzipping one, he fishes out two small plastic pill containers and a small glass ampoule, then returns.

'Here,' he says, handing me one of the bottles. 'Take two, and chew, hold it on your tongue but don't swallow. Let it completely melt on your tongue, and keep your mouth closed for a moment afterwards. Watch me.' He demonstrates, exaggerating his movements for my benefit. After about a thirty-second demonstration—time, doctor, time—he sticks his broad tongue out for me to inspect, showing that it's empty.

'Your turn: two, chew, melt, hold,' Gren diligently instructs, and I follow his orders to the letter, sticking my tongue out afterwards.

'Excellent, perfectly done!' He reaches up to pat me twice on my shoulder in praise. Gren has been my doctor for the last two years and I have grown entirely accustomed to his pats-for-good-behaviour reward; another doctor who was even a hair less sweet than our little Gren would not receive the same good graces from me.

'Okay, now to test.' He snaps the ampoule, breaking it in half at its tapered middle, and holds it out before us. 'What do you smell?'

I give a good and proper sniff to the air. 'Nothing,' I indicate, feeling apprehensive about that response. I'm well and truly nose-blind now, and it's not at all a pleasant experience.

Gren follows suit with a series of deep nose sniffs. 'Same. We should be smelling putrid oilyfish guts, according to the label. I think we're good for suiting up, Captain.'

I nod, and the pair of us scramble to don our helmets, then gloves, checking ourselves then each other's clasps and buckles to ensure they're all locked down properly. Green confirmation lights trigger inside our helmets as our suits verify their sealed integrity. We're good to go, and we fetch our gear.

Due to the involvement of Pryok'tel in this incident, I'm insisting that we're both armed during this rescue—though the Pryok'tel are not often known to linger after a kill, it has been recorded that they will sometimes wound a single foe, and then wait in the shadows to see if anyone comes looking for him. It's not likely in this situation, given the speed of the attack and the Pryok'tel's subsequent departure—this was a 'planned hit' from my perspective, but I won't take that chance. Though we have only detected one life form, it is possible that the Pryok'tel are falsifying the signal, while masking their own—life-sign detection does have limitations and there are known ways to fake a signal, so I won't take it for granted that our readings are an absolute guarantee of our safety.

However, we are a civilian mining vessel, and our choice of weapons is limited accordingly: coil-gun pistols, capable of firing a hundred rounds of super-heated, molten non-ferrous slugs at devastating velocity; they are simple to use, reliable, and easily punch through Pryok'tel body armour with even a halfway decent shot. It is a perfect weapon for both novices and veterans, a standard sidearm throughout the OSS due to its consistent performance and relatively simple care and maintenance. Still though, I'd prefer my OSS Naval Forces plasma sniper rifle, where a single well-placed shot will vaporize an opponent down to the atomic level, from up to a half kilometre's distance. Definitely not a safe weapon in the hands of a civilian, and I had to turn mine over when I left the navy.

But I have brought my own plasma-powered, molecular-lattice carbon-steel sabre, whose twin blade-edges are honed to within the width of a few molecules. When it's unpowered, these edges are merged, creating a single blade that's sharp enough to slice through light body armour and whatever else is underneath. For tougher jobs, like hull-plating, blast-doors and mech-armour, powering the sabre will split the blade apart by a centimetre, and a beam of plasma surges between the two parallel blades, with an energy output that's enough to get whatever I need cut, cut. It's a lightweight beauty too, reaching a metre and a half long, with a power supply that will last a full hour before needing to recharge. It was a bond-gift from my baron, Cralren, and I've enjoyed nearly forty years of service with it, downing a battalion's worth of Pryok'tel against its edge.

As I hand the coil-gun to Gren, I'm surprised how easily he accepts it, reconfiguring its grip to fit his littler hand, then holstering it smoothly with a professional's dexterity, only needing a quick glance in order to do so. Little suncoat is full of surprises, it seems. He's also armed himself with a portable scanning device, and quickly resumes adjusting its settings to his satisfaction.

'Got him,' Gren's voice tells me, over our suit's comms, and he shows me his scanning device, where a white blip is pulsing on a grid-display, the number twenty-five just under it. 'Ready to depart on your order, sir.' Seems that getting suited up has put Gren's nerves in the rubbish bin; it's not uncommon—

something about how the clothes make the man—but I'm still pleased to see it.

'Confirmed. Verifying seal integrity—check. Verifying docking bridge integrity—check. Opening port side hatch.'

We step into the docking bridge and are greeted by the faint blue glow of the wreck's emergency kinetic shields on the opposite end. I can see only a darkened interior beyond the shield, sometimes quickly illuminated by pulsing emergency lighting—and in between those pulses, it's apparent that the Pryok'tel have had their way with this ship. Gren and I approach the shield, and he spots and points out the exterior controls that will release it—they're in lockdown mode but it only takes a few punches on the control panel before the shield blinks out. There's a swoosh of air as the wreck's atmosphere rushes into the docking bridge's, sending various detritus billowing along with it.

'North by north-west, twenty-one metres ahead,' Gren advises, pointing with two fingers inside. 'One and a half metres down, sir.'

'Confirmed. Entering site. Hold for my signal to enter,' I order, and proceed when Gren provides his confirmation.

I am thankful for the experience my service in the OSS Naval Forces provides me for times like these; I know how to proceed in a safe, efficient manner, checking perimeters, verifying the site, constantly assessing for danger. What I see between the pulses from the emergency lighting tells me that this was a civilian vessel; there are domestic items strewn haphazardly around in an awful jumble, both from the Pryok'tel's looting and the subsequent tumbling through space, as it seems the wreck's gravity plating is no longer able to do its job properly in stabilizing the interior.

After checking this first entrance corridor to sufficiently feel, to the barest minimum extent, that it is safe, I signal Gren to enter. My suit's chronometer tells me that we've got about fifteen minutes to locate and retrieve our survivor before the wreck's power goes offline, and the emergency kinetic shield that's blocking the wreck's other wound, the one that formerly connected this aft section to its bridge, gives out. When that goes ... 'rooosh!', as Gren so eloquently described.

'Stay here. If I don't return in ten minutes, get back to the shuttle and seal the access port. My suit will keep me alive if this wreck depressurises, but I want you on board the shuttle in that case.'

'Confirmed, sir,' Gren replies, his voice strong but I think I hear nerves creeping in, and I'm reminded of his inexperience. He is still doing a top-notch job for a recently graduated doctor's first time in space, and I have every confidence that he'll be able to handle whatever happens next with skill, though I acknowledge I have no choice but to feel this way. 'Survivor is sixteen metres ahead, one and a half metres down, from our current position. Still north by north-west. Good luck, Captain.'

Though there's a risk in doing so, I've no choice but to proceed rapidly into the interior; it's cramped for someone of my size, and that is made worse by constantly having to bypass various pieces of strewn furniture, cargo and personal belongings that did not meet the Pryok'tel's standards for looting. Still, though, I'm making good progress, but I soon reach a corridor whose ceiling supports have collapsed, blocking my passage.

'Gren, how far am I away?' I ask into my suit's comms.

'Three metres, sir, and one metre down.'

I get busy at clearing the collapsed beams as quickly as I can; I'm not worried about nicking my suit, but I do need to be somewhat careful lest one of the damn dozen or so seals on it pops. When I've cleared a path sufficient for me to squeeze my bulk through (maybe I should switch to a salad, instead of *cerret* pie, for tonight's dinner), I check in with Gren again.

'One metre by one metre; he should be right in front of you!'

I look around desperately, unable to see anything resembling a person: there's only flooring, damaged ceiling and wall panelling ... I see it then: one of the wall panels is slightly ajar, but there's a collapsed beam blocking it from opening further. I push the beam away, and the wall panel swings open, spilling its contents out before me.

*****

I am no poet.

I like to ramble, and sometimes, as much by chance as by design, it results in a clever string of words coming together that can make my listener laugh, or when I try and I'm lucky, to look away bashfully. I'm not an eloquent man by any means, but at this moment, I wish I had spent my life studying the best words our people use to describe our world, because only those best words could suffice to describe what I see now.

Beautiful.

He is beautiful; whatever that word once meant to me, its meaning's been reset to a new standard, now and forever more. Its inadequacy is almost insulting, but it is the only word I know that even comes close—the only one my mind can think. The word repeats in a loop as I behold who is before me: I am staggered, unable to breathe. Shocked, and humbled, by who I see.

Every romance story worth its print has a moment like this, and it's always made me laugh at its ridiculousness. 'He's so pretty he stole my breath away' or 'he's so gorgeous my heart skipped a beat' or 'when I saw his lusty beauty, I went rock-hard in my trousers.' Pure rubbish, the lot of it, I've always thought; the words of the inexperienced attempting to oversell the impact of a moment.

And yet ...

I am a well-practised lover; I enjoy my den-time as much as any man, maybe a tad more, and I have had the excellent fortune to share time with a wealth of handsome men, many of them very truly so. I've been a sire too, for my Cralren, though I am not his anymore, either in law or his love. Midnight-black hair with an inky lustre, intensely brown eyes that heated your soul with the faintest of glances, brushed bronze skin, a delicious cock generous in both form and offerings, and an arse that took all I had to give with hunger and want, Cralren and I made an excellent pairing. His slight frame melted together with my heavier one in a way that sent us into a shared ecstasy that only a baron and his chosen sire can experience. Despite his dismissal of me, all those years back, his beauty has not been diminished in my eyes nor in my heart, not even for a moment.

And yet ...

I will go to my grave, twice over, never speaking this thought out loud, even under the worst of tortures: by comparison to the man before me, Cralren may as well be Murth. Forgive me, father of my children, forgive me for that most despicable insult.

But he is *that* beautiful.

*****

'Did you find him?' Gren asks desperately over the comms. 'Captain? Report? Captain! We're running out of time! Captain Toar report!'

I am forced back into this universe, out of the one in my head, where this man and I are tangled together in the deepest of embraces, sharing our bodies, our hearts and our souls as one. I'm exaggerating my chivalry here, though; be assured that most of the words running through my head right now are vulgar three-to-five letter terms, with a particular repeat of 'fuck' in all its variants; they're fuelling me to conjure a lust-soaked fantasy world with a ferocity I did not think I had in me anymore. As I've said, I'm not an eloquent man.

Snapping back to this universe, with all of its panic, danger and impending disaster, is a jarring experience though, and it takes one more imploring 'Captain!' before I reply.

'Yes ... survivor located,' I stammer, then more firmly, 'Attempting retrieval.'

With what little care the direness of the situation allows me, I reach into the storage unit that this radiant man had managed to hide himself in, and gently pull him out and free. I immediately see his injuries; there's a nasty gash in his left side that bleeds again from my effort to retrieve him, and I'm almost sent to shivers at the thought of being the one to cause this. His left leg looks injured too—it's not lying properly, and there's a small gash and welt on his forehead. But his eyes are closed, and he doesn't stir from my efforts; I can tell he is alive from the shallow breaths his chest still provides him, so wherever he is right now, he's not in pain. I sweep him up into my arms; he's not at all heavy, only slightly more than Cralren ever was, and so it's no problem for me to carry him in both arms, safely cradling his head with one hand while I turn around.

'Retrieval successful, returning to the shuttle now. Gren, take the helm and begin the sequence to disengage the docking bridge—hold until I'm on board.'

'Is he hurt?'

'Yes.'

'Take him directly to the triage in the back of the shuttle on your arrival, Captain. Is he ... human?'

67

I pause before replying, momentarily remembering the consequences my answer will bring. 'I believe so.'

There's no response, and I'm carefully picking our way back through the debris, ensuring that my Baro ... the survivor, the survivor is kept from being further harmed as I bounce off too-close walls in my haste to get to the exit. I can see the access hatch getting closer when the gravity under my feet begins to falter, sending me bounding with each of my steps as lighter junk begins to float off the floor.

'Captain, the wreck's power is going to give out any minute, you need to be on the shuttle!' Gren orders; there's an urgent, panicked but unshakable insistence in his voice. 'I've prepped propulsion but you need to be here now!'

I'm trying, you bossy little suncoat!

I can see the exit clearly now, and the sound of groaning metal can be heard as the wreck and our docking bridge wrestle to stay together. I'm leaping now, using the reduced gravity to partially sail over the remaining distance, every glance I have shared equally between my destination and my precious cargo. He's still completely out to the world, which I'm briefly envious of as I realize how bleak our situation is becoming.

I'm nearly at the exit when the last of the wreck's emergency kinetic shielding blinks out for a moment, sucking us back into the interior of the vessel as its atmosphere explodes out into space. I hear the shield snap back in place, but the vacuum effect has moved me further than I can afford. I may not make it. Oh Great Oarth I may not make it. *Please, please I need to make it. Save your son, please oh Great and Eternal Oarth, in his moment of terrible need, shine your glory into his heart and let your strength be his, let your love see him through his dark times and on to succour, oh Great Oarth save your wayward son ...*

With a final bound my boots hit the first floor-panel of our docking bridge, and I'm able to close the narrow remaining distance in one giant leap, landing on the hard titano-aluminium plate of the shuttle's floor. Gren's wide-eyed expression at my arrival is quickly followed by a slamming of his fist on to the hatch's controls, and the shuttle seals tight.

I gently set our survivor down in the nearest alcove that forms the port side benches that our miners sit in; there's no time to get him to the triage but in the three or so moments I must spare for this task, I manage to slap and secure a few restraining buckles around him. It's going to have to do.

'Gren, release the docking bridge,' I order, and quickly take my position at the helm, but I'm not yet fully seated before the last of the wreck's shielding gives way and its atmosphere flees into space with tremendous fury, the force of which rockets our tethered vessels backwards—all while our docking bridge is still attached. There's a terrific screaming of metals being wrenched as both the wreck and our shuttle are sent hurtling through space under the explosive force of the escaping atmosphere.

I've managed to grip the seat of my chair in time, so that I'm not launched crashing into the front of the shuttle, but it's taking all my strength to just stay in place. Gren squeals in fright, but he is desperately trying to break the connection to the wreckage, pounding its release command repeatedly.

'Take the helm!' I blast. 'Gain control of the ship!'

His hands, awkwardly gloved, are nonetheless frantically scrambling over the surface of the control helm, and he's trying with all his might to stabilise us and get us to safety. A nasty jolt staggers me to the ground as our docking bridge finally gives way and tears free from the wreck, but we're now sent spinning out of control, a whirligig gone rogue, as I inadvertently predicted.

I hear Gren give a frightened whine and I forgive him immediately for it, for despite his fear he is not giving up, and is still desperately adjusting and correcting to get us stabilised. The front cockpit of the shuttle consists of three panels of reinforced transparent carbon, as hard as diamonds, and so we're treated to a streaking blur of stars spinning around us with a vomit-inducing intensity. I had almost got myself into my pilot's chair before the g-force from the spinning hit, but now I feel my claws ripping the seatback, trying to keep hold as tightly as I can, as my feet begin to lift from the ground.

I can only spare a moment to think about the state of our survivor, and whisper another quick prayer to the Eternal Oarth on his behalf.

Gren is not giving up though, tilting against the force with all his strength to try and maintain his position at the helm, still entering commands to the propulsion unit to slow us down; his poor sweet face tight in a teeth-clenched grimace, portraying both terror and the refusal to give into it. His defiance is an inspiration to behold; in this moment, he is the handsomest he will ever be—the true spirit of the Eternal Oarth radiating from him—and his valiant efforts are beginning to show the first signs of success; I can feel the forces lessening, and I'm able to haul myself slowly into my chair.

Once my fat arse is properly sat, I manage to jam one of my restraints on, and then take over the controls to hit the starboard retrograde thruster, rapidly cutting our spin, and then gain full control as I pull us out and away, stabilising our flight-path with a well-rehearsed series of corrections and alignments. Soon enough, we're level, flying away from the wreck site. I see the aft section of the wreck hurtling away into the infinite void, its fate unknowable as it spends the rest of eternity wandering the stars. A cold shiver slithers its way down my spine—that would have been the fate of our survivor, had we not intervened in time.

Gren doesn't respond, and when I look over at him, I can see he's in shock— his eyes are wide and glassy, and there's an unfocused quality to them. His face is slack, his tongue lolling out his mouth.

'Dr. Gren?' I ask, carefully.

His eyes move towards me, and I can see them focus on me, and for a moment it seems he'll be okay. But then his face scrunches closed, his mouth opens, and the front interior of his helm is obscured by a spray of vomit. It's not a funny moment, if I have described it as such, it's a matter of real concern— he could be choking, or the vomit could cause a short in his suit's internals, cutting out the power and his breathing apparatus.

I unbuckle the pair of us immediately, helping the suncoat up, but he vomits more forcefully again and it's a struggle to keep him on his feet. He needs to come out of that suit, now, but with our survivor on board, I know that's against our doctor's orders. I cast a look towards the human, and, by the grace of the Eternal Oarth, somehow, he has managed to get himself thoroughly tangled in the bench's restraints, which held him firm against our rather rough departure, and he's in no worse shape than when he boarded.

Gren sobs, probably from embarrassment and the rush of exhaustion that comes after surviving a harrowing ordeal, but I only lift him to his feet and half drag, half carry him towards the rear of the shuttle.

'I am so proud of you, I am so proud of you,' I say with all my heart as I gently guide him back to the storage area. 'You saved our lives, my wonderful chap, well, well done.' It's not the most professional words a captain should offer in this moment, but they are the ones that are the truest in my heart, and I feel no shame as I say them.

I sit him in the triage area, close the door behind me, and help him to remove his helmet. He takes a deep rushing gasp of air as it comes off, and looks as miserable as any man ever could be. I will spare my little Gren the embarrassment of describing his current condition in detail—it's rather a tight fit in our helmets, and the spattering has gone up and everywhere—but it's no trouble for me to grab a nearby cloth and help tidy him. I have three sons, all adults themselves now and older than Gren, but I shared in raising them as soon as they were weaned from their baron father; I've cleaned my fair share of vomit, and worse, and it is no bother to me now.

'You're getting a commendation,' I advise him, as I wipe away the last bits from his face. I look at him deep in the eyes, my expression serious. 'For heroism and bravery. That was amazing, for anyone, to have accomplished, let alone a doctor on his first away mission.'

He smiles weakly. 'Leave out the vomiting part, will you, sir?'

'What vomiting?' I reply, and smile. In a fatherly gesture, I reach out and cup the side of his face, using my thumb to stroke above his eyebrow. I nod though. 'I'll bring you one of our spare suits; you need to change—we've got a patient needing your help.'

'Yes, yes of course. Load him into the shuttle's auto-doc, secure him in, then press the big green button. It will start a scan; it should be done by the time I'm done. Be gentle with him.'

No need to advise Gren that his question isn't necessary; I will always be gentle with our survivor. I have no choice but to be.

CHAPTER 8

Rowland

*D*oleo ergo sum. I hurt, therefore I am.

I can hear faint growling. Quiet woofs. Gruffs, huffs, and hard rolling r's. I sleep again, wondering what monsters will catch me while I do.

I wake, and this time I'm barely able to see a dim light in front of my eyes, from some source that's above me. More growls, more huffs, another woof. I sleep—they're getting close, they'll catch me soon.

It's the third time that does the trick; when I wake, this time it's because my biocomp is piping its diagnostics into the far-left column of my vision—its systems are fully operational, but it's reporting that my own systems are not quite as peachy—'injuries have been sustained'.

More concerning though is that it has recorded an auto-doc's attempt to repair those injuries. Auto-docs are CAPS tech, meaning that whoever ran that scan knows their patient is wired with illegal cybernetics, and so the auto-doc won't make the repairs until they are removed. Not a good start to the morning.

Some awful memories come rushing back suddenly, focusing on the auto-doc: Bryce. He is quickly followed by Bett, Cor, Ivan and Mia—they all need my help. I have one teetering moment trying to convince myself that I'm dreaming, that everything that happened didn't *really* happen, right? They're fine, this was just a stupid nightmare, but this hope is vanishing from my mind like smoke through a grasping fist. No, they're all in danger—terrible, terrible danger. I need to get up, get moving, help them, now!

I try to sit up from my prone position, but I've been strapped down across my chest. My hands are free, though, and I reach up to rip whatever's holding me in place, only to hear a quick succession of alarmed grunts and woofs coming from the right of me. I turn my head quickly to see the source of these sounds and …

And I'm looking at a bear in a spacesuit.

I *am* dreaming after all. Thank God.

But I'm not dreaming. The bear has two gloved paws up in front of itself, and it's taking a step—wait bears don't walk upright, do they? In long-ago circuses, maybe, on a ball?—towards me, slightly waving its paws in a side-to-side gesture. It's repeatedly making the same sound at me: *rer, rer, rer,* and its eyes are locked on me—wide with apparent surprise, but non-threatening.

It's not a bear, I think, as my vision focuses on this strange figure, and more details are becoming clear: its face is more narrow, more refined, than a bear's is, but there's still a muzzle, straw-coloured fur, and I can see rounded ears on the upper sides of its head—just like a bear's—and it's definitely got the 'all the better to eat you with, my dear' sharp teeth.

But I think it's smiling at me. It's lowered its head slightly, and its approach is obviously slow and cautious.

It's about my size, in terms of height, but it's much broader across the shoulders than I am; I can see well-rounded muscle under the spacesuit and its chest is a solid wall. It's definitely heavier than me though, for its middle section looks much rounder than mine is—I would risk saying 'plump' but that's prejudicial, as this could be a part of its natural morphology. Its hands are huge, with particularly long fingers that seem to curve inwards at the ends, though they are currently gloved. Thick thighs too, but its legs are somewhat squat compared to the rest of its frame, and unless this species is very differently built than I am, based on the rounded bump in the front of its pants, I suspect my 'it' is in fact a 'he', even though that assumption has got me into trouble before.

The spacesuit that he's wearing though is archaic: a single-piece jumpsuit, made from a glossy material with a metallic bronze sheen, covered in a complex series of straps, valves and seals, topped with a fish-bowl style clear-dome helmet. Air supply regulators connect the helmet and the suit with two tubes, and though I can't see it, I'm pretty sure there's an air-tank stored in the back. There're emblems, I think, on his shoulders and chest—a series of weird scratch-marks that are definitely in a pattern, but if it's a language, it's not one I have installed on my universal translator. Thick gloves and dark brown boots complete this 'my first spacesuit' ensemble—the last time I saw something this old was in a museum. By comparison to the suit I was wearing when hacking the derelict, a mid-range fully-enclosed carbon nanofibre suit with auto-air scrubbing capabilities (and a sexy combination of steel grey shades with electric blue trim, to match my ship), the suit this bear is wearing might as well be a potato-sack.

Equal amounts of fear, confusion and bemusement course through me. He's a giant blond teddy bear in a centuries-old spacesuit, and there's this terribly baffling conflict in me between his adorableness, strangeness and possible threat-level. Remember how I mentioned about 'just because something is fluffy and cute …?' Yeah, that doesn't mean it's going to like you; every fuzzy thing from a full-sized polar bear to a pissed-off chinchilla can be dangerous.

'*Rer, rer. Grul kreth ultan kir,*' he soothes, his voice calm, and gentle in tone. He points to himself.

'*Oar Gren,*' he indicates, patting his chest with one paw, all the fingers splayed. '*Gren,*' and pats again. He extends that paw towards me, and raises his brows.

'Rowland,' I reply; there's no way to be sure *Gren* is this bear's name, but it's as good a starting point as any. I follow up quickly though, 'I don't understand your language. Do you understand mine? Nod your head if you do.' I nod my head up and down from my reclined position, and watch the bear —

No, that's not correct at all anymore—the physical differences are growing more and more apparent the closer he comes. It's like he's a bear just into the first few evolutionary steps into becoming human—just enough for me to say 'that might not be a full-on bear, but I'm sure it still shits in the woods'. His obvious intelligence though, demonstrated by his language, gestures and facial expressions—and the fact he probably gave me his name—quickly banishes any idea that this is an animal; he's obviously sapient-level, though from a species I've never seen before. Bear-man? Man-bear? Werebear it is. It'll have to do.

When the werebear nods enthusiastically at my question, I explain further. 'Then it looks like your translator has my language installed, but I don't have yours installed on mine. If you've got the language file somewhere, I can upload it, and we should be able to speak.'

Gren nods again, understanding, and turns from me, heading for the exit.

'Wait, wait Gren,' I call out, and he turns back to face me. 'I was with five other people: four humans like me and a Harculcorian. Are they here?' I ask urgently, holding up one of my hands with all my fingers splayed out to get my point across.

He shakes his head from side to side, then looks behind himself with an unsure glance.

'I need to find them,' I tell him, then resume my efforts to free myself from whatever is strapping me down.

'*Rer, thrane Rowland ...*' the werebear indicates in a nervous-sounding tone, turning back, and moving quickly towards me, likely to try and stop my escape efforts.

'No not *rer*, Gren, I need to find them. We were attacked by the Pryok'tel, they were taken prisoner,' I say. This has to be my truth. It has to be. I'll risk insanity if I use a different term than "prisoner". 'They're still alive and I need to find them.'

'*Thrane Rowland, kettereck tarkrel cinercoth,*' this Gren fellow starts nicely, but his voice has gone up in tone. He's stopped a few steps from me, and I'm suddenly aware of just how big he is—he's a hulking mass just out of the corner of my eye, and I know that if he wanted to, he could hold me down with just one hand. I'm strong, I work out and have my own set of well-built muscles, but this blond dude has at least fifty kilograms on me, with arms as thick as tree limbs, and I've been badly injured.

'Gren, I need to go.' I look at him right in his amber eyes: lovely, bright and obviously filled with concern.

'*Hulth,*' he answers. '*Hulth, ur grolother cer toar kreclanthan.*' Again he makes the double-handed wave-motion to me, and starts stepping away. '*Hulth. Hulth.*' Wait, I assume. He walks backwards, slowly, still making his hand-motions, then exits through a heavy cabin plate door, closing it behind him. He gives me a quick look through the door's port-window, and then I hear the sounds of the lock-bar sliding into place.

Left alone, I have the chance to focus and assess my physical state more closely. My left side is searing hot with pain, and it's now I notice I've been bandaged, rather professionally too. The under-suit I was wearing—I didn't get the chance to change out if it before I went to speak to Bryce—is gone: I'm naked beneath a thick pale beige cloth, warm and smooth against my skin, and I feel like I'm resting on a raised bed, a gurney perhaps, though if it is, it's the widest gurney I've ever been on—I've a great deal of room to myself.

My left leg feels pretty good though, and my right arm has full mobility. Head hurts somewhat, and I touch an area above my forehead, feeling the newness of recently formed skin there. Dermal regeneration—any common first aid kit has one of those, and they can't detect my unauthorised cybernetics, so it will still function on me.

It'll have to do. I can't stay here. They all need me. I'm their captain, I promised them they would be safe. I resume my efforts to free myself, forcing the band that's been holding me down off, and then make the effort to sit up fully. My left side squawks in protest, and my biocomp recommends I discontinue my current activities, but both are ignored.

Gren still hasn't returned, so there's a chance to survey my surroundings, and I try to get a better idea of where I am and what's available that could help me out of this situation. The best way to describe where I am boils down to a rectangular box, about six by ten metres, with metal walls, no windows and only one discernible exit: the large, square door that Gren just walked through and locked behind him.

Looking around, the words 'functionally utilitarian' quickly come to mind, judging from the unadorned walls, which have few notable characteristics other than some black scuffmarks here and there, and some neatly-done repair-work to a couple of panels, all of a uniform solid metal-grey colour. The most prevalent feature in the room is the unmistakable odour of unrefined kelmisite—a smell best described as an unhappy three-way between copper, cheap soap and, oddly, woodchips. It's heavy in the air too—this room must be used to store it or process it, and it makes me wonder exactly where I am.

I can feel the room's gravity: it's slightly off the Earth-centric norm I'm accustomed to, and so things are feeling heavier for me in general—not unbearably so, but noticeable. This, and the distinct and ever-present hum of powered engines in the background, lead me to guess I'm on a space vessel—which makes sense given that Gren was in a spacesuit—but then, why am I not? The air, other than the smell of kelmisite, is perfectly breathable for me, oxygen-rich enough so that I'm neither light-headed nor giddy—it's possible Gren can't breathe the same atmosphere, though, and they've configured this room's environmental settings to accommodate me.

Definitely on a gurney, I confirm—rather, it's a portable anti-grav bed that's been erected for my benefit—it's far larger than I need though—almost enough space for two of me, if we were snuggled close—but it's surprisingly soft under my fingers, as is the blanket that's covering me. Well-made, I can see—both the blanket and the gurney—the material under my fingers is tightly woven, and feels as strong as it is supple.

I recheck the room, and this craftsmanship can be seen elsewhere as well, from the tight fit of the room's single door, to the perfectly joined wall-panels, to the neatly sunk lights above my head, all glowing with a white light sufficient to provide illumination but without a harsh glare. Bare, minimal and unadorned, this room is nonetheless of quality, at least from a purely space vessel engineering perspective.

There's a set of what look like storage lockers though, five along each wall beside me, and I've just managed to swing my legs off the gurney to go take a closer look when I hear the heavy *fee-fi-foe-fum* of approaching footsteps.

The lock-bar is lifted, and as the door swings open, I can immediately tell it isn't Gren coming in. I crane my neck as I try to take in the juggernaut entering the room. Some instinctive part of me clutches that warm blanket closer against my chest as my eyes strain to get the entire image in at once.

This one … this one makes Gren, and therefore myself, look puny. He's a towering whopper, just barely fitting into the room without needing to stoop, though he had to in order to fit through the doorway. Well over two metres tall, and easily more than a metre across his heavily bulked shoulders. His frame is a mass of brawn beneath his spacesuit: his chest a broad barrel, his torso a solid keg, and hulking arms that look strong enough to bend metal beams. His legs, tree-trunk-sized with thick quads and calves, are in proportion to his frame, and each of his hands and feet looks big enough to squash me flat with one blow. He's immense, at least double my weight and then some, and it's the powerhouse kind of weight, not the 'I should really hit the treadmill one of these days' kind.

His massive head looks at least twice the size of my own, and through the fish-bowl space helmet he's wearing, I can see his face—surrounded by thick grey fur, the colour of an angry thundercloud, with a stout muzzle ending with a broad black tipped nose; he's got those unmistakably ursine features as much as Gren has, but his grey fur is not quite as—fluffy? fuzzy?—looking as Gren's is. There're other differences as well: his muzzle is squarish, where Gren's is rounder—maybe this grey one's a carnivore and the blond one's more of an omnivore? Maybe I should stop judging a species I just met by comparing them to an Earth animal? I'm sure I wouldn't appreciate them comparing me to a gorilla, even though I am technically an ape too.

But it's his eyes that really capture my attention—my God, they're a brilliant shade of blazing cobalt—zaffre blue, I've heard it's called—vibrant and almost electric, unlike any I've ever seen on a human before, filled with intelligence, emotion and, somewhat understandably, caution; eyes that are watching mine, gauging me as much as I am him.

Corculhorhan is a big man, and I remember similar feelings of surprise when I first met him—but this giant before me dwarfs my memory of Cor. This stormy werebear is easily the largest person I have seen in real life—I have viewed images of the Wenverti giants, and they are all well past three metres in height—but the goliath in front of me is all too in the here and now. It takes all of me not to look at the bump between his legs either, but I fail quickly—curiosity and cats—and that's when I'm sure my eyebrows lift to the skies; he's bigger than Gren in more ways than one. Clearly.

It is fair to say that if I find Gren moderately intimidating but still kinda adorable, then his friend is truly overwhelming and genuinely awesome, emphasis on the 'awe' part. I can tell by his posture that he knows it too; he's got that confident stance you earn from being the biggest kid in the class. This observation is supported by Gren, who is standing to the man's side, but also a step back—not like he's hiding but clearly giving the grey behemoth the spotlight. A son with his father, maybe, given the differences between the pair? Probably a junior officer and his superior, given their spacesuits. Or is it that Gren is the one that does the soft talking, and he went and fetched his big stick?

What they do share, though, is the obvious intelligence that animates their features into the clearly sapient-level category, which have changed this grey one's initial cautious look into one of surprise when he clearly caught me sneaking a look at his goods. The faintest curl of his lips occurs at one corner, and this could be the pain I'm in talking here, but I'm sure I see those rich blue eyes twinkle.

This giant holds up a small touchpad—well, small in his massive hand but normal-sized for me—and waves it briefly at me, then holds it out, before cautiously approaching. I swear the room is shaking with each of his footsteps, but that's not the case—it's just my heart rate that's speeding up. He stops and extends his arm to its full length, stretching so as to hand the touchpad to me, which I accept.

'Thank you,' I mutter. I don't mean disrespect by my muted tone, but I am in awe of this man. There's fear, there's curiosity, there's desire, there's anxiety and there's apprehension—oh shit, there's desire?!—rolling over my thoughts in a constant back-and-forth battle to take centre-stage in my brain. He sees all of this, I'm sure—I'm too stunned to mask the feelings churning in me—and I only hope there's enough of a cross-species behavioural gap that he hasn't seen through me entirely. I doubt it; these werebears seem more on the 'were' side with each passing moment, but the 'bear' side isn't going anywhere soon.

I read the touchpad; it's written using the same characters that are on their spacesuits—their language is one that I don't recognize, a series of sharp punctures and furrows of varying width in specific patterns—almost like katakana, except more 'gouge-y'. The touchpad is clearly not CAPS tech—their logo is nowhere to be seen, and they do love their corporate branding, but the jack in me knows that I could interface with this device directly if I wanted to. I don't want to risk using my cybernetics in front of the werebears though—I don't know how they would react, so I decide to go old-school instead, and it's a few simple clicks of the interface before I've switched whatever they're showing me into CAPS Standard.

Greetings from the Oarthecan Space Services. I am Captain Toar Grithrawrscion of the Lurcaster's Claw, *and our doctor, Grenrethar Harnthscion, is with me. We would like to ask you how you are feeling?*

I pick out the proper names Oarthecan and Toar, thanks to Gren's—whose full first name appears to be Grenrethar—previously successful communication. I start to type in a reply, but about a quarter of the way in, I remember they can understand me.

'Thank you for saving me, Captain Grithrawrscion, and Dr. Harnthscion. Did you find any other survivors, four humans and a Harculcorian?'

He shakes his head, and beckons for the touchpad. He slash-writes a few words and returns it to me.

No. I am sorry. Let's have us communicating properly; our language is loaded on to that pad you've got there. Just touch it to the back of your neck and your universal translator should pick it up from that point. Also, please feel welcome to call me Captain Toar, and my friend here is Dr. Gren; thank you however for your courtesy.

'Yes ... of course,' I say again, dully. His 'no' answer is a hard pill, and it's sticking in my throat as I try to swallow it. I can't meet his gaze for some reason—my emotional state is running away from me; I need to find my crew, it's the only thing that matters. I need to focus, and the grey werebear's—Toar, he is Captain Toar—hulking presence is a looming distraction.

I follow his instructions—ones that I haven't done since I had my cybernetics wired in—and my biocomp picks up that the touchpad has only this one language file and a basic operating system installed. That's odd—touchpads like this are used for all kinds of reasons: log entries, personal correspondence, storing and playing media files, but this one just has the one language file.

The Oarthecan language file transfers quickly enough; it's a moderately complex language that uses lots of imagery and specific noun references, and their sentence-structure can sometimes be grammatically reversed, but it's no worse than CAPS Standard. It takes a moment to fully instal, and I hold up one finger to show that I'm waiting for that. Toar's returned to the far end of the room, by the door, and is standing with his hands clasped behind his back, next to Gren and his frequently anxious looks at me.

'Okay,' I say, when the installation is complete. 'Try saying something,'

'Are you able to understand me?' Captain Toar asks; his voice is terrifically deep and clear, but it's got a friendly, helpful tone to it.

'Yes, you're coming through fine, Captain,' I confirm, and then quickly, 'Are you sure there weren't other survivors? Our bridge got ripped away during the attack and two of my crew were on board, there were also two crewmembers who may have been outside the ship when we were attacked.'

'Yours was the only life-sign we detected in the vicinity, and we scanned both sections of your vessel, which would have included the surrounding area,' Toar explains, and he avoids my gaze for a moment. 'I'm very sorry, Baro ...' he stammers, then adds '— uh, Mr. Rowland.'

'We were ambushed by the Pryok'tel, and they're known to take prisoners for slaving. It's possible that there's still a chance to save them but not for long; the Pryok'tel are cannibals and if my crew is alive, they could be in terrible danger.' I'm unable to keep out the desperation in my voice.

'The Oarth have had a long history with the Pryok'tel, and so when I say I understand your concern, please know how deep that understanding is,' Toar replies, sombrely. He lowers his head again, and when he looks at me next, his expression is pure apology. 'But I'm sorry to advise that we're in no position to help, Baron Rowland,' he explains, almost sounding embarrassed, but his tone's not what is confusing me.

'We're a civilian operation and have no means of attempting a rescue with the resources we have. I know the danger you're talking about, I've seen, first-hand, the depravity of the Pryok'tel, and so when I say that I'm sorry, please accept it in the truest sense of the word.'

We regard each other for a moment, our wills battling: Toar's expression is one of regret and sympathy, and his immense stature is in a posture of respectful contrition, but he is not moving. I can't accept his answer, and there's no way sitting here is going to save my family. Every problem has a solution, if you're smart enough. If you care enough. I will be both of those things for my crew—my family—I will break my body in half if it means there's a chance to save them.

Also, don't think my new title of 'Baron Rowland' has gone unnoticed, by the way—I'm not sure what it means but my translator is working correctly with the term; UT's don't supply context, just a direct translation if there's a possibility the word can be translated—which yes, can sometimes lead to either a hilarious or disastrous result, depending on the word. If there's no direct translation, the UT substitutes the closest equivalent word or words that convey the meaning. Baron is coming through 'as is', but last time I checked, I don't recall being a part of Earth's ancient nobility. But it appears Toar is comfortable using the term, and I'm not sure of the etiquette of correcting him, or even if he needs to be corrected—"baron" may be the nice way of saying "stranger" or "person in need of help" in Oarthecan.

'I need to leave,' I state, and dismount the gurney. This causes an immediate stream of chiding and reprimands to spout from Gren, but I ignore him and stand up—only to feel a searing pull in my left side, causing me to wince, turn and falter, but it doesn't stop me. After some fussing, I've managed to wrap my blanket around my middle in a makeshift kilt, and start scanning the room for something slightly more practical to go and rescue my friends in.

'Where's my clothes?' I demand, but my voice isn't as strong as I want it to be—the pain in my side is alive and getting out of the bed has woken up all its teeth. My leg isn't as solid as I want it to be either; there's weakness in it when I put any weight on it, and my knee feels like it might buckle if I take a step.

'You're bleeding.' Toar points to my injury, his expression tight with worry, but I've noticed he's not moved from blocking the door.

'That's enough, that's enough,' Gren says with a kindly authoritative tone, stepping forward. He's moving towards me like I'm a wobbly toddler about to fall, all concern and caring. 'We just finished sewing you back together, no need to undo all that work, Baron.'

'I'll be fine,' I mutter crossly, but even *I* think that's an exaggeration. My head isn't as fixed as I first thought it was, as I'm seeing stars around the edges of my vision. My biocomp is flashing a new set of warning messages at me now too. God, is the entire room against me here?

'There, there, let's have me help, shall we?' Gren says with an irrefusable sweetness. He's at my side, his arms hovering around me, ready to catch me if I topple over. I glare at him, challenging him to try and stop me, but he has this impenetrable kindness that just deflects my stare—I'm obviously not his first difficult patient.

'Listen to our good Dr. Gren, Baron Rowland. Please. You're hurt,' Toar urges, and his tone is just as kind, but carries a lot more gravitas—he's used to his orders being followed, that's for certain. I've noticed that he's also come closer into the room, his posture seeming ready to act if he needs to, but his expression is one of sincere caring, so I don't feel threatened at all. Even though he is encased in his spacesuit, I can clearly see empathy in his eyes: they're full of compassion, blotting out any lingering thought in my mind about him being a bear: he is a man, a furry, sharp-toothed werebear of a man—but those blue eyes of his—they're marvellous, impossible not to be comforted by. To be caught by, I'm finding, and that's causing me some confusion that I just don't have time to deal with.

'Captain Toar, they'll *eat* them,' I whisper, locking his eyes with mine, imploring him, but my fear and exhaustion is getting the better of my voice, straining my words. 'They're my family; good God, they're all my family.'

'I swear to you, Baron, I'll do everything I can think of to help. Just rest now, please, we'll talk more when you're able,' he assures me, as Gren continues to encourage me onto the gurney; I'm moving slowly and under my own power as much as possible; he's helping and while I have the feeling he could easily just lift me up and place me on the bed, he's letting me set my own pace.

I'm tired, I'm weak, and I'm not going to win. I don't think I'll be able to rest so long as my family is in danger, but as soon as my head sinks into the softness of the gurney, my body betrays me, the last of my reserves ebbing. I've lost this round.

Gren attends the side of the gurney and gives me the sweetest look—his adorableness is irresistible and gnaws down my anxiety despite my need to hold on to it.

'There there, good Baron, you'll be all right, just a bit of a lie-down, and we'll have you proper in no time, I promise,' he soothes, adjusting my blanket around me, tucking here and there, placing the strap back over my chest, but it's just a light fit, not a restraint.

'I can't ...'

'That's right, you can't help your family in your current condition, that's very wise of you,' Gren agrees, kindly. With the slightest of touches, he places the back of his hand against my forehead, like he was taking my temperature. I'm not sure if he's accomplishing that, given his hand is gloved, but he seems to be taking as much comfort from the gesture as he's giving. 'We'll get you back up, right and well, in no time.'

Gren gives his captain a direct look. 'I'll come get you after he's had a rest?'

A look of disappointment momentarily appears on the captain's face, but he nods once quickly. 'Of course, Doctor. I'll return to the helm; please see to Baron Rowland's recovery, and advise if he requires anything further,' the grey furred giant instructs, and then turns and leaves the room, stooping again to exit through the door.

79

Sleep is rapidly creeping over me, I can feel it pulling me down and wanting to take hold, but I have enough energy to say. 'I have to … I promised …'

'There, enough of that,' Gren kindly chastises, but his smile is all sweetness as I fade back to my slumber.

CHAPTER 9

Toar

Captain's log, OSSM *Lurcaster's Claw*, currently on board our shuttle. The date is 28.13.221 and the time is 02h00. Captain Toar Grithrawrscion reporting.

The survivor of the CAPS-S *Brunhilda's Grace* (see previous log entry) continues to recover, with Dr. Gren reporting that his vitals are strong, and he is expected to make a full recovery, in time. Though the survivor's initial reactions are centred on finding his missing family, he seems to be otherwise cooperative and communicative. Dr. Gren and I remain in good health and report no physical side effects from being in proximity to the survivor, and always remain under olfactory suppressants and in our spacesuits while treating him. See Dr. Gren's medical logs, included in the transmission to the *Grolthon's Spear*.

However, our investigation continues into why our auto-doc refused to treat the survivor, outside of the reason indicated as illegal cybernetic implants. Though neither Dr. Gren nor I can determine the nature of these implants, nor what capabilities they provide the survivor, I plan to discuss the matter further with him pending his further recovery.

I have dived the shuttle out of the kelmisite field to transmit a request for assistance to the OSSN *Grolthon's Spear*, approximately fifteen hours out from our position. I have encoded the transmission directly for their captain, advising that our survivor is a human male, and we will hold our position and await their assistance. However, Science Officer Threng indicates that the *Grolthon's Spear* may only now just be receiving that transmission.

Next log entry scheduled for 06h00. Toar logging off.

Never thought I would write a log entry like that one.

I blink, rubbing my eyes to keep them open, and store my written log into my personal touchpad. I usually dictate my log entries, but I've ordered Gren to get a kip in while he can, and he's currently dozing softly on the miners' benches. My helmet's off but nearby, and I'm glad not to be breathing in the stuffy confines of its regulated interior, but I'm still being chafed by this damnable suit something fierce; I can't take it off though, as I may need to head back to the storage area for some reason. Gren needs his rest, so I'll give him a few more hours before I try and catch up on my own. Long and interesting day, indeed, and it's nipping at my ankles.

It's about two hours since my conversation with Mr. Rowland, and I find myself in a battle between my obvious attraction to him (not made any easier by his not-so-sneaky look at my trousers, mind you; don't think I missed seeing that) and my equally growing concerns.

To start, there's the auto-doc's refusal to treat Rowland—I'd pressed the green button, like Gren instructed, and had barely turned my back before the whole machine burst into tears about 'illegal cybernetic augmentation detected'. Not 'unknown', not 'incompatible'—*illegal*. The auto-docs were traded to us by the CAPS—well, donated really—so having this machine clearly understand whatever Rowland has is illegal, and then refuse to treat him because of that, it just doesn't speak well of either Rowland or the CAPS, in my opinion.

Then, as we were getting him out of his bloodied clothes so that Gren could treat his injuries, I had a good look at what Rowland was wearing—there were no markings indicating he was a part of the CAPS-S, and from what I've heard of the CAPS, they're enormously proud of their logos and emblems and such. I only knew to look for this because during my brief and frantic search of his vessel, I noticed how domestic everything seemed, like it was a home rather than a workman's craft: there was a whole hodgepodge of things left behind that have no place on a salvage-ship, at least not one that actually wants to salvage anything. It looked like it was built for comfort, like for a family, as Rowland said.

My suspicions were the reason the touchpad I handed him only contained the Oarthecan language file; though he is terribly pretty, even more so once we got him tidied up, there's a part of me that knows things are much more complicated with Rowland than first appearances would have me believe. I don't entirely trust him, and regardless of how I'm attracted to him—which, I admit, I am quite strongly so—when he looked me over, I got a bashful tingle in my tummy, something I've not felt in years—but I still have enough common sense left in me not to be completely struck blind by his physical appearance alone.

Now that I'm thinking of him in this way again—I'll mention I did see Rowland fully out of his kit, having to help strip him out of his damaged clothing and assist Gren in treating his injuries and all. It'd be proper for me to say that I averted my eyes and focused on the task at hand, but I couldn't just not look, so I can only hope I struck a good balance between indulging my curiosity and helping Gren.

Rowland is simultaneously very much like our barons, and very much unlike. His basic form and general appearance are the same, you know, standard head, arms, legs, and all, but he's much broader than barons generally are, with properly thick muscles all over him, especially his good solid chest and shoulders. And his arms, and legs, and bum … yes, well, suffice to say where our barons are trim and often svelte, Rowland is much more robust—I particularly liked his tummy, which is not as slender and sculpted as our barons' but slightly rounder and more comfortable-looking—I suspect he's a man who enjoys a good meal but not to excess. Odd though, there's this little hole in the middle there—I didn't get a real chance to inspect it but it caught my eye and made me curious.

I very much liked his colouration too: he's got a light skin tone, a warm pinkish colour, like some of our woodcoat and stormcoat barons have, and his hair is this charming shade of light brown, almost blond. It's like Rowland got the best colours of woodcoat and suncoat mixed together—I've seen his hair-shade only a few times before, I've always thought it special. A very interesting detail is that lots of this same shade of hair grows over his chest and belly, and that's unheard of for a baron; they're naturally glabrous, with hair only atop their heads. I admit that when I saw that Rowland also had hair peeking out from his armpits, around his crotch and just above his marvellous bum, I found it strangely, but highly, erotic.

And yes, lovely cock and balls, while I'm mentioning things. I only sneaked a few glances, both because it's impolite to stare and I'm not sure he'd appreciate me doing so, and because I didn't want to rile myself up too much while I was supposed to be helping Gren get Rowland fixed. Yes … he's quite well put together down there is all I'll say—nice proper shape, right proportion to his body, perhaps erring on the more generous side, and a little overhang on his sheath, which I do enjoy. His balls are not as big as our barons' usually are, but that's not an issue for me, and I liked that there's some fuzz covering them too. I bet he tastes marvellous though—I could fit all of him entirely in my mouth, feel his lovely cock grow full and hard against my tongue, have him push himself down my throat, licking and suckling him until he bursts …

See now this is a perfect example of what I've been saying about that battle my mind's been waging non-stop: I think of Rowland, I get excited, I get concerned, I think about why I am concerned, and that leads me to think of Rowland … and it's been like this for hours.

Rowland. What a lovely name though—it's got such nice bite to it—feels good in my mouth every time I say it. I wonder if he's 'Row' and his sire dad is 'Land', like how us drones are named, but I suspect it's Rowland, one name, like a baron's. Regardless, it suits him—strong, solid, but still graceful and easy to say, to the point and yet with so much hidden potential and …

I'm doing it again. Here I am, seventy-seven years old, three grown sons, over a half-century of service in the OSS … and I'm daydreaming like a man fresh from boyhood, when his scent first kicks in, and he's ready to start denning. Maybe I can add to my log, focus my mind on work again, go scrub the privy if that's what it takes to stop me from mooning over the gorgeous passenger we've got on the mend in the backroom.

I've caught myself idly scratching the surface of the helm with my claw-tip, sketching out a portrait of Rowland—not hard scratches though, there's no damage done to the console, but I find myself drawing the details of his beautiful face as they swim in my mind. Such truly rich features he has—broad, squarish, but refined too, and nice symmetry and proportions—his nose is the exact right shape for his face, and his little round ears, flat against his head, look like they were picked out just for him. A lot of my attention centres on his dashing, clever eyes and firm, kissable lips, of course. I wish I had some of my drawing supplies, but all my things are back in my quarters—I used to carry little scraps of paper and a graphite claw cover for just these moments—but I've not done that for years.

Got to clear my mind or else risk him leaving footprints on my brain, so I decide to update my log with additional details, but then I hear Gren stirring in his sleep—he's muttering to himself, caught in the jaws of a bad dream. He's shaken off the emergency blanket we found to cover him, which is almost as itchy as the spacesuit, but he was at least able to get out of that for a while.

I go to pick up his blanket, but his mutterings increase in volume, and then he's sat bolt upright on the bench, and saying with alarm, 'Pills! Pills!'

'It's all right, Dr. Gren, we've taken our pills,' I reply, softly, holding out his blanket for him. 'Just before you nodded off, remember? Only about two hours ago.'

He looks at me, sleep-confused, but reaches for his blanket easily enough. He takes a good strong whiff of it, then says, 'Nothing. Good.'

He's wearing the simple lightweight attire that normally goes under the suit— little more than a thin one-piece garment that zips up in front, and that blanket will do him good—it's only about five degrees in the cabin, since I'm trying to conserve the shuttle's energy as much as possible, and keeping the back storage room at a balmy twenty degrees for our guest is a power drain. Temperature-wise, drones are comfortable in the low teens, but I know enough about barons, and their lack of fur, to understand they need things warmer.

'Don't forget your pills, though, Captain. You're bigger than me so they'll go through you faster,' he instructs. Gren wraps his blanket over his shoulders, but he's not lying down.

'Not forgotten, don't you worry. Back to bed, then,' I encourage.

'No, I'm awake now. Too much on my mind!' He gives me an apologetic look.

'Fair enough. A strange day, for certain.' I motion for him to shove over, and when he does, I take a seat beside him. 'You did really well, Gren. I meant what I said; I'm putting you up for commendation when we get back. You really nailed the 'above and beyond' today—well, well done.'

He gives an embarrassed but grateful look. 'Thank you, Captain, that means a lot to me. You did amazing though! You totally found our Baron Rowland and got him back in time, and were all 'leave no man behind!' when you jumped into the shuttle, then stopped us from spinning out of control and crashing ... just ... *raur,* just *raur!*'

I chuckle and ruffle the fur on his head. 'We're only here because of you, but I'll take your praise, good Doctor. And Baron Rowland, *he's* only here because of you. That was a tricky thing you pulled off, stitching him up like that.'

Gren furrows his brow. 'Yes, that was ... unexpected, for certain. I mean I looked over his injuries, briefly, and thought "no worries, those are easy fixes", but when the machine refused to heal him, and that reason ...'

'I know. I don't know much about this cybernetics stuff at all. Seems unnatural to me, sticking robots in your body,' I say, absently. We Oarth do know about cybernetics, but only second-hand from our contact with the CAPS. Certainly, outside of our UTs, there's no Oarth I know who'd be in for having his body all mucked up by bits of wires and such, or whatever is used.

'Well, we do have our UTs,' Gren counters, reading my mind.

'Yeah, but they're just little and don't do anything too serious. Don't have a clue what Baron Rowland is capable of. Bit of a concern, really.'

'Should we ... should we be calling him Baron, Captain?' Gren asks, nervously, pondering I suspect whether another honorific for our guest would be insulting. I've been feeling the same way, myself—calling him Mr. Rowland seems so ... low, almost derogatory, and entirely against my instincts—but nevertheless, true. He's human, not Oarth, meaning Baron Rowland is Mr. Rowland, despite every outward appearance telling me otherwise.

'I think Mr ...' the word feels wrong in my mouth, '... Rowland would be what he'd prefer, now that you've mentioned it,' I agree. 'Let's try and keep that in mind—he may look like our barons do, but he's not one.' But even as my words leave my lips, I can't say I feel entirely sure I'm correct.

'Yes, true, but still ... he's not at all like they described them in our lessons,' Gren observes.

'Oh, how's that then?' I ask, giving him a curious look.

'Well, for starters, he is rather pretty, isn't he? Like, *insanely* pretty, really ... all that lovely fur on his tummy and chest, so soft a brown it's almost a blond, like I am, but his eyes are just so ... *raur* ... beautiful.'

I snort a small laugh at Gren's guilty-sounding acknowledgement, but I'm curious about what he said. 'Textbooks didn't mention that, then? His looks? You said there were pictures of them?'

Gren nods. 'There were, but they were mostly either illustrations or simple diagrams—you know, body shapes and arrows pointing to parts and the like—medical diagrams. Any real pictures of humans all had their faces pixelated out—to maintain privacy and anonymity, I assumed, but ... now? After seeing Mr. Rowland? Now I think that obscuring served a deeper purpose.'

'How so?' I ask, curious about this little conspiracy.

'I've said it before, but didn't really understand how true it was at the time: a race of super-barons. I've been thinking non-stop about the decree, and why the punishment is so severe. It makes sense with what I understand now.'

I nod, following along. 'A race of outrageously beautiful men, all with overcharged Allures that are constantly armed ... what did you say? Us drone Oarth would just melt in their hands?'

'Worse than that, Captain,' Gren warns. 'Our whole society, our whole species, functions as a small number of barons directing a large number of drones. Our entire existence has operated like that, since, well, forever. There are about thirty billion humans, with half that number being males—more than enough so that every individual drone could choose from thousands of humans if he wanted to. Imagine what will happen to us if that suddenly becomes a possibility? Can't find a baron? No problem—here's a galaxy full of human men to choose from instead.'

'Yeah, but can Oarth and humans even have kids together?' I ask, not sure myself.

Gren shakes his head. 'No. Humans have two sexes—and their males are not the child-bearers like our barons are. I mean, we're capable of the physical act of mating with human males—our external parts are pretty much identical—but human males don't have the internal parts that are required for conception. That's all with their females. It *might* be possible that our barons could choose a human to be a sire, but that would just make things worse for our species, in that case. There's so few barons as it is that having one choose a human would cause a riot, if not a full-out war.'

He sighs and gives a small, disappointed frown. 'That, and, well, from what I understand, most human males will only engage in sex with females.'

I frown now too. 'Not even if it's just for a bit of fun?'

'No,' Gren remarks, glumly. 'I've heard that *some* of their men do, but it's rare. And there's no way to tell the ones that will from the ones that won't.' He stops now, mulling a thought over. 'Which I'm sure must be terribly frustrating for them.'

'Indeed,' I reply, though I recall now that Rowland did give me a solid, thorough looking over—perhaps he's one of the sensible ones, maybe? 'But then, that's a good thing, I mean, for us Oarth, right?' I continue, thinking on this topic. 'If human men won't respond to us Oarth, then it's not like we're going to waste our time pursuing them, are we?'

'Except that their permanently charged Allure might not give us the chance to be so clear-headed about that. I mean, you've been Allured yourself, Captain—how much were you able to resist your baron?'

'Didn't want to resist him, Gren, he was my Baron and … *oh*,' I finish, seeing the point Gren's already worked out.

'I'm pretty sure the CAPS must have come to the same conclusions, too,' Gren continues. 'I mean, they only let either human women or non-humans talk with us, and we're not allowed near their men—they probably don't like it when we go all primitive on them like that.'

'I think it's for our protection, more than theirs,' I suggest, and Gren looks at me curiously. 'Well, think about it—what would happen if the CAPS decided that Oartheca was ripe for the plundering, like the Pryok'tel did? Who do you think the CAPS would have on the front lines in that fight?'

Gren's eyes go wide. 'Dear Eternal, we … we wouldn't stand a chance. They'd just send their prettiest human men, and we'd give up without firing a shot!'

'We wouldn't just give up, Gren—we'd willingly hand Oartheca over, plus our lunar colonies, and the outposts on Marden—the entire system. We'd be on our knees without them having to ask.'

We're both silent now, contemplating the conundrum that our guest in the storage area poses, even if Rowland is completely innocent of such intentions. I wish I were exaggerating my worries, here, but I'm sure there'd be no way us drones would fight human men anywhere near how we fought the Pryok'tel. Especially, you know, if those men showed up without their shirts on. And they asked nicely, or worse, demanded it, all bossy-like and such. A domineering baron is a common drone fantasy, after all—even Cralren and I role-played that on a handful of occasions, and his nature is a gentle and sweet one.

And I doubt that a drone's biology would give two tail-wags about it being an infertile pairing; the drive would be there, even if the destination could never be reached. I mean, to be upfront, if Rowland wanted me to, I'm sure I'd be his sire—I'd love to be, actually, it'd be wonderful, amazing even—and I wouldn't care we couldn't have kids. Maybe the fact I already do have children is leaning me closer to not being bothered by that, but I doubt it would matter to most other drones in the long run—most of us don't have children of our own to begin with—there's just not enough barons to go around—and the competition for a baron's favour is intensely fierce.

And human men? They'd destroy that competition—burn it right down to the ground—the very foundations of our society, and we'd be the ones holding the torches. We've just started to recover our numbers after the Pryok'tel occupation, we're working hard but we're nowhere close to the half-billion or so of us that were all over Oartheca before the triple-mouth baron-spites arrived— and the introduction of a super-charged, plentiful but entirely infertile class of pseudo-barons would completely derail us. The decree ... the decree makes sense. And here I am, breaking it and everything. Oh, Toar, you damn fool.

But he is that beautiful, and I find myself not bothered by my foolishness in the slightest.

'Should we tell Mr. Rowland about the decree?' Gren asks, gingerly. 'I mean, he's got to be wondering why we've separated him from ourselves, like we have. He must be terribly lonely and sad all by himself back there.'

'Let's not overwhelm our guest, Doctor. He's had a far rougher day than we have—a topic like this is the last thing that he needs.'

'Yes, it's quite awful. Awful. But I thought you were so well-spoken with your words to him, Captain. Very kind, even though the situation does not look good. I think he knows that, however.'

'Yes,' I agree, gravely. Hope is the last thing to die, normally. With the Pryok'tel, it's often the first.

'Can we do *anything* to help him?' Gren asks, tentatively.

I shrug. 'The OSS may choose to investigate the Derresion system if they're not already aware of it. But because there's no direct Oarthecan involvement with this, there's no official cause for them to. It *is* the Pryok'tel though, so, that may be reason enough—but it would be a purge in that case, not a rescue. I'll recommend that they contact the CAPS of course, to let them know their citizens have been taken, but ... I'm not sure Mr. Rowland is with the CAPS, if I'm honest.'

At Gren's surprised look, I fill him in on my observations and suspicions. He nods, following along.

'Best not make a big issue of it, yet,' Gren advises, after a moment's consideration. 'I don't want him stressed if we can help it. I'm not familiar enough with his metabolism to feel comfortable in giving him pain medication, so he's just dealing with all his physical pains, and his emotional ones, on his

87

own. Thank the Eternal Oarth that the bone-mender worked on his leg though, or else I'd have to keep him sedated; it would be a cruelty otherwise.'

'I agree, Doctor, best to keep him comfortable, as much as we can. When we meet up with the *Grolthon's Spear*, they'll get to the bottom of whatever mystery Mr. Rowland presents, if they see fit to do so.' Using 'Mr.' instead of 'Baron' here is leaving a terribly unnatural taste in my mouth, but I'm forcing myself.

Gren nods in agreement, then sits quietly with me, each of us with our own thoughts on the matter. I find myself not entirely looking forward to the arrival of the *Grolthon's Spear*, they'll take Rowland aboard, and out of this system, for certain—meaning that our short time together will come to an abrupt and permanent end.

'One question though,' I ask, hopefully, and Gren perks up with interest, which I'm glad for, because I've had this curious thought ever since seeing Rowland out of his clothes. 'That ... hole, on Mr. Rowland's stomach, just above his belt line. What's that?'

Gren's entire expression lights up, and I can see the tidal wave of information forming in the depths of his eyes.

'It's his *navel*, isn't it fascinating?' And at my blank expression, he proceeds to unleash the flood. 'Human babies don't grow like we do—they live in their female dad's insides for like nine months or so, then come out when they're mostly done. Sort of. Anyway, while they're in there, there's this feeding tube that connects their female dad's system with theirs, passing nutrients and stuff along, and when they get born, that tube needs to be chopped off. The little hole that's left over is called a *navel*, but they sometimes call it a 'bellybutton', which is just so unbelievably cute!'

I'm now somewhat uncomfortable, trying to imagine along with what Gren is saying. 'So, they ... they don't mature in their barondad's pouch?'

'Well their dads don't have a pouch. Think of it this way; their female dad has a built-in pouch in her insides, whereas our baron's pouch rests on the outside, atop his tummy, as you know. You remember when your kids were born, how they were ...'

'Yes, I remember,' I interrupt, now obviously embarrassed. The birth of children in Oarthecan society is a sacred event; it's an entirely intimate experience only shared between the sire and his baron, the details of which are simply not discussed, not even between close friends, even if one of them's a doctor and already knows the details. It's considered highly crass to even mention it, but I forgive Gren because he's just being his expressive self, not insensitive. Cralren and I ... well, I will just put this simply: I have never felt more love for another, nor by another, in my entire life, than the moment when our children were born. It's a deeply special, almost holy, event—one that is just not talked about openly.

'Yes, well, you know the rest,' Gren says, catching my discomfort. 'Suffice to say that human offspring don't continue their development in an exterior pouch, they mostly develop inside their female dad. That's why you didn't see a pouchline either; humans don't have them because they have their bellybuttons instead.'

I grin at him; Gren is so delightful to be with, when he's not saying things that embarrass me. Just the right combination of intelligence, kindness, and curiosity. Plus a bravery and conviction that rivals the heartiest of warriors, which I had no idea he possessed and am so wonderfully surprised to discover.

'You know Gren, without you today, all of this would have gone down in flames. Normally, I would have brought along a co-pilot for assistance, but I just didn't want to expose additional crew members unless it was necessary. Turns out you were the one man that was needed for the job. I'm proud of you, Gren.'

Gren smiles shyly, pleased by my praise. 'Well, it's your example that I drew inspiration from, Captain. The way you knew exactly what to do, and even when the pressure got really high, you stayed in control. It's easy to see why you're the captain, and ...' He pauses, seeming to struggle with what he wants to say next. He looks me square in the eyes, his courage coming to the surface again.

'And I don't think what OSS Command and the Assembly of Barons did to you was right, Captain, kicking you out like that, over what happened all those years ago,' he says, firmly, bravely. This is a taboo topic he's bringing up—almost as severe as the child-birthing—and my face takes on a wary look, indicating my discomfort. I'm about to reply in some way that changes the subject, but he continues before I can think of what to say.

'It's obvious that you're supposed to be in command, and not of a mining station,' Gren states with conviction. 'You should be at the front of this war, at the front of securing Oartheca from the Pryok'tel—like you used to. You've got the instincts and the know-how, but more importantly, the right heart for it too. If you're going to take the time to make a commendation for me, then I'm going to do the same for you—I will write the OSSN directly and let them know that reinstating you would be in Oartheca's best interest.'

'Gren, that's kind of you, but you'll buy more trouble for your efforts than it's worth,' I explain, cautiously. He frowns immediately so I continue. 'I'm happy to be where I am, and given the chance to provide service, still.'

'You're not happy. You're depressed,' Gren replies, not unkindly but still a little too bluntly for such a diagnosis. 'I'm speaking as your doctor, now, Captain; I've looked after you for the past two years and you show a lot of the signs ...'

'My punishment wouldn't mean much if I was happy about it, Gren,' I interject. 'It's supposed to be unpleasant, after all.'

'Yes, but I doubt the intent ...'

'I'm fine, Doctor,' I interrupt again, more forcefully but not nastily, and I give him a reassuring squeeze on his shoulder to show that I'm not angry with him. 'Things just have to be the way they are, for now at least. Honestly, I'm fine, but thank you for thinking of me.'

He eyes me disapprovingly, and the tone of his next words reminds me Gren is a spitfire, when he needs to be. 'You're not fine, but I can see we're not going to agree on that for the time being. When you're ready, one day hopefully not too far off in the future, we can talk about ways to help you cope with what you're going through. As your doctor, your mental health is as important to me as your physical health, and … as your friend, if you think of me like that, it's doubly so.'

I smile. 'I do think of you as my friend, Gren. It would please me no end if you thought of me that way too.'

'I do, and I'm glad to tell you that,' Gren replies. 'And … unless you directly order me not to, I will let the OSSN know that reconsidering their decision in your regard would be not only wise, but fair. I'll be smart about it, you know, nothing demanding, just an invitation to reconsider. It can't hurt your case.'

'My case is over,' I say, looking over my nose at him. 'But if you want to write to the OSSN, I won't stop you. I'll thank you, instead.'

'Well, you're welcome then,' Gren replies, and he wraps his arms around my torso as I give him a good hug over his shoulder. Our little cuddle dispels the tension of our conversation, but just to be sure, I give the top of his head a fatherly kiss.

I do believe Gren will follow through on his intention of pleading my case to the OSSN; I just don't believe it will do any good. Perhaps I am depressed, as Gren says, because any hope that I'll one day return to being in command of a proper OSSN frigate died in me a long time ago. My statement about being happy to be of service is true, in the sense that were I not the captain of a mining station, then I'd be nothing. It was all I was allowed to be.

Gren is also correct about my depression in that most of us are—the war we've been waging against Pryok'tel aggression takes as much out of our hearts as out of our bodies. There's no end in sight, either, at least not in my lifetime, perhaps not my sons'—we just don't have the resources to push them back; it takes everything we have just to keep them out of the Oarthecan system.

And so, when I pit my little worries against the worries of my home, there's just no contest. So I get a mood on me occasionally—I'll survive it.

There's no choice but to.

CHAPTER 10

Rowland

I've been awake for a couple of hours now; hard at work.

Shortly after Gren finished tucking me in, he placed that band back over my chest, snug but not constricting, and I gave my best performance, pretending to be asleep, trying to get him to leave as soon as possible. I couldn't see what he was doing, but he stayed in the room for a few more moments, before I felt his gloved hand very gently touch my forehead, and then softly pet the top of my head.

'Poor fellow,' he murmured softly, and I actually felt better from his comforting words. 'What an awful day for you.'

He then departed, turning off the main lights, leaving the one directly above me dimmed. I got to work as soon as he left.

Remember the touchpad Toar handed me, with the Oarthecan language? Toar and Gren didn't, and thanks to some lucky sleight-of-hand when I transformed my blanket into a kilt, coupled with the distracting excitement from my 'dramatically heroic' attempt to insist on finding my crew, they forgot about the device, which I slipped beneath the mattress. I've been lying on top of it the entire time, waiting for Gren to leave.

I wait a good twenty minutes at least, though it feels like an hour, before fishing it out. As soon as my left hand touches it, I've jacked into its primary interface, the first command I give being to dim its output light to near blackness—there's a porthole window in the door and if they check on me, I wouldn't want the touchpad's illumination to rat me out.

It's a rudimentary device, little more than an electronic book, but it has what I need, which is wireless connectivity—there would be no way to transfer the language to my biocomp otherwise. I've been worrying that the device would be limited to just transmitting protocols, but a quick check dispels these fears—while it appears the touchpad was purged of any data, the operating system is intact, and capable of sending and receiving transmissions. Which means these good Oarthecans, as kind as they are, have just inadvertently handed me the keys to any connected electronic device within range.

It's child's play to find the local network, but they have shown basic common sense by using an encryption protocol that's blocking me. So, it looks like I'll need to take a trip to *Bow-Ties* again, to see all that can be seen.

I could describe the steps required to hack this encryption, discover the network, and all the devices linked to it, break into those devices, and become the administrator of each, but it would be like describing a sixth-year's triumphant defeat of a pre-schooler on the playground. Once upon a time, the security protocols the Oarthecans use would have been considered excellent, it's just that that time came and went before I was even born. They are in desperate need of a cybersecurity consultant, and if what I plan to do works out, I'll offer my services for free by way of apology.

Suffice to say, I'm soon in *Bow-Ties*, meeting all kinds of new people, one of whom is the smarmy and stubborn auto-doc, who after a brief conversation with its operating system, is now convinced that my cybernetic implants are entirely legit, and she can't wait for my next appointment, would I be so kind as to stop by?

I also meet the operating system of the shuttle craft I'm apparently on, who is an absolutely foul-tempered misanthrope—my subconscious represents it as a hobo with rotted teeth filed to sharpened points. I can't say a computer system can be actively mean-spirited—I mean they have no emotions—but this one comes close with its sheer reluctance to help with even basic commands.

It's a simple spacecraft—basic short-range vessel, standard inter-planetary Under-drive, not bad propulsion capabilities though, better weaponry then *Lucky* has—*had*, damn it—and pretty decent scanning systems, especially for metallurgy detection, analysis and topographical identification. Of course, this shuttle must be used for mining—Toar had mentioned the OSS Mining Division in his initial communication to me. It also explains that lingering smell of kelmisite that's been bothering my nose.

The shuttle's systems also have a delightful amount of log files stored on them, everything from six weeks' worth of mission reports, personnel logs and the entirely helpful flight records, which quickly catch me up on where I've been and am currently. We're out just past the kelmisite asteroid field, likely so that we can make long-range comm transmissions—and there those transmissions are, in the hands of a helpful old-world switchboard operator—copies are ready for my perusal when I get the chance, because I'm going to need to know more about this shuttle and where I am, if I'm to have any hope of rescuing my family.

Otherwise, the navigation system has a moderately decent map of the surrounding star systems and spatial features; there're some gaps, especially nearer to the CAPS borders, but I do notice they have better mapping of the Pryok'tel Hegemony's space than the CAPS does. I deduce this means the Oarthecans are not a part of the CAPS, but more than that, there's no treaty, either—or else they'd share star charts with each other. Some tech sharing, what with the UTs and auto-docs—but the CAPS gives those out like candy to children at a playground—so this means the Oarthecans are new to the CAPS, maybe? I'd never heard of Oarthecans, but that means nothing—a new sapient-level species is discovered at least every year, and I've not been keeping up since my departure from the CAPS.

Environmental controls, sanitation controls, life support, cabin monitoring, propulsion—all the standard components are present, and all are highly maintained for a ship that from what I can tell is ... two hundred and twenty-three years old? This causes me to pause and reconsider things for a second. If this shuttle, at first glance, appears primitive to me, its age indicates that at the time of its construction, it was at a more advanced level than ours were — it even predates the foundation of the CAPS. Why the lack of upgrades since then? I mean it's obvious the Oarthecans value the shuttle—according to the numerous maintenance logs, it's looked after like a beloved pet—but why so far behind the times? It's something I will need to ponder later.

It's time to face the hobo now: turn its spiky frown upside down and get it to see me as its new owner. It resists in the form of encryption, command code confirmations, verification passwords and the like—but it's a toothpick fence in front of a hurricane, I'm afraid. It bends to my will, and the first thing my subconscious does is reformat its image to one more pleasing to me. The familiar blue god begins to coalesce from the hobo's ashes, a beautiful phoenix that solidifies into ...

An Oarthecan. A cobalt-blue Oarthecan giant, no less, but one who appears to like his gym time. While naked, it seems and ... rather happy to see me, too, by appearances. His eyes are not a mirror of the galaxy, either—they're the colour of storm clouds, a wonderfully moody grey, with electric edges crackling with life. He's got a wide happy smile on his muzzle, his expression cheerful and keen to help.

I'm going to have a word with my subconscious about this. I get that it would be an Oarthecan, but ... *this* particular Oarthecan? I mean yes, I know, the blue god is obviously based on Toar, I'm not stupid—I mean I am stupid to even be imagining this to begin with, but I mean, I thought I'd only had a twinge of interest—not this ... blatant, er ... why can't I imagine pants for him? What's with that? I ... why's he so ... eager ... to help me? Later, later—there are things to do that need doing.

'Hello there, Mr. Administrator. I am Shuttle Craft A for the OSS Mining Vessel *Lurcaster's Claw*. Awaiting your commands.'

It said hello to me. I know that it's my biocomp working with my subconscious to interpret the operating system, manifesting its command line and responses in a way that's easier for me to understand, but ... why would I make it say hello? I usually interpret it as the polite but innocuous 'Greetings' followed by its identification protocols ... why am I making this one so friendly?

The first thing I establish with this 'Blue Boy' is whether I have complete control over the entire vessel; he cheerfully replies that I do. I don't want to trigger that yet; taking over the vessel will consume almost my entire concentration and resources to manage, and I need to learn more about my situation to devise a plan for what happens next.

My next step is to instal a rudimentary AI overtop of the shuttle's existing operating system, based on a pared-down version my own biocomp uses. The AI's necessary here: while I could manage the ship using my own internal resources, all the little bells and whistles that'd need looking after would hog my system resources, forcing me to concentrate on operating the ship rather than interacting with the outside world. Given all that I will need to do out in that world, I can't spare those resources, so setting up an AI will take care of the ship while I look after the rest of my plans. I slap a heuristic learning algorithm protocol on as well, which should help the shuttle learn faster and become more responsive to my commands.

Finally, I switch on the shuttle's monitoring capabilities—there are cameras in this room, and the main area outside, where I can see Toar at the helm and Gren asleep on some benches, and exterior cameras show us currently out in the middle of space, with nothing but the wide starry void surrounding us.

Toar appears to be writing on his personal touchpad—a quick electric sniff in that direction and I can tell that I could access it easily. He's still wearing his spacesuit, though his helmet is off, and Gren is in what I guess is the under-suit they wear beneath. Why they're in spacesuits is a question I've already pondered, and I figure that we don't breathe the same kind of air, and since I'm injured, they can't treat me if I'm the one wearing the spacesuit. It works in my favour, but I'll need Gren back in his for my plan to work.

I'm going to vent them into space and steal the shuttle. I don't want to hurt Toar or Gren at all, let alone kill them—I mean, I'm obviously forming an initial attraction to the authoritative yet primally handsome Toar (yes, no one is more surprised than me—I usually buck at authority figures), and Gren is a living teddy bear full of cuddles and kindness—but this idea formed in my head when I first thought about why the Oarthecans were wearing spacesuits to begin with.

They'll be fine—I'd never consider this plan otherwise. Out they go in a quick puff before they even know what is happening, then I'll contact their mining station and have them send another shuttle over to pick them up. In the confusion while that's happening, I'll fly my new pet shuttle over, then deep-jack the station, and use its Under-drive to go after the Pryok'tel.

It's not the most detailed of plans yet, nor the noblest, I'll admit. All I can think to say is that I will play every card I have to rescue my family—every card. I owe them that. I can't let goody-two-shoes bad feelings about upsetting a pair of Oarthecans I've just met stop me from doing what needs to be done. I could never forgive myself if I did. I won't hurt them, that'd be going too far, but making them suffer the minor inconvenience of an impromptu spacewalk is a small price to pay for getting my family back.

Even if Toar and Gren saved my life, fixed me up and have been nothing but kind, courteous, and … fuck, *gallant* towards me since we've met. I've said that I'm not one of the good guys. I've never been able to afford that.

Okay, self-justification for endangering the lives of others over; the shuttle is mine, and I've got an eye on his crew. I set up a trigger to notify me if they get too close to the camera nearest the door to my room, because I'm going to need to start reading and researching my next steps, and that means going through records, logs, communications—everything, trying to find the answers to the many details I need to resolve.

I spend a good amount of time—real world hours I think—studying what I can find, not only from the shuttle but also a comms buoy that we're linked to, still back in the asteroid field. One of the first surprises I discover is the Oarthecan stellar communication method—Under tunnelling—which is again about fifty years behind the times. They open micro-dive portals between themselves and a series of comm buoys they've got spread out all over their territory, then transmit their messages as light waves, which are basically massless, between their buoys until they reach their intended destination. The time that it takes a message to cross distances via Under tunnelling is relatively short, as compared to, say, the speed of light itself, which could take years to communicate between locations, but it's an absolute snail's pace compared to modern CAPS comm methods.

It must take them hours, possibly days, to send communications between themselves; I can't imagine this level of frustration because I've lived my entire life under the CAPS's comm method. We use quantum entanglement to send binary pulses between coupled particles—basically, instantaneous messaging across the entire known system, so long as you've got access to one half of the paired entangled particles. Because of its near-instantaneous speed, it's possible to have live conversations, even if you're on opposite sides of CAPS space. Most CAPS ships have hundreds of particle halves, with their other partnered halves being kept in various centralized repositories spread over our territory in a quasi-public communication network.

I'm able to obtain all the information the buoy gathered from where *Lucky* had her final day—and can confirm that there were no other life-signs detected in the wreckage. The bridge section is still tumbling where the attack occurred, but the aft section, where I was, is nowhere to be found, likely due to its explosive venting sending it off into space. The buoy recorded the scene of my rescue— Toar is one damn fine pilot, I will give him that; anyone watching the footage would be left amazed that we made it out alive.

I'll shed a tear for the *Luck of the Draw* later; right now, finding my family is the only thing that matters. I did love my ship, but it was a thing, and I'm not obsessed with things, either in the collecting or the having. Maybe one day I'll come back to this spot, see what I can salvage from the bridge, see if I can find the aft section, but it's unlikely—*Lucky*'s gone, but there's still hope for her crew.

Once I think I've gathered all I can from the buoy, I dig through the shuttle's brains, and discover a dossier on a mining station named the *Lurcaster's Claw*, which is the name Toar mentioned, and I receive its entire crew contingent: names, ranks, careers—yes, they're a civilian outfit, Toar told the truth again. He's been in recent contact with them, and so it's these communications I listen to next:

'Mission successful, First Officer, one survivor rescued and secured: Dr. Gren is seeing to the survivor's injuries. No other casualties to report,' Toar's voice indicates; he's definitely a captain, has the officialness and authority part so smoothly blended into his words that it becomes part of his natural speaking. I've tried to wean myself off using that voice, but there are times when it's extremely helpful.

'Congratulations, Captain. Is he ...?'

'Maintain your position. I'm taking the shuttle outside the asteroid field; have Threng locate the nearest OSS Naval vessel and transmit their coordinates and comm channel to me. Resume mining operations as per the schedule, and you remain in command pending my return. Captain Toar out.'

Hmm. That cutting off was strong and Toar doesn't seem like he's the gruff kind—granted I've spoken maybe two dozen words to him, so what do I know? But my first impression—other than 'holy fuck that's a giant bear'—is that he's civil and compassionate. Something's not quite right with how he's speaking to his First Officer.

Toar's next communications are from his science officer, a Threngdral Drellriscion, who's got a young-sounding eagerness to him as he provides Toar with the coordinates and comm frequency for the OSSN *Grolthon's Spear*. Soon enough, I'm privy to the transmission that Toar sends the *Grolthon's Spear*, and that's when things get weird for me.

*****

TO: Cpt. Derrarvral Henthrothsire, OSSN *Grolthon's Spear*
FROM: Cpt. Toar Grithrawrscion, OSSM *Lurcaster's Claw*
RE: URGENT REQUEST—Immediate Assistance for the Care of a Human Male

On 27.13.221.21.13 we responded to an automated distress call from the CAPS-S *Brunhilda's Grace*, which was the victim of a Pryok'tel ambush and was destroyed. See enclosed logs detailing our observations of this encounter. Life-sign scans of the wreckage detected one survivor, and we were successful in our attempt to retrieve him. We have rescued a human male, who identifies himself by the name 'Rowland'.

Though Mr. Rowland's current condition is stable, we are unable to fully see to his injuries, and given his nature, lack the facilities to adequately provide long-term protection for either him or ourselves from the known biological incompatibility that exists between our two species. Consequently, we request immediate assistance to release him into your care.

We are aware of the decree governing the interaction with humans and have taken all reasonable precautions to ensure we have no direct physical contact, including remaining in enclosed spacesuits in his presence, at all times. As Dr. Gren is aware of a human male's Allure, we have taken additional precautions in the form of olfactory suppressants to prevent any unintended exchange with Mr. Rowland.

It must be said that Mr. Rowland is exceptionally striking in appearance, to the point that his presence may compromise the effectiveness of your crew, even if they are under suppressors. It is with my highest recommendation that he is kept secured, with the fewest number of people knowing he is aboard, for everyone's safety.

It is necessary to state that I do not find Mr. Rowland is to be entirely trusted, yet. He appears to have illegal cybernetic implants, as identified by the CAPS's auto-doc system. Additionally, his vessel's call sign was registered with CAPS-S credentials, but my initial inspection indicates the vessel was civilian class. Finally, the arrival of the Pryok'tel, and their subsequent attack, leads me to believe he has a level of involvement with them that requires further investigation, even if he is their victim.

However, Mr. Rowland has taken no action against us and has been cooperative and forthright. My opinion is that he is a conscientious person whose primary concerns are with his family, and who has suffered a recent and terrible loss at the hands of the Pryok'tel. He reports five of his family members are missing and is desperate to locate them.

For that reason, I humbly recommend that you please treat Mr. Rowland with the utmost kindness and hospitality, for if there was ever a person who needed it from us, it is him. I further recommend that you consider contacting the CAPS, to see if they can help locate his family, if that is a course of action unavailable to yourselves. I am including the extrapolated breach point for the Pryok'tel vulture, in the Derresion system, for your further consideration.

We will hold position at the enclosed coordinates, awaiting your most expeditious arrival.

*****

Well, that was an interesting read. It poses more questions than it answers, such as 'what is an Allure?' but the key words of the day are 'the Derresion system'. That's over three light years from where we are, according to the shuttle's star map. Can't get there in the shuttle, but I'm certain a vessel the size of a mining station has an Under-drive that can.

But then they would be stuck in that system, their Under-drive drained and needing to be recharged. With a Pryok'tel vulture lurking about. That's a problem—I can't leave an entire mining station's crew hanging out in space under that kind of threat—that card's not even in my deck. I love my family, but they would never forgive me if I got others killed on their behalf—I mean Ivan probably wouldn't mind that much but the rest would never speak to me again, I'm certain of it. I wouldn't speak to myself.

I'm changing my mind about venting Toar and Gren into space, not unless there's no other choice. It seems Toar's communication, imploring for my care and safety, even though I present a biological risk to them, has touched the better part of me. His comments about my appearance were … flattering, but they're not the reason for my change of heart—anyone who would show me this level of consideration while risking themselves deserves a better solution—if I can find one.

I scan a few more files quickly, but there's not much more that's immediately useful. I'm interested to learn about this Allure, a power I possibly have, and how I could use it to my advantage, but I need to lock down the details of my plan to get myself to the Derresion system first. If Toar turns me over to this Captain Henthrothsire, I'm going to lose any chance I have of saving my family—there's no way I could deep-jack a vessel that's frigate class size, and as soon as the CAPS gets involved, I'm off to prison and my family is dead—they will not risk their personnel to rescue criminals.

Criminals. We were doing crime, when the Pryok'tel attacked. There was an extremely specific reason we were in the asteroid field to begin with: the automated transport. There's no mention of the transport in Toar's communications, nor of the scans recorded from the shuttle—where's it gone? Did the Pryok'tel ...

My entire universe of worries narrows into a single point in my brain in a terrific rush, a black hole of realisation sucking everything into one inescapable point of doom. I need to speak to Toar, now. There's no more time for planning, I need to act.

That's when my motion sensor beeps in my brain; there's movement in the shuttle's main cabin, and when I check the internal cameras, I can see Gren is awake, and Toar is sat beside him, having a conversation. Using the shuttle's internal monitoring system, I tune in, hoping for some additional information they may be sharing that I can use as part of my plan. No such luck, but I get to be included on a fascinating topic my two new friends are discussing.

It's pretty clear they're very curious about me, which is understandable, but my ears burn when Toar and Gren start making compliments on my appearance. From what I piece together of their following conversation, it sounds like the Oarth are a single-gender species, all males, with the ones being referred to as barons being the primary child bearers.

This isn't a problem for me to understand—I've encountered single-gendered species before, as well as trinary-gendered, shifting-genders, parthenogenitors, parasitic reproduction and even benevolent symbiosis. The universe is fantastically diverse when it comes to ways to reproduce—but my embarrassment hikes up a couple of notches when I discover exactly why the Oarth have been referring to me as 'baron'. I don't mind the misunderstanding, I'm actually quietly amazed that the universe allowed for this parallel to form, and yeah—it's nice to be admired and all—but it's that they're backing the wrong horse, and that's making me feel guilty. I wonder if the Oarth would show the same courtesy to Betts or Mia, let alone Cor, as they've been showing me. I'm going to need to make it clear that calling me Mr. Hale is the most honest way to address me.

Which, from the next part of the conversation, seems like the right thing to do—this decree they're mentioning, an enforced ban preventing Oarth and human men meeting, seems like a good idea. The CAPS is not an empire, officially—we're supposed to be building a community, but I wouldn't hedge my bets that at some point in the future, the CAPS wouldn't leverage this Allure thing if the Oarth had something worth taking.

Then the conversation turns quite interesting as they get into the nitty-gritty details of things—xenobiology has always fascinated me and I've never been shy about sex stuff. But Gren is definitely behind the times regarding current inter-species reproductive options—it's highly probable that Oarth and humans could have children—perhaps not in the traditional Oarth method, whatever that is—

but thanks to technology, I can think of at least a half-dozen sure-fire methods, readily available, that can allow a person to become a parent with practically anyone else who wants to be one, including—thanks to CAPS legislature that guarantees the rights of clones—themselves.

There are some restrictions, such as if there's a fundamental core difference like carbon-based versus silicon-based, organic versus artificial, or cellular incompatibilities (or not having cells at all)—but those are just a handful of exceptions in comparison to the whole. More often, it's cultural restrictions that prevent people from different species having children, and there are always ways around those too.

It's when their conversation switches to the topic of Toar's punishment for something he's done in the past, and the resulting depression because of that, that I realize my surveillance has turned into full-on eavesdropping. From the sounds of it, Gren is Toar's doctor, and so I'm now clearly breaching their doctor-patient confidentiality, and I cut off my monitoring so that I can return their privacy to them. I'm saddened to learn that Toar's not doing well in the brain box; he seems like a decent kind of guy, first impressions and all, but that's not going to stop me from doing what I need to do.

There's no more time to waste, it's time to bring my new Oarth allies into the fold, and I will need all the tricks, cajoling and, if necessary, outright begging, to accomplish that. My plan is risky, but it's the only one I can think of that will work. Standing, and being careful of my wound, which actually isn't all that bad—I was hamming it up for the distraction benefit—I tie the blanket into a reasonable kilt, using the strap that was holding me down as a belt, and walk carefully to the door. I can hear them speaking to each other, making plans, and so I know that it is now or never.

I knock solidly on the door, and say in a cautiously friendly voice, 'Hello?'

CHAPTER 11

Toar

The knock from the storage room door gives both Gren and me a bit of a start, and we pull back from our hug like we've been caught by our dads still up past our bedtime. When I hear Rowland's tentative 'Hello?', I'm on my feet quick enough, heading to the door's porthole window.

Rowland is just on the other side of the door, and he smiles apprehensively when I approach. I have to admit, for the first few moments, I just goggle at him, his beauty getting the better of me, not helped by the fact all he's wearing is that blanket—his wide shoulders and broad chest, plumped with hefty muscles, that delightful, slightly rounded tummy with its fascinating 'bellybutton', and all that light brown fur leading down, down, down—but he's out of bed, which is worrisome because he's still injured, and I can't help but furrow my brows in concern.

'Everything all right, Mr. Rowland?' I ask, rather more loudly than I intend, but I've at least ensured my voice carries through the door.

'All is good,' is his friendly-sounding reply. 'Just would like to talk, if there's a chance.'

I look over my shoulder to Gren, checking with him to see if that would be permissible.

'Should be okay,' Gren indicates, looking around for his spacesuit. 'If he's well enough to talk, then there's no reason not to. Here, you go in first, and I'll get ready and join you as soon as I'm re-suited.'

I nod to Gren, then turn back to the porthole. 'Mr. Rowland, if you'd be so kind as to go to the back of the room there, I'll come in just as soon as I get my helmet on. Won't be a moment.'

'Sounds good,' Rowland responds cheerfully, perhaps overly so, and then starts to walk back. It's then I see he's wrapped his blanket about his middle and I feel a terrible pang of guilt—we've taken his clothes, and he's not got anything to preserve his modesty other than that little blanket. Have to fix that—I'd be jailed if I ever treated a baron the way I'm treating Rowland—and while I know he's not a baron, there's this very strong part of me that just can't see him otherwise.

I fetch my helmet quickly and secure it in place, noticing Gren's managed to get the bottom half of himself back into his suit, and then return to the door. Trying to salvage at least something that resembles courtesy, I knock, asking if it's okay to come in; Rowland's reply is again cheery, but there's definitely a sense of apprehension in his voice. He's still sitting on the gurney, and he's running his hands along that touchpad I'd handed him before, nervously. Hmm—I'd forgot about that touchpad, and my inner voice warns me about idle hands being playthings.

However, at the sound of the door unlocking, he lifts his head, and I'm struck right in my heart by just how lovely his hazel-green eyes are, but he only holds my gaze for a moment before looking back down at the touchpad.

I enter the room, slowly and without making myself appear too menacing—I've been told that I can seem menacing, though I don't mean to, so I've mastered the skill of making subtle entrances when they're called for, like now.

'How may I help, Mr. Rowland?' I enquire, pleasantly. He again looks up for just a moment before he returns to looking at the touchpad.

'Heh, actually, it's just Rowland,' he replies, kindly. 'If you feel more comfortable with it though, it would be Mr. Hale. Hale is my family name. But you're very welcome to use Rowland, or Row, if you like.'

'Right, then, Rowland. Sorry for that,' I reply, again trying to be as courteous as I can. My word, he's such a good-looking baron—such wonderfully expressive facial features, like the gentle slope of his cute nose and those terrifically rich, inviting lips—but why's he not looking at me? Can't see anything on that touchpad he's clutching—not that there'd be anything to see, what with only having our language file on it. 'What can we do for you?'

'Well, I'm feeling much better, and there're some things I'd like to explain, and I'm sure you have many questions, too.' He pats the gurney, and I step forward without a second thought. I stand closer to him, an arm's reach away, but I can't quite yet bring myself to sit on the gurney—seems too forward, and I want him to see me as a proper, respectable drone, not some street-cad on his first sight of a baron that's not his dad.

His eyes are bothering me though; not his actual eyes themselves—they're a beautiful, green-soaked hazel—reminds me of being deep in the forest on a sunny day, just magical to look at—it's that he's not keeping them on me for anything longer than a moment before they dart away. It's like being bathed by wonderfully warm water and then having it switched to icy-cold just as you're enjoying it. I want to address his obvious concern, but in an effort to appear as helpful and non-threatening as I can, I'll need to let him take the lead with whatever he wants to talk about.

'Well, only if you're up for it—wouldn't want to overwhelm you, so, we'll just have ourselves a nice chat, at your pace, as long as you like and about anything you like. Sound all right?' I offer, and I catch myself lowering my head to look in his eyes when I say it. I pull back, appearing like I'd planned my behaviour, but I'm still left with this feeling that I've done something wrong, something to offend him, and I'm scrabbling to think of it.

Maybe he's upset that we've taken his things and left him naked and alone? I'd be, after all, if I woke up on a ship with a bunch of strangers who need to always remain in spacesuits around me. He's probably furious that I won't help him find his family, which I empathise with, but I really can't do anything other than what I've done; I know it's not enough—if I were still an OSSN captain I'd dive into the Derresion system full speed, guns blazing, dear Rowland, I really would ...

'Why is it that I call you Captain Toar, and not Captain Grithrawrscion?' he asks, all of a sudden, but in a polite tone. 'Is Grithrawrscion not your family name, or do Oarthecans just go by one name in conversation?'

'Oh, well, that,' I begin, just as politely. 'Grithrawrscion is a clan designation, uh—not really a formal name. Us Oarth—that's what we call ourselves—Oarth, just have our one name, really, since our clan designation can change over time— Toar Grithrawrscion is just a short way of saying "I am Toar, Scion of the High Baron Grithrawr XXI". So that's why it's "Captain Toar", otherwise it would be "Captain Scion of the High Baron Grithrawr XXI", which wouldn't really make sense, because my dad has many scions, see, one of …'

He is looking at me now, fully, as I ramble on, and he's got a cheerful glint in his eyes as he listens to my foolishness. It's brilliant to behold. He's smiling a small smile, and I automatically return it. He's so lovely to me, right now, his charming face and his perfect eyes—so full of character, and intelligence, and beauty. I'm sorely missing my graphite claw and paper scraps now—I could spend hours capturing every one of his beautiful expressions, from the way he's turned his head over his shoulder as we talk, to his downwards glance when I first saw him holding the touchpad. Such noble features too, even though he's much broader than our barons are—both in terms of his impressive physique and general facial structure—but still carefully sculpted and shaped, like the Great Oarth himself built him from the clay of the Grand Shores of Mighty Yorturen, breathed His divine breath into His creation and brought forth this miracul …

For a terrible moment I think my pills have run out—Gren did remind me that I needed to take them more often than he did, and I'm scrambling to remember if I have—it was, two hours ago? More? I give a good sniff through my spacesuit. I still can't smell anything. I better …

'Go on,' Rowland says, kindly. 'Your dad has many scions … you mean your siblings?'

'Oh yes,' I confirm, rather proudly. 'Dad's got thirty-one kids, two of whom …'

Rowland's eyebrows lift, and his mouth drops into this gorgeous expression of amazement, revealing perfect little white teeth, barely fanged at all; teeth that would make our barons burst from sheer envy. How much I would love to run my tongue over those teeth, feel their smoothness, taste each one of them, then invite his tongue to taste mine, feel how sharp they are, long and at the ready.

'Your dad has thirty-one children?' Rowland asks, and as I nod my head, he chuckles this lovely little laugh. My heart does skip a beat now, at this delightful sound.

I think of all my brothers: my two sire-brothers, who were born with me from our shared sire dad, Cullergrath, and my twenty-nine baron-brothers, one of whom is a baron himself, the Baron Grithrawr XXII, spread out amongst Dad's seven other sires. Our family used to be larger, but we've lost some of my brothers along the way—eight at last count. We're luckier than most families though—we pay for the protection of Oartheca with our very lives, after all— but I don't want to share this sadness with Rowland, not when he's starting to like me, a bit at least.

'Yes, and grandchildren too—three from me, plus more from …' I tell him.

If I thought his small grin was beatific, then the grand smile he beams at me now nearly knocks me off my feet. Rowland's little cheeks puff on each side, and there's such a joy in his eyes that it's obliterated any of the concerns I had about him.

'You're a dad? That's awesome!' Rowland cheers, genuinely thrilled. 'Are they with you, at your mining station, the, er … *Lurcaster's Claw*?'

Good memory this one, but I don't recall if I mentioned it was a mining station. I'm about to reply when Gren comes in, carrying one of the drawers from our unofficial galley, turned into a makeshift tray. A suncoat-sized ceramic mug, a thermos and an assortment of our protein bars, the ones from the emergency supply kits, are all included in the tray, and he's managing not to tip any of it as he carefully steps inside.

'I brought you some drinks and snacks, in case you were hungry, Bar … Mr. Rowland,' Gren announces. 'Not sure what food of ours you can eat, but these are just basic proteins and carbohydrates, should be safe for you, if you're hungry. I've got some hot water, and if you're feeling brave, I could make you some *dulian* tea—it's very mild and shouldn't be a bother for you.'

The kind expression Rowland provides Gren makes my heart swell with affection; I can see the caring and gratitude radiate from him, and it's taking a lot of my control not to reach out and touch him, just to prove to myself he's not a dream. What a wonderful, sweet man this is, to show such gratitude for the smallest tokens of courtesy we're able to offer him. If there was a chance, I'd serve him the first harvest of *arenlan*-blossom nectar, in a fine silver chalice, and then …

I am not Allured. I'm not. Being Allured is a significantly more powerful sensation, there's an urgency when you're Allured—to bond, to protect, to sire, and serve, and I'm not feeling that at all—well, the siring part for sure, but it's not got that same level of absolute 'must' with Rowland—it'd be great if we did—wonderful, even, truly—if he'd have me—but it's not like I feel I might turn feral if we didn't. I'm definitely deeply attracted to him, that's obvious—I mean I cannot think of anyone that wouldn't be, save for the Allure-blind, but those poor blighters wouldn't want Rowland anyway.

I know that my judgement is being affected, though, and Gren's presence reminds me that I need to be professional, so I stuff my fanciful feelings down and resolve to bring my role as captain to the front. In a nice way though, I mean Rowland is still a lovely creature, no need to scare him away or intimidate him.

'Thanks, Dr. Gren, that's great of you. I'll try that tea. You not knowing if I can have it is sorta connected to what I'd like to talk to you both about—I'm sure my care has been very tough for you, what with the auto-doc not working on me.'

Both Gren's and my eyes go wide. Gren sets the drawer down somewhat shakily but doesn't stop himself from starting the tea. He gives me a quick look though, uncertain.

'It's all right, I'll explain,' Rowland says, 'The auto-doc told you I have illegal cybernetic implants; I know because those implants told me that I was put into an auto-doc. They start here,' Rowland explains, and then reaches out with his left arm, lowered, and opens his palm, touching the centre of it with his right index finger, 'where I've got a direct neural systems interface port installed, just under my skin. That's linked to my entire nervous system, then all the way up to my biologically integrated computer—my biocomp—which is right here,' he indicates, touching the back of his neck, where our own universal translators are installed. 'It's sort of like your UTs, but more powerful.'

He looks at Gren, and then me, and he still has his smile on, but it's forced. He's nervous, and his eyes are once again not able to hold mine for more than a moment.

'What do these implants allow you to do, Rowland?' I ask. My tone is clear and non-confrontational.

'Well, before I explain that, I would like a chance to say a few things, just so we get off on the right foot,' Rowland requests, and regards me expectantly, waiting for my permission.

'Go on, then,' I reply. My voice is flat now, cautious, but I'm still trying to sound nonchalant. All those little happy tingling feelings that I was enjoying pause mid-flight.

Rowland breathes out a big sigh. 'Okay, first and foremost: I mean you no harm, at all, in any way. I promise you, and I know you've got no reason to trust my promises. Just know that I'm hoping, really hoping, that we can be friends. I'm counting on it.'

Neither Gren nor I respond, and so Rowland continues, his eyes still switching back and forth between mine and Gren's.

'The second thing is that I have nothing to do with the Pryok'tel—their attack on my vessel was entirely unprovoked—we had no idea they were coming. But it's obvious they knew we were there; the time from when they dived in, to when they dived out, means that they were close by and waiting for us—this was a set up.

'And that leads me to my third point—going forward, you need to know that anything I do, or have done, is solely to get my family back. They mean everything to me—and the thought of them in the danger they're in is driving me crazy.'

He takes a pause, sighing again. He gives Gren a look, specifically at the tea that's been brewed, and after a quick confirmation from me, Gren hands it to him. Rowland takes a small sip, thanks Gren with that sweet little smile, and continues.

'With those things in mind, let me continue by saying I'm not with the CAPS-S, as you've deduced. I'm not even a salvager—I am ...' He pauses to search for his words, shrugs, and says, 'A criminal. A thief. I specialize in breaking into complex security systems. Which is why I have this,' he holds up his left hand.

'My cybernetics are used to directly connect to those systems, disarm them, take them over, and then the thieving starts. So, you may ask yourselves, what was an illegally cybernetically enhanced thief doing in the middle of an asteroid field past the farthest section of his known space? Well, he was thieving, of course.'

He takes another sip of his tea before he continues. 'Not long ago, my friend Corculhoran, the Harculcorian I mentioned, finally got the last piece of a puzzle he's been trying to solve for the past six years: the disappearance of a highly valuable CAPS-T automated transport, which was declared lost, twenty-some-odd years ago.

'Its disappearance has always been a mystery—those transports are designed to ship goods across war zones, and one had never gone missing before, nor since, I think. So finding this missing transport has become a quest of sorts—a 'holy grail' or 'city of gold' or 'fountain of youth', something so amazingly valuable but lost so completely that finding it was considered a fool's errand.

'But Cor ... Cor is a smart man—he knew better. The man is a genius mathematician, with the patience of a saint and a banker's greed. He'd been gathering every fact he could about the transport: where it started from, where it was supposed to end up, what path it was taking, what was going on in space during the time it got lost, every little fact or detail went into his giant brain, and stewed there.

'So then, he found an old astrometric report from a Jylrelanrian stellar cartographer, which indicated that a previously undocumented comet had passed within a portion of the transport's dive path. The comet contained high volumes of rare radiogenic materials, which would have corrupted the transport's dive-point calculations—meaning its Under-drive nav system got fucked up, and dived to a point it wasn't supposed to.

'Figuring out the maths involved with calculating the comet's volume of radiogenic materials versus the corruption factor versus a thousand other variables is so far beyond my brain's ability to understand that even my biocomp can't do it. Not Cor though—patience of a saint, greed of a banker—he did it. Tracked it all out—found out that it dived too close to a star, which would have screwed its stellar nav drives, and so it drifted. He plotted its drift course, through several sectors, and found its most likely position was back in the kelmisite field, where any long-range distress calls the transport would have made to get itself rescued would have been blocked.

'Now, we had no real proof that it was here—but these transports are known to carry extremely valuable cargo, so just even coming out to see if we were right was worth it. Plus Cor would not let up, it was his own *magnum opus*, and he swore it was here. And ... he was right. We arrived in the asteroid field two days ago, and after sending out a series of short-range comm requests, pretending we were the transport's owner's—well, early yesterday morning—we get a reply: beep beep beep, here I am, come get me. With me so far?'

He stops and looks at us both. Gren is sat cross-legged on the floor, listening, but he's got his thinking face on. I'm still in front of Rowland, my arms folded across my chest. Thief indeed. Foolish old man, you really know how to pick them. But he is that beautiful …

'Go on,' I say, bluntly.

'So we found the shuttle, and broke into it, and the treasure was ours. For a moment, like, just a moment, the entire universe was perfect. Then the Pryok'tel attacked and everything came crashing down to shit. They knew exactly where we were, and not only that, knew exactly when I had cracked the transport—I hadn't even been back on board for more than an hour before the first volley hit. But this is not the worst of it, not by a long shot.'

He breathes out another long sigh, and I can see him steeling himself for something we're not likely going to enjoy hearing. Not that I've enjoyed hearing any of this, mind.

'See, the contents of the transport are valuable, but not nearly as valuable as the transport itself. It's got a full veil, a Variable Energy Intensive Lightwave & Electromagnetic Distortion Device. Completely disarmed, ready to be removed, reverse engineered, mass-produced, and ...' he sighs again, deeply, at his own next words, '… deployed on every vessel across the entire Pryok'tel Hegemony.'

*****

I've never had my manners tested before as much as this man's testing them now.

'A *veil?*' I'm unable to hide the disbelief in my voice. 'You're just saying that so that we'll send everything we've got to go and rescue your friends.'

'I really wish I was,' Rowland replies, dully, 'but I'm not. It's the reason I agreed to Cor's idea to begin with—a chance at an actual veil? It's worth the price of some star systems.'

'Ah, yes, how silly of me—this is about money then, is it?' I accuse him, nastily.

Rowland frowns at my words, and for a half breath, I'm cowed by my appalling rudeness, but I'm finding it difficult to believe his story—not the attack by the Pryok'tel—witnessed that first-hand—but the idea that a veil's involved is too farfetched. I mean, I hope it is—the complete conviction Rowland's putting into his words is difficult to fake, but he's admitted he's a thief, so who knows what he's capable of?

'No, it's not about money,' Rowland retorts, calmly but there's an edge of irritation to his tone. 'At first, yes, absolutely it was—but now? I think we both know the danger our people would be in if the Pryok'tel arm their fleet with veils. And if you don't believe me when I say they've got one now, and can do just that, then by all means, Captain Toar, let's waste what little time we've got arguing with one another about it. It's not like there're the lives of my crew on the line while you figure out whether or not I'm telling the truth.'

'As I've said, I'm doing all I can in that regard, Mr. Hale,' I reply, not rising to his goad. 'I don't think you could expect me to risk the lives of my crew to save yours. You're a captain as much as I am; would you do the same if our situations were reversed?'

'Yes, because there's a goddamn veil on the line!' he snaps, and then appears to regret his outburst immediately, scowling as he looks away, embarrassed. He's flustered, understandably so, and I'm quite aware I'm coming across as the villain here, refusing to believe him. Seeing his distress is uncomfortable for me—Rowland may not be a baron, but my more primal instincts disagree, and there's a whisper in me telling me I'm doing something profoundly wrong by upsetting him. But there's no proof of anything he's saying about the veil—and I'll have him bawling like a baby before I even consider the smallest fraction of an idea that puts my men in the firing sights of the Pryok'tel.

'I don't expect you to risk yourself or your crew, Captain,' Rowland continues, once he's settled himself. 'I'm not asking that—I got myself into this trouble, and I'm the one that needs to fix it. All I'm asking is for you to let me borrow this shuttle for a day or so; I'll fly off to the Derresion system, assess the situation …' He pauses in his explanation, seeing what must be a very dark look forming on my face.

I lower my head and level my gaze at him, face to face so he cannot look away. He recoils, somewhat, a fearful look in his eye, and I feel a stab of shame for having put it there, but it does not stop me from continuing. 'How is it you know about the Derresion system, then?' I ask, as calmly as I can manage. I know I did not tell him about that.

This catches him, and he goes silent. Gren stands and takes this moment to step between us. 'Baron Rowland, Captain Toar, let's take a moment to resettle here,' he starts, nervously. His slip in using the incorrect honorific is carried through to his next statement, and he's not even aware he's doing it, from the state of his worried tone. 'Baron, you told us you wanted to be friends, and …'

'You're dismissed, Doctor,' I state.

Gren raises his eyebrows, and Rowland's eyes move to regard our doctor, his brows coming together with concern. No doubt because his only ally in this room is about to be ejected.

'Sir, I …'

'Mr. Hale does not appear to be in any urgent need of your services. Return to the main shuttle compartment and write your final report on his assessment. Have it readied for my inspection within the hour.'

When Gren does not immediately move, I add with a cool terseness, 'You have your orders, Doctor. Dismissed.'

To his credit, Gren only provides me a neutral look of compliance, then turns and leaves the room without a backwards glance, shutting the door behind him. I'm sure that later, I'll feel badly for my rough treatment of him, but at this moment, I cannot have him as a distraction. Rowland has moved to take a position behind the gurney, putting it between us. Again, perhaps I will later regret making him feel he needs to take a defensive position with me, but not now.

'I asked you a question, Mr. Hale,' I start, failing entirely to remain calm—my tone is not kind and I don't care, but it's still taking mental effort for me to refer to him as 'Mr. Hale' instead of 'Baron Rowland' ... would it be 'Baron Hale' instead, I wonder? I push these nonsense thoughts down and return to my point.

'The Derresion system—there's no way you could have known that on your own. When you say that you're a thief and can breach security systems—is that what's happened here? You've breached us?'

'Yes,' Rowland admits. He is looking at me; his gaze is unwavering, but I can still see the fear there. He's been caught and there's no way out.

'To what extent?' I ask, pointedly.

'End-to-end. I have complete control over this vessel,' he says steadily.

My jaw hardens and my eyes narrow. Unconsciously, my fingers have splayed and hooked, preparing for a fight. I correct myself immediately, reminding myself that it's not just that Rowland's half my size and no match for me physically, but that the idea of harming even a hair upon his beautiful head is sickening.

'I see,' I manage to say. 'And by end-to-end you mean what, exactly?'

'Life support, environmental, comms, propulsion—all of it. I can even stop the toilet flushing,' Rowland states, trying to sound humorous.

'Well we wouldn't want that,' I respond flatly. Again, there's no proof in his words—just his unshakable conviction when he speaks them, and that's starting to wear down my resolve.

'Am I or Gren in any danger from you, Mr. Hale?' I ask, forcing a calm tone. I don't suspect we are but I'm more interested in his reaction to the question.

'No, no,' Rowland hastily assures me, and takes a hesitant step forwards, one hand extended, perhaps wanting to comfort me, but he catches himself and stops. 'No, none at all. You saved my life and I owe you big-time for that.'

'Odd that you'd show that gratitude by taking over my shuttle, then,' I retort, but he's faster with his reply.

'Not really, Captain. I'll do anything to save the ones I love. Taking over your ship isn't something I'm proud of, but it's not a problem for me either. A ship the size of that vulture's got about a fourteen-hour Under drive recharge cycle, meaning there's *maybe* ten hours remaining until they dive from Derresion to God knows where, and I lose the chance to find my family. I have to save them, and if you can't help, then for crying out loud, at least don't stand in my way-the clock is ticking.'

That same damn conviction in his voice. He's not wavering for a moment and it's becoming increasingly difficult to sense if he's lying or not. And he's right about the vulture's rechange cycle-it's been just over four hours since the attack, and unless the vulture's got other business in the Derresion system to keep them there, they'll be gone before lunch-time today. But I can't let that sway me here.

'How do I know you're not being crafty, Mr. Hale? You've said you've taken over the shuttle, but last I checked, I was still in control at the helm.'

'*Blue Boy*,' Rowland says aloud, and there's an electronic chirping noise that springs out from the room's comm panel—almost like a cheerful little *terk-terk*—and it's not a sound I've ever heard this shuttle make in all the time I've been aboard. 'Raise the temperature in this room by five degrees, and provide confirmation when complete.'

At my puzzled and now worried expression, Rowland explains casually, 'I've installed a rudimentary AI on the shuttle's systems. Based on my biocomp's, and voice-activated. Helps when you want to get things done with a limited crew.'

Though not exactly thrilled by what I just heard, nevertheless, I begin to feel that it's getting warmer in the room, and as the temperature rises, so too does my temper. There's another electric chirp from the comms panel, and a voice I've never heard before—but one that still sounds familiar somehow—speaks.

'Temperature is now twenty-six point six two degrees.'

'So you can make it warmer,' I remark, trying to sound unimpressed by this new development, but feeling entirely the opposite. 'Environmental control ...'

'*Blue Boy*, spool the Under-drive and calculate a dive portal one hundred kilometres off the *Lurcaster's Claw*,' Rowland orders, and after the electric chirp states it's complying, I hear the distinctive hum of our shuttle's Under-drive engine begin to power up.

'Enough!' I bark, angrily. Great Oarth, he's got our engines!

'*Blue Boy*, disengage Under-drive and power it down. Clear dive portal calculations.'

'Complying. Completed.'

It takes a long moment while I force the thunder brewing in me back down my throat; my fingers splay wide again for a quick moment, but I breathe out through my nose, unclench my jaw, and give Rowland a hard stare. His point's been amply proven—Under-drive access is limited to only authorized personnel—and now this game's changed into an unpleasant reality.

'Can't let you have this shuttle, Mr. Hale,' I start, firmly, 'and I can't negotiate with you when you've got me in such a bad spot. I don't think ...'

'We're not negotiating, Captain Toar. I can't negotiate the lives of my family, that's not something ... I mean would you, if you were in my situation?'

I raise my eyebrows. 'If I was in your situation the last thing I would do is bite the necks of the only people who can help me.'

'And how is it that you can help me? By contacting the *Grolthon's Spear* and hope they go after the Pryok'tel, if they feel like it?'

He cuts me off before I can stammer out asking how he knows about the *Grolthon's Spear*.

'End-to-end, Captain—all your communications, your scans, your records—everything that's been through this shuttle that was stored in its memory. It's not important right now.'

I want to disagree, rather loudly, but he continues before I get a word out.

'What is important is stopping the Pryok'tel, getting the veil back and rescuing my family. Because Toar ...' he stops, and hesitantly steps further around the gurney, so that it's no longer between us. 'If I can't save them, then there was no point in saving me. They're everything to me—without them, I'm nothing.'

I study him, sternly—that conviction he's been wielding is only getting stronger. His lovely forest-coloured eyes—*he is that beautiful*—are locked on mine; they're imploring me, compelling me to give in. But I won't, despite the growing part of my heart that's telling me I'm wrong. He's not a baron, I'm forced to remind myself, and I'm not Allured, he's just pretty and sweet, and that's all.

'I can't do it, Rowland. Not … not without real evidence there's a veil.' I relent, mollifying my heart if not him. 'And you have to return my shuttle to me—I won't consider helping you if you're a threat of any kind to us. See it from my side, if you want me to see it from yours.'

He sighs wearily and lowers his head, shaking it. There's a part of me, a small but still vocal part, that has the urge to hug him—to physically comfort us both—it's part of my culture, part of my nature, after all, to connect in a very tangible sense to help resolve conflicts and restore good feelings. Plus, he does look terribly upset, and I've been a brute towards him—I'm feeling the need to make amends and soothe us both. It's his damn, beautiful, not-a-baron-but-tell-that-to-my-heart appearance that's messing my head up, making me unsure of myself.

'What proof would you accept?' Rowland asks, giving the first sign this situation might be on the path to peaceful resolution. 'I have records on my ship that show the plans we made; I can access my bridge from here and download them for you—schematics, security assessments, tech manuals, maps, our flight paths, our tactics … everything that will prove we've been planning this for months.'

'And my shuttle?' I ask, making sure I sound collaborative—I do not want to force him back into conflict mode.

He looks pained. 'You … you understand that your shuttle is the only way I can save my family, right? So long as I'm in control of it, then I have the power—and therefore the responsibility. But if I return your shuttle, then you become the one that must make the decision. The decision if they live or die.'

'I do understand that,' I answer, decisively.

'Are you sure, Toar? I'm offering you a way out here—I'll take you and Gren back to the station, you can say I stole this vessel—which will be easy to do because that's absolutely what's happened—and you're off the hook from that point forward. I don't want you to get involved in something you're not at fault for, something that's going to be extremely dangerous.'

I pause for a moment. 'See, that's where you're wrong, I think. I'm involved already. I became involved when I saved you. I made that choice, and, well, I need to see it through. I will do what I can, and if there's some plan you have, I'm willing to hear you out. But we need to trust each other, Rowland. It's the first step in saving your family.'

That gets to him, and I can see a battle forming in his mind.

'You promise?' he asks. Demands, more accurately.

'I do. I promise.'

*****

The next half hour is difficult to listen to. Though we have restored ourselves, in terms of civility if not trust, Rowland explains everything that he's done while we thought he was resting, and I'm both amazed and frightened by how thoroughly he's compromised us. In addition to completely taking over the shuttle and having it obey his every spoken word, he's also been able to get into every scrap of electronic documentation we have aboard.

I doubt he's given up his control of the shuttle; one does not simply hand over the last arrow in one's quiver so obviously, and so easily. Rowland, despite his beauty, is a manipulator, and a scoundrel, but I remember his words that everything he's doing is to save his family, and so while I don't like what he's done, I suppose I can understand why he's doing it. I'm forced to admit that I might do the same, more if I could, if I was in his position—I'd hope any captain in charge of his crew would do his best, like he's doing. I also doubt that I could stop Rowland from retaining his access, given the degree of his success to begin with, and so I'm going to play along with his apparent contrition to see where it goes.

He's not boastful of his achievements, I'll give him that—if anything, he apologises for his violations against us and makes no comment on our woefully vulnerable systems—I know the CAPS is more advanced than we are, I just never realised how much more—part of me now thinks that if Rowland were able to completely take us over using a simple touchpad, what could the CAPS do to us with a fleet of these cyber-thieves with all their toys?

Rowland's named our shuttle '*Blue Boy*', explaining that for the voice commands to function, the shuttle's operating system would need a prompt to listen for—something unique so that it knew it was being addressed. I can't pronounce that name at all—the best I can manage is '*Vlue Voy*', which is all wrong, so Rowland tweaks our shuttle's understanding to accept the Oarthecan equivalent as well: *Cres Gur*. When I asked him why he chose that name, he smiled vaguely and said 'it came to him in a dream' and that the shuttle appears to 'like the name due to its highly recognisable phonetic structure'.

I've no idea what he is on about, and I begin to realise, that I have no idea who Rowland is. I took him as the prettiest baron I had ever seen, and that was just another crushing example of the monumentally poor judgement I have been showing today. Terrible example, for Gren, for all of them. I don't regret rescuing Rowland, not in the slightest—that was absolutely the right thing to do, but my actions after that? Poor. Should have kept him sedated as soon as the auto-doc alerted us to the illegal implants—but I didn't. Because he is *that* beautiful, I wanted him to like me. Stupid, old, lovesick fool that I am.

Gren joins us again, and I give him a look that I hope tells him I'm sorry, and everything is good now. He doesn't seem to be particularly bothered by my snarling at him, and his demeanour quite improves when Rowland advises him that the auto-doc should be more cooperative, but it's with a very crisp professionalism that Gren reminds me that it's time for my pills, simply handing the bottle to me. We all move to the main shuttle compartment, so that Rowland can continue his retelling while having his session with the auto-doc. I'll need a moment to smooth things with Gren, but for now, we both continue to listen to Rowland.

From his research, Rowland's pieced together an excellent picture of his, and our, situation—it's not just the shuttle's records he's obtained; he's managed to download the buoy's records as well—and were it not for the distance to the station and the surrounding kelmisite, I'm certain he'd have gained access to the station's log—somehow. All that he knows about the attack, about us, and how we're planning to transfer him to the *Grolthon's Spear*—everything that he says that I can confirm from my own knowledge—is true.

He's also patched into the file system on his *Luck of the Draw*—and while the systems are damaged, he's managed to obtain an undeniable set of documents showing the details of the veil they were after. Precisely articulated technical specifications of the transport it was installed on and the veil itself, along with strategies for disarming and removing it. Meticulous records on discovering the transport's location in the kelmisite field, which match exactly with what Rowland explained previously. Flight paths, a series of Under dive portal coordinates—the lot. If this is a ruse, he's gone to incredible efforts to ensure its realism—efforts that wouldn't make any sense since our rescue of him was entirely coincidental—he had no idea we were also in the field. He had no idea who the Oarth even were.

Which means, on the balance of probabilities and the consequences thereof, it is more prudent to believe he is telling the truth about the veil than to deny it. While I'm sure he has the genius, charisma and appalling lack of morality required to fabricate a story like this, the highly specific details he provides about the device, and the speed at which he provides them—are just too clean for me to risk accepting that this could be a ruse.

I'll need to shove all my other worries—Rowland, Gren, my own blundering at how I've handled this—aside, because if the Pryok'tel have a fully functional veil, we need to act. Rowland is correct—if they dive from the Derresion system, we'll lose them for good—and then it will be just a matter of time before Oartheca is re-invaded, and we will literally not see them coming.

CHAPTER 12
Rowland

Despite my trip through the auto-doc, I still feel like shit. Yes, my side is healed, my head is fixed, my leg's fine and some cuts and bruises I hadn't had the chance to identify are looked after, too. Haven't had a full-scale auto-doc cleaning in years, so it's even managed to smooth out some old scars from past adventures and fix a cavity in my back molar I had no idea about. As a side bonus, after Gren ran a query, the auto-doc said that it looks like human and Oarth physiology is highly compatible—we can breathe the same atmosphere, eat the same foods, shake hands and get married if we want to.

I don't say this as a joke, either: determining cross-species compatibility is a priority for an auto-doc—knowing whether or not, for example, the saliva from another species will, say, wind up pre-digesting your tissue (never, ever kiss a Myliorian, even though they're beautiful purple hued elves with solid ebony eyes—and the inability to store body fat—they're cut like diamonds as a result), or possibly cause a fatal allergic reaction (Brolocons—shame, their dorsal tentacles look like they'd be a lot of fun), or result in you experiencing psychosis induced-rage (Pelprotrals, who developed it as a natural defence—they're slurred as 'crazy-spits', which is really unkind).

So, given that, I was hoping to get a hint as to what this 'Allure' thing with the Oarth is all about, but the auto-doc is silent on the subject—it literally displays a green check mark when the request for 'human versus Oarth' is finished. Gren, watching out of the corner of his eye, also gets a momentarily confused expression at the result, but he's been on the subdued side after getting verbally bitten by Toar.

Who looks miserable, by the way. He's tired, at a minimum—I don't know Oarth facial expressions entirely yet, but drooping eyes and sluggish movements are a pretty good indication of fatigue, for many species. His massive frame seems to be sagging under its own weight—he's taken position at the helm, and is slumped in the chair there, resting his helmeted head against an arm he's propped up on his elbow. His other hand looks like it's doodling something on the surface of the console he's closest to—his gloved fingertip making little scratching motions in a deliberate way. He still wants me to go over everything I know, trying to find out just how far I got into their shuttle's systems. Nothing I'm saying is improving his expression, either.

'All done,' Gren says to me, kindly, but I can tell he's tired as well. He helps me out of the auto-doc, and hands me a coarse-fibre under-suit, similar to the one I saw him wearing through the cameras. I'm grateful to receive it; it appears that the Oarth enjoy much lower temperatures than humans do—the main shuttle cabin is below ten degrees and it's hard for me not to shiver in my ad hoc kilt.

'Found this in the back lockers,' he mentions. 'It's for a woodcoat, so, it might be big on you, but I'm sure you'll like it better than a blanket.'

I nod, and thank him, then say to him, 'Look, now that I'm all fixed, why don't I go in the spacesuit instead of you two? I know that there's this Allure thing to worry about, but …'

'What do you know about the Allure?' Toar groans. His eyes are closed and there's a pained look of exasperation on his face.

'Nothing, other than its name, and that it's the 'biological incompatibility' problem you mentioned in your communication to the *Grolthon's Spear*. That's it,' I lie. I'm not yet ready to admit to overhearing their conversation, where they had mentioned I was 'over-endowed' with this Allure ability. We've had enough truth for one day, and there's plenty of hurt and distrust between the three of us to see us through a good long while.

Toar doesn't say anything further, just keeps his eyes closed, shaking his head slightly as it rests on his arm, so I turn to Gren, 'It would at least give you guys a break, you both look like you're dead on your feet.'

'It … I'm …' Gren stammers, and then looks to his captain.

Toar doesn't respond for a moment. When he does open his eyes, there's a bored look of resignation in them, and it's almost dangerous to behold. He's suddenly on his feet, marching to us, and both Gren and I shrink back. But Toar stops in front of me, lowers his head so that we're eye-level, gives me a curious look, then straightens back up and proceeds to remove his helmet.

'Captain, be careful!' Gren warns, reaching out to put his (by comparison) very little hand on Toar's very big arm in an attempt to stop him. It doesn't work.

Toar's helmet comes off and I realize this is the first time I'm actually looking at him, rather than through the clear dome of his helmet or a camera. Though tired, and still miserable-looking, he does seem much more … emphasized, than he did before—his features are clearer now, and he just looks so much better for it—I can see the fur colour around his squat muzzle is a lighter grey than the rest of his face, his ears are more pointed than Gren's are, and those incredible blue eyes of his shine even brighter now.

But Toar doesn't appear to be quite done ignoring his doctor's orders. He returns to my eye-level, and for a moment the size of his massive head, full of numerous sharp teeth, triggers my fight-or-flee instincts, and if it was not for those eyes of his, assuring me, I probably would do one of them. Hopefully flee, if it came to it—because a physical confrontation will not end well for me—but then my nose catches a strong, spicy aroma that is somehow both new to me and yet familiar on a level I don't understand, and I inhale deeply, just as I see the end of his broad, black nose twitch at me, giving a good whiff of the air near me too.

'Nothing. Can't smell a thing. Let alone him,' he mutters, then turns to head back to his chair.

'Captain, you mustn't …' Gren starts loudly, but Toar just flatly replies, in that bored tone, 'Damage done, Doctor. No sense in worrying about it now,' as he slumps solidly back in place. 'I've got a feeling Mr. Hale and I will be spending a lot of time together, in the near future. Can't do it while living in a spacesuit all the time.'

Gren and I share a look before he replies, 'I ... I think I will just stay in mine, just in case, if you don't mind, sir.'

'Probably the wiser course of action,' Toar grumbles.

'Look, let's ... let's start again, can we?' I ask. 'You guys saved my life, and so far the way I've paid you back for that has been kinda on the shitty side. Even though the guy you saved is a sleaze-ball, that doesn't take away from the fact you did the right thing.'

'It's nothing to do with you personally, Hale,' Toar replies, and not unkindly either. 'It's what you've done that's bothering me.' His voice is so much nicer to listen to without that helmet, I think, even though what he's saying is not. There's a deep rumbling timbre in his voice, which makes sense considering his massive size, but I find that I like the way he almost sing-songs some of his words—pulling the vowels out if he wants to emphasise his meaning. In particular, how he says my name makes me grin, 'Rooowland', with a plunging 'o' that hikes back up at the 'land' part—Gren doesn't do that when he speaks, and I'm wondering if the difference I'm hearing is an accent or a difference in their ethnicity.

'You ever hear of skip-diving, Hale?' he asks. The look he is giving me makes me think he already knows my answer.

I nod. 'That's my plan. It's the only way, all things considered.'

He grunts, looking off into the distance, saying nothing more. He's already figuring out my plan, and he knows it's not a good one, even if it's the only one.

Gren pipes up, 'That's a new term for me, skip-diving. Is it like little dives, one after the other, like skipping a stone? I thought you could only do that if you're not travelling very far between dives.'

Toar does not lift his chin from his hand but gives me a look and a nod in Gren's direction.

I turn to Gren and explain, 'It's when a smaller ship, like ours, flies through a dive portal that a larger ship, like the station, creates. Because the dive portal the larger ship creates is calibrated for a higher mass, it can catapult the smaller ship, letting it "skip-over" its own dive-range limitations. That way, I can fly to the Derresion system, and leave the *Lurcaster's Claw* safely behind.'

Gren puts on an overly-enthusiastic smile, looking to Toar. 'Oh well, that's wonderful then, right?'

Toar looks over his nose at me, and then raises an eyebrow. I've left out a very significant detail about skip-diving. I don't want to worry Gren, but I can see either I tell him, or I'll force Toar to, and that's not fair.

'Well, it's got some risk to it,' I continue to Gren. 'There's a lot of maths and planning involved ahead of time, you know, when calculating exactly where the smaller ship will end up.'

'If it ends up anywhere at all, that is,' Toar remarks, dryly.

Gren's brows knit together so vigorously that I worry he'll sprain a muscle, so I quickly counter Toar's point, 'Which it does, when the math is done correctly, Captain. But yes, Gren, if there's a mistake in opening the portals, either the entrance or the exit, the littler ship could under- or overshoot its exit portal, and … well, not come back.'

Gren's expression is a testimony to the word 'aghast'. 'Stu … stuck in the Under? How do you get out?!'

'You don't,' I reply, trying to smile as kindly as I can at him.

'Needless to say, not recommended procedure,' Toar adds, but he gives me a resigned look. 'But needs must, and all.'

'No, no, no there's got to be a different way—we can wait until the *Grolthon's Spear* gets here—they can make that dive all by themselves, easily. We'll just go on board, ask the captain, and we're off, safe as your baron's den!' Gren insists, looking from Toar to me for confirmation.

'The Pryok'tel aren't going to stay in the Derresion system, waiting for us, Doctor,' Toar says, and now speaks more gently. 'Much as I'd like them to, mind. No, if I were them, I'd be on my way back to Hegemony Headquarters with a new toy that's going to take over the galaxy, as soon as my Under-drive was charged.'

'The Captain is right, Gren, we can't wait,' I add. 'The *Grolthon's Spear* may not even get our transmission for another few hours, and even then, they'll need time to recharge their Under-drive from the dive it takes to reach us—and the Pryok'tel will be long gone by that time.'

'Dive the station then!' Gren says, and to him this is a new idea. 'We can park just outside of the system, and then use the shuttle …'

Both Toar and I are shaking our heads, but it's him that speaks. 'Can't risk the entire crew, Doctor. We'd be stuck there waiting for the station's Under-drive to recharge, and that vulture could come by and pick us to pieces.'

Gren is still wearing that expression of horror. 'But … the alternative … stuck, forever, in the Under? That's … that's … no. No!'

'Needs must, Doctor,' Toar repeats, with an affectionate look at Gren, one that I think truly shows his sweeter side. 'The risk is not unmanageable, but yes, the odds are about fifty-fifty, from the reports I've seen of past attempts. Eternal spare those poor souls who found that out the hard way,' he adds, solemnly.

'I can get better odds than that, Captain,' I say immediately, making sure my tone sounds optimistic, not argumentative. 'Remember I told you Cor was a maths genius? He's got a formula that puts success well into the mid-eighties' percentile. We've skip-dived twice before, successfully—dived seven light years when my ship's on-spec limit was three.'

'Suppose you wouldn't be here to say otherwise if it hadn't worked,' Toar retorts, trying to sound funny, I suppose, but failing in my opinion, and my optimism fails as well. He catches himself though, and by way of an apology, adds, 'But I'm glad you understand the risks, and any help you're able to provide will be put to good use.'

'Certainly,' I indicate, but I'm beginning to doubt myself. Cor plotted those skip-dives; I may have his formula, but I don't have his brain, and it was always him who put both of those to use to ensure our success. I feel like Da Vinci's charity case apprentice—the one he had to hire to shut his family up—when I think about me having to plot those portals.

'Dr Gren, take Mr. Hale back to his suite and help him with that suit, it's too cold for him in just that,' Toar says, flicking his gaze at me in my blanket. He turns in his chair, silently dismissing us, and returns to staring at something off in the distance that doesn't exist. I've a feeling continuing this conversation may aggravate things, and Gren and I dutifully follow through with the plans to see me better dressed.

*****

'Sorry for all the trouble I've caused,' I apologize, lamely, as Gren unfolds the under-suit and shakes it out for me. We've returned to my 'suite', as Toar put it, and Gren's taken the time to close the door behind us.

'It's all right, just been a bit of a day. For you more than anyone. Here, one foot, then the other, both your arms, and then it just zips up in front. We can adjust the collars and cuffs for a better fit,' he smiles, but tiredly, and then turns his back politely so that I can dress.

'You won't be going with me, you know, Gren. I couldn't put you in that kind of danger. Otherwise who else would I have to fix me up when I get back?' I ask, trying to lift the mood.

Gren turns his head to see that I've got myself zipped sufficiently, and proceeds to help adjust the under-suit. He's right—whoever this suit belongs to has much larger shoulders than I do, and a much broader midsection, but a couple of tugs here and there and it's not looking so bad. It smells sort of like Toar did, but not as strongly—that vaguely familiar, definitely pleasant scent I don't recall encountering prior to meeting Toar—kind of musky but warming and comforting. Suit itches though, and I can tell the fellow who owns it has a rich shade of chocolate-coloured fur, since the interior of the suit has caught many stray tufts between its coarse fibres.

'Well, that will be the Captain's decision of course, but I think he'll agree with you. The two of you will need to plan out ...'

'He won't be going either,' I remark, my brow furrowing. 'Is that what he thinks?'

Gren blinks. 'But you asked for his help, didn't you?'

My eyebrows rise as I realize my own error. 'Just to help me open the *Lurcaster's* dive portal—that's all. He can't come with me—Jesus, no, it's suici ... it's going to be really difficult. I gotta straighten this out with him.'

'Not a good idea, right now, Baron Rowland, he needs a chance to think things over.'

'There isn't time, Gren, and ... it's just Rowland, if you like—I'm definitely not a baron, at a minimum. Kinda thought we could be friends, though, what with you saving my life and all.'

117

He smiles weakly. 'Sorry ... Mr ... Mr. Hale, I'd like that too, and I hope we can be one day. I won't stop you, if you think it's best to speak with him. Just ...'

He steps forward, so that the distance is close between us, and reaches out to gently take my hand. 'Be careful with him, please. He's ... you ... you have a lot of power over us. Do you understand?'

The sudden serious turn to his usually cheerful demeanour is a signal I need to pay attention. 'The Allure?' I ask. 'I don't know what that is, even.'

'No, not just the Allure, it's simpler than that. I suspect, like me, and probably most every other Oarth, the Captain may be attracted to you.' He gives me a momentarily bashful look, his cute little ears lowering for a moment, and squeezes my hand. I squeeze back, appreciating his candour.

'Despite what we both know about you not being a baron, you certainly still look like one,' Gren continues. 'Barons, in Oarth society, are our mating partners, the ones drone Oarth like Toar and me have children with. And you ... you are very much a baron, in our eyes at least. Somewhat on the extreme side, too, if I'm being honest. So I'm afraid it's plain old biology you're up against, Mr. Hale; our reaction to you is instinctual, and it's powerful, and I think the Captain is wrestling with that as much as anything. I just want you to know.'

'I thought it was something like that,' I reply, not letting Gren know that I overheard their conversation. Gren's usage of the word "drone" to describe both himself and Toar is also uncomfortable for me—there's an association of inferiority, but Gren seems fine with the term, and I remember that the UTs provide a direct translation of words, which does not always mean the connotations are transferred over. It just seems somewhat derogatory to me, that's all. 'Is there something I can do to discourage these feelings, other than being an asshole?'

He snorts a laugh and gives a look that says I should stop being silly. 'Just be clear with him regarding your intentions, is all; he'll not pressure you if he understands you. And maybe ... be careful with touching. We don't understand how your Allure works—it could be transmitted dermally.'

'What is the Allure, exactly?' I ask, directly.

'Oh, well, that's the mating signal our barons produce when they want to have children. Pheromone-based, stemming from scent glands in their necks, armpits and groins. Normally, even though most Oarth are sexually active with each other, to one degree or another, it's usually just for fun and all. But not with a baron; when a baron wants to have children with a drone, he'll mark the drone with his Allure, transforming him into a sire. It's a true biological change in both of them—makes them both fertile when they're otherwise not. And, understandably, very interested in putting that fertility to immediate use—the need to procreate becomes kind of irresistible at that point; a need that is only satisfied by the deed,' he explains, with a slight grin, but it's a sad one.

It takes me a moment to reply. 'I see. Humans can't do that—I mean many of us are horny most of the time—but our fertility isn't trigger-based like yours is—we're able to make babies even when we don't want to. I think we produce pheromones too, but our sense of smell is pretty basic, so I don't think we even actively notice them, let alone have control over producing them.'

'Well, we don't even know if it is your pheromones, to tell you the truth. It could be your hormones that we're able to smell, but are misinterpreting, or even something simpler—do you sweat to keep cool, like our barons do?'

'Yeah.'

He shrugs. 'Could be that. The point is, we don't know, so just be mindful. Please don't get me wrong—you are perfectly safe around any of us, even if something should inadvertently happen—drones will never hurt their barons, or force them, even if they're Allured—that's part of how the Allure works—we become extremely protective and focused on our baron's well-being. But I think it would be quite stressful and confusing if it should happen between you and an Oarth. I know most human males are only interested in mating with human females, so, I can imagine it becoming uncomfortable having a loyal-to-death Oarth following you around whose heart's desire is to sire children with you.'

I guffaw. 'I'll keep that in mind Gren. I don't want to affect either you or Toar, that way. Or anyone, for that matter.'

'I'm glad to hear that, Mr ... Rowland. I'm glad to hear that, Rowland. It's not like us Oarth are mindless, sex-starved beasts, please don't think that.'

'I don't think that about you at all,' I reply. 'You both seem like good, decent people—I think I'm quite lucky you guys found me, actually. But just in case, if this Allure thing does happen, is there a way to make it stop? Like, take a shower or something?'

Gren shrugs. 'No, once it hits, it hits. Distance and time will quickly end the fertility part, but the feelings never really go away, not altogether. Once an Oarth has been Allured, both the baron and his sire, their lives are changed for it.'

'So, what you're saying is "forever in love"?' I ask, and when he nods, I add, 'That's ... I see what you're saying. That's too powerful, Gren.'

'Yes, which is why I want to warn you. Toar knows all this, but if you're going to work with us, you need to know too. Keeping you in the pouch is as much a risk to us as it is to you.'

'More so you than me, from what you've explained,' I acknowledge. 'I'd never use it, the Allure, if that's its price.'

'Yes. I'm glad you're able to see it that way,' Gren states, giving me a very deliberate look. It's clear his warning was more for their benefit then mine.

*****

I leave Gren and return to the main compartment of the shuttle, where Toar is in nearly the exact same position as he was before. He regards me with an uncertain look, and the tension in the air hasn't lessened during my absence.

'That suit seems large on you,' he offers, after giving me a look over. 'Are you okay with it, for now? When we get to the station, I'll try and have something more on the suncoat side found for you.'

'It's fine Captain, thanks, but speaking of the station, you've brought up a point I need to clear up.' I take a seat on the nearby benches, and make sure my posture and expression are relaxed and open. Which is how I'm hoping this next conversation goes, but not betting on it.

Toar's expression darkens for a moment, likely thinking what else I could say that's worse than a stray veil in the hands of the Pryok'tel, but he puts on his captain face, and asks, 'What's on your mind, Mr. Hale?'

When I start, I make sure to sound calm, and clear. 'When I asked for your help, all I meant was for you to open the *Lurcaster's* dive portal for me—that's it. My plan was that I take *Blue Boy*, alone, through to Derresion; it's the reason why I took the shuttle over, so that I could pilot it and manage all the systems, on my own. You coming along wasn't what I had in mind, at all. I'm willing to take the chance with skip-diving, but I can't ask anyone else to—it's too dangerous, and I don't want anything to happen to you.'

He raises an eyebrow. 'That's kind of you, Mr. Hale, but I can't have that. At a minimum, turning over OSS property to a known ...' he stops, catches himself, and starts again. 'To a party outside of the OSS is a violation of Oarthecan law. At a maximum, asking one person in a little shuttle to go off by himself to save the galaxy seems foolish.'

'Fair point,' I agree. 'Two would be better than one. But not you.' I look him in the eye, and say directly, 'You have kids, and I don't want to be the one who takes their dad from them.'

Suddenly I find myself with a lump in my own throat—I managed to get what needed to be said out, but there's a kickback to my heart I wasn't expecting. Fuck, where's this coming from? I know where, of course; my own Dad, unfairly dead before his prime leaving Mum and me alone, but that was a quarter-century ago.

For a moment it looks like Toar is going to stand, but he changes his mind. He addresses me with a quiet, sincere tone, 'Again, that's very kind of you, Mr. Hale. My sons know their dad has a sometimes dangerous job, like all OSS personnel do, and they know that if something happens, I love them, and I was doing my best for them. I've been in service all their lives, and each of them has been in the services too. They understand sacrifice, as well as anyone can.'

'They won't understand when it comes to you,' I argue. 'They never will.'

Toar considers my words; I can see that I've said something that's touched him. After a moment, he leans forward in his chair, places both hands before him and knits his fingers together, and regards me with a kindness that makes him the most handsome I have ever seen him.

'Perhaps not. I'll tell you what—when you and I get this job done, you can tell them how silly their father was for even trying it, and then all four of you can scold me for being a dim-witted old man. Deal?' he asks, with a mischievous grin.

I actually laugh for a moment, but the seriousness comes back too quickly for me to enjoy it for long. 'Jesus, Toar ... it's too much to ask from someone I've just met. Too much for you to do for a person you've just met.'

'Well, never say I'm not a generous soul, will you then?' he asks. His sudden good mood was not how I was expecting this conversation to go—I was expecting a battle, fireworks, but he's gone in the complete opposite direction. And that worries me—is this what Gren was referring to, the power I have over them?

'Gren,' I begin, then take a moment to formulate how to say what needs to be said. 'Gren told me about barons, and how I look like one of them. He said that you Oarth are attracted to barons—you know, for like, sex and reproduction. So I gotta ask you this upfront, and I'm not going to think badly about you either way, regardless of your answer: are you attracted to me, and if so, is that messing with your judgement?'

Toar looks downwards, ears lowered, obviously embarrassed. He pulls back into his chair and rests his muzzle against the hands he's lifted. It takes him many moments before he speaks, but when he does so, he sits up with his back straight, and looks me clear in the eyes.

'Yes, I am attracted to you. You're the most beautiful creature I have ever seen,' he states, calmly. 'Yes, it's part of the reason why I want to help you—to say otherwise would be a lie. All I can say is that it's not the only reason nor the main reason. It won't be a problem between us, I can promise you that.'

I've mostly lost track of what was said after 'you're the most beautiful creature I have ever seen'. It wasn't the compliment itself—which was obviously sweet, but it was how he said it. He fucking *meant* those words, from somewhere deep down inside him. It's taken me aback; it's been a long time since someone has bared their heart so directly with me. While the timing and the circumstances are the shittiest this universe could possibly ever imagine for me, coupled with the knowledge that I'm entirely responsible for causing all of that shit to happen, Toar's words have given me hope that maybe I still have some worth, to someone.

I'm not responding, and Toar appears to be becoming uncomfortable with the silence, because he reaches up and scratches his head before placing his hand behind his neck.

'Sorry for that,' he says, sounding self-conscious. 'I know human men only like women; I didn't mean anything by it. Just, just being foolish, is all, I suppose.'

'I don't think that,' I reply, coming back from my thoughts. 'I'm flattered, actually. Deeply. And, for the record, not all human men are only attracted to women. Some of us do like men.'

His expression lightens, and he gets that charming little grin on his face for a second, but quickly switches back to his captain mode.

'I don't expect anything from you, if that's worrying you,' Toar explains, with too much resolve. 'We've only just met, and with bad timing, to say the least. And, you know, I must be quite … uh … strange-looking to you. You look like our barons, certainly, so my attraction is understandable, but … I know I'm quite, er … different from what you're probably used to.'

There's a part of me that wants to share with Toar that I do find him genuinely attractive, and that attraction is steadily simmering with every moment we're together. That yes, we're different-looking, but not alien. That I admire his stature and the way he carries himself—he's quite the blue-eyed behemoth—and that I've been imagining what he'd be like out of his spacesuit. That I find the colour of his fur really quite becoming, I have been wondering if it's as soft as it looks. That his ears look fun to play with and that I wonder if he's got a tail too, since the under-suit I'm wearing appears to have a particularly placed pocket in the backside I'm unable to find a reason for otherwise. That if eyes are the windows to the soul, then his soul must be as deep as the ocean that's painted his.

More than that though, I find that I'm drawn to him for the strength of his personality, admittedly what little I know of it. He's kind, sensitive, and good-natured, but not without the occasional fire when he's pushed, just like myself in that sense. We seem like we're both passionate about the things we care about—both of us are captains—yes, I know, only one of us is now—and it takes a strong will to handle that title. Plus, that whole charging in and saving me from the out-of-control wreckage of the *Luck of the Draw*—can't really ignore something like that, after all.

If it needs to be said, if it came to sex—which, yes, I've been thinking about, when there's a moment's reprieve from the constant fear for my family—then with half-hearted humility I can say that Toar's not even close to the most exotic sapient I've been with (though, he would be the largest—and figuring out the safety of any encounter is something I'm puzzling out in the back of my mind). I don't consider myself to be especially xenophilic—just androphilic, and there's a lot of variety with men these days.

Humans have found that this universe is a big place, and if, sexually, we limit ourselves to ourselves, we'd miss out on a lot of fun and learning—better to stay safe at home instead. Humans have always been sexually adventurous, and we took that adventure along with us into the stars. Finding an attractive werebear that digs you is not the weirdest thing this universe has to offer, by far—it's practically tame. Let's just say that if Toar and I were a couple, none of my fellow humans would even bat an eye. Well, possibly not—he's about two and a third metres tall and built like a barge, and I am sure they'd share my safety concerns.

But there's no chance to pursue anything like that with Toar, not while my family is in peril. If it somehow appears that I've not been thinking of them throughout all of this, that's a very deliberate choice on my part. They're the whirling panic that I'm barely holding back, their beloved faces are always just behind my closed eyes, and I'm not exaggerating when I say that if I think about them too long, I might go mad. Take the example where I'm risking a twenty-some-odd percent chance of eternal stasis in an infinite void and thinking 'yeah that wouldn't be so bad' as proof.

Toar is about to ride hand-in-hand with every risk I'm about to take, and while his reasons are not what I think they should be, he's not wrong when he says one person will fail. If I leave him behind, then that failure is practically guaranteed; if I take him, there's a better chance, slightly. Barely.

'We're not that different, Captain,' I answer. 'And you don't look strange, let's be clear on that. But it's good that you don't have expectations. You know that everything I do from this point out is to find my family. Everything, and the only thing. I owe them that. You understand?'

The look of disappointment on Toar's face is like a magnesium flare: hot, bright, but over before you blink. Then he shoves on his captain's face again, before I get a moment to regret what I've said.

'Yes, that's sensible. Understandable,' he says, with professional, and I think rehearsed, courtesy. 'I appreciate that we're clear, so thank you for that.'

'Sure thing. If you want to rethink your offer to help, I understand,' I say.

'No,' he says flat-out. 'It wasn't an offer, but it's kind that you'd allow me to, if it were.'

I smile in defeat. He's determined, and there's no point arguing. Our time is better spent elsewhere.

I start to stand, but there's a part of me that feels that I've cheated Toar; he was so candid with me, and I've given him the 'let's just be friends' speech. It's not the truth—I can't be more with him, but that doesn't mean I wouldn't want to. Toar saved my life, and so at the very least, I can pay him back with some of the honesty he's given me.

'It would've been nice, though, getting to know you, Captain, if things were different,' I offer. 'Outside of all of this shit I've got myself—and I guess you now too—in. I've always been a sucker for the big brave type, and you've definitely got that going for you. Being handsome on top of that is just a bonus, I guess.'

Maybe that was too much to say, but that amazing twinkle in his eyes comes back, and I feel better for having said it.

CHAPTER 13

Toar

There is much work to be done, and little time to do it.
I've dived the shuttle back to the *Lurcaster's Claw*, and we've arrived just after 05h00, meaning we've got just over six hours left before the vulture dives again. I've managed to convince Gren that I can dock the shuttle inside the *Claw*, since Rowland came up with the brilliant idea that he goes into a spacesuit instead of us.

This will allow our crew a chance to get the newly-named '*Blue Boy*' retrofitted for a cross-solar system adventure, without our entire crew needing to take olfactory suppressors to stop Rowland's Allure while that's being done. There's a laundry-list of upgrades we'll need for me to feel the even slightest tickle of the idea we're prepared here, and I've only given my crew two-hours to complete it all. They can do it, but I'm going to need to lean heavily on Yar's whip-cracking abilities to accomplish it.

Since there's going to be crew coming and going, Rowland's also taken to raising his helmet's radiation visor, which hides his face behind a one-way gold tint that he can see out of, but no one can see in through. And he'll remain on the shuttle at all times, as both Gren and I feel that actually allowing him to step on to the *Lurcaster's Claw* is too risky, and to his credit, Rowland agrees entirely.

I admit, I've got muddled feelings about Rowland; he seems to be a contradiction between a man who cares immensely for others and a man with no compunctions about doing as he pleases. Part of me admires him, and not just because—oh how did I put it then?—'he's the most beautiful creature I've ever seen'—well he is, actually—I could go on for hours describing him and think it's the best use of time imaginable. And he's smart, resourceful and obviously deeply loyal towards those he loves, plus he seems to know a thing or two about forming strategies and executing plans.

But it's his self-admitted criminal side that's bothering me something fierce. I don't hold with bad boys, never have—find the whole idea of furthering yourself at the cost of others repulsive, and so I hope there's more to him than that. As pretty as he is, I can't see myself getting on with a thief very well.

I've not spoken with Rowland much since our last conversation, you know, the one where I all but admitted that I was a lovesick whelp, and he told me to start doing my job. In a nice way, mind you; I'm not bothered about his request that we keep things on the professional side—thought he was kind about it, and it did drive home the urgency of the situation. Hurt a little, true, but I did appreciate that 'handsome' comment. Greatly. More than I should have. It's nice to feel worthwhile, is all I can say; it's been a long time. But that compliment keeps popping into my head whenever there's a spare moment, which isn't helping, so I've turned my attention to things that have a more immediate need to be solved.

Yar has been an absolute champion in that department, must say: he's been coordinating my every request, and not one prying question about any details he doesn't need to know. Before I arrived at the station, I had let my bridge crew in on that yes, Rowland is a human male, and that there was a matter of urgency that required our immediate attention in the Derresion system. I've kept the details truthful but sparse, as the less they know, well, the less trouble they'll get into, I suppose. All that I have said boils down to that the Pryok'tel attack resulted in them stealing a piece of valuable technology, and the recovery of said tech is rather on the important side. Left out the bit that it's a fully functioning veil—can see that causing a panic—but I did include this pertinent detail in my communications to the OSS.

I've also kept my mouth closed on the skip-diving part too—giving Rowland a chance to work out the equation necessary to make this step more palatable than 'there's a pretty good chance we'll fail before we even start'. I know Yar's guessed at the necessity of a skip-dive, possibly others too, but if they have, they're keeping it to themselves.

In the meantime, the shuttle's retrofitting is underway: I've ordered *Blue Boy* to be stocked to his gills with a full battery of both rockets and heavy-duty mining charges, plus upgrades to the navigation, targeting and scanning software to give us something that could pass as a tactical station, if you closed your eyes and believed hard enough. I've assigned our Chief Foreman to improve the medium-watt laser cannons as well, and to make sure our rocket and charge-firing systems are in full working order. Even Murth is helping—Eternal be praised—by coordinating a series of communications upgrades that will allow *Blue Boy* to intercept and possibly jam another system's comms, though he's warned me it will most likely fry our own comms if we try.

Gren has departed our shuttle, co-ordinating an update to the quarantine lab with some of his equipment; he has an idea that will help manage Rowland's Allure better than pills. It'll be nice to smell things again, so I was more than happy to give him the resources he needs. His departure was rushed, but he's assured us that he'll see us off—he seems less fierce with his Allure worries now that Rowland and I've been sharing the same environment without any immediately apparent effects. The 'no-direct-touching' rule remains in place, and both he and I have been good about that. Don't want to be, when I ask myself, but again, I'm seeing it as a way to help respect Rowland's request for us to keep it professional.

I've shut the entire station's mining operation down and pulled all available crew to help with *Blue Boy*'s last-minute retrofit, to keep the crew who are not immediately involved with the upgrades off and out of our way, giving them extra rec time and full use of the mess, all at full pay. I've tried to keep Rowland's identity limited to as few people as possible, but despite its physical size, the *Lurcaster's Claw* remains a small ship when it comes to rumours and gossip. Yar's been my stern voice though—any unauthorized personnel in the docking bay will lose two shifts worth of pay and be confined to their barracks for the remainder of the journey, and that threat seems to have done the trick.

One of the small kindnesses though that's really touched my heart is dear Rey, who volunteered immediately to help with the retrofit. He's a junior miner, so his technical skills are limited, but he can lift supplies, scrub laser banks, load mines, and do whatever task's set before him with enthusiasm. I caught up with him, in a private moment, and made sure that he understood how much his visit to my cabin meant—I kept it polite, mind you, just a good pat to his shoulder, maybe one sneaky kiss to his muzzle, and told him that I was flattered that he'd even think of me. He's invited me for a second attempt, at my pleasure, but …

But Rowland. I really cannot waste any more time with these daydreams of him. Doesn't matter that they're making me feel that maybe my life can be something like it was once. When I had someone who loved me, and it was more than just a fun encounter that's not meant to last past an evening. I told you, I'm a lovesick fool. Seventy-seven is by no means terribly old (for an Oarth, at any rate), but it's well and truly past young, and I need to stop acting so daft.

Focus, as Rowland asked me to do; that's what he needs from me, so that's what I'll give him. His entire family is in peril, and he can't be bothered by some faded old coat chasing his tail—even though he's not got one, just two wonderfully firm looking buttocks, with a slight dusting of that same light brown hair that's on his chest and tummy—Eternal, I would love to give each of those delightful globes a right proper squeeze. And more, with my tongue and such, but I can't think of that right now.

While my crew scrambles to fit all the upgrades in the two-hour window I gave them to do so, Rowland has been working on his formula for pulling off this skip-dive, which I unabashedly admit I'm nervous about—terribly so. I've done hundreds of normal dives, possibly over a thousand, since the start of my service with the OSS—but not one skip-dive. Regular diving is essentially perfected, these days: you can't open an entrance portal without simultaneously opening the exit portal—your dive system simply won't allow that to happen. There's never been a recorded incident in all of our time Under diving where there's been a problem with losing a ship—certainly there's been times when the portals don't open properly, but if that happens, your ship's system immediately collapses both portals so nothing goes through.

Skip-diving, however, is entirely different—the ship that's travelling is not the ship that opened the portal, and so you need to suppress the travelling ship's safety systems for it to just 'go with what you've got'. That's why it's entirely against procedure—the risk is high and the consequences extreme, and I don't know of an actual successful skip-dive attempt, though I've heard rumours of failed ones. The OSSN *Korthron's Arrow* was lost, a few years back, and talk around the fleet was it was due to a failed skip-dive. Great Oarth, I hope it wasn't—the thought of one hundred and sixty-seven men stuck for all eternity in the Under, never knowing it, sends a black shiver all over me.

But there's no chance for me to indulge such worries; if the skip-dive does work, we're going to need to have a plan in place once we get there. Based on what we know of the new model vultures, we've got about six hours remaining before the Pryok'tel's Under-drive finishes recharging, and they can dive to another system. These vultures have a five-lightyear dive limit range, and given that radius, there are eight other star systems they could reach from the Derresion system, if they chose to dive to a system at all. Far too many systems to try and send an OSSN frigate to investigate.

While Rowland's been busy, I've called Yar, Chresh and Murth into a conference, going over every available detail we have on the Derresion system: a red dwarf sun with four main planets, three gas giants and one rocky terrain planet that's tidally locked. The gas giants have dozens of moons each, with the largest, Derresion Three, having over a hundred whereas the smallest, Derresion Four, has a scant twenty by comparison. Most of the moons are of a standard composition of rocks, ice and various common metals abundant throughout Oarth space, but with so many moons recorded, it's possible that there's a hidden treasure among them that would draw the Pryok'tel's interest.

Derresion Prime, however, the tidally locked terrestrial planet that orbits nearest the sun, was once noted for having an abundance of primitive life in its marginal habitable terminal ring—the narrow stretch of surface between the planet's constant light side, and dark side, measuring about fifty kilometres wide only, but extending the entire circumference of the planet. A simple multicellular alga has completely overtaken this surface, choking out the possibility of any other life forming. Though the records we have of Derresion Prime are mostly from the Nurcillices, the OSS Science Academy did send a research team out there seven years ago, only to report that the planet was unfit for possible colonization, with the extremely blunt description of 'it's all slimy and gross' being captured in the notes of one researcher.

Given Derresion's lack of immediate value, save for the interesting side note of having a slime planet, and its relatively distant location from Oartheca, the OSS has shown no interest in further exploring the system—nor has any other of our spacefaring neighbours—it remains unclaimed as of our last records. Derresion is also far from the known borders of the Pryok'tel, however, so why they've chosen to dive there is an unpleasant mystery we're left having to guess at—it's entirely possible that there's something both the Oarth and the Nurcillices missed.

Both Yar and I think that Derresion Prime is the most likely destination for the vulture, but Chresh is interested in Derresion Two, particularly its vibrant ring of crystalised salts containing high quantities of bromine, which creates a vivid blood-red circle around the planet's methane rich blue atmosphere. Bromine is a dietary necessity for the Pryok'tel; they require large quantities of it to survive—which if they stuck to eating each other like their damnable evolution told them to, they'd have in abundance—but since they've started sinking their teeth into other less bromine-rich species, they often have to have it as a supplement. They sprinkle it on their meals as you would salt. It's revolting and only further confirms how unnatural the Pryok'tel are in my eyes, but that does not take away from Chresh's good point: an entire planetary ring of bromine would be valuable to the triple-mouths.

Once we've established the mission's field of engagement, I move the discussion towards defining mission objectives, and this part is going to be hard, given what's at risk versus what we're capable of accomplishing. I address my war council for ideas, but there are some hard facts that need to be discussed, and so I'm currently in the shuttle's back storage area, tele-meeting with Yar, Chresh and Murth over a touchpad, so that I can see them as well as hear them.

'This mission has two priorities: prevent the Pryok'tel from escaping the Derresion system with a piece of stolen tech, and the rescue of Mr. Hale's missing crew members.

'Without needing to state the obvious problems of one little shuttle going up against a vulture,' I begin to my assembled team, 'I want us to come up with a plan that accomplishes both. Starting from the point that we've successfully made it into the system, give me your best ideas, lads, on what can be done to accomplish both the rescue and the prevention—any ideas will help. I'll mention that it'll be only myself and Mr. Hale involved here: Dr. Gren will stay on the station and return to his duties once he's cleared quarantine.'

There is silence, which I hope is due to minds being put to the best use and not stupefaction from the sheer lunacy of what I'm suggesting. The silence goes on for a period that's becoming worrisome, but it's Yar that speaks up eventually.

'Can't speak to the rescue, Captain, but I do have an idea for preventing the escape, though truth be told, it's not that good,' he says.

'Any idea is better than none, most of the time,' I reply.

'If you're determined to do this, I would recommend throwing everything the shuttle's got directly at the vulture's Under-drive, preventing their escape altogether. It's heavily shielded, but if you're able to breach the shields with the cannons, launching your entire battery of rockets at the drive should damage it enough to at least force them to make repairs. Those rockets are designed to punch asteroids apart—they pack enough of a wallop to do serious hull damage, possibly breach it if you're a good aim. But they'll do next to nothing if the vulture still has its shields.'

'Not nothing,' Chresh says. 'But not a lot either: Yar's right, the energy disruption from the lasers needs to do the bulk of the work breaking the shields. But the rockets can help with the final blows if needed: the shuttle carries twelve in total. I could tweak their payloads, overcharge some of them, make for a bigger bang. Once the shields fail, the rockets could do some pretty good damage to their hull, but you gotta be careful—unless you're planning to blow up the vulture. Need to be a dead-eye shot, Captain, if you want to just disable them.'

'Captain Toar used to be a dead-eye, for certain, all them years back,' Murth interjects, and it sounds like he's actually complimenting me. 'Top of the roster in confirmed kills. But that was with a starclaw attack fighter; I don't think our ratty shuttle can compare.'

'It's all we have, but you're right Murth—it'll be tricky, for certain,' I agree.

During my early years in the OSSN, I was an ace fighter pilot—Star Rangers we're called—with over fifty-five confirmed kills in my starclaw. Nowhere near a former den-mate of mine though, the living legend Eractur Craggurscion; that snowcoat was a deadly hunter during our time together on the *OSSN Star of Oartheca*—over a hundred and twenty confirmed kills and more since then—but I'm still considered by many to be one of the best Star Rangers in the OSSN stable. But that was, what, forty years ago? Before my sons were born, at a minimum. Let's hope it's a skill one doesn't forget.

'I don't want to risk destroying the vulture,' I continue, 'so long as there's a possibility that we can find and rescue Mr. Hale's crew. Can we modulate some of the rockets' warheads to deliver less of a yield? I can use those for more precision disabling once the shields drop.'

'Yes, that's easy. I'll configure a third of the rockets on overcharge, another third at regular, and the final third under regular yield. You can pick and choose as need be,' Chresh confirms.

'You'll need to overcharge the lasers too, though, so watch your shots accordingly. Sustain their fire as long as you can, but you'll likely drain them before the shields fall—use your rockets as a last resort,' Yar adds.

'Good. If this is an option that presents itself, the risk is worth the payoff—disabling their Under-drive will give the OSSN plenty of time to get to the system, and they can finish the job from there. Now, on to the rescue part of the mission.'

Another silence falls from the team.

'*I'll* say it then,' Murth grumbles, after a while. 'With respect, sir, his crew's already dead. We all know that. From what I know about these humans, they're too weak to work as slave labourers—the Pryok'tel only take the strongest; the rest become food. It's an ugly thing, sir, but we're all thinking it. Maybe that reptile fellow's still alive, if they decided he's worth the bother. Maybe they just ate him on the spot, like the others.'

I don't respond immediately because this is the same suspicion I've been having. Saying otherwise is naïve, so I choose my words carefully.

'I'll not disagree with you, Murth. But there's got to be some hope, here, somewhere still. Mr. Hale told us he saw one of his crew members being taken away—so we can't say for sure they're dead at this point. Pretending for a moment that there's some entirely unfathomable reason they're still alive, how do we get them?'

More silence again, but then Chresh pipes up, tentatively, trying to think things out even as he speaks. 'Their gravity system is close to their Under-drive, at least on their older model vultures, the ones we built. If ... if you took that out at the same time as their drive, there'd be no way they could make repairs in space. They'd be forced to land somewhere.'

'Yes,' Yar agrees. 'and once they've landed, you could ...' but he stops, unable to see his way through the overwhelming odds.

'Go on, Yar, let's hear it—everything on the table, after all,' I remind him, kindly, though if I follow the idea he's tentatively presenting, it would definitely not be considered a good one.

'Storm their ship?' Murth asks, and that snide mocking tone of his has returned. 'One Oarth and a little human against an entire vulture's worth of triple-mouths? Might as well go for a dip in the bromine fields first, Captain; they'll thank you for it when you hand yourself over as dinner.'

'Aye, Murth, respect if you wouldn't mind,' I growl. 'No bad ideas, and so what's yours then?'

'Sit and wait for the back-up,' he retorts immediately. 'If you've blown their drive, and their gravity, they're not going anywhere. Wait for the OSSN to show up and finish the job. If these humans are still alive—which they're not, by the way—then …'

'They'll kill them for sure at that point,' Yar interjects. 'They'll never hand over what they've taken.'

'They're already dead!' Murth snarls. 'I'll not have the Captain risk his life over some fool humans who were out where they're not supposed to be doing Eternal knows what!'

I'm momentarily surprised by Murth's sudden outpouring of concern on my behalf. We are clan-related, but this is the first time I've ever heard anything from him that even remotely sounds like we are.

'Murth, my kin, please,' I ask, hoping to leverage this sudden new regard for me by using a subtly affectionate term with him, the first time I think I've ever done so.

'No!' Murth barks, and he's suddenly more worked up than I thought him capable of being on my behalf. 'Toar, you can *not* risk your life like this, your father would skin me clean if you died on some fool's errand, you're my son by law and …'

The rest of us are stunned, and it seems even Murth is surprised by his own outburst. He has never publicly acknowledged our relationship in such a profound way. As a sworn clansman to my father, he is correct: I am technically his son, by law. Yet he has never called me this, ever.

'…and you're still too valuable to the OSS to discard,' Murth finishes, feebly, embarrassed.

'You could try and negotiate,' Chresh speaks up, and then because of the lunacy his idea entails, he quickly adds; 'If you manage to disable the vulture, you could try and exchange the lives of Mr. Hale's crew, and this stolen technology, in exchange for not destroying their vessel. The Pryok'tel are not suicidal, after all—what with them thinking they're the universe's only real living things—they could see it as the exchange of goods for their lives, which is more valuable to them.'

'That … is a possibility,' I murmur, unsure. I don't recall any instance where a negotiation with the Pryok'tel was even considered, let alone successful. Though they are not suicidal, as Chresh indicates, fighting to the death doesn't appear to be too much of a bother for them either.

'Or just blow the whole thing up and be done with it,' Murth growls. 'I'm sorry, Toar, to be the one that says these horrible things, but if this stolen tech is so important—and I believe you when you say it is, you've always been good at telling the truth—then you need to destroy them. Nothing on that ship is worth your life, Toar, nothing. Not some strangers, not some toy, nothing. If the Pryok'tel cannot be allowed to escape with this prize, then kill them all and be sure.'

'He's right, Captain,' Yar replies.

'I know,' I agree.

Another round of silence before I state, 'I will attempt the negotiation, and if that fails ... I will wait for OSS back-up to arrive. If it seems likely that the Pryok'tel will escape by some other means, I will destroy their vessel.'

There's a sinking feeling in me; I've just damned Rowland's family, if they're not dead already. It seems so cowardly of me not even to try a rescue—but I can't see how! Murth is right, the Pryok'tel would not take humans as slaves, they're too weak—they only ever took the strongest of Oarth as slaves, our suncoats and nightcoats were only ever fit for their larders. Rowland's family is most likely gone and risking my life for their ghosts is foolhardy!

But Rowland. This will devastate him, and he'll not understand nor forgive my cowardice. I'm not sure I can, either. I'm ashamed of my own inability to help him, hiding behind odds and probabilities when the most important thing is to try and help. The veil is not as valuable as his family is, and risking my life for the chance at saving others from a fate I would not wish on anyone but the Pryok'tel themselves seems like the right and decent thing to do. I just don't know how to do it!

I thank my team and dismiss them back to their assignments, but Murth stays on the touchpad while the others drop.

'I'm sorry for my outbursts there,' he mumbles, over the channel.

'It's quite all right, Murth,' I reply, even-toned. 'I'm surprised by your caring, actually.'

His response is fast. 'Easy, you. I know we don't get on most of the time Toar, but you are my kin, and I do...I do love you, you damn fool. Sometimes it's because I have to, granted, but I still do.'

This is flooring me. Murth has never said he loved me, even during his clanship ceremony when he technically had to—mind he didn't say it to any of my brothers either, I wasn't singled out for exclusion—but I'm still shocked to hear it now. I try to make sure my face doesn't show it.

'I love you too, clanfather,' I reply, using the official designation he holds for me as my family member. I'm not sure I do love him, but because I'm not sure that I don't, it's technically not a lie. Before I can even contemplate how this makes me feel, Murth grumbles his response.

'No, you don't, and I don't blame you. I'm a miserable old shit and you know it. I'm fine with that—your dad didn't offer me clanship because I've got a winning personality. He took me on because he wanted someone to keep tabs on you. I accepted not because of the great honour of serving a High Baron, nor because there'd be a chance I'd become a sire, which your dad's made clear will not be the case, but because if I help him, he'll give me a place in his barony and a pension that'll see me through.'

'I suspected as much,' I say flatly, and any feelings of love for him are being crushed just as they're being born.

'Aye, you're not stupid,' he snaps back. He doesn't mean this as a compliment. 'But what neither of us suspected is that it turns out I do actually love you. All right? I do—watching you these past few years, seeing you make the best of a bad situation, seeing how dedicated you are to a job you're entirely overqualified for, and yet still do with pride and dignity, every day throughout … it's hard not to love you, clanson, you make it damn hard not to love you.'

The smothering of my feelings for him slips, and they blossom instead. My eyebrows have risen to their limits and I'm left speechless. Murth continues, a dam having burst in him.

'And it's because I love you that I need to say this: they won't take you back, the Navy, even if you succeed with this fool's plan you're dreaming of. None of us will, because none of us can, my boy. What you did was unforgivable, Toar. The death of a baron can't be erased, ever. Not in my eyes, your dads', anyone's. None of us can take you back as you were, and this won't change that. If you're doing this because …'

There, Murth's said it, the thing that I've hinted at but is still too damn painful for me to admit to. He's referring to the incident that resulted in me losing my officer's commission with the OSSN and becoming clan-kicked. Yes, under my command, one of our barons died. Except that … that's not accurate, if I'm being forced to think about this. Under my direct order, one of our barons—the total of whom make up about one percent of our total population—died. Not … not died—was killed, if I'm to stay accurate, again as much as I hate thinking of this. But despite the immense shame these thoughts flood me with, it doesn't undo the fact that Murth is correct: it's a crime that I can never be truly forgiven for.

'I'm not,' I interject. 'Baron Thursk's death happened under my command, and there's no coming back from that. I understand that, clandad, I do.'

'Then why are you doing this, you gigantic clod?' he insists, sounding worried for me now, which is again something I have never heard from him. 'Risking going up against the Pryok'tel in a *mining shuttle*? Great Oarth, what will I tell your dads? Please tell me it's not because you've got hard for the human, is it? You're always so quick with your pecker that it's got me wondering.'

'No, it is not!' I spit, quickly, then calm down. By nature, Murth is not a nice man, and this is just another manifestation of his sourness. I don't actually think he intends to be insulting, I just don't think he understands how to be loving, in the way I understand that term.

'And if you do need to tell my Dads something, it'll be that I did my best to understand all the risks, made plans to reduce them, and still made the decision with a clear mind. And not with my pecker, thank you very much!' I growl.

Murth grunts with a disbelieving tone. 'Can you tell me, at least, what the triple-mouths took?'

I sigh. 'It's so dangerous, clandad, that telling you is a risk. Just … just know that it's that important. My Dad will pressure the OSSN, and they'll tell him, and if it helps, you can let him know I'm okay with you knowing, if he feels it's safe to share. He won't though, Murth—it's really that bad.'

He's silent for a moment, thinking. 'Well, I do trust you, Toar. If you say it's that important, then I'll believe you. But just barely, mind you, because what you're doing is stupid. Plain and clear. But if you do it, give it your all, son, because I'll want to bawl you out when you get back. I'm going to spend all the time you're away coming up with the exact way to let you know just how much of an idiot you are.'

'Wonderful, that's the missing bit of motivation I needed to succeed. Was worried otherwise, now it'll be a success for sure!' I'm trying to keep the snarl out of my voice but it's still getting in there, though Murth just softly snickers over the comms channel, and I realize now that he's teasing. Perhaps this is how he shows love. Miserable way to do it, but we're all different, I suppose.

'You're too good for this job, Toar,' … and now he does sound like he loves me. 'You should be back in the Navy. I wish that could happen for you, clanson, I do—but it won't, and I won't do you a false favour by lying to you saying otherwise. Trust me, having you back on a proper ship would do me a world of good—I'm tired of your too-handsome face taking all the good men here to your den, and leaving me nothing but the scraps. I want you out of here so that life can go back to normal for me.' He ends his statement with a mock huff, and I just shake my head. He's wrong about me taking all the good men, but perhaps from his own success rate, I am by comparison.

'Nothing on Oartheca could improve your den odds, but I'll still come back, regardless. I promise, clandad,' I say, and he nods. 'But there is one thing you could do for me. Tell my Grath, Hars and Reth that their Dad loves them, will you? That I'm thinking of them, that they're with me, always.'

Murth doesn't respond for a moment, and when he does, there's a sadness in his tone. 'Of course, Toar. I'll tell your dads the same, right?'

'Yeah. Don't think Culler will listen,' I mutter. My sire-father Cullergrath is a proud man, a retired OSSN captain himself, and takes his oath to bar me from his family, as part of my punishment for getting a baron killed, seriously. He's a stormcoat too—both of my Dads are—and the shame I've brought our coat-clan is not something he'll ever forget.

'He will. I'll make him. He can be a stubborn old den-lurker all he wants, but he's got nothing on me,' Murth says, and he's actually smiling at me now, in full.

'True enough, you old fleacoat. Get on with it, then,' I reply, smiling back at him. 'And thanks, clandad. I do love you, too.'

'Aye,' he agrees, pleasantly. 'It's good to hear that. Won't change how I treat you, but it's still good to know, I suppose.' He huffs again, and I laugh, witnessing his personal brand of humour for the first time since I've met him. We end our call, and I feel better for having learnt Murth really was my clandad all along.

*****

Our little war council wrapped up, I send an encoded message to the OSSN and the *Grolthon's Spear*, detailing the plan to pursue the Pryok'tel and the reason for it, and to meet in the Derresion system with all due haste. VEILEDD technology—the 'veil'—is unused, but not unknown, by the OSS. When I was part of the Navy, I was privy to the defence strategies we designed to counter vessels under a veil—all of which boiled down to 'none to speak of'. The threat of the Pryok'tel having access to this technology should get all the OSS alarm bells ringing, for certain.

I check in with Rowland, who's sitting at our newly designed tactical station, a series of complex graphs, schematics and flow-regulator diagrams splayed out on the viewscreens in front of him. Since there's crew coming and going in the shuttle, he's still got his rad-visor up, but he talks to me through his suit's comm unit, and I can hear the tension in his voice.

'I can get it to seventy-six percent success, that's it, on my own. I've worked in Corculhoran's equation but the numbers aren't coming out like he makes them. I've missed something, or I just don't get it. Is there anyone I can work with on your station who's familiar with dive physics?' he asks.

'Outside myself, it would be Threng—he's our science officer—ah but you know that. He's working on some installation requests for the shuttle, but I can reassign him, over the comms—send him what you have and work together. I can sit with you too, and see what the three of us can come up with.'

'Yes, let's do it,' Rowland agrees, 'but there's one thing more I'd like to offer, that could help.'

His choice of words leads me to believe I'm not going to like this. 'Go on, then.'

'Well, with your permission, using my cybernetics, I could interface directly with *Blue Boy*'s Under-drive system, and, simultaneously, directly with the *Lurcaster's Claw*'s systems.'

I refrain from immediately saying no, but I'm sure that's going to be my answer anyway. 'And what would that accomplish?' I ask.

'I would be like a third regulating system between the two, better able to make adjustments when the portal's forming, because both systems would be able to allocate their entire resources to work independently, but, through me, we could achieve a better synchronization to predict and create a more stable exit portal. If you're worried about me gaining that level of access, I can show you safeguards that can keep me isolated to just the Under-drive systems, and …'

'I'm not worried. I trust you, Rowland,' I say. I'm not sure that I do, and I think I'm saying this for both our benefits. Given that I'm near to telling him that I've not figured out a way to save his family, anything I can do to get him on my side seems like a good idea.

He stops speaking for a moment, perhaps forgetting that I can't see his expression, which is causing my heart to feel distinctly cheated, at the moment.

'Would you be at risk in any way?' I ask, after more time passes.

'No, not at all, really. Nothing that I can't handle. Thank you, Captain. With me acting as the regulator, I'm able to get us to an estimated seventy-eight percent success probability. Between that and the three of us working together to solve this equation, I … I think we might make one Harculcorian.'

I page Threng; he's not been made aware of our plan to skip-dive, and I suspect he'll be on the upset side when he finds out. Turns out that's not the case at all, as when Threng joins us on the comms, it's apparent that he did in fact guess it, all by himself.

'See, here, you've missed accounting for the dimensions of the *Lurcaster's* entrance portal, you've generated one that's the size of the mining station itself, but we can modulate it to match the shuttle's easily enough,' Threng points out, after having reviewed Rowland's calculations for a solid while.

'Yes, but if we do that, the exit portal would also need to be correspondingly reduced, which increases the probability that we'll miss it, which, you know, I kinda want to avoid if possible,' Rowland counters.

'Not entirely, there's nothing that's stopping us from keeping the exit larger,' Threng advises. 'I mean it's inefficient fuel-wise and will drain our drives like we're diving ourselves, but it's not like we're going anywhere anyways. Plus, you'll make a spectacular bang on your exit, but … if you tweak your variable here, and then carry that all the way through, that should result in a …'

'No, can't have that,' I interject. 'If our exit into the Derresion system creates too large a breach wave, the Pryok'tel will be sure to detect us—and we'll lose any element of surprise we might have.'

'I could re-calibrate the exit portal to be just outside of the system itself,' Rowland offers. 'It would mean some flying time into the system, say a few hours, but we would remain undetected. I know we can't afford the time but I'd rather take my chances with a safe exit than rush and well … not have to worry about anything, after that.'

'How much time's left until the vulture's Under-drive recharges?' I check.

Rowland shrugs. 'Given the guess of a fourteen-hour recharge cycle, a little less than five hours, if our estimates are right.'

'It seems like the better option,' I remark. 'If they see us dive in, they'll be on us, and our little shuttle's no match. I know time is precious, here, Mr. Hale …'

'No, no, I agree. Rushing in where angels fear to tread,' Rowland replies, a tad on the defeated side, but nevertheless begins to update the equation to factor in a dive exit further back than was originally planned.

I struggle a bit with his idiom; my translator substitutes the words 'divine spirit beings' instead of another word Rowland used—but I understand his sentiments. Rowland completes his updating and there's a dramatic pause as the Under-drive systems recalculate the odds of success for the simulated dive scenario, and when it finishes, it flashes seventy-nine-point-eight percent. There's a disappointed groan from Threng over the comms, but I notice something's been left out of the equation.

'Mr. Hale, I can't see where you've accounted for the shuttle's shape, here,' I say, knowing that I'm about to be chastised for my controversial opinion, which is not an opinion at all but a tried and tested fact.

There's no immediate reply from either of them, but it's Rowland who responds respectfully; 'That's not typically a consideration when working with portals, sir; the mass is important, as we all know, but the actual configuration of the diving vessel's never been proven to factor into the overall success of a dive.'

'Generally, no, it doesn't matter, when you're talking about a vessel diving itself,' I explain. 'But as I understand it, skip-diving needs to consider every possible variable. If you re-factor this part of the equation, here … account for the dimension of the shuttle there, realign the entrance portal while keeping the exit as wide as we can make it, then …'

I run my revised scenario through the simulator, trying not to feel too proud when the calculation breaks the eighty-percentage barrier. By a whopping zero point three of a percent, but it still does it.

'Well done sir!' Threng cheers over the comms.

Rowland places his hand on my knee and gives it a good squeeze. I think my heart stops at his touch.

'Good job, Captain. I stand corrected,' Rowland says. He's not yet removed his hand. The urge to tear that helmet off his head and claim a kiss for my reward is overwhelming.

'Yes, well, age and experience has to count for something when working with you younger lads, I suppose,' I say, trying to sound casual. If he moves his hand up my leg I'll have him on the floor, here, now; I'm sure of it. No, no, settle down, go slow with him, if this goes at all, don't muck this up because you're desperate …

But he takes his hand away, and returns to the equation, running through the scenario again to see if there's another variable. While he and Threng are speaking, and I'm trying to get my head out of some truly lusty scenarios that are causing my crotch to take interest—focus, Toar, you promised him—I notice that Rowland has keyed a private message to me.

Is it okay if I tell him about my cybernetics?

By way of an answer, I interject into Rowland and Threng's current conversation. 'Mr. Threng, Mr. Hale has another factor that needs to be accounted for. He's got the ability to directly interface with both the shuttle's and the station's systems, and coordinate the two through his own internal computer systems. If he does that, and we're able to get him successfully connected, what kind of effect would that have on our little problem?'

'Oh *raur!* You're a *jack*?' Threng asks excitedly. 'That's so—I mean *raur* what kind are you? I've heard that the CAPS has all kinds of cybernetically enhanced people—like mech hunter-killers, or cyber-assassins, or blackweb spiders, or …'

Rowland laughs. 'Nothing like that—just a bit more than your average comms officer. I can definitely link the shuttle's and the station's drives together, though. Captain Toar's given me permission to do so, but I might need your help, Mr. Threng, to get connected properly.'

'Of course! I'd love to help you!' Threng exclaims, and there's almost a squeal to his enthusiasm, but he brings himself under control quickly. 'Uh, if I may, Captain?'

'Yes, proceed at Mr. Hale's instructions. Mr. Hale, if you'd like to update your equation factoring in your involvement?'

Rowland does so, and we all hold our breath as the simulation dances its way through the new calculation. There's an explosive cheer from Threng, a good 'whoop!' from Rowland and a hearty chuckle from myself when the result comes back: eighty-two-point-seven percent success.

None of that matters to me though, to be honest. He's put his hand back on my knee, and when I take his hand in my own, to give it a good squeeze, Rowland doesn't pull away. I wish so much to see his face right now it's causing my chest to go all tight. All I can do is see my own grinning mug reflecting in the gold tint of his visor. I look happy, at least.

'Excellent, just excellent,' Rowland crows. 'That's more like the numbers I'm used to. We can do this, Captain, we can do this,' he assures me, and I know he means it.

I don't reply with words, I just give a quick three pumps with my hand on his. I love holding his hand. Oh Great Eternal, I love it. I don't want to ever let go. I've known him for less than a day and don't understand my own level of need for him, but it's there nonetheless. It clicks for me then—I *will do everything I can to save your family*—I think to myself, in that moment. If this man loves his family so much that he's willing to risk his life for them, then I don't care if he's a thief. The love for his family, that's noble, that's who he really is, at his core. Helping him is the right thing to do.

Maybe … maybe I am Allured? I don't care, I just don't right now—his hand in mine makes me feel right about myself for the first time in years. It's made me remember what it was like to love and feel loved. I'm not so foolish as to think I love Rowland—that's not the case—but it's this first little spark that helps me remember what it was like to be warm.

'Uh, hello?' Gren's voice interjects, and Rowland and I've been caught, each of us taking our hands back quickly. I turn to see our doctor standing in the port-side hatch entrance, his arms full of an assortment of items. He's got a kind, caring look on his face though, a knowing smile after seeing Rowland and me; I dare say it even looks happy too.

'Brought you some things for your journey,' he says, holding his bundle up. 'You first, Captain, if you can be spared.'

I give Rowland a look, and he replies, 'Yes, Threng and I can take it from here, Captain. Good to see you, Gren.' He waves to our doctor, who beams a giant smile in return.

I stand and walk over to Gren, beckoning him to join me on the alcove benches, which I've noticed are all cleaned now, and it looks like some very decent mending has been done too. Gren sets his items down and the first thing I notice is my regular uniform; the light grey tunic set atop the navy trousers and jacket, along with a set of sturdy boots, a clean tailcatch, socks, a vest and my official captain's hat, its dark leather brim polished brightly.

'Ah cheers, Doctor. I'm getting chafed bald in this spacesuit,' I say, holding up my hat, and placing it on my head. It's just a bit of apparel but I do immediately feel more confident putting it on.

'Well, I'd prefer you stay in it, but in case you feel otherwise, I thought you'd enjoy your uniform,' Gren replies, smiling his all-too-knowing smile again. 'Managed to find Mr. Hale a spare set of miner's overalls and such too, just in case—they're for a suncoat so they should fit better than what he currently has. First Officer Yar wants me to tell you he's putting together a set of gear for you both as well, but the commissary doesn't have much for this kind of adventure, I'm afraid. Food, emergency supplies—I think there's a survival shelter, too, but it'll be snug.'

'We'll take what we can get, thank you, Doctor.' My eye catches another one of the items Gren's brought: a set of powered fur clippers and I give a questioning look.

'Oh, yes, made a better solution than the pills, if you're up for it: a transdermal patch. Should keep you safe without you having to remember. Would you like to give it a try?' he offers, holding the clippers. 'I'd need to shave a small section of fur from your forearm, nothing too drastic, I promise.'

I dutifully hold out my forearm, and he flips it over so that my palm is facing upwards. Halfway between my wrist and my elbow, he buzzes off a section of my grey fur, exposing the darker grey skin underneath. Gren takes his new patch, removes its backing, and sticks it on. It immediately begins to tingle, and at my concerned expression, Gren explains.

'That feeling should fade, soon. Effect's not as instant as the pills, so be sure to change it every twenty-eight hours or so, before the one you've got on runs out. I was able to make a batch of ten, so, unless you're planning on an extended vacation together, you should be fine until you get back,' Gren remarks.

I grin. His optimism is a major boon to me, and I'm thankful for it. The thought of a vacation with Rowland is only briefly entertained; even if we do succeed, the decree against contact with human males is still there, and that's going to be more formidable than some filthy Pryok'tel vulture that needs to be dealt with. I've deliberately not thought about what will happen after this mission, though I imagine that the best outcome will be Rowland departing to the care of the OSS, and most probably, back to the CAPS.

I turn to look at Rowland, and feel a twinge of apprehension. I've not told him of our plan, and it's likely he's going to be angry with the decision to only disable the vulture, rather than rescue his family. There is a part of me that wants to find them, but I cannot see a way to do that which doesn't end with us in a

Pryok'tel larder, which—and I will never say this to him—is where I think his family now is.

But remaining silent will not make the telling of the tale any easier. Best get on with it, I suppose. In a tone as cheerful as I can muster, I say,

'Mr. Hale, Gren's come by with some things for you, come and say hello.'

CHAPTER 14

Rowland

I'm not one of the good guys.

If there's any doubt about that, know that it was all smoke and mirrors when I appeared to turn over control of the shuttle to Toar and delete my admin account. There's no way I could give up my last chance to save my family, not that easily, and appearing to surrender to win Toar's confidence was the simplest method to get the station's dive portal open, which was my goal all along. I could have done it myself, but the time it would take, and the risk of it backfiring, was too high. Getting Toar to trust me was the easier solution.

Yes, I leveraged his attraction to me to further my own ends; that's a small price to pay, and for it, I've bought a fully armed shuttle and a stable(ish) skip-dive portal, which I plan to use to its fullest potential against the Pryok'tel. That's why I originally set the skip-dive exit portal directly in the middle of the Derresion system; I want them to find me, I want them to come for me, and now that I've got *Blue Boy* armed, I want them to attack. I can't wait another six or seven hours to fly into the system and then play hide-and-seek with the Pryok'tel—not only should they be just about ready to dive by then, it's another massive amount of time my family sits as the daily special on their dinner menu.

But my entire plan is in jeopardy because Toar is stubbornly insisting on coming along. I get it—his priority is the veil, which, granted, is fundamentally the most important aspect of this, were I to view this mission from a rational, objective viewpoint—but since my family is going to be eaten, I think I'm entitled to a smidge of irrationality. Toar's presence … complicates things.

It turns out that part of the price I paid for leveraging Toar's attraction is that I'm now attracted to him in return, and despite my efforts to not let it bother me, what I'm doing to him is making me ashamed, on multiple levels. I don't use people like this; I mean, yes, I do use people, but they're always on the deserving side of it, at least from my perspective. Comeuppance is a major satisfaction point for me, and Toar's a complete innocent.

I guess it comes down to having my cake and eating it too, and that's never going to work; either I drop my manipulation and start working with him honestly, which I fear will end up costing my family their lives, or I commit to my deception all the way, in which case there's a shot at rescuing my family but at the cost of ruining any possibility of something happening between Toar and myself. The former is worth a thousand times the latter, except … it just isn't, and that's what's making me so ashamed. He seems like a really decent guy, and I'm screwing him over.

It's when he said he trusted me that I really felt a dagger stick in me: one edge laced with triumph, the other covered in guilt. Normally, I would have congratulated myself at winning a mark over so fully, but with Toar, I feel like a sack of shit about it—and then I feel worse because I'm even bothering to feel that. I can't let my feelings for Toar stop me. If my family dies because I delayed their rescue, what would I tell their ghosts? 'Sorry I couldn't save you from being eaten but I didn't want to upset my hot new boyfriend that I met yesterday?' It's not a joke. They come first. They must.

But then I went and put my hand on his knee, and made the whole situation worse for both of us. I did it as a silent sign of appreciation since he couldn't see my face and I didn't feel right about praising him in front of Threng. I could see that my touch thrilled him, and that wound up thrilling me too—and the momentary break that little second of happiness provided from the constantly increasing sense of panic and doom was like water in a desert; I was parched for it, I drank it down, and it revitalized me. His face—that little one-sided grin of his—told me how much he enjoyed it, and that just ... healed me, for a moment, while I was there with him. And then we held hands, and that calmed me down so much my mind could focus on the task, instead of the panic. It just felt good, and I feel like shit for that too.

He's become a safe haven for me. And I like him: physically, emotionally, mentally. I'm not in love with him, but I'm interested in knowing more about him, because ... because I could see myself loving him, if he'd accept me and all my tom-fuckery. It's so fucking selfish of me but I'd be lying if I said otherwise—there's this magnetism he has, and I find that just being with him, just holding his hand in mine, matters to me, even though it shouldn't. All of this just adds more to the pile of shit I've become for doing what I've done to him, and at the same time, not doing more to get my family back. I have to put Toar aside, I have no choice.

Since I have full access to the shuttle, and, thanks to Toar, the station's Under-drive systems too, I technically have everything I need to get going. Threng, the station's science officer and one smart little cookie, has tied me into the systems I need—and I've noticed that he's set up a monitoring system to watch that I don't stray outside into other station components. I've no intention to, but I'm still impressed by Threng's caution here—his enthusiasm for me being a jack apparently did not trump his caution. Good on him.

I'm wrestling with what to do about Toar. I've got to come up with a way to convince him to leave and let me make my way on my own, because when I put myself in his boots, the safest thing to do would be to find the vulture and signal for back-up. It's a good plan, but it's not the one I can afford. I'm still in this mental trap of how to resolve the Toar conundrum when I hear him speak up, sounding chipper.

'Mr. Hale, Gren's come by with some things for you, come and say hello ...'

I smile, but then realise Gren cannot see my face, so I stand and go over to greet him. Gren is holding what looks like a pair of clippers, and Toar is rolling down the sleeve of his under-suit. He's now wearing a dark navy brimmed cap with an OSSM—*Lurcaster's Claw* emblem embroidered on it. It has a striking resemblance to an old-Earth navy commander's cap, black brim and all, so much so that I'm wondering about the numerous parallels between our two species, especially ones that evolved essentially on opposite sides of the galaxy.

Regardless, his hat suits him entirely.

'Dr Gren, I've been meaning to ask,' I say, sounding deadly serious for a moment, and the blond teddy bear's face takes on a worried look. 'Now that I'm in a fully sealed spacesuit, would it be okay if I gave you a hug?'

'Oh!' he laughs, and then looks away embarrassed for a second, then to Toar, who is grinning that handsome grin of his. 'Well, I guess so, just a little one though.' He holds out his arms wide, meaning he has no intention of just a little hug.

I give him my best bear—wait, that's species-ist of me—I give Gren a great big hug, wrapping my arms around his back, and a hearty squeeze, which he returns. We're forced to manoeuvre around the bulbous helmet I'm wearing, but we manage. He is just as cuddly as he appears but there's firm muscles too, which is wonderful to feel against me. It's a solid, friendly hug, of a kind I realize I've not had in quite some time, and I find myself not wanting to break from it— Gren's embrace is comforting and reassuring.

I'm beginning to feel guilty again, and so I pull back, but not in an awkward way, and give him two pats on his shoulder as we part. 'Thanks again for everything, Doc. I owe you my life. I won't forget this.'

'Oh, never mind that, all in a day's work,' he says, but I can tell that he's secretly beaming from my thanks. He also seems reluctant to back away from me for a moment or so, and there's a star-struck look in his eyes. I remember his warning about the power I have due to an Oarth's natural attraction for me, but I thought being in a spacesuit with a domed helmet would have prevented that.

'I've brought you some extra clothes, too, for your adventure. I figure the spacesuits may burden you down some, and so I've got you this nice clean miner's suit—it's on the drab side but it's comfortable and won't get in your way. Loads of pockets and such,' Gren explains rapidly, and reaches down to a pile he's placed on the nearby bench, handing me a neatly folded navy-blue bundle. 'Plus some clean underclothes and everything—it should all fit close enough.'

'Thank you, Gren, it's just perfect. Very kind of you,' I reply, accepting his gift.

'You're welcome,' he answers, and that same little shy smile's returned. I wonder if he wants me to try them on now, but we've still got some of the crew coming and going in the shuttle. None of them are currently here though, so I take a quick moment to drop the rad-shield on my visor, and make sure the first thing Gren sees is my appreciative smile.

'You've been a champ, Doc, and I owe you a lot more than my life,' I say, sincerely. 'I hope one day I get to repay you. You're still up for being friends, once we get back?'

Gren nods heartily. 'Yes, I'm holding you to that. Good … good luck, to you, both.' His voice falters. 'Please be safe, as much as you can, please. I know that finding Rowland's family is important, but you're important too. I know at least one person who really cares for both of you and will be terribly upset if something should happen.'

I see Toar give a quick look around, and seeing no one but the three of us, he puts one arm around Gren and squeezes him close, kissing him atop his head. 'We'll do our best, my good Gren, I promise.' My heart melts at this. 'Now, let's say our see-you-laters, I've got some ideas I'd like to share with Mr. Hale here, and there's not much time left.'

'Of course, yes. Farewell, Rowland, and farewell, Captain. Come back soon because I can't wait to hear all about it.'

'Take care Gren, we'll see you soon, for sure,' I say, and give him another quick hug.

'Be good, Doctor, you still owe me a report, mind,' Toar grins, and pats Gren on the shoulder, turning with him to walk him towards the shuttle hatch. I wave and so does Gren, and then Toar and I are alone. He closes the shuttle door, and as the latch clicks, he turns to me, with a look of forced confidence.

'Got some ideas I'd like to run by you,' Toar offers, but sounding as though he's trying to convince himself of something. 'Been with my team coming up with a plan, but I'm not convinced it's the best one. Would like you and your cleverness to help sort some things out, if you're up for it.'

'Yes,' I say immediately. Again, he's surprised me—I thought he'd go all captain on me and tell me what we were going to be doing.

'Good, good—look, I need to get out of this damnable under-suit, and I'm sure you'd like to as well. Why don't you go in the back there and change, and I'll do the same? Just give a knock when you're ready and I'll tell you if I am too,' Toar suggests, and I can tell that in addition to being tired, he is also uncomfortable.

'Are you sure, Captain?' I ask, but not confrontationally. 'The Allure thingy ...'

'Won't be an issue, I'm sure. Go on, then, I can tell you're as scratchy as I am.' He nods in the direction of the shuttle's back storage.

'All right, I'm not going to argue, these things are at least fifty percent made of itch.'

He chuckles, and I exit. When I arrive in the room, its former contents have almost all been entirely replaced—there's still two crates marked as emergency supplies, and my gurney has been collapsed and neatly stowed, but now there are four long metal containers, in rows that stretch to the back of the room, and nearly as high as I am tall. Each row is clearly marked in Oarthecan with numerous danger and warning signs—these are mining charges. Enough to dent a moon. Fuck, someone means business. Hope flickers when I see these—whatever Toar's plan is, he's not going in under-armed, it seems. There's been a lot of work done on the shuttle while I was busy with the skip-dive equation; I've not had a chance to check in with *Blue Boy* to see what's been done, and I'm eager to find out what other new toys we've been given to play with.

Gren is correct: the navy-blue mining uniform is both simple, and comfortable—it's made of finely woven, smooth material that reminds me of cotton twill—with a good heft to it but it still breathes, and yes, it's loaded with pockets on the sleeves, chest, sides and hips, with a ventricle zip running from below my neck right down to my balls. The undergarment I've been provided with is a set of loose-fitting trunks held in place by a pull-cord waistband, of a much thinner version of the material the mining suit is made from, but in a nondescript grey. Still of excellent quality, it comes with another of those reversed-out pockets in the back, and given how that pocket aligns right up to my tail bone, I'm guessing the Oarth do have tails—stubby ones, given the length of the pocket.

I knock on the door to let Toar know that I'm ready, and he replies the same, so when we join up again in the shuttle's main compartment, he's now fully dressed in his dailies—and he's quite the sight to behold: bulk and muscle, grey and tall, and the navy-blue of his uniform just highlights the powerful bright blue of his eyes. I can't get over just how massive this man is—and as my eyes roam all over him, I notice that his eyes are roaming over me as well. He's wearing an appreciative expression that he's trying, but badly failing, to hide.

'What?' I say, turning around in a small circle with my arms extended. 'Not my colour?'

He gives a short laugh, and that charming, crooked grin returns. 'Not that, Mr. Hale. Just it's the first time I've ever seen a baron in such, uh ... a workaday outfit. They normally dress quite fancy. Looks good on you, though,' he replies, and I can tell he means it.

'Thank you, you're quite the dapper captain yourself, too. Not that I'm a baron, though, Captain. Remember.'

'Right, right,' he answers, guiltily. 'Never mind me then, let's get on with it,' he continues, but his eyes keep scanning every centimetre of me, and I can't help but feel a flush of pride at being so obviously appreciated. 'Have a seat, and we can talk,' he offers, extending his hand towards the helm.

'Holy shit, you have claws,' I remark, seeing the two centimetre or so thick, black nails that curve slightly at the end on each of his fingers. I immediately hear how rude that sounds, but I'm surprised—this is the first time I've actually seen an Oarth's ungloved hand, and to see that they're basically armed at all times is both unusual and concerning.

'Oh, yes, we do,' Toar replies, inspecting his wicked manicure like it's the first time he's ever seen it. He sees the look on my face and quickly adds. 'Don't worry, I'm very careful with them.'

They're fascinating for me, so I ask if I can see them closer, and he steps towards me and offers his hand. I take it in both of mine, turning his palm over and getting a good look. These are not for show—these are real weapons, slightly pointed and quite sturdy-looking—he could tear chunks out of someone if he put his mind to it. I find them oddly appealing—having that kind of power literally at your fingertips must give you a sense of pure not-to-be-fucked-with-bad-ass-ness.

'Okay if I touch them?' I ask, and when I look at him, I see interest in his eye, and wonder if this is arousing for him. I'd like to find out, actually.

144

'Of course, if you like,' he replies, almost dreamily, and extends his index finger for my inspection. I grip the tip of his claw carefully between my own index finger and thumb, being careful not to apply too much pressure because I don't know if his claw is sharp or if this is uncomfortable for him—neither is the case, but the tip is pointed, and it's quite solid in my grip. He could definitely do some damage with this. It's then that I see a small, blue piece of thin plastic adhered to the middle of his forearm, and my brow creases with curiosity.

'It's a smell-blocker,' Toar explains. 'In patch form, so that I won't need to remember to take pills. Stops your Allure, we hope.'

'And stops you from smelling anything at all,' I deduce, and look at him with sympathy. Nature's given him a large, broad snout, and I'm certain he's accustomed to using it.

'Not a bother, I really don't notice it,' he lies, kindly. But then his eyes soften, and he looks at our clasped hands fondly.

'You know, I liked it a lot when we were holding hands, back there. And now. Feels … right,' he gently flirts. He curls his index finger slightly, so that it hooks mine.

'It does, doesn't it?' I meet his gaze, interlacing the rest of his fingers with mine, and giving his hand a good squeeze, which he returns with care—he'd be able to break every bone without a second thought, but here we are, my little pale hand in his massive dark mitt. I want to do more—this moment seems to call for something more meaningful—but I just can't. It seems … disrespectful, with things as dire as they are, to be taking a break from it all to see if Toar's a good kisser, which, with the way he's looking at me right now, I'm sure he'd be happy to show me.

'You know, when this is all over, and everything's not so crazy, would you like to go out to dinner with me, or something? Get to know each other better, doing something that resembles normal?' I ask.

Coward, I chastise myself.

Toar's expression transforms to one of utter happiness. 'I'd love to,' he says without a moment's thought, and again, it's said with such sincerity that it's as though I've given him more than he could've hoped for. 'I'd really love to.'

But then he pulls me into a hug, and he is so wonderfully firm and strong it just makes me feel immediately like things could actually turn out all right. And when I say strong, it's not a crushing embrace but I feel his power. Like Gren, Toar's got a layer of cuddliness to him, but then it's solid muscle underneath, and his are much bigger than the blond doctor's. Somehow, though I don't recall when, I've put my free arm around his trunk-like waist—I can barely reach far enough to touch the sides of his back—and he puts his free arm over my shoulder, pleasantly heavy against me and bringing us still closer together.

As we're pressed against each other, that deep, hearty, warming smell that I first encountered is now all around me, strong and welcoming. It's both a comforting and enticing scent that reminds me of a spice I can't quite place, only darker, richer and wondrous to experience. I don't know if Oarth wear cologne, but if this is just how they normally smell, it's an intriguing natural fragrance, and it makes me push up even closer to Toar, which he happily accommodates.

It's then that I become intensely aware that I'm right up against his crotch—and Jesus he's got a lot going on there—I mean it's arousing and kinda intimidating all at the same time—but he's definitely feeling me down there as much as I'm feeling him. I should pull away; this is getting too hot for me, and as much as I'm enjoying it, there's a world of work that needs to get done.

It's then I hear Toar's stomach gurgle tremendously, and I stifle a chuckle, while he looks skyward in embarrassment. Our little moment's been thwarted by the call of a different nature, but neither of us breaks the embrace.

'Hungry?' I ask him kindly.

'Aye, all that talk of dinner and such,' he replies, patting the sides of his broad stomach to silence it. He takes a quick look around the interior of the shuttle, before returning to address me, still close against him. 'Care for a bit of breakfast, Rowland? We still have some time before the upgrades are done—how's about having us a short break?'

It's been close to a day since my last meal, and while my nerves are so frayed I can't feel hunger, I know that I'll need something to keep me going—the end of this day is a long way off and the last thing I need is to face it on an empty stomach. That, and Toar looks like he needs to recharge—there's still that sleepy look in his eyes, and I can tell he's forcing himself to stay alert.

'Yeah, that's a good idea, Toar—while we're at it, do Oarth drink coffee? Something with caffeine, to wake me up?'

He nods. 'Don't know what that *coffee* thing is, but I'm certain a nice hot mug of *stôl* would do us both wonders.'

'*Stôl*?' I ask, quizzically.

'The beverage of choice of the Eternal Oarth himself,' Toar says, with a twinkle in his eye. 'You'll see.'

CHAPTER 15

Toar

Oh that was a marvellous hug we had, let me tell you! Rowland's so strong—he wrapped his arm around my waist *and* gave me a good and proper squeeze, too ... just, *raur*, just *raur*! Our barons don't do that, they let themselves get held, and they put their arms around your neck, or rest them on your chest, or something, but they don't have the strength to really give a solid hug like Rowland did. It's his big muscles that give him that edge, and they're just as genuine as they are gorgeous. It's like Rowland's got the beauty of a baron and the strength of a drone—well, a suncoat maybe—but it's still the best of both worlds—it's all deliciously erotic, I'm finding. Had to think of unpleasant things towards the end of our hug though, 'cause I was getting a bit too excited, emotionally and physically, from all that bumping up against him.

But he certainly was bumping against me too, there was intent there—and that, oh that—was so amazing. Then my stomach had to go and get all talkative, and well, that was likely for the best—I did miss dinner and Rowland's suggestion that we get some *stôl* sounds like just the cure for some of my simpler ailments. So I've put in an order for a small meal for us to share, directly to our galley, and as this will be Rowland's first taste of Oarthecan food, I want to make sure he's impressed.

Our Galley Master, Drezcruth Morthenclan, a kindly old woodcoat who celebrated his one hundred and thirtieth birthday last month, has served in the *Lurcaster's Claw*'s kitchen since the age of thirty-six, and there's every indication he'll make it an even century before he considers retiring. This is not a career decision that is widely cheered by our mining station, mind you—there's been loads of not-so-subtle requests from the crew that he's encouraged to retire—with one nasty suggestion that we just leave him at the space dock next time we depart—as his tongue's dulled with age and now almost everything he makes for us tastes odd in some way.

I love a good chunk of roasted *nartholor*, but Drez always manages to get it on the overdone side, which I still enjoy but there's a lot of chewing involved, and I end up picking my teeth for hours afterwards. His *lathanan* stew, which is supposed to be a savoury dish made from carefully smoked and aged fish, is somehow sweet—nearly like a sticky fish jam, if that horror needs to be imagined. And his *kennrol*, which is a finely blended legume that's spread over thick slices of bread, is so obnoxiously spicy that you end up feeling the burn more on the way out than going in. I hate *kennrol* day, I do.

Sadly though, the House of Morthen is not a wealthy barony by any means, and I've not got the heart to replace dear old Drez because of that—his income, meagre as it is, goes entirely to support the Baron Morthen, who, for what he lacks in coin, more than makes up for in children; I think Drez told me he's got over a hundred clansons these days, and it doesn't look like Baron Morthen is going to stop anytime soon. Removing Drez's little income from the pot, especially for a Baron that's gone above and beyond with helping to repopulate Oartheca, just doesn't sit right with me.

That, and, well, at his age, Drez isn't quite as fussy as our younger lads can sometimes be when it comes to making den decisions. He's old enough that traditions, customs and rules don't quite have that same sense of importance they may have once held for him. And so, on those occasions when I'm nearly starved to soreness for a den-mate, Drez'll always make room for me in his—and not make me feel bad for it, either. He's good to me, that way: a kind den-mate, docile but still attentive, and though his fur's more grey than brown these days, he's still on the easy-to-look-at side. Happy for our time together, too, and that's more than reason enough for me to keep eating his *kennrol*.

However, if there's one thing our Drez is still a master of, it's his *cerret* pies. It's the best thing we've got on board: our Drez's never made a bad one yet. *Cerret* pie is drone food, though—you'd never serve it to a baron, even the most humble—it's just too mundane, and I'm not sure Rowland will enjoy it, but it's the safest bet. So it's two of these I order, plus a bowl of crunchy *kortuk* stalks— just so Murth can tell Dad I had my greens for the day, mind. I don't know if Rowland likes desserts, but I do, so I've also asked for a *kelberry* cream pudding and some preserved *dulian* sweeties, which always makes for a nice after-dinner treat. That, and a large thermos of *stól* of course, a thick, inky, viscous drink made from the roots of the *stólenhock* shrub, somewhat savoury and best served piping hot, but with that nice kick of the caffeine Rowland and I most definitely need.

'Our snack shouldn't take long, in either the getting or the having,' I tell Rowland, joining him on the miners' bench, where he's taken a seat. 'We'll have ourselves a short break, then be back at it, soon enough.'

He nods, and then gives me a very straightforward look. 'This doesn't count as our dinner, though, in case you're wondering—I plan on making that a lavish experience, to thank you for saving my life, and everything.'

'Heh, no need for fancy on my account,' I reply, grinning, and, after a needed moment to screw up my bravery, I add, 'I know any dinner with you would be wonderful.'

He gives me a shy grin, his forest-coloured eyes twinkling, and I offer him my hand, which he accepts right away again—so that we're now sat together, hand-in-hand, and my whole heart is humming with happiness for it. Great and Eternal Oarth, how I wish I could smell right now though—having this sniffer-blocker is driving me near to lunacy—Rowland's right beside me and while I can see, hear and touch him, there's a part of him that's entirely invisible to me, and my heart keeps telling me that's probably one of the best parts, too. Still, smelling Rowland would lead us into trouble that neither of us can afford, so I remind my heart to enjoy what it can, or else have naught to enjoy at all.

'So, it appears we're going to ignore that whole speech of mine to keep things professional, right?' Rowland asks casually, and I immediately start to pull my hand away, but he holds on, gently. 'It's fine—no sense in pretending there's not something between us.'

'No, suppose not,' I agree, but I look cautiously in his eyes. 'You're … you're all right with that, are you? I'll keep it light-hearted, best I can—and I know I'm being selfish, here—just can't help myself, really.'

He makes a small frown, and sighs heavily. 'No, it's me who's being selfish. I feel like a second I spend with you is a second I could be spending trying to figure out how to get my family home. Feels like I'm betraying them, somehow.'

I put my arm over his shoulder, and gently squeeze him close. 'Having a quiet moment with a friend isn't betraying your family, Rowland. It's normal to need a reprieve, to give yourself a chance to gather your strength. That's all that's happening.'

'Except for the part that I'm enjoying it, and that doesn't sit right with me,' Rowland replies, sombrely, his gaze down and his shoulders slumped.

'Nothing wrong with a bit of comfort, when it's needed; no one would begrudge you that,' I reply, gently. It's taking a tremendous amount of restraint not to kiss the top of his head, or comb my claw-tips carefully through the short hair he's got there, that rare colour just between brown and blond. Give him that comfort I'm used to providing a fellow-Oarth who's down in spirits like Rowland's feeling—but he's not an Oarth, and I don't want to make him feel even guiltier for accepting that comfort.

He straightens his back and squares his wide shoulders, and I get the impression he's got something on his mind that he wants to talk about, so I take my arm away, and give him my attention—but we're still holding hands, so what's coming can't be all that bad, I hope.

'There's something that's concerning me, involving what we're doing,' Rowland remarks, a note of caution in his voice.

His words are worrying me, but I invite him to continue. Best to get it out, I feel. 'Go on, what's on your mind, then?'

'Just after my auto-doc session, Gren and I had a conversation about how the Allure works, and what effect it has on Oarth like you and he are,' Rowland starts, and he's got a serious look in his eyes. 'I'm worried that if we go down a path like the one we're on, Toar, something could happen where I inadvertently Allure you … and I don't want that. It's too much, for both of us, to have you change like that.'

Not been looking forward to this conversation, at all, but I knew it had to come sometime. I open my mouth for a moment, not sure of what to say, close it, then try again. 'What did Gren say, exactly, about how the Allure works?'

'That when it happens you become fertile, and that you sort of need to have sex at that point, and well, that you wind up being "forever in love" afterwards. That's … too much for me, Toar—I mean I like you, a lot, but having that kind of power over you kinda unnerves me.'

I huff in annoyance. I am going to have a word about this with Gren, for certain!

'That's a bit of an exaggeration,' I start, trying to be patient but there's a low growl to my tone. 'Yes, the Allure is used when you want to start a family, and yes, there's certainly a desire to procreate—granted, a mighty intense one—but it doesn't take away choice. It's like … a very strong word of encouragement, but it's far from an order, let alone a directive—you *want* to do it, you don't *need* to.'

Rowland gets a puzzled look on his face, so I continue, hopefully providing a better understanding.

'See, when my baron—the Baron Cralren IV—and I were together and decided to become Allured—which is a choice we both made, after a good while of knowing each other—it wasn't him poaching me randomly off the street— both of us remained free-willed, always,' I say, ensuring that my tone is clear. 'We both chose to go forward, together, having children—neither of us was "forced" or "compelled" to do so—Eternal Oarth, that'd be horrible, if that was the case.

'Now you can argue that yes, our instincts were in overdrive during that time, and … yes, the fertility part does add a sense of urgency to the matter, but I can tell you flat-out that either of us could have changed his mind at any time. It's an instinct, strong as I said, but like … I dunno, being hungry I suppose—just because you feel hungry doesn't mean you lose the ability to decide what and when you're going to eat. Well, maybe that's a bad example because you do eventually have to eat … where *is* our snack by the way? Cook's taking forever …' I grumble.

'So … what about the "forever in love" part?' Rowland checks, peering carefully at me.

I roll my eyes. 'Also a bit of an exaggeration, I'm afraid. Gren's a good doctor, don't get me wrong—but he is young and maybe under a fantasy about how being with a baron actually is, versus what's in our stories.'

I pause, trying to find the right words. 'I mean, yes, I will always have a deep love for my Cralren, but that doesn't stop me from living my life, Rowland, nor does it stop him. We're not slaves to each other, we're family.' I stop at this point, because that last bit about family isn't true anymore—it's against the law for me to even suggest that it is, since Cralren formally ejected me from his barony— and so I elect to try a different tack.

'See, I was not Cralren's first sire, and he's had two other sires since me. That's how barons are—many sires over the course of his life and rarely the same one for longer than a decade or so. Sure, he may have a favourite sire from time to time, but it's almost unheard of that he'd ever only have one on a permanent basis. If the Allure made a baron "forever in love above all and others", well, he'd just stick with one sire, and that'd be bad for us all. Now don't get me wrong, though—we will always share a love, he and I, but it's a gift that we both happily keep, not a collar around our necks.'

'Oh, I had thought that maybe you and your husband—sorry—your baron— Cralren—were still together?' Rowland asks, curious.

That question dances too close to why I'm no longer a part of the Barony of Cralren IV, and I'm not wanting to share that reason with Rowland just yet— finding out I got a baron killed is likely not going to be a boost to his confidence—so I have to step carefully when I answer.

'No, not in that sense,' I start, cautiously. 'I was his active sire for around eight or so years, up until the first few years after our sons started school. That's the typical length of time for a baron-sire relationship, at least for a physical union—once our sons entered their second year of classes, I switched from being Cralren's formal sire to being one of his clansires—meaning I was still a part of his barony, but he and I were no longer denning together.'

Rowland nods along, thinking on what I've said, but his next question reminds me what a sharp memory he has, as he's already puzzled out what I've been trying to avoid addressing.

'The captain of the *Grolthon's Spear*, his last name ended with *sire*— Henrythinsire?' he asks, uncertain.

'Henthrothsire,' I correct, and a sinking feeling settles into me as I begin to dread what surely is going to be the next question—how come I'm not a Cralrensire, then? But Rowland's giving me a thoughtful look—I think he senses my reluctance here, maybe because somewhere along the way, I've hunched my shoulders over and my voice's gone all low.

'Does that mean he's the Baron Henthroth's currently active sire, then?' he asks, considerately.

I nod. 'It could mean that, but normally, even if Derrar wasn't, he'd still be referred to as Henthrothsire, afterwards,' I reply, quietly.

There's a silence between us now; I think Rowland's caught on that I'm uncomfortable and is picking his next question carefully. Which isn't right—he's just being curious, after all, wanting to know more about me, which I should be grateful for, but I just … don't want to risk him refusing me because of my awful crime. Not him. Not now, when we've just started.

'So does that mean, now, that Cralren has a different sire, that if you wanted to, you could look for another relationship, as well?' Rowland asks. 'Become another baron's sire, maybe?' he says, and gives my hand a very gentle squeeze.

I smile broadly, my mood changing almost immediately. 'Another relationship, yes—but not with another Oarth baron though; drones like me are only allowed to be the sire for one baron, traditionally—I mean we could, from a physical perspective at least, but that's heavily frowned upon—have to share, give others a chance to have kids, and all.'

'Better for your population, too, in the long run,' Rowland remarks, his thinking face on. 'Creates a more stable gene-pool.'

'Exactly,' I concur. 'That's actually important, at the moment. We've not got a lot of barons, you see—never had but today it's even more dire—so making sure there's lots of diversity in our bloodstock is a real challenge for us. And it stops a lot of fighting between drones that would happen otherwise—hogging a baron is viewed quite badly—I mean wars used to get started for doing that— unless of course, the baron chooses it to be so—in which case, that's his choice and all the drones need to respect it.

'But again,' I continue, having a think on this while I'm speaking, 'that's very rare; I mean I can't think of a case in all the time I've been alive that it's one-sire-one-baron, forever. Usually, other drones will begin to vie for a baron's attention around the seven-year mark, and that only escalates as more years pass. It's best for everyone that a baron finds a new sire—when and if he wants to, mind. We never force our barons, ever, to choose against their own wishes.'

'And that frees Oarth like yourself, to find a relationship, afterwards?' After I nod, he adds to my delight, 'Is that something you're hoping to find?'

I nod enthusiastically, my smile only getting broader as I find myself gazing contentedly in his eyes. 'Oh, yes, that'd be just lovely, it would. You know, when there's time for it,' and add, rather bravely I think, 'and the right fellow, certainly.'

He eyes me for a moment, then chuckles as he looks away. 'You're a flirt, aren't you, Captain?'

'Not all the time,' I protest, feigning injury, re-catching his gaze with mine. 'Certainly, when there's cause to be, though.'

Must mention, briefly, how badly I want to kiss him now—I mean we're shoulder-to-shoulder, close as you can be, holding hands still—and he's giving me this look that's so hard not to see as an invitation to do so—but I've got to let him be the one who makes that decision—it's got to be his choice, after all— but maybe with just a tad more flirting …

I'm about to press my courage further by asking if a relationship is something Rowland's looking for too, when an electric alert sounds from the port side hatch, and the voice of a steward comes over the comms systems. 'Your meals are ready, Captain.'

I sigh heartily. Think it's the first time I've been disappointed by the prospect of a meal, but the timing is probably for the best, all things considered. We both keep looking at each other, leaving the steward likely having to guess at what's going on, but it's Rowland who drops his hand first, and I follow along.

'I'll go in the back storage room,' Rowland replies, standing.

'Yes, and I'll get things set up here,' I say, likewise getting to my feet. 'Then I can continue to help you get a better understanding of the Allure, if you like. You really mustn't be too worried, Rowland—even if the worst did happen, I'd never be a bother to you, ever.'

He smiles his charming smile before replying casually. 'Don't think you could ever be a bother to me, Toar, but I'm glad you're helping me to understand better.'

*****

I've downed my *cerret* pie, and Rowland is picking little pieces off the last half of his. We're both sat cross-legged on the floor of the shuttle—I've spread out one of our emergency blankets, and then folded two more into makeshift cushions for us to sit while we eat. He catches the direction of my gaze, centred directly on the untouched portion of his pie, then laughs as he passes it over.

'Did you not like it?' I ask, concerned. *Cerret* can have a gamy taste to it, which I love, but Cralren always detested—barons have different palates than drones do—we only ever had *cerret* when it was a special occasion for me.

'It was excellent,' Rowland says, genuinely—and that's a wonderful little surprise—and then adds with a chuckle, 'It's just that's a gigantic portion for me!'

'Oh, well, then, can't have it go to waste,' I reply, taking his leftovers, but then I do remember something of being a half-way respectable man. 'I mean, if you're certain you don't mind, that is?'

He laughs again, that lovely sound making me smile instantly, and invites me to proceed. He places one of the *dulian* candies in his mouth, sucks on it for a moment, then raises his eyebrows with delight.

'Gotta say, Toar, you Oarth know a thing or two about good grub,' Rowland says, raising the back of his hand to cover his mouth, a subdued belch behind it. I have never in my life heard a baron do that, and there's something in me that finds it ... intriguing. The best parts of an Oarth drone, and all—an appreciation for good, honest food, and no need to be so dainty about it, neither.

'Got you some dessert, too, if you like, a nice pudding with ...'

He holds up his hand in surrender. 'That pie was more food than I usually eat in a day, Toar—I'm stuffed, good man. Will take some of that Oarthecan coffee you mentioned before, though ... stout? Stole?'

I nod, reaching for the thermos. '*Stôl.* It's on the strong side, so, just sip at it—you might not like it at first but trust me, stick with it—it'll grow on you.'

I pour him a good-sized portion into a mug, and chuckle at his expression as the thick dark liquid slowly fills it. When I hand it over, he sniffs at it, crinkling his cute nose, double-checking with me if he should proceed. A small gesture of encouragement is all he needs before he takes the plunge. He grimaces on his first sip, and he smacks his lips together, disapprovingly, but it doesn't stop him from taking another sip. By his third, his expression has relaxed, and then it's like he's been drinking it all his life.

'So, have I got you better sorted about the Allure?' I ask, a hopeful tone to my question. 'That even if it did happen, it can be managed, and it's not quite the end of the world as our dear Gren made it out to be?'

He cocks his head. 'I think I'm more on board—I got the impression from Gren that it was a compulsion that couldn't be refused, but from what you're saying, it's closer to an intense feeling, and you still have control.'

I nod, relieved, and take a solid bite out of my bonus portion of pie, continuing to nod as I chew. When my mouth is free, I add, 'Gren's a great doctor, but he's not been a sire—it's hard to understand what it fully means unless you've gone through it yourself. I think I've done it more justice than he's done, but still, nowhere near perfect. It's an amazing thing, Rowland, to be Allured—a very meaningful, very special time—and I agree that it wouldn't be the best thing if it did happen between us, but even if I mess up completely and for some impossible reason it does happen, I'm not going to become your thrall or anything. You'd not be responsible for me, or obligated to me—it just won't be an issue.'

'Hmm. I think it would be a good idea if we prevented it, Toar. You'll let me know if you do start feeling like it's happening, though, right?'

'Of course,' I say. I'm not sure that I will, to be honest. If I do somehow end up fully and properly Allured, the last thing Rowland needs is to feel beholden to me. I'll keep it quiet—he doesn't want it to happen, and so for him, I'll make sure it never will, even if it does.

'One thing, though,' I ask, grabbing a couple of *kortuk* stalks. 'You had a word that you used for Cralren; it didn't come through quite right on my translator … I was given the term 'legally bound male partner?' Is that how humans have their relationships with their males? Legally bound?'

Rowland frowns. 'That … that's not really a good translation. Sounds very … uh, heavy-handed. The term I used—*husband*—often refers to a male partner, yes, but it's much more than just "legally bound"—though there's a legal aspect to it, most of the time. It's got a much deeper emotional connotation though—think of it as a partner you choose to share your home with, your life with, sometimes have children with, if that's what you both want.'

'Oh, so, like a sire,' I check, spooning a good-sized portion of the *kelberry* pudding into a bowl, and he nods. 'So does that mean human women Allure human men, then?' I ask, holding out his pudding for him. He shakes his head, and so his portion goes to me instead.

'No, not in the way you think of that term,' he answers. 'We flirt, and date, and things like that, but there's no biological …' he pauses, thinking. 'Well, there might be a biological change in us, I'm not entirely sure on that, to be honest. If there is, it's nowhere near so pronounced as an Oarth Allure, like you and Gren explained—we definitely don't need the Allure to be procreative, in that we're pretty much fertile for most of our adult lives, in most cases.'

I nod, sagely, trying to ignore the slight but entirely unnecessary salty taste to the *kelberry* pudding. 'Sounds a lot like the Nurcillices; they don't use an Allure either—they've got, uh, breeding seasons, I think they call it? Like their women are ready to have children at certain points in the year, then somehow their men catch on to that, then a courtship starts, and then nature takes its course, and all.'

Rowland thinks on that for a moment. 'Eh … we're a little different. Normally for humans, courtship can be undertaken by anyone, at any time, and there's no hard and fast rule as to who starts things off—either can initiate a relationship, and if the other one's interested, they'll go along with it.'

'What about the case where it's two men?' I ask. My bravery is on fire today, it seems.

He ponders for a moment, while I finish my pudding. 'Same rules, for all intents and purposes. It's … not really a distinction, in the case of same-sex pairings, though I guess there might be some differences—humans are very individualistic, after all, so I can really only speak for my own experiences. One of us will try to catch the attention of the other, and if he's interested—he'll let you know.'

'Sounds like us Oarth, then—between drones at least,' I remark, casually, but there's a singing part in me that hopes Rowland holding my hand is his way of letting me know. 'With a baron, there's a lot more formality and all, proper ceremonies and such, but when it's just us drones, and we're looking for either a den-mate or a possible bond-mate, then yeah, sounds like we're the same as humans are in that regard.'

Rowland furrows his brows. 'What's the difference between a den-mate and a bond-mate?'

'Hmm ... intent, I'd say,' I respond, trying to think on the distinction. I refresh Rowland's mug of *stôl*, and pour myself one, as I try and come up with the best way to answer his question. 'Den-mates are, you know, for fun and stuff—short-term, is the best way to think of it, but still enjoyable and meaningful. Bond-mates is more for long-term, more ... *husvand* ...'— I stammer over that word, there's that tricky sound in the middle I can't manage— '... material, to borrow your word. An Oarth will have many den-mates in his life-time, but if he's lucky, only a few bond-mates.'

Rowland raises an eyebrow. 'How many is 'many' den-mates?' he asks, curious.

I look perplexed for a moment. 'Oh, uh, many. Even the most ragged of us can still expect not to be left out, most nights—someone's usually up to help a man out of the cold. Us Oarth like to den, after all,' I say, grinning. 'Helps to keep everyone in good spirits, and to get along better. Otherwise, we're prone to fighting—well, not so much these days, but certainly in our past, before the Pryok'tel. Back then, there was a lot of clanship rivalries, as I understand it, but nowadays we mostly just den-up to resolve any major issues. Nothing settles a grudge better than a good solid round or two with your cocks out.'

He laughs, loudly and generously. 'All of us could probably benefit from that idea. Humans are different, though—we fight a lot with each other, and with outsiders, too. Maybe we should adopt the Oarth way of life and just get it on to settle our differences.'

I nod. 'Does wonders, trust me, you. And it's not just for settling disagreements, it's also a way to make friends, get to know your neighbour, build teams, and the like.'

He smiles. 'Build teams? Are you saying that Oarth are into the group-scene?' he asks, a cheeky glint in his eye.

I feel my heart sink—the Pryok'tel express deep disgust at what I'm about to explain, and I wonder if humans have the same prejudices, but Rowland seems like he's not bothered by the idea. 'Well, yes—drones often get together in groups to have some fun. Most of our social events involve at least one collective gathering—usually at the start, to get everyone settled, and sometimes at the end, just to make sure we're all still friends.'

'Really?' Rowland says, amused and surprised. 'That's ... not very common at all, in human culture—we're usually more reserved about something like that. I mean, yes, I've been to an orgy—an event where lots of men get together for the purposes of having sex—but that was the only purpose to it.'

'Nothing wrong with that either; I've been to many high dennings—hundreds of fellows, all together, just having a good time.'

Rowland blinks with surprise. 'Hundreds?'

I nod, but I'm beginning to worry I'm overwhelming Rowland with too much detail—even the Nurcillices found that aspect of our culture to be a bit much, expressing the same surprise at how open us Oarth are with each other, sexually. The Pryok'tel hate us for it—they think intercourse outside of the purposes of conception to be a waste of resources, which to them, is the highest crime imaginable. I personally think eating defenceless children is worse, by a large degree. But Rowland doesn't seem put off by this topic—surprised, but not repulsed—and, given what he's said about having been a part of this 'group scene' as he puts it, I elect to open up more.

'For us Oarth, Rowland, sex is a way to help keep us together, as a people. It's not just for fun—though granted, it *is* a lot of fun of course ...' I fumble, trying not to sound apologetic but it's coming across that way. Our centuries-long subjugation at the hands of the Pryok'tel really drove the point home that the rest of the universe does not think like Oarth do, and that we're lesser for being the way we are. Animals, they call us. 'It's more of an enjoyable social fix-all, and ... ah ... I mean ...'

Rowland raises his hands. 'Not criticising, Toar, not at all. Just highly curious—it's fascinating, actually—I mean it when I say that the universe would be a much better place if we just dropped our pants instead of pulling a gun. It's just unusual for me; please don't get me wrong. And—forgive me if I'm prying—but when you say making friends and forming groups, would that include ... does that mean, you and Gren ...?'

I shake my head, taking another sip of dark, luscious *stôl*, already feeling my eyes brighten as the caffeine hits my tummy. 'No, no, Gren's my doctor. We have some rules about denning when there's an issue with power, responsibility or authority over another man. Normally, the only rule for us drones is making sure there's eager consent from all concerned parties, but in the case where there's a chance for abuse of social or authoritative position, there're some guidelines about ensuring the person in the lower position of power is kept safe. In Gren's case, since a doctor's first responsibility is to make the best decisions for his patient, a den-based relationship could mess that up. So there's no chance Gren and I could den together. Wouldn't mind, he's a sweet fellow and all, but no, that wouldn't be proper.'

'But ... the rest of your crew?' he checks, his tone reflecting his inquisitiveness.

I sip from my mug. 'Yes, a few of them. And they're denning with each other too—it'd be highly unusual if there wasn't at least a couple of lads together somewhere on the station, at any given point of the day.'

'That's very different than humans,' Rowland remarks, on the contemplative side. 'Especially on a vessel. I mean it happens, but it all has to be clandestine—it's got to be wonderful to be so liberated from that kind of nonsense.'

'Well, it's not like we den out in the open, during shift,' I reply, though I have caught my crewmen doing just that, on many occasions—they get told off for the first few infractions, and repeated occurrences are met with a temporary ban from their shift-work, where one hopes they spend that time getting it all out of their system. 'But yeah, we've not got the same, uh … restrictions … that we've seen in other species. Pretty much if you want to den, there's usually someone who'll be happy to join you in that, and on a larger vessel, you're never stuck for choice.' *Mostly*, I correct myself, silently.

'So polyamory is the norm for you guys then—having many different partners at the same time,' he clarifies, seeing my expression.

'Yeah—that sounds about right,' I concur, having a last big swallow from my mug of *stôl*. 'Even bond-mates will still den outside their relationship, either on their own, or as a couple, or however they both feel it best suits them. In the case of our barons, it's different—normally the sire won't want anyone other than his baron, but there's been exceptions—after all, if the baron wants to roam or add to the pile, then by all means have at it. Is that how it is for humans then, or are you like the Nurcillices instead—you know, just one life-mate, for always?'

Rowland shakes his head. 'Not usually. I mean, well—we're sort of all over the map, really, though I think many of us are monogamous, at least on the surface. I myself just like to be with one guy, if we're in a formal relationship, but if I'm only casually dating, then I'll play the field, so to speak.'

He goes quiet now, a sombre look in his normal bright eyes, and his mood changes from light-hearted inquisitiveness to bleak introspection. I reach over, placing my hand lightly on his knee, and he gives a small puff of air through his nose, trying to appear casual.

'Just thinking about Bryce and me,' he says, downplaying his feelings but I can tell he's upset. That name sounds familiar to me; I can't quite pronounce the first part of it—the best I can manage is 'Vryce', so it stuck in my head.

'He's … he's one of your family members, on your ship today, right?' I check, and when Rowland confirms this, I ask, 'He's your bond-mate, then?'

His expression see-saws before he answers. 'Sort of. Not, not really, from his perspective, but I still love him. Kinda like how you and Cralren are—we're not together but there's still that affection, that love for him. We'd been fighting a lot, you know, and had sort of got to an okay place like … just *seconds* before the Pryok'tel attacked us—like literally seconds. And then I saw him get … hurt, and …' He stops now, putting his elbows on his knees and then his head in his hands, shaking his head back and forth.

I immediately scoot over to his side and wrap an arm around his shoulder, drawing him near, that feeling of his unusually firm, muscled, drone-like body wonderful against mine. I so badly want to kiss the top of his head right now, soothe him, comfort him, but I must be restrained. I offer him my best words instead.

'We'll find him, never you worry, we will,' I say, hugging him close to me. 'My crew and I've been working on a plan, and, well, I think there's something we can try. Let's finish up here, and I'll fill you in on it. Don't worry, Rowland, don't worry.'

157

He sighs, but gently pats my arm that's holding him. 'Yeah, we'll try. I owe him that, at the very least, after all.'

CHAPTER 16

Rowland

Toar and I've cleared the remains of our 'snack', and while I know from just living my own life that big men eat big meals, I had no idea what that could really mean, until today. While the savoury meat pie that Toar ordered for us was excellent—deeply hearty with a generous layer of flaky pastry, it was immense—one of them could easily feed an entire fireteam of the butchest marines the CAPS has to offer, with plenty of leftovers.

At least forty centimetres in diameter and easily half that in depth, plus absolutely crammed to capacity with seared cubes of meat that come from whatever a *cerret* is, all in its own private bathtub full of rich, unctuous gravy, I had bravely chowed down half of my pie before being completely defeated by the other half. Toar ate his like he was eating a sandwich—giant bites that made short work of the pie, with his long and intriguingly dextrous tongue ensuring not a drop of that gravy was missed, whereas I had been given an odd set of metallic utensils which I can best describe as a fondue skewer, a thin stiletto and a curved spoon with a wide-bowl—all of which were awkward to use but I figured it out.

Gotta say though, *stôl* is definitely an acquired taste—there's just no comparison that would do it justice—maybe if you smoked a cherry and blended it with overdone steak, then added something you've never encountered before that made your mouth slightly pucker—odd, certainly, but not horrible after the first few swallows. Once you get over it though, it certainly has an excellent caffeine kick—two mugs of the stuff and I'm completely awake. It's kinda weird drinking it too; the cooler it gets, the thicker it becomes, almost to the consistency of gelatine, but adding one of those little purple candies that came with our meal really made a difference in helping it go down while it was still hot.

Despite the downwards turn in my mood near the end of our meal, what with remembering Bryce's imminent peril, I did brighten afterwards, mainly because Toar and I got into a light-hearted argument when I tried to help tidy things up—despite him acknowledging that I'm not an Oarth baron, he can't help but see me as one, and apparently barons do not help in tidying. When I still insisted, I received a firmly polite 'guests don't clean' admonition, with him literally holding the dishes up and over his shoulder so that I couldn't reach them. I finally let him win, and his little triumphant huff of victory was impossible not to find adorable and amusing.

While I'm on the topic of his adorable side, Toar is indeed very huggable, that much is unquestionably true. Soft but firm, gentle but strong, all at once. Comforting and ... alluring, for lack of a better word. I can tell he's a genuinely sensitive kind of guy, too—quick with physical affection, expressive with his emotions, and obviously a man who feels things deeply. I remember when we were talking about barons, and how a drone inherits a surname when he becomes a sire, Toar's entire demeanour changed—for whatever reason he's not called

159

Cralrensire, it was painful for him to talk about—and to see the shame in his cobalt eyes made me so sad.

It'd be impossible for me—or anyone in my boots, I guess—not to enjoy his attention, and it did help me get a better handle on what I'm dealing with. I'm electing to heed his words about everyone needing a reprieve to gather their strength, but there's a guilt in my soul that refuses to be mollified. I need to find my family, and then, well, me and Toar can have all the hugs either of us could ever possibly want. If I'm still alive to give them.

So it's time to get back to business, and when he's finished tidying (with my surreptitious help), I move and take the co-pilot's seat at the helm. Toar takes the pilot's chair, but as soon as he's sat he immediately extends his hand for mine again, and I take it without a second thought. It's crowded here at the helm; Toar is too big for this shuttle, and I notice how often he has to hunch and stoop to move around in it. He's practised at it too, navigating the limited space with a rehearsed dexterity, but it's got me wondering—why would the Oarth design a shuttle in such a way certain Oarth couldn't use it? Even here at the helm, he's barely able to sit properly in the pilot's seat—it's just too small for him, but he doesn't seem to mind—and, well, it does put him within easy reach of the co-pilot's chair, which I'm finding is actually kinda cosy.

'So, hear me out, first,' Toar begins. 'My crew and I've worked out that the best plan for us—and I mean Oartheca, here—is to observe the Pryok'tel and get their next dive coordinates, if they're planning on continuing back to the Hegemony. Obviously, this means that there's no rescue attempt, and I don't like that. What we could come up with in that regard is to engage the vulture and take out its Under-drive, then try and negotiate the return of your crew when the OSSN shows up.'

'Do you think that's possible? Either taking out their Under-drive or that they'll negotiate?' I ask, sceptically. My knowledge of the Pryok'tel is limited but their reputation for ruthlessness is known across the systems.

'No. No I don't,' Toar says, and he gives my hand a gentle squeeze for this next part, because he's become solemn. 'Now, Rowland, what I'm going to say next is awful, but I need to say it so that we're both on the same page. I don't think … I don't think we can be very hopeful that your family is still alive. I'm absolutely willing to go with you and find out, for sure, but it wouldn't be responsible if I set up false expectations for you.'

His words echo the most logical parts of my own thoughts, which also happen to be the darkest and most maddening: the ones I've been refusing to listen to. I'm fairly sure Bryce was dead the last time I saw him—holy fuck, thinking that is like a white-hot needle right in my heart—but his body was at such a bad angle after we were slammed into the med-bay floor—but Ivan, Mia, Bett and Cor? I need to believe their fates are still not so certain.

'I understand, Captain. It's likely true—I mean I'm not stupid, I know what the Pryok'tel are capable of—but I hope you can understand how I need to know? Either way? This Schrödinger's Cat's got to be put to rest, or it'll drive me crazy.'

'Who's what now?' Toar asks, uncertain of my idiom.

'Schrödinger's Cat. A little animal in a closed box, that could be alive, or dead, and so it's technically both until you open the box and find out. So long as I don't know my family is dead, they could be alive, and ...'

Toar nods. 'Yes, I follow you. So let's say they are alive: even if we take out the Pryok'tel's Under-drive—which is not very likely, being honest with you again—it's still not a certainty they'll negotiate, but it's a possibility. Pryok'tel think they're the only living beings in the universe, so they could view your family as goods to be bartered with—sorry that's awful again of me to say—but they've also been known to fight to the death—it's part of their way of life. Eat, or be eaten. Nasty baron-spites, they are.'

'Yes,' I concur, though I don't need to.

'All that being said,' Toar continues, 'I know that you've been working on your own plan, and so I thought that maybe you could share it with me, and we put everything out and choose the best.'

I nod, ready to spill my plan, which involves Toar staying behind. Rather than mince words, I speak directly, as he's been doing. 'You stay here, and stay safe. I take the shuttle, dive into the system, get the Pryok'tel to capture me, hack into and take over their ship, find and secure my family, cut life-support to the rest of the ship, make sure all the three-mouthed bastards are dead, then fly the fuck home in the vulture, never to return.'

Toar gives me an appraising look. 'I see. And you ... you can do that, take over their ship like you took over *Blue Boy* here?'

I shrug. 'Possibly. I won't know until I try.'

'And if you can't?' Toar asks, concerned.

'Then I remotely detonate *Blue Boy* with his entire payload, while he's in their cargo bay, and blow us all into chunks,' I conclude, and Toar scowls terribly.

'No, that's not the way ...' he starts fiercely.

It's my turn to squeeze his hand, and I'm looking into his beautiful eyes as I do so. 'They cannot have the veil, Toar. My family is the most important thing in the world but if the Pryok'tel escape with that veil, we're all dead in the long run, and it will be directly my fault. Millions—possibly billions—of deaths. There's no way that can happen, Toar, and I can speak for everyone in my family when I say they'd trade their lives to stop that.' Again, I think of Ivan protesting me being so magnanimous on his behalf.

Toar is quiet while he contemplates my plan, but he nods eventually. 'No, they can't have the veil, I agree. So there's some sticky points with your plan, such as how do you get on the vulture, and how do you prevent them from killing you outright?'

I've thought of this. 'Pryok'tel are harvesters, as I understand it—*Blue Boy*'s got some pretty decent worth to him, so I'm sure they'll take the bait there. As for killing me, they have to find me first, and I can hide pretty damn well, even from life-detection scans. It's why they didn't find me back on the *Luck of the*

Draw—I was able to corrupt my biosignature long enough for them to overlook me.'

'You can do that?' Toar asks, amazed.

'Yes, for a short time. The longer I do it, the riskier it is, but I should be able to have them inspect the vessel, figure there's no-one on ...' Then I stop. There's a gaping hole in my plan. Toar's already caught on, though, and he speaks it out loud.

'If they don't find a pilot, then how did the shuttle get there?' he asks, and I reluctantly nod my head along.

'Yeah. Bit of a sticky point, as you said,' I agree. Damn it, I had thought out everything but this one pivotal detail.

'That's where I come in, then,' Toar says, and he puffs out his heavy chest comically, jamming his thumb on his chest three times. 'They'll certainly believe an Oarth is the one for creating all the fuss with the shuttle. And they'll likely take me prisoner, what with me being the perfect slave for their mines and all, especially if I don't put up a fight—well, much of a fight—got to make it believable.'

I shake my head. 'I can't ask this of you, Toar, it's just too ...'

'Enough of that,' he interrupts, squeezing my hand and placing his other one on my knee, leaning close. 'You're not having to ask me, I'm insisting. I've got to make sure that veil doesn't leave in their hands either. Don't want to end up a slave, mind you, so ... blowing up *Blue Boy* remains our last course of action. I've chocked him full of mines, so, that should do it.'

I have to say it one last time, just to be sure, 'You understand this could all backfire badly, and ... you might not come back from this one, right? I need to know you understand death is a real possible outcome.'

'I do,' he nods. 'And you needn't worry about me being smitten and doing something foolish to impress you. I'm not Allured, and I know what I'm getting myself into. Don't know if you know this about me, but this isn't my first "no-hope-but-let's-give-it-a-go" mission, and I know the risks, and I accept them. The price is too high, Rowland, we've got to give it our all. Besides which, I've got myself a real dinner date coming up soon—and I won't be missing that, let me tell you.'

I can't resist him. Everything he's done for me, everything he's willing to do for me—it's just too much. I bring his hand to my lips and kiss the top of it, tickling my mouth against its grey fur—and I am pleased to discover that yes, his fur is very soft, and that incredible smell of his fills my senses to the brim. 'Thank you, Toar, thank you. I'll give it my everything, I will, I will.'

There's a starry look in his eyes from having watched my lips touch the back of his hand, and I wonder if he is actually Allured, because he's somewhere far away in his mind at the moment. Now is a good time to tell him that I'm one of the bad guys, while he's riding this emotional high.

'I still have access to the shuttle,' I confess, quietly.

'Of course you do. You're too clever to have given it up that easily,' Toar replies. Hesitantly, he takes his hand from my knee and brings it near my cheek, unsure for a moment if he should proceed. When I don't pull away, he places it there, with the lightest of touches. His palm is padded in slate-coloured skin, which is coarse against my cheek, but wonderful to feel all at the same time.

'You trust me from here on, though, all right?' Toar says. 'We're a team now, you and me, and while everything we do must be for the mission, we'll do it together. Whatever happens, Rowland, I'm going to be on your side. No more secrets, okay?'

'Okay,' I answer, even as I can feel the very tips of his claws just brushing the short hair on the side of my scalp. He's right, he can be careful with his claws, as his touch is equal parts ticklish and soothing. He's looking at me with such fondness right now that if I don't put an end to our touching, I'm going to start taking this miner's outfit off, and there's just no time for that at all.

I turn my face to the side, so that my lips touch his palm, and that same delighted, mesmerized expression returns to his face. I take his hand in mine, and bring it back down to our knees, trying to steer the conversation where it needs to go.

'We need to do an inventory check: supplies, gear, weapons, all of it. Find out what we're missing, get it if we can.' It's the only thing I can think of to say to break this moment. I actually just want to sit here a while more—together with Toar, keeping at bay the awfulness that the rest of this day is going to bring.

'Right, got that done, this way,' Toar directs, and stands, offering his hand, which I take, and leads me over to two of the supply crates. He pops open one of the lids, and lists its contents.

'Emergency rations, water, med and hygiene kits, sleeping gear—Eternal I could use that, bit peaky if I'm being honest—plus an emergency shelter, comms beacon, survival gear—well, sort of, nothing fancy—but we'd be okay if we need to get by on our own for a while. That's in this one.' He then opens the next storage unit, and this one has the goodies I've been looking for.

'And here we've got our war chest, such as it is,' Toar begins, and reaches in to remove a standard coil-gun pistol, in its holster, turning the grip end towards me. 'You know how to use these?'

'Yes, I've four years' training in the CAPS-N academy—I'm familiar with hand pistols, single pulse energy rifles, and even a shoulder-mounted plasma-cannon, if you have one of those. Also stun-batons, close combat weapons and plasma-infused blades. Basic hand-to-hand, and some training with light explosive ordinance, though not much.'

'Impressive!' Toar beams, and claps me on the back in praise. 'You're military? I thought you said you were a thief?'

I give him a quick look from the corner of my eye. 'Long story. We can chat about it at dinner, okay?'

Toar immediately understands my reluctance to continue the conversation, and nods. 'Right, well, we've got the pistols, and I've got my plasma sabre— there.' He points to one of the lockers. 'And, well, I've got you a solid workman's blade here, if you like.' He holds up a decimetre long standard utility knife, simple black handle, in a sheath. 'And outside of some smaller mining charges,' he says, indicating a series of small token-sized discs, about the size of bottle caps, in a padded box, 'that's what we have in the way of offensive weapons.'

I hold up one of the charges, by its edges, carefully but confidently. 'Press and delay, or remote activated?' I ask.

'Both. Timer can be set from ten seconds to ten minutes, depending on how much you turn the top part there—it'll tell you the countdown on top. Remote's just inside the lid there—and we've got six boxes of these.' He gives me a reassuring look. 'There're some benefits being on a mining station, it seems.'

'Indeed. String these along the corridors of the vulture, and we could do some pretty serious damage,' I say, inspecting the disc in my hands appreciatively.

'Perhaps—they're meant to shatter rock, so the interior of the vessel will likely be able to absorb a lot—it's kinetic force rather than energy-based—but for anti-personnel purposes, you're bang on about that. Otherwise, we've got some basic handheld scanning equipment, and Gren recalibrated this one to detect life signs. Plus, there's some more workmen's tools—a pocket myriad there—everything you need to fix a mining station from the inside, at least manually that is,' Toar concludes, eyeing the contents of the chest, a disappointed look on his face.

'It's good, I mean I'd prefer some AI-powered combat drones, a plasma launcher and carbon-nanofibre full body armour, but hey, mining station—you did good here, Toar,' I say, and clap him on his back.

Toar gives me a puzzled look for a moment—I think I've used some terms he doesn't understand—but shrugs it off and adds, wistfully, 'I'd love having a plasma-launcher, aye. That, or my sniper rifle.'

'Sniper rifle? You're military, too?' I ask, checking what I've suspected for quite some time. A military background would explain the expert level of piloting I saw from him while watching the buoy's recording of my rescue.

He mirrors the look I gave him previously. 'Long story, we'll talk over dinner,' his reply echoes, and then he starts reaching into the storage unit, but I pull his hand back.

'Just the pistol, Toar. Remember, you're supposed to be getting caught. They'll just take everything from you. Me, on the other hand ...'

I grab my pistol, a box of the charges, the knife, the pocket myriad, a med kit—but my eye passes over the hygiene kit and I stifle a laugh—it's a cleaning kit for your back passage, which, given that Oarth are all male, makes sense to have on hand as part of any survival scenario, when I think about it. I don't need to take one of those—mentally noting that they're there, though—but I take the life-sign detector. Those pockets Gren provided me turn out to be extremely useful; I've got space for everything and then some, and am entirely comfortable even though I'm now as fully armed as I'm going to be.

'And the sabre,' I say, heading towards the locker Toar indicated.

'Hey now, steady on,' Toar replies, sounding proprietary, adding with a note of authority, 'That's my sword.'

I reach the locker, open it, and find the weapon hanging in its scabbard, charging. This is a fine weapon indeed, and I can see why Toar is possessive here; I've seen plasma-powered blades before but this one is a work of art, judging by the quality of the hilt and the detailing on the scabbard.

'It's beautiful,' I say appreciatively, and turn my head to look at Toar, who's got an apprehensive look about him. 'May I take it out?'

'Yes, but please be careful about it,' he replies, and comes over to stand beside me. I no longer find him as looming as I once did, but I still feel a sense of awe whenever he is close like this.

I reach into the locker and reverently remove the weapon; its hilt is a black metal embossed with fine silver grip marks, and is curved slightly downwards with a silver-toned guard and minimal basket, while the blade itself has a slight upswept curve to it, near its end. The scabbard is also a power recharging dock, and its display indicates the weapon is fully charged, ready for use. At what looks to be about a metre and a half in length, it's almost too big for me; I'd need both hands to wield it properly, but I imagine Toar uses it as a single-handed weapon. This is a professional swordsman's instrument, not some foot-soldier's machete, and I'm wondering if I have the skill to wield it.

It's remarkably light in my hands, though—must be molecular lattice carbon in construction, as a metal weapon would be much heavier. I've not yet grasped its hilt—I mean there's the obvious sexual connotations here that I'm sure we're both experiencing, on some level. Instead, I hand the blade to him, and he takes it by the hilt with an ease that shows his proficiency. With his thumb claw, he begins to purposefully trace patterns along the silver etching on the back strap, and in response, a series of lights on the quillion respond—first red, then switching to green, in pattern.

'Here,' Toar says, softly, 'take it by the grip, using your sword hand.'

I do so, getting a good proper hold of it with my right hand, and Toar asks me to keep my hand there for a moment. The green lights fade, one by one, then blink three times before the hilt goes dark.

'There, it's keyed to you now, too. When you need to ignite the plasma, there's a switch your thumb should be able to reach, just under here,' Toar indicates, showing me the spot under the quillion. 'Lasts for about an hour, the plasma, which should get you through whatever you need getting through. Careful though, it's got a conductive heat output in the ten-thousand-degree range, at the edge—touch it, you'll break its thermal barrier, and you'll lose a finger.'

I give him a frown. 'I know, I've used them before. In practice, but still.' I put the fine weapon back into the locker and close it.

My last comment has caught Toar's attention, however, and he scrutinises me. 'You've been in a fight, then, a real one? With those that are trying to kill you?'

I shrug. 'Not a real one, no. My training was all VR simulations—high quality, next-to-life realism, but no, I try and stay out of actual combat. I'll know what to do, if it comes to it.'

He nods once or twice, then looks over the bridge of his nose. '*When. When* it comes to it. Your plan works out, and there'll be shooting, maybe even swordplay, too. You're prepared for that, aye?'

I look him square in the eyes, but the answer is for myself. 'Yes.'

He nods once more and pats my shoulder firmly. 'Good,' he starts, but then his voice takes on a darker edge. 'You need to understand, Rowland, that the Pryok'tel are merciless sire-spits; they'll fight to the death, and they don't back down. Surrender is death to a Pryok'tel—that's part of their nature. Don't give them a chance for a peaceful resolution, because they won't give you one, and if you do, they'll remember your kindness with scorn, when they're having a good chew on you later.'

I nod, but don't reply otherwise. Killing is not my forte—as in, I have never killed another person. Ever. I don't want that to change, but Toar is making it clear that might not be an option.

'Right then, we're nearly ready to get going,' Toar replies, inspecting the shuttle's interior. 'You recalculate the skip-dive's exit portal for your original coordinates—no need to be sneaky, with us wanting to be caught. All I need do is address the crew, and then we're off.'

'Aye, Captain,' I state, mock-saluting. I meant it as a joke, but even I hear the ruffled feathers in my tone. Toar catches this as well, and turns his head to the side.

'Suppose that does need to be worked out, which one of us is the leader here,' he says, but he's just being polite. We both know that.

'You are. You've got the experience, both in combat and with the Pryok'tel. Just ignore my chipped shoulder—I apparently have issues with authority that I need to work on. It won't be a problem, sir,' I reply, ensuring I sound authentic. I don't have a problem with authority, so long as authority knows what the fuck they're doing and aren't there just for the ego rush. Hence why I lasted less than a year in the CAPS-N.

He regards me earnestly for a moment or so, but then nods. 'That's the better option; not being boastful here, but you're right—I do have a lot of time logged in fighting the Pryok'tel. Mind you, as the leader, I'm going to be counting on you for your advice and suggestions, so you speak when you feel you need to, especially if it's to do with your area of expertise and such. You know, robots and security systems and … you know … that thing you do with your hand you said.'

I give him a smile. 'Hacking, sir.'

'Yes, that,' he says, but I'm not sure he understands the term, by how hesitantly he says it. 'You're not OSS, I'm not your captain, so you can call me Toar, if you like.'

'Captain when it's about the mission, Toar when it's about us, sound good?' I offer, and he grins, apparently liking the idea we're going to talk more together about things other than the mission.

If there's a chance, but I suspect the odds don't favour that.

CHAPTER 17

Toar

Ah, Rowland kissed me, he did!
Yes, I know, I should be going over the details of what I'm doing to get
our mission underway, but he did kiss me—*twice*—and even though they
were just little ones on my hand, both times were lovely. Truly lovely—so sweet,
so endearing—and he's got such soft little lips, all warm and lush, and it took all
that was in me not to kiss him back on those lips. I thought maybe I should've—
I'm no novice to romance and I could see that he wanted me to, maybe, but he's
got to be the one to initiate that, I mean, if he wants to, which I do think he
does—what with three proper hugs and two little kisses under our belts already!

Great Oarth, I wish I could smell him though—I bet he's like a slice of the
Eternal himself. I bet his scent is all over him too, and I so want to find out if
that's the case—I'll start with the traditional spots of course, his neck, then his
pits—I can't wait to lick his pits, he's got hair there too, little bit darker than on
his head, and that's going to be fun. Lick him all the way down his big furry chest
and nicely curved tummy too—I wonder if he likes his 'bellybutton' licked? I
can't wait to find out. But I bet he likes his cock licked though, and I so much
want to feel his length down my throat, drink him deep while we get ready for
our first time joining up proper like.

Dear me, that's getting on the explicit side, must admit—and that's the
politest thought that I've been thinking, while I'm at it. I've been imagining all
kinds of scenarios between Rowland and me, since we met, but after those little
perfect pecks, my daydreams are taking on a much more, er, *detailed* quality—you
know, combinations and positions and all that—fantasising about what I'd want
to do to him, and have done to me. If he fancies the top pie, or the bottom one,
or like myself—either, depending on the mood that hits—I take on all comers.
And while it's good to know my imagination hasn't dulled after all these years,
these fantasies are becoming somewhat of a bother—there's quite a lot of work
to get done, after all. Pardon my coarse pun, but if I keep this up, I'm going to
need a private moment in the head to tend my own den, and that'll be awkward
having to explain. It'd definitely help to clear my own head, it would.

Tricky to work out if this is a basic level of attraction or if this is the first
symptoms of an unintended Alluring, though. Been having a think on what I told
Rowland about our Allure, and am wondering if I downplayed it to assure
Rowland that he'd be all right. Have to admit that even though I've been Allured
in the past, I'm not an expert on the subject (still slightly more qualified than
Gren, though) and I'm definitely not qualified in my opinion when it comes to a
human's Allure. I don't *feel* Allured, honestly, maybe—I mean I'm definitely on
the riled-up side, but that's an entirely normal and natural reaction, all things
considered—Rowland is delicious to behold, after all—the most drone-like of
barons, the most baron-like of drones, an erotic hybrid that's making it hard to
think and having to think while hard. Maybe it wasn't such a good idea to take

my helmet off, after all—Gren did warn me that we don't understand how Rowland's Allure works, and it's possible I've gone and done something stupid.

Whatever the case may be, I can't let it become an obstacle, so I've returned to getting back to it. The shuttle's upgrades are finally complete, though it took more time than I budgeted, I'd rather be running late than running unprepared.

Currently, I'm sat at *Blue Boy's* helm, trying to form the right words to say to the crew of the *Lurcaster's Claw* about my imminent departure. I don't want it coming out as a 'farewell' but more as an 'all's well, see you soon'. I've been putting off thinking about the consequences of failing here—Rowland's right, we'll be dead—I mean that's the better alternative, to tell the truth. I know first-hand that Pryok'tel slave pens are the Eternal's blighted hellscape—I've been on too many liberation missions and well know the ill-treatment Oarth receive—worked to the bone and then eaten when they finally fall. The survival rates are less than a quarter, from the accounts of Oarth we've rescued, and those survivors are never the same afterwards. I've even heard terrible, terrible rumours that the Pryok'tel have slave barons, setting them up as breeding machines—which cannot be true because a baron can only have children if he chooses to—but still, the idea is the fuel of nightmares. So none of that can come out in my speech to my crew, even though it's lurking in the back of my mind.

Although the *stól* I had during our break has done wonders at keeping me awake, I'm still tired—and between that and my brain constantly returning to den-thoughts with Rowland, my speech-writing is starting to suffer: all my words are getting jumbled and overlapped, repetitive even. I've got to push through, because we need to get going—the deadline for the Pryok'tel's Under-drive recharge is getting closer and closer, and we've still got to find them even when we hit the Derresion system. I'll speak from the heart; I think I'm best when I do that, after all. We're going to depart at 08h00, which gives us nearly four hours to find the vulture before it dives at 11h41, and so I have Yar coordinate an all-hands meeting just prior to our departure.

'Attention crew of the *Lurcaster's Claw*, this is Captain Toar Grithrawrscion. As many of you know, at approximately 20h10 yesterday evening, we observed an attack on an unknown vessel by the Pryok'tel, which resulted in the destruction of said vessel. We were able to rescue one survivor, who revealed that the Pryok'tel stole an article of valuable technology. In accordance with OSS guidelines, I will be undertaking a mission to pursue the Pryok'tel.

'During my absence, First Officer Yarenthir Relthorclan will remain as acting Captain; please show him the same level of professionalism, support and incredible work ethic that each of you shows me every day. I know that I can count on each of you, both to carry out our original objectives, and to keep the situation calm, contained and, at all times, confidential.

'In preparation for this mission, you have all worked with extreme proficiency to complete the upgrades to our shuttle, and for that, you have only my best gratitude and appreciation. Please know my goal is to return to you and resume my captaincy with all due haste. You are, each of you, amazing and talented individuals, and I know that regardless of the outcome of this mission, you will all continue to be so. It is a pleasure and a privilege being your captain, and so I look forward to being with you all again, soon. With my best to you all, Captain Toar out.'

There. Good and relatively to the point, for me. Didn't gush and kept it upbeat and positive, which is as important for the speaker as for the audience, in this case. I turn and see Rowland with an approving look in his lovely hazel-green eyes, and he walks over to put his hand on my shoulder, patting it twice.

'Well done, Captain. I'm ready when you are,' he states, and takes his seat to my right, at the new tactical station. We strap in, and I'm beginning to feel the nerve mites starting to bite. This first part of the mission—the skip-dive—is the worst part; I could have gone my entire career without having done one and been all the happier for it. My anxiety must be showing, because Rowland immediately takes my hand, giving it a good squeeze again.

'It'll be fine. It's just a regular dive, Captain. We've got it covered,' he says, and his voice is completely calm. He's done this before so I guess he's got the confidence I'm lacking, and so I try and hike my balls up and get on with it. I squeeze back, then return my hand to the control console—I will need all my attention, and both hands, for this next step.

Rowland and I go through the series of pre-check items needed to launch the shuttle, and I'm surprised by his efficiency and skill—he's obviously had formal shuttle-pilot training, as he indicated, since he's able to match my request for confirmations and sequence initiations step for step. For a moment, I do feel as though I'm back in the Navy, leading an away mission with my fellow Rangers—Rowland shows such proficiency that I'm beginning to get a confidence-boost. That, and he's purposefully shifted his leg over, so that our knees are touching, which I'm sure wasn't part of his training but is nonetheless most welcome and helpful.

'All systems checked. Initiating launch. Clearing docking bay doors in five, four, three, two, one ... we're clear. Moving to pre-established portal coordinates.'

'Connecting to Under-drive system—Captain, I'm going to be directly interfacing with *Blue Boy* now,' Rowland advises, his tone instructive. 'From your perspective, it will look like I'm meditating or sleeping—you can still speak to me normally, but there may be a delay before I reply ... that's normal too, and I'll be speaking back to you over the comms system. I can still hear you, and feel you, but it's best not to move me around too much. I'll stay connected until we're on the other side.'

'I understand,' I say, but I don't. I've never seen this 'hacking' thing, and it's making those mites bite again. There's no training for what we're about to attempt, but there's plenty of risk, and I get this sudden image in my head of my Dad, weeping at the news his son is lost forever in time and space.

'How are you so calm, about this dive?' I ask Rowland, trying not to sound envious.

He thinks for a moment before answering, his handsome face taking on a cute expression as he ponders. 'Well, the way I see it, there's only two possible outcomes: either we succeed, or we don't. I'm only going to be aware if we succeed; since if we don't—well, I'm not going to be able to know if I'm stuck in the Under, am I? So, in that sense, since I can't perceive that outcome—it doesn't exist for me. And so if only one of the two possibilities can exist for me—the one where we succeed—I guess that means when we try it, it's going to work, because that's the only outcome that I can be aware of.'

I think on what he's saying, and there's a certain logic to it, albeit a fatalistic one. 'But our families will know otherwise, if it doesn't work.'

'Well, we won't be able to perceive that either, so, it also doesn't exist,' he replies, but gives me a dry smile. 'At least, that's what I'm telling myself. I figure if this doesn't work, and we're stuck in the Under, the next moment that we're going to be able to perceive is the moment when we exit, if that ever could happen. It could take a trillion, trillion years for that to occur, but to us, it will be an instant.'

'Oh, that's not making me feel any better,' I grumble.

He chuckles. 'I can think of worse things than being stuck in the Under all that time and not knowing it,' he says, turning to me with a tender smile. 'Especially if you've got a good friend along with you.'

I grin but turn away, bashful for a moment. He can be very sweet, Rowland can be.

'Let's hope it's the instant instead of the next iteration of the universe, eh?' I remark, and Rowland nods in agreement, reaching over and patting my knee.

'We'll be fine, Toar, the math is perfect. You just worry about getting us in, and what'll happen when we're out,' Rowland says, and then places his left hand on the console, his open palm running over its surface.

'Where are you, where are you?' he mutters absently to himself, and then his hand stops just near the edge of the terminal. 'Ah, gotcha.'

He regards me with a determined look. 'Okay, I'm ready to jack. See you on the other side.' Turning to face forward, he closes his eyes, and takes two steady deep breaths: one, then another, and then he's perfectly still—a peaceful, sleeping, beautiful statue.

'Rowland?' I ask, but there's no response. He's so still it's beginning to concern me, and I fight the need to reach out and check if he's okay—he had specifically said not to move him, and I don't know enough about what he's doing to know if what I'm seeing is normal.

The voice of *Blue Boy* suddenly speaks to me, startling me.

'I'm connected, Captain. I'm in direct interface between the shuttle's and the station's Under-drives, and they're in working order—we're good and everything is ready when you are.'

'You're all right, then?' I ask, a note of worry in my voice.

'Perfectly fine. I can see you, by the way. Wave to the camera? Give me a good smile.'

I turn the corner of my lips in a small grin and lazily wave one of my hands. This is really bothering me, actually—there's an element of in-Oarthness to what I'm seeing—of not being alive—and I want him to stop what he's doing and come back to me. I've never considered myself a technophobe, by any stretch— we're still discovering new stuff about the technology we've liberated from the Pryok'tel, even two centuries later. My son Rethtoar—*tsk*—Rethculler—is an engineer, and he's told me all kinds of new things that make me terribly excited for the future of Oartheca—but what I'm seeing now gives me a bad twist in my stomach. This, what Rowland's doing, is too much for me. I want to take him out of that chair and hold him in my arms, to make him stop.

But that could wind up fouling the dive, and so I'll just have to swallow my feelings and trust what he's doing. I turn in my seat and take my controls, entering the series of commands that will get this show on the road, and get Rowland back to me sooner. 'Right, spooling the shuttle's Under-drive. Signalling the station to initiate its spool.'

'Drive systems spooling. Cross-relaying dive metrics. Synergizing portal stabilization,' the robo-voice of Rowland indicates.

'Portal formation detected; coordinates zero mark zero-two-two, point two-five kilometres,' I reply.

'Hold for drive alignment confirmation. Alignment at thirty-two percent efficiency. Increasing shuttle's drive calibration. Fifty-five percent and rising.'

'Portal formation nearing completion.' I look out of our cockpit and I can see the faint blue-white ring of the portal forming; it's only a hair's breadth wide to my perception, but I can see the space it encircles beginning to distort. So far, it appears to be a completely normal portal.

'Alignment achieved; both systems report stability. Proceed at your discretion, Captain,' Rowland directs. He's so Eternally-blessed calm. How, how is he managing that?

I take in a deep breath, hold it for a moment, and let it out. I feel Rowland's leg push harder against me. I want to reach out to touch him but I still need both my hands on the controls, and I don't want to risk distracting him and sending us into eternal oblivion.

'Portal formation complete. Charging propulsion. Setting course for the portal,' I indicate and watch the propulsion system rev up. With my coordinates laid in, once I see we're at full charge to our engines, I do now find myself taking a hold of Rowland's knee before I execute the command to enter the portal.

I am frightened as the ship lurches forward and I see the rush of the dive portal coming at me, and that fright escalates to genuine terror, even as I wonder if my last words are going to be:

'Brace for dive in three, two, one … diving Under, Great Oarth save our …'

*****

'... souls!' I shout, as we're spat out on the other side.

There's a terrible cacophony as the ship's internal alarms start blaring howls of alerts. We're spinning; I can see the stars outside the cockpit whirling around us, and I immediately try to gain control of the ship, punching my terminal to engage our retro-rockets to get us under control.

'Damage sustained to Under-drive system,' Rowland's voice states calmly; I don't have a chance to look over at him, I'm desperately trying to get the shuttle to come to a stop but the controls are resisting my input.

'Propulsion unit offline; re-initializing,' Rowland replies. 'Proximity alert, multiple unidentified objects within current trajectory, recommend engaging avoidance protocol ... ah, Jesus fuck!'

I can see it now—gigantic red rocks flash across our cockpit's view as we keep spinning. I fire our main thrusters at specific intervals to break out of our tumble, pulling us away but at nowhere near the speed we need to avoid smacking right into them. Got to buy us some time or we are going to impact in moments.

'Get my propulsion back!' I command, and quickly check my sensor grid— we've got about three seconds before *Blue Boy* collides with a fat red rock the size of the *Lurcaster's Claw* itself, directly in our path.

'Re-initialization in three, two ...'

'Now!' I yell, and slam my thumb claw on the retro-rockets command; they fire at the last possible moment, slowing us enough for me to gain control, and plunge us downwards along the length of the rock in front of us. There's pinging noises in the ship as we clip off some smaller outcroppings along our path, but in a few moments, my board lights up in confirmation that our propulsion has been fully restored, and I'm able to fire our retros to flip the shuttle ninety degrees, our stern to the rock, and blast our engines full force—launching us out of harm's way and into the deep of clear space.

It takes me a few moments flying straight into inky darkness before I'm able to come down from the terror I've been experiencing, and I'm so numb right now I'm not aware that I've stopped breathing. I do hear ragged breathing though, and have enough sense in me to pull back on the engines, and establish a standard orbit. I turn now to see Rowland, his left hand off the console, and vice-gripped on my leg instead. I'm not even aware that he's done that, but his hand is shaking, and his grip is getting uncomfortable.

His eyes follow mine to his hand, and his grip lessens. 'You're amazing,' he mumbles, and then looks at me deeply. 'You're truly amazing.'

I laugh, nervous and giddy, coming down from my high. The truth of the matter is that I'm feeling more alive than I have in years—yes, I've missed the danger, the excitement that can only come from exploring the vastness of the universe in a starship. I never considered myself as the type who enjoys trouble, but I can't deny that the past few hours of my life have been full of a thing that I apparently crave, and have been starved of. Not much to do on a mining station other than whittle away the hours in idle chat and writing reports that, at best, will get a half-arsed once-over before being filed away and forgotten. I've lived more in the short time since I met Rowland than I have in years.

I've got to check on our tactical systems, to see if our breach has been detected and there's a Pryok'tel vessel en route to ruin our day, and when I turn back to advise my co-pilot that all looks clear, I catch him gazing out our main viewing window, a wistful light in his eyes and a small smile on his face. I turn to share in what he's looking at, and when I see it, I too am struck silent.

Derresion Two is a vibrant, nearly electric blue in colour, with bands of cerulean clouds constantly swirling and streaking across its surface. Now from this distance, the bright ruby red of its bromine ring, set against the massive blazing blue background, is a marvel for the senses—the contrast between the two colours makes them both throb with intensity and the entire picture is truly breath-taking to look upon. I've missed this too, awfully—the indescribable thrill of discovering new planets and other astral bodies, seeing them up close with my own eyes, marvelling at the infinitely complex beauty of every corner of the galaxy. Or, sometimes, right beside you.

'It's incredible,' Rowland whispers in awe. His eyes dart back and forth between the details he sees, but he lets them rest for a moment, and his lovely smile returns in full.

'Aye,' I say, my eyes turning to him. 'Not the most beautiful sight I've seen today, but still.'

He looks over at me with a darling expression of embarrassment and appreciation at my little flirtation. I've scored a bigger hit than I thought though, because only another moment goes by before he leans over towards me—and my heart jumps now, 'cause I'm fairly sure from the look on his lovely face and his half-closed eyes, that he wants to kiss me. It takes all that's in me not to leap from my seat and sweep him up—in my mind, that's how our first kiss starts and all—but I mirror his actions instead, showing as much restraint and civility as I can, so as not to spook him. I'm still much quicker when I lean over, however.

A nasty bit of nerves bites me when he hesitates, just before our heads are close enough together, and I think he's going to change his mind—and I have an awful moment where I think he's backing out, and that I'm just too different for him, that I'm too much of a brute where he is just that beautiful ...

And then his lips touch mine and ...

... (*bliss*) ...

I mean ... I just ... oh and then he's ...

... I hear a small huff of satisfaction, a moan of pure joy—it could be from either or both of us. His lips are on mine and I'm beyond myself with happiness. I want so badly to keep this first kiss of ours slow, affectionate, to savour it entirely—I've been thinking about this moment since I first found him—and the reality of it is far superior to my best imagining of how it would be. He is precious, this perfect man before me, and I'm both humbled and elated just to be in this moment with him.

But my body and soul are demanding more, I'm craving him and all he is, and my tongue darts out to lick his lips, seeking permission to enter his mouth and meet his. He provides that permission, quickly, without hesitation, placing his hands on my cheeks, stroking them softly as he gently holds my head in place, turning his own slightly to the side so that we can connect deeply together. I'm careful only to put the tip of my tongue in because I'm not sure if he's had a tongue as big as mine before, and I don't want to overwhelm him with it—but as his tongue matches mine, lick for lick, I can feel my cock thundering to attention.

I'm only slightly aware that I'm pulling Rowland towards me, eager to feel his body push against me once more. He's matching my efforts, coming closer willingly, drawing us together, leaning into our kiss. Then each of his hands touches the spot under my ears where my jaw connects, right where my scent glands are, and the explosion of sweet tingling that follows forces a deep, urgent groan of pleasure right from the core of me.

I stand now and Rowland does the same, in near tandem, and as I press us together, my now fully swollen cock thuds right against his delightfully rounded but still firm stomach. It's terribly crass behaviour on my part—such a thing would never be permitted with our barons—but I want Rowland to see, to feel, how much he's affecting me—how much I want him—and, yes, to feel him against me too, to learn if he's as excited as I am. It's taking all that's in me not to vulgarly grind against him, as much as I want to. I've put one hand around his waist though, resting it just above his bum—there's something about knowing there's a slight dusting of light brown hair just above that perfect arse of his, just a few centimetres from my hand now, that's causing me to soar with lust, and then I feel his hard swell against me—firm, generous ... Eternal damn these trousers!

But he pauses now and I suspect I've been too bold, too rushed with him—he's human and kissing a lumbering lout like myself is all new to him. My eagerness, my ... need for him, has got the better of my manners and consideration; had I behaved so coarsely during my first encounter with Cralren, I doubt he'd have deigned to continue with me. Barons must be wooed, they must be deferred to, and they must be the ones to not only initiate a physical encounter with their sires, but to set the course for how that encounter unfolds.

The instant I feel Rowland's hesitation, I make sure to relax the grip I have on his rear—I don't let go but I stop the pressure, and just let my hand rest there, stroking the small of his back lightly with my claw-tips. He's still kissing me though, so that's good—that's so, so good—but I want to make sure he knows that we're going to go at his pace.

He pulls back now, looking me in the eye, with an expression halfway between desire and uncertainty. He kisses me again, quickly, then pulls back, hesitates, and we resume a deeper kiss a third time before he forces himself to take a step back. I let him go, but I'm slow to return my hand to myself.

It's a moment before he sorts himself out, and he's not shy about needing to adjust himself in his mining suit in order to do so. I elect to stay as I am, tented and all, to ensure there's no chance of him mistaking my feelings in this moment, and I rumble, 'Well, that's made all this worthwhile,' and I can't help but feel a pure joy as I see a pleased look in his lovely eyes. He is so, so beautiful.

He gives a short laugh, and then kisses me again, quickly, before stepping back to sit in his chair. He's not looking at me, seeming to need a distraction to settle himself, and after clearing his throat, he offers tentatively, 'Heh, maybe with all we need to talk about, perhaps we should follow that dinner we've planned with breakfast the next morning?'

The skin around his neck and cheeks flushes, and my response to his offer is quick and clear.

'That sounds right,' I agree, heartily. I have to cut that sentence off though, as the urge to add "my Baron" may be too much for either of us now, even though it's how I feel at this moment. "My sweet Baron" would definitely be too much.

'Good, good' he replies, busying himself further but still wearing his little grin. 'I'll run a ship-wide diagnostic, Captain, if you can get us a picture of where we are.' He's taken on a business-like tone, but still sneaks appreciative, interested looks my way, top to bottom, and especially around my belt area. I must truly have a fascinating belt buckle.

'Yes, of course,' I reply, and need a moment to adjust my own self before I sit—Rowland's eyes follow all my actions, though he's trying to be coy about it—but I'm back at the helm soon enough, accessing our navigation system to see where we are and what's going on around us.

'Well, we've made it to the Derresion system, that's for sure. We're about fifty-two million kilometres off course, though. Right in the ring system of Derresion Two, as you can see. That's its bromine ring we nearly hit.'

Rowland gives an apologetic look, then shrugs a shoulder as nonchalantly as possible. 'Skip-diving is an art as much as a science,' he explains, lamely.

'I see,' I reply, also trying to sound nonchalant as I double-check my readings. 'If we'd been just a hundred thousand or so kilometres more artistic, we'd have dived right into the planet itself.'

'Psssh, plenty of room,' Rowland says dismissively, but he does not meet my wary eye. He's reviewing his display console and there's a bothered look about him. 'Under-drive system is damaged,' he remarks, 'but *Blue Boy* says the repairs are pretty straightforward. You wouldn't happen to be an engineer as well as a pilot and a captain, would you?'

'I can take a look, but no promises. I'm scanning for other ships within our radius—nothing's showing up at the moment, but keep an eye on that while I take a look at the dive engine? The Pryok'tel have better scanners than we do—they may have detected our breach wake.'

'Understood—we've got some other little glitches too but I can work those out from here. All in all though—gotta say, I think we're good here, Toar. Congratulations, you've just survived breaking the laws of Under dive physics.'

I grin happily at his comment, but I don't really register what he's saying on a deep level. I still feel his lips pressed against mine, still feel his tongue caressing mine, still feel his hips in my hand. His cock against mine too—I want to be chivalrous here, but I am proudly Oarth, and my needs can't be glossed over so easily.

I stand from the helm to start towards checking the Under-drive, which is situated under the floor panels near the galley, but Rowland reaches for my hand as I do so, and I take his. He doesn't say anything, but from the gentle stroke of his thumb on the back of my hand, and the soft, somewhat shy look on his face, I figure he's trying to show me his feelings—I'm not sure what they are specifically, but it's still lovely for me, him holding my hand. He gives a few more thumb pets, then pats my hand, releases it, and turns back to his console.

As I make my way towards the Under-drive, I find that my thoughts have nothing to do with the shuttle and are all about Rowland. It's at this point I suspect I may be Allured, at least to some degree. The lovely kissing we've been doing—my feelings surge each time, from the first sweet peck he gave me on the back of my hand to our recent extended session. Gren's voice haunts me, reminding me we don't understand how the human's Allure works—we've only guessed it's smell-related, but it could be physical contact too. If that's the case, then, well, there's no going back for me now. My tongue can still taste his, after all.

I don't care, though, not one bit. I've been on my own for over fifteen years now—with my family barely able to speak with me, and certainly, no bond-mate in the works. And it's been awful for me, as it was intended to be. Yes, there's been many den-mates during that time—but it's been out of pity as often as it was actual desire. That I'm still considered worthy of a fuck every now and then is more than I can rightly hope for, and I know that. I consider myself lucky that I even get that attention—I did, after all, get a baron killed. I doubt I'd stay past a night with a drone who did that, if I bothered to den with him at all.

But with Rowland, there's this hope—he wouldn't care about my past, he's from a different culture, and what I did might not carry the same damnation in his eyes. So if I'm Allured by him, so be it. I'll not let Rowland know, it'll be all right. I won't burden him, not with all that's happened to him, and all he still has to go through. I'll just do my best to make sure he makes it out the other side of it all, and take it from there, wherever 'there' turns out to be.

I crouch to pull up the floorboard just underneath our makeshift galley and expose the secondary interface module for the Under-drive. Leaning down, I can see the diagnostic display console, which is currently not in alert mode, which is a very good sign, and so I start to run a scan to discover what the problem is.

'Ugh,' I hear Rowland moan, and turn to see him holding his fist just below his sternum, a sour look on his face. 'That *stól* isn't sitting too well with me,' he says, ruefully, and winces as he suppresses a hitch in his chest. 'Heartburn and then some.'

'Heh, poor lad,' I sympathise. 'That happens to me sometimes, if I've gone and had too much.'

'I'll check the auto-doc, see if it's got some antacids, or something,' he states, standing to head over to the unit. He casts a concerned look down at the exposed floorboard. 'What's the problem?'

I turn back and check the first read-outs on the diagnostic module—though the system scan is still running, the initial results are all coming back as positive, which is good news I think because a glaringly serious problem would have shown up immediately. I take a closer look though because from my perspective, there's nothing wrong with the system at all—there are various indicators that are all lit in their positive state, and there's no discernible damage to any of the hardware, at least none that I can see. It's possible that our tumbling dislodged a connection or something, which is an easy fix, but it does mean pulling up more floorboards.

'Can't see anything,' I indicate, frowning, and Rowland comes closer to peer over my shoulder. 'Everything is looking fi ...'

There's a quick flash of pain on the side of my neck and a short hissing sound. I turn to see Rowland hopping a step backwards. He's holding a small metal device in his hand—I can't tell what it is—but the apologetic look on his face tells me he knows what it is.

'Sorry, Toar,' he says regretfully. 'You'll be fine, though. I promise.'

'What did you ...' but my words are beginning to slur, and my vision is doubling. A massive wave of fatigue hits me, hard, on top of the exhaustion I'm already carrying. I try to stand but my entire body is weakening, and all I can manage is to put my hands out to stop myself from falling flat on my face.

'What did ...' I try again, reaching for him. But there's a blackness seeping quickly into me, and Rowland's image is fading as fast as I am.

'You're all right, you're all right, just sleep now ...' he coaxes.

I've no choice in the matter. I obey.

*****

I wake up, groggy, confused, and increasingly furious with every moment that passes.

My head is pounding and there's a weakness throughout my entire body; it's fading but it takes me a moment or two to realize that I'm lying on my back. It's initially dark, but there's a light coming from somewhere, yet my eyes are taking their time to adjust. The air is damp, hot, and unpleasantly unfamiliar; I still can't smell anything but I have the feeling that if I could, this air would stink.

I've got a blanket on me though—one of the scratchy ones from the shuttle—and my head's resting on something soft. As my eyes adjust, I find myself looking at the craggy surface of a rock ceiling, and the source of the faint light is somewhere to my left—as I turn my head, I can see that I'm indeed just slightly inside of a cave, a few metres from a rough open wound that forms its entrance. I can see a dull red sky, cloudless but oppressive and heavy.

I pull my blanket off and sit up, slowly—realising that I'm desperately thirsty in addition to being discombobulated. As I do so, I find that I'm lying on our shuttle's gurney, collapsed so it's resting near to the ground, and my head had been resting on another blanket folded over to form a pillow. I've obviously been placed here with a degree of care—and as I look around the small rocky foyer where I was laid down, I can see that I've been left with most of the supply crates we had on board as well. Our comms beacon is resting on top of one, and on one side, propped in front of it, is my personal touchpad. On the other side is a sachet of purified water from our emergency supplies. This little shrine's been set up directly in my line of sight out of the cave, so I wouldn't miss it.

Despite his obvious care to make me comfortable, it's hard for me not to be enraged at Rowland for what he's done to me, wherever the Eternal-damned place he's left me is. I should have known not to trust him—he's proven time and time again that dealing with me honestly is just not a possibility—this is his third betrayal of my trust in as many chances I've given him to earn it: he stole my ship, he lied about giving it back, and now he's drugged me, when my back was turned, no less. True colours, indeed. Crafty, deceitful liar. The little thief, as much as I didn't want him to be.

I grab the water and puncture the top of it with my claw-tip, guzzling its contents down in a few mouthfuls, trying both to wash the stale taste from my mouth and parch my thirst. I grab the touchpad, momentarily tempted to thwart whatever plan Rowland has for me by launching it out of the cave with all the force I can put behind it, but I think better of it, and instead follow his wordless instructions and turn the damn thing on. I'm not surprised to see I've a message left for me, the subject line being, 'Sorry, but hear me out.'

Rolling my eyes and giving a hefty, irritable sigh, I play the message, and discover it's a recording made by the little thief himself, where from the background, I can tell that he's in the shuttle pilot's chair and yes, there I am, passed out on the floor just behind him. Rowland's got a small, sad smile on his face as he addresses the camera recording him from the helm's display monitor.

'So, hear me out, Captain,' he starts, his tone already apologetic, and I'm disgusted with myself that at the sound of his voice, my heart yearns for him, and that the first layers of my outrage are already being eroded with just these few opening words. Oarth-damned Allure …

Rowland sighs and looks skyward, before continuing. 'First off, you're safe—you're on Derresion Prime and if I've done my job properly, somewhere out of harm's way and resting comfortably. I've left you all the supplies we had, and programmed the comms beacon to start transmitting a distress signal just before the *Grolthon's Spear* is expected to arrive in the system. They'll find you, but just in case, I've also sent your coordinates to the *Lurcaster's Claw*. Just sit tight, you'll be rescued before you know it. You've got food, water and supplies to last you a long time. I've also downloaded some entertainment from *Blue Boy* to keep you occupied; sorry, it's mostly training manuals, but there was some light fiction as well, and some kind of matching game, for when you stop being angry at me and start getting bored,' Rowland explains, and gives a lame grin.

'Also, that was just a mild tranquilliser I used to take you down—well, mild for you, I'd be in a coma if I took that amount—but I had the auto-doc calculate the right dosage to get you down for an hour or so. Hopefully you're feeling rested but the auto-doc says you'll experience dehydration and headaches, so if you've not done so, please drink the water I'll leave out for you, and I'll put some analgesics in the med-kit for you too.'

Rowland looks away from the camera for this next bit. 'I hated doing that to you. Ambushing you like that. Fucking ... awful of me.' He sighs deeply and shakes his head. With a shrug of his shoulders, he continues. 'But it had to be done. There's just no way I could risk you, Toar—I've lost five people that I care about and losing another is just ... not going to happen. You've already done more than could be expected of anyone. Especially for a worthless two-bit shit like me.'

He faces the camera again and gives a quick twist of his lips. 'Between that and knowing you have kids, well, the decision becomes irrefutable at that point. We don't know each other, at all really, but if we did, you'd likely know that I lost my father when I was younger, and it fucked up my life. My Dad died while following the orders of an idiot who thought he knew better—sort of like what you're doing with me, if you'll notice—and I never got over it. I don't want your sons to have that in common with me, Toar. They'll never forgive me if I let something happen to you. Never.'

'Also,' he continues, reluctantly though, 'I think we need to acknowledge that there's a lot of emotions that are affecting both of our judgements—and I need to take responsibility if it's the Allure that's affecting yours. I don't know if it is, but I'm not willing to take the chance with your life to find out.'

He gives a thoughtful look to the camera. 'I know you would have gone with me to the end. Through the worst of it, right beside me. I can tell you're that kind of guy. I can also tell you that I'm not worth that. I'm ... just not, Toar. I'm not a baron. I'm not even a good human; just look at what I've done to you since you've known me. You deserve someone who's on the same level you're on—and even at my best, I can't match you at your worst. But the least I can do for you is not be your Schrödinger's Cat, Toar, so let me open that box for you instead—this is how our story goes, and how it ends:

'I fly off the slime world, and through a daring and clever series of ruses, treachery and good ol' fashioned skulduggery, I trick the Pryok'tel into giving me back my crew. They're all alive, and somehow, together, we overtake the vulture and claim it as our own—I want to jettison the Pryok'tel crew into space but my friends talk me out of it. In the meantime, my crew and I fly back to CAPS space, shaken by our adventure but none the worse for wear.

'Betts, my best friend—God, I would love to introduce you to her—goes back to the CAPS-N and is reinstated—and promoted—for all her awesomeness over the years. Ivan keeps being a bastard, but a noble bastard, and takes a job as a security consultant, earning his credits legitimately—at least at first glance. Mia has had her fill of cowboy space antics and follows Betts to the CAPS—two years later, she's the lead engineer on the best ship in our fleet. Bryce and I resolve our differences, and we part as friends, but his next boyfriend is nowhere near as sexy as I am and that pleases me no end. Cor returns to Harculcor, and becomes a diplomat-slash-scientist-slash-politician triple threat, where his incredible brain is put to use solving the galaxy's biggest problems. A millennium of peace soon follows.

'As for me? Well, I earn myself a broken heart, having left one of the best men I've ever met stuck on a slime world, but I'll know we're both going to be all right. I've turned the veil over to the CAPS as a peace offering, and having learned my lesson, start a new life where I put my criminal tendencies to good use. Still not going to be a part of the fucking CAPS, but I'll consult for them—which means I get paid double. Everyone is successful and safe. We all live happily ever after.

'As for you? Well, after being mad for a while, you have a good think about why I did the things I did, and somehow, you find it in your heart to forgive me, even if it's just a little. The *Grolthon's Spear* shows up in orbit, and celebrates you for saving your station from the evil human terrorist who threatened to blow it up unless you helped him—you are given a parade when you return to Oartheca and your name becomes synonymous with 'hero'. On those rare occasions when you think of me, you know that I'm safe, and happy, and a better man for having met you, but you don't think of me that often. See, you find someone …'

He stops now, looking downwards as a terse grunt escapes him, and he clears his throat. It takes him a moment before he continues, and when he does, his voice is rough, but he speaks as though he's giving me an order. 'You find a bond-mate just as goddamn amazing, brave, and noble as you are, and you kiss him just like you kissed me. You take his breath away, and he loves you from that moment on, every day of your long, happy and prosperous lives together. Whatever troubles you've had, they're all in the past—it's nothing but a happy-ever-after for you too.'

He pauses, and a wry grin casts a shadow across his lips. 'You do learn one thing from me though, and that's if something or someone gets in your way, you say fuck it, and do what needs to be done. Why? Fuck why. You know better, that's why. You don't let others tell you how you're going to be—You. Tell. Them. Whatever gets in your way, you're the winner. Every time.'

'And that's how our stories end, Toar. Happily ever after, for the both of us. There's no other possibilities that can be perceived.' He winks. 'Take care of yourself, my big man—the universe needs more guys like you in it. Now, go make your story come true. For the both of us.'

He gives me a friendly salute, then kisses the tips of his fingers, presses them to the screen, and the recording ends.

It takes me many moments to speak, and when I do, I find I can barely manage a whisper. 'You daft fool. I already found the one I want to kiss like I kissed you.'

But it turns out I've lost who I found. I sit back down on the gurney, and just stare out into the rust-red sky, unsure of what to do next other than wallow in a deep despair that's churning in me. It's not for myself that my mood turns to such sorrow—it's Rowland's words that are causing my eyes to go all leaky. How he said he was worthless, a 'two-bit shit'.

The certainty behind those words is breaking my heart—and that he genuinely thinks so poorly of himself—let alone believes it—is devastating me. It's so far from the truth that I wonder at how awful his life must have been for him to think that. As upset as I was, or perhaps still am somewhat, I can still see that everything he's doing is to save those he loves—I can't be that angry, especially since I'm unharmed and only mildly inconvenienced while he's flying into a battle he cannot win for a chance to save those he loves. I would trade everything, save for my own family, to have someone who loved me that much.

He knows his clever plans won't work. He's going to blow up the shuttle to stop the Pryok'tel, just as he told me. Because he doesn't think he deserves to live after what's happened to his own family.

It's his punishment as much as his victory, and my eyes spill over with that awful thought.

CHAPTER 18

Rowland

Yeah, I know.

Turns out the hardest part of my plan to safely remove Toar from the equation was not how to render him unconscious—that part was pretty straightforward actually—the auto-doc had ample solutions to choose from to incapacitate an Oarth of Toar's size for the short-term, without causing damage.

No, the hardest part was moving him—he easily weighs half a tonne and, being unconscious, he was a dead-weight too, like a gigantic floppy cat who refuses to move. My muscles are mostly for show, and although they do come in handy on many occasions, I could barely drag Toar more than a few metres before becoming exhausted. Deciding that the better muscle to use would be my brain, I cut power to the shuttle's gravity plating, floated my sleeping buddy over to the gurney in the storage area, then used its anti-gravity setting to gently float him out of the shuttle after having landed on Derresion Prime.

I know, I'm deflecting—minimizing my ugly behaviour—because the hardest part was watching the few seconds of betrayal in Toar's eyes before the tranquillizer took effect. God, I hated having to do that, even if it was for the best, but when I weigh it against him getting killed, it's by far the better call. I hope the message I left him at least partially gets him to not hate me; I'll hate myself enough for us both.

Not that how Toar feels about me will matter in a few hours; as all outcomes of my plan result in me no longer being a problem for him. But if I'm only to be a memory to him, I'd prefer it was at least not a horrible one. I meant every word I left for Toar—I do think he's a great guy and it would have been well worth it to know him more, but only from my perspective—he's too much an upstanding gentleman for a lowdown grifter like me.

As for our make-out session—well, it was simultaneously the best thing I've had in years and like nothing I've ever had before. I will admit experiencing a moment of doubt before I took the plunge with him—and I'm ashamed to say it was nothing to do with being too worried for my crew, or needing to stay on mission, or anything remotely that sensible or wise.

It also had nothing to do with his physical appearance—which I'm kinda worried he might think is the case; he'd previously mentioned that we're very different—but at this point, that's not how I feel about him—we've got more in common than we don't, in ways that both baffle and intrigue me. Toar is a man as much as I am, and I'm just as attracted to his complex soul and gentleness as I am to his impressive physical self—I think I've made it clear his stunning cobalt eyes make my knees weak. And that crooked grin of his—the one he gives me that tells me he's pleased or when he's being clever—it's just irresistible.

I hesitated because I knew that I had to remove him from this scenario—that decision was made when Toar told me he was going to get captured as a slave, just to give me a shot at my plan. There was no chance of that happening, but

Toar is stubborn—a trait I share and admire, by the way—and I just had no more time left to convince him otherwise. So I hesitated, because if I kissed him, in that moment, I was worried he'd think it was just to seduce him, get him to lower his guard. God, I hope he doesn't think that—*I* would, in his boots.

But I did kiss him, not because I'm a manipulative asshole, or because my curiosity and desire get the better of me, or because at the end of the day, I'm just a horn-dog who likes big soft-hearted guys—I wanted to kiss Toar because I wanted to, and that's all.

And ... woah, it was ... I don't know the right words to explain it. Great? Fantastic? They seem kinda lame in doing our lip-lock justice—'perspective-changing' is nearer the mark. The best part was I could tell immediately how much he wanted to kiss me, how absolutely thrilled he was that it was happening, and that spurred me on like a fire underfoot. When your partner's enthusiasm matches yours, it's all the more potent, and Toar made sure I knew just how *abundantly* eager he was—what with him standing there, showing off his undeniably hot version of 'wearing your heart on your sleeve'.

I think I moaned — maybe it was him, maybe both of us—because he felt so damn good against my lips. Then that aphrodisiacal scent of his hit me, full on, and to borrow an Oarthecan expression—that was just *raur*. Between the sensation of his dextrous lips, coaxing tongue and that delicious scent, my cock made sure I understood what real instinct was all about. When I touched just below Toar's ears and heard that primal grunt of his, I thought for sure we'd be getting naked in a matter of moments. I could tell he was letting me take the lead, and so when that fucking mountain he's got down his trousers bumped against me—damn, feeling him fully against me flicked my overdrive—and I needed to choose: stop, or go all the way, then and there.

I chose to stop ... reluctantly. Not just because yeah, we're in the middle of a soon-to-be hostile situation, and my family's lives are on the line—you know, the smart thing to do—it's that I don't want to fuck Toar. I mean, *just* fuck Toar—I've got nothing against fast encounters with guys I've just met—some of my best hookups took less time than learning the dude's name—if there was a chance to learn it, that is. It's that I want to *be* with Toar, fully: all of him, unrushed, where we can spend our time discovering, sharing, savouring. He's so deeply into me that he deserves more from me then just a quickie on *Blue Boy's* floor. No, no: Toar's that level of extra-special to me, and I feel he deserves to be treated extra-right for our first time, if we have one—I so want that for him ... for us. After that, yeah, we can fuck fast and furious, all primal instincts let loose to run wild.

But there won't be a first time, or a next time, because it was then that my plan to incapacitate him solidified—I was debating whether or not I'd go through with it, but kissing him made the decision for me. He's truly a special guy—rare, and important not just to me, but to his family and his people. There's no way my tom-fuckery is going to get him killed. So sleepy-time it was, then off to find a place to keep him safe while I go risk my life. The only logical destination was

Derresion Prime—the tidally-locked slime planet with a breathable atmosphere.

Derresion Prime is actually beautiful, in an absurd sort of way. The surface of its habitable zone is almost entirely covered by this purple alga, and when you're flying over it, it's an ocean of grape jelly as far as the eye can see, with only marginal outcroppings of black rocks here and there where the alga hasn't climbed up yet. It was on one of these rocky 'shores' that *Blue Boy* detected an entrance to a suitable cave system that could be a shelter for Toar—it seems the alga only grows where the constant dull red rays of the Derresion sun hit the surface, and so this covered area seemed the ideal place to keep Toar comfortable and safe.

Leaving Toar was the best thing to do—I mean I know he'll be fine, but I already miss him—his hulking size close by is somehow comforting, and his absence is surprisingly sorely felt. Being around him makes me feel better, and leaving him behind makes this the first time since the destruction of my *Luck of the Draw* that I'm on my own.

Which I'm finding disturbing, since there's been no sign of the Pryok'tel since we arrived in the system. Our breach-wake, exiting our dive, was surely large enough for them to detect, and I've dived twice since then—once from our position in the rings of Derresion Two to Derresion Prime, and from there, to a position midway between Derresion Three and Four—and there's not been a peep on *Blue Boy*'s sensors of another vessel coming to investigate my activity.

But then again, why should the Pryok'tel come after me? They've got what they came for, so why risk a further confrontation when they can just hide and wait for their Under-drive to recharge so that they can get back home? They don't need me, I need them—and my entire plan hinges on them being brainless scavengers. I've forgotten that villains are never so black-and-white as to behave the way you predict. The Pryok'tel had a purpose today; they've nearly succeeded at getting away with it, and I need to stop underestimating them.

This thought forces me to address a topic I've been hiding from, one that I briefly mentioned to Toar but didn't elaborate on; the Pryok'tel knew exactly when and where to strike us. There's no way that they just 'showed up' out of the black and stumbled across us—they knew we were going to be there, and the only way that could have happened is if someone let them know we were coming. And that awful thought leads to the inescapable conclusion that this someone was a member of my crew.

It wasn't Bryce, I'm fairly certain; he's got no motivation for it—I mean we weren't getting along but nowhere near the point of wanting me and the rest of us killed. Bryce is non-violent to begin with, being a doctor and all. For him, the best outcome would be the one we planned: he'd get his new life and the funding he needed, and that's all in the shitter now. Besides, both of us were caught completely off guard by the attack—if Bryce knew it was coming, he did nothing to protect himself—in fact, given his state the last time I saw him, it's unlikely he's survived the initial volley—I'm holding out hope, but I've never seen a person get back up after landing the way Bryce did on the med-bay floor.

I can't see it being Betts either: she's space-savvy enough to know that dealing with the Pryok'tel is like juggling razors barehanded—no matter how skilled you are, it's just a matter of time before there's blood. Putting aside our nearly decade-long friendship—the one that she chose over the career path that had been so carefully laid out since she was old enough to see spaceships racing over the skies of her home world—I can't see any benefit for Betts in betraying us. *Lucky* was as much her home as it was mine—she cared for each of us as much as her own family—and there's nothing for her to gain from working with the Pryok'tel that she would ultimately want more than keeping us safe. That and well, I love her; she is my big-sister, and I know she thinks of me as her baby-brother.

Ivan. See, now, I've described Ivan as being something of a clod, but he's not—he's got enough smarts to see the potential in a deal with the devil, but not the danger. And he's got a river's worth of greed running through him—I've caught him doing side-deals that put us all at risk, just to turn a few extra credits for himself. But the man's deliberately ignorant, and slow to trust—I doubt that he would have listened to the Pryok'tel to begin with. Unless … unless they were acting through another agent, one Ivan would have trusted—and that's a rabbit-hole of conspiracies I just don't have time to explore.

I have to admit I'm biased in Mia's favour; she's young, vibrant, enthusiastic, and I don't feel she'd have it in her to do this kind of dirty against people she so obviously loves. Granted, I have known her for six months—tops—and it's entirely possible she's the one who sold us out. I took her as a starry-eyed novice on her first adventure in space, but was any of that actually true? I did vet her, and her records matched her story: she was a teenage refugee who had enough smarts and drive to get herself an apprenticeship at the CAPS-T Guild, and when she graduated, took the chance to explore the stars while time and opportunity were on her side. Her records checked out front-to-back, but it's still possible she got an offer that was too good to pass up. Young doesn't always mean dumb, but sometimes it does—and I could see myself at her age being tempted to turn traitor on a bunch of people I barely knew in exchange for a lifetime of creds.

But both Ivan and Mia were likely not on board when the attack occurred; they were on the derelict, out in space—and that seems the most dangerous place to be when a ship dives in and starts opening fire. If either of them knew of the impending attack, they certainly chose the worst place to be when it came.

Which leads to one last candidate: Corculhoran. The man with the plan—as in, every single detail thereof: times, location, schedules—exactly what the Pryok'tel would need for such a precision strike. The one who mentioned how pleased he was at my consistency and predictability—all the little cogs falling right into place, on time. The one who was on the bridge during the attack—where the bridge was miraculously spared, despite being the first place I'd attack if I wanted to incapacitate a vessel.

I don't want it to be Cor; not just because it would reinforce the bullshit stereotype that all Harculcorians are stone-hearted bastards, loyal only to their brood-mothers. That their species is bloodthirsty, warmongering and cruel, because five years with Cor showed me the incredible depth of their souls, their beautiful intelligence and wondrous creativity and caring. That he's an alien, the only one of us that isn't human. That it's him, because he's different from us.

This is an awful thing to admit, but it's true: with the exception of Betts, I would rather have our betrayer be anyone other than Cor. I love that man the way you would love your brother, or your best friend, or your favourite teacher—all three at once, really. He's been a constant source of wisdom, humour and comfort to me all these years—they say Harculcorians cannot laugh but I've heard Cor's throaty crackling many times, and he tells the most bizarre, intriguing jokes that the universe has ever heard. Were Harculcorians interested in sex outside of reproduction, then yes, I think Cor and I may have been more—as it is, Harculcorian men are essentially asexual until they're near Harculcorian women in season, which only occurs for two weeks a year—but the relationship we do share is one I value beyond understanding.

It would shatter me, if it turned out to be either Betts or Cor. I think I can recover if my family is dead—as blunt as it is to state that, I've done it before and while it was an agony I'm not yearning to repeat, I know that I can come out the other side—maybe this time without an ocean's worth of alcohol and a med-ship's supply of drugs. But to be betrayed so absolutely by someone you love? That … that would break me and my understanding of how this universe should work. I wouldn't be able to … I don't know … continue existing? I just couldn't.

I think of Toar, now, and miss him with a sudden intense fierceness. Sure, I betrayed him, but from a place of caring, from a place of … love, maybe? No, not love, but possibly the first sliver of it. Definitely affection. He's obviously important to me, though I've just met him, but I don't have the time or desire to dive too deep into why; all I can think of is that it's something to do with his sincerity—I know his attraction to me is Allure-based, at least partially, but there's also something unbreakable about it, and that strength can't just be written off as a biological reaction. There's absolute intention, behind those blue eyes of his. Maybe if I do pull through what I need to do next, I'll swing by Derresion Prime and pick him up. Apologise. Start anew.

Assuming I can get any of this started—right now I'm cruising blind in space looking for a ship that does *not* want to be found. Doubt is winning a battle in me: it could be that the Pryok'tel aren't even in the system; I could have miscalculated their Under-drive recharge times, and they've already dived out, or their dive extrapolation was off and they didn't even arrive here, or they didn't resurface at all and they're stuck for all eternity in the Under. A thousand things could've happened in the hours they left the kelmisite field and I'm betting my entire stake they're here.

But the vulture wasn't the only thing that left that kelmisite field. The derelict was nowhere to be found—Toar's buoy confirmed it wasn't present during its scan of the battlefield—meaning that I'm fairly sure the Pryok'tel took it with them—given the speed of their strike, then departure, it would have made sense to take the entire transport with them rather than try and salvage the veil on the spot, out in space. So they took it with them. The derelict that I'm still the sole system-administrator for.

There's a chance here, a slim one, if I can get in contact with the derelict itself, instead of the Pryok'tel. I disengaged all of its primary systems, but I didn't delete its backups and archives—it's possible, and here I'm crossing every body part hoping that this is the case, that even though I restored its operating system, the backups were left intact—meaning that I could reset its systems using those backups. Particularly, its defensive systems—and I'm sure that when that derelict wakes up and finds itself in the middle of a hostile's cargo bay, it's going to take every action it can to escape.

The issue though is that the emergency transmission range to the derelict is exceedingly short—maybe fifty thousand kilometres, which in space means I essentially need to be shoulder-to-shoulder with the derelict for it to receive my transmission. I don't have the time or the fuel to fly to every corner of this system where the Pryok'tel could be hiding, and with them not wanting to come out to play, I'll need to think further about how to sniff them out.

Sniffing. *Blue Boy* is a mining shuttle, designed to sniff out expensive minerals—he's spent the last two centuries hunting kelmisite, and his sensor systems are primed for it—he's essentially a giant metal truffle-hog for unrefined kelmisite. Raw kelmisite is uncommon in the universe, and you either find none of it, or like the asteroid field, massive amounts all at the same time. The Pryok'tel vulture was wings-deep in that kelmisite field, and it's possible there were enough particles floating in the field that their ship got painted—you need to scrub that particulate off, too—there's still a lingering odour of it inside the shuttle and Toar had his crew polish *Blue Boy* spotless. I doubt the Pryok'tel had the time to stop by a detailing shop for the necessary scouring required to make them invisible to *Blue Boy*'s honed sensors.

'*Blue Boy*,' I state, and the shuttle chirps its recognition response, awaiting my instructions. 'recalibrate external sensor array to scan for unrefined kelmisite. Send a scanning pulse out every ten seconds, and report any rate higher than one part per ten million. Disregard any source that is yourself.'

It's about a minute before *Blue Boy* indicates the sensor array's ready, and the first pulse is broadcast. I eagerly watch the display monitor, hoping that my first shot is lucky, but it's not. Nor is my tenth, as I make my way from Derresion Three to Four, at full speeds. It's frustrating; despite *Blue Boy*'s impressive scanning range, it's nothing compared to the breadth of emptiness that comprises your average stellar system. This could take hours, mathematically speaking, to get a hit, if there's a hit to get at all. I just don't have that kind of time. I really need a break, here—come on, Universe, you owe me for the shittiest day possible you threw my way …

It's half an hour later, when I get within sensor range of Derresion Four, that the first ping comes back, and I bolt upright in my seat to check the display for confirmation. Ten seconds later, the ping comes back again—strong, solid— with *Blue Boy* indicating the source at fifty parts per million. Definitely unrefined

188

kelmisite. It doesn't mean it's the vulture though; they could've spent time there and all *Blue Boy* is picking up is residuals, but the next pulse reports quadruple the saturation levels. I strap myself in and start running another systems check. When the next pulse reports back ten-thousand parts per million, it's got to be the vulture—otherwise it would be another asteroid field full of kelmisite, and that's definitely not the case.

I'm suddenly not sure what to do. I hadn't actually planned the fine details out if I got this far—and I find myself turning to look at Toar's position at the helm, his empty chair still just as empty as it's been since I dragged him off the shuttle. Despite my attempt at being noble, the decision to go this alone is now appearing to be the stupidest thing I could've done—Toar's experience as a pilot, and his experience with the Pryok'tel, would really come in handy here—and he's stuck looking at a purple ocean.

But he's safe. He's safe, and whatever happens next, he'll stay safe. He won't be another tally on the death-register I've made today.

I'll be in ship detection, and therefore hailing, range in about three minutes, and I'm likely within theirs already. From the locations of the blips that are coming back, cross-referenced against my map of this system, the vulture is hanging out on the furthest moon of Derresion Four—the very edge of the system. It dawns on me that the maps I'm counting on are Oarthecan in origin, and seven years out of date—the Pryok'tel could have a station at that moon now, and I'm flying in with one little shuttle to do what, exactly? Attack? Negotiate?

Bargain.

What little I know about the Pryok'tel reminds me that they're harvesters—resource gatherers. It's something to do with their home world; it's resource-poor, and the Pryok'tel evolved to gather everything they can to survive. I think that's the reason they're cannibals, too—there's nothing else to eat. I can use that against them—their need to harvest—it's not just the shuttle I can offer, either. A lifetime of underhanded deals has netted me a nest egg—not much, but it should be enough to wet a Pryok'tel's whistle—especially since most of my wealth is in the form of non-traceable, non-CAPS credit-related valuables.

And that's just *my* nest egg—Cor's a wealthy man, far more than I am if his investment portfolios are even partially legitimate, and Betts has some goodies stashed somewhere I'm sure. It'll be enough—it has to be enough.

I take a steadying breath, ready myself, and open a comms channel, targeting the area where the kelmisite signal was the strongest.

'To the Pryok'tel. My name is Rowland Hale, captain of the vessel you destroyed in a kelmisite field ten hours ago. I have an offer of goods to make in exchange for the people you took from that vessel. Respond.'

No response. I try again, hoping my next attempt doesn't communicate my anxiety and frustration.

'Hale to the Pryok'tel vessel orbiting the moon of Derresion Four. I am not affiliated with the Coalition of Allied Planetary Systems. They have no knowledge of this transaction. My offer is of high value, hard currency commodities untraceable to the CAPS.'

At first, there's still no response, and I'm formulating my third attempt when *Blue Boy* registers a reply from the Pryok'tel. They're requesting visual communication, and I quickly accept before they change their mind.

I can count the times I've seen a Pryok'tel in person on one hand: I know what to expect in terms of their physical appearance, but I'm nonetheless surprised for a moment when the image of my responder is displayed on my screen. As I've explained, other than their mouths, they're remarkably human looking, but the man on my screen bears no resemblance to the raiding pirate cannibal I imagined him as.

His features are quite refined—with white, pointed quill-like thingies on top of his head, currently lying flat against his skull like a thick set of hair, to the sharp, angular features of his rich orange skin, to the dark rust colour of his lips and the vibrant amber of his eyes, he's quite striking in appearance. From the centre of his lower lip to about where his Adam's apple would be, were he human, runs a dark bronze line—the seam of his third mouth, and I can see the same lines on either side of his primary mouth, though they're much fainter.

Though I can't see much of it, he's wearing a dark mossy green—almost black—uniform. I catch the Mandarin collar and squared shoulders, each ending in burnished copper epaulettes. There're some emblems in the same metal on his lapels that my translator is at a loss to explain, but given the amount of them, I'm guessing he holds a prominent position within the Pryok'tel Hegemony.

I wouldn't say this man is handsome in a traditional human sense, but he is stately, almost regal, even though he's wearing a quietly curious expression, and I can see wheels turning behind his bright eyes as we assess each other. There's a good solid moment as we size each other up over the monitor, but it's him that speaks first.

'Captain Hale, I am Primus Suren'thos, captain of the Pryok'tel Patrol Vessel *Sh'hyzen-shi*. I must admit, I am surprised to see you—we were not able to locate you during our rescue attempt, and were quite saddened at the thought you had been lost to us. I am pleased to see that's not the case.'

Suren'thos' words are smooth, calm, and genuine-sounding. His voice has that practised cadence, the one I refer to as 'captain-y'; authoritative, in control, voicing demands without actually speaking them.

'Rescue attempt?' I ask, incredulously, before I'm able to stop myself. 'You can rescue someone you tried to kill?'

He holds up his hand, gloved in a dark, shiny material that matches the colour of his adornments, his palm outward. 'That was not our intent, Captain, and we regret the outcome of our attempt to neutralise your vessel. We were acting under information that was obviously incorrect regarding your combat capabilities— had we known that you were civilian class, we would not have employed such measures. As it was, we detected that your vessel was at least corvette class, and we responded accordingly.'

190

Corvette class? How could he have thought my *Luck of the Draw* was a battle vessel? Even the most rudimentary sensors would have detected that … and then I remember. I'd ordered Mia to alter *Lucky*'s energy output signature to trick the derelict transport. The Pryok'tel appear to have fallen for the same deception. My stomach twists in on itself as I realise my part in the attack that followed … but it still doesn't explain how the Pryok'tel knew we were there—what information were they acting on?

'Is my crew alive?' I ask, again before I can catch myself. I'm showing too many of my cards, and that's stupid of me. But I'm desperate, and confused by this Suren'thos, who is acting with diplomacy and civility, when all the past information I have regarding Pryok'tel indicated they were bloodthirsty monsters. That's far from what I'm seeing and hearing now, but their past aggression towards me is impossible to ignore.

'Some are,' Suren'thos confirms, nodding once. 'They're safely on board and in no danger, I assure you.'

'Some?' I press. The twisting feeling in my stomach reaches an agonizing level, and I can feel my legs beginning to shake from the nerves—Schrödinger's Cat just multiplied into five versions of itself, but not all of them are going to be alive when I open their boxes. Some will be, from what I'm being told, and not knowing who is threatening to override what little remains of my composure.

'Perhaps it's best you come on board, Captain,' Suren'thos offers, calmly. 'This situation was never meant to unfold this way, but there's still an opportunity for it to be resolved successfully.'

'Successfully for who, exactly?' I ask, attempting not to let my emotions show overtly. The knowledge that only 'some' of my family are alive is corroding my soul, but I have to push it down, process it later—if Suren'thos sees how badly this news is affecting me, he'll use it to his advantage, which will only further endanger my surviving crew. It's taking almost everything in me not to react, and if there was some way to shunt my feelings to my biocomp's buffer for processing later, I would take it.

I'm still out of range for a comm attempt with the derelict transport, but that distance is closing with each passing moment. I'm not sure what my next steps are—disabling the vulture by activating the transport, or saving my family by playing along with Suren'thos? It has to be disabling the vulture—the Pryok'tel cannot have that veil—but the Pryok'tel will certainly kill whoever they've 'saved' from my family if I do that.

'All parties. You must believe me when I state that we have no intention of harming you or any of your crew, Captain Hale. What's happened has been a terrible mishandling of events—for which you have my honest apologies—but there's no need for the situation to continue that way. Please, come aboard, peacefully, and we will conclude this amicably.'

I use this opportunity to look downwards, pretending to consider his offer— in reality, I am checking *Blue Boy*'s outputs—I'm still ten minutes out before I reach the minimum possible distance for a successful comms attempt. All I have to do is agree to Suren'thos' plan, to come aboard his vessel, and I'll reach his ship without incident. Yeah, right.

But I need more time! Prolonging the conversation, I ask, 'Why are you even doing this to us? We had nothing to do with the Pryok'tel, why did you come after us?'

'I will answer all of your questions, Captain, and allow you to see your surviving crew members, if you come aboard peacefully and surrender yourself to our custody. If you are concerned for your well-being, I assure you, you are in no danger from us; you will be unharmed.'

'You mean, you won't eat me?' I ask, bluntly. It's the most important question, when it boils down to it.

A momentary look of tedium flashes on Suren'thos' face. 'No, Captain Hale. We will not eat you. Perhaps we may even have the chance to correct you on that slander.'

I have heard far too many consistent accounts of the Pryok'tel's consumption of sapient species for it all to be brushed aside as 'slander'. My disbelief must be showing on my face, because Suren'thos continues.

'Yes, Pryok'tel eat the dead,' he starts, and there's a weary tone to his voice: this is not his first time explaining this. 'We've done that since the dawn of our race; it is as natural to us as breathing is to you. Yes, we eat the dead of other species—as do humans, as I understand it, though the morally comfortable restriction against sapients you have is not shared by us. No, we do not hunt down and murder other sapients for the sole purpose of consuming them. Yes, we have, in the past, consumed other species without understanding those species have death customs that conflict with ours. We have made mistakes, we are working to undo them, and will remind our fellow stellar neighbours that none of their histories are free from cultural misunderstandings that have led to blood, tragedy and death.'

Eloquently spoken, but I'm not buying it. It's the slickness—a rehearsed quality that has a faint tinny sound—he's toeing the company line. He's trying to assuage my fears, luring me in, though he's not aware that getting close is exactly what I want.

'Why won't you tell me which of my crew members are alive?' I demand, knowing he'll avoid answering my question. Eight minutes out.

'Because I do not want to provoke a violent reaction from you,' Suren'thos replies, quickly. 'Pardon my racism, but you humans are well known for your temperamentality, and are prone to reacting poorly when you feel that you've been wronged. It's a shortcoming that I'm trying to dissuade you from, though I will admit that I'm not familiar enough with your people to be entirely sure I will succeed. It is my hope that I can appeal to the common ground our people do share, such as the need to know our loved ones are safe, with a view to resolving this situation without further unnecessary violence.'

I barely manage to refrain from retorting that I'd rather be known for a short temper than cannibalism, and instead I say, 'Which one of them betrayed the rest of us?' Six minutes.

He shakes his head slowly. 'No, come aboard. I will answer everything then.'

I make a show of pondering for a moment, spending precious seconds that need spending while I race ever closer, before I try another avenue. 'What about my original offer? To trade for my crew? What could I offer you that's worth your time? Pardon *my* racism, Primus Suren'thos, but you Pryok'tel are known for your ... how do I put this? "Non-traditional resource-gathering practices"? I will admit that I am not familiar enough with your people to know if you're keen on bargaining, but I am hoping to appeal to the common ground our people do share, such as cutting a better deal than the one you've been offered.'

The quills atop his head rise slightly, and that shit-eating grin on his face is wide enough that the lines of his second mouth are more prominent. I've caught his interest, for certain.

'You amaze me, Captain Hale. Here you are, out in space, all on your own with nothing but a stolen fren'zalth class shuttle, and you're attempting to make a counteroffer on the multiple outstanding bounties on each of your crewmembers' heads? You yourself are worth a million and a half Alconalc round-coins, after your visit to their automated weapons manufacturing plant last year. They've still not managed to purge that virus you installed, by the way— you've cost them billions in lost revenue.'

I further refrain from snorting my indifference to the plight of the Alconalc. Cor and I built the virus Suren'thos is mentioning; it's a lovely bit of recursive code that essentially causes the Alconalc manufacturing plants to randomly insert a self-destruct sequence into their line of otherwise top-quality automated proton turrets, making one in every dozen or so trigger at an unknown point in the future to first target any other turrets within the vicinity, and take them out, then take itself out in the most spectacular way available to it.

The virus is exceptionally difficult to detect too, taking precious hours to scan each turret or else risking the entire production batch becoming unsafe for sale. I installed the virus and added a tickling little trick that ensured each time the virus was successfully identified, it would instal a hidden copy of itself under the detector's own system. Sounds like they've not figured out that the detectors now also need to be scanned, because each time an infected detector scans a clean system, the virus propagates, lies dormant, then activates at another randomly determined interval. Good times, good times—I did that job on the cheap too, after having learned that the Alconalc were selling the turrets to both sides in the Purdo civil war, reaping a fortune for years as the Purdonese brought themselves to near extinction.

Best of all, letting me know about the Alconalc bounty is a serious fuck-up on Suren'thos' part; he's spilled the reason why he wants me so badly, and alive to boot: I'm the only one that knows how to purge the Alconalc virus. My bounty will be worth exactly zero round-coins if I'm dead.

'They can afford it, what with the skulls of millions of Purdonese adorning their bank accounts,' I remark, coolly. 'No, I can't offer you my weight in bounty, but I do still have some worthwhile resources for your consideration: wonderfully anonymous elements and ores—fully tradable across the system— and I can offer you, say, highly lucrative information opportunities, if you're brave enough to take them.'

'No, Captain Hale. The Pryok'tel do not deal in whispers. Hard currencies only, I'm afraid.'

Four minutes, I just need more time.

'Well, what if my offer was just for my surviving crew, not myself? The young female engineer, Mia, she's got nothing serious on her, and the larger male Ivan is likely more trouble than he's worth. The smaller male, Bryce ...'

'Your attempt at discovering which of your crew is alive is commendable, Captain, I will grant you that,' Suren'thos patiently interrupts. 'That won't work, but I do admire your efforts, and you've earned this first offer then: I will agree to listen to your proposals, with fairness, if you come aboard. It's all I can provide you at this time. You'll need to come up with something more tangible than promises.'

'What if I threw in this shuttle? It's top of the line, chock-full of valuables, as I'm sure you've detected—surely it's worth the price of one of my crew?'

'It is indeed,' Suren'thos agrees sincerely. 'Though I don't know if you can trade something that already belongs to us.'

I frown. 'What do you mean?'

He smiles. 'Well, according to the shuttle's registration, it was stolen from the Hegemony two hundred and eight years ago, along with its parent mining station. Stolen by the Oarth, during one of their many raids against us during that time.'

He's caught me off guard now; I knew from Toar that the Oarth and Pryok'tel had an unpleasant history, and I should have inquired more about that, in retrospect. Yet another reason Toar should be here, now, I admonish myself.

'Did you meet the Oarth, Captain Hale?' Suren'thos asks, with what I think is mock interest. 'I'm sure you'd remember them. Large, hairy, stinking, brutish things—primitive and space-clumsy—but useful under the right conditions. I'm sure they would have loved meeting you, Captain.'

There's now a prickly feeling that crawls up my spine to match the twisting in my stomach. When Suren'thos refers to the Oarth, I can see that he's not the suave, urbane diplomat he's pretending to be—though physically, his first mouth remains in place, his words are so full of his teeth he might as well be using his warmouth to speak them.

'The Oarth?' I reply, confused. 'If you mean the crew that first rescued me, I didn't catch their names. I just jettisoned them into space at the first chance their backs were turned.'

'Murder, Captain? That's out of character for you,' Suren'thos remarks.

'Didn't say they're dead, Primus. At least, they weren't when I left them in the kelmisite field.' Two minutes out, but I dislike the direction this conversation is taking. I don't want to involve the Oarth at all here—Toar was clear that he had no love for the Pryok'tel, and now Suren'thos' words indicate that hatred runs both ways. He's drawing information out of me that I don't want to share—but it's obvious he knows the Oarth are involved and I've no clue how that's going to factor into things.

'I wonder what they were doing there, in that kelmisite field, in a shuttle that belongs to a mining station?' Suren'thos ponders, but again, it's with a mocking undertone. 'We had no record of Oarth activity in that area, so it's a surprise to know they're this far out. Perhaps after we've got you safely on board and have our business sorted out, I'll return to the field and say hello to the Oarth. Thank them for helping find you.'

'Suit yourself, Suren'thos. I don't know anything about these Oarth you're mentioning, but don't let that stand in your way.' I'm trying to sound indifferent, trying to convince Suren'thos that I don't know about the Oarth, but his eyes are narrowed, and I can tell he's on to me.

'Kind of you to offer. I'm sure that your dealings with the Oarth went smoothly, but it would be valuable to us if you could provide any information on your interaction with them. Very valuable.' Suren'thos now fixes me with those bright yellow eyes, burning with triumph.

'Whatever information I have, I'd be happy to trade,' I lie immediately.

'Excellent. I can see that you're less than a minute away, and I am preparing your crew for your arrival. Now, according to the dossier we have on you, you're not known for violence, Captain Hale, and I'm sure we can keep counting on that. With your crew under our care and attention, I feel sure you wouldn't risk something foolish, say, oh—an altercation to rescue them, for instance?'

'I'm not sure what you'd think I'd be capable of doing in that department, with this little shuttle here,' I reply. 'I mean, if you ask, I might be able to laser off some of the kelmisite residue from your hull, if you held still and let me.'

Suren'thos nods. 'Good, I am glad we're agreed on that. Prepare the shuttle, Captain; we'll take you aboard the moment we've confirmed the weapons are offline, and you've dropped the entire arsenal of mines and rockets you've brought along with you. Though I'd be loath to do so, for the safety of my crew, I will be forced to destroy you if you enter weapons range before completely disarming, as per my instructions.'

'Of course, that's agreeable. See you shortly, Primus. Hale out.'

I cut the transmission, and scramble to think. I've got about thirty seconds before I'm in transmission range, and about thirty-five seconds before I'm in weapons range. Suren'thos will have no problem destroying the shuttle—I think *Blue Boy*'s shields could take one hit from their particle weapons, but the next would obliterate me. Yet anytime I try to form a meaningful plan of action, my thoughts immediately centre on Toar. Suren'thos' words regarding the Oarth have unnerved me—it's obvious that his interest is in capturing me, and now I'm wondering if it's got something to do with the Oarth. Do they know I look like an Oarth baron? I mean, if their species have history together, surely they do ... is that a factor here?

Before there's a chance to examine this possibility, *Blue Boy* alerts me that I'm within transmission range of the derelict. That gives me five seconds to decide if I'm going to go through with my plan to activate the transport's backups, or forfeit that idea and try to strike a bargain with Suren'thos. It's the thought of Toar being put in danger that wins that decision, without another second of thought spent debating it. One deep breath in, then out—and I send the reboot transmission to the transport.

God, I hope it's listening.

CHAPTER 19

Toar

There's not much to do on Derresion Prime other than brood and feel poorly.

When I was raising my sons, one of the house rules was if you were feeling angry and such, you were allowed five full minutes to get all those feelings out (safely, mind you) but then you had to calm down and be willing to talk it out. It worked, usually, though Grath often managed to push his five minutes well past the deadline—he's the hot-tempered one of my trio, but also the most determined and passionate—first out of the pouch and all.

So I've been trying the same approach on myself, but it's not working. It's been close to an hour since I started—the sun doesn't move in the sky, so it's tough to tell how much time's passing—and I'm just as muddled as when I started, a mess of anger, guilt, and despair all bubbling in me like a brewing poison, topped over with an ugly scum of sadness that's just eating up my insides.

Shouldn't be feeling this way. I'm seventy-seven and been through some truly awful things in my life, much worse than this. War is misery's sire, and it's brought me the death of kin and clan, of the Baron Thursk, and of so many friends and comrades in arms that it shames me that I've lost count of them all. Survived it all though, so the impending death of one man should not be bothering me so badly. Except, that man is Rowland.

I've no right to be so torn up. Had no idea he even existed when I woke up this morning, and if I'd followed the law and not got involved with his rescue, I'd have gone to bed still not knowing him. The only way my feelings for him make any sense is because I went and got myself Allured, partially. Maybe. But if that's all this is, it'll fade quick and things will get back to normal, soon enough.

You know, the normal where my sons are barely keeping in contact, where neither my Cralren nor my own sire father will speak to me, and all have stripped their names from mine. The one where my baron father has sent a spy to keep tabs on me because that's the only thing he can get away with under the law. The normal where men like Rey will den with me for a night, maybe two if I'm extra lucky, then move on, never to return. Can't wait to get back to that.

Selfishly, I was hoping Rowland could be my way out of all that, even if it was only a fool's hope, mind. When we were snogging in the shuttle, it was like the entire ordeal of the past fifteen years suddenly never existed, and I felt genuinely normal again. Happy, even. And then he left that recording where he tells me to go and find someone that I can kiss the same as him—and I just … there *is* no-one like him.

I'm still angry about what he's done of course, but I've at least worked out I'm not angry about *why* he did it—I mean, granted, can't say I'm tickled to giggles at being knocked out and dumped on a slime world, but I accept that he did that because he was trying to keep me out of danger. After all, I am entirely safe for the time being, while he is not, so it's hard to argue with his reasoning.

197

No, I'm angry because his actions have endangered himself, and ... the thought of him getting hurt ... let alone killed ... while I'm stuck here contemplating poor old Toar is just driving me to a black misery.

And that recording—where he says he's worthless—oh Great Oarth, that was a stab in my sides. Not ashamed to admit I had a bit of a cry listening to that—partially because I called him a little thief, reinforcing an insult masquerading as an opinion, and that shames me so deeply. Called him a criminal to boot, even though under Oarthecan law, I'm a worse one than he is. Then learning that his own Dad is dead, coupled with the likelihood his crew family is now too—och—I'd need to be made of stone not to feel awful for him. That I can't do anything about it just darkens the misery.

There's a part of me though, that same foolish part that pretends Rowland and I can one day be the cure for each other's ills, that thinks he went and left me a secret message in his recording. That last bit, where he says when something gets in your way, say fuck it, and do what needs to be done, the 'You. Tell. Them.' part. He's left me on this planet without a clear plan on how I'm to eventually leave it—but was he challenging me to try and get around that? If I'm to take what he said to heart, then maybe he wants me to find a way back to him?

'Could've made it easier for me, though, if that's the case,' I mutter.

My five minutes are more than up, and I've resolved that I will follow Rowland's last bit of advice to me. I stand, stretch, shake, and try my hand at saying 'fuck it', and get on with doing what needs to be done.

In any survival setting, the first thing to do is assess where you are and what you have. The cave I'm stuck in is, to my untrained eye, a cave, much as any I've been in on Oartheca or other worlds. The ceiling is rough rock, with the floor somewhat smoother, though both are peppered with bumps and crags and such—no hanging stalactites I notice, though. The stone walls are a dull, unappealing blackish colour—they look volcanic, maybe? Whatever the stone is, its colour is quickly swallowing up what little light enters from the mouth of the cave, making the rest of the interior pitch dark. I press my hand against the surface of the nearest wall, finding the stone strong and cool to the touch. I'm no geologist, but my best guess is that this cave appears to be naturally formed, without any signs of being altered by a deliberate hand.

I've got twenty or so square metres to move around at the mouth of the cave, and after configuring the touchpad to illumination mode, I can see that it extends further back, sloping down slightly. Might go exploring, if I get too bored, though that seems a bit daft to do on my own—when you're lost, the fastest way to be found is to just stay where you are.

Cave entrance explored, it's time to find out what else Rowland's provided for my hopefully short stay. There's the comms beacon of course, which according to him, will activate automatically in the next few hours and transmit my position to the *Grolthon's Spear*, and I move that off the storage crate, so that I can see what else has been left for me. Opening the crate, the first and most obvious items I see are my sabre, carefully laid on top in its charging scabbard, and placed neatly beside that, my captain's hat and one of the coil-guns.

I collect my sabre, strapping on the scabbard; its familiar weight pressing against my thigh is comforting, as is donning my hat. I at least look the part of a captain, and trust that soon enough, I'll begin to feel it too. The coil-gun, along with its holster, is similarly secured.

The rest of the supplies in the crate are familiar: med-kits and the like, extra water and rations, more blankets, four boxes of the charging mines, two scan …

'Are you an Oarth?'

*****

I've never considered myself easily spooked but the voice coming from behind me straightens my spine with such speed that I'm surprised I've not snapped my own back. Whirling, my sabre drawn instinctively, there's already a snarl on my lips as I face whatever just spoke—but all my bravado is snuffed out the instant my eyes behold what's before me.

A figure, large and vaguely Oarth in shape, stands in the cave's mouth. With the only light coming from the sun streaming in from behind it, I can't make out any distinctive features, like fur-colour and such, but the general outline is there—the ears atop the sides of the head, the prominent chest and shoulders, stout arms and legs, the former resting at its sides. It's not doing anything other than standing there. Then there's this faint but still unpleasant squishing noise as the figure moves, raising its arms slowly out from its sides but still below its waist, palms towards me, in a gesture of peace.

'You are safe. I will not harm you,' it speaks, though the sound it makes doesn't emanate from the being's head, but from the entire form. As these words form, I see the outline of the figure vibrate ever so slightly, pulsing in time with the sounds.

It's a rare moment when I've not got anything to say, but what I'm seeing now has sucked all the words right out of me. I'm absolutely gobsmacked. I do manage to lift my touchpad up, and as its light falls on the figure, I hear myself quietly gasp, 'Eternal's balls!'

It's not an Oarth at all. It's an entirely purple, undulating mass in the shape of an Oarth, but there's no real features—no eyes, no mouth, and only the general idea of a muzzle. The lack of details extends to the rest of its body as well—there's no claws, no fur, no clothes—just a rough shape whose entire surface moves under the light, quivering, rearranging itself. Looking this thing over, I'm torn between curiosity and repulsion, and I find that I've gripped my sabre hilt tighter, my thumb claw hovering close to triggering the plasma blade.

It's a good moment or two before the figure 'speaks' again. 'I am Derresion, and this is my home. You are welcome here, Oarth.' It still has its 'arms' extended out from its sides. There's about ten metres between us though, and it's not moving further into the cave.

It's speaking perfect Oarthecan to me—my translator isn't needed, but its voice is distinctly non-Oarth—though the tone is robust, there's a faint buzzing sound that worsens with every hard consonant, and whatever regional accent it's using is one I've not heard before.

'What do you mean, you're Derresion?' I finally manage.

The figure extends one arm behind itself, indicating the endless expanse of purple alga. It's now that I see its legs are connected to this ocean by a narrow line of purple slime creeping along the ground.

'I am all that you see, when you look out across this world. The ocean. That is me,' it explains.

'You're ... you're all of that ... purple stuff?' I check, not understanding the magnitude of what it's trying to tell me.

'Yes,' it confirms, simply.

From what I remember of Derresion Prime, the purple alga is everywhere— it encircles the entire habitable ring of this planet, which is about one percent of the planet's surface area. If what this thing is saying is true, which I've got no proof of, mind, then it's one organism with an approximate surface area of ... let's see, four-pie-r-squared times one percent ... about thirty-eight million square kilometres. My sabre suddenly doesn't appear to be the most effective choice of weapons, if this Derresion fellow is speaking the truth.

'If you are similar to the first Oarth I met, you will have many questions, and I will answer them all, but I must know one thing first: can you leave this world?' it ... well, Derresion, asks.

An odd question, and my hackles, already on edge, tingle with warning. 'Why do you need to know that?' I demand. I'm at a loss as to what to do or say, and while this purple fellow's not making any threatening moves towards me, I keep my sabre aloft, at the ready.

'Oarth cannot survive on my world—there is no sustenance here for you, there is nothing to eat or drink. What water there is cannot be extracted for you, and I am the only organic substance on the planet. Oarth cannot digest me. You will perish unless we return you home.'

'I'll be fine,' I answer, curtly.

'That is my hope,' Derresion replies.

There's more silence between us, and while the figure lowers its arms, I don't lower my sabre.

'You are much like Orlintack, the first Oarth I met,' Derresion starts, after the silence between us becomes too long. 'He did not trust me at first either. We became friends, though, and he taught me much about the Oarth and Oartheca. Please tell me, are your people free from the Pryok'tel? Orlin so wanted that, it was his hope that the occupation of the "three mouthed corpse fuckers" would end, and Oartheca could return to being free.'

I snort a laugh despite my distrust of this purple pseudo-Oarth, the polite tone it uses for such a fine but still crude pejorative getting the better of me. But only for a moment.

'I don't trust you,' I reply, bluntly.

'Is it my form?' Derresion asks, sounding apologetic. 'This is how Orlin and I communicated together, as he found it easier to speak to me this way. If it disturbs you, I can take another shape.'

The figure begins to shift then, squirming and melting upon itself with the most disgusting noise I've heard in some time, like the sound of the worst upset tummy you could have, and the grip on my sabre tightens as I ignite the plasma blade. Derresion immediately stops and returns to its Oarth shape.

'Apologies,' it states. 'I see how you could interpret my actions as hostile. Please, tell me, what could I do to put you at ease?'

'You could leave me alone,' I reply.

It takes its time before responding. 'If that's what you want, I will comply. I only want you to be safe, and to not die here, as Orlin did, because we could not find a way off this world for him. It was awful, to see him suffer. I do not want that to happen to you.'

'I'll be fine,' I repeat. The blue light of my sabre's ignited plasma helps me to ensure my words sound firm.

The figure bobs in what must be a 'nod'. 'Then I will return to the ocean, and leave you be, but know that I'm here if there is a way that I can help you, after all. When you return to your home, please, share with Orlin's family that he is here, and that he did not die alone, and that his last thoughts were of them and how he loved them.'

The figure begins to move away from me now; not walking but just sliding backwards out of the cave. I watch it exit, and as it moves further away from me, see it shift its shape into an ambiguous blob. I'm relieved to see it's going, to tell the truth, but there's this nagging little buzzing in my brain about Derresion's last words to me.

I step closer to the cave's entrance and watch as the blob breaches the first real edge of the ocean, where it collapses entirely in on itself, and I'm left only with the sight of the murky red sky, dull black rock and the vast, endless expanse of purple that takes up the entire view of the horizon.

I sheath my sabre—there's no real threat I could ever make towards this Derresion entity, but it seems to respect that I was at least making one. I have this horrible realisation that if it wanted to, this purple monstrosity could flood the cave, pouring itself to fill it entirely, engulfing all within, myself included.

Yet, it didn't do this. It spoke to me, it chose to let me know it existed, and made no threat towards me. The only thing it wanted from me was to know that I would be all right—it did not want me to die.

'This Orlin fellow,' I call out, perhaps against my better judgement. 'What was his Baronsname?'

There is a shifting in the ocean, and a small blob rises, slowly, from the surface. 'Kerthsclan. Orlintack Kerthsclan,' it speaks, and the vibration noise it uses for speaking is coming directly from this blob.

'Kerthsclan? As in the Baron Kerth?' I check.

'The High Baron Kerth VII, yes,' Derresion replies. The blob is much smaller than its Oarth form, but its voice is of the same intensity, and, if I'm being kind, still sounds friendly.

Hmm. Chresh, my tactical officer, is a Kerthscion, though my memory tells me his baron is not a High Baron—meaning Kerth is not a member of the Assembly of Barons, the leaders of Oartheca. And I think he's Baron Kerth IX, or was it XI? Maybe Kerth's dad was a High Baron though? Barons are named after their baron fathers—the name is carried down across generations, to keep track of lineages. It's possible that this Orlin fellow is a relative of Chresh's, though I've not heard of this Orlin's sire, Tack, either.

'I may know of the Baron Kerth, and I will deliver your message, when I get home. Where is Orlin buried, then, if he's dead? His family will likely want his remains back, if he's one of them,' I explain.

'His remains are here, with me, below. Safe. I did not want him to be lost to the elements—the winds can be fierce at times and his body would be ruined by them, so I keep him with me.'

I make a face at the thought of this, and Derresion immediately adds, 'I promised him he would not be alone, that he would always be looked after, and that he would be with his family one day, if it was possible. Keeping him here with me was the only way. If you can leave this place, would you be able to take him with you, to take him to Oartheca again? He wanted so much to be with his sire, Tack, and his bond-mate, Hauz, who lived in Alther's Grove.'

I don't recognize the place, but the name Alther is immediately identifiable—he was the baron who rallied our people for Oartheca's first truly global rebellion against the Pryok'tel, and while he died in the initial skirmish, his death galvanised all Oarth to continue to fight. Were it not for His Exaltedness, the Arch-baron Alther, Eternal Beloved, we might still be under Pryok'tel rule, if we had survived that long. More likely, we'd be extinct.

'I … I'll see what I can do,' I reply, not wanting to share more of how I'm planning to get off this planet. My instincts are telling me not to trust this thing, this sentient ocean, but all it's asking of me is to look after this Orlin.

'When you are ready, I will bring Orlin's remains to you; you need only ask. I wish you well, and am thankful for your help. Orlin was very dear to me and knowing he will be with his family again fills me with much happiness. Thank you, good Oarth.'

'Toar, my name is Toar. Toar Grithrawrscion,' I reply, before I let my distrust spoil the courtesy being extended to me. I've been told that Oarth are slow to trust, and I can see that's exactly how I'm behaving. We've good reason to be slow, mind you, but that shouldn't mean we ignore basic friendliness.

'I see. Then thank you, Toar. Peace to you, and all your kin,' Derresion replies, using the formal Oarthecan farewell, when we want to be polite. The blob begins to melt again.

'Wait, wait,' I request, looking skywards. The blob solidifies, awaiting my words.

It's a risk, what I'm about to do, engaging an unknown alien entity whose nature and intentions are not entirely clear. I've been trained for this situation—all OSS captains have training in first contact situations, and while I'm rusty, I recall those lessons easily enough. Establish similarities to gain trust, use open dialogue to gain understanding, be willing to share information to gain facts, but don't over- or under-share, either. Determine intent, and establish good foundations. So far, this Derresion has shown nothing but good faith, and all I've been is suspicious and rude. Mind you, he's the size of a planet, and I'm one man with a sabre. My caution is justifiable.

But I'm never one to shrink from a challenge, and with that caution in mind, I elect to start an earnest attempt.

'How ... how did you come to know Orlin?' I ask.

*****

It turns out that Derresion is a rather chatty fellow, which is saying something, coming from me. I don't know if it's because he's got no-one to talk to otherwise, but he's been sharing everything he knows about Orlin, Oarth, Pryok'tel, and answering every question I've put to him with apparent forthrightness and honesty.

I've returned to the cave to have a seat on one of the storage containers, and Derresion has resumed his Oarth shape, standing at the mouth of the cave as we have our conversation. If what he says is true, then Derresion is the sole occupant of this planet, and has been since the time his consciousness first formed, 'back when the world was still turning'. He estimates that he is over seventy million years old, and although he admits that this is an approximation, I'm nonetheless dumbstruck if it turns out to be the case. The enormity of this concept—having lived longer than the entire recorded history of Oartheca, by a factor many times over, is beyond my ability to understand, and all I can do is just accept it for now and ponder its meaning when I've not got much more immediate issues to sort out.

Derresion estimates he met Orlin about three centuries ago, when Orlin managed to survive the destruction of a Pryok'tel slave vessel he'd been a captive on. The vessel had suffered a catastrophic malfunction while orbiting Derresion, and Orlin had made it to an escape pod in time, arriving on the surface uninjured, but with no supplies, no communication and no means of escape.

'Our first encounter happened when he tried to eat me, since I am the only organic substance here. I cannot be eaten, though—Orlin just vomited the part I allowed him to take out, though he did say I tasted "not that bad, actually". But hunger was not the problem so much as hydration was. I tried to bring forth water from myself, but I don't work that way; what little water there is in the atmosphere I absorb without thinking, and it does not rain here, as it does on Oartheca.'

'So, he died of thirst?' I check, grimly.

'No,' Derresion replies. 'We agreed that fate was too awful to be allowed. At the end, he chose to let me stop his suffering.'

That admission draws another sour look from me, and seeing me tense up, Derresion continues. 'Orlin persevered for many days, Toar, while we tried to find an answer. But he grew weak, and then frightened, as he sensed his end approaching. I never knew despair before Orlin, Toar, but I learned it then. It was terrifying, to see him hurting so, and be unable to stop it. Terrifying for both of us, but Orlin was truly brave about it—much braver than I was. He knew his death was inevitable, and he asked me to help him meet his fate on his own terms, rather than time's.'

'How did you help him end it?' I ask, solemnly. It's difficult to gauge Derresion's emotions—what with no real face to speak of, and his voice being an approximation of a voice and all, but his demeanour seems diminished as he speaks about Orlin, and I can tell it saddens him to relive this memory.

'He entered my ocean, submerging himself, and his breath ran out. I was with him, every moment. He was never alone. It was quick, and painless as possible. For him,' Derresion concludes.

'I ... I'm sure he appreciated your help, Derresion. You did him a great service by showing him that mercy. Thank you for being brave yourself—for facing something you probably never had to face before, and making the hardest decision anyone could make. I'm glad Orlin found you.'

'I am glad, beyond my understanding of that word, to have found him,' Derresion states, and I absolutely believe him.

I have this sudden worrisome feeling that I might be faced with Orlin's choice, and my eyes inadvertently fall upon the comms beacon, still blinking, its countdown slowly ticking away.

'Why did your baron leave you that?' Derresion asks, 'seeing'—though I don't know how he manages that, not having any actual eyes—the beacon I'm looking at.

'My what?' I ask, confused. Cralren is currently on Oartheca, last time I checked.

'Your baron. He put you here, in this cave, and left you your things. I could not understand what he was doing, especially since he seemed so sad doing it.'

Rowland, he means Rowland. 'Oh, he's ... he's not my baron. He's just a friend,' I mumble, finding myself looking downwards in embarrassment for a moment, then looking back up at Derresion, my expression curious. 'Orlin told you about barons?'

'Yes. Orlin shared all his knowledge of himself with me, and that included everything he knew of your people, world and customs. All of it.'

'He taught you everything about us, including our language, in such a short time?' I ask, unable to prevent the suspicious tone from re-entering my voice. At best, a man can survive about seven days without water, and I doubt Orlin had the chance to discuss barons while he was desperately trying to find a way to survive.

'Yes, it was a side-effect of his attempt to feed on me. When he consumed my form, I learned of his, in entirety. All of him. Neither of us knew I could do that—he was the first other life form I have encountered in such a manner—but the effect was beneficial for us both. For a moment, we were one being, and so he shared his life with me.'

'What?' I ask, sceptically. 'You learned his entire life because he tried to eat you?'

'In a sense, yes. When my form came into contact with his, I learned how to mimic his form—his body, his organs, his cells—all of him. His brain, and all of its structures, in particular. So when I mimicked his brain, I learned all about him—everything he knew, thought, felt, sensed and dreamed about.'

'And he let you do this?' I ask, trying not to let my distaste for such an overwhelmingly intimate invasion be too apparent.

'No, neither of us knew this would be the outcome. But as he said when he discovered my ability, "no point cheering at an empty stage", which I knew meant that whatever happened was over, could not be undone, and so there was no point being distressed by it.

'The benefit though is that I did learn everything he *knew*, and that made our time together even more valuable, but also, his death much more poignant. Our bonding changed the nature of my being. I learned more about this universe from his life of forty-nine years than the seventy million I spent on my own. I had no idea I was even on my own, until Orlin. I miss him, badly.' Derresion sounds genuinely bereft.

'So that's how you're able to speak Oarthecan, and know so much about us, then? You're drawing on Orlin's memories?' I check, perplexed.

'More than his memories—I am able to mimic his brain structure. Part of me can be as Orlin was, process information as he did, draw on his experiences to ponder and think and feel. That is not the same as him, though, he was so much more complex than I am able to mimic; I am just his shadow.'

'You ... you can be Orlin? Er, a shadow of him?' This is fascinating.

'I can think in the same manner, but what he thought, the ideas he had, the feelings he had, those were all of his own making. I can mimic him in a physical sense, but anything I think of is mine—it comes from me. I am not Orlin, I am Derresion. Does that make sense?'

I nod slowly. 'Your brain works like Orlin's did, but whatever you come up with is your own.'

'Yes. He and I sometimes disagreed, even though we were both using the same structure—the format of his brain—to form our arguments. His experiences shaped his views, my experiences shape mine. Imagine a sponge, where a thought is a drop of water. There are a million different paths that water can take through the sponge: he took his path, I took mine.'

'That's amazing, Derresion,' I acknowledge. 'To be able to learn all that a person knows just by mimicking their brain—I mean, you could learn all there is to learn, if you mimicked everyone you met.'

Derresion is quiet for a moment. 'Possibly. I am not sure if that is something

I want, however. There is a difference between learning and discovering, and just knowing. I know some experiences Orlin knew, but I do not understand them, because I did not experience them for myself. The love for his family, which was so important for him; I understand that he loved them, but I do not know why. These are things that cannot be comprehended without experiencing them. I would rather experience, so that I can know.

'Unfortunately, I cannot experience such things—I am alone here, and will always be. I cannot leave my home, and there are few chances to experience things when there is no-one to experience them with.'

'I see,' I remark, but then remember the survey team that reported on this planet, seven or so years ago. 'Other visitors do come to your planet, though, from time to time?'

'Yes, though it is rare. My last visit was from the Pryok'tel, four years ago. They harvested some of me, performed some tests on the environment, took some samples of the rocks that I live on, then departed. I have not seen them since.'

'Did you try to make contact with them?' I ask, curious.

'No. Orlin hated the Pryok'tel. His brain had many, many memories of the tortures they had visited upon him. The harm they had done his family, his home. I remembered everything that had happened to him when I first saw the Pryok'tel. I will admit, there was a part of me that wanted to destroy them for their crimes, but I refrained, because they were not the ones responsible for the injury to Orlin—the Pryok'tel who were are long dead, I suspect.'

I bite my tongue before I can tell Derresion he should have destroyed these Pryok'tel; while the Oarth are at war with the three-mouthed baron-spites, I'll not drag another into our conflict. Derresion needs to make his own choices about that, if it comes to it, but I'm comforted to know that Orlin's memories would likely be a part in whatever decision Derresion makes.

'A few years back, we had a team here to survey your planet, too,' I start, and Derresion 'nods'.

'Yes, four Oarth,' Derresion confirms. 'I did not approach them, because they did not look to need my assistance, and I was keen to discover their purpose. They too took samples of me, and my home, and made many notes about their observations, and I did not feel it was right to interrupt them. They needed to make their own discoveries, and I wanted to give them the chance to learn without my interference.'

'Hmm. Well, they didn't learn about you, I'm sorry to say,' I reply. 'They only reported that you were alga, and that was it. They should have paid closer attention, it seems.'

'They discovered what they discovered, and that is all that can be asked of anyone. I wanted to speak with them, but it seems that a part of Orlin's distrust of strangers lingers with me—and I refrained because of it. They were what Orlin knew as suncoats, and he disliked them, since he was a woodcoat. His memories affected me, and I was unsure of how to act.'

206

Derresion is referring to a long-abandoned prejudice my people had for each other, based on the colour of our coats. Suncoats were despised by the woodcoats. Stormcoats and nightcoats hated each other, and no one liked the snowcoats. Well, except for the embercoats—they were loved by everyone. But thanks to Pryok'tel viciousness, our red-furred cousins are now extinct—they've all been dead since around the time of my great-grandfathers, killed to the last by the Pryok'tel, in retaliation for the first Oarth uprising, soon after their initial invasion. The death of the embercoats broke the spirit of Oartheca himself— but it was not the only weapon the triple-mouthed butchers used against us.

Three hundred years ago, when Orlin was alive, our coat-colour bigotry was used by the Pryok'tel to further subjugate and murder us. If there was one good thing that came out of our near-genocide, it was that we killed and buried that prejudice just as thoroughly as we killed the Pryok'tel themselves. Today, we are all one people, and the difference in our coats is celebrated and cherished by all Oarth. That the cost of this celebration is that we've lost our beloved embercoats has never been forgotten, and has never healed.

'However, you are a stormcoat, and those distrustful feelings were not as strong with you. When I saw you, alone and under such curious circumstances, I decided not to repeat my past hesitation. If I may ask you, why did your friend leave you here?'

I frown. 'He says because he wanted to keep me safe.'

Derresion does not reply immediately, and when he does, his tone is cautious. 'Safe by leaving you alone on a planet with no food, no water and no way to escape? I do not understand.'

'No, no, he left me some supplies, and has contacted some of my other friends to come and get me in a while,' I explain. 'I'll be fine. And when my friends turn up, we'll be able to take Orlin back with us, see him home, to be with his ancestors, and all.'

Although Derresion does not smile, I can sense his pleasure at my response. 'That will be just proper. Thank you, Toar.'

'And if you wanted, I'm sure I could have some more Oarth visit you, now that we know about you,' I offer, hopefully. 'There're many scientists who'd love a chat with a seventy-million-year-old super-being like yourself, I'm sure of it. But only if you want to of course; we'd want to be your friends, but only if you wanted to be ours. We'll leave you alone if that's what you'd prefer.'

'I want to be your friend, yes. Toar, though how you arrived was unusual, I am glad you did. You must thank your friend for me, he has given me a gift by leaving you here, even though it upset him to do so.'

I find myself kicking the stone beneath my feet. 'He was upset, was he?' I ask, trying not to sound too interested, despite how much I feel it.

Derresion 'nods', meaning he shifts the top bit of his form up and down with those same squishy sounds that I'm probably never going to enjoy hearing. 'Yes; I understand from Orlin when a baron is upset—how their faces look, how they behave. Your friend was sad when he was laying you to your slumber; he made great efforts to ensure you were comfortable, checking and adjusting you many, many times to make sure your head was supported, and your body protected. He kissed you, too, and held your hand for many minutes. That is why I thought he was your baron—he looked and behaved as the barons Orlin remembered.'

'He's not a baron,' I reply. 'He looks like one, but he's not Oarth. Rowland— that's my friend's name, is a human—a different species.'

Derresion is quiet again. 'Fascinating, truly. An entirely different species near identical to your barons. This universe is a wondrous place that such a thing could happen. It would be quite interesting to meet Rowland, one day, and discover more about him.'

I look away now, my frown hardening. 'He might be dead, now, for all I know.'

'No, your Rowland is currently on his ship, near the last planet in this system. There is a Pryok'tel vessel there too—is he on his way to meet them? He must be careful if that is the case—the Pryok'tel are unpleasant people—do humans …'

'How?' I ask, amazed. 'How … how do you know that? That he's on his ship?'

Derresion is silent for a moment. 'I feel the energy pattern emanating from Rowland's ship, still. I sensed his vessel coming and kept track of it when it departed. His vessel is still emanating that energy, and I can still feel that energy as it eventually makes its way back here. It is not too far away, only near the edge of this system.'

'You … you can feel his ship? All the way on the edge of this system?'

'Yes. He is travelling now.'

At my confused expression, Derresion elaborates. 'It is no different than you seeing light with your eyes. Imagine that your eye is the size of this planet, and you were able to see all forms of energy wavelengths—cosmic, light, microwaves, radio waves, and electromagnetic, gravity, sound, temporal, Under waves. Electricity in all its forms and ways to generate it. Forms of energy the Oarth do not have words for, yet. When you can sense all of that, a little ship is easy to keep track of when it is so close by.'

'Close by?' I ask, incredulously. 'It's hundreds of millions of kilometres away!'

'Billions,' he corrects, nonchalantly. 'Three hundred and eighty-seven billion kilometres, at this moment. Very close.'

'Great Oarth!' I breathe as I try and wrap my head around the magnitude of what Derresion is saying. He has the capability to see billions of kilometres away?

But he misunderstands my exclamation, and asks 'Are you worried for your Rowland?'

'Yes, quite!' I reply, emphatically. 'He's in over his head, and he's going to get himself killed.'

Derresion is quiet for another moment, then asks, 'Do you need to go to him?'

It's my turn to be quiet. 'Yes, but … don't see how that's possible; my other friends won't be arriving for hours, and unless you've got a spaceship stored away somewhere, I'm stuck here until then.'

Derresion bobs. 'Not a spaceship. But close enough, I think.'

CHAPTER 20
Rowland

Silence. Nothing but silence.

My attempt to contact the derelict transport has gone unanswered, and it's been a good five minutes. Back on *Lucky*, when we first arrived in the kelmisite field and transmitted this same request to find the derelict, its response was nearly immediate. I fear that by purging its systems, I may have disabled its communications—but I'm transmitting on the derelict's emergency channels, and those are hardwired into its base operating system. I'm racking my brains to see where I've gone wrong, what I've missed, when Suren'thos' smooth voice snaps me back to the moment at hand.

'Everything going well, Mr. Hale?'

'No,' I reply, sounding frazzled—easy enough, because I truly am. 'I'm having trouble figuring out how to disarm these systems—they're all new to me, sorry. Just a moment more.'

'Oh?' Suren'thos remarks, casually. 'You've not jacked into the shuttle? I would have thought that was how you managed to overtake it to begin with?'

Damn it. He knows I'm a jack.

'Yes, I have, it's just wrestling with me,' I assure him, with as much honesty as I can muster. 'Shouldn't be much longer.'

'I should think not—it appears you triggered a random communication request in your attempt to do so, from what we've been able to see on our sensors. Don't worry, we blocked the transmission—no harm done,' Suren'thos mock-assures me, with that oiliness that makes me want to shove his head quills down his throat, one at a time.

'Ah, sorry for that—just, one second here …' I reply, and with great reluctance, I initiate *Blue Boy's* disarming sequence—taking the lasers offline, ejecting the missiles, and dumping the entire storage bay's worth of mines out into space. I can hear the back wall of the storage room opening, and *Blue Boy's* warnings and sequence steps for depressurising that section and dropping the mines.

'Good, you've sorted it out, I see. Well done, Mr. Hale, our thanks for being so compliant,' Suren'thos oozes. 'Please feel welcome to join us on board; our starboard docking hatch is ready to receive you.'

'Understood, Primus Suren'thos. Initiating automatic docking procedures. See you soon. Hale out.' I end the transmission and let out the desperate 'FUUUUCK!' that's being welling inside.

Well, it appears I'm royally screwed. Not only did my plan completely fail, but Suren'thos has me dead to rights, basically stripped naked and spread-eagled out in front of him for the worst fucking over of my life. And as a delightful bonus, he knows I'm a jack, which means he's no doubt doubling his cybersecurity systems in preparation. Another plan down in flames.

I look over at Toar's empty chair. I didn't make a mistake there, at least. Had he been here, Toar would be in even worse circumstances than I'm about to be in—seems there's no love for the Oarth in a Pryok'tel's heart, and I doubt Suren'thos' cordiality would extend to Toar. This fact doesn't stop me from selfishly wanting to have Toar with me, even if it's only to have someone to vent my frustration to. He'd give me one of his amazing hugs, tell me it'll be all right, give me that boost of confidence I sorely need right now to figure a way out of this. As it is, I can sense myself panic-spiralling—all my escape paths are being blocked.

There's still a chance Suren'thos will negotiate. I'll make him an offer for my crew so valuable he'd be a fool not to take it. Make it so that whoever is still alive will have a chance to start over—from scratch, most likely, but they'll be free. As for myself, I'll figure it out—I always do, I assure myself, but my words seem hollow.

Blue Boy is dutifully following my docking request, aligning himself to the vulture's starboard hatch. I can see its black, angular entrance, and the docking bridge extending for me. In a few minutes, I'll be docked, and either go out guns blazing or surrender. Since I left Toar one of the coil-guns, I only have the one myself, and even with its hundred-shot capacity, I doubt it'd be enough to survive a battle, let alone win it. Surrender it is then.

And that's how I exit *Blue Boy*—carefully stepping out, my hands raised, only to be greeted by a squad of fully armed Pryok'tel troopers, in head-to-toe tactical combat armour, pointing plasma assault rifles, charged and ready.

'Hey now, I'm here by invitation,' I remind them, without lowering my hands. They don't lower their rifles—instead, the one in front, his armour sporting extra bling, advances towards me, rifle pointed right at my face.

'Where is Prim ...' I start, but this troop-leader suddenly flips his rifle and rams it into my stomach. I see the blow coming and have a second to brace for it, but I'm not going to lower my hands and give them an excuse to open fire. The butt slams hard in my guts, and I double over, to my knees. The trooper immediately 'helps' me down, shoving me to the floor with his boot.

'I've surrendered ...' I start, but with a free hand the trooper clouts me hard against the side of my head, stunning me. I'm still able to make out one of the others stepping over to me, a metallic device in his hand that looks like a chunky bracelet. I sigh, internally, as I see what it is when he gets closer: a dead-jack.

Dead-jacks are cyber-muzzles, a device that forces an interface with a person's cybernetic system, and either interferes with them to the point of uselessness or, if it's one of the nastier ones, fries the jack's system fully, usually causing neurological damage in the process. The result is the same in both variants though—the jack is nullified—but I get to experience the terror of waiting to find out if this nullification is temporary, or painfully permanent.

The one holding the dead-jack immediately goes for my left hand, splayed out in front of me as I tried to brace myself from smashing into the floor plating. He roughly grabs my wrist and snaps the bracelet on—and an instant later I feel the access point in the centre of my hand go numb—and that sensation rockets up my arm, right to my biocomp. I've got about a millisecond to brace myself for what comes next—a complete wipe of my biocomp. Rendered offline and emptied of its entire contents—all my hacking algorithms, my internal file systems, Mia's bespoke bio-signature corrupter, my interface software that allows me to dream of *Bow-Ties*—all of it. Fuck, they even take my language files. But they've not fried my system, just taken it offline—I'm still a jack, just a useless one. Even if I manage to get the dead-jack off my wrist—it locked with a clearly audible click—I'll still need a complete system reinstal to get back to normal, and I doubt the Pryok'tel have that in mind for me.

'*Zjur fa-teth, ortu'clis,*' the lead boot-stomping trooper tells me; there's a sneer in his voice but I have no way of knowing if that's intentional, or if that's how Pryok'tel normally speak.

'I don't understand you,' I grunt, not adding 'you dumb fucker', because they can still understand me.

'*Hek,*' is the reply, and Boot-Stomper finally removes his offending appendage from my back. He and his jack-killing buddy force me to stand. I glare at Boot-Stomper and get another smack for the look on my face. It staggers me for a moment, and when I look back at him, he gestures with his rifle, further down the hallway.

'*Zar'zen,*' Boot-Stomper orders. Not wanting to risk another cheap shot, I turn and proceed in the direction he indicates. His remaining friends, four more plus Jack-Killer, still have their rifles trained on me as I walk fast but cautiously down the hall.

Jack-Killer takes the lead, and I follow at his pace as we leave the docking bridge. The first thing that surprises me is how elegant the interior of the vulture is: clear, sharp angular architecture, pale grey walls with shiny black contrasting trim, sparkling white panelled floors and ceilings, smooth lines and bright illumination throughout. Stark, but exceptionally clean and organised, bordering on sterile, but there's a minimalistic aesthetic in what I'm seeing. I was expecting a blood-soaked abattoir with the remains of past and future meals hanging from the ceiling, the futile wails of the doomed echoing in the distance. The difference is jarring—these Pryok'tel are not living up to their reputations, and while I'm grateful for that, I'm not entirely sure if it's a good thing.

There's some display units situated at regular intervals, their digital outputs now completely unintelligible to me. The Pryok'tel's written language—built on highly detailed hieroglyphs, which up until a few minutes ago I understood—is now gibberish—pretty, but gibberish nonetheless. I'm looking for any glyph that could represent where we are—like two ships connected by a line, but no luck—the construction of the glyphs doesn't appear to use literal imagery.

I see other Pryok'tel now, travelling the hallways in what I assume are their normal daily activities, meaning that none of them are paying me a moment's notice, but seem completely unfazed that I'm being marched through their vessel. Just another day at the office, but I suppose I should be grateful they're not giving me hungry looks and licking their lips … yet.

Jack-Killer makes a series of determined turns as we head towards wherever I'm to end up. I keep seeing the unintelligible hieroglyphs over doorways and additional display units—the Pryok'tel do seem to be organised and structured in their ship design, at a level equal to, if not better than, the CAPS, and again I'm impressed at the organisation, cleanliness, and crisp professionalism I see everywhere. There's nothing out of place, or scuffed, or worn in any manner—it's like this vulture's just flown straight out of the shipyard.

Eventually we stop at a sliding door to a room with a short series of glyphs illuminated above it—I don't see any skulls, cooking instruments or torture devices represented in the glyphs, thankfully—but when Boot-Stomper and Jack-Killer lead me inside, it's quickly apparent I've not been given the guest quarters. It's the examination table, inclined at a forty-five-degree angle, that's the first giveaway that the rest of my day is going to be par for the course. There're other devices in the room as well, though these are not quite so menacing in appearance; a series of terminals and consoles, storage cabinets and the like—all tidy and clean, of course.

There's another Pryok'tel in this room, standing next to the table, a detached look on her stoic face as she regards me. Her uniform is a lighter green in colour than Boot-Stomper's and his buddies', and she's only armed with a touchpad—given her appearance, I assume she's medical personnel, or something like that—for all I know she could be the food inspector. She exchanges some words with Boot-Stomper, whose replies are short and to the point, and as he finishes, she nods tersely, seemingly satisfied with whatever she's been told.

'See-l'zet clis,' she orders, firmly, and Boot-Stomper gets to work, roughly grabbing my shoulder while Jack-Killer steps in front of me, yanking the zip of the mining suit I'm wearing down hard. I keep quiet and compliant as they strip me naked. I'm a CAPS-N graduate, so I'm long accustomed to being nude in front of other soldiers and medical personnel, but I find myself angered at how shabbily they're treating the clothes Gren so kindly found for me; the expression on Jack-Killer's face as he handles them is clearly disgust. I make sure, however, that mine remains as expressionless as the doctor's.

I don't see the benefit in struggling, making a show, even as Boot-Stomper thrusts me roughly towards the examining table. There's nowhere to run and fighting is not an option—even my new doctor looks like having the chance to beat me into submission would make her day—so I comply, as it seems it is the best, if not the only, course of action. The one thing that's keeping me somewhat calm is knowing that Suren'thos needs me alive to collect the Alconalc bounty, so whatever these Pryok'tel are planning, it probably won't involve my death. Probably.

As I'm strapped in and held down by both wrists and ankles by a set of gravity-clamps, spread-eagled as I somehow inadvertently predicted, what follows for the next fifteen or so minutes is a thorough, yet thankfully painless and non-invasive examination, performed by a series of green and orange lights that emanate from a sensor module in the ceiling. As the lights dance up and

213

down over every centimetre of me, making multiple passes, Doctor Mean barely looks up, her attention either on her touchpad, which she sometimes taps and interacts with, or on outputs from the displays nearby. No-one says a word, but both Boot-Stomper and Jack-Killer keep their rifles at the ready.

The light show ends, unceremoniously, and after one last check on her touchpad, Doctor Mean takes her leave, her two goons following close on her heels, with Jack-Killer taking my clothes and boots along with him. The room's normal illumination remains on at least, as I'm left to contemplate my next steps, limited as they are.

There's no way out of the gravity-clamps; the more I strain against them, the higher their gravity becomes—I'd need inhuman levels of strength to even get one limb free. I do get a better look at the dead-jack that I'm wearing though and am pleased to see it's a black-market knock-off of a readily available commercial unit I've encountered before. If I can break it off, its nullification effect should be disabled soon thereafter. That my biocomp will remain useless is another matter though.

I'm still scanning the room for anything that could help me out, when the doors slide open and none other than Primus Suren'thos marches in, intentionally I think, as though he's running late for a meeting that he'd rather not attend.

'Captain Hale, so good to meet you in person,' he speaks, in nearly perfect CAPS Standard. His accent is not an Earth accent I recognize—he over-gutturalises the 'C' and 'H' in my title and name, and there's a weird uptick on some vowels, but he's more than understandable.

'Likewise, Primus Suren'thos. I'd shake your hand and all, but …' I explain politely, indicating my shackles.

Assuming an overly apologetic look, he sits at a console, looking over the output. 'Oh, that, just a precaution. Your reputation for escaping confines precedes you, Captain; we just want to make sure there's a chance to dissuade you from that, until we get to know one another better.'

'You seem to know quite a lot about me already.'

'Correct,' he agrees, still reviewing whatever data is on the display, likely the results of my examination. Or he's playing a power game with me, trivialising my situation to show he's the one in control, but not in a grotesque, obvious manner. This one likes his appearances.

'You speak CAPS Standard quite well, Primus,' I compliment him falsely. 'I'm flattered you would take the time to learn our language; I would have thought learning another species' tongue was beneath a Pryok'tel.'

'Nonsense,' Suren'thos replies, dismissively, still focused on his terminal. 'Just another prejudice about my people you appear to be suffering from, Captain— we are highly interested in resources like you; learning your language is a pleasure for me—a truly bizarre and wonderful way of speaking, so full of inefficiencies and contradictions, but endless opportunities for expression and creativity. A wasteful language, ultimately, but interestingly so.'

I'm struggling to keep my face neutral: the contempt Pryok'tel have shown others has been on record, across the known systems, ever since we first encountered them a century ago. Sure, there's been CAPS propaganda, it's a tried and tested form of keeping your enemy's villainy alive in the hearts and minds of your populace, but there's also live video feeds of Pryok'tel harvesters devouring civilian outposts they raid—I've seen those myself—and the only interest the Pryok'tel appear to have for other sapient species is how they taste.

Finally, apparently satisfied with the readouts, he faces me, a fake look of concern on his face. 'You seem to be in good health, none too worse for your mishaps today. I do apologise'—lie—'for what happened; we acted on the best information we had at the time. I regret discovering that information appears to have been falsified.'

'Where are my crew members, Primus?' I ask. 'You said you would tell me if I joined you on board. Here I am.'

'Yes, yes, here you are, demands and all,' he remarks, in a laughing tone, but I can tell he doesn't like it when I put him on the spot. 'Well, let's get right to it, then. Two of your crew members died in the initial encounter; the male Ivan Vasilyev and the male Bryce Winston. Vasilyev suffered severe cellular destabilisation from being directly in the path of our breach-wave, and Winston received fatal blunt force trauma to the base of his skull. Our assessment indicates Winston died instantly, whereas Vasilyev survived no more than a few minutes. It is unlikely he was conscious for that period.'

My universe shrinks to the size of a pinhead. They're … they're … oh God, oh God, don't cry don't cry don't cry …

'I am sorry, Captain Hale. This was not what we wanted. We share your pain.' Suren'thos speaks convincingly enough that I can't quite tell if he's lying.

'Where …' I stop, having to kick the frog in my throat back down. 'Where are Bethany, Mia and Corculhoran?'

'The female Bethany Ortez and the male Corculhoran of the Twisting River are safely secured in resource storage, in hypno-stasis, awaiting delivery for collection of their respective bounties,' Suren'thos informs me, with exaggerated sympathy. 'The female, Mia Ong, is here, on board, also safe.'

'And the remains of the others?' I demand, not knowing if I want to hear the answer.

'Also safely in resource storage, also awaiting delivery. Not eaten, as I'm sure you meant to say,' Suren'thos simpers, so wide that the corners of his mouth split slightly. 'Ivan Vasilyev has a marginal dead-or-alive bounty for him in the Terhosh system. Your doctor, Bryce Winston, has no worthwhile bounties, and so whatever trade opportunities you propose will be for their remains.'

'State your opening offer, then,' I say tersely. I'm done playing whatever game Suren'thos wants me to play.

He steps out from the console now, and comes to stand over me, his yellow eyes glinting. 'So forward, all of a sudden, are we? Where's this cavalier charm, this roguish banter, I've heard so much about? Hmmm?'

'I guess I'm all out of good manners, Primus. It's been a long day,' I remark, coldly.

He laughs, and it's the most artificial sound I've heard an organic being make. *Blue Boy* would laugh more convincingly.

'It's only just begun! You see, Rowland ... I can call you Rowland, now that we're friends, correct? You see Rowland, I was *so* pleased you arrived. You represent a full twenty-one percent of this mission's net value, and losing you cut deeply into our profits.

'Granted, the veil you located—and so helpfully disarmed—will benefit the Hegemony for decades to come, but you ... you are still a most lucrative resource. The combination of your multiple bounties is truly impressive: nine star systems—*nine*—are paying fantastic sums for your head.'

He leans forward now, and roughly grabs the short hair on top of my expensive head, tugging it as I try and turn away from him, so that I'm forced to look at his smug face. 'You must be so proud to be so wanted. But I'll tell you a secret, shall I?'

He leans closer now, and his breath is fetid, hot and awful as he whispers close to my face. 'None of that is worth as much to me as what you know about the Oarth. Don't lie to me, human, not now, not when I can smell their stench so heavily upon your flesh. You reek of them. It's eye-watering. I would have the first layers of your skin scrubbed from you if I thought it would do any good.

'So I will tell you how this negotiation will go: you will tell me all you know about the Oarth, from the moment you met them in the kelmisite field, to the moment you let them mate with you—you filthy degenerate—to the moment we are now. You will tell me everything, and you will tell the truth.'

Now he leans all the way over, his lips brushing my ears. 'Or I will eat every single one of your crew members myself—dead, alive, both and either, bounties be damned. And I will make you watch. I may force you to join, if you really test me.'

He returns to his standing position, letting go of my hair so that I can finally wrench my head away from him. He makes a dramatic gesture of wiping his hands on a nearby cloth, an exaggerated look of disgust on his face, and then returns to his seat at the console.

'So, now that we're clear on the terms for our negotiation, tell me of your first encounter with the Oarth—exact location, number of crew, type of personnel. Proceed when ready, Rowland.'

It's a wonderfully crafted threat. Quite frightening, actually, and I have no doubt he'll follow through—he's got the veil, plus he'll keep me alive, but Betts, Cor and Mia will become 'acceptable losses'.

And so, I spill everything I know about my time with Toar and Gren, I'm ashamed to say. I'm not a good guy, remember. I try to be clever about it, being vague where I can be, but this is not Suren'thos' first time interrogating—he's a master at asking direct questions, then subsequent counter-questions to validate my responses. I do have some interrogation-resistance training, but this man is a virtuoso: cunning, calculating, and surgically precise. I'm also certain the console he's looking at is monitoring my vital signs—he can tell if I'm lying.

Suren'thos learns about the stormcoat Captain Toar Grithrawrscion and his suncoat doctor Grenrethar Harnthscion, plus the science officer Threng, though Suren'thos accepts I do not recall the enthusiastic young man's baronsname. He learns about the *Lurcaster's Claw*, its position in the kelmisite field, my assessment of its defences. He learns about the skip-dive, and is delighted to learn how we accomplished it, his second mouth becoming clearly visible as I describe the formula to him.

'And where are these Oarth now?' he asks.

'They're on the station, still,' I reply, dully. We've been at this for nearly an hour, and my shame at betraying the people who saved my life is draining me.

'All of them, incl ...'

He's too close to having me reveal Toar's location; I need to throw a wildcard out to divert his attention. 'Let's stop these pointless questions, shall we, Primus? Why don't we get to the heart of what you really want to ask? Why don't you ask me about the Allure?'

The wildcard scores a direct hit: I see the interest in Suren'thos' eyes; they sparkle with delight even as he narrows them with anticipation.

'Ah, so, you know about their Allure, do you?' he remarks, sounding indifferent but this is the biggest lie he's told so far. 'I've heard rumours about humans and their Allure—that the Oarth are helpless against it, to the point of mental incapacitation.'

'I didn't see that. I was in a spacesuit for a large portion of my time with them,' which is a true statement, so I'm sure Suren'thos' monitors will not snitch on me. 'They think it's smell-based, and so I was either kept encased in a spacesuit when I was near them, or they were in suits,' which is also true, since I was only ever outside of my suit when I was with Toar alone, singularly and not 'them'.

'I see,' Suren'thos states, checking his output. He looks slightly disappointed. 'Pity, I would have loved to know their reaction to you. You know what a nuisance they are for us, I think? Even two centuries after we graciously returned administration of their planet to them, they still pester us with petty raids, open piracy and acts of terrorism at every turn.'

'You have my sympathies,' I remark, mimicking Suren'thos' previous tone.

'Thank you,' he graciously acknowledges. 'They've been a long-standing annoyance to the Hegemony, and so any opportunity of finding a way to suppress their activities is of course of high value. Which one of them mated with you, by the way? I assume it was the stormcoat—their primitive hierarchy would not allow the smaller suncoat the first opportunity.'

'Neither of them mated with me, Suren'thos. If you're smelling Oarth, it's because I was wearing their spacesuits and clothes—mine were destroyed when I was rescued.'

He checks his read-out, and raises an eyebrow. 'You're telling the truth. I am amazed. The Oarth are mindless, sex-starved beasts—I was certain they'd have raped you the first chance they got. Your resemblance to their barons is remarkable though; perhaps that is why they refrained.'

Mindless, sex-starved beasts. That's the second time I've heard that description—originally it was from Gren, asking me not to think of the Oarth like that. I wonder if the Pryok'tel taught the Oarth to think of themselves in that way—I understand Oarth society is sex-positive, perhaps to a more prevalent and enthusiastic level than other societies—but I doubt they thought their way of living was shameful until they were told otherwise.

'I will admit, I'm glad to learn you've not been degraded by them in such a manner,' Suren'thos continues, and he sounds civil now. 'They're brutish creatures, Rowland. Primitive, stupid and dull. When we first arranged to administer their planet, some four hundred years ago, they hadn't even discovered basic electricity yet—they were dressed in the skins of animals and wielded clumsy iron-based tools against us. They prayed to imaginary beings and fought endless tribal wars with each other. They were thousands of years behind us in terms of social evolution, let alone technological. We tried to enlighten them, teach them higher concepts and new ways of thinking, but they are coarse, vulgar, bestial things. Barely into the category of sapient, really. Agreeable-tasting, however, and highly nutritious.'

I will not acknowledge the last part of his rambling, and instead focus my response on a point Suren'thos has deliberately ignored. 'They seemed to have a decent enough understanding of your technology,' I remark, trying to keep my temper. My impression of the Oarth is that they are courteous, caring and empathetic. I was sorta falling in love with one, after all.

'Oh, that,' Suren'thos says, absently. 'Yes, they're capable of picking up the bare minimum of understanding, if you give them enough time, and beat it into them. We used their labour to build many of our vessels, and after centuries of being exposed to our technology, I suppose they did manage to figure out how to turn the lights on.

'Still, we should have just exterminated the lot of them before we released Oartheca. Small investment for doing the galaxy a long-term favour,' he states, and then sighs disappointedly. 'But resource decisions must be made, and we must adhere to them, for the sake of all,' he finishes on a grandiose note.

He regards me with a curious, interested expression. 'So, returning to what I was saying, before your excellent distraction, you had mentioned that either you were in a spacesuit, or they were, for the entire time you were together?'

I nod. 'They had no way to smell me,' I reply. Another truth, despite not being the actual answer he's looking for. This is not my first time under interrogation, though I will admit, this is my first time being so fucking frightened.

'I wonder, I wonder,' Suren'thos muses, still eyeing me, then gives me a fake grin. 'Look, Rowland, you've been so helpful, telling the truth, providing so much valuable information, I am wondering if you would do me one small favour, just as a courtesy for keeping your crew alive?'

I refrain from spitting on him. 'Ask away, Primus.'

'Would you mind meeting an Oarth, as you are now? Without the barrier of a spacesuit between the two of you? I am sure it would be a highly informative experiment.'

I can't help but raise both my eyebrows, and am positive the console that's monitoring me is recording the rise in my heartbeat and blood pressure.

'To what end, Primus? You want to see me get raped by an Oarth?' I ask, disdainfully.

'No, of course not,' he replies, with equal disdain. 'Both you and the Oarth would continue to be restrained—your continued safety is my pleasure to provide.'

'You don't seem to need my permission, Primus,' I answer, weary of this farce.

'That's the spirit,' he replies. 'Here is my offer: you participate willingly— meaning you do whatever I say needs doing during this experiment, and I will reward you for your cooperation.'

'I will not hurt the Oarth,' I interject, firmly. 'Kill me, kill my friends. Lose our bounties for the sake of your experiment and report that to your superiors. See if they agree with your resource decisions.'

The sullen, deathly glare he gives me lets me know I've broken his façade, finally. But I pay for it, as he lashes out and strikes my face with a resounding slap, hard enough to cause my ears to ring and stars to burst in front of my eyes.

'Address me with that tone again and I'll remove your tongue with my own teeth,' he states, deadly calm. 'The Alconalc do not need you to speak when I turn you over to them. They don't need you to walk, they don't need you to use your right arm, they don't need the nose attached your face. They don't need the skin covering your body nor your reproductive organs. They need your brain, your nervous system, and your left arm. That's it. Everything else is just extra meat, waiting for the harvest. Keep that in mind the next time you address me.'

'Of course, Primus, I apologise,' I say, making sure I sound cowed. It's not difficult. 'You were saying you would reward me for my cooperation?'

He continues to glare for a moment, then that fake charm returns like he's forcing on an ill-fitting suit. 'Yes. If you cooperate, in entirety, I will bring Mia Ong to see you. You will be allowed to say your farewells. I will also allow us to discuss plans for the remains of Vasilyev and Winston. If you offer sufficient resources to cover the costs in doing so, we will arrange for transport of their bodies to a location where whatever corpse-processing ritual you can afford may take place. This is my only offer to you—do you accept?'

'And Bethany and Corculhoran?' I counter, and brace for another smack.

'Non-negotiable,' Suren'thos states. 'We have secured agreements for their return, there is no counteroffer you can make for them. The Pryok'tel standard of excellence for adhering to our commitments cannot be traded away, for any price.'

Again, I'm baffled by his answer: when the fuck did the Pryok'tel start caring about how they're perceived by others? This is a worry—a minor one, all things considered—but it still gets planted into my brain. Apart from the cannibalism talk—a point which has been made amply clear is still the case—this entire encounter with the Pryok'tel is nowhere near what I was expecting—they're behaving almost entirely opposite to their past reputation. What's going on?

'And if I refuse?' I ask, sounding curious, because we both know I would never risk such a thing and am just idly speculating, right?

He shrugs. 'Then dinner is served early tonight.'

I shake my head, unable to stop the annoyance from appearing on my face. Suren'thos' eyes narrow with that impatient, offended look he wore just prior to smacking me, so I hastily reply, 'Fine, bring your Oarth in. Let's get this disaster started.'

This causes him to chuckle, more earnestly this time. 'Your enthusiasm is sure to pay off. Now, let's see, let's see, what's available here …' he muses, and I'm beginning to see that Suren'thos has that unfortunate combination of sadism and megalomania that makes him truly dangerous; a violent drama queen that makes dealing with him precarious and ultimately futile, since he will only be satisfied when he gets his own way.

'Ah, yes. Resource 114-C2. Expendable, but should still do nicely. Currently in hypno-stasis but waking him up will just make that all the more educational for us. What a surprise it will be for everyone.'

Suren'thos resumes masturbating his ego while he makes the arrangements to have this resource delivered, asking me questions that seem to have no real purpose other than to belittle me, or the Oarth, or exemplify his own magnanimous and superior self. I'm really not paying that much attention to him anymore; so long as I'm able to form my answers in a way that suits his fantasy, he's pretty content to keep jerking it. This does spare me some brain-space to think, but I'm torn between finding a way to escape—which there still isn't— mourning the death of Bryce and Ivan, which if I think about for more than half a moment causes my eyes to water, and wondering if Mia, Betts and Cor are okay. Oh and yes, the impending visit from a new Oarth, where I'm going to find out just how 'overcharged' my Allure is. Can't wait for that.

All too soon, another Pryok'tel trooper enters the room—she's not familiar to me, though I've only got half a moment to assess her before she steps aside, and another examination table, this one on a gravity lift, floats into the room, guided by the not so sorely missed face of Boot-Stomper. On the table, a red-furred Oarth has been set out on display, strapped spread-eagled and as naked as I am, though by how his head is lowered, resting on his chest, it looks like he's still under stasis-sleep.

He's taller than Gren, but nowhere near as big as Toar—but he's thin— ragged even; Toar and Gren are cuddly—both in looks and in feel, as I can attest, but this poor guy is haggard—he still has muscles, but he's taut, stringy-looking. I can see signs of abuse on him everywhere—there're patches in his coat, his feet are chafed and cracked, almost bald of fur, and all the claws on both his hands and feet have been clipped to nubs. One of his ears looks like it's been damaged and healed in a terribly scraggly line. Poor man, poor poor man. I have this sinking feeling that however hard his life has been, today's going to be much worse.

Suren'thos addresses his troops in Pryok'telish, and Boot-Stomper provides a succinct report. Suren'thos seems pleased, and directs his troops so that Boot-Stomper remains by the poor Oarth, while the other takes her place behind me, off to the side, out of my field of view.

'It seems that 114-C2's stasis is taking longer to dissipate then predicted,' Suren'thos starts. 'Easy enough to remedy, but you do have my apologies for the dela ...'

The Oarth grunts, groggily, lifting his head, the black end of his nose twitching at first, but in a moment, inhaling mightily. His eyes spring open and I see green irises vanish as his pupils go to their full width, wild and frantic. He is looking directly at me, but I can't understand his expression—it's like he's waking from a nightmare into an even worse one.

An ominous sound emanates from him, primal, furious, starting deep in his chest before escaping him first as a whine, but increasing rapidly into a thunderous growl. He shakes at his constraints, testing them at first but when they resist, his struggles escalate, as does his howling. He does not take his eyes from me, but when it becomes apparent he can't free himself, he casts a desperate look to his bound wrists, trying to understand what's going on.

'Say something to him,' Suren'thos orders.

'Like what?' I ask, but the sound of my voice is sufficient. The red Oarth snaps his attention back to me immediately, doubling his efforts to escape. His frustration mounts with each passing moment, as does the sound of his bellowing. His whole body is beginning to strain to get free, his wrists and ankles crushed terribly against the restraints.

'Stop ... stop that,' I say, trying to sound soothing—he's really beginning to injure himself, but the sound of my voice is only further agitating him. He flashes me a desperate look, almost apologetic, and then tries again to escape, pushing against all four of his bonds simultaneously, curling desperately from the effort. His grunting is now turning plaintive, into short, clipped whines that are breaking my heart.

'Interesting,' Suren'thos remarks, checking his readouts. 'But I think we can do better.'

Suren'thos addresses the Pryok'tel trooper beside me, giving her an order I don't understand, but soon learn anyway as she digs one of her fingers cruelly into my sides, the tip of her fingernail sharp enough to draw blood and cause me to yelp in surprise.

That's when the real bellowing starts. The Oarth sees me squirm, eyes the Pryok'tel who hurt me, and flips the fuck out. He opens his mouth and one of the loudest sounds I've heard echoes in the confines of the room—a gigantic roar that reverberates off the walls—it's as deafening as it is ceaseless! Now his efforts to escape are becoming dangerous to himself—his eyes, berserk with intent, never leave mine, and he's focusing all of his strength to pull one of his arms out of his restraints. I can see all his muscles, through his entire body, bulging as he pulls his arm with everything he's got—and his hand is being squished against the restraint to what must be an agonizing degree. He's going to rip his arm off to get to me. I know it. He will rip his own arm off to get to me.

'That's better!' Suren'thos crows, his gaze moving between this poor Oarth and the readout from the terminal. 'All his vitals are dramatically rising—stimulate the subject again, Secundus Vay'auh-ta.'

I get another needling jab; I try to keep my face still, try not to register it, but it doesn't matter—the Oarth bellows anew—and this time, I do hear a sickening pop—the poor man's pulled his own shoulder out of its socket—and is still pulling.

'Remarkable!' Suren'thos celebrates, but I have had more than enough of this. 'His adrenaline levels are spiking, his endorphin levels are at never-before-seen heights—I doubt he even feels the pain he's causing himself—oh but this can't last long—his blood pressure will burst his own heart!'

I give Suren'thos a baleful glare, but he's too focused on his readouts to notice. I have to try something to save the Oarth, and so I force a gentle look, despite my own thundering stress levels.

'Shhh—shhh,' I say, quietly, calmly, looking into the Oarth's hysterical eyes, giving him the friendliest expression I know how to give. He regards me for a moment, hesitates, then resumes his pulling, but his bellowing has returned to that frustrated whine at least.

'No, no, you must stop. I'm all right,' I coax, and he looks at me again, uncertain, but only for a moment, before he resumes pulling—somewhat less frantically, but still with all he's got.

'He doesn't understand you,' the Pryok'tel behind me states, her voice emotionless.

'That's correct,' Suren'thos remarks, casually, still engrossed by what's on his display. 'We don't bother with translators on these ones—waste of time.'

I rack my brain—there's plenty of ways to communicate without words—there's got to be something that will work. I try 'shhh, shhh' again, but it's useless—for all I know it's an irritating noise to an Oarth, as it seems to just cause the red Oarth to pull harder. I try and remember my first conversation with Gren, when I first woke up on *Blue Boy*—I hadn't had Oarthecan installed on my translator, and he was speaking to me ...

'*Rer,*' I say, softly, remembering. '*Rer.*'

The Oarth looks at me and stops. His eyes are still wild, still full of pain, confusion, and anger.

'*Hulth*' I try, but I've said it wrong—even to my own ears, I can tell it's not how Gren said it. Gotta ... gotta think more like I'm a bear—more four legs, less two legs—my god that's awful for me to think but I need to try something.

'*Hulth*,' I try again, woofing—*tsk*—the 'ulth' part ... and it works. He stops pulling immediately, his eyes on mine, searching, frantic still, but searching.

'*Hulth*,' I repeat again, the same way. He's breathing hard, his brow furrowed in confusion, in fear, in pain, but he seems to be gaining marginal control over himself.

'*Grol kern relther rahl thrane!*' the red furred Oarth implores, desperately. His voice is hoarse from all his bellowing, but it's still full of terror.

'He says "You are in great danger baron",' the Pryok'tel, Nails McStabby, indicates from behind me. I think her name might be Vay'auh-ta, but I'm not sure and don't give a shit.

'Tell him to stop hurting himself,' I ask, and after a moment, Suren'thos nods once.

Nails speaks Oarthecan to the poor fellow, but he just bares his teeth at her, and the pulling starts up anew.

'*Hulth, hulth*,' I repeat, soothingly, and he stops again. 'Tell him *I* said to stop hurting himself.' I try to keep the irritation out of my voice.

She repeats herself, and I catch the word '*thrane*' in her words, which I had heard this Oarth say before. This time, he looks at me as she says it, and at her words, his body seems to ease slightly, but this reprieve does not last long. His nose remains in overdrive—his nostrils flaring as he continues to sniff the air vigorously, and his eyes wild, the pupils huge and dazed. Whatever madness is gripping this red-furred Oarth surges back, and his howling resumes at an ever-increasing volume, as does his thrashing and arm-wrenching. His mouth begins to foam at the sides, and his breathing is now just a series of rapid-firing pants between his desperate baying, and when I do manage to see his eyes, he's ... he's not there, anymore—all that made him himself has been burned away by the Allure.

'Are we done here, Suren'thos?' I demand, raising my voice loudly over the Oarth's, as best I can. 'Get what you were looking for?'

Suren'thos eyes me with that cold expression. Perhaps the futility of this is getting to him, but I suspect it's more that the sound has moved beyond entertaining and is now painful.

'For now,' he concludes. The bellowing is unbearable, and he gives Boot-Stomper a terse order, who then takes the poor Oarth from the room, increasing his frenzy. He snarls and thrashes mightily as Boot-Stomper leads him away, piloting the gravity table back out of the room, and it's many moments before I can no longer hear the pitiful bellowing down the halls. My god, this is an awful day.

'We'll dispose of that one and bring another on the vigorous side.' Suren'thos announces when the volume returns to normal. 'I really wanted to see if he'd tear himself apart to get to you. I'm sure a healthier sample will provide what I'm looking for.'

Dispose of him? 'I will trade for his life,' I state, immediately. 'Third Bank of

223

Lerenthar, Account number Alpha-ninety-six-beta-gamma-nine. Two thousand Lerenthar fets. You get the password when you assure me of his safety.'

Suren'thos eyes Nails, still behind me. I can't see her response, but Suren'thos answers. 'Are you certain, Rowland? The resource is damaged—a waste of good currency.'

'Then fix his arm,' I add. 'Plus enough time for him to heal properly. And give him a fucking meal already,' I snarl, unable to control my temper.

Suren'thos ponders, then responds, 'I suppose there's a reason for the human expression about fools and money. Fine, deal struck—I'll return him to stasis and when he reaches his delivery destination, he'll be healed, fed, then rested for a period of sixty consecutive hours.'

'Your word?' I demand.

Suren'thos nods. 'Pending payment in full. I'll let Secundus Vay'auh-ta complete the transaction.'

I wonder if Suren'thos will follow through on his deal—for my own sake I decide that he will, though I have no proof of this 'Pryok'tel standard of excellence'.

'Well, that's enough entertainment for me, I think, as enjoyable as it has been,' he remarks, stepping away from his console and towards the door. 'Secundus Vay'auh-ta, conclude our negotiations with Rowland, and when complete, secure him in hypno-stasis for his trip to Alconalc. We depart within the hour, and I expect this to be resolved,' he orders, but he is looking at me.

'Primus, you said I could see Mia if I cooperated. Deal's a deal, correct?' I insist, and I am proud of myself that my voice is strong, not betraying my desperation.

'Of course,' he says, looking reproachful—but it's all an act. He gives this Secundus Vay'auh-ta a meaningful look.

'We Pryok'tel always follow through on our promises.'

CHAPTER 21

Toar

I'm not quite sure what I'm looking at, if I'm honest.

When my sons were young, six or so I think, Cralren and I made sure their education would be the best we could offer. Given that we both come from well-off families, we had the means to provide our children with a chance for learning that is not always available to others.

Typically, most sire fathers will enrol their drone sons in the same academies they went to as boys, partially due to tradition but for those families where means are tight, their dad's alumnus status guarantees their sons a spot. In our case, we had the chance to send Grath, Hars and Reth to a special pre-academy assessment school, where each of my sons' individual talents and interests could first be discovered, cultivated, and then directed into the appropriate training academy based on areas they were both interested in and naturally excelled at.

These assessment pre-schools allow your children to explore many different types of activities to see where they excel. Turns out our brave Grath is a soldier through and through—no surprise there—he's keen on physical learning, competition and challenging his body, while our sweet Hars is a born artist with a brilliant imagination and cunning hands to bring his wildest ideas to life, and quick, clever Reth is an engineer that sees not only how things go together, but how they come apart, and what else they can be transformed into.

What we also learned were the areas our sons are not particularly interested in: Hars cannot stand hurting others and, uh, I do say this with a father's love, is a lot fonder of his sweets than his exercise, being on the extra cuddly side—still looks good on him, though. Reth is socially awkward and prefers the company of machines and gadgets over other people, and, again said with love, he's not in any danger of becoming a sire—I'm quite worried he's Allure- or even den-blind, but if so, he won't talk to me about it. Grath ... well, I've mentioned his hot temper, and that temper refuses him the patience required for managing fiddly, delicate things, such as is needed for artistic challenges.

One day, when the three of them came home from their studies, each of them presented me with a blackclay sculpture—that day at school was ceramics day, and this was their first experience trying their hand at moulding the stubborn but beautiful material into any shape their minds could imagine. This was the day we discovered Hars' talents—he made a highly articulated figurine of our pet *terk-terk* Nosso, complete with the little fuzzball's twin tails coiled high over his back. Reth made a puzzle game, with spinning gears that would only turn properly if you put them in the right order, and if you did, rotating them turned the puzzle into a smiley face.

Grath ... well, when Grath presented his gift to his dads, for the life of me, all I could think of when I looked down at the oblong, black, roughly textured and slightly chunky thing was 'that shit must have hurt coming out'. Had the sense not to say that aloud, thankfully, and was grateful for Cralren's experience as a parent when he immediately cooed and asked Grath how he felt about making it, rather than what it was. Grath said he hated it, that it was supposed to be a dagger, that he altogether hated blackclay, that all art was stupid, and could he go play with his practice sword now?

I of course still have all three gifts, safely stowed in my quarters at my Dad's house, but I'm now experiencing that same loss for words when I look at what Derresion has brought up from his depths and laid out on the shore in front of the cave. What's worse is that I'm picking up this sensation of pride beaming from his squishy purple form—at least Grath had presented his gift without any illusion of its merit—but here, Derresion is actively waiting for my assessment of what's been put before me. I'm not sure if "That's lovely, Derresion, how did you enjoy making it?" is the best thing to say.

'I see, how … how does it work, then?' I ask, and make a mental note to thank Cralren for his lesson. What I'm looking at is again another oblong object, this time in an absolute mess of colours, shapes and random bits and pieces sticking out of it. It looks like it started life as some sort of spacecraft—and then I remember Derresion mentioning that Orlin landed here in an escape pod, all those centuries back, but what I'm seeing now wouldn't even pass the laxest safety inspection to qualify as an emergency spacecraft.

'It works well. It is Orlin's escape pod, but I have improved it,' Derresion explains, confirming my guess, but I'm curious what 'improvement' actually means here. 'Now, it can travel the stars, through the Under, and return you to Oartheca.'

'It does what?' I ask, giving this ugly thing a closer inspection. In my opinion, this escape pod will never see the stars again—if anything, it's a warning to do the exact opposite. In fact, from some of the Pryok'telish scribblings I can see on a few of these grafted-on parts—one of which clearly indicates 'Caution—extreme radiation'—I find that I'm taking a step back from the thing.

'It shall travel the stars,' Derresion continues. 'I have given it all it needs, augmenting its existing capabilities to support life, generate propulsion, navigate systems, send and receive communications, and open Under dive portals. It is also quite comfortable.'

'Look, good Derresion,' I begin, trying to sound kindly but I'm skirting the lines of rudeness. 'I'm sure you tried hard but … this doesn't look safe, to me. Maybe if you explained how you even know how to build something like this, that might help me to understand?'

'Of course! That story is important!' Derresion exclaims. 'When I bonded with Orlin, and mimicked his brain, I discovered all that he discovered. Not just the things that he *knew*, but everything he had encountered in his life.'

'During his enslavement, his abductors forced him to learn how to fix their ship—they made Orlin responsible for the "biological resource reclamation systems"; he had to keep them clean, keep them working. He learned how that system worked, how it connected with other systems, and how those systems worked. His Pryok'tel abductors did not know how intelligent Orlin was, so they did not care where he went, so long as he did his tasks. He went all over the ship, every day for years, seeing and hearing along the way—he did not *know* much of what he perceived, but he *remembered* it, deep down in his brain. He remembered all of it.'

'Okay, right—so Orlin learned how to keep the toilets flushing,' I confirm, and Derresion nods. I carefully add, 'Can you help me understand how that leads to sticking an Under-drive on an escape pod?'

What follows from Derresion is possibly the most thorough lecture on ship systems and design I've ever listened to. For a solid fifteen minutes, he goes on (and on) about the equipment parts, energy flows and structural components Orlin encountered during his time aboard the Pryok'tel ship, and how while Orlin himself may not have understood what he encountered, Derresion, with three centuries to think and experiment, puzzled it out. He explains the finer workings of vessel parts I never knew existed—I'm no novice at ship mechanics, but Derresion has got this down to naming specific nuts and bolts.

The overall picture is that Derresion has spent all this time not only learning exactly how these parts work, but how they work *together*—explaining complex processes that my poor brain just cannot follow, so after a bit I'm just nodding along and mumbling 'yes, of course's and 'mm-hmm's every so often so as not to appear entirely stupid. It sounds quite impressive, his knowledge—I've no way to validate it, but it is impressive.

Time is precious though, and I think Derresion catches what my bridge crew often refers to as the 'wrap-it-up' look in my eye. 'You can deduce the rest. Orlin himself did not *know* the entire intricacies of these connections—but he *remembered* them, and so I learned from his memory. After Orlin died, I set myself the task to discover a way to ensure that his fate would never be shared by another. At first, I thought as Orlin did, using a mimicked copy of his brain—but that did not result in a solution. So I made another copy of his brain, to think about ...'

'I beg your pardon?' I interrupt, not understanding. 'You made another copy of Orlin's brain?'

Derresion holds up his two 'hands' before me, cupping them together. Then he begins to pulse, causing waves of his purple self to fill the space in between his palms, until he is 'holding' an object, created out of his own being, that is unmistakably the size and shape of an Oarth's brain.

'This is a copy of Orlin's brain, one like those I made discovering the solution I needed. One brain on its own could not puzzle out everything, so I made another to help. That also was insufficient, but now I had two brains thinking two different ways to discover the answer—and this made thinking easier for me—more productive, more efficient. So I made another brain. And another. Fourteen million copies of Orlin's brain, in total. Thinking in fourteen million different ways, sharing ideas, checking and rechecking each other, all to find a solution. It took the next two hundred and seventy-six years to discover this solution, with many trials and errors, but I succeeded.'

I'm again stunned into silence. The expression I'm wearing must be ridiculous. I just cannot understand what's being told to me.

'You ... you made fourteen million copies of Orlin's brain and had them all thinking about the same problem, but in different ways, for nearly three centuries?' I check, unknowingly asking the silliest question I will ever ask.

'Yes,' Derresion confirms, re-absorbing the copy back into himself.

I sit down with a giant thump on the rocky shore, my stare shifting between the cobbled-together escape-pod-cum-starship and Derresion. At our last population count, there were just under two-hundred million Oarth—nowhere near our pre-Pryok'tel estimates, but we're all trying to fix that. Except, that estimate is not entirely true now, in a sense—apparently, there's been fourteen million versions of the same Oarth hanging about all by themselves out here on a tidally-locked planet nobody else even bothers with, thinking about one problem, for the last few centuries. No-one is going to believe this when I tell them. No-one. I don't believe it myself, and I'm staring right at the proof.

'Where did you get the parts for all of this, then?' I manage to ask, finally, trying to distract myself from the overwhelming concept that a being like Derresion presents—that he can become an entire race of people simply by willing it.

'In orbit. The Pryok'tel vessel Orlin was on was destroyed, but there was still enough salvage for me to find the parts I needed to make the craft,' Derresion explains. 'Most of what I found was damaged, but I made repairs, eventually. Bits and pieces, here and there, tested, modified, and tested again. Until all of it fit together, until all of it worked.'

'You've tested this craft, then? It works?'

'Yes, forty-seven tests of all systems, except the Under-drive, with one hundred percent success rate. Three tests with the Under-drive, one hundred percent success rate—but I cannot test any more as there will not be enough kelmisite fuel left to reach Oartheca.'

'But could we send it to reach my friend, instead?' I ask, the first glimmer of hope springing in me.

'Yes. I will show you how. Your friend's vessel is now at the fourth planet, just next to the Pryok'tel vessel. You will easily reach him, but you will not have enough fuel to reach Oartheca if you do.'

'That's all right—there's another place we can travel to afterwards that's much closer—not Oartheca but there's a lot of other Oarth there, and they'll help us.'

'Then you may go to your Rowland, when you are ready to do so. May I show you how this works?' Derresion invites, sounding eager to show off his handiwork.

It's the thought of reaching Rowland in time that makes the decision for me to trust this little, uh, life raft Derresion's made. I suppose if I were truly the professional captain I claim to be, I'd give myself more time to think about the situation, make a decision based on a careful assessment, ample consideration of outcomes and a proper review of other possibilities. Instead, though, I do exactly what Murth accused me of—I think with my pecker. Well, no, that's being unfair—I think with my heart, if I'm being kind to myself, but my pecker does get some choice comments in.

I find myself nodding my head even before I've spoken. 'Yes, I want that—give me the grand tour, Derresion—spare no detail,' I say, then remembering that Derresion likes to talk even more than I do, hastily add, 'that I'll need to know to operate your … escape pod? Emergency craft? What's the name of your ship?'

'I have named him *Orlin's Hope*,' Derresion responds, in his typical matter-of-fact manner.

Aww. I am deeply touched upon hearing that name. Oarth vessels are almost always named after a baron, coupled with a noun that describes their basic purpose—*Lurcaster's Claw*, *Grolthon's Spear*, and such. This is a tradition we had even before the Pryok'tel appeared over our skies. To name a vessel after a drone is not unheard of—*Terakcoar's Eye*, a science vessel named for our leading astronomer, for example—but this is only bestowed when the drone has provided extreme service to all of Oartheca. That this little makeshift vessel is named for Orlin is just so perfectly appropriate that I find myself getting misty-eyed. It's such a noble tribute and speaks volumes about just how much Derresion understands and values not only his friend Orlin, but Orlin's people as well.

'That's a wonderful name, Derresion,' I say, sincerely. 'Orlin would be very honoured that he's been so fondly remembered and thought so well of.'

'It is his memory that honours me. Often, I think what I would be like if I had not met Orlin, and it saddens me that I would have continued experiencing the universe in the way I once did. Meeting him unlocked an entirely new way of being for me—an entirely new universe of possibilities. If helping you pays tribute to Orlin's generosity, then I'm pleased to provide for such a worthy purpose.'

'Spoken like a true Oarth,' I say, smiling broadly. 'Orlin would be proud.'

*****

What Derresion lacks in ship design aesthetics, he certainly makes up for in functionality and ergonomics.

He pops the front hatch of the escape pod open, showing its interior, which is almost like the cockpit of one of our starclaws, though much roomier and with a series of touchpads on either side instead of a flight stick between your legs. Derresion explains that as he had no way of predicting the skill level of his next stranded visitor, he's designed *Orlin's Hope* so that much of the ship's operations are automated, and only minimal inputs are required to pilot the vessel.

I note with a tinge of envy that the entire interface is designed specifically with an Oarth in mind too—the touchpads are claw-sensitive, which is something us Oarth haven't yet fully worked out how to do, consistently. That, and the single occupancy seat is large enough for a snowcoat to fit in entirety—with Derresion's reasoning being to ensure any Oarth could escape, not just a woodcoat like Orlin was. This pleases me entirely, not only because it shows just how much Derresion cares for us, but also because there's enough room that I'm sure Rowland and I could squish in together—meaning we could use *Orlin's Hope* to get back to the *Claw*, when it comes to it. It'd be a tight fit but I find that thought doesn't bother me in the slightest. Quite the opposite actually.

As Derresion explains how each of the systems works, I've noticed that there's a few systems that aren't immediately apparent.

'Are there any weapons, if something goes badly?'

'No, the increased mass from weaponry would limit the range of the Under-drive,' Derresion replies. 'However, there is energy-shielding sufficient to absorb several direct hits by the laser cannons I discovered in orbit. I have also provided superior manoeuvrability to assist if that scenario occurs.'

'Ho-ho, that's nice to hear,' I chuckle. 'What's its speed?'

'One quarter of light speed, sustainable for twelve hours. Once you rescue your Rowland, I would recommend you do not attempt to fly to your next destination, however—use the Under-drive to get you there. The drive itself has a nine-hour recharge.'

'You've really gone all-out on this, Derresion,' I state, pleased. 'You've given me everything I'll need.'

'Almost. It has only short-range transmission capabilities,' Derresion apologizes. 'The long-range systems on the destroyed vessel were beyond salvage. Also, there is no planetary lift-off or landing capability—instead, I will lift you into space, and …'

'Stop, stop,' I interrupt, again. This Derresion fellow says the damnedest things! 'You'll lift me into space?'

Derresion regards me for a moment, then regards the ocean—which is himself, mind—behind him for another moment, and regards me again. 'My planet's atmosphere extends only sixteen kilometres before you can reach space suitable to create an Under dive portal. Sixteen kilometres is a meagre fraction of my total volume. I will lift you into space. If you want to land on a planet, you will need to find assistance when you get there, though.'

He stops for a moment, like he's considering something, before he asks, 'Toar, please tell me, is Oartheca safe? Are the Pryok'tel still there?'

'No, we kicked the triple-mouths out a long time ago; in fact, next year we'll be celebrating the two hundred and twenty-second anniversary of the day we won our home back,' I beam, proudly. 'Maybe you can come for a visit, and help celebrate with us?'

'No, I cannot leave this planet. The light of my sun is what sustains me—it is my energy source—my food if you will—and without its constant rays, I would soon perish.'

'Then we'll send a contingent of revellers over, and celebrate here with you, if you like,' I offer enthusiastically.

Derresion's face shifts to form an approximation of a mouth, stretched comically wide, trying to mimic me. 'Yes. I would like that very much.'

He falls silent, and I feel that our time together is nearing its end—*Orlin's Hope* is ready to go, and time is not on my side—I'm going to leave soon, and he's going to be all alone again. Given his chattiness, emotional reactions and his desire to help others, Derresion seems like a being who enjoys good company—and I wonder if Orlin's responsible for that. Most Oarth enjoy good company, save for our snowcoats but even then they'll seek it out if too much time passes—and the idea that Derresion is going to go back to being by himself makes me feel poorly.

'Look, may I ask you a question, Derresion?' I ask, and after he eagerly agrees, I do so, 'If I gave you a hug, if you wanted one … would that result in you learning how to mimic me, and my thoughts? I want to give you a hug but I'm not ready to share myself like that … that would be too personal for me.'

Derresion's whole body vibrates as he responds, and when he speaks, it's with tremendous excitement, 'Yes, you may hug me, and I will refrain from learning how to mimic you!'

Another part of Orlin coming through, I realize—a bit late I am ashamed to say—the need and desire for physical affection and comfort. Derresion has been thinking like an Oarth, fourteen million times over, for the past three hundred years now—with no-one to hug him, no-one to even touch at all. No-one here to comfort him after Orlin, his only friend—the only other person in his universe—had died. He's been alone ever since.

I immediately step forward and wrap my arms around his squishy form, which no longer seems alien to me in the slightest. He may be purple and made of alga, but Derresion is an Oarth, and has been for centuries. At my touch, all of Derresion ceases quivering, and he puts his arms around my back, his head resting on my shoulder, squeezing with a good strength to show how much this moment means to him. I hear him whispering, 'A gift, a gift, a gift', over and over.

When we part, Derresion invites me to take my seat inside the shuttle and explains what the next steps are going to be: once the hatch is closed, and seal integrity confirmed, he'll take me and *Orlin's Hope* into his ocean, then lift us upwards until we break atmosphere. He continues with demonstrating how the controls work—even if I were not already a pilot, the simplicity of the system is so straightforward I think a child could operate this craft.

'I will update the Under-drive's portal calculation system to automatically open a portal near to your Rowland's current location,' Derresion indicates. 'As soon as you reach free-space, the system should create the portal itself and dive you there.'

'Wait, if Rowland's shuttle is close to the Pryok'tel vessel, I don't want them to detect my breach-wave,' I remark. 'Although this ship is cleverly small, if I dive in too close, they'll see me coming, and I want to avoid that for as long as I can. Are you able to set the coordinates for the exit portal further back? Say, about a megametre? Should be enough for me to avoid detection if I coast in under my own inertia.'

'Yes, I can do that, but your Rowland's vessel is no longer close to the Pryok'tel vessel—the two are now one.'

'Then I'm running out of time,' I say, urgently. 'Derresion, it's time for us to put your hard work to good use. Let me get my things, and then I'd best get going.'

I hurry back inside the cave while Derresion updates the Under-drive's navigation system; I ransack the supplies Rowland left me, gathering my sabre, captain's hat, the coil-gun and one of the scanners, holstering or jamming these items on me as quickly as I can. My eyes fall on a box of the smaller blasting charges, and I take these too, along with their remote detonator—suspecting they'll come in handy once I find a way to board the vulture. As I near the bottom of one crate, my hand touches a smooth, curved surface, and I discover that Rowland's packed my spacesuit as well—including the helmet and under suit. This is a good turn of luck, even if it does mean I have to strip down to my tailcatch and suit up. I head back outside when I'm ready, where Derresion stands near the escape pod.

'I'm leaving you my signal beacon, Derresion—that blinking thing on that crate there,' I indicate, heading towards *Orlin's Hope*. 'It's programmed to send a signal in a few hours, to my friends on board the *Grolthon's Spear*—a frigate that should be turning up to help out here. If I've not come back to you before then, when the landing party from the *Grolthon's Spear* arrives, don't be afraid to talk to them—even if they're suncoats or nightcoats—we're all the same now. Just be like you've been with me; tell them you met me, where I've gone off too, and tell them I said you're to be trusted. Tell them about Orlin and how you want to help him get back home—they'll understand and know what to do.'

I board *Orlin's Hope*, settling into the reclined seat—Derresion's right, it's quite comfortable—with my hands naturally falling to the sides within easy reach of the touch panels. If I survive my upcoming adventure, I'm going to suggest to the OSS they have a nice chat with Derresion about interior ship design—he's got a knack for it and there's a lot of features here that, in all seriousness, I would love to see become a part of how we build ships. Maybe with Derresion having to consciously form his own body, he understands how bodies are best made comfortable? I don't know—it's a thought that I'll ponder when I get a moment.

'I wish you success, Toar, and hope that we will see each other again, one day if not soon. Please use *Orlin's Hope* to the best of his ability; I hope you rescue your baron, and are seen safely to better times.'

'Rowland's not my baron ...' I start.

'Rescue your baron, Toar,' Derresion interrupts, and that mimicked grin of his returns.

I look away, bashful suddenly, seeing the futility of arguing with the perception of an aeons-old super-being that can think fourteen million thoughts for every one of mine.

'Right, well, yes, that seems like the best plan. Better get on with it,' I reply, embarrassed.

'Once the hatch closes, the automated systems will come online. All you need do is relax; I will have you in orbit shortly thereafter, and you will be on your way.'

'One last question, Derresion, if I may? Did … did you have a hand in the malfunction of the Pryok'tel cruiser Orlin was on? I can't think why a ship like that would suddenly have a catastrophic incident right over your planet—it's very coincidental.'

'It was not coincidence, it was sabotage,' Derresion clarifies.

At my intrigued expression, Derresion explains. 'As I said, Orlin did not know all things, but what he did, he knew well—how to maintain and repair the vessel's biological resource reclamation system. He knew that he was to maintain its power relay connections, or else risk a surge occurring if the system encountered a sudden spike in power usage. He knew that if a surge did occur, it had to be vented away from the relay—or else there would be risk of overload. If that occurred, the overload would need to be directed elsewhere, to be safely absorbed across multiple non-critical systems. Certainly not redirected entirely to the propulsion system.'

I begin to chuckle, seeing where this is going, and I'm right as Derresion continues. 'The Pryok'tel are strict in enforcing routine—a routine that resulted in a shift change occurring at the exact same interval, every nine hours. When a shift change occurred, Orlin noted that the resource reclamation system experienced a dramatic increase in usage. So he timed the unit to purposefully malfunction at the moment of its highest power consumption peak. Since he knew when that moment was going to occur, he ensured that his duties took him near the escape pods at that time. All those escape pods were tied to the same power relay system, save for one, which Orlin disconnected.'

'And so when the malfunction happened, right after shift change when everyone needed to use the head …' I predict and am again correct.

'Yes. The resulting power-surge quickly caused a cascade reaction in the propulsion unit—causing a massive, and spectacularly explosive, ship-wide systems failure. Orlin's timing was very nearly miscalculated—he had only a few seconds to launch his escape pod before much of the vessel was destroyed.'

I laugh, perhaps inappropriately at the news of so many dying at once, but it is a wonderful turning of the tables that Orlin managed to blow up a ship by having a toilet flush, and such cleverness should be cheered. In our war against the Pryok'tel, their own arrogance is one of the chief weapons we use against them—they think we're stupid animals, and we're more than happy to maintain that illusion since it results in so many Pryok'tel being proven permanently, violently and deservedly wrong.

Derresion and I conclude our goodbyes, with him thanking me and wishing me well, hoping to see me again, and with me promising that I will when the first chance presents itself. I sort of rush this part, mainly because I'm feeling I've grown attached to my new, er ... purplecoat? *Dulian*coat? I'm stuck to think of a proper coat name for him—I'm hungry so all I can think of is purple food items, which is no good for a coat name—but regardless, I will miss my new friend, and look forward to seeing him one day, soon.

As I settle further in, Derresion gives me one more of his silly, but still sweet, smiles as he closes the hatch, and I hear an airtight seal being formed. There're no windows or anything like that for me to see out of, but the entire interior illuminates brightly, so I can see properly all around me. The inside of the hatch doubles as a display monitor, with camera views to the front, sides and back—Great Oarth, we need to get something like this for our starclaws—we're still relying on domed cockpits after all—and there's another display that's relaying information to me (all written in perfect Oarthecan, thank you very much again, Derresion) about what's going on.

Through these monitors, I can see a great wave of Derresion's ocean engulf me, and while the monitors indicate I'm moving, I don't feel the pull—it looks like *Orlin's Hope* has a solid set of inertia dampeners protecting me, and this helps tremendously as I can see that I've changed direction, and am quickly ascending into the skies, surrounded by Derresion's mass as he lifts me upwards.

I feel obligated to do something here, the pilot in me instinctually saying to check read-outs, adjust gauges, or fiddle with controls—push a button, at least—but there's nothing required; Derresion really built his ship so that anyone could be rescued, regardless of his space skills. If I wasn't so geared up to rescue Rowland, I'd probably wind up having a nap—the cockpit is quite comfortable after all, fitting me next to perfect and I'm reminded I'm well and truly past my regular bed-time.

I've a moment to myself to think on something Derresion mentioned, about what he'd be like if he'd not met Orlin. What if instead, it was a Pryok'tel who had managed to get in the escape pod? That thought is a cold one indeed—a massive, complex and exceptionally powerful super-being whose personality is a mimic of the Pryok'tel mind. How different my encounter with Derresion would have been if that was the case—me being dead as the most likely outcome, there.

What's more, I wonder if Derresion would cast his exceptional gaze across the universe not with a cautious, curious and compassionate eye, but a ceaselessly hungry one that cares for nothing but its own self. How different his universe, and consequently, the universe as a whole, would be. I avoid thinking too much more on this though, just thanking the Great and Eternal Oarth for the good fortune that allowed events to unfold the way they did.

Soon enough I've been lifted into the outer atmosphere, the dull red sky fading quickly into the starry blackness of space—it's only just a short way past this, where the gravity of the planet fades enough for portal formation to occur, that my monitors tell me that Derresion's ocean begins to recede, and *Orlin's Hope* is under his own power. Then there's the sound of what I hope are the primary power systems coming online, a deep thrum through the cockpit that's only moderately concerning, but then this noise is soon joined by the much richer and unmistakable tone of the Under-drive spooling—a sound I've heard hundreds of times before but never this close to my ears. Can't say I enjoy it, really, but there's nothing to be done for it.

One of the monitors off to the side of my main viewing screen indicates the coordinates for the portals to be opened—the exit one being about a million or so kilometres from the Pryok'tel vessel, as per my request. It will take me some time to fly there, but I assume that given the small mass involved with my dive, the exit portal will be too difficult for the Pryok'tel to detect from that distance—even if they're actively scanning for portals. I mean, I hope that's the case. Don't much care to put the shields to the test, unless there's no choice.

It doesn't take long before the entrance for my dive portal forms—it looks stable enough to me, and *Orlin's Hope* automatically starts to rev its propulsion. Just another dive, Toar, and not even a skip-dive at that, you'll be fine, you'll be fine, you'll be …

… fine, my thought concludes, as I breach out the other side safely. Test four, and still one hundred percent success rate—thank the Great Oarth for fourteen million brains getting it right so consistently. My velocity is still maxed out, so I enter the commands to cut main power, and just let my inertia carry me towards the vulture—given my relatively small size and the fact I'm not using any real power, it's possible they may not see me coming. With the Pryok'tel's fetish for preserving resources and being efficient down to the atom, I doubt they'll be scanning—there's just no reason to—but I'm not so sure as to start feeling anywhere near comfortable.

This gives me a chance to work on a plan, save for one somewhat significant point—I've lost sight of the reason I'm supposed to be here, which is to stop the Pryok'tel from escaping with the veil. I mean, I know in my head that's what I should be focusing on, but I'd be a liar as much as I am a fool if I said I didn't feel my priorities shifting to rescuing Rowland. The soldier in me tells me that can't happen—the veil is the only reason I came along. Except that it wasn't the reason, it was the excuse—and that's not allowed to be the case anymore. I promise myself that while I will make every effort to try and save Rowland, he cannot be …

He is that beautiful, though.

… he cannot be put before Oartheca; he himself said it—millions if not billions of lives at stake. Rowland's own plan was to destroy the vulture if he failed to take it over, and he wasn't optimistic about his chances of doing that. He knew what needed to be done.

Whatever my plan is, I've got just under half an hour to work it all out—and the first part is swearing an oath to do my duty: stop the Pryok'tel, then save Rowland. It needs to be that way, even if there's a very loud part of me that's fighting back. If I need to sacri … oh Great Oarth … sacrifice Rowland to stop the Pryok'tel, that's what's best—it's what he'd want as well. Because no-one that beautiful would put himself before others.

I just hope I'm as strong as he is beautiful.

I'll need to be.

CHAPTER 22

Rowland

Sometimes, I really don't like getting what I ask for.

As Suren'thos departs, Secundus Vay'auh-ta makes her way around from behind me, walking slowly at first, then turning to face me directly.

Yes, I get a moment or two of is-she-or-isn't-she, but it's not a terrible shock when it turns out she is. Yes, the orange hue of her skin, nearly the opposite to the blue shade I'm used to, causes a moment of doubt, but it's only a moment. The bob-cut hair, which I remember changing colours every other week, is missing now—there're the rows of small bone-white quills instead, resting flat against her skull. Her roundish cheeks are still there, though. The curve of her small nose. The dark, deep brown of her eyes. They're all there, still, even if the woman I remember as my little sister is technically not anymore.

The faint lines on the sides of her once small mouth are visible, as is the seam that extends from the centre of her lower lip to her throat: the tell-tale signs of her second and third mouths. And those dark eyes of hers, once full of laughter and bright wit, are cold and dead things now, looking at me with no more interest than one would pay to an empty wall.

She is my Mia, but she is not. Behold the power of genetic recombination, in all its wicked glory.

Yes, there're dozens of emotions wrestling in my brain—and the ones you'd expect, like betrayal, disappointment and heartache, are all making themselves heard, but there's one overriding them all. That's the one that gets to speak, and when it does, I find it's the one that best represents how I feel.

'I'm glad you're alive, Mia,' I say, simply. 'I was worried about you.'

She doesn't reply immediately. She just keeps looking at me with those dispassionate eyes—assessing me, I suppose, but I'm not sure what for. I couldn't be more thoroughly at her mercy than I am now. Finally, though, she turns and takes a step towards a nearby counter, and from a cabinet underneath, she removes a folded sheet, which she tucks around my middle section, so that I'm no longer openly dangling my goodies in front of her. She is efficient, and emotionless, as she does so, and she does not meet my eye as she finishes her task. It's only when she returns to her spot in front of me that she looks at me once more.

'The password for your Lerenthar account?' she asks, plainly.

'Mia, you …' I start, but she closes her eyes with a deliberately bored expression, before slowly opening them again.

'The password,' she repeats, with that same uninterested tone. She removes a touchpad from her belt, opposite the plasma pistol she's carrying, and holds her finger over it, awaiting my response. I give it to her, repeating the sixteen-character password, which she records dutifully. Silence as she enters additional commands, and then she returns her attention to me.

'It will take approximately seven hours to receive a reply from Lerenthar.

When we get the response that the funds have been transferred, the Oarth you purchased will be seen to, as Suren'thos agreed.'

'Enough. Look, just … be Mia, just … please, for a moment,' I request, exasperated. 'I know you're not. I know you're probably some high-level infiltration specialist who's the herald for the forthcoming Pryok'tel invasion of the CAPS. Or some other off-the-wall, double-crossing genetically recombobulated secret-agent-ninja working for the greater glory of god-I-don't-fucking-care-what. Just be Mia—just for a second—you fucking owe me that after all of this.'

For a moment, it looks like her boredom will get the better of us both, but instead, her eyes soften, her face brightens, and she tilts her head in that shy, sweet look she used to give us when she'd done something clever that wound up saving our asses.

'Why Captain Hale, you know I'd do anything for you. You only need ask, just the one time even!' she beams, and adds that little giggle at the end, for good measure.

I laugh, relieved and heartbroken at the same time. Silence between us again, as my thoughts battle in my head—one side wanting to rage at her, the other desperately sad for her.

'It must have been awful, for you, being away from your home, being among people who would …' I start, but she cuts me off cleanly.

'Captain Hale, your sentiment is wasted,' Mia—Secundus Vay'auh-ta—informs me. Her voice is flat, bored again, but not nasty. I get the impression we're having this conversation only because she's been told to, and she wants it to be over, now. 'I am a professional, and this was an assignment. There is no need for your emotions; better to save those for yourself. If you can take comfort from that, then do so.'

'Why us, then? The *Luck of the Draw*, specifically?' I ask, not hopeful she'll reply, but she surprises me.

'Victim of your own success, Captain. Primus Suren'thos mentioned it, I'm sure—you're a lucrative endeavour.'

'I find it hard to believe the Pryok'tel have taken up stake in bounty-hunting,' I scoff. 'Surely a galactic empire has better things to do than pick stray credits up off the pavement?'

'We do,' Vay'auh-ta replies. 'And if it were just you, you're correct, you would be beneath our notice. As would Cor, on his own. And Betts,'—I catch her use of our nicknames, by the way—'but the three of you together? Your continued success rate? Now that's slightly more attention-worthy. Add the prospects of recovering a fully functional VEILLED system, and well … here we are.'

'I wish I was flattered,' I reply. 'But there's far more lucrative opportunities in the galaxy than catching the bounty on a bunch of small-time crooks.'

Now she smiles, but it's not in triumph, it's more the smile a patient teacher reserves for the dullest student. 'It's not just the bounties, Captain. That's just the marrow in the bones. The veil is a sweet prize, for certain, but the real meat is learning how you did it all—every scheme, every plot, every little adventure and heist you managed. The learning opportunity you and your crew provided—how the CAPS's internal structures work, and even more valuably, how to bypass them. Well worth the effort.'

She turns from me now, to sit in the chair in front of the monitor reporting on my vitals, giving the information a closer examination. 'It appears you've recently benefited from some medical assistance. I take it you were injured in our initial attempt to neutralize *Lucky*?'

Another nickname. I wonder how much of my Mia remains in the woman I see, and whether there's a way I can bring her out to help me.

'Nothing that an auto-doc couldn't look after,' I reply. Given her captain's disdain for the Oarth, I'm not sure I want Vay'auh-ta knowing that it was Gren's services that saw me back to health. 'How is it you survived the attack? Weren't you on the derelict when your buddies showed up?'

'No,' she replies, still studying my read-outs. 'I deliberately sabotaged my spacesuit to make it appear that it had malfunctioned, and remained on board while Ivan proceeded to the derelict.'

I am quiet for a moment. 'You knew the attack was coming and you still let Ivan leave the ship?'

Her eyes slide over to me when she answers. 'I did ask him to help me sort out the problem, but you can likely guess my success at dissuading him. Something about receiving an extra share and a quarter,' she adds, benignly enough. 'The plan was for him to remain with me in the cargo bay, but there was no stopping him.'

'Well, except for telling him about the impending ambush.'

She nods and turns back to my read-outs. 'That may have worked, but it would have placed the operation in jeopardy. There was no choice but to leave him to his fate.'

I want to argue, but she's made it clear that's going to be a waste of time. 'Did he die as Suren'thos said?'

She hesitates before replying, but at least looks at me when she does. 'His explanation is one of the possibilities. Our doctors' knowledge of your bodies is not yet sufficient for absolute certainty. The autopsy did indicate Ivan died of massive cellular destabilization, but we cannot be certain how long it took, nor if he was conscious.'

'And you feel nothing about that?' I finally snap. 'You share six months of your life with that man, and you feel nothing that he's dead now? A fucking end-note in a report is all he was to you?'

'Do you want me to be Mia, again?' she asks, almost politely. 'I can keep that deception going for a while longer, I suppose. Or I can treat you like an adult and tell you the truth. Your choice.'

'You can stop pretending that the death of a person you knew for half a year means noth …'

'It does not mean anything to me, Captain,' Vay'auh-ta interjects, the patient teacher making a reappearance. 'Ivan's death does not mean anything to me, nor to any other Pryok'tel. You are not alive to us, Captain; none of you are. You are animate, you are sentient, but you are not alive. The best I can offer you is that Ivan Vasilyev's termination was a preventable loss of resources. Out of respect for the loss of his value, I will not pretend Ivan had meaning to me beyond that. He did not. You do not. None of you do. To the Pryok'tel, to me, you are a resource. A valuable one, but a resource still. Nothing more.'

'You people are insane,' I mutter, my frustration getting the better of me, 'and anyone who has the idea that someone other than themself has no value, is themself without value.'

'Yes,' Vay'auh-ta sneers, 'as though your species doesn't exhibit the exact same behaviour, just on a less efficient, less honest level. But I will not argue with you, Captain, it is a waste of what little time remains.'

'Then get on with it, Secundus. I was hoping that there was something of Mia left in you, but after three minutes of knowing you, I'm glad Mia died in the ambush as well. The thing that's wearing her face is an insult to her.'

Her first mouth turns slightly upward at one corner. 'Mia is alive and well, Captain. She will live again, after I've been debriefed and sent on to my next assignment. Granted, she will go by another name, but take comfort in knowing that Mia Ong survived the destruction of the *Luck of the Draw*—the sole survivor, I fear.'

I narrow my eyes. 'Suren'thos said that Betts and Cor would be turned in for their bounties.'

'And that was true. Unfortunately, we both know Cor's brood-mother will either execute him for his failures and the shame he brought to her name, or she'll turn him into a mindless thrall to guard her clutch until the end of his days. The Harculcorians are not known for mercy, and even less so when it comes to themselves. A foolish species, to waste such a resource for the worthless idea of "honour".'

I remain silent, because everything she's just said is true.

'And as for Betts, her injuries were severe, Captain,' Vay'auh-ta continues. 'Cranial impact and lacerations to her frontal lobe caused by a piece of shrapnel piercing eight centimetres into her skull, just above her left occipital bone. Without the attention of a CAPS medical professional of the highest calibre, I doubt she'll regain consciousness—and if she does, she won't be Betts. It's unlikely the agent offering her bounty will invest in her repairs. I would not.'

The news of Betts' condition takes another chunk of what little restraint I've got left—but I refuse to give Vay'auh-ta the smallest degree of satisfaction. She's also flat-out wrong—the CAPS-F is amongst the best medical practitioners in the galaxy, and I know full well that taking a piece of metal to the brain won't be that big a deal to fix—but it seems Vay'auh-ta doesn't know that. No need to share info—we're no longer friends.

'And me?' I ask, forcing myself to sound casual, but I've already guessed my fate, and she confirms it.

'I've just checked that the muzzle you're wearing hasn't damaged your core cybernetics, so you will be taken to Alconalc as planned. However, after you repair their manufacturing operations, I cannot see a way that they'll let you leave the planet alive. You cost them billions, Captain.'

'Oh I'm sure they'll find some way to extract every round-coin I've cost them,' I remark, but again, I can't argue with her. If I land on Alconalc, the chances of me spending the rest of my life in a concrete box with a strictly controlled wireless access point are basically guaranteed.

'You will look after Bryce though, right?' I check.

'Provided you turn over sufficient assets, yes. Dr. Winston's death was exactly as Suren'thos explained, if that is of value to you. A terrible waste, regardless— his value as a medical practitioner placed him in a high acquisition category— Suren'thos will be required to compensate the Hegemony directly for Bryce's loss.' She looks at me, and something in her demeanour changes—she seems less cold towards me with her next words, and her tone is respectful. 'That is the closest I can come to expressing condolences, Captain.'

I actually believe her; maybe because I want to, but there's something about the choosing of her words and how she spoke them that rings true. It's being made abundantly clear that Pryok'tel do not value life in the same way humans do, but I'm able to see that in the ways they do determine value, Bryce did matter to Vay'auh-ta. 'Thank you. I've got three rare-form Telro crystals—worth about nine thousand CAPS credits on the right market—will that be enough to send his body back to his parents on Titan?'

'Ample,' she remarks and makes another note on her pad. 'I will also include Ivan for that—my understanding of his death ritual was to vaporise his body by tossing it into the nearest star. Another waste, from my perspective, but it was what he wanted.'

'And what would you do with him, Vay'auh-ta? Eat him, I suppose?' I goad, cruelly.

'Yes; there's no higher way to honour him.'

I make a disgusted noise, but she continues. 'I do not understand you, Captain—of the humans I have been assigned to, you are by far the most generous in terms of cultural understanding and tolerance—to the point of foolishness on many occasions—and yet the honourable act of consuming the fallen, to ensure that their last contribution to this universe is one of value, remains repulsive to you. Why is that?'

I look at her incredulously. 'You're asking me the reason why I find eating people repulsive? As in, accepting the hunting down and murder of another sapient being for the purpose of eating them is … a matter of cultural tolerance?'

'I did not murder Ivan nor …'

'Don't try and wash your hands of this, Mia—their blood is all over them and no amount of mentally licking them clean is going to work. You set us up, you got them killed—doesn't matter if you didn't mean it, you got them killed. You may as well have been the one to snap Bryce's neck.'

'False,' Vay'auh-ta counters. 'You put them in danger more than I did. You tempted them, you cajoled them, you put them in our path. All of it was you, you were the Captain. You took the risk. You failed.'

The pain in my heart at these words silences any reply; they're echoes of exactly what I've been telling myself since the first shot hit *Lucky*. I know Vay'auh-ta is leveraging my weakness against me to win this argument—I'm sure she received my full psych eval along with whatever intelligence dossier on me she was provided for her assignment, let alone travelling with me for the past half year. Goddamn, her words hurt, and she knows it, but at least she has the decency not to rub it in.

I find that I need to swallow a couple of times before I can reply, and I switch back to a previous point she made, so that I can at least carry the conversation on without my voice cracking with grief.

'Humans … humans find cannibalism abhorrent,' I begin, patiently. 'I understand Pryok'tel evolved with no other choice but to eat each other, but that wasn't the case for us. It's disrespectful to the memory of the person when you treat their body as food. After six months with us, Mia, I'm sure you figured that out all on your own; not sure why you want me to explain it to you.'

'For the chance to explain that I do not share your views and hold the opposite ones instead. To me, the idea that Bryce and Ivan are to be discarded, to be prevented from becoming a part of my life, to provide me with sustenance that allows me to live and carry on, is a disgrace.'

I smirk. 'Careful, Mia. You're almost sounding like you do care.'

'That a valuable contribution to the succession of life is being tossed into the nearest star, or stuck in the ground to rot away? Seems to me you're the one that doesn't care.' There's a hint of fire in her voice now, the first one she's given since our conversation started.

I tilt my head to the side. 'Would you like to …' I stop, trying to find a way to make cannibalism sound positive. 'Take Bryce and Ivan into your life, like you said?'

Vay'auh-ta doesn't reply immediately. 'My orders were to secure additional funding from you in exchange for processing their remains.'

'That's not my question.'

She regards me with a sullen expression before she sneers, 'Yes. Yes, I want to honour them. They were valuable people and …' She stops, her eyes widening at the betrayal of her own dogma.

'I won't tell Suren'thos, Mia,' I reply, after giving her a moment to let her own admission sink in. 'I won't tell him that you've been compromised by your time with us. But I think we both know that this was your last mission. Can't go around sympathising with the enemy, after all.'

She turns her back quickly on me, but not before I catch her scowling face. With a little more time—just a bit more—I can swing her back over to my side.

'We're not enemies,' she remarks, still facing away from me. 'We're trying to prevent a war.'

I frown in confusion, but she continues before I can get a better understanding of what she's trying to tell me.

'The Pryok'tel are not the CAPS's enemies. Not yet, at least, but we both know that's going to change, if both sides remain on their current course. Our borders are too close. Our people, too different. Our estimates predict when war breaks out, it shall last centuries, with the Hegemony winning what would at best be a pyrrhic victory.'

She turns to face me again, her eyes now alive with passion. 'We Pryok'tel value life, Captain Rowland—whereas your people have no concept of what life even is. My actions here are to save my people, so even if I am compromised, as you need to pretend, I will still serve them. That's the real difference between us, so much more than our diets. I do what I do to save lives. You do what you do to line your pockets.'

Another devastating blow to my heart, but I'm still winning, I think. A pyrrhic victory indeed.

'How are you saving lives, then, Mia? Help me understand,' I ask, genuinely.

She paces the room for a few moments before replying. 'Capturing the veil. The CAPS are using VEILEDD technology to undermine our borders, to spy on us and send aid to our enemies. Tear our Hegemony apart, bit by bit, from the inside. If we can find a way to break that veil, we can re-secure our borders, stop the incursions, and ensure we're not brought into a conflict that will destroy billions.'

'And not use the veil for your own invasion, right?' I remark, dryly.

She waves her hand dismissively at me. 'Stop being stupid. You think the CAPS built a veil that they themselves cannot pierce? There's a way to break it and thanks to you, we'll find it. Take comfort in knowing we are not the aggressors here, Captain. By nullifying the veil, the onset of war could be delayed long enough that a diplomatic solution can take place.'

My eyebrows lift and I'm unable to stop a laugh from escaping. 'Diplomacy? Now who's being stupid? Hate to burst your bubble Mia but in case you missed it, you Pryok'tel are despised from one end of the known systems to the other— I mean in some languages the very word Pryok'tel is considered an insult. Can't really see people changing their minds about a war simply because you figure out how to break the veil.'

Vay'auh-ta shakes her head and gives me a tired look. 'Piercing the veil is one of hundreds of steps we're taking to ensure we prevail. We can see that your CAPS is keen to keep their aggression contained to the shadows; open warfare with us would risk fragmenting your political structure, and so any decent peace treaty we offer will be gladly accepted.'

'And then what? What's the end game?'

'We wait you out. The CAPS is doomed to failure, you know that as much as I do. Too many differences, not enough resources, too much distrust. You are not Pryok'tel; the CAPS is foolishly wasteful, embarrassingly gluttonous, and terminally short-sighted. It's a matter of time before you collapse. We are patient.'

243

Her words are a direct reflection of my own ideology; the CAPS is corrupt, it is weak, and it's not going to last—not without a major overhaul so that it starts living up to its own ideals of fairness and prosperity for all, instead of those in power. That's one of the reasons I left the CAPS—it's all a charade, and not a very deep one at that—a case of the emperor's new clothes on a galactic scale.

'Well, if it's peace you're after, why not turn us over directly to the CAPS instead? Nothing says "let's be friends" more than handing over a mutual enemy.'

Her lips tighten. 'That was one of the scenarios discussed, Captain. It was discarded by a resource recuperation assessment. I do not agree with that assessment, but that does not change that I am bound by it. Your capture was expensive, and that cost must be recovered. There's no alternative.'

'Now who's being short-sighted?' I retort, but she doesn't acknowledge my comeback. 'At least, at least get Betts to the CAPS, Mia …'

Vay'auh-ta shakes her head, firmly. 'I have no authority to negotiate with you on that. None. The assessment has been made; not even Suren'thos can break it. Unless you tell me what your plan is.'

I give her a confused look, but Vay'auh-ta just rolls her eyes. 'Captain, I've worked side-by-side with you for half a year. You scheme with a recursive level of contingency—you have backup plans within backup plans. And yet, you walked off that shuttle with both your hands in the air, easy as you please. Suren'thos accepted your surrender because he's just arrogant and ignorant enough not to see you as a threat. Me? Not so much.'

She steps towards me now, smiling sweetly, batting her eyelids at me. 'Let's stop pretending that you've got nothing up your sleeve, and you tell me how you plan to get out of this. Nothing is ever straightforward with you.'

'In case you're not paying attention, Mia, there's nothing up my sleeves—you've taken the shirt I was wearing, literally,' I remark, trying to sound nonchalant, which is difficult because Mia is absolutely correct, I do have things up my sleeves—in the metaphoric sense—let's hope whatever lie-detector technology the Pryok'tel use gets fooled by allegory.

'I have been paying attention, and I think it has something to do with this useless conversation you've dragged me into,' Vay'auh-ta retorts. 'You're stalling for time, waiting for something. Please tell me it has nothing to do with the Oarth, does it? We both know you're not the type to jettison innocent 'people' out of an airlock, especially ones who would have been so infatuated with you.'

'I'm here on my own,' I state, firmly. This is an easy truth.

She looks back and forth between my eyes, trying to see if I'll break under her scrutiny. I will not. I cannot.

'I'd avoid them, the Oarth, if I were you, Captain,' she warns me. 'They're filthy, degenerate things. Animals, really. You saw that red-furred beast—he would have torn you up if he had escaped his restraints.'

'He was starved, scared and abused, Mia. I'd have ripped my own arm off if it meant I could get away from whatever hell you're putting him through.'

Her eyes keep scanning mine. 'You've always had a soft spot for broken things—it's your greatest weakness. It's why the Mia Ong personality was crafted just for you—a poor refugee, lost, left alone—we knew you couldn't resist. Don't let that same weakness cloud your judgement regarding the Oarth; they're violent, dangerous savages and the galaxy is better off without them.'

'Funny, they have the exact same opinion of you,' I reply, smiling helpfully.

She shrugs. 'We can be reasoned with, if there's sufficient worth in doing so. Like now for example—tell me what you've got planned, and I'll arrange to get Betts back to the CAPS-F. Otherwise, I'm going to have to take advantage of that weakness of yours.'

'Mia, I've got nothing up my sleeve,' I reply, hoping my tricky words keep working on the lie-detector. I doubt they will—even I can tell that the threat of getting caught is causing my stress levels to mount.

Vay'auh-ta continues shifting her gaze back and forth between my eyes. 'You're lying,' she concludes, and then returns to the monitor snitching on my stress responses. 'I see a demonstration of my intentions is required.'

'No, wait,' I back-pedal, trying to figure out something to say that will satisfy her but not jeopardize my last hopes.

'You're wasting my time, and that's an insult no Pryok'tel will suffer.'

I brace for whatever torture is about to come my way: electric shocks through the restraints on my wrists and ankles immediately come to mind, but I also wonder if those scanning beams that initially assessed me have a 'cook' setting too. Maybe she'll bring back the Oarth, make him suffer in front of me, and at that thought, I can feel my own heart speed up in my chest.

Instead, she only enters some commands on her terminal, and then from above me, another display monitor descends on a mechanical arm, to rest about a metre in front of me. It will be the torture of the Oarth, broadcast from some location where my voice cannot comfort him, that she'll use against me. I don't know if I will be able to withstand that, but I will have to—if I crack, it's all over for all of us anyway. Vay'auh-ta is right, I am stalling for time, but there's no way enough has elapsed for even the smallest part of my last-second, hail-Mary, cobbled-together-with-dreams-and-wishes plan to succeed.

But instead of a live-feed image being presented to me, all I see is a command line, the cursor patiently awaiting instructions. Vay'auh-ta begins entering the commands on her terminal, and a string of glyphs appears.

'I'm going to display the current Resource Storage inventory, filtered to show only active sapient biological assets,' Vay'auh-ta explains, and a list of about twenty rows displays. 'Now, let's just translate this to CAPS Standard ... and, here we are.'

There're no names, but I do see designations, one of which is a series of numbers and letters that ends with a hyphen suffix of 114-C2. There are additional characters in other columns for this row, but I can't figure out their identification system—however, there's enough commonality with other rows for me to deduce that there are other Oarth currently in stasis, and possibly other species as well. As I'm scanning the list, the rows for 114-C2, and two others, ending in 195-A1 and 089-B3 are highlighted on the screen.

'Your Oarth friend, Betts and Cor,' Vay'auh-ta explains, seeing my peering expression. 'Currently all safe in hypno-stasis, along with eighteen other assets. Tell me your plan, or I will have the computer randomly choose one of these assets and terminate it.'

I know she will, but I've got to try something to steer her off this path. 'I doubt your Hegemony will appreciate you killing off their resources, Mia, seems … wasteful.'

She enters some commands on her terminal, and a row gets updated, the single character value in the far right of the field changing from a one to a zero. It's not one of the highlighted rows; it was two above Betts' row though.

'Oarth. Deep mine labourer, forty-nine years of age, noted for his endurance—stormcoat too—shame; they're quite valuable,' Vay'auh-ta starts, and then looks me dead in the eyes. 'Resource terminated.'

Her eyes don't leave mine. She's telling the truth, and I know it. A stormcoat. That could have been Toar; it would have been, had he been with me. My stomach hitches at this thought, and I fight to suppress the urge to vomit, gagging a couple of times.

'Care to try again? 114E-1's death was painless captain—I had the system overload his neural energy, so he died instantly, under stasis, never feeling a thing. The next one will not be as fortunate. They'll be awake, and I will make it slow. You still have a seventeen in twenty chance of it not being someone you know though, so, maybe your luck will hold for another round?'

'The missiles,' I mumble, trying to fight back another stomach heave. I can't look at her. Her coldness, her utter coldness. Mia … Mia was never here. I've been played, and now someone is dead. That poor man.

'Go on,' Vay'auh-ta encourages, calmly.

'The ones that Suren'thos made me jettison prior to coming within range of your ship. I've programmed them to fire as soon as they detect your Under-drive spooling,' I admit, painfully. 'Your shields will be down in order to open the portal, and there's enough to disable you completely. You won't be able to stop them all in time, they'll blow your drive and you'll be stuck here.'

Her brows arch. 'And then …?'

I sigh, heavily. 'The Oarth. I've been working with them, and they've dispatched a frigate—more than enough of a match for a vulture, let alone a disabled one. If you turn me, my family and the veil over to them, I'll convince them to let you escape with your lives.'

'And you will convince them of this how, exactly?'

I give her an exasperated look. 'They won't risk letting me be harmed. Even without the Allure, I've got enough pull with them to make them listen. You'd only need to pretend to risk my life, and that'd be enough.'

She nods and is quiet as she contemplates my words. 'When do the Oarth arrive?'

'Not sure. Few hours, at a minimum. Likely more.'

She returns to her monitor, the read-outs no doubt verifying my words. 'I see. Well, Captain Rowland, you do not disappoint, I will give you that. Clever, though ultimately futile. We have no fear of the Oarth.' She enters some commands on her terminal, and two more rows in the display in front of me highlight.

'See there? We have our own barons. The Oarth would have let us depart with you, the veil, and the rest of the Oarth in exchange for even one of them. Your plan was going to fail, even if I hadn't forced it out of you,' but she doesn't sound happy about it. She almost sounds sympathetic. 'You've lost, I'm ...'

There's a distant booming noise, and we both turn in the direction it came from. Another boom, closer to us, quickly follows. Vay'auh-ta regards me with a questioning expression, but I just shrug, baffled. The missiles were only supposed to go off when the Under-drive was spooled, and I would have heard that. Whatever is happening now has nothing to do with me.

A third boom goes off, much closer and very loud, and the room shakes violently, the power going out and plunging us into darkness. For me, the plunge has a more literal effect, as the restraints holding me to the examination table blink out for a moment, dropping me to the ground before they can re-establish themselves.

When the emergency lights kick in, I've leapt in Vay'auh-ta's direction, and with the last moment possible left to spare I manage to knock her drawn plasma pistol from her hand, following up as fast as I can with a solid punch to her face. She moves her head back in time so that my knuckles just graze her chin, but my momentum carries me forward so that I crash into her, pinning her to the wall. Her knee comes up between my legs and I've got enough sense in me to close my thighs before my lower bells are rung, but her distraction works long enough for me to forget to cover my face, where the long nails of one of her free hands rake my eyes, forcing me back in pain.

I do hate being right sometimes, as I've said: turns out that Vay'auh-ta really is a secret-agent-ninja, because the elbow she drives into my sternum hits me with enough precision, speed and force to topple me backwards, winding me terribly, giving her a chance to look for her pistol. She spots it a split second before I do, and again I'm left to grab for her as she dives towards it. I'm able to catch her by one of her arms, and this time, I'm prepared for her counter-attack, blocking first another strike to my face, then moving my foot just out of the way to avoid a crushing heel strike from her boot.

We're in it now, facing off against each other. My hand-to-hand training is amateur at best, and rusty as fuck, but I've got mass on my side and the ever powerful need to stop her or else I'm dead. My main problem is that I don't want to hurt Vay'auh-ta—just overpower her, incapacitate her—and she knows that. Vay'auh-ta has training, patience, and doesn't appear to be suffering from any hang-ups about me being her former captain, either—she's not pulling her punches, and she'll quickly win this fight if I'm sloppy.

Her strikes are fast and precise, and I'm on the defensive in a matter of moments. My blows are brutish and clumsy, but I'll only need one of them to land properly and that will end this fight without hurting her too badly. Easier said than done though, as she dodges with skill and grace—but I'm forcing her away from the pistol, backing her into a corner, where her agility will be hampered and my size will gain the advantage.

Vay'auh-ta knows this, and so her assault is focused on my soft bits—eyes, throat, armpits, groin, and I'm doing my best to keep her at bay, but she lands a couple of solid whacks and I'm having to favour defence over offence. I've got a feeling one of our lucks is going to run out, and I damn well hope it's hers.

She's finally forced back far enough where I'm able to overwhelm her with my bulk, taking a glancing knee strike too close to my testicles in the process, making me see stars in the corner of my vision, but I get her in a solid bear hug, pinning her arms, and slam her hard into the back wall, her head making a satisfying thud that must be causing her own stars to form. I lean back, preparing for another slam against the bulkhead, and this is where I completely fuck up.

It's the banshee's shriek that startles me, but that's soon replaced by utter terror as Vay'auh-ta unleashes her warmouth. A giant, red, gaping hole filled with needle sharp teeth, a handsbreadth from my face, and wider than my entire head. I can see the back of her throat vibrating with the force of her wail, I can see the saliva forming, getting ready for her next meal. My face. She is going to bite my face off!

I drop her and stagger back—I'm not ashamed to say that I'm truly terrified; between her wild, blazing eyes, that relentless, piercing scream and the hundred or so little daggers lining the blood-red cavern of her splayed mouth, it's like nothing I've ever seen before—a horror monster come to life, right in front of me.

I'm not really paying attention to how she manages to knock me down—I think it's a kick that catches me on the side of my head, sending me to the floor in a heavy whump, which is then quickly followed up by her foot connecting solidly with my face. All I can see is stars now, stars and a bottomless mouth with endless teeth.

I think she steps over me, I'm too dazed to really figure out what she's doing, but I see her casually stoop to pick up the pistol as she closes her deadly mouth. She returns to the monitor station and enters some commands—but I make out that there's no power, since the monitor that was listing their Resource Storage is black.

Vay'auh-ta regards me coldly as she levels her pistol at me, moving towards the door, which slides open to reveal the inky shadows of the hallway now barely lit with emergency lighting. My vision is getting blurry though; her boot to my face has left me dazed and fighting for consciousness.

'If you move from that spot, I will kill you, Rowland. Stay here and—*hrk*—'

It's the sabre that sprouts from the centre of her chest that cuts her final words off. Vay'auh-ta manages to look down, a puzzled, pained expression on her face, now illuminated by a thin blue line of bright plasma between twin blades, as she tries to figure out what's happened, but she's dead on her heart's next, and last, beat.

CHAPTER 23

Toar

Half an hour isn't much time to come up with a plan, when the pressure's on.

I reckon my best bet's to try and use *Blue Boy* as the main way into the Pryok'tel vulture—from what Derresion told me, I'm assuming that *Blue Boy*'s been docked with the vulture via a connection bridge.

If this turns out to be the case, there's a chance I could land *Orlin's Hope* directly in *Blue Boy*'s storage area—Derresion's little craft's only slightly bigger than a normal single-occupant escape pod, after all—then see if I can board the vulture via the tethered bridge. Lots of 'ifs and buts' with this plan, mind you—may need to scrap the whole idea depending on the situation when I get there, and even then, once I've boarded the vulture, I'm not particularly keen on my chances of taking on the entire crew while I try to find Rowland …

I mean, while I look for a way to disable their Under-drive. It's shocking how easily I'm allowing myself to centre this mission on Rowland—I do understand how stupidly selfish that is, but that's how the Allure works—putting your baron first, at all costs. I'm fighting Oarth evolution at every turn, and I fear I'm my own worst enemy. Well, other than the triple-mouths. I'm not *that* muddled.

One thing in my favour is my experience with those needle-mouthed ghouls, which includes a solid understanding of their combat strengths and weaknesses. Outside of their arrogance, ignorance and phenomenally foul breath, the Pryok'tel's greatest disadvantage is that they're very poor at thinking outside of the box, being so bound by the need to be efficient that they're predictable and don't adjust well to the unexpected. They are exceptionally talented warriors, true—I can't fault them there, their competence is enviable, and I'd be the arrogant one if I pretended otherwise—but only so long as you play by the rules. Change things up, come at them from different angles, and they're slow to adapt.

If I could surprise them, throw them off-balance, then there might be a way to reach their Under-drive and disable it—there's no shielding that would stop these mining charges from reducing it to ruin. The problem then becomes getting there and back, all while trying to avoid at least fifty Pryok'tel.

One thing not going for me is my size; no-one's ever mistaken me for the sneaky type. Stealth is better suited for our littler suncoats, and nightcoats do have a natural advantage with their coat colour, but us stormcoats don't make good spies at all (our strength lies in seafaring)—meaning I'm likely going to have to fight my way through the decks. The combat part doesn't worry me, I mean so long as the Pryok'tel keep their plasma weapons holstered. That's asking a lot. In a tight squeeze, such as the interior corridors of your typical vulture, I'm quite the easy unarmoured target.

So I need to work out a way to create enough of a diversion to get to Row … och! … to the Under-drive, disable it, then find Rowland, return to *Orlin's Hope*, then dive back to the *Claw*—all without a single shot from the Pryok'tel taking either my fat backside out—or worse, hitting Rowland—in the process. It'll be a challenge, looks like. Maybe if I attack at chow time? I'm desperate enough to think that might actually work.

Too soon I'm within range of the vulture, and I'm glad to see the first part of my plan's already in place—*Blue Boy* is indeed tethered to their docking port. So far, it doesn't appear they've noticed me, so I risk sending power to my engines, reducing speed so that I can assess the situation properly. There's no response from the vulture as my engines power, thank the Eternal, and I'm able to get a good look.

First thing is to check if *Blue Boy* is still an option, so using some of the new comm range frequencies that Murth installed, ones that the Pryok'tel don't typically scan for, I send a hail. The response comes immediately as that little electric chirp followed by that odd voice Rowland gave him.

'Hello, Administrator Toar, your hail is acknowledged. How may I help you?' I've got to admit, hearing that robo-voice is quite satisfying now, despite my vague dislike of it before.

'Where's Rowland?' I immediately ask. Priorities be damned after all.

'Administrator Rowland is currently on board the Pryok'tel vessel, Deck B, Asset Processing Room Four.'

I raise my eyebrows. That's … an awfully specific location. Last time I checked, we didn't have the interior layouts for these new vultures in our tactical databanks. 'How do you know that?'

'Interior schematics obtained with internal sensor array recalibration completion. Active monitoring of Administrator Rowland continues. Result: based on available information, Administrator Rowland is currently located on Deck B, Asset Processing Room Four.'

Ho-ho! *Blue Boy*'s taken over the vulture's internal sensors, if my robo-speak is any good. This changes everything!

'What other recalibrations have you done then? Why are you recalibrating the vulture?'

There's a short delay, and I'm forced to remember that my shuttle only sounds like a man—it doesn't think like one and I may have overwhelmed him by asking two questions at once. I'm about to repeat my first question, but *Blue Boy* responds.

'Recalibration progress report: fifteen-point-six percent complete. Mission parameters: recalibrate all Pryok'tel vessel components and overwrite existing operating system. Disable current permission matrix and set Administrator Rowland as exclusive main user. WARNING!'

I wince at the volume *Blue Boy* uses for whatever he needs to say next.

'Current mission parameters in jeopardy. Estimated time to Pryok'tel Under-drive availability: fifty-two minutes. Estimated time to Under-drive recalibration: six hours forty-seven minutes. Probability of success to recalibrate Under-drive before activation: zero percent.'

'I see,' I reply, grimly. Rowland told me he was going to try to take over the vulture, but from what *Blue Boy*'s explaining, there won't be enough time for that to work before it dives.

'What can I do to help?' I don't know if our shuttle is clever enough to work that out, so I'm also trying to come up with a way, but *Blue Boy* replies almost immediately.

'Proceed to exterior hull location four-two; disable access port nine, arrive at destination: Deck C, section five. Proceed to Server Room Three: disable secondary computer processing unit, designation C-9. Proceed to Deck B: disable primary power relays, sections three, four and six. Obtain additional recalibration processor: Administrator Rowland, located on Deck B, Asset Processing Room Four. Return to Shuttle A, designation "*Blue Boy*". Designate Administrator Rowland: primary recalibration processor.'

That was *very* specific, but a better testament to 'easier said than done' I cannot think of. Ambitious little fellow, our *Blue Boy* is.

'Look, *Blue Boy*, I can get to the access port and open the hatch, but the moment I do, I'll get swarmed by Pryok'tel ...'

'Incorrect assessment detected. Counter assessment: Internal sensors have been recalibrated. Active monitoring of access port nine: disabled. Active monitoring of depressurisation detection: disabled. Active monitoring of secure ...'

'Disabled, got it. You've blinded them, and they won't know I've opened the door and invited myself in. I'm going to also assume the Pryok'tel won't be able to monitor me walking through the halls, not unless they use their own eyes, right?'

'Hypothesis assessment complete: correct. WARNING:'

I wince again and this time I do order, 'Not so loud, please!'

'<warning>:' *Blue Boy* stage-whispers. 'Pryok'tel personnel active on Deck C, sections one, two, three, four ...'

'Yes, there's lots of them, I'll need to fight my way through.'

'Recommendation: Administrator Toar avoids engaging Pryok'tel to prevent high probability of injury or death occurring.'

I tilt my head: I'm not sure if there was real sentiment behind *Blue Boy*'s last statement—he's a shuttle after all—but he did sound concerned. Rowland mentioned he'd given our shuttle the ability to learn things on its own—and while that did not sit well with me at the time, it looks like that's coming in very handy at the moment—but I wonder if *Blue Boy*'s gone rogue and taught himself how to feel. That ... that's a worry for another day.

'Right, well, I'm going to need you to be my eyes and ears on this, *Blue Boy*. Link up to the comms channel in my suit and keep a watch on me. Let me know—quietly, mind you—if it looks like I'm in trouble of running into Pryok'tel while I'm making my way through the ship.'

'Confirmed.'

'And keep me updated if Rowland moves from his current location, or if something that's out of the ordinary—outside of what we've planned or expect—occurs.'

Now there's a longer pause, and I wonder if I've been too vague—Rowland would be so much better at this—but *Blue Boy* eventually replies, 'Confirmed.'

'And keep your recalibration mission ongoing.'

'Confirmed.'

'And …' I pause, swallowing against the ramifications of my next necessary order, 'and if I give you the command to do so, or Rowland does, or you see both of our life signs, uh, stop … then I want you to detach from your mooring, proceed directly to the vulture's Under-drive, and collide with it at maximum possible speed, timing an overload of your laser banks at the moment of impact.'

Another lengthy pause.

'Because if …'

'Confirmed.'

Oh, I am nervous now. My shuttle hesitated at being ordered to take out the Under-drive—I felt that—there's no mistaking he was making up whatever mess of circuits and wires comprise his mind. I wish I could say that I was proud *Blue Boy* made the right decision, but the thought that he made a decision at all is not sitting well with me. I swear I was not a technophobe before today, but then again, I never met a quasi-sentient mining shuttle before today either. Between him, Rowland and Derresion, today's been quite the day for meeting all sorts of incredible new people—my log entry tonight is going to be an epic.

*****

Never liked zero-g.

Being in the OSS for over half a century, I'd have thought that taking space-walks would be easier these days—but I suppose that all my time amongst the stars has instead instilled in me a powerful respect for its sheer infinite size. Being outside of a spacecraft, with only the thin layer of my spacesuit and the little glass bubble to see out of, reminds me that I'm one tiny speck in a limitless void. One misstep, one slip or loose grip, and I'll be lost to that void, forever.

Hoping to avoid that, I've programmed *Orlin's Hope* to respond to my comm signal, and home in if something does go wrong. Nonetheless, I've had to override his safety procedures and pop the hatch, ten metres or so from the vulture's hull section four-two. I can see the access port I'm to use directly in front of me and give thanks that the Pryok'tel don't instal transparent panelling along their hull—otherwise, they'd be in for an exciting show.

Have to make the leap from my little escape pod to the port hatch, which means I'm about to experience free-falling through space, without a tether, for about ten seconds. Compared to today's other activities, it's somewhat on the simple side, but nonetheless I'm having to dig deep into my courage reserves. I've magnetised my gloves and my boots, so I should 'stick' when I reach the vulture, but I could still bounce off if I hit too hard. My jump must have just the right amount of strength.

Whispering a prayer and then holding my breath, I focus on the destination hatch, and then … I'm out of the escape pod, floating, drifting towards my destination. I've done a good job on the leap, am proud to say—I've cleared the escape pod properly, but my pride falters as my flight is faster than I planned. I refuse to look at anything other than the hatch I'm rushing towards, especially not a quick look over my shoulder to that infinite black void that's waiting for me if I fail.

My hands are the first to hit the hull, and I feel the gentle but quite sufficient pull of my magnetized gloves making contact, quickly followed by my boots. There's only a slight rocky moment when my inertia gets transferred along my arms, but I do come to a stop quickly enough. Now I look back, seeing *Orlin's Hope* with his hatch wide open, and realise the distance was further than I thought—I reckon the size of the vulture messed up my depth perception—but that's fine. I'm here.

'Toar to *Blue Boy*,' I signal over my suit's internal comms system. 'I'm at the hull. Do the Pryok'tel know I'm here?'

'Negative. Impact detection signal suppressed. Proceed to access hatch nine.'

'Right, proceeding.' I make slow hand-over-hand, foot-over-foot motions as I crawl across the vulture's hull, but my aim was good so it's only a few moments before I'm at the target access port.

'Attempting access,' I advise, and then draw my sabre, powering it on. One quick clip from the plasma blade severs the casing for the hatch's manual override control, and then my hand is on the big red handle that will pop the hatch. Here goes nothing …

I half expect the vulture to light up with alarms as I push the handle downwards, but there's nothing other than the pressure chamber on the other side—and that doesn't even light up, which it's supposed to do when the hatch is opened.

'Access to hatch nine detected: signal suppressed. Proceed to pressurisation chamber and signal for re-pressurisation protocols when ready.'

Seems I'm better at sneaking with an entire shuttle's worth of AI looking out for me. I scoot inside as quickly as I'm able, then re-seal the hatch.

'Hatch secured, *Blue Boy*. Okay for re-pressurisation.'

There's a hiss as air rushes back into the chamber, and I feel the vulture's artificial gravity kick in—Pryok'tel use a lower gravity than we do, but I'm more than accustomed to it—I think this is the sixth Pryok'tel vessel I've boarded? The seventh? Well, the first one in fifteen years—let's hope I remember how things are supposed to go.

'Re-pressurisation complete. Proceed five metres to junction twelve, rotate ninety degrees, and proceed six metres to Server Room Three. <warning>:,' *Blue Boy* dramatically whispers, and I roll my eyes. 'Pryok'tel crew members detected in Sections One and Two. Recommendation: Administrator Toar avoids detection.'

'Thanks, *Blue Boy*, I'll try my best. Proceeding.' I remove my helmet and clip it to my belt, then demagnetise my boots and gloves—don't want to be hampered by sticking unnecessarily.

I step out into the familiar hallways of a Pryok'tel vessel. Much like their fighting skills, I cannot begrudge them their cleanliness and order—it's one of the few things we now try to live by as well, though our ships are never so barren and hollow-looking. We like our comforts, and our colours and trappings, so our ships, the ones we've built ourselves at least, and not recovered like the *Lurcaster's Claw*, are much cosier than this sterile, unimaginative, 'efficient' style the needle-mouths favour. We also build bigger hallways, while I'm comparing things—a snowcoat would have to hunker down to make it through this ship, and I'm feeling the cramped confines creep in on me.

I pick my way carefully through the halls, scanning for Pryok'tel constantly, my sabre drawn and ready. Wish I could smell—be quite useful now, but I'm wearing the patch Gren gave me—Pryok'tel have a *very* distinctive whiffiness that lingers. In all honesty, it's not a bad smell in and of itself—sort of citrusy like with a faint hint of bitter bromine, and whenever I smell it I know there's going to be a fight—but it's strong on them and terribly useful when trying to keep track of where they're going, where they are, and where they've been. I'm keeping my coil-gun holstered for the time being—one shot will draw the entire deck right to me, so if I'm to fight, I'd prefer the clean silence of my sabre and a free hand to smash skulls.

Which it turns out, there happens to be, sooner than I'd like. I've just made the ninety-degree turn towards my goal when a Pryok'tel crewman exits from a room to my left; he's looking down at his touchpad, doesn't know I'm even there, but he will in the next second. When my powered sabre lashes out in a tight arc, it catches him under his left arm and exits out his right shoulder, hewing him cleanly—he doesn't even get a squeak of protest out.

Based on his insignia, this unlucky fool was a *substratus*, the lowest-ranking personnel in the Pryok'tel chain of command, and one who likely never saw combat—except for today, briefly, mind. I take neither pride nor shame in cutting him down: all Pryok'tel are my enemies, and my only concern for this former corpse-thief is that his body is not spotted by his friends, who may decide to report his death prior to having a snack. I immediately push the body into the room, following along to check if there's any other Pryok'tel that need looking after; there isn't.

'*Blue Boy*,' I whisper into my suit's comm system. 'I've just taken out a Pryok'tel; any change to the rest of the crew's behaviour? Was I detected?'

'Analysis complete: No change to crew behaviour detected. Recommendation: continue to Server Room Three.'

'Are there any Pryok'tel there, or near in adjacent rooms?'

'There are no life-signs detected in Server Room Three. There are two life-signs detected in the adjacent room. Recommendation: repeat Pryok'tel neutralisation procedures before entering Server Room Three. <warning>: Combat procedures required.'

'I'll be fine, *Blue Boy*, don't worry. Just keep me updated on other Pryok'tel movements.'

I scan the room I'm in—it looks like a records processing room—a simple terminal on a desk, with a simple seat, and a few wall-mounted cabinets most likely containing servers. I stuff the corpse of the crewman under the desk, shoving him hard so he'll fit properly and be out of direct line of sight from the doorway, and then return to the hallway.

I'm not sure if taking out the two Pryok'tel is a good idea: one missing crewman creates a risk of someone asking where he is, and so three missing crewmen triple those odds. Plus, while I am fast, any skirmish risks drawing attention, and me getting shot—Pryok'tel put up a good fight, as I've mentioned—even that recordkeeper I cut down probably would have made for a decent round or two, had he been looking where he was going.

I make the decision and creep as quickly as my newfound stealth abilities allow me, directly to Server Room Three, helpfully marked in Pryok'telish right above its door. It's then that my eyes catch the display panel beside the door, indicating it's currently locked. I'm about to signal *Blue Boy* for help, but he's already on it, it seems, because the door suddenly opens. In I go, on the hunt for the computer in question.

Secondary computer processing unit C-9, also clearly marked, is a tall white box of blinking lights and humming power, with a small monitor in front with a tiny black touchpad interface underneath. According to what I'm reading on that monitor, there appears to be an electronic battle going on—there're frequent lines of commands flashing by, which are attempting to execute specific instructions, which are refused, which are then counter-refused, back and forth and so on. Every once in a while, I see one of the instruction lines get answered with a 'Completed' response, but they're very few and far between—most of the replies are 'Request denied' or 'Insufficient privilege' or 'Failed to connect'. I even see one that says 'Permission revoked', all in red—and that's never a good response from a computer.

'How do I disable this thing, *Blue Boy*?' I ask. 'I'm no good at that hacking stuff, like you are.'

His instructions are wonderfully clear, 'Insert Pryok'tel neutralisation device into primary interface panel, ten centimetres. Fully rotate device, then descend twenty centimetres. Rotate one-hundred-eighty-degrees, then remove device and retain for future usage.'

'Is it going to blow up if I do that?' I ask, nervously eyeing the machine.

'Do not proceed more than twenty centimetres downwards to avoid explosion possibility. Recommendation: increase processing speed; Pryok'tel detection probability increasing.'

Right, on with it then—let's hope I'm as precise with my measurements as I'll need to be. One steadying breath, then a quick thrust of my sabre pierces the interface panel—I'm not sure that it's ten centimetres deep but the resulting flying sparks make me feel I've done a good enough job. I twist in a full circle, then a fast thrust downwards, to what I hope is twenty centimetres—I think I've gone over but there's no kaboom—definitely a lot more sparks however and now black smoke's puffing out. One more half turn then I withdraw. I'm glad I can't smell anything at the moment—that smoke looks thick.

'Update: access granted to secondary computer processing core. Update: internal deck controls, Deck C and Deck B—granted. Long range communication control—granted. Inventory management system—gran ...'

'Glad you're winning your fight,' I say, smiling. I swear *Blue Boy* sounds happy.

'Recalibration progress report: thirty-nine-point-four percent complete. Probability of success report: unchanged. Recommendation: ...'

'Yes, hurry up and get Rowland, I know,' I reply, but then stop. I can hear movement from the other room, and I regret not following *Blue Boy*'s recommendation to take out the two Pryok'tel there. Gripping my sabre, I power its plasma on, and go take care of business.

I catch another *substratus* exiting the adjacent room—another quick slash from my sabre relieves him of his head, his last expression one of surprise. His body makes an excellent projectile as I pick it up with my free hand, before it hits the ground, and launch it at his companion, who is only now standing up from her desk as I enter the room. She manages to get a squeal out before her former co-worker collides with her full-force, knocking her into the wall before they both tumble to the floor. I don't give her a lot of time to realise what's going on, having cleared the distance between us in a single bound, landing just in front of the entangled pair, driving my sabre down on the two in a vicious chop. Now there's four quarters of Pryok'tel I'll need to hide—oh, and the head—that's still out in the hall. It's a good thing my sabre's plasma blade cauterises as it cuts, else I would find myself painted in the pale-yellow liquid the Pryok'tel use as their blood.

'Which way to Deck B?' I ask *Blue Boy*, stuffing the head into a nearby drawer. I'm eyeing the plasma pistol the other Pryok'tel officer's carrying—she was a Tertius, based on her uniform—an officer and likely the one in charge of the two I've killed—and so she was permitted to carry a firearm. Unfortunately, Pryok'tel do not craft their weapons with a stormcoat's hand in mind—the thing's too tiny for me to use properly—and even if I could, the Pryok'tel use DNA verification on their weaponry, meaning that it'll definitely not permit me to fire it, even if I cover my hand in their blood—learned that the hard way, from past adventures.

'Exit room and rotate two-hundred and seventy degrees. Proceed ten metres to junction ten, turn ninety degrees, proceed two metres to Lift Three. <warning>: Pryok'tel personnel active. Recommendation: avoid detection while en route to Lift Three.'

I'm really starting to like my new shuttle friend—even if he sometimes overstates the obvious, I'm getting the impression *Blue Boy* really does have my back. I follow his instructions, quickly but as stealthily as I can. I hear an automated door further down the hall from me start sliding open for a brief second, then stop abruptly and shut, with the surprised words of the Pryok'tel crewman on the other side complaining that it's broken. *Blue Boy*'s remote handiwork, I'm sure—he mentioned he had gained access to this deck's operating controls. I make my way past that door quickly, and as soon as I'm out of sight, *Blue Boy* releases his grip, and the irritated Pryok'tel isn't any the wiser I've sneaked by.

I reach Lift Three, which, I'm happy to report, is waiting for me, doors open—you always get that panicky moment where you're waiting for the lift, risking capture, but *Blue Boy*'s done his job and taken care of that little potential hiccup. But that's as far as my luck goes, as there's a double-quick electric chirp over my comms suit: I've been discovered.

'<warning>: Pryok'tel alerted—casualty detected in Asset Record Room A. Communication request to main bridge: denied. Communication request to security: denied. Denial bypass attempt initiated: countermeasures deployed. Recommendation: Administrator Toar increases progress completion rate.'

'Understood—keep blocking them, *Blue Boy*, you're doing great. Make sure no-one gets off C-deck to alert the rest of the ship.' I shake my shoulders, getting the stress out of me, and grip my sabre tightly. This next bit's going to be tricky.

'When I get to Deck B, *Blue Boy*—lock all the doors and block all inter-ship comms,' I instruct, calmly as I can. 'When I near one of the target power junctions, call it out—I'll plant the charges, then you tell me where to go after. When all the junctions have been properly mined, I'll detonate them, then point me to where Rowland is.'

'Confirmed. Recommendation: Administrator Toar receives increased positive outcome probability percentage.'

Did ... did *Blue Boy* just wish me good luck? If he did, I appreciate it, because I'm most certainly going to need it.

'Update: Deck B lockdown completed. <warning>: Pryok'tel crew detected in Deck B interior hallways. Combat probability assessment: maximum probability.'

So it's to be a fight, then, is it? I'm ready. The doors to the lift open, and Deck B is before me. Here we go.

*****

Another Pryok'tel head sails from its owner's body as I catch two troopers off guard, having come around the corner with *Blue Boy* snitching their position out to me. The other one, also a Tertius, manages to get his assault rifle up and gets a shot off; I've barely managed to use his former pal's body to block the plasma blast, which is powerful enough that there's a good portion of my 'shield' obliterated, and a second shot misses my head by only a few centimetres, scorching the wall behind me.

I throw my meat-shield in the path of the gunslinger, but this one's a proper trooper, not an easily-spooked recordkeeper—he dodges aside, and his rifle comes up for a killing shot. The tip of my sabre clips the end of the barrel off though, a good nick in the nick of time, and I spin quickly on my follow-through, hoping to cut this baron-spite in half with a decent arc. He flattens himself against the wall and I only manage to catch his chest plate, searing it clean through but leaving him unharmed. He thinks he's lucky to be alive, and that foolishness fuels his bravery as he swings out with his ruined rifle, using it as a club. That mistake costs him his life: I use my height advantage over him, literally, in that I lean over him, jaws extended, and snag the entire top of his quill-covered skull between my teeth.

Many novices would bite down here for the killing blow, their instincts shouting to go for it—but I know better—not wanting either the taste of Pryok'tel brains in my mouth nor a head full of quills to ruin it. Rather, I clamp down with enough force to get a proper grip, then lift and shake my head sharply to the side. I hear the Tertius' neck bones snap and his body go limp before I spit his remains out. I can taste my own blood on my tongue—and gingerly remove one of the barbed quills that still managed to get jammed into the roof of my mouth, thankfully not too deep. Bit painful as it comes out, but still, I'm better off than its former owner.

I see the decapitated one's assault rifle and squash an envious feeling; I'm best with a sniper rifle, mind, but no amateur with assault weaponry either—and having that heavier firepower, with its essentially limitless ammunition supply, makes my little coil-gun seem woefully inadequate.

But I do have my mining charges, and those are being put to good use. *Blue Boy* calculates I'll only need two per power junction to disable them, so that will leave me with fourteen to use however I like. With proper timing, these charges can double as grenades, with enough concussive force to shatter bone, even through armour.

I get primary power relay three dressed, and four only a few moments later, but the last one's further down a hallway, near the end. I make my way down as quickly as I can, but a frantic interruption from *Blue Boy* breaks my attention:

'Warning!: Pryok'tel override successful, two metres ...'

A doorway to my left opens, and a Secundus emerges, rifle drawn and sweeping as he checks the halls. I've got nowhere to take cover, so my only option is to charge full into him—he gets a shot off and I feel the blast graze my shoulder, scorching me fierce, but I tackle him head-on. It's then I see his friend in the room, rifle also raised and about to fire. I grab the Secundus and roll him and myself to the side, past the line of sight of his friend, coming up on top of him. He's drawn a blade from somewhere and makes to jab it into my side, but my weight advantage comes into play—I'm a heavy boy, if I've not mentioned that, and I'm crushing the Secundus to death just by sitting on him—he can't get his arm free to make his thrust.

But this smothering is too slow; his friend is already coming out to take his second shot, so I pull back my arm, claws splayed and swipe with all my strength down at the Secundus's face. Now I'm painted in yellow—half of the Secundus' face, and his entire jaw, hits the wall beside us, and he instantly goes limp under me, the remains of his head at a very sharp, unnatural angle against his shoulder.

Meat-shield refreshed, I roll off in time to block two blasts of the other Pryok'tel's rifle, then launch the corpse at him. This is the Sub-Primus—the second in command, what's he doing off the bridge?—and more than a match for me. He nimbly dances back into the room, avoiding his former friend sailing down the hall, but by the time he pops back out for another shot, I'm on my feet. As his rifle turns the corner, I've grabbed it by the barrel and yanked it out of his hands, flinging it down the hallway like useless trash.

The Sub-Primus retreats further into the room, and I follow—both of us knowing only one of us will be leaving. From his holster, he draws his kino-baton; a collapsible weapon that, when extended and powered, hits with a gravity-induced kinetic distortion effect, crushing its target with more force than its wielder could ever provide. A match for my sabre, for certain, and this fight is going to be one of luck as much as skill—one hit from that baton and it'll break any bone it connects with, just as one hit from my sabre will sear apart anything it contacts.

But when I enter the room, something from the corner of my eye causes my heart to clench painfully; a *Lurcaster's Claw* mining uniform, crumpled and discarded on the floor, with a pair of suncoat sized mining boots tossed on top.

'WHERE IS HE?' I boom, the volume of my voice tremendous, but the Sub-Primus is not impressed. Lesser Pryok'tel tremble and shake at our heart-bellows, yet this one's heard an Oarth's promise of death before, and survived to hear another. He will not after mine, though, I swear that.

'Your baron?' the Sub-Primus taunts. 'Dead and gone, friend Oarth—and what a meal he made too. My first human—eating the flesh from his rump was … how do you beasts put it? *Raur, just raur.*'

Well that's gone and infuriated me, just like it was supposed to. My first swing is wild, brutal, a reflection of my temper, and he counters it easily, the kinetic force from his baton smacking against my sabre, sending wicked shock waves up my arm and nearly knocking the blade from my hand. It's thrown me off balance, too, and I'm not fully able to get out of the way of his next swing—an overhead wallop that catches my singed shoulder, the impact of which causes my entire arm to go numb with pain. I grunt and am forced to step back, and he advances immediately, coming from another side and forcing me to turn away from the door, exposing the exit to him, while I'm pushed further into the tight confines of the room.

That smug expression he's wearing lasts only another moment—I've still got enough movement with my free hand to pull my coil-gun and aim it at his face. He swings out and I'm forced to pull back or have my hand shattered, but he's exposed himself from his efforts, and my sabre lunges, catching him in his mid-section, but it's only a glancing blow, and he again dances back in time. I did catch him though—not very well, but he's wounded now—then again, I am too.

My coil-gun is levelled at his head—I'm a real soldier, not a storybook hero—I've no fancy morals that prevent me from shooting him rather than sticking to a proper duel—and he's forced to close the distance to me—after all, you always rush a gun. His baton is low, blocking the upswing from my sabre, but he crashes into me, knocking at my hand holding the coil-gun—he's not strong enough to disarm me but it does buy him a half-second to get out of my sights.

I lunge with my jaws extended, aiming for his face—but he's fought Oarth before, and he keeps his head as far back as he can—but now he's fucked, and realizes it too—I just storm forwards, my size overwhelming him as I force him up against the wall, using my torso as a battering ram. He slams into the wall behind him, trying to escape, but I drop my gun and grab his throat, hauling him off his feet. He lamely tries to swing his baton, but I block with my sabre, pinning the baton to the wall. It's over, he knows it, and I'm more than prepared for his last, desperate act.

His warmouth inflates, wide, howling, terrible, separating the lower halves of his jaw apart, down to his throat, exposing that gaping red maw of white needle teeth. But just as he's survived a heart's bellow, I've seen my share of warmouths—they no longer frighten me in the slightest (I'm still thoroughly repulsed, mind). As his diabolical pucker prepares to give me a fatal kiss, I drop my sabre, and reach into his mouth, grabbing one side of his jaw, careful to avoid the worst of his teeth. Our palms are tough—a thick set of skin we've retained from when our ancestors walked on all fours, millions of years ago, and that skin offers me good protection against those little daggers he's got, all the better to eat me with. I let go of his throat and use that hand to grasp the other half of his jaw. His eyes widen as he realizes what's about to happen next, and his shrieking takes on an extremely eerie pitch, which only stops when I finish pulling his head apart.

The silence of the room, and a couple of seconds, allow me to catch my breath again. The Sub-Primus' remains are slumped on the floor, what's left of his head a disgusting mess, and I'm forced to shake bits of him off my claws, my face and the front of my spacesuit. Shoulder hurts, a lot, but it still sort of works. He's tagged me worse than I thought; Gren's going to have some work to do, next time I see him.

'*Blue Boy*, report on Rowland. Where is he?' I snarl into my comms—I'm still livid after this fight, not finding any comfort in victory, not with the Sub-Primus' jibe still ringing in my ears.

Blue Boy repeats the exact same location as he did previously, and when I ask him to tell me where I am, I'm relieved to hear it's a different room. I double check *Blue Boy*'s information, asking him to confirm it's Rowland's life-signs he's tracking, and our shuttle patiently repeats himself. So the Sub-Primus was lying about having eaten my baron, which I would be relieved to hear if I didn't feel so embarrassed about having let his taunt get the better of me. Nearly lost that fight because of it.

I'll hold the after-action report on my behaviour for another time; right now, there's one last power relay that needs to be decorated with mining charges. Then on to Rowland—who, I work out, must be naked again—poor fellow seems to be having trouble staying dressed today—so I sweep up his clothes and boots, storing them on myself as best I can, then retrieve my sabre. I take one last look at the Sub-Primus before exiting—was a good fight, he nearly won—and I'll remember the lesson he taught me about staying cool the next time someone threatens my baron—but he'll never learn the lesson I taught him. Never mock a baron within earshot of his sire—a surer way to death the universe just does not know.

Returning to the hall, the last power relay being right at the end of it, I plant the final two charges, then return to the room where the Sub-Primus rots. I let *Blue Boy* know that I'm ready to blow the relays, then press the remote for the charges. A moment later the first boom shakes off in the distance, then the second one soon thereafter, then the third, just down the hall from me, is quite loud—and winds up plunging me into darkness as the power to the deck is cut. It takes a few seconds for the emergency lighting to power on, and now there's plenty of klaxons singing.

Blue Boy chirps before updating me, and I swear I hear excitement in his voice, 'Progress report: disruption to Deck B power supply has disabled vulture's entire secondary computer processing network. Recalibration processes improved by sixty-seven percent. Recalibration progress report: forty-seven percent complete. Success probability report: fifteen-point-nine percent. <warning>: Pryok'tel counter-recalibration resources allocated. Recommendation: Administrator Toar proceeds to obtain Administrator Rowland.'

'On it,' I reply, shaking my neck and rotating my sore shoulder, before heading back into the now dimly lit hall. With directions piped to me by *Blue Boy*, Rowland's just down this hall, turn left, and at the end of that hall. A few minutes, at best, but I find myself running to cut that time further. I arrive just before the door to Asset Processing Room Four opens, and I hear a Pryok'tel threaten from the other side.

'If you move from that spot, I will kill you, Rowland. Stay here and …'

My sabre ensures that threat will never come true.

CHAPTER 24

Rowland

I'm about to find out if it's possible to feel crushing sadness and overwhelming joy at the same time.

Turns out, you can—as the lifeless body of Secundus Vay'auh-ta crumples to the floor, I see the massive form of Toar step into the room, and I'm caught in an emotional Lagrange point as I try to take everything in at once. Mia is truly gone now, if she ever existed at all, and—despite what I was certain was a sure-fire way to prevent it—Toar is here, like a storybook hero come to save the day.

'Toar?' I ask, striking a tone that's a mix between ecstatic, surprised, and confused.

My big brave buddy looks down at me as I'm only now trying to get myself up, his cobalt blue eyes roaming over me, and his expression changes from grim-faced stoicism to unmistakable relief.

'Rowland!' he calls, taking one step over Vay'auh-ta without a backwards glance and reaching me in the next. He immediately crouches to one knee, using his free hand to help me up, patting me here and there gently to see how badly I've been injured—I'm not that bad, my face must be swelling from the two solid impacts I took, plus a couple of decent fists here and there, but I've gotten up from worse, and I do so now.

'I'm all right, I'm all right,' I assure him. Maybe there's shock setting in, because I can't gather my thoughts to form anything that makes sense: Mia is dead, her crumpled body is just behind Toar—small mercy her face is turned from me—and the man who killed her, who I left stranded on a slime planet with no apparent way off, is now crouched beside me, fretting over me like a long-lost lover. I try telling myself that Toar doesn't know it was her, my Mia, that he's cut down: at the very least, he was able to do something I could never have—see her for what she was, and deal with her accordingly. It's the ugly truth that I'm not brave enough to face, possibly ever: she was a liar, a Judas, and a stone-cold killer. But she was my Mia.

'Rowland, *grontel utur sevseren*,' Toar says quietly, his free hand gently stroking the small of my back, deep concern in his eyes.

'Toar, I can't understand you, my language files got wiped from my UT. But if you said so, it's good to see you too, man. So fucking good.' Despite my ambivalent feelings, the automatic part of me punctuates my words to Toar with a fast, fierce kiss, and he responds in kind—but it's a brief union, as we both understand the danger we're in. Still, to have him here, no matter how impossible, is a much-needed reprieve from the dark and miserable things I've seen in the last hour.

Toar nods, helping me up, brushing my shoulders and patting me to make sure I'm stable on my feet, searching every centimetre of my body with a determined look as he does so—there's nothing amorous about his actions, even though that bedsheet I'd been given to keep me modest has long since fallen away—he's all terse efficiency. Finally, he takes a step back, fumbles with the items he's carrying, and produces the mining suit and boots I'd been wearing.

'You've thought of everything!' I accept my clothes gratefully. Looking over at poor Mia—who I must stop thinking of like that, because Mia never existed—I address Toar.

'Please, can you put her on the examination table there?' I ask, starting to dress. He looks at me quizzically and I explain, 'Just … long story, but I don't want her left on the floor like that. She … she … sorry, just please?'

He stoops and picks her up without another word. He's seen these examination tables before, as he taps the controls carefully, lowering it into a horizontal position so that the body of Vay'auh-ta stays where I'd like her to. He gives me an uncertain look, but remains quiet as I finish putting my boots on. I retrieve the sheet she found for me.

'She was the spy,' I explain tonelessly, looking at my former ship-sister. 'Mia. A Pryok'tel deep-cover agent. She's the one who betrayed us, signalling for the attack.'

I move her arms over her chest, covering her fatal wound, and arrange her so that she looks like she's just sleeping. I should feel hate for her, but I just don't—sorrow and regret, certainly, but bluntly, a sense of justice as well—she got Ivan and Bryce killed, Betts terribly injured, and she killed an Oarth just to prove a point. There is only so much sympathy I can afford her.

Still, with her death, I'll try and forgive her, but it's likely my anger and despair will be with me for a long while—those feelings will just have to be crammed atop the pile of delayed misery I'm stuffing into the furthest corners of my mind, to be swallowed by later. As I cover her with the sheet, I think a silent goodbye, and hope that if I see her again in the next iteration of the universe, it'll be as friends.

'Rowland,' Toar says, a warning-note in his voice. When he sees that he's got my attention, he points down the hallway, then makes a walking gesture, his fingers wiggling back and forth rapidly.

'Yes … we need to get going. Where, exactly?' I ask.

He thinks for a moment, then makes another gesture, curling his hand into a fist, then extending his thumb and pinky outwards, then moves it up and down, waggling it side to side. Like a bumblebee flying. *Blue Boy*.

'If that means getting back to the shuttle, that's the best plan, but first, can we get this thing off my wrist?' I ask, extending my arm with the dead-jack attached, pulling back my sleeve so that the shiny black metal band is clearly visible. Toar eyes it carefully, then takes my hand with his free one, pulling my arm gently so that it straightens out. Cautiously, he inserts the tip of his de-powered sabre in the narrow space between the dead-jack and my wrist, then gives me a meaningful look.

'Ready,' I answer, not turning away as he jerks the sabre quickly, still holding my extended arm. The sharp blade, and his strength, ensure the band is severed cleanly, without the need to power its deadly plasma. As soon as the dead-jack falls away, my cybernetic systems begin to re-boot, and diagnostic metrics run along the left-side of my vision. They're not saying a lot—my system's been wiped, and all that I'm looking at is the rudimentary operating system, waiting for commands. All my customized interface software is gone, but there's a way to get it back—and we just happen to be on the path to that very solution.

'Thanks,' I reply, rubbing my newly freed wrist. 'That thing cleared out my entire biocomp—language files, all my security system overrides—everything. I had a feeling that the Pryok'tel had something like that in mind, so I installed all my systems on *Blue Boy* and made a backup of everything I had—he's been using that to hack the vulture's systems since I got here. If we can get back to *Blue Boy*, I can do a system restore from his files, and then help take over the ship.'

Toar nods, tapping his collar where his suit's comms system is installed.

'You're in contact with *Blue Boy* now?' I ask, and he nods.

'Oh, you are so fucking amazing,' I beam, stepping closer immediately. Toar must think I am going in for a hug, so he's put his arms out accordingly, but I must disappoint him here—I lean over and speak directly into his suit's system instead.

'*Blue Boy*, Admin Rowland here—status update on the recalibration of the vulture?'

'Recalibration progress report: decreased to twenty-six-point nine percent. <warning:> Anti-recalibration procedures initiated by Pryok'tel systems administrators. Estimated time until complete system reversion: seventeen minutes. Recommendation: …'

'We need to get to *Blue Boy* now!' I urge.

Toar speaks into his system, and *Blue Boy* responds for him. 'Administrator Toar indicates he is aware of the plan and instructs you to "follow his lead".'

Toar speaks some more, and *Blue Boy* follows up, 'And indicates that he is happy to see you.' Toar gives me an expression of unsure hopefulness, checking my reaction to his translated words.

'I've never been happier to see anyone in my entire life, Toar. Never,' I respond sincerely, smiling the best I can with a face full of pain, then give him a look that's easy to interpret. 'Let's get this all over with so that I can spend the next couple of days thanking you.' I lower my brow further, so that my gaze is narrowed on him. 'In every way we can imagine. Repeatedly.'

Toar's face goes slack, his eyes widening, then he nods eagerly, that lopsided grin of his slowly spreading. But then his expression turns serious, and he puts his fingers to his muzzle, making a closed gesture, then points to his ears. Right, time to pay attention, and I nod. He unholsters his coil-gun, handing it to me, gesturing towards its grip and making a pulling motion. Figuring out his instructions, I adjust the coil-gun's grip to fit my hand, then remember Vay'auh-ta's plasma pistol is still lying on the ground—when I reach for it, Toar just shakes his head—pointing to the pistol, then crossing his palm out, frowning. Guess he means that, for whatever reason, I'll need to make do with the coil-gun, and Toar with his sabre.

We enter the hallway, now just barely lit with emergency lights, and head back towards what my memory tells me is the way to *Blue Boy*. A turn of a corner later, and I see the body of Jack-Killer, I think, or what's left of him, lying discarded in the corridors, beside an open door—his face is a gory disaster, but I recall his general size well enough to guess that it's him. Yuck, but it's nothing to what I see when I peer through the doorway, into the room—based on his chest-bling, this is what's left of Boot-Stomper, slumped against a wall. As my eyes scan his remains, suddenly my own face doesn't seem to hurt as much.

Something from the corner of my eye moves from down the hall, and I give a hard shove to Toar, pushing him towards the open doorway—but I'm barely able to move him before two other Pryok'tel troopers turn the corner, their rifles raised and at the ready. Toar sees them the moment before they're able to open fire, hauling both of us into the room just as two plasma blasts scorch the ground where we were. I'm on my feet, covering the open doorway with the coil-gun, ready to fire at the first thing that steps into view, and I can hear the pair barking orders.

Toar sneers and takes a mining charge from a pocket, arming it. He looks at me, signs that I should scoot from my position, then raises his other hand, all five fingers displayed. He counts down to zero, aims the charge at an angle, and launches it through the door, against the corridor wall, sending it ricocheting down toward the Pryok'tel. There's a squawk of alarm from the troopers and then a tremendous blast, and Toar is back out into the hallway, his drawn energized sabre casting a blue glow into the darkness.

I lean out of the doorway to cover him, but his bulk almost takes up the entire hallway, and any shot I'd take would hit him—I'm decent with a coil-gun but not *that* good. Doesn't matter though; he's cleared the distance to the Pryok'tel, and cuts one down cleanly as they're just getting back to their feet, slicing him nearly in two with a perfect slash so fast I barely see it. The other raises his rifle and I fire, clipping his shoulder and throwing him off, his own shot hitting the ceiling just above Toar's head—who spins and chops down hard with the sabre, but the trooper manages to skirt away in time, raising his rifle for a point-blank shot, with Toar dead-to-rights and nowhere to take cover.

But foolishly, the Pryok'tel has placed himself almost directly in my line of fire, and it surprises me how fast I take my shooter's stance and fire off three rounds—*vrreep! vrreep! vrreep!*—in rapid succession. I guess the hours spent at the virtual firing range have paid off, as all three of the super-heated slugs slam into the centre of my target. His armour takes the first shot but the next two—there's no chance, those molten slugs are heated to over a thousand degrees and travel at ungodly speeds—blow a smoking crater first through his armour, then through his chest.

He cries out and is blasted backwards, slamming into a wall before toppling to the ground in a heap, the stench of burnt flesh mixing with the metallic-smelling discharge from the coil-gun. He's the first person I've killed, I realise, with a hollow and distant understanding—like I've not really done that to him, even though I'm looking right at his body. Didn't even know his name. I don't know if this should matter to me, but it does.

Toar's alive though. Whatever my sins, they're washed clean by a simple nod of his approval.

We're back down the hall in the next heartbeat, my first victim forgotten for the moment, but I suspect his ghost will be hand-in-hand with Vay'auh-ta when she comes to haunt my dreams tonight. From the direction we're heading, we're making good progress back to *Blue Boy*, but his alert coming over Toar's suit throws a great deal of rain on our parade.

'<warning>: Anti-recalibration will result in Deck B controls being returned to hostiles in twenty seconds. Counter lockdown measures imminent. Recommendation: proceed immediately to Lift Three.'

Toar changes direction and we sprint down the corridor, heading to what I hope is the lift. As we pass through the vessel, the overhead lights suddenly switch to full illumination—the Pryok'tel are re-establishing control of this deck: we'll be swarmed as soon as they get the doors unlocked. Unless they decide not to bother with that at all—keep all the doors locked, except the one to an exterior hatch—then pop that and send everything in the corridors hurtling into the cold dead vacuum of space. My sprint turns into full-on panic-fuelled flight.

Turns out being vented into the void is not the Pryok'tel way, as I start seeing various panels next to the doorways we're passing switch from a red state, to a yellow state: they're unlocking, and we're still not at the lift, though I can see it at the end of a short corridor, doors open, expecting us. Toar sticks two more mining charges to walls as we pass, their arming lights blinking. Only a few more steps before we reach the lift, but a door slides open ahead, and a Pryok'tel emerges.

It's Dr. Mean, and her confused look quickly turns to terror as she sees Toar and me barrelling down at her. I raise the coil-gun in her direction, and she stumbles back into the room, falling backwards in her attempt to escape; I spare her a quick glance as we charge by—she's cowering up against her desk, shielding her face, calling out some gibberish that I don't understand. Toar doesn't even bother looking her way; he just keeps us moving towards the lift.

We make it into the lift and as soon as Toar's in, I raise the coil-gun, searching the corridor for any signs of movement; Dr. Mean is still hollering something, but she's staying put, and I can still hear others coming from further down the hallway. As the doors begin to close, Toar presses the trigger on the charges' remote, blowing them, ensuring our exit from this deck isn't hindered by last-minute reinforcements as the hallways erupt in deafening blasts, cut off only when the lift doors finish closing, and we are on our way, downwards.

We're both breathing hard, but I only allow myself a moment's respite before I'm against Toar, speaking urgently into the comms.

'*Blue Boy*, we're cut off from reaching you on Deck B—list available alternative routes.'

'Proceed to Deck D—Primary Docking Bay. Establish control of Primary

Docking Bay and await arrival of shuttle craft, designation *Blue Boy*.'

'Understood—lock down Deck C and establish fractal-based encryption keys for all currently recalibrated systems, then discontinue recalibration. Re-deploy all recalibration resources to establishing control of Deck D.'

'Complying. Estimated time for Deck D recalibration with current resources and currently deployed counter measures: four hours thirty-seven minutes. <warning>: Mission parameters in jeopardy.'

'You're telling us!' I complain bitterly, but Toar interjects, speaking into his systems. It's a long stream of Oarthecan, but he's got a plan from the sounds of it.

'Complying. Disabling lift access to all decks. Hypothesis extrapolation complete: Flooding Deck D with high-frequency magnetic particle distortion will result in all plasma-based weaponry becoming inert. Recommendation: prioritised Deck D recalibration to target environmental safety controls, then proceed with magnetic distortion.'

Toar nods enthusiastically, waiting for my agreement, but I can't provide it. 'Toar if we flood the deck with magnetised particles, it'll interfere with my ability to interface with *Blue Boy*—and I won't be able to help him take over the ship. It'll also take out my coil-gun.'

Another stream of Oarthecan is followed by the translation, 'Administrator Toar indicates: "I'll secure the deck while you get *Blue Boy* into position. Once that's done, we can clear up the distortion and you can get your files back from *Blue Boy*—we then make our stand on Deck D. *Blue Boy*'s mucked up the lifts so they'll have a right problem getting to us, but they will eventually, so I'll keep you safe while you do your thing. Sound good?"'

'Taking on an entire deck's worth of Pryok'tel? Even without their weapons, they're still going to fight you with anything they get their hands on,' I respond, uncertain.

Toar gives a 'not-to-worry' expression and taps his sabre; even de-powered, that edge is honed to a near molecular level—and with Toar's massive strength behind it, he'd be able to cut through just about anything the crewmembers could throw at him, including themselves. I do pity the Pryok'tel—I mean that sincerely, by the way—Toar has repeatedly shown he doesn't have my hang-ups about killing the enemy, but I still would rather they all surrendered so that we could just go home and carry on living our lives.

But that won't happen, not today, and I can't let my squeamishness interfere with what needs to be done—the only way Betts and Cor, let alone Toar and I, are getting out of this alive is to eliminate the Pryok'tel threat. If that means killing every last one of them, then … then I guess that's what that means.

'Well, if there's anyone who can do it, it's you. Rip them a new one for me, but keep your ass out of trouble, all right? Come get me if I can help turn the odds,' I state, firmly, perhaps with too much bravado.

Toar's expression softens, and he puts his hand on my shoulder, and I step forward and wrap my arms as far as I can around him, and he immediately pulls me in closer, hugging me with a good strength. I lean my head up, and he lowers his so that we get to share another short, but nonetheless deeply meaningful, kiss—and this time the tip of his tongue sneaks into the mix, which I find is just exactly what's needed. Feeling the press of his lips against mine is just the boost to my courage I'm looking for, and as his hand cups the nape of my neck, drawing me closer, I get the impression Toar is happy to provide it.

'For luck,' I reply, as we break, and then sneak him one more quick kiss as the lift comes to a halt. 'We're going to need it.'

Toar speaks more to his suit comms, then places both of his hands on my shoulders, locking eyes with me as the translation comes through. 'Administrator Toar indicates: "No, we've got this, you and me. Never you worry. We're the winners, every time. We. Tell. Them."'

'You're fucking right we do!' I beam, proudly. Damn he knew just what to say—I pound his chest hard, twice, enforcing my point, and he puffs it out so that my strikes make a mighty thud against him. He gives me a firm swat on my rear, too, coupled with a mischievous glint in his eye.

Toar speaks again into his suit's comms, and then when his translation comes through, he extends his sabre towards me, handle first. 'Administrator Toar indicates: "Use this to get to the Docking Bay—let me go first, but if someone gets by me, you look after them, right?"'

I hesitate, uncertain that I could use the weapon—not from lack of skill, but of conviction. I don't kill—prior to today, I had never taken the life of a sapient being—and I don't know if it's something I could do again, especially so up close and personal. Simulated combat scenarios do not prepare you for the screaming, the blood, the smell and the fear—even the CAPS's most advanced virtual realities don't hold a candle to the gruesomeness of real combat.

But all it takes is another nod of Toar's head, and I take his sabre in hand. He needs me to do this as much as I need to do this. His life is on the line as much as mine is. I won't let him down, not just because of all he's done for me, but because I'm not going to let him do this on his own—he didn't let me, after all.

'You're sure?' I check with him, and he just nods again, with certainty. For emphasis, he holds up both of his hands, and hooks his fingers, wriggling them to show me his deadly claws. Point taken—nature has given him his weapons, and unless I plan to beat my enemies with my bare fists, I'm going to need the sabre more than he will.

'*Blue Boy*, keep these doors closed until the magneto-distortion takes full effect,' I instruct. 'Once that's happened, open the lift, then disengage your moorings and proceed to the Docking bay. Continue to call out enemy positions while en route.'

'Confirmed. Increased successful probability percentages, Administrators.'

I give a confused look at *Blue Boy*'s last words, but Toar just shrugs, then faces the doors, flexing his fingers, rolling his head on his neck, shaking his shoulders out—it's then I see he's injured, a dark burnt line, about the size of my hand, singeing his left shoulder. Doesn't look too bad, and it doesn't appear to be bothering him, but the sight of Toar's injury galvanises me, and I grip the sabre's handle hard, taking a ready stance while we wait for *Blue Boy* to work his magic.

'Update: magneto-distortion field achieved; estimated time to plasma nullification in ten, nine, eight …'

I let out a deep breath, then inhale, preparing myself in the few seconds remaining. I look over towards Toar: his eyes are narrowed, his jaw clenched, and his upper lip curled to show his deadly teeth. He's taken a runner's stance, directly in front of the door, and I'm just behind and to the left of him, sabre at the ready—Here we go, here we go …

'… two, one. Plasma nullification achieved. Disengaging moorings and proceeding to Docking Bay,' *Blue Boy* alerts, and then the doors open.

They're waiting for us on the other side, and I've a split second to see their looks of horror as they discover their weapons are useless, and their death, in the form of a grey giant with claws and fangs bared, is barrelling towards them with the speed of a thunderbolt.

Describing the carnage that unfolds in the first few moments seems almost too pornographic to detail specifics. What I will say is that I've mentioned Toar's size but not really had a chance to communicate his strength—but I see it now, as he literally tears the Pryok'tel squad apart in front of my eyes. Limbs are ripped away like they'd been attached with nothing more than thread. Heads are caved in, either by a massive swipe from one of Toar's fists, or in the case of one unfortunate soul, between his enormous jaws. I could have lived my entire life without seeing a man eviscerated alive, his guts splattering the floor and walls. It is a slaughter. A bloody, brutal slaughter delivered with a precision that belies its ferocity.

I … I can see now that for all my efforts to treat others fairly and without discrimination, I've discriminated against Toar, in the worst way. I'd been referring to him as a werebear, and that's an insult of the lowest kind: he is not a bear, nor a human, nor some halfway make-believe monster I need to describe him as to make sense of him—to think of him like this denies him his true identity. He is Oarth. Proud, powerful, deadly and utterly, utterly unstoppable.

I don't even need to swing the sabre, not even once—though I advance out of the lift, ready for the melee, the single Pryok'tel I engage quickly abandons our duel, as Toar's unbridled savagery forces him to ignore me entirely, desperately trying to hold fast against a relentless Oarth death-machine in overkill mode. I could've stabbed the Pryok'tel as he turned from me, but that seemed as underhanded as it was unnecessary—he fell, they all fell, to Toar. I find myself respecting their resolve—they didn't flee, they didn't cower—they did their jobs, right to the inescapable, bitter, bloody end. It's over in a matter of minutes, the final act being Toar pulverising the head of the last trooper with one tremendous stomp of his boot.

The formerly pristine halls are now soaked in bright yellow blood and viscera. Toar is covered in it, head to said boot, along with other unidentifiable bits of our enemies. There are multiple corpses scattered around us in heaps: ripped, mangled, shredded or broken apart. The smell is heinous—a combination of blood, vomit, and other body fluids, painting every surface of the corridor, and the sight is … I want to say something snarky here, for my own benefit, to minimise the impact this is having on me—some glib comment that brushes away the horror I'm seeing—but I can't. It's obscene. It's …

I centre my attention on Toar, the only good thing in this forsaken slaughterhouse. He appears to be all right, and is licking his hands clean from the gore, then spitting what he's managed to wash away out of his mouth with a disgusted expression. His eyes meet mine, and there is a shadow of emotion colouring them—he doesn't want me to see him like this, and so he lowers his head, looking off to the side, trying to avoid my gaze. But he is still Toar, he is still my friend. And I still want him.

'Tastes pretty bad, huh?' I manage, after a few heartbeats. There's the glib comment. It's so inappropriate, but it has the marginally positive effect I was hoping for. Toar's blue eyes return to me, and a small, reluctant grin finds its way to the surface of his lips, as he nods.

'Okay …' I say, trying to sound like the last few minutes were only a minor interruption instead of a grisly battle that will leave long-lasting scars on my psyche. 'Which way is the Docking Bay?'

Toar looks over at some glyphs posted on a wall, and after wiping away some yellow fluid, points down the corridor once, and then to the right. He squares his shoulders and starts off in that direction, signalling for me to wait, until he gets further down the hall, to a four-way junction. He checks each direction, then signals me to follow. I reach him, and together, we turn right, him taking the lead, as we hurry towards the Docking Bay.

Toar speaks to *Blue Boy*, and our shuttle replies, 'There are currently three Pryok'tel crewmembers stationed in the Docking Bay. Estimated time of arrival: three minutes. Recommendation: neutralise Pryok'tel threat and secure Docking Bay.'

'Just like before?' I say to Toar as we approach the doors to the docking bay, and he nods firmly.

When the doors open, I make sure that I'm ready to use the sabre when there's a need to, and the two of us enter the room with a grim determination. The Pryok'tel crewmembers have taken position behind a makeshift barricade of crates and storage units, their plasma pistols at the ready, pointed at us. The bafflement on their faces when they open fire, and nothing happens, is pitiable.

These are not soldiers—well, they don't appear to be, based on their uniforms, which lack the body armour our previous adversaries had—they seem like regular crewmembers. But man, even when they realise their weapons are useless, they do not back down, stepping out from behind their barricade, picking up nearby tools to use as last-minute weapons—one poor man is left with nothing more than a hyper-spanner to wield.

'Surrender,' I call out—I don't want to see unarmed crewmembers butchered, not like the troopers were. 'We just want the Docking Bay—we're not interested in you.'

Toar turns towards me, wearing a hard expression, his eyes dark and unkind. He shakes his head, side-to-side, twice.

'Toar, these aren't …' but he just shakes his head again, and I notice that the Pryok'tel have not stopped advancing towards us—they will fight to the death. They're blood enemies, from what I can tell, after all—and I recall Toar's words about the uselessness of showing Pryok'tel mercy. The most merciful act I can do here is return Toar's sabre to him, which will help end this encounter quickly and cleanly, and he accepts his blade, facing his foes with a hard look of determination. There's no malice in his eyes, no hate, but no thrill for the kill either—just the grim look of a man who needs to get an unpleasant job done. He is a soldier, doing his duty, putting his life on the line so that I can do my part without interference, so I turn away from the impending massacre, trying instead to locate the primary control system for the docking bay. I see it, to the far left of the room, and hurry over just as the screaming starts.

The controls are easy enough to figure out, even in another language—there's a simple interface with straightforward icons I can understand. I study the display panel—pretending that I can't hear three people meeting their deaths just a few metres from me—it seems to be a series of commonly used commands that I'm familiar with from having worked with my own cargo bay on *Lucky*.

Toar joins me after a few minutes; this time, he's found a random bit of cloth to clean himself and his sabre with, and eyes the panel I'm looking at while he does so. He points to a series of icons, then repeats it in the exact same order, and another time just to make sure—he's indicated the necessary steps to secure the docking bay, open the doors, and initiate what I think is an automated process to assist with landing a shuttle. I nod, understanding.

'*Blue Boy*, what's your progress?' I ask.

Our shuttle advises he's nearing his approach, and recommends that I initiate the auto-landing process. While I get busy with that, Toar learns from *Blue Boy* that there are still four other Pryok'tel on this deck, and heads towards the docking bay entrance, taking position to ensure that whoever risks interrupting us will regret it. I send the signal to *Blue Boy* to disperse the magneto-disruption effect here in the docking bay—I'll want to be able to link up with him as soon as he lands.

The main exterior bay doors begin an alert, signalling that they're about to open, and an energised shield winks into place, ensuring that the docking bay's interior remains protected from the vacuum of space that's about to be exposed. Soon enough, the bay doors start to slide open, and I can see the stars of the Derresion system come into view. *Blue Boy* takes centre stage in the next moment, and approaches, slowing his speed as the docking bay's automation begins to guide him in.

Then there's a shrill squawking from Toar's direction—I'm too far from him to hear what his comm suit blurts out, but he's immediately on his feet and rushing towards me—I turn back to look at *Blue Boy* and see him attempt to shift out of his locked position, trying to break free from the automated control—but in the next second a blinding pulse of light slams into his starboard stern—it's got to be a Pryok'tel torpedo of some kind—and the following explosion launches our shuttle like a fireball directly into the docking bay.

Toar tackles me in time and we roll together, tumbling on the ground as the blazing *Blue Boy* careens through the docking bay and slams full-force into the opposite wall, a sickening cacophony of crunching metal, shrieking hull-plating and shattering glass echoing into the room's confines. The smell of burning quickly fills my nose, but the docking bay's automated fire suppression system comes online and encases the burning wreck that was *Blue Boy* in a containment shield, cutting off the oxygen and snuffing the fire out. Toar and I both survey the devastation with hollow looks.

'No,' I whisper, untangling myself from Toar and getting to my feet. 'No, no, no …'

Toar grabs my wrist, carefully, to prevent me from rushing towards *Blue Boy*, who is a still smoking ruin—but there's still enough left of our shuttle, I hope, that I can access his main processors—but time is running out, if he loses power, it's a full system shut down and then I'm absolutely fucked.

'Toar, I need to get to him now, there's still a chance!' I say, urgently, and he releases me, but follows close on my heels. We reach the smouldering ruin of *Blue Boy*—his starboard and stern are essentially obliterated, but his helm, where his main processors are located, is still somewhat recognisable—I mean it's smashed to shit and scorched, but at least it's not melted slag like his aft-end is.

His cockpit windows are a shattered ruin, which is a silver lining as I wiggle my way through them—I burn my cheek on a too-hot piece of debris, but I ignore the pain and push deeper. He's upside down, too, which is not making this easier—but when I reach his interior, I can see there's still power, the lights flickering but still strong, for the moment. My left hand immediately reaches up to find the spot on the co-pilot's terminal, the one I found before, and there's a few seconds of panic as I pat the area frantically, unable to locate the spot, but I finally feel that familiar electric tingle in the middle of my palm when I hit the right point on the terminal, and my cybernetic command line comes into view.

I turn and find Toar peering at me through the broken windows, still in the docking bay, a look of expectation on his face. I give him some quick instructions, 'Toar, gonna need a few minutes here to copy my backups over—cover me and I'll make it as fast as I can.'

Another single nod, and he turns to let me get on with it. I've not got any software installed on my biocomp other than its most basic command system, so I need to enter commands manually using eye movements on a virtual keyboard. It takes precious seconds we don't have, but I manage to establish a connection to *Blue Boy*, and enter the command: *RESTORE SYSTEM FROM PROTECTED ARCHIVE 'FUCKUSURENTHOS_01'*. The relief I feel as my biocomp proceeds to access *Blue Boy*'s archives is so palpable I think I can actually taste it on my tongue—the files are being copied, and are automatically starting to instal, and lines of beautiful cyan blue command confirmations begin to trickle down my interface view, like mana from heaven.

The initial core interface system starts to instal, and the first thing I do is check on *Blue Boy*—his damage is catastrophic: a core system shut down is imminent as a power supply failure is projected in four minutes. That's still enough time to copy my archive over, but losing *Blue Boy* is a devastating blow to our plans—without his recalibration efforts, not only will I be on my own in attempting to take over the vulture's systems, but any recalibration he did achieve will quickly be undone by the Pryok'tel. Meaning we will lose control of Deck D's environmental systems, their comms systems, their internal scanning system—everything. Two men against the entire remaining crew of the vulture. Not very favourable odds.

But there's still some hope—*Blue Boy* has anticipated his own demise, and has executed a series of encryption protocols against the systems he managed to recalibrate, creating a labyrinth of overly complicated procedures that will likely result in the Pryok'tel needing to perform a full reinstal to purge completely. Regrettably, he was not able to disable their Under-drive system, but he was able to affect their navigation systems—meaning he's bought us at least another hour before the Pryok'tel can undo his handiwork and get their Under-drive portals to form properly. Maybe that will be enough time for the *Grolthon's Spear* to reach the system—but it's impossible to tell. I'll need to finish what *Blue Boy*'s started.

My archive finishes copying—and I've got enough of my system restored to send *Blue Boy* a final message before I disconnect—and for some reason I don't fully understand myself, I choose to send him a message of thanks, telling him that his performance was admirable, and we would never have made it this far without him. Again, I don't know why I'm doing this—*Blue Boy* is not sentient, his AI is rudimentary, and he cannot understand even the concept of thanks, let alone what it means and why I'm saying it, but it just feels like the right thing to do. In a sense, *Blue Boy* was my friend—and maybe since I've lost two of my friends today, and the remaining three are in the worst danger of their lives, *Blue Boy*'s loss is getting the better of me—and so saying goodbye properly seems like the only way I'm going to be able to deal with it.

It's time to go—Toar and I need to get out of the docking bay—once *Blue Boy* powers down, the Pryok'tel will re-establish control, and I'm fairly certain the first thing they'll do is drop the protective shielding separating the interior of the docking bay from the void of space, flushing us pesky intruders out once and for all. I disconnect from *Blue Boy*—one more goodbye before I leave—and then scramble out of him as quickly as I can, finding my way back to Toar double-time.

I see Toar, who's taken position back at the main doors to the docking bay, sabre ready. At the sight of him, I execute the commands in my biocomp to reinstal the Oarthecan language—already noting that my internal interface software has been fully restored—and by the time I reach him, I receive a confirmation that we'll once again be able to converse without the need for hand signals.

'Should have my languages back—mind saying hello?' I ask him, hopefully.

'You all right?' Toar asks, his brows coming together, checking over me.

I can't help but give a short laugh of relief. Hearing the deep rumble of his voice, and understanding what he's saying, is filling me with confidence as much as it is with happiness—I've missed his sing-song words. 'Yes, I'm fine—you're coming through perfectly. Are *you* all right? Your shoulder looks like you took a bad hit.'

He scoffs. 'It's nothing—little burn is all—had worse making my own dinner, once. How's our *Blue Boy* though?'

'He's done his best, but his systems are shutting down, and we're going to be on our own, pretty soon. We need to get out of this docking bay, and find me a terminal I can connect to. Somewhere that we can secure—that's where we'll make our stand.'

Toar thinks for a moment. 'Opposite hallway was marked as Resource Management Control—likely they'll have what we need there; might need to clear the room, though.'

I nod. 'We better get moving—the magneto-distortion won't last much longer, and I don't like the idea of a fire-fight next to the terminals I'll need. Lead the way, big man.'

We've just exited the docking bay and are returning down the hall when a highly irritating screech of electric static comes over the comms—the Pryok'tel are trying to break my control over that system, and the awful wail I heard was the first sign that they're getting close to doing so. I will need to reinforce my control, but I can only do that when I've jacked in.

'Toar, they're going to gain control of this deck any moment—they'll be able to break the locks on the lift shortly afterwards. Expect the welcoming party soon after,' I warn. Toar considers my words, stops in our march towards Resource Management, and lays down a couple more mining charges in the path behind us. I notice he's running low in his supply, though—the box is more than half-empty.

When we reach the doors to Resource Management, Toar hands me his sabre again, and we enter, him in the lead, and me following—but the room is deserted—whoever was supposed to be at their post has made the wise decision to retreat. The room is medium-sized, larger than where my interrogation happened, and with a prominent bank of terminals dead centre. The biggest problem is that there're two entrances to the room, the one we came in through and another on the opposite wall—two points to cover, and only one of us able to do so—I'll be connected to the larger of the four terminals in the room, fighting on a virtual battlefront.

It takes Toar only a few moments to scan the room, making the same assessment.

'Where do you need to be?' he asks, and I approach the central terminals—there's plenty of access points for me to choose from—so I pick the one that

James Siewert

would be the most protected from the doorway that we entered, but not the other.

'Right,' he states, and begins to salvage what he can from the room to form barricades—literally ripping chairs, containers, tables and whatever else he can get his hands on and dislodge—his strength is almost too amazing to fully comprehend: his muscles bulging with tremendous effort as he breaks bolts, rips moorings and tears down cabinets. If he ever grows tired of being the captain of a mining station, he'll easily find work as a one-man wrecking team.

I, however, have other plans—remembering that the plasma nullification will soon be lifted, I let Toar know I'll be right back, then hurry back to the lift, to the blood-stained walls of our first encounter with the Pryok'tel team who tried to hold us off. I find their weapons—a large assault rifle, looking undamaged enough that it may still work. Toar's previous gestures indicated that it would not work in our hands—and that makes sense—locking a weapon so that your enemy can't use it is a well-known practice—so common that the ways to unlock it are just as well known. As soon as my left hand touches the interface panel on the rifle, I'm able to access it—and changing the setting from 'only allow Pryok'tel' to 'only allow non-Pryok'tel' is child's play for me.

'Here,' I say, tossing him the assault rifle when I return to our stand. 'Fixed this so it'll work for us.'

Toar takes a break from his fortification—of which he has done an impressive job, having completely blocked the other exit, and built blinds for himself to protect him while he covers the main door. He gives me an appreciative glance as he picks up his new rifle, pleased with having the larger—and significantly more powerful—weapon in his hand.

'Right, this will do, this will do,' Toar says, appraising his work—I get the feeling he wants to add "it'll have to", but he doesn't—no need to state the obvious. He then regards me. 'You ready on your side, then?'

I take my position at the central terminal. 'Ready. It'll be just like before—I will go still, appear to be sort of out of it—but I can still hear you. If you get into trouble …'

'No,' Toar commands, sternly. 'If I get into trouble, you keep going. You've got to stop them, Rowland—they can't leave this system with that veil. However you do that, however you need to get that done—do it. Don't stop on my account, don't stop to try and save me, don't stop for anything—not until you're done.'

I try to form words, to assure him that's what will happen—my throat is constricting here—so I nod firmly, making sure my eyes are directly locked with his. He needs to know I will not back down. He needs to know that if he has to sacrifice himself, it will be worth it. And with that thought, I say with conviction:

'We. Tell. Them.'

'That's my baron,' he says, proudly, and then meets me at my station. We share a last kiss before this final battle; it's a mixture of tenderness with urgency, hope with fear, comfort with confidence, as we're nearing the few seconds we have left together. It's us versus the Pryok'tel—winner takes all. Still a good kiss though—Toar really is quite the talented lip-wrestler.

As we part, he takes his position, crouching behind an overturned storage locker, and I take mine at the terminal, my left hand interfacing with its access port, that tingle telling me I'm ready as I'll ever be. One deep breath in, one out, and the lovely face of my mother, smiling kindly, as she wins me a giant grey teddy with bright cobalt blue eyes … wait … that's not how …

CHAPTER 25
Rowland

I'm not in *Bow-Ties*. Far, far from it.

My first confirmation that all is not as it should be is the blank white room that forms in front of me. That's bad news—my system files have been restored enough so that my custom interface software—the *Bow-Ties* representation—should be up and running. That it's not means one of two things: either the software wasn't installed properly—which would mean that whatever I'm about to try will fail in a couple of seconds—or that my attempt to hijack the system is being actively countered by real-life Pryok'tel jacks—and that they're able to suppress my software interface is their way of telling me 'you're fucked, buddy.'

Not good, not good—but not the end, just yet. I'm not without my own tricks—ten years of breaking into some of the galaxy's best security systems wasn't achieved through sheer luck after all. If Toar's a battlefield warrior, then I'm a cyber-field warrior.

First things first—put my armour on: a round of fractally-generated request algorithms to shield my identity, scattering my presence in the system as an unidentifiable mass of millions of users bombarding the system with petty, rudimentary access requests from millions of different sources. I'm the only legitimate source, but like a school of sardines that changes shape and size every nanosecond, it's going to be pretty tough finding me among the army of phantoms I've created.

The Pryok'tel response is classic and effective—giant swipes of denial protocols, refusing and locking out the request source—but these denials must be logically based, not fractally, and so it'll take them a long time to break down my ruse and find me. They will eventually, but it sets the stage for the battle that's unfolding—if I hijack the vulture first, I can lock the Pryok'tel jacks out permanently, and I win—if they find me first, they'll do the same to me, and I lose.

Next is to start pecking away at the sub-systems *Blue Boy*'s managed to secure, randomising their operating parameters so that the vulture's main system will need to actively prevent a ship-wide disaster—things like setting oxygen levels to four particles per million (denied), setting gravity to three hundred percent above normal (denied)—randomly generated system settings that the vulture must protect against to keep the crew alive. That will keep most of the main system busy, but the secondary processing system will …

… not be a problem! It's been physically taken off-line! Like, when I try to check its status—it's completely dead; no power, no responses, nothing, and that thing was responsible for handling overflow from the main system, which is currently nearing maximum operating capacity from all the bullshit requests I'm dumping on it. I would say that this is my lucky day, but yeah, it's so not been the case—more like this is the one diamond of good fortune in an avalanche of

278

bad-luck coal. That secondary system is also responsible for ensuring system security access, which means all I'll need to do is mimic an existing account on the system, decrypt its security settings, enable permissions and …

Voi-fucking-là, I'm now an authenticated user. I only have read privileges—no updating, no creating, no deleting—but I've been authorised as a legitimate user account. And guess what, you three-mouthed-bitches? All my sardine buddies are getting the same credentials—we found the hole in your hull, and we're all swimming in. It's party-time in the vulture's system.

But the Pryok'tel jacks are not yet done with me, and start performing mass purges of accounts, using a brutal set of protocols that will likely clear some of their own personnel's access to the system, but yeah, their accountants can always have access restored later. It's a good tactic, and I need to start taking them seriously. From what I'm seeing, there's at least three separate admin users fighting me, each taking separate actions to stymie my progress: one to handle the bullshit requests and phantom user accounts, one to re-take the sub-systems I currently control, and one to shore up defences to prevent my continued penetration. Three versus one. I'll need to even the odds.

I direct a portion of my sardine school to start making requests to access whatever they're permitted to access: library files, personnel records, inventory registers—anything and everything, and repeat these requests, taxing the system admins in an attempt to find out what I'm doing—their response is the same: shut non-essential systems down and lock them out, but I'm noticing they're protecting some areas in the system, likely its core operating procedures, which can't be shut down or else it would result in an eventual system collapse.

My read-only role is not going to cut it here though, but while the Pryok'tel are busy blocking what attacks they can, I've located encrypted user logs, and start scanning these for what I need: access credentials. This is what I've been hunting for, and I launch the first salvo of my decryption algorithms—they chew through the possible security combinations for one particularly powerful account, possibly one of the system admins themselves, but I send another salvo to lesser accounts as well—all I need is one with write-ability to the system, and this first foothold I've established will become a trench.

It's when I unlock one of the lesser accounts that I hear the real-life sounds of plasma weapons fire—it's distant, like fireworks that are too far away to see, and I hope Toar is okay as he fights to keep us alive. My unlocked account does have marginal abilities, one of which is installing software, and so the first thing I have it do is instal a complex account deletion protocol—forcing the system admins to verify every step manually when they try to delete one of my sardines. Dirty trick, but it works—they either have to take real-world seconds to process each account they want to neutralise, or abandon the attempt and let my sardines swim wild. Either way, it's a solid punch to their defences.

And with my write-ability, my environment begins to change before my eyes—*Bow-Ties* is forming, but the familiar entranceway is guarded by an orange-furred Cerberus, each of its three mouths splayed wide like a Pryok'tel's warmouth, snarling and shrieking at me. It does not like me at all—stepping towards it, which is the virtual equivalent of submitting my user credentials, I'm met with baleful howling and spit-drenched snarls. I'll need to pacify it somehow, convince it that I'm legitimate—but the three-headed dog doesn't look like he's going to go to sleep anytime soon.

Whereas I launched a salvo of decryption algorithms before, now it's a full-on orbital strike—I throw everything I have at the security system, a million command requests bombarding it simultaneously—but the damn dog is counteracting everything. Even my best, most devious tricks are being thwarted by tight loops of identity verifications, authentication re-validation protocols and flat-out denials—I pass the eight-hundred thousand mark of my algorithms and the monstrous hound still hasn't lowered even one of its three sets of saliva-dripping jaws. Not good.

I'll need to adapt my algorithms on the fly, reforging them in real-time to create additional weapons—but that's going to eat my entire resources, already stretched to capacity maintaining my sardine shield. I need more power—more resources to handle the vulture and its Pryok'tel sysadmins' attempts to counteract me—I'm not making any real progress and I know I won't succeed at this pace; either the admins will finally locate me, and lock me out, or more likely, Toar will get overrun, and I'll get to experience a 'hard-disconnect' a few moments later. Hold on, Toar, I'll get this done, I promise.

I throw the vicious dog a Gordian knot puzzle—a clever algorithm that's a logic trap in contradictions—it doesn't do anything other than force the dog to pay it some attention to solve it, but it buys me a moment's reprieve while I figure out what I can do. I scour the systems I still have control over: internal sensors is mine, and I use that to locate any available computer source that I could take over.

I'm an idiot. Well, I'm stressed, and I am experiencing the first signs of anxiety about failing, so my forgetfulness is understandable, but I realise that while I'm not the administrator for the vulture, I'm still an administrator. To the derelict automated transport, and all its high-tech, wonderfully unlocked system resources. And since I'm now situated inside the vulture and still have access to the internal comms system—albeit for the time being—contacting the blue goddess shouldn't be a problem.

I broadcast my communication request on the secured channel the derelict monitors—the one we used to find it to begin with, all the way back in the kelmisite field, and include my deeply encrypted credentials in the transmission. It's only a few heartbeats before the beautiful voice of the derelict responds, like honey in my ears.

'Greetings, Administrator Rowland: how may I …'

'Transmitting file FUCKUSURENTHOS_01, instal and initialise on priority one basis,' I tell her urgently. 'Apply heuristic learning processes to all enclosed decryption algorithms; randomise and verify uniqueness. Link all available system resources to Admin Rowland, then proceed with recalibration of system target:

Pryok'tel Patrol Vessel, designation *"Sh'hyzen-shi"*. Initiate.'

'Receiving file. Please stand by,' she acknowledges, and to my delight, I see the first trace of her form beginning to take shape—and my subconscious has taken the liberty of arming her fully. She appears before me as an angel, fiery-white as a neutron star, adorned in golden plate armour, immortal and perfect. Each feather in her gigantic kaleidoscopic wings represents a re-factored algorithm, and I can see millions of them. The spear she holds—my interpretation of her system access protocols—is forged from the cosmos itself, and her galactic eyes blaze with a benevolent confidence.

'Processing complete. Recalibration of target system initiated. Please stand by,' my Cyber Seraph states, and steps forward to face the Pryok'tel Cerberus without hesitation.

The beast shows her only rage and hate, but she is resolute and undaunted by its display. Her spear thrusts forward and the right head of the beast bites down on it hard, snarling as it ravages it between its teeth, but the Cyber Seraph seems unfazed. Her wings extend to their maximum length, the tips spreading wide and fully, and she launches her attack—millions of colours streaming through her wings, over her body, through her hands gripping the spear, and right smack into the gob of the Cerberus. Its face turns from orange to white-hot, but it does not relent nor let go—it just bites down harder, shaking its head, and I notice that some orange returns to it, and even starts seeping back along the spear. They're locked in a battle, from which only one will emerge.

One head down—well, otherwise occupied—two to go. I can take one of them myself, but the remaining one would have the chance to gnaw me and the Seraph to ribbons while doing so; we could hold out but it would just be a matter of time, which we do not have. I need more power—and I keep desperately searching for anything that could help.

'Alert: protected file directory located,' the Seraph states calmly. She takes one hand off her spear, pulling an orb of energy towards her, its pattern coming directly out of the dog's mouth, whose face is a picture of hatred as it's forced to give it up. She holds out her hand to me, and I see the directory now: a small, blue sphere that glows brightly in her outstretched hand, with dark grey electricity crackling over its surface. Alive. Waiting. 'Encryption protocols detected: Administrator Rowland or Administrator Toar, please provide access security credentials.'

'Credentials provided!' I yell triumphantly, and God I think tears are forming in my real-world eyes as my *Blue Boy* is returned to me. Somehow ... somehow he knew his demise was imminent, and managed to copy himself into the vulture's systems. I fucking bet those Pryok'tel jacks are shitting themselves now—that's what they were hiding from me, that's what they were desperate to protect—his copied-over system was locked behind a file directory and the Seraph managed to rip it from the Cerberus' clutches and break it open.

The Cyber Seraph releases the orb and the giant cerulean Oarth takes shape—and this time, he's not in his birthday suit. I've adorned him in a suit of medieval plate armour—I don't know if there's such a thing as an Oarth Knight of the Round Table, but that's how my subconscious interprets my new *Blue Boy*, complete with a bear's head emblem emblazoned on his shield and breastplate. His sword ... his sword is a sabre ... and it's drawn and at the ready, grey-toned lightning dancing over its blade.

'Hello Administrator Rowland,' King Oarthur states—as he's definitely no longer just a boy, though he is still wonderfully blue—'Recommendation: resume recalibration mission. Awaiting confirmation.'

'Initiate!' I cheer, and King Oarthur immediately spins to face his enemy, his sabre slashing at the left head of the beast—it cuts deep into its mouth as the beast clenches down on it. Thundering electricity rips along the blade's edge, enveloping the beast's head in a lightning storm, attacking it with a fury that exceeds even its own rage. King Oarthur seems to have a grudge to settle.

That leaves the centre head for me, and I launch myself at it, my fists slamming into its maw. I don't armour and arm myself as I have my two compatriots—for some reason, my virtual avatar is always just regular old Rowland—but that doesn't mean I haven't power here too. I grip the monster's ugly mug with both of my hands and pour everything I've got into breaking that hideous face apart—I imagine the last time I saw Boot-Stomper and that's what I'm going for—I will rip this thing in two!

But ... but we're at a stalemate. The beast cannot win, not with all three of us, but we can't win either—all we're able to do is keep it occupied and stop it from overwhelming us. With time, I am sure we could eventually break it apart—but time is not what we have. All the Pryok'tel are doing is keeping us busy, too—they know that their real-world buddies are going to overtake Toar, and me soon thereafter, which will end this fight and hand them their victory. We could win, we could ... but there just isn't time for it.

'Seraph, Oarthur, scan for additional system resources—anything that we can take over and utilise—I don't care if it's an unattended monitoring station, a misplaced touchpad, or somebody's personal comm device that's been left on—anything that has any kind of processing power that I can connect to—locate and advise.'

'Searching,' my comrades indicate, and I join them in the attempt, reaching out with broadcast requests to anything within my vicinity. I find Toar's suit comms, but they're nowhere near powerful enough to help; it would take more resources to configure than they'd be able to provide in return. I encounter other systems as well, but they're all still under the beast's control—his jack masters know that I'm hunting for additional allies, and they're doing a damn fine job ensuring I don't find any. I'm scrambling here, trying to find anything—I locate one of those touchpads I asked for, but the beast senses my discovery, and shuts the device down with a remote command. Damn it ... I've got to find ...

'Additional resource detected,' King Oarthur suddenly indicates. 'Vessel Identification: unknown. Designation: *Orlin's Hope*.'

Huh? Another vessel in the vicinity?

'Requesting connection protocols,' Oarthur states. 'System connection established.'

'Additional system resources available!' an unknown voice pipes up, and as our connection is finalised, my subconscious interprets this new entity as a purple ball of energy, shapeless and small but still entirely at my disposal. Its operating system is—*bizarre* would be the kindest word I can imagine, closer to pure chaos held down with duct-tape being closer to the truth—but it is connected, available—and just might be enough to turn the tide.

'Transmitting file FUCKUSURENTHOS_01,' I start to instruct, launching my installation file at the excited grape. 'Initialise on priority ...'

'HOSTILE SYSTEM DETECTED!' the purple gremlin screams, *throwing* itself right into the middle of the beast's back, landing on it with a splat that sticks to the monster like an exploded aubergine. 'ESTABLISHING CONTROL OF BIOLOGICAL RESOURCE RECLAMATION SYSTEMS!'

I blink in surprise—our new ally completely disregarded my file transmission; I know I've not set myself up as its Administrator, but I mean ... it could at least try and listen, right? Nope—perhaps its own systems are too alien to interface with mine successfully—that does happen, especially when first encountering new species and attempting to access their computer systems—but there's something about how this purple puff-ball works that's too unstable for my liking. It really, really wants to gain control of the vulture's sanitation sub-system—like making sure the toilets flush properly is the sole key to solving all the universe's mysteries. Maybe it is? I don't know—if I survive this battle, I'll give that idea its due—but right now, there's a three-headed dog that needs putting down, and if my overeager grape wants to take over the toilets, have at it, buddy.

I resume my hunt for additional resources to take over and use in the battle, but I've picked the field clean—we're trying our best but it's still a stalemate. Thankfully, my electric allies do not tire, but there's an ever-increasing dread in me that the sand left in my clock is running low ...

And then the death-knell of our defeat tolls. It's Seraph who advises us, and I'm envious that she has no emotions to understand the depth of what she announces. 'Alert: Under-drive systems initiated. Spooling protocols engaged.'

'Estimated time to portal formation: two minutes, ten seconds,' King Oarthur adds. '<warning:> Mission failure imminent. Recommendations: no recommendations available.'

'Divert all recalibration efforts to Under-drive systems,' I instruct, but am immediately met with twin 'Failure' responses from my comrades. The vulture is going to dive, out of the Derresion system. We're going to lose unless I think of something now!

'BIOLOGICAL RESOUR ...'

'Ignore!' I reply, irritably, but I notice that the purple gremlin has cracked open the door to *Bow-Ties*—it's a sliver, but he's managed to take over the sanitation systems. A small victory, and as revenge I will make sure that the

Pryok'tel have a miserable time at the head, but it's nothing that I can use.

I scan the systems I still control: internal sensors—generally useful, but not helpful in shutting the Under-drive down. Same for internal comms—the Under-drive is command-line interface-capable, and the Pryok'tel navigator is directly entering coordinates. I've got some environmental controls capabilities for Deck D still—but the worst I could do is set the gravity levels to maximum permissible values, or make it too cold for everyone's liking—nothing a decent sweater couldn't fix …

'BIOLOGICAL RESOURCE RECLAMATION SYSTEMS AVAILABLE!' this *Orlin's Hope* repeats—and my subconscious shows him hopping up and down at the sliver of the door. I growl with annoyance—I can't see the benefit of accessing the ship's plumbing system—whether the toilets are going to flush is not going to stop the portals from forming!

Then I see the Seraph drop to her knee as the beast snaps the tip of her spear between its relentless jaws, and its orange light begins to poison the length of her spear. She's losing her access credentials—they'll be able to neutralise her soon—but she does not relent and continues her attacks. The same happens to King Oarthur—his shield has a devastating crack running down its centre, and his sabre is no longer alive with his fury, though he remains determined and keeps the fight going. I'm all right, but if my two friends fall, the dog-heads they were battling will turn on me instead—and that's a fight I'll not win.

'BIOLOGICAL …'

'FINE!' I snap, and pay attention to *Orlin's Hope*, whose constant jumping up and down has finally got the better of my patience. He points to the sliver he's made, and I peer inside—making sense of the systems he's compromised and recalibrated. My interpretation of the vulture's waste reclamation systems is predictable: a tidy looking little janitor, nothing too original I'm afraid—though he is well and truly willing to help with whatever request I want to make. Seems that in addition to controlling the lavatories, this system is also responsible for a general set of commands under the ship's sanitation protocols, which controls recycling of biological waste from other sources around the ship, as well as general recycling—wow, the Pryok'tel are recycling deities—I'm *so* stealing these protocols, they far exceed anything the CAPS has. There's also sanitisation routines, automated cleaning schedules, ship-wide decontamination proto …

Oh, you fucking idiots. You stupid, predictable, germo-phobic, slaves-to-efficiency idiots. I've been handed my victory, thanks to Orlin's efforts, but my chance at claiming it is running out.

'Open a comms channel to the bridge,' I instruct King Oarthur, and he does so at my command.

'I've won, Suren'thos,' I declare, my voice strong, undeniable. My message is carried out to the entire crew. 'Surrender control of the vessel, and I promise to spare you and your crew.'

There's that artificial laugh of his in reply. 'Such dramatics, Rowland! You're nowhere near victory I'm afraid—you've got further …

'I've won. No tricks, no gloating, no way out for you unless you give me full access—now!' I demand. The chance to win is slipping away, but I will not initiate my coup d'état without giving them a chance to save their own lives— their defeat will be entire, bow to stern, otherwise.

'You're delusional,' Suren'thos sneers in reply. 'We will never surrender, least of all to you.'

I pipe a message directly into Toar's suit's comms systems. 'Toar, seal the door. Top priority.'

'Right, on it,' he confirms.

'Last chance, Suren'thos,' I warn. 'Don't be an idiot—you can't see how I've done it but I've ...

I'm interrupted by the worst sound I've heard today, maybe the worst in my life. Worse than the bellowing of the poor red-furred Oarth. Worse than the last gasp of Vay'auh-ta. Worse than when my *Luck of the Draw* took that first hit, signalling the end of the life I knew and loved. Worse than the dragging of my beloved Bryce. It's the sound of Toar's hard grunt of pain, followed by the escape of a terrifying, rattling gasp—and then silence. I pull up a view of the Resource Management Room we're in—the door is closed but Toar's slumped against it, collapsed and holding his left side, his face twisted and grim. Blood gushes from a large wound on his side, about halfway down his torso—I can't see directly how bad it is but from the red pool that's slowly forming underneath him, it looks bad. Very, very bad.

A coldness steals over me, a void that silences my doubt at what needs to be done. They shot Toar. They may have killed him. There is only one answer to that. Without another thought, I initiate the first step of my Armageddon, sending the appropriate commands to the automated sanitation system, over which I have entire control.

My reply to Suren'thos is flat, hard and final, 'Executing automated decontamination protocols. Target parameters: All non-specified locations. All safety verifications: Verified. Initiate.'

Suren'thos' final words are cut off before the first syllable even gets past his lips.

CHAPTER 26

Rowland

E arth's greatest war strategists, past, present and likely future, will all give you this one well-known piece of advice for victory: use your enemy's greatest strengths against them.

The Pryok'tel are fearsome opponents—ruthless warriors, efficient tacticians—they didn't form their Hegemony by asking politely after all—and that ruthlessness and efficiency carries through to their daily lives. Probably a much-needed survival strategy on their resource-poor planet—they do not waste efforts, resources, or time—Vay'auh-ta herself said wasting time is the highest insult to a Pryok'tel. Anything that can be streamlined is streamlined, anything that can be made efficient is made efficient. It's a cornerstone of their way of life, and it affects how they interact with this universe, how they design their tools, and unfortunately for them in this case, their ships.

I understand now why the vulture looks impossibly clean: the Pryok'tel frequently run an automated sanitisation protocol that uses a lethal type of modulated radiation that breaks down organic matter to the atomic level, transforming it into its most basic parts. What this amounts to is that periodically, a merciless kill-pulse sweeps designated sections of the ship, disintegrating any unshielded organic matter. The results are 'spotlessly clean'—no amount of manual cleaning could ever accomplish the same level of sanitisation as quickly and, you guessed it, as efficiently. And the pulse can reach every section of the ship, bow to stern—if you're going to do things, do them right, and completely, the first time.

Now obviously there are numerous safeguards in place to prevent the inadvertent activation of this sanitisation process while crewmembers are around. There needs to be confirmation that there are no personnel within a certain distance from the section being sterilised, and there needs to be double-confirmation from authorised personnel to initiate the process, and there needs to be a final check ensuring the pulse does not target any section outside its set parameters. You would need to have full access to the internal sensor array, the comms system and at least two authorised accounts, one of which is the administrator for the sanitation sub-system, to run the kill-pulse on, say, the entire ship all at once. I've all three of those components.

And that's what I feed the automated sterilisation protocols: the entire ship—every deck, every room, every nook and cranny. Save for two rooms—in this case, Resource Management, and just for safe-measure, Resource Storage. Yes, please accept this recently-run sensor-scan confirming all other sections are empty of personnel—and here's the confirmation that you need, signed-off by two authorised users, including the system admin, and yes, you are authorised to proceed. Initiate when ready.

I don't hear the crew of the vulture dying en masse, thankfully—I'm not sure how the modulated radiation works to be honest, but I think the effect is nearly instantaneous. I hope. Certainly I heard no screaming from the comms channel—just a sharp intake of breath from Suren'thos—his last, it seems. The internal sensor array confirms the only lifeforms detected are two in Resource Management, plus twenty in hypno-stasis in Resource Storage—all other rooms are devoid of even the most basic forms of life. Sixty-eight Pryok'tel crewmembers unaccounted for, though. I murdered at least fifty of them. Jesus.

The Cerberus has transformed, now that its masters have been reduced to elemental building blocks, from a three-headed monster to just a large dog with that splayed Pryok'tel mouth. Not a problem for the combined efforts of the Seraph, King Oarthur and the purple hero who won our victory, though he seems happy just being Captain Clean. It's a matter of time before they'll break the last of the vulture's defences, and I can instal myself as the primary administrator. That means I can disconnect, and return to the real-world, where—with everything left in me—I hope to find Toar alive.

I break my jack to the terminal, and rush over to him. He's slumped against the doors, his head lowered, chin resting on his chest, right arm covering his side. He doesn't lift his head at my approach—bad sign—and it takes a gentle hold on his uninjured shoulder before he knows I'm there.

'Got myself shot,' he mumbles, adding remorsefully, 'Sorry. Door's closed though.' His eyes are glassy, his expression slack.

'Yes, yes it is—you saved the day Toar, fucking well done,' I tell him, in what I hope is an optimistic tone, even when I follow up with a lie, 'You'll be fine, don't worry.'

Up close, I can see the extent of his injury—there's a fist-sized hole in his left side, a plasma shot sinking deep in him, burning the edges of his wound but demolishing his insides. *Fatal*, my past combat instructors would say, but I can't accept that. He's still here, there's still got to be a chance.

'Nah, it's bad,' Toar grunts, but looks me in the eye. 'Won though, right?'

'Yes. Just you and me now, Toar. Can you move? We've got access to the entire ship—we can get you to a med-bay.' I put my shoulder under his arm, trying to help him stand, but he gives another hard grunt of pain and I've got to stop. Goddam he's heavy, even with him trying to help me, my muscles bulge painfully, but we've at least got him off the door he managed to close, in time to shield us from the kill-pulse—and he's now resting against the wall.

'*Blue Boy*, where's the nearest med-bay, and how far?' I ask, and our shuttle—well, our vulture now I guess—answers:

'Deck C, one hundred sixty metres.'

Toar and I exchange looks. We both know he won't make it up one deck, let alone one hundred and sixty metres—it may as well be light years. But I refuse to give in. This is Toar—he wouldn't give up if it were me lying on the floor.

'Easy as a walk in the park,' I say, trying to stay positive. 'I'm just going to check the hall, make sure we've got a path to take—just sit tight, I'll be right back'.

He grins, weakly, and nods. I touch his face quickly, then get myself into the

287

hallway. It's a fucking disaster—scorch marks, blast impacts, the remnants of exploded mining charges all around—Toar put up a hell of a fight. Then I see uniforms, armour and weapons further down the hall—all that remains of the unshielded Pryok'tel forces, after the kill-pulse hit them—I count nine empty husks. Toar held back a full squad of heavily armed soldiers with nothing but a borrowed assault rifle and a box of mining charges—no armour, no support— the man is a fucking legend.

'Okay, we're clear, just going to get …'

I hear doors sliding, down the hall—the lift is opening. Suren'thos staggers out, his pistol drawn, his eyes weeping blood, his face a horror of partially-dissolved skin, his flesh twisted and ruined. Somehow, he's managed to survive the kill-pulse—barely, by the looks of it—but enough so that when his one still functional yellow eye sees me, he's fast to fire, and I barely manage to get back into the room to take cover on the wall opposite Toar.

'YOU FAILED, ROWLAND!' Suren'thos screams—his voice high and berserk, manic and drenched in fury, in pain. 'COME OUT SO I CAN REWARD YOU!'

I draw my coil-gun, back against the wall, and exit cover for a moment to get off a shot, but yank myself back just in time as a plasma blast screeches by, right where my head was—I barely got a glance but I could see Suren'thos shuffling like a zombie toward me. Whatever his ailments are, they don't seem to be affecting his aim, and I have a feeling that if I risk another shot, he just might give me that reward he's offering.

'How'd you do it, Suren'thos?' I call out, behind cover. 'Survive the kill-pulse? Thought I got all you cannibal sons-of-bitches in one go.' If I taunt him, enrage him enough, he may just make a mistake—that's my best shot.

'Experience, whore-trash—you don't survive on Pryok'tel long without it!'

'Well, I guess you're like roaches then—one always survives the bug-bomb.' My jibe is answered by another shriek and two more plasma bolts tearing into the room.

'I will not eat you,' Suren'thos calls, insanity soaking his words. 'I am going to strip your flesh from you, and feed that to your broken Earth bitch instead, then let that crazed Oarth beast have you—rape you until you are nothing but rags and ribbons.'

'Yeah, yeah, yeah, and your mother made your brother into porridge. Guess with half your brain now sludge that's the best you can come up with, but cut the Oarth rape comments, Suren'thos—one would think the Primus doth protest too much.'

I hear a weak chuckle from Toar at that, but another two blasts rip into the room, one right after the other, telling me that Suren'thos is closing the distance. Injured as he is, a coil-gun is no match for a plasma pistol—the split second it takes for the coil-gun to charge is all the time Suren'thos will need to turn me into Swiss cheese from his pistol's near instantaneous plasma fire. At close range, there's no chance for me.

Toar must know this too, because he grunts to catch my attention, his eyes moving down to his sabre. The sabre could even the odds—in the hands of an expert, which I am not. But I also see he's got one last mining charge—and that might be the deciding factor.

I hit the button to close the door—it'll buy me a few seconds before Suren'thos is on us. It gives me the chance to drag Toar further down the wall, straining with everything I've got but I get him away from the door, then collect what I need from him. I reconfigure the coil-gun to fit his hand, then press it into his palm.

'Do not let him leave here alive,' I say, staring into Toar's fading, beautiful, blue eyes. 'If I lose, do not let him win.'

He blinks, once. It's all he can manage. I kiss his forehead fast, and then slap the last remaining mining charge against the door, setting it for ten seconds. I step back further, behind the console I was first jacked into, and take cover.

The door opens and another three plasma blasts hit the console; I can smell the stench of heated metal and ionised particles, but I can't see Suren'thos—I can hear him though, wheezing, shuffling towards me. If he turns his head to the left, he'll see Toar, and that cannot happen.

'Personal shield? Emergency force-field? How'd you do it, Suren'thos? Or did you just hide under the melting bodies of your bridge crew?' I call out, drawing his attention. Another blast screams by me, scorching the back wall.

'Shield,' he hisses. 'Took the brunt of it, enough for the opportunity to pay you for what you've done. You'll not win, degenerate, I'll make ...'

...two, one—boom! The charge detonates, and Suren'thos is launched into the room, sailing by me—but I catch the faint amber outline of that fucking personal energy shield—the one that likely masked his life-signs when I checked for them—snapping into place, protecting him again, both from the worst of the explosion and the corresponding impact into the wall. He hits it solidly, bouncing off, dazed, and lands in a heap, still holding his pistol.

I leap from my cover, both hands on the sabre, lit with blue plasma, ready to finish what the kill-pulse started, lunging forward to impale him as he stands—but I strike the energy shield, one of the few things a plasma blade cannot penetrate in a single blow.

The impact is enough to knock Suren'thos' aim off, and his shot just misses my left ear—I can hear the air around it crackling as the blast slams into the ceiling. My momentum has knocked him back, and I take a step back, chopping directly where his neck connects to his shoulders—only to bounce off that damned shield another time. He angles his pistol for another round, and I step into his outstretched arm, blocking him, but I've stepped too close—he ducks his head under my own arm, gripping it with his free hand and then hoisting upwards, me momentarily on his shoulders, and I am suddenly ass-over-tea kettle as he judo-flips me hard into the floor.

Still gripping my arm and now standing over me, he lands a boot solidly against my throat and chin, pressing down, twisting my head, and I am straining

to look back—his pistol is levelling ... he's taking aim, it's a point-blank kill-shot
...

I hear the *vrreep!* as the coil-gun fires, and his shield springs to life to block the shot—Suren'thos turns in the direction of the firing, just as another two shots hit—half of his blood on the floor, and Toar is still an excellent marksman. I see the shield finally snap as its energy reserves are exhausted when the last slug hits and ricochets off harmlessly ... but then the firing stops. I twist as much as I can, just in time to see Toar slump to his side—he's out, or worse.

That unnatural laugh of Suren'thos fills the room. He presses his boot harder against my throat, cutting my air off, as he shrieks that hideous sound. He glares down at me, his one good eye filled with hatred, the other eye now actually burst and dripping from its socket.

'So that's how *you* did it,' he cackles. 'Your Oarth inseminator? Really, Rowland, such a disappointment! Oh, but I will see us equal for what you've done—the pain ... the pain you will experience ... it shall make this universe shudder!'

That boot comes up and slams into my nose—twice—I grunt in pain and feel my body go limp, my consciousness threatening to flee at any moment. Seeing me stunned, Suren'thos turns and advances toward Toar.

'Animal. Filth. Pervert,' Suren'thos taunts gleefully, continuing his advance— God this bastard loves to gloat, even half-melted as he is. 'Degenerate. Primitive. I shall visit every agony that my crew experienced upon you, you incestuous beast, you waste of flesh.'

From the side of his belt, he removes a small blade, and through the blurriness of my vision, I can just make out an orange glow springing around it—a plasma dagger.

'Let's see, how to start my restitution—ah, but that's a big word, "restitution", too big for your dull brain—"grrrr, me make it you pay" is more your level. I think I'll take your testicles, here and now, and shove them down your pretend-baron's throat—that should give us a good start.'

The. Fuck. You. Will.

Half dazed, half enraged, I force myself to my feet—grabbing Toar's sabre. Confused, unable to see clearly, and certain my nose is broken, I somehow manage to hoist the sabre, two-handed over my head, even as I sway on my feet. The image of Suren'thos doubles before me, and the room swims, but with everything I've got, I launch the sabre, tomahawk-style, directly at Suren'thos. It cartwheels through the air, end-over-end, a deadly blue halo as it flies towards its destiny—but I fall to my knees before I can see if it hits.

There's a deeply satisfying thud, but when I look up, Suren'thos is still standing. The sabre ... I've missed ... it's buried hilt-deep in the wall directly in front of him, just above where Toar has collapsed. Suren'thos appears to be looking at it, his arms slightly outstretched on either side of him. At least I've caught enough of his attention to stop that stupid laugh of his ...

And then he splits, down the middle, from the top of his head to the middle of his back. He hovers on his feet for another moment, a gory letter Y, before falling forward. Seems I didn't miss after all. Come back from that, you sadistic cannibal fuck.

There's no time to savour my victory—Toar isn't moving, and I race with all the strength in me to get to his side, lifting him up and propping him against the wall.

'Toar, Toar buddy, you still there?' I ask, desperately, patting his face, smoothing his fur, shaking his uninjured shoulder carefully. He groans, and his eyes flutter open—thank God.

'Yeah,' he slurs, and drifts in consciousness again. 'Just ... just sleepy ...'

I lift his chin—gently—so that we're eye-to-eye. 'No, Toar, you're not sleepy, you know that. You're getting up; we're going home.' Fuck, my voice cracks on the word 'home'. 'You have to get up, now, come on, you're too ...'

'S'okay, Row, it's ...' he drifts again, but manages the hint of a smile. 'Yer safe. All that matters.'

'I'll bring something,' I state, standing. 'A med-kit, something to stabilise ...'

He reaches out with his free hand and takes mine. 'Too far. Just ... stay.'

'No, Toar ... please, no ...'

'Sorry ... sweet Rowley. You'll be fine ...'

'Not without you,' I choke out, bitterly, wiping at my eyes.

He grins weakly. His beautiful cobalt eyes are meeting mine, but I can see him fading—oh God if he dies it'll kill me too—Toar you can't do this!

'Yeah, you'll be fine,' he manages, but is stronger with his next words. 'You tell my boys ... Daddy loves them. You tell my dads their Toar loves them. They're ... they're all here ... with me ... now.'

He slowly reaches up to put his hand on the side of my face, his fingers curling on the back of my head, just like he did in the shuttle. 'Everyone ... I love ... is here ... with ...'

He fades.

CHAPTER 27
Rowland

Not Toar. *Not Toar!*
God-damn this! God-damn this all!
I think I'm howling in grief; I don't know for sure, there's this sound erupting out of me—I can't control it. That dam I built that's been holding back all the terror, misery and agony I've absorbed since this whole disaster started cracks mightily when my Toar drops his gaze and his face slackens.

'Toar!' I yell, but there's no response from him. 'Toar!'

He's gone. This incredible man, gone. There're no words—just this enormous void where my soul once was—it's rushing out of me and …

But his eyes are closed—dead people don't usually get the chance to do that, the last clever bit of me pipes up. They die with their eyes open—he could have just lost consciousness—also, he's not soiled himself—dead people do that when they're really dead, remember? Check him, you fucking idiot, check him while there's still a chance!

I snap back to reality, and check Toar's vitals: he's still breathing—barely—the black tip of his broad nose puffing shallow breaths, and there's a weak pulse my fingertips discover through his massive wrist. For how much longer I don't know, but whatever time is left to us is escaping while I dither and moan. Fucking get a hold of yourself, moron! You're always crowing about how fucking clever you are, always gloating how you manage to find a way out—so dig fucking *deep* here and find a way, or was all that bullshit you fucking loser? Find the way, find the way, FIND THE FUCKING WAY NOW! You let Bryce die, you let Ivan die, and now Betts is …

'Stasis. She's in stasis,' I say aloud, stupidly. 'In Resource Storage. On Deck D, where we are.'

A whisp of a chance. My last one. His last one. If I can get him into a stasis chamber, there's a chance it'll halt his death long enough for us to reach a medical facility—the exact same situation Betts is in, but at least I won't have to take Toar to a CAPS-F hospital fifty light years away.

'*Blue Boy*, how far to Resource Storage?'

'Twenty metres.'

I can do that. I can move Toar twenty metres. Fuck that he weighs more than half a metric tonne. I can do it. I will do it.

'Prep a stasis chamber, enabling emergency medical stabilisation procedures,' I command and add, 'Cut power to this floor's gravity plating, *Blue Boy*,' hoping that my previous success at moving Toar can be repeated.

'Unable to comply—full access to Deck D environment controls is incomplete. Estimated time until access obtained: twenty-seven minutes.'

Damn it! I doubt Toar has seven of those minutes before I gain access. I need another way.

'Sorry Toar, this will hurt like a bitch,' I say gravely, then grab him under his armpits, and start hauling his ass across the floor. He doesn't even groan at my attempt, which isn't a good sign—he's too close to crossing life's finish-line to feel pain.

It's taking all we've got, but we're moving, slowly—thank God smooth, even flooring is the Pryok'tel's preferred choice in ship design—Toar is sliding across the floor but it's a major effort just to move him a few metres—eighteen metres left, I can do this—we can do this. Ignore the blood trail—ignore the blood—nope, stop, get something to bind his wound—you're leaving half of him on the floor.

I set Toar gently down, as best but as fast as I'm able to, and scour my surroundings for something to use. I see and grab the nearest two Pryok'tel uniforms, shaking out a fine powder from each of them—the remains of atomically deconstructed Pryok'tel, I guess—and return to Toar. I bundle one up in a giant ball, press it against his injury, then wrap the other one tightly around his middle, binding him close. At least the uniforms are sterile, all things considered.

I resume hauling but I've noticed Toar's breathing is erratic, and I only get to drag him another metre or so before I see that he's stopped breathing. Please let what I remember from my mandatory CPR course work on an Oarth—please please please I beg as I squat beside him and begin pounding on his chest. Thirty compressions, then two resuscitating breaths—I have to avoid his teeth but I manage to make a good connection on his muzzle, enough so that I see his chest rise on its own, but only once, twice … he's leaving. His injuries are too much, and seeing him lying on the floor, limbs splayed, the logical part of me asks to let him go, to stop trying to prevent what has already happened. I can't. I won't.

'Just wake up already!' I yell at him in desperate fury. 'We're almost there, just wake up, Toar!'

My words echo in the corridor, heard only by myself. Oh Toar, no—not like this—*we're so close*. But it's no use, and I just lay my head on his chest, begging him quietly to just wake up, please.

Stupid, stupid waste of time, but if he's going to leave, I'll be with him to the very end.

*****

My eyes see it then, since I've got my head on his chest.

There on his forearm, where his suit's been torn. A blue plastic patch. The one he wears so that he can't smell me. Because of my Allure. The Allure, the one that sends Oarth into a frenzy. If there was ever a time where that would be a good thing, it would be now. Sorry Gren, looks like I was wrong—turns out I will use my Allure. I just hope it works. It has to. This is really the last chance.

I rip the patch off, tossing it aside and rubbing Toar's slate-grey skin underneath—I even spit on my fingers to try and scrub off the last of whatever drug was suppressing Toar's sense of smell. When I think I've done all I can, I

293

return to the CPR. Breathe Toar, breathe and let's see if my damn Allure is powerful enough to resurrect the dead.

Nothing happens. Either there's still too much of the olfactory suppressor in his system, or he's not taking enough of a breath for my Allure to reach him. It took a moment or so for my red-furred Oarth friend to get hit, so I'm not giving up—I try more CPR, then check his pulse—thready is too generous a term, but at least it's still there. Two more breaths into him, and I see his chest rising and falling from my efforts—but when I stop, so does he.

'No, Toar, come on … I need you to breathe. You can smell me now after all—come on, take a breath!' I plead.

I remember that he likes a spot just below his ears touched—when we were smooching on the shuttle, I only just lightly tickled there, and he responded immediately. So this is what I do now, leaning over his chest so that my fingers graze that same spot on both sides of his neck, and I make sure that my neck and chin are pressed right up against his nostrils—I think that's where humans smell best—I've always enjoyed giving a good sniff along my lovers' necks, and certainly, even over the smell of fresh blood, spent mining charges and discharged plasma fire, Toar's own spicy scent is coming through strong in my nose—vetiver! That's the damn spice he smells like … no, wait, not quite, but close—funny what runs through your head in a moment of intense panic. But even as my fingers dance all over the area just below Toar's ears, there's still no response—he's either not able to smell me, or … or he's dead, and he'll never …

There's a huff. It's not from me—I feel a blast of hot air hit just below my right ear, right where I've put the tip of his nose. No mistaking it—it's powerful enough to move my hair. Another blast of breath, this one strong, is quickly followed by Toar's chest expanding under me as I lie over him.

'That's right, that's right—get me into you,' I whisper to him, and carefully take hold of one side of his stout muzzle, while I rub my neck up and down the other side. I crane my neck so that my forehead brushes the spot under his ear, tapping it with a good bump, and then there's a groan that escapes Toar—I can't tell if it's from pain·or pleasure, but I don't fucking care—it's a groan. Dead men don't groan, I recall.

When I pull my head back up, I see his eyes open—his pupils are giant black holes, nearly eclipsing his cobalt irises entirely. They're sharp though, clear, and when they lock on to mine, that groan of his turns stronger—a full on 'woof' coming through. His arm, on the uninjured side, begins to curl up to reach me, but I back up and off his chest, keeping just out of his reach.

'You want more? Come get me,' I say, making sure my eyes are staring directly into his.

A low, frustrated growl escapes him, and he starts to turn towards me, swinging his massive arm over, reaching for me with a solid movement. I back up more, further down the hall, in the direction of the stasis chamber which I hope *Blue Boy* is getting prepped for us.

'Almost got me there, big guy. You'll need to do better though if you want to catch me,' I taunt, and scoot further back still.

That growl turns deep in his throat, an exasperated edge to it, and his eyes take on the determined look of a predator. He rolls himself over, pushing himself up—shakily, but he's doing it. Suren'thos said that the red-furred Oarth's endorphin levels spiked because of my Allure, and that it was likely he couldn't feel the pain he was inflicting on himself—but that was only after Vay'auh-ta needled me in the ribs. Seeing me in pain was what really flipped his switch—but I've got a feeling Toar may respond to a different kind of stimulus.

Shamelessly, I lower the zip on my mining suit, halfway down my chest—Toar's gaze follows it all the way down, and when I stop the strip-tease, another woof grunts out of him hard, a clearly annoyed sound to it.

'Two steps, Toar—I'm just two steps away.' I don't care if I must strip naked and wave my bare ass like a flag, I'm getting Toar into that stasis chamber. I have exactly zero other options coming to mind and this is working—so on with the show.

He lumbers to his feet, pain flashing on his face, and grips the padded wad of uniform pressed into his side. His expression is one of exhaustion, but his eyes, still huge with black pupils, don't lose track of me, and don't change in intensity. He takes a clumsy step in my direction, and I get to my feet before he has the chance to take his next, backing up again down the corridor.

Still facing him, I lower my zip further still, and when he sees my bellybutton, Toar gives another lusty grunt, taking that second step, his free hand reaching for me for a moment before he winces and returns it to his side. He stops, and his eyes close, his expression going slack, and he looks so tired. I need to get his attention back, now—get that adrenaline spiking, get him to stop feeling the pain.

'Hey, hey, you've not yet caught me. I'm going to get away,' I tease, pulling open the front of my miner's suit, exposing my chest further for him. His eyes reopen and return to looking at what I'm offering, but he's hovering in place, swaying slightly. That all changes when I flick my thumbs over my nipples and give each of them a good tweak —

Now he takes a proper step towards me—full strength, staggering slightly, his eyes huge and his jaw clenched with determination. That injured side doesn't seem to be bothering him anymore either, and he reaches out now, the tips of his fingers grasping for me. I keep advancing backwards, in the direction of Resource Storage, and he follows along at a slow, staggering gait. We're halfway there, we've got to be by now, it was only twenty metres away. I turn my head and catch the signage the Pryok'tel are so fond of—our destination is the next left at the four-way -junction. So close!

Toar and I make it around the junction, but he stops against the wall, breathing hard. I'm still just out of his reach, a lewd carrot on a stick, but he's tiring—I can see a dark red spot on his side as his makeshift bandages have been soaked through, and his eyes are only halfway open now, still locked on me, but getting glassy. I give him a moment's respite, but then we've got to get going—

he's fading again and I don't think the Allure's going to bring him back twice. We're so close though, so close, ten metres, maybe less, then I can save him.

But when I take a step back, Toar doesn't move; he looks so tired, so defeated, and in so much pain. I lower my zip further, hoping that maybe a flash of my crotch hair's going to help here, but he only gives a dull grin and stays where he is, puffing hard, slumped against the wall.

I dash over to him, pulling my zip up so that I don't fall over myself, and put my shoulder under his free arm.

'Come on, we need to get going,' I urge, but Toar just huffs, and does not move—except, I notice, that his hand does still manage to land on my butt, rubbing me weakly. Next to death, and he still cops a feel—you have to admire that.

'All that and more if you get off that wall and come with me,' I tell him. 'Now move it, soldier, ten metres—now!'

I pull on him to get him off the wall, but he's not coming. He grunts, clearly hurting, clearly exhausted. I peer up at him, and he's looking down at me with those same huge eyes, where I can see he's no longer got the strength. But I'm not out of tricks just yet.

'I command you to get moving,' I order him, my voice forceful, strong—making sure he understands. 'You are forbidden to disappoint your *thrane*.'

Got him. His face takes on a shocked expression, his eyes widening and his mouth closing like I've slapped him.

'I said move it!' I bark at him, and yank him off the wall, on to my shoulders—this time he comes, and together—God damn he is so fucking heavy!—we stagger the last few metres down the corridor towards Resource Storage.

It's a slow, arduous haul in the literal sense; as we near the door, I'm straining with everything I've got in me just to keep him semi-upright; he's half walking, half being dragged, but as we get to the automated doors, which slide open to meet us, his legs give out from under him, and we crash together in the doorway, onto the floor. I manage to stop the worst of the fall but we still land in a terrible jumble. He lets out a low, mournful moan at his failure, and after I've managed to extract myself, the look he gives me is one of fearful apology.

'No, you're doing great, you're doing great,' I say immediately, showering his face with fast kisses, stroking his head, rubbing his ears to comfort him. 'It's just a little more—a few steps is all.' I turn and look into the room—and there it is, the stasis chamber *Blue Boy*'s prepped, slid out of its alcove and waiting. Thank God—more likely *Blue Boy*'s nascent intelligence actually—that this chamber is large enough for Toar. It's so close.

'Come on, we're there, we're there—a few more steps!' I implore, and pull on his arm to get him to stand—but he's stuck, now, on the ground—his exhaustion, his injuries, his pain too much for him. I can't let him give up though—I won't—we're here, it's right here—

'No, come on, get up …' I beg him, but he can't even raise his head anymore. He's already given more than any person could—I've spent his reserves, and then some—cheating to get the last possible bit out of him, and it still wasn't enough. Last card. Last desperate card. The deck is empty after this.

'Toar, about six steps in front of you is a stasis chamber,' I tell him, as calmly as I can manage. 'If you get in, I can use it to save your life. I'll go get Gren, and he'll fix you, good as new. But only if you get in the chamber.'

I lean down, and whisper right in his ear, so that I know the last bit of him that's still there can hear me, 'And if you get in that chamber, you will go to sleep as Toar Grithrawrscion. When you wake, you will be Toar Halesire. I promise you.'

Not sure if it's Rowlandsire or Halesire, but it's not important—the effect of my words is instantaneous, and exactly what I was hoping for. Toar's head immediately lifts from the ground, and his eyes blaze, returning to look at mine with an intensity I've never seen before in any person I've known. I don't know what I see there—a fire? A light? Something—something from the core of him. Something that's been locked away, and in even more pain than he's in now, has found a way free, finally. He jerks his head in the direction of the stasis chamber, eyes it, then returns to me, giving me a last look.

A deep, dark rumble starts in his chest, then the first low hum of it escapes his mouth, and as he rises to his hands and knees—his bellow starts, his teeth gnashing at his pain, biting it, destroying it, defeating it. His eyes shut tightly against it, his expression is anguish and triumph in one. I back up, clearing his path, and his bellow truly blasts into the room, loud, deafening, powerful. He will not be stopped; I know this beyond anything I've ever known.

Like a punch-drunk boxer, he forces himself to his feet—and takes those last six steps at a run. He charges the chamber, bellowing so loudly that I need to cover my ears against it, but I'm right beside him as he crashes into the unit, throwing the top half of himself over. He struggles to get himself in, but he's losing that battle. I'm there beside him in the next heartbeat, and see what needs to be done to finish this one last, awful hurdle.

They say that adrenaline can make miracles happen, and I'm going to put that theory to the test. Squatting down, my back to the stasis chamber, my shoulders bumped right up against Toar's broad backside, I take two fast breaths in—and push up with my legs, with my shoulders, with my very soul—I will get him into that chamber, even if my heart bursts from trying.

I don't know what the current world-record for a human's squat-lift is these days—between genetic alteration, cybernetic enhancement and various forms of drug and hormone therapies, it's impossible to determine exactly what humans are genuinely capable of. I've got none of those fancy augments myself though— just regular old me with my regular old muscles—and my record for a squat-lift is three hundred and fifty kilos. I know Toar weighs more than that, so today is either going to be a personal record for me, or an abject failure.

I push. God-damn it, I push up, up, up—my entire body burns with the effort, my jaw is clenched so tight my teeth are gonna shatter … I will not fail Toar, I will not fail Toar …

'GET ... YOUR ASS ... IN THERE!' I yell at the top of my lungs, my leg muscles bulging and starting to shake as we near the crest of the lift.

One last helpful scramble from Toar, and then he's over, his crushing weight releasing suddenly from my shoulders as he ungracefully—but entirely—plops into the stasis chamber. I don't give myself the moment I need to catch my breath; instead, I scramble to adjust Toar, getting him on his back then aligning his arms and legs. I'm not gentle here, but he's too out of it to complain—in fact, his eyes are closed, and he's taken on a stillness that signals that he's got nothing at all left. His chest is still rising though, slowly, shallowly ... he's done more than anyone else could ever have done.

'*Blue Boy*, initiate hypno-stasis procedures for unit number ...' I scramble to find this chamber's unit number. 'DF-891-B. Provide biometric assessment when complete.'

'Processing, please stand by,' *Blue Boy* responds. The hatch to the chamber closes, and I manage one last pet to Toar's cheek before it comes down fully, creating a seal. As the unit withdraws back into its alcove, I scan the monitoring screen, watching intently as the first few lines of Toar's hypno-stasis procedure is run.

'<warning>: Resource significantly damaged—stasis procedures are not recommended,' *Blue Boy* alerts.

'Override,' I say, firmly.

'Processing resumed. Initiating emergency stabilisation procedures. Processing. Processing. Override failure, re-attempting.' My eyes bulge at this, and I step as close as I can to check the monitor—there're lines of warning about Toar's severe internal damage, but *Blue Boy* is pressing forward, allocating additional power to create the hypno-stasis field. There's no progress bar or other indicator to monitor—either the stasis will take effect in entirety, and save Toar by suspending all but the barest minimum of his metabolic processes, or it will not, and Toar dies, bleeding out from his injuries, alone in the chamber, in the dark.

'Processing complete. Stabilisation achieved. Hypno-stasis field confirmed—all life signs suspended.'

I collapse against the wall of the alcove, sinking to the floor so that I'm sitting on my butt, head in hands. I got him, I got him. *Blue Boy* continues to make recommendations that I seek medical assistance prior to waking Toar, but it's just background noise to me. My heart is thundering in my chest, my pulse a deep drumbeat in my ears, and I'm taking huge breaths of air to steady myself. I get myself enough oxygen so that the spinning stops, and calm myself down as much as I can. Is this over, finally? Have we won, at last? Or does the universe have one last dirty trick up its sleeve?

I lift my head, staring off into the distance, hoping that this is the end to this day—the worst day of my life, save for it bringing Toar and me together. What a price to pay for that though—what an awful price.

It's then that I see it—there, across from me, just beside the door we staggered through and collapsed in the middle of. I start to laugh, low at first, but then with increasing volume as I contemplate the dark humour of it all. An anti-grav lift. Like the one the Pryok'tel used to bring my red-furred friend in to see me with. Right there—ready to use, ready to lift Toar up with no more than the press of a few buttons. Right there—stored efficiently.

I laugh louder, but it soon turns to sobbing as all the emotions I've been refusing to experience force themselves out of me, finally. It's okay, no-one but *Blue Boy* can hear me—if a man cries alone to himself, that doesn't count as crying, does it? Shouldn't matter—I've got every right to it, after all. My poor Bryce. My God, Bryce, he's gone. And Ivan—so unfair, so wrong, so very wrong that he should have died. Mia, who never existed, except in my heart—gone too. Betts and Toar, suspended on the precipice of death—a stray power fluctuation, and they could slip over. Cor should be all right though, at least there's that. I'd wake him up right now but Harculcorians have a bitch of a time coming out of this type of hypno-stasis; they need medical monitoring and I don't think I wanna risk that just so that I can have a friend to talk to. Besides, he's never seen me cry—I wouldn't want to embarrass him.

So I sit, weeping, laughing, seesawing between the two, a man in misery and a man in pain, but a man who's won. We did it Toar, we fucking did it—beat those cannibal fuckers to the very last of them. They're ash and dust now—no chance that their bodies will be honoured by becoming a meal.

Forgive my pettiness, but that last bit is so darkly satisfying—after all they have taken from me, it just feels *so* good to pay them back.

CHAPTER 28
Toar

Halesire. I'm Toar Halesire now. Even while I dream, I know that fifteen long years of pain have come to an end with just those words.

'... Toar, are you with us, then?' a voice beckons me. Heard that voice before, somewhere in my memory.

Fuzzy-headed, for certain—I feel too light for my own body. Where am I?

'He's coming around, Captain,' that same voice states. Doctor ... Doctor Pokey? Nah, I'm still dreaming—Dr. Pokey retired, he's on Oartheca, not here ... with me. Where's that again?

'Toar, this is Captain Derrar, you're onboard the *Grolthon's Spear*—can you hear me, my good man?'

I open my eyes—well, I squint—there's a harsh white light above me, and it's too much right at the moment. Feel weird, all floaty and such, but I think I'm on my back—there's something soft underneath me at least. That's twice today that I've woken up with no clue as to where I am.

'Rowland,' I mumble. 'Rowland, where ...' I drift, confused, but still with it enough to ask where my baron is, which is what any proper sire should do.

'He's safe,' that voice—Derrar—states. 'How are you feeling, Toar?'

'Odd,' I manage, opening my eyes further. I'm able to make out the first features of two faces looking at me—an old stormcoat and a mature woodcoat, about my age, but my vision's too blurry to make out any real features, yet.

'Here, I'll give him another shot of ...' the stormcoat starts.

'No,' I reply, shrinking back. That's definitely Dr. Yozthren Letherclan; old Pokey's not lost his tricks. 'I'm good—just need a moment.'

My head clears somewhat—I'm still feeling too woozy to pretend that I've got all my wits about me—things are too bright and there's that unpleasant, too-clean smell of sterilisation and medical supplies, that vaguely fruity and entirely artificial smell that you only ever find in a med-bay. It's never a good time when you smell that.

Great Oarth I am smelling! I reach up to cover my nose—if Rowland's here, I'll get Allured—I can't have that because ... wait ... my memory says that's ... ooooh, that's a good smell-memory I'm enjoying now—that ... oooh, that ... blazing fire, pure sugar, darkest of oceans, brightest of sunlight, rapture and ... fucking, breeding ... lust drenching me, desire seeping into every part of me, filling me, overflowing through the very tips of me .... I am his ... .and he is *mine.*

'I mustn't smell,' I say, shaking my head. 'Rowland's Allure—too powerful, he can't control it ...' Oh but I want to smell him again—and by the Eternal Oarth himself, I will—I will bathe myself in Rowland's Allure, it will cover every hair on my body, every cell inside me, every drop of my blood will be soaked in it. Even if it means I'll be destroyed by it.

'It's okay, Toar, Captain Hale ...' Derrar starts.

'*Baron Hale*,' I snarl, my teeth bared, my upper lip curling. 'He is the Baron Hale.'

I start to sit up, but Dr. Yoz gently places his hand to prevent my efforts—he only needs to apply a feather's touch and I'm held fast. But my vision's cleared now, and I look directly into the face of Derrarvral Henthrothsire—a man I knew as a friend in years past, but if he calls Rowland by any other title than Baron again, I will bite that woodcoat fucker's face off without a second thought.

'He's safe,' Derrar assures me, with a compassionate look. 'He's not far away, and you'll be able to speak to him soon, but we need to have a talk first, Toar—you, me, and Dr. Yoz.'

'Didn't you retire?' I ask, nastily, eyeing Dr. Pokey. 'Or was sticking your patients with needles too much of a fucking thrill for you that you had to come back?'

'Irritability and rudeness. Previously unknown side-effect of a human's Allure. I'll make note of that, I will,' Yoz grumps.

I'm about to snarl again that he should do just that, but the better part of me prevails. 'Sorry, Dr. Yoz. Forgive me. It's good to see you—just out of sorts.' I reach out with my hand to just touch the Doctor's, showing I mean no real harm, and he gives me a fast but gentle squeeze—apology accepted.

'That's understandable, Toar,' Derrar soothes. 'Let's give you a moment to fully come to, get you comfortable and all. There's no rush.'

'Rowland is really safe?' I ask, again, needing that confirmation. That he's not here is driving me to a type of frantic anxiety I've never experienced before, but these men are my friends, supposedly, and I've got no reason to distrust them, yet.

Derrar and Yoz help me to an upright resting position against the back of the med-bed. 'Baron Hale is currently on board the Pryok'tel vulture the two of you captured,' Derrar explains, then continues. 'We've got an away-team helping him keep the ship afloat. We're back in Oarthecan space, awaiting the arrival of a CAPS vessel to come and retrieve him and his crew. Everything is fine, Toar—everyone is safe.'

'The away-team's in spacesuits around him though, right—and they can't smell him?' I ask, concerned.

'All precautions are being followed,' Dr. Yoz confirms. 'Though it's not just his smell, Toar—they're not allowed any physical contact with him at all. The Baron Hale has secured himself in a separate deck on the vulture—so there's not been even a chance to get a look at him. By his own choice too, mind—the right one, in my opinion—and it shows he's got a brain in his head, and a light in his heart, taking the Allure seriously. We've kept in contact with him over the comms—he's fine, so he says.'

He's not fine. He's all by himself with people he can't even talk to directly—and no-one who's gone through what Rowland has would be 'fine' after that. I choose to keep this to myself, since I've got no way to solve it.

'Says he misses you,' Derrar adds, kindly. 'We'll let him know that you're awake and in recovery, and that'll make his day, for certain.'

'Speaking of recovery, Toar, that's something I'll need to talk to you about, after the Captain here's said what he needs to,' Dr. Yoz adds, looking at me sternly. 'But before that, I'd like to do some basic cognition tests with you—simple questions, if you don't mind.'

'What for?' I ask, suspiciously.

'To see if you're addled from being smacked in the face by Baron Hale's Allure,' Dr. Yoz asserts. 'Got to make sure you've not popped a brain strut and gone all crazy on us.'

'I'm fine,' I remark, darkly, giving Dr. Pokey an unkind look.

'Sure you are, now let me just prove that,' Dr. Yoz replies, with a patient expression that can't hold a torch to the one Gren uses on me.

What follows for the next ten-minutes or so is a series of easy questions about my past, things like my birthday, where I was born, who my Dads are—standard fact-checking questions that I assume are being asked just to make sure my brain is still working. There's a couple of—trickier—quizzes about what I remember about my time in the OSSN, and why I left, and my time as captain of the *Lurcaster's Claw*. Then there's some standard behaviour questions, 'what-would-you-do-if' scenarios that the OSS uses to determine whether you'd be a suitable officer—almost verbatim from the actual tests I took, and I remember all those answers so it's easy to provide them again, especially since I still believe them.

'And now about Baron Hale,' Dr. Yoz continues, and keeps looking down at the touchpad he's holding, purposefully avoiding my gaze. 'How do you feel about him?'

'What do you mean?'

He looks up and plasters a smile on—I get the impression that even asking these questions is going to be awkward. 'How do you feel about him? Do you like him, are you angry at him, are you wanting to be with him?'

'Well, I want to see him, to make sure he's okay,' I reply, vaguely. That statement is true, in the sense that it is the most trivial portion of the immense feelings I have towards my baron. That's the answer that Dr. Yoz is looking for, by the way—that I'm Allured, and that I consider Rowland to be my mate. I'm havering about concealing this, but I was once an OSSN officer, and still consider myself as one, on the inside—officers do not lie, they do not shy from the truth—it's better to face ruin than perpetuate a lie that could get others harmed.

'And yes, I do think of him as my baron,' I blurt out. I won't mention the part that my title is Halesire now because I want to check with Rowland first on that—I mean he said it to save my life, I seem to recall, but I'm not entirely certain he understands what those words could mean for us, if he meant them. 'But I know that he isn't. I know that he's human, and that he's not an Oarth baron. I feel that he is, certainly, but I know that he's not.'

Now I've lied, I realize. Rowland *is* a baron. He is *my* baron, too. I've not been awake more than fifteen minutes and I've already denied him. I should be shorn bare and beaten bloody for what I've done—that's still the traditional punishment, after all—never seen that, and there's no record in my lifetime of it being done—because only the worst, ugliest and vilest of drones would ever deny their own baron. Like I just did.

'I do think of him as my baron, though,' I repeat, trying to absolve myself in case the Eternal Oarth is listening—which He always is. 'I do. I just also know that he's human. I don't know what that means fully but that's how I feel about him.'

Dr. Yoz has been taking notes on everything I've said, nodding along.

'Would you protect him as if he were a real baron?' Derrar asks, considerately.

'Yes,' I say, immediately, then add with firm conviction, 'And he *is* a real baron, Captain, just not an Oarth one. To me, at least.' Why? Fuck why. I. Tell. Them. That's why.

'Even though he's going to be returned to the CAPS, and it's likely you'll never see him again?' Dr. Yoz asks.

'We don't know that,' I respond, strongly but not aggressively. 'I can't see him until this Allure thing is fixed—fully, you know, where I could smell him.' Great Oarth I want to smell my sweet Rowland! 'But that doesn't mean I will never see him again. There's a way, if you care enough, if you fight for it enough, and I will find it, one day. If he wants me to, that is.'

'I think he wants that too,' Derrar assures me, but Dr. Yoz scowls.

'So long as Baron Hale's Allure remains a threat, then I cannot allow you to come into contact with him, Toar. I'm sorry,' Dr. Yoz adds, firmly but not without a degree of respect.

'But if I've the smell-blockers on ... and we're in spacesuits ...'

'Toar, it's not just his smell, you fool boy. We've confirmed his Allure is transmitted dermally as well; you absorb it through your skin just by being in proximity to him. It gets up your nose, through your pores, in through the surface of your eyes—right down into you, and there's no drug on record that will block all of that. Sure, a spacesuit *could* prevent it—but we both know you won't keep one on when you're around him.'

'But I'm already Allured, Doctor. At least, partially—what more could happen now?'

Dr. Yoz's eyes widen with astonishment. 'Insanity for a start? Permanent damage to your brain? An overload to your endocrine system? Irreparable damage to your nose, skin, entire Oarth-blessed nervous system ...'

'He gets it, Doctor,' Derrar interjects, holding his hand up against Dr. Yoz's tirade.

'No, he doesn't, Captain. He got hit by the very tail-end of Baron Hale's Allure—just a whisp of it, just a fraction—there was still enough of the olfactory suppressant in his system to prevent the worst of it, and even then, the Allure very nearly fried his brain. Full force? It will shatter him—you only need to check on our patient down the hall if you want confirmation of that.'

Derrar shakes his head, signalling for the doctor to stop. 'That won't happen, Doctor. That won't happen.'

I look back and forth between the two men—something is going on, and I've been left out of the loop—I'm not even in the same star-system as wherever that loop is.

'He understands. Seeing Rowland is dangerous,' Derrar states, but gives me a fast, distinct look. 'Toar's seen enough danger to last a lifetime, I'm sure he wouldn't risk more over this.'

Derrar knows full well that I will. I can tell from the look that he just flashed me that he absolutely knows this.

'Yes, well …' Dr. Yoz starts. 'Even for a man in prime health, risking being near a human's Allure is simply not allowed. For you, young man, it's beyond prohibited. The physical trauma you've experienced is going to take some time to undo, and the last thing that will help you is getting another whiff of a lethal Allure. I absolutely forbid it.'

'What are my injuries?' I ask, wanting to change the subject—Dr. Yoz is doing his job with all his blustering and such, but there's no force in the universe that will stop me from seeing my baron, other than my baron himself. So switching Yoz to talk about my injuries will at least get him off my back—I've not been feeling them, but I think that whatever's making my head fuzzy must have something to do with that. I'm not in any pain, even though I do recall taking a too-close plasma blast to my left side—I remember seeing a ragged hole where I used to have proper skin and flesh, and of course, the blood—*my* blood— pouring out of me like a bucket with a hole in the bottom. 'You can tell me, with Captain Derrar here.'

'Humph!' Dr. Yoz snorts, eyeing us both. 'Well, for starters, your busted shoulder's been fixed—that was the easiest part to remedy, mind you—but you'll still need some physical therapy to get it back in good working order. The hole in your left side's a different story though: I've got you patched and stable for now—but we're having to grow you two new kidneys—your other two are holding out, but the ones you had were in direct firing line and were missing when we found you. Your gall-bladder will also need to be replaced, and we're growing you a liver-graft to patch up the one you've got. That, and replace a bit of your large intestine, plus you've downed five litres of transfused blood and may need another.'

'I see,' I say, grimly. 'How long am I out for, then?'

He shrugs. 'Organs will take a couple of days to fully grow—we'll transplant them in a series of separate surgeries over the next couple of weeks: intestine, kidneys, gall-bladder then the liver-graft, in that order. You'll need about a month's worth of recovery after that, plus a course of meds to help stave off infections and the like. About two months, give or take, and you'll be on your feet.'

'Two months?' I ask, disappointed.

'On a liquid diet too I'm afraid,' Yoz instructs. 'At least until we get your intestines sorted fully. Good thing you're a little on the hefty side, Toar—you're going to lose some weight from all this—silver lining I suppose.'

'What about, you know, my lower bits?' I ask, hesitantly. It's a question every Oarth who's been seriously injured asks.

'Might have a tad bit of trouble passing water, but that'll be the extent of it. No denning with another though, just to make sure the patch job I gave you has a chance to stick—at least two weeks.'

'*Two weeks?* I've not died, Doctor!'

His eyebrows rise. 'You very nearly did, Toar—if it weren't for your clever baron, I'd be having to ship your body back to your dads. From what Baron Hale's told us, he used his Allure to get you into that stasis chamber—and that saved you by the fluff of your coat. First time I've ever heard of an Allure bringing a man back from the dead, must say.'

'What about returning to work?' I ask. 'My first officer is holding the fort— I'm sure he can keep doing that, least 'till I return—I'd like to give him an idea of how long that will be.'

Yoz and Derrar briefly exchange concerned looks, but it's Yoz who replies. 'I'll let the good Captain here talk to you about that. In the meantime, Toar, I'll be your primary physician during your stay with us—*the Grolthon's Spear's* got a top-of-the-line med-bay, no need to send you to Oartheca for the surgeries. You can recover at your Dad's estate, when you're ready for that—and have his doctor look after you from there.'

'Well, I know I'm in good hands while on board, at least,' I say, hiding the disappointment at weeks' worth of unnecessary needle jabs while Dr. Yoz has his way with me. I'm being unkind; Dr. Yoz is a fantastic physician—just behind the times, and rough around the edges, and no desire to change that. Gren certainly wouldn't stick me with needles, and I'd have got at least twenty pats on my head by now, what with having survived a plasma blast. 'What about, uh, side effects, from Baron Hale's Allure?'

He grumbles even before he starts. 'From what your blood chemistry indicates, you are fully and truly Allured, Toar—right down to your wrigglers all going into active baby-making mode, so, keep that in mind if you're planning to tend your own den, in the next few days—you'll ejaculate ...'

'Yes, Doctor, we know,' Derrar interrupts, patiently. 'We've both been sires and know what to expect.'

'I know that,' Yoz remarks irritably, but then eyes me again. 'But it's best he knows ahead of time before I get a call with him in a panic from having soaked his den.'

I stifle a laugh. Extended and voluminous orgasms are one of the more pleasant aspects of siring with a baron—highly and rightfully so—as are the back-to-back ones, which can leave a sire writhing in ecstasy, depending on how much his baron wishes to keep him riding the wave. Cralren often had me so drained I thought I'd been hollowed out from the inside, taken to the point of perpetual bliss and held there for—oh, until I stopped being able to tell time? We love our barons for many reasons, and while having kids together is one of the greatest—the act itself is ... well, if denning between drones is great, denning when you're fertile with a baron is what legends are written about. I would be telling the worse lie imaginable if I didn't think that sharing a den with Rowland wouldn't reset all of those legends.

'I'll let a den-mate know what to expect, if there's one in the works for me,' I promise.

Yoz shakes his head. 'Sorry Toar, it'll fade before you're ready to show it off, I'm afraid—distance from your baron, and all—though possibly not right away, given the strength of Baron Hale's Allure. But as for den-mates in your near future? Once you're able to, and given everything you've recently accomplished, you'll need a scheduler to keep track of the requests you'll be receiving. If I weren't your doctor, I'd be on that list myself.'

This obviously catches me by surprise. Not that Yoz wants to den with me—I mean, he's quite handsome, even as grumbly as he is, and we've always had a thing for each other—maybe we came close to crossing the line when he was giving me a physical, once—perhaps twice—he's talented with his hands down there is all I will say—but that the idea that I'm to think my den-card's going to be full is perplexing. Not that I want it to be full—all I want is Rowland—but to hear that my desert might be getting more than a partial spitting of rain is causing me some understandable confusion.

'I'll bring him up to speed, Doctor, when you're done with your medical advice,' Derrar says, giving the doctor a distinct look.

'Which I am,' Yoz indicates. 'Except to remind you, Toar, that you're in my med-bay now, and I like things a certain way. None of the too-soft fur-stroking that suncoat tyke you've got on the *Lurcaster's Claw* does.'

'Oi, Dr. Gren's a fine ...' but Yoz just gives me a mischievous wink, and pats me on the top of my thigh, near my crotch. I don't mind that—quite nice actually, and all this talk about dens, fertility and the like probably has us all thinking of things—but I'm more curious about why I'm suddenly prime den-mate material.

'Right, well, I'll turn the floor over to our captain here, and you and he can have a chat. No more than an hour, mind—you need to rest, Toar, and if you feel like a nap, the Captain can always come back.' Yoz reaches over and provides me with some of that too-soft fur-stroking he accused Gren of, running his hand over my forehead and top of my head.

'If you don't mind this old saw-bones saying so, I'm glad you survived all this, Toar. Don't think a lesser man would have, to be honest. And it'd have been a shame if that had been the case—that baron of yours saved your life, what with his Allure, and I'm mighty grateful to him that he did. But another dose will likely take back what he gave you—so don't you muck about with it, or you'll both regret it. Mind me on this, lad. Please. I know you want to be with your baron—I do—but his Allure is like the sun—it will *seriously* harm you, if you get too close.'

There's something too sincere about Yoz's expression right now, something too imploring about his worry, that makes me take what he's saying to heart. But I also know Rowland is in my heart, and I will find a way to be with him—safely. 'I will stay safe, Doctor. I promise.'

'Good,' he agrees, then addresses Captain Derrar. 'He's all yours, Captain. You be nice with him, he's come through a war, after all.'

Yoz pats my knee, carefully, twice, and then departs the room, leaving me alone with Derrar, who has a calm, considerate expression as he watches Yoz depart.

'He came out of retirement, you know, just because I asked him to. Short on talented doctors, as always, but he's done his time and then some. Still, didn't take a word of real convincing to get him aboard—seemed that after a few months sitting at home, he got bored, and re-enlisted the moment I asked.'

'Shame about the needles, though.'

'True,' Derrar replies, nodding, then turns to face me. 'Speaking of painful pricks, I'll give you the bad news first—but remember, there's good news at the end. Let me know when you're ready.'

I breathe out a sigh. 'Best get on with it. I'm fired, aren't I?'

He nods. 'Yes, you've been dismissed from your position as captain of the *Lurcaster's Claw*. More than that, though—and remember, hear me out—you've been charged with being in breach of the decree.'

'Meaning?' I say, dreading the response.

He reaches out and carefully places his hand on my shoulder, giving it a tender squeeze. 'Meaning, Toar Grithrawrscion, you are hereby under arrest for actions contrary to the official Proclamation of the Prevention of Human-Oarth Contact, and are in my custody, pending your recovery. Once you're on your feet, you are to be released to your father, the High Baron Grithrawr XXI, to await trial at a further date.'

I nod, silently. I had hoped this wouldn't have been the outcome of my rescue of Rowland, but it was always a possibility.

'And my crew? Have any of them been charged?' I ask, not really wanting to hear the answer.

Derrar sighs. 'Dr. Gren is under investigation, and has been temporarily suspended from duty, without pay, pending the results.'

I grimace hard at this, and Derrar is quick to follow up. 'It's just an investigation, Toar, he's not been charged with anything—it won't even show up on his record, if it's found that he was following orders and was genuinely compelled to provide aid under medical circumstances. From what the Baron Hale has told us, that's entirely what happened, and so I'm sure Gren's going to come out of all this unscathed.'

'But there'll still be a stain,' I remark, angrily. 'Maybe not an official one, but there'll be rumours. He was a candidate for sireship, Derrar, and this will be enough to disqualify him in any baron's ...'

Derrar shakes his head, firmly, and his grip on my shoulder increases slightly. 'No, Toar—remember, you need to hear me out in full. Don't start down the path of guessing what will happen, not until I've given you all the facts.'

I nod, then signal for Derrar to continue. My heart is hurting too much for me to risk saying something, because I might start yelling.

'The rest of your former bridge crew were interviewed, and no further action was taken—you did a good job in keeping them out of harm's way, Toar, all things considered. And that's the worst of it. Now, ready for the good news? There's quite a lot of it, I'm happy to say,' Derrar hints, and his smile tells me he's eager to share whatever this news is.

'Not yet, Captain. What's going to happen to my Rowland?' Another question I'm dreading the answer to.

Derrar's previously happy expression fades. 'We're meeting up with the CAPS-N cruiser *Assiniboine* tomorrow, and we will turn his care over to them, along with his two surviving crew members.'

My face twists with pain, not just at the news that Rowland is leaving, but that only two of his family members have survived. He must be devastated, and not being able to comfort him hurts worse than anything Derrar has told me so far.

'You've got to let me see him, Derrar,' I beg, my voice weak in my throat. 'It … it would be a cruelty not to, a cruelty. You've no idea what he's lost, and how badly he's been hurt by it. Please, for the love of the Eternal, you've got to let me see him.'

'You will Toar, you will. I've been chatting with him ever since we've rescued him, and I can tell he's in deep pain, despite how he tries to hide it from me. He's also worried sick about you.'

'But Doc Yoz said …'

'Dr. Yoz has never been a sire, Toar. We are. We know what it's like, we know what needs to be done. I will arrange for just the two of you to meet, in a private place, where you'll be able to help him, and say your farewells. I've not met Baron Hale face-to-face, but even just speaking with him, there's no way I'd allow him to be ripped away from you like that, not without having a chance to say goodbye.'

'You can't risk that for us, Derrar. The decree applies to all Oarth, and if you're caught sneaking him on board to see me, they'll come down on you like a meteor.'

The hand that's been on my shoulder now strokes the top of my head, petting with care. 'We all need to do things so that we can sleep properly at night— finding a way to bring you two together is one of the better things I can do to help with that. Besides which, even if I'm caught—I'm fairly sure no court in the land would ever convict me—letting two heroes of Oartheca reunite one last time will be seen as the right thing to do—we're a romantic bunch, after all.'

'Heroes of Oartheca?'

'The good news I've been referring to. I'd love the chance to share it, what with all this gloom I've had to spread.'

I nod my head, turning so that his hand brushes my ear—his touch is a comfort, right now, helping as much as the pain meds I'm on.

'So, the most straightforward news,' Derrar starts, excitedly. 'Baron Hale is turning the vulture over to the OSS, pending your approval—he says that you're the key system administrator and that you'll be able to gain access to all of the records on board the vessel. That's a huge prize, Toar—not only will the OSS be able to find out about the new model vultures—port to stern—but Baron Hale says that there's a full manifest of where the vulture's been for the past six months. What we're going to be able to mine from its databanks will keep OSSIS busy for years.

'That, and we've confirmed that the CAPS's veil's still in its transport—the Pryok'tel were just in the process of removing it, but they didn't get it done before you won it back. Took loads of information out of it, but Baron Hale couldn't find evidence that they sent a transmission back to the Hegemony about what they discovered—meaning he's pretty sure that any secrets the veil had are still safely out of Pryok'tel hands.'

He now places his other hand lightly on my chest, near my heart, patting twice. 'And that's just the tip of it, Toar. See, the real prize was what the vulture was carrying—nineteen Oarth, of whom two were barons.'

I turn to face him, my eyes wide. 'Two *barons*?' I ask, shocked. 'How? Where from?'

'We're in the process of finding that out—they're just out of stasis and are resting, and well …' his face relaxes, and he gently rubs my ear between two of his fingers. 'They've been slaves all their lives, Toar—they don't know who we are, and they don't trust us, yet. From what Yoz can tell though, they're both fathers … many times over, in fact.'

My face crumples. 'No … no that's …'

Derrar just keeps rubbing my ear, comforting me. This is horrifying news—I mean it's wonderful they've been rescued, but that they've somehow been forced to bear children … nightmare-fuel, as I've said.

'So it's true then?' I ask. 'The Pryok'tel have found a way to get barons pregnant?'

'Yes, we've always suspected that, and now, well, we have proof of it,' Derrar replies sombrely. 'Once we win over our recovered barons, we'll find out how they came to be fathers, and when that report reaches the Assembly of Barons, I suspect they'll redouble our efforts to track down any other captive barons. Your vulture is going to play a huge part in that, what with us now having access to all those fine, detailed records the triple-mouth baron-spites are so fond of keeping. All of that is going to work in your favour Toar, when it comes time for your trial—had you not rescued Baron Hale, we'd have never recovered these Oarth; they'd remain lost to us.'

Now Derrar stops stroking my ear, and grasps one of my hands instead, wrapping it in his and bringing it close to his chest, holding our clasped hands on his heart. 'And yet, even the rescue of two barons and the drones is still not the best news I have to share with you. All of that will make you a hero in the eyes of Oartheca, but this last bit—this last bit will make you a legend—a true champion for us, you and the Baron Hale both.'

His eyes get misty, and he needs a moment before continuing. 'One of the drones you found—is an embercoat.'

I gasp aloud and my grip on Derrar's hand tightens involuntarily. I stare at him, dumbfounded. Of all the impossibilities I've encountered today—enough for a lifetime, I'll add—this by far is the most pronounced. There *are* no embercoats—there's not been any for centuries—but I can see in Derrar's eyes that he's telling the truth.

'You're … you're sure, Derrar?' I ask. I just cannot believe this—if it's true, it would mean … it would mean we could be a whole people again—a cure to a despair that Oartheca has never been able to heal from.

'Yes, we've confirmed it on a genetic level. That, and well, his red fur—he's just beautiful. Seen him with my own eyes. The colour of fire, just like the history books said they were. I never … never even dreamed …' He looks away from me, not wanting to show his sorrow, his elation, but I pull gently on his arm, bringing us together to share a hug at this impossible, miraculous, news.

They were dead and gone, our embercoats. Killed to a man by the Pryok'tel—a punishment for our first attempt at winning our freedom. Their extinction broke us, kept us broken, until Prime Baron Alther's rebellion, but that was a century later. No living Oarth has ever seen an embercoat—we've only ever had stories of them from our great-granddads, and their remains buried in our crypts. Until today, it seems—and that, that is … a joy beyond my ability to understand, even as I'm experiencing it.

I kiss Derrar's cheek, hugging him close to me—such a joy needs to be shared, an end to a grief our very bloodlines carried, for so long. He returns my affection, kissing me—carefully—on the bridge of my nose.

'So you see,' he continues, when he's caught his breath, pulling back and wiping his eyes quickly, 'that the rescue of an embercoat will likely go a long way in your favour, Toar, when it comes time for your trial—if there is one, after all. Everyone thinks it's just going to be a formality, mind you—something to show that the law has weight, but that it's justice that prevails.'

I am lost for words. All I manage is, 'A real embercoat?'

He laughs, and nods, kissing me on my forehead. 'Real. Very, very real.'

'Can I meet him?' I ask, hopefully.

He sobers now, that happiness draining from him somewhat. 'Yes, you can see him, but … he's not well, I'm sorry to say. He … Baron Hale … told us that the Pryok'tel deliberately exposed our embercoat, unprotected, to his Allure.'

'Oh, Great Oarth,' I whisper. 'What happened?'

Derrar retakes my hand. 'There's a reason for the decree, Toar. Yoz wasn't exaggerating when he said a human's Allure is lethal. Our poor, red-furred cousin's been permanently damaged—all he does is howl for his baron, refusing any attempt to reach him—we need to keep him sedated or else he starts to hurt himself, or anyone within reach. That, and well, Yoz says if he keeps going on like he is, it's just a matter of time before some blood vessel or something in his brain bursts, and kills him. There's talk about returning him to hypno-stasis, to buy us time while we find a way to fix him—but yes—the human's Allure. Not to be messed with, Toar. Ever again.'

310

'So we'll need to stay in spacesuits, if I'm to meet Rowland, before he goes,' I say, but Derrar doesn't immediately reply.

'That's for the best,' he states, carefully. 'It'd be my official recommendation, at least if what I was doing was official in any capacity. You know the risks, Toar—I trust you also know how to handle them.'

'I do understand,' I reply. It's all I will say—Derrar knows that I will take that risk again—there's no keeping a sire from his baron—but I will be cautious; should something happen to me because of the Allure, Rowland would blame himself—and I won't have that. But I will be with him, however I can manage it, even if all that we can do is hold hands again.

'Now, regarding my official capacity, I'm to obtain your statement about your involvement in all this, from the moment you made the decision to start this adventure you've been on,' Derrar continues. 'You'll have the benefit of an advocate at your side, and I'll recommend my first officer, Commander Huer, to provide you that assistance.'

Two careful pats to my chest, and Derrar stands up. 'But we can do all that in the next couple of days; give you a chance to rest up, and remember all that's happened. In the meantime, I'm sure you'd like to get a hold of Baron Hale—he's quite eager to know how you're doing.'

'Yes, please, that'd be proper,' I say, sitting up further at this news—which causes a slight twinge in my side—that patch-job Yoz mentioned makes its presence known, and I remind myself to be more mindful of it.

'Thought so—I've brought you a touchpad with a private link established with him,' Derrar replies, reaching over to the nearby bedside table, and handing me the device. 'You'll be able to see him in addition to hearing him, which he'll appreciate—he's been on his own on that vulture for two days now, so I'm sure getting to see you face-to-face, so to speak, will be a welcome treat for you both.'

'Two days? Is that how long it's been?' I ask, disappointed as I take the touchpad from him. It's just been a few minutes for me.

'You were at death's door, Toar—took a while to bring you back from that. Welcome back, by the way.'

'Heh, thank you, it's great being here. Truly, Captain Derrar—thank you for saving us, and for helping Baron Hale all this time, when I couldn't—I'm sure he's incredibly grateful; I know I am,' I say, touching his hand with mine, petting the back of it.

'Pleasure, Toar, pleasure. Just ... curious though,' Derrar says, a shy note to his voice. 'I've only spoken with Baron Hale over the comms—not had a chance to see him myself ... if you didn't think I was being rude, what does he look like? Is he as beautiful as I've heard rumours he is?'

'More so,' I reply, absently, as my memory draws my baron's face for me in my mind. 'More than your best understanding of what that word means. He's ... best of both worlds, really. Just ... here, find me some paper, and a graphite claw or something—charcoal dust even—I'll make you a sketch.'

'Hmm. Decree's silent about *drawings* of a human male ... good idea, Toar,'

Derrar replies, and it's only a few minutes till he's had one of his crew bring me what I'm looking for—good thick paper, just a shade or so off white, and a small set of graphite covers for my claw-tips—and I pick the one that best fits my drawing finger.

Though I'm still on the muddled side from both my injuries and the pain-meds I'm on, between my years practising little drawings like this and the hundreds of glances I've sneaked of Rowland during our time together, it takes me only a short while before a very passable portrait of my baron appears on the paper—it's like my finger almost guides itself, tracing the daydreams I've been having of him since we first met. Pleased with my work, I turn it over to Derrar, who regards it with a long, slow, appreciative gaze ... one would say lingering, with the amount of time that's passing.

'I say Toar, if this is even half accurate—that's ... well ... he's one lovely-looking baron, isn't he? Just ... perfect,' Derrar remarks, continuing to gaze longingly at Rowland's portrait. I'm not jealous—all barons are beautiful and having a drone express desire for a sire's baron is entirely to be expected; after all, they may become that baron's sire themselves one day. A sire never 'owns' his baron—that's as offensive as it is ridiculous to suggest—and so being proprietary is viewed quite poorly. Still—with that dreamy, faraway expression Derrar's currently got smeared all over his face, can't help but feel somewhat territorial. If he stares at the portrait much longer, he'll drool on it!

'Yes, well, thinking of giving that to Rowland, you know, as a memento of our time together, and all,' I say, reaching out. Derrar looks at my hand, at first unable to fathom what I'm asking for, then mumbles an 'of course' and returns the picture of *my* baron to me.

'Now,' Derrar starts, making to take his leave but still casting quick glances at my drawing. 'I'm off to give you a needed rest, as per our good Dr. Pokey. I'll check in with you later today, to let you know how I'll manage to get your baron to you ... bit tricky, having to figure that out, and not get caught.'

'Oh, have a word with Rowland,' I reply. 'He's very clever, Derrar, as I've said—he's likely thought of something already—even if you've not mentioned your plans to him. Fast as a whip-crack, he is.'

Derrar raises an eyebrow. 'Is that so then?'

I nod. 'He's the cleverest man you'll meet, Captain—you'd be a fool to think otherwise, even for a half-moment. It wasn't just his pretty face and his super-charged Allure I fell for, after all. Man's got a brain the size of a planet ... oh!'

Derrar starts at my exclamation, and I quickly follow up with what's just popped into my head. 'Derresion! Did you get to Derresion Prime, and pick up the beacon?'

'Yes,' Derrar says, 'We had a good chat with our new purple friend, albeit briefly, what with us needing to leave for Oartheca as soon as we could. We've got the remains of Orlintack Kerthsclan safely on board too—we'll bring him back to his family, soon—sure they'll appreciate having their ancestor back, even if he's three centuries late. We've also arranged with Derresion to receive an official Oarth delegation in the next few weeks—he's terrifically excited about the whole idea. Quite the achievement, there, Toar—making friends with an entire planet. That's another one for the record books.'

'He's a true Oarth, Derrar—don't let his outward appearance tell you otherwise,' I say.

Derrar laughs and pats me on my good shoulder. 'We'll have lots more to talk about, after your rest. Now have your chat with our good Baron Hale—send my regards and let him know I'll be contacting him later today.'

Derrar leans down to kiss the top of my head, then smooths out the fur there, and around my face. One more pat on my hand, and he leaves the room, and me with the touchpad. The door has barely closed when I've already keyed in the commands to connect to the vulture.

'Rowland—this is Toar, please respond, if you've got the chance.'

And in the next second, all the pain in my body flees before the sight of him— my sweet baron Rowland, and his wonderful smiling face.

CHAPTER 29

Rowland

Two days of worry vanish when my eyes fall on the bright, happy face of Toar.

I've just received a signal on the touchpad Captain Derrar sent me, to keep contact with the *Grolthon's Spear* while I'm stuck on the vulture. There is an Oarth skeleton crew helping to man the ship, but they're restricted from Deck C by direct order—and I'm trying to play nice by not getting in their way—so I've been mostly on my own for the past two days.

It's … not been easy. Between worrying over Betts, Cor and Toar, and speculating what will happen to me with my impending return to the CAPS, I've not been sleeping well. When I do sleep, that's when the nightmares come to keep me company, and it's not just Vay'auh-ta paying her respects—it's her, the entire crew of the vulture, and an extra-special appearance by both halves of Suren'thos. Other than Betts getting into the qualified hands of the CAPS-F, if there is one thing I am looking forward to when the Oarth eventually hand me over, it's that whatever sentence I'm facing will include a mandatory therapy stint. The CAPS does not fuck around with PTSD, which is good, because I'm gonna need it.

But I have made good use of the time during my waking hours—decrypting files, unlocking extra ship systems—the vulture is well and truly under my control, but I'm going to give it to Toar, as a way of properly saying thank you, and I assume he'll turn it over to the OSS.

I've not been entirely alone though—Captain Derrar frequently checks in with me, and he likes to talk as much as Toar does, so what he promises are only going to be quick calls to see how I'm doing often extend well past an hour. I'm glad for his time—though we're only able to share an audio connection (the touchpad is capable of visuals, but you know, the decree and all), he's been telling me more about Oarth culture, Oartheca's current state of affairs, and its history—both before and after the Pryok'tel occupation.

From what he's told me about the brutality and cruelty of the Pryok'tel, and their very nearly successful attempt to exterminate the Oarth—I don't hold any bad feelings for Toar killing Vay'auh-ta, whom I no longer think of as Mia (mostly). To an Oarth, all Pryok'tel are enemies, and while I myself don't subscribe to that kind of black-and-white thinking, I've never experienced an entire segment of humanity being wiped from the universe, such as Oartheca experienced with their embercoats—so I can't really judge.

Yes, Captain Derrar's explained that my red-furred friend is an 'embercoat'— an Oarth variant previously thought extinct, who've not been seen for more than three centuries. He told me why, too, and there's an outrage I feel on behalf of all Oarth at this cruelty, but I'm not surprised by it—it would be the most efficient way to quell an uprising, after all. So the discovery of an embercoat—a young one, no less—is a miracle, one that will be celebrated across all Oartheca.

It takes me a moment before I'm able to actually say hello to Toar—seeing his brilliant cobalt eyes again, with the right amount of blue iris instead of the giant black pupils like the last time I saw them, is such a relief that I'm just enjoying that sight again.

'You look good, Toar, you look good,' I tell him—because he really does, given the last time I saw him. 'I miss you, bud.'

'Me too, a lot,' he replies. His eyes scan me, and he smiles contentedly at the start, but then he takes on a concerned look. 'You're all right then, are you? Your face, your jaw there … it's all … uh … dirty?' he asks, his brows pressed together.

I feel my jaw—I'm not sure what he's talking about—my hand slides over my chin, feeling the couple of days' worth of stubble. Last time he saw me, I'd been clean-shaven, so is that it?

'Do you mean my beard?' I ask, unsure.

His expression goes still. 'You … you grow fur on your face?'

'I do—I can try and find something if it bothers …'

'No,' he orders. 'Leave it.'

I chuckle. 'Okay then, I will for you.'

'Good. You're all right otherwise, though, are you?'

'Yeah,' I answer, simply. He knows I'm not, but I won't bother him with that. 'Sorry I couldn't be there when you woke up, but you know—the decree. When do I get to see you though?'

'Captain Derrar will be having a word with you about that, later today,' Toar says, with a wink. 'Might be tricky, as per the decree, but I told him you'd have an idea about how to handle that, if needed.'

'I've got some suggestions,' I say, a small grin creeping over my lips. 'You know me and my challenges with following the rules.'

'I certainly do,' Toar chuckles. 'Rather useful, at times, that is.' But then his smile falters slightly as he says, 'Don't tarry too long though—we've not got much time left, together. I've heard that you're leaving us, tomorrow, back to the CAPS'. His tone is trying to sound upbeat, but there's a distinct melancholy to it.

'But I'm coming back,' I say firmly—and Toar's eyebrows rocket upwards, his whole face lighting up.

'I don't know when,' I add, cautiously, 'other than to say as soon as I can. Might be a while …'

'Doesn't matter,' Toar says, dismissively. 'That you are is more than I could ask for. We'll work it out, you and I, never you worry. We. Tell. Them.'

'You're damn right we do,' I answer. 'You're damn right. Look—this comms channel is fine for saying hello to each other Toar, but there're things I want to say to you in person, and tomorrow is coming faster than I'd like. Let me get a hold of the Captain, and we'll get things in motion on my end. It'll take a few hours, but I'll be there.'

'That's fine. Gives me a chance to get a rest in, so I can be bright and ready

315

for you, and all.'

'Speaking of which, I'll need to stay in my spacesuit—Derrar's mentioned the decree ...'

'Won't be a problem. It'll just be so good to see you, dear Bar ... uh ... Rowland,' Toar says, looking a bit embarrassed, a bit uncertain to use that title.

'You can call me Baron, Toar Halesire. I think that'd be right for us.'

He starts with another smile, but then stops before he can finish it, his lower lip slightly wobbling, and his eyes glistening.

'That would be. That would be quite proper indeed.'

*****

Orlin's Hope is an awesome little ship.

Though perhaps not at the top of the class in terms of overall appearance, its little size belies its usefulness—it's highly manoeuvrable, child's play to pilot, and quite difficult to detect unless you're actively scanning for it. That, and well, it's not registered anywhere in the universe—there's no record on any database that this little ship exists—it's a phantom amongst the stars, and now that it thinks of me as a system administrator, I'm more than capable of taking it out for a spin to, say, ... the port-side docking hatch of the OSS *Grolthon's Spear*.

Which, Captain Derrar assures, will be undergoing a full systems validation test on its operating procedures—making any ship-docking requests appear as part of a testing cycle, along with any resulting procedure that, say, extends the connection bridge, establishes a seal, and allows for someone to board the *Spear*. All that would just be a part of the testing, after all—entirely expected.

Apparently, another set of tests is being run on the adjoining quarantine chamber—and that will take what, oh, four or five hours to complete? Have to be thorough. Thankfully it's all automated, so no crew will need to be there to check that it's running—results can be picked up in the morning. There might be a glitch that corrupts the results though—it's being tested for a reason, you know.

Speaking of quarantine requests, Captain Derrar thinks that maybe Toar didn't have a chance to get a full cycle run when he first arrived—an oversight that needs to be corrected. Toar will be taken to the other quarantine chamber, on the port side of the ship—I mean the starboard side—oh, was there some confusion there? Mistakes happen, from time to time—but the worst result would only be that poor Toar is left all alone to his own devices in the wrong quarantine room for a few hours. Shame—but these things do happen.

How'd I manage all this? Well, Captain Derrar has been a real friend these past couple of days, taking time out of his busy schedule to check in on me, making sure I've got supplies and such. The kill-pulse wiped out all the food on board the vulture, not that I would have eaten any of that anyway, so he sent me a care-package filled with an assortment of Oarthecan foodstuffs, all pre-checked with their doctor to make sure I'd be able to eat them. A lot of it was preserved, ready-to-eat meats—the Oarth definitely put their sharp teeth to good use—but

I particularly like *dulian*, which is a purple citrus, about the size of a grapefruit but with that pleasant sweetness and subtle tang that makes *stôl* all the better for me. Captain Derrar was delighted to learn that I knew about *stôl* and made sure my care-package contained all the supplies I needed, with instructions, so that I could keep my caffeine levels in good repair.

And the Captain was further pleasantly surprised when I asked him about his baron, the Baron Henthroth, and if they had any sons he could tell me about—which he did, four in fact, and would I like to learn about them? Of course I would! They're in their early teens—my, how fast they grow up—and did that mean that the Baron Henthroth had taken on another sire? It certainly did—but the Captain hadn't found a bond-mate yet—he gets busy, with having to keep Oarth space secure. Lonely, too, I bet—not that I wasn't absolutely sure he'd have his pick of den-mates—yes, I know all about denning, Captain, seems like a very sensible practice, and I'm sure such a handsome-sounding man like yourself must have to fight off all the requests you receive—ha ha ha! You're sure you want to keep talking Derrar? I *love* chatting with you, but it is getting late in the evening, after all, must be time for your bed—oh, what about me? As in, what do I look like? Well … let me tell you …

It was my first time playing the vamp, and I think I did a good job of it—I've not made any promises I'm not going to be able to keep of course, but yeah—maybe I comms-seduced the Captain into thinking it wouldn't be such a terrible idea if I had one last goodbye with Toar. Let's just say when I heard Derrar's heavy breathing near the end of last night's chat session, I was pretty sure he was going to help me today, especially if it meant he could catch one quick glimpse of me. Hey, if you've got it, use it—especially if it gets you a chance to thank the man who saved your life in person, rather than over a vid-screen. Of all the terrible things I've done in the past few days, this is the least of them—plus I think Derrar actually enjoyed it, so …

I must say, I like the look of the *Grolthon's Spear* as I fly over—the Oarth have gone the exact opposite direction with their ship designs to the Pryok'tel, probably as a giant 'fuck-you' to their former enslavers. Where Pryok'tel vessels are dark, angular, devoid of markings and sinister in appearance, the *Grolthon's Spear* is a gleaming white, highlighted with bright blue markings and lights, with Oarthecan scratch-mark lettering proudly displaying his name right across his bow. He's a curvy boy too, a rotund main section with gently curved wings on either side, plus another oval shaped deck stacked on top, with a ring of transparent panelling, giving the crew a full three-sixty view as they explore the stars. Armed, though, that's for sure—I count at least four heavy particle cannons, front and rear torpedo bays and there's twin swivel-mounted ion gunneries on either side of the observation deck. Every component has a smooth, curved flow to it—no harsh lines, no jutting pieces—it's all blended and fits together perfectly. It looks sort of how I think Oarth are: comfy, solid and deadly when they need to be.

Captain Derrar holds true to the plan: I've docked at the hatch, and have exited *Orlin's Hope*, waiting patiently in the attached quarantine chamber. It's a good-sized room—I notice that the general interiors of the *Spear* provide for wide halls and tall ceilings—I bet Toar wouldn't have any problems roaming around here. That curved theme also applies, as far as I can see—the doorways are ovals, the corridors are tubes, and even the seat I'm sitting on is more a lounge than a bench. Again—it's all very comfy—lots of tasteful colours, particularly pleasant greens, easy purples and cheery blues on what looks to be walls built from carefully shaped and polished wood—that's the first time I've ever seen that material used in a ship's interior. I get an immediate impression of being at peace. If their quarantine chamber is this relaxing, then I wonder what their dens are like.

I'm not left alone for too much longer to ponder this though, as a short bleep from the entrance alerts me that my Oarth friends have arrived. Captain Derrar himself pilots Toar on his med-bed into the quarantine room, where I'm waiting, dressed head to toe as a Pryok'tel space trooper—with my helmet on clear mode, just so that they can see it's me of course.

Seeing Toar is a mixed pleasure—that he's alive is sending me over the moon but that he's obviously injured is hard to cope with, even though he does look significantly better than at our last encounter. He's sat upright on his anti-grav med-bed—which is much larger than the one I was on, giving Toar plenty of space to be comfortable. The rich grey fur of his hefty upper torso is on display, but I notice that there's a bald-patch on his shoulder, exposing his slate-grey skin underneath—I recall that there was once a scorch mark there, but it's entirely healed, save for the fur that will need to grow back. A blanket—again, almost identical to the one I had when I first awoke on *Blue Boy*—rests just under his massive pectoral muscles, likely placed there so I won't see his more serious injury, and extends right down past his feet, all neatly tucked in.

But he's beaming his crooked grin at me, and I can't help but to return my own smile at this—the cheer at seeing him is warming my heart so much, I'm able to put aside my worries and just enjoy this moment with him.

The man I assume is Captain Derrar, however, is straight up wide-eyed staring at me, his mouth slightly agape. He's a pretty decent-looking fellow, about Toar's age—I think, not as fluffy as Gren, at least—but with a thick coat of dark bay fur with a few tuffs of white around the sides of his muzzle, and his eyes are a paler baby-blue, but with intensely dark rims. Somewhat taller than I am, and heavier set like Oarth generally are—but not into the stormcoat's range—sort of half-way between me and Toar is accurate. Close to how I imagined he'd be, but judging from the look he's currently wearing, I'm nothing like he's imagined. He just keeps staring at me, and it's not until I tilt my head expectantly that he responds.

I catch something he quickly mutters to Toar about having to practise drawing before Derrar steps forward and places his left hand over his heart, all of his fingers splayed, and bows low from his waist—which I'm fairly certain doubles as an opportunity to get an eyeful of my crotch.

'Baron Hale, I am Captain Derrarvral Henthrothsire. Please allow me to welcome you aboard the *Grolthon's Spear*,' he croons, and I see the slightest narrowing of Toar's eyes upon hearing these suave words.

'Pleasure is mine, Captain,' I reply, equally charming—I mean I don't purr when I say it, but there's a rumble to my tone that I don't think I've ever actually used before. 'Thank you for having me aboard—unofficially, at least.'

He rises from his bow and I blast him with a dazzling smile, the sight of which causes that stunned expression to momentarily reappear before the captain returns to his charm-mode.

'Of course, though one day I hope we can make it in an official capacity,' he offers, all honey-toned. 'I'd love to host you, Baron, and treat you to the very best of Oarthecan hospitality.'

Not sure he means to use the word 'host' there, and I can't help but give an encouraging laugh at his brazenness, which causes him to grin ever so slightly.

'Four hours, you said?' I ask, and he knows I'm referring to the window of time Toar and I will have together.

'Closer to five, but we'll need some time to see you safely back to the vulture. I'll give you a fifteen-minute warning, when it comes to it,' Derrar confirms, nodding once.

'Then, again Captain, please let me thank you,' I answer warmly. 'I'll remember you for your kindness.' He can't help but give a bashful look in return.

'A better reward I cannot think of,' he responds, giving me a deliberate wink before bowing again deeply. 'By your leave, then, Baron.'

'Take care, Captain,' I reply, graciously—again, this is the first time I can recall behaving this way.

He straightens, and then turns, taking a moment to give Toar a gentle squeeze on his uninjured shoulder, and then departs. Toar and I regard each other. I can all but see the air distorting from the intensity between us.

'You've got protection?' I ask, simply. His answer is to show me the blue patch on his forearm, a replacement for the olfactory suppressant I ripped off him earlier. It's all the answer either of us needs.

My helmet has barely finished retracting by the time I've crossed the distance to meet him, his arms outstretched, eager to have me in them again. I don't crash into him of course—he's hurt and the last thing I want is to make that worse—but when my lips meet his, the fire between us ignites with delicious intensity. His tongue is immediately in my mouth, and I'm keeping pace as best I can, wrestling with his, darting into his mouth when he gives me even a small chance to do so. His teeth are long, and sharp, but I've already figured the right way around them, and we each turn our heads so that we can get right down and deep.

He pulls back, catching my eye, and then runs his tongue over my chin, my jaw—I can hear it scraping against my stubble, and the look on Toar's face is ecstatic. I get the feeling Oarth barons don't grow beards, because Toar is loving this sensation as his tongue-tip tickles me. He follows with a broad, flat lick on

319

my throat, running up the side of my jaw, over my cheek, before stopping at my ear, sending pleasant shudders all the way through me. Then he returns to my mouth, hungrily, and I'm eager for us to resume our wrestling.

I prop my torso against his uninjured shoulder, and he's got one hand behind my head, gently pulling me close with those careful claws of his stroking the base of my neck, tickling and soothing at the same time. His other hand finds the one I've got resting on his chest, and grasps it tenderly, while my spare hand finds his ear and traces its outline, or catches it between thumb and forefinger, rubbing and caressing it softly. It's when I slowly move that hand downward, just to that little sweet spot under his ear, that Toar moans in pleasure, the sound wonderful in my head with our mouths still connected, his hot breath filling me.

I break the kiss, his lips and head chasing after me for a moment, so that I can give myself space to get out of this Pryok'tel S & M gear I've been forced to wear. Toar likely does not have good memories of these spacesuits, but if he does, he's not said anything—his brilliant blue eyes never leave mine for a second—and they reflect the only thought that's currently running through his head: *more*. I debate for a microsecond whether this could become a sexy strip-tease and discard the idea immediately—there's no time for that; I want to get back to kissing Toar, and while holding his hand is nice and all, I think we're both ready for more than that.

I release the front sealing clasps on the suit, and there's a hiss of air as it depressurizes, then releases its bindings so that I can peel it off. These suits are modern enough that an under-suit isn't required—in fact, they work better with direct skin contact—so as the suit opens to expose my chest, Toar's eyes soak in the view, and he gulps.

'Ma ... may I?' he asks, reaching up with his hand, extending it slowly towards me, but stopping, looking at me achingly, seeking my permission.

'Yes, absolutely,' I reply. His trepidation is as adorable as it is irresistible—man's the size of a mountain but as gentle as a breeze.

His claw-tips just touch the centre of my chest, and he curves his fingers so the curls of my chest hair dance between them, a wistful, enigmatic smile on his face. After a quick glance to my eyes to see that I'm still good, he places his whole palm against my skin, moving his hand slowly across, stroking and petting as he goes. The claw-tip of his littlest finger just grazes one of my nipples, and it quickly perks from his attention, so he grips it—again, carefully—between his thumb and finger, and gives a satisfying tug. I respond with a happy huff of pleasure—and so he tweaks me, sending a pulse of sweet sensation up to my brain and right down to my cock.

I part my spacesuit further, with Toar's eyes following down as more of me becomes available to his lustful expression—once again when my navel is displayed, there's this flash of intrigue from him, and he can't help but slowly drag his claw-tips downwards, circling my bellybutton carefully with one claw. When he gets too close to the centre, a short laugh escapes me and I pull back slightly—and Toar's hand immediately stops, rising off my skin—a look of worry on his face.

'Just feels funny, a bit ticklish,' I say. 'I've got something else you can play with though, if you like.'

Another swallow. 'Okay,' he answers, trying to sound brave, but there's a hint of a wobble to his voice—either desire, or nerves, perhaps both, getting the better of him.

The rest of my spacesuit comes off quickly enough—I've had practice getting out of similarly constructed suits, so I'm even able to manage getting the boots off without too much of a delay. When I stand finally, fully on display, I take a small step backwards to let Toar see as much of me as he wants to—and his eyes fall everywhere on me, repeatedly: not one centimetre of me is regarded without anything other than pure desire. It's thrilling for me, and humbling too, to be so appreciated.

'You're magnificent,' he tells me, his voice full of tenderness and want, his expression one of reverence and longing. I return to his side, and his hand is back on me in an instant, caressing my chest, my stomach—slowly moving downwards. I'm half-hard already but that's quickly upgraded to a full-on salute when Toar, after first getting another visual confirmation from me, gently traces the tips of his claws over my balls, then up the length of my shaft at a tantalizing pace, his touch like electricity. I let out a shaky breath as that claw-tip finds my foreskin's entrance, then dips in to circle my sensitive cock head, causing those shivers to force a pleasurable sigh from me.

'You're stealing all my lines,' I growl, leaning over to kiss his lips, which he hungrily accepts before our tongues resume their interrupted tango. When there's a break, I manage to tell him, 'You're handsome beyond measure Toar. It means everything for me to be here with you.'

'Same ... oh Eternal, the same,' he murmurs deeply, and our kissing resumes—for a short while, at least. I part so that I can place my lips just under his ear, and as soon as I kiss him there, that deep, urgent groan of his rumbles out of him. Looking down his length, I noticed that his blankets are quickly taking on a life of their own, what with all the movement going on down just below his waist.

I continue kissing down his neck, that formerly warm, spicy, contented smell of his now full-on hot and arousing—like the tweak to my nipples, the signal courses through me and lands squarely in my crotch, causing my cock to surge hard, the head poking almost fully out of my foreskin. I'm determined to give Toar some much-needed tenderness here though, so I keep on my way downwards, sweeping over his broad shoulders, feeling his soft fur and the dense muscle underneath, my kissing tracing a path down his neck, over his collarbone, and further over his thickly furred chest.

I reach one of his nipples to repay him the treat he gave me, only this time using my lips and teeth—and a flash goes off in my brain: if Toar has nipples, then do barons have tits? I'm sure I'll find out one day, but for now, I'm curious if Oarth enjoy their nipples being sucked on, teased between teeth, lapped with the tip of the tongue. Toar's grunt of pleasure and push forward of his chest confirms that yes, indeed they do—they really do, especially when my hand finds his other nipple, and tugs and tweaks that one in tandem with the one I have in my mouth. This teasing, this tugging continues until another quick glance downwards tells me that Toar's at full sail; the blankets poking straight up at an impressive height.

But as I let go with my hand, and start moving down Toar's broad, firm chest and towards the blanket that's covering the rest of him, he reaches and takes my hand in his, holding it still.

'I'm … I'm not supposed to den,' he tells me, quietly, sadly.

I release his nipple, and look up at him, an *oh?* expression on my face.

'I mean, I can't … I shouldn't do anything too serious—something that could pull on my wound, is all. I'm sure it's okay if we just, you know, keep using our hands and stuff—is that okay with you?' His look is one of pure apology, heavily peppered with hope.

'Of course!' I assure him. 'I'd love to do more but I still love what we're doing—you want to keep doing that? I know all kinds of things we can do that won't involve you moving around too much.'

'Yes, yes I'd love that!' Toar exclaims, happily. 'But I want to share with you too, not just be stuck here.'

I look at him firmly. 'I'm having an excellent time, Toar.' I lean up and give him a hearty smack on his lips. 'Don't you worry about me, there'll be another time for us when everything's the way it should be, and we can do whatever our imagination can come up with. Let's think of this time as a practice-run—a preview of all that's to come. And come, and come,' I add, with a mischievous grin.

He chuckles, then adds with a tilt of his head, 'Speaking of that, just … there's some extra cloths and such to help keep us tidy, if there's a need to, just on the side of the bed here, under me.'

'How did I know you'd come all prepared for this?' I ask, exaggerating a suspicious tone.

'Comes pre-installed with every unit, I swear,' Toar protests, feigning innocence. 'But on a serious note … my doctor says that your Allure went and made me all, uh … fertile, and the like.'

'I can't get pregnant, Toar. Don't have the parts,' I say, reassuringly.

His eyes widen and he adds quickly. 'Oh, no, don't mean that. Didn't even … no, what I mean is that … well, uh … I'll, uh … spurt, rather a lot, if that's where we're headed. Not that we have to, I love what we're doing, and if we just want to … uh, so anyway, you know when, oh wait—do humans, you know—when it comes time …'

I save him. 'I think we work pretty much the same way in that regard.'

He looks relieved. 'Oh good, good. It's just that for me, I'll cum buckets now, and I don't want to spook you if that happens.'

I laugh, unable to catch myself in time, and Toar joins in with his crooked grin. 'Some benefits to being fertile, after all,' he adds.

'Thanks for the heads up,' I say, and we kiss again, problem solved. 'Speaking of head, okay if I take a look at what you've got under your covers? He seems like he wants to meet me.'

'Indeed he does,' Toar states, grinning. He tugs at the tucked in blankets, and I help out, quickly loosening them from his uninjured side. Once there's enough slack, I manage to slide my hand underneath, atop his stomach, and give long, circular rubs over his firm, hairy belly—and I notice the fur there is softer than what he's got on his chest and shoulders. His grin widens, and he closes his eyes, enjoying the tummy-rub—but I'm careful to stay clear of his injury—his fur's been shaven there too, so as soon as my fingers feel his bare skin, I detour around that and keep my fingers well into his fur. A few more tummy laps is all I can afford though; my curiosity is demanding I continue exploring this massive hulk of a man, and that flagpole he's waving at me is nearly calling out, demanding the same attention. The circles I'm making increase ever wider, until the tips of my fingers are just there … just there …

When I do finally reach his cock, I notice two things immediately—hot, as in thermal, and thick, as in 'holy fuck'. My hand spreads wide before I'm able to get a grip, and Toar lets out a short whistle at this first touch—*Christ* I can feel his pulse through his shaft—thump-thump, thump-thump—but if I thought his cock's girth was impressive, as I keep moving my hands down to his balls—good God they're each at least the size of my curled fist, likely bigger still, firm and heavy and covered with thick, soft fur. As I tickle my fingers over his fat sack, petting and stroking him, Toar hums contentedly, scooting his hips up slightly to allow me improved access to his nethers. Enough of this damn blanket, let's see this beast in all his glory. And Toar too, of course.

I carefully lift the blanket up from his uninjured side and lay it slowly down on the other, to keep his injury concealed—I do notice that there's a little of that shaved patch on his stomach exposed—and I discover what I overheard was his pouchline, almost like a barely visible scar in the shape of a semi-circle across his tummy, sealed over, but the main goal has been accomplished—Toar is now proudly, and absolutely fully, on display.

Now, to preserve Toar's modesty, I'll not go to *great lengths* with precise physical dimensions—no detailed measurements other than those in the *broadest* of terms. I will say one thing right off the bat, though: every man I've been with has had a perfect cock—every one of them—big or small, I like them all, fat or thin, just put it in—and Toar is no exception. Though I have no source of comparison with another Oarth, Toar seems equipped on the proportional side of the scales, a trait he shares with me—nothing obnoxious, but nothing to feel shy about either—with the exception that, well—he's a big man, quite thick in form—let's just say that he's pretty consistent all over.

I don't normally go into details describing my lovers' genitals, but Toar is a new species for me after all, and it's always a surprise how creative nature can get when designing a cock—I mentioned that Jylrelanrian's have two (forked, not stacked) and a Brolocon's is flexible, he can control it just like he can his dorsal tentacles, but it turns out Oarth are basically identical to humans in the penis department—which is great because that means I'll know what to do to completely undo Toar. Nice chubby cock head with a well-pronounced rim, and a comfortable length that ends above his pendulous testicles. His slate-grey foreskin's ample; even at full mast it covers all but the very tip of his cock, which is a similar grey but with a very slight scarlet tone to it—I know Oarth blood is red so that make sense. As stated, he's perfect—every man is, after all.

'It's you who are magnificent,' I state, quietly, earnestly, my eyes trying to gather all of my handsome Toar in at once, top to bottom but yeah, lots of his lower middle—I mean, come on, he's all new for me, after all—but I do make sure I'm looking at him in his cobalt eyes when I say, 'My God, Toar—you, all of you … you're perfect.'

He gives a shy smile, then looks like he wants to say something, but gets bashful, looking up at me through his lowered brows. 'Thank you, Baron Hale. I'll treasure your words, I will. Always.'

'I've a feeling I'll be saying it often, so I hope you've got a big treasury,' I say, approvingly.

Speaking of big, I must admit I'm feeling slightly intimidated by the prospect before me—excuse my crudity, but Toar's cock is *girthy*—I mean desire is desire, but logistics are logistics, and some of my feelings must be showing on my face, because he's quick to say:

'I'm very careful with him too, if you're wondering.' His grin is kind but his eyes are making promises he knows how to keep.

'Well, not *too* careful, I hope,' I say, bravely, stepping forward.

'Never you wor … aah!' he starts, but I've stolen his words when I place a kiss directly under the head of his cock, right on that part that's most sensitive on me, and, it turns out, on him too. A firm lick over the ridges sends a shudder through him and another gasp escapes him when I circle his entire tip with my tongue. Two more of these swirls, and he's gripping the sheets of his bed, and when I run my tongue downwards, to bathe his length and then his balls, his breathing is ragged. Yeah, this won't be a problem after all.

I'm able to get the first part of him in my mouth, but my jaw's stretched to capacity and I'm gonna nick him with my teeth—I'll have to practice on something of similar size to try and get him in further, next time—not that he cares though—that ragged breathing is turning into low, long exhales and sharp intakes, as between my hands, tongue and mouth, I savour and explore all he's giving me. I'm pretty sure that I could push him over the edge now, which would be a lot of fun … but there's one thing I've been meaning to find out …

I slip one of my hands to his furry thigh, and make more circular petting motions, while my other hand and my mouth keep Toar's cock entertained, every so often taking a break to place kisses, licks and suckle on each of his massive balls—yeah they're bigger than my fist, by a good margin—he must need to be careful when he sits down—before returning to his cock to find a new way to make those gasps of his keep going. My other hand, though, circles wide now, then grips his buttock, kneading the firm flesh between my fingers, and Toar sighs happily, raising his leg slightly to give me better access to his ass cheek. I keep pushing my hand further under him, and he raises up even more, thrusting his hot cock into my slicked hand and eager mouth. I finally get my hand far enough down so that it can slip under him … up to where his spine meets his butt …

Yep, he's got a tail. The short, stubby, furry appendage I can make out is most definitely a tail. I glance up to make sure me touching this isn't an equivalent to getting your bellybutton poked at, but no, that's not the case at all.

'Yeah fucking tug my tail,' Toar demands, throatily. Well there's my answer. He's raised his hips up enough to give me good access to said tugger, and I take a decent grip, giving a short but firm pull down towards me.

'Fuck yes!' Toar growls, thrusting his cock harder into my grip as I give him more of these short, firm tugs. 'Just like that, just like that … Eternal that's so fucking good …'

Gone is Toar's sweet shyness and angelic nature—seems his tail is his horny devil-switch. Mental note taken. As he pushes the tip of his cock into my mouth, I start to taste the first of his pre-cum—tangy, quite sweet, and plentiful—I lap up a stream of it, loving its taste. We're both having a fantastic time: Toar is growling a low, pleasurable rumble, as I keep tugging his tail, and he keeps thrusting, but I'm getting concerned with his angle here; he's leaning too much on his injured side, and if something goes wrong there, that'll be the end to our fun—and we're not done by a long-shot. I wanna see this 'cum bucket' I've been warned about.

I give one last tug, then release, tapping his hip to get him to settle back in a safer position, then give a few good licks and spits on to his cock, slicking it up so that my fist slides up and down on him with a good speed. I return now to kissing up his stomach, one hand stroking him at a good clip, the other running over his muscled frame, kneading, petting, caressing as I make my way further up, returning to his mouth. When I get there I'm instantly met with his tongue pressing against my mouth—he's still hungry for our deep kissing, but now his breathing is coming in short, hot blasts between our lips. He's wrapped one arm around my back so that his claw-tips graze my butt, and his other is pressed tenderly to the side of my face, gently caressing my hair.

He's close now—his cock is rock-hard in my hand, swollen to capacity, hot as a fire poker, and he's unable to stop with these short thrusts of his hips, extending each of my strokes, stretching him to his fullest length. His kisses are like he's starving for them, moving his tongue with mine in a way that demands more with every lick. Yet there's one last little trick I'm eager to see before I take him over the edge—as I keep kissing and stroking him, my other hand snakes its way along his chest—stopping to pinch his nipple of course, and Toar rewards me with a sharp approving grunt—before continuing its journey slowly, languidly along his neck, up and up ever higher, just right to that sweet-spot he's got under

325

his ear ... and just when I start to dance my fingers back and forth right on the exact spot ...

Toar breaks our kiss before roaring tremendously—not that terrifying bellow he launched at the Pryok'tel during the battle in the corridor, but close—that right-from-the-centre of his soul rumble of sound that vibrates the space between us. At the same moment—his cock spasms forcefully in my hand—it fucking jumps with real strength, and I can feel his ejaculation surging under my fist even before he blasts full force, his opening volley arcing high into the air.

So does the next volley, and the next—his seed thick, white and fucking copious as his orgasm hits. He's clenched his eyes shut tightly and his teeth are bared, that sharp bellow transforming into a series of hefty grunts that match the timing of each of his voluminous blasts—three, four—nine? ten? —*fifteen! sixteen!*—fucking Christ he's still going! I'm keeping up my pace on his wild-firing cock, and soon my hand, arm and shoulder are drenched with Toar's thick cum—*holy shit this is fucking hot!* My own cock is all but about to burst my load from the sight of this, and I've not even touched myself—this is the hottest thing I've seen in my life—and he's still pumping like a fountain gone haywire!

It's about half a minute or so before he's finally taking steadier breaths, and the last of his orgasm begins to taper off—not stop—taper off—and I slow my fist's rhythm so as to give him a chance to savour this sensation fully. His jaw unclenches and he immediately reaches for me, pulling me close so that we can resume our deep tongue kissing while I wring the last drops from him. I'm so fucking on the edge just from having witnessed all this that all I'll need is a kind word and I'll blow my own load.

'Mount my chest, cock forward,' Toar orders firmly. He nods towards me.

'You're sure ...'

'Yes,' Toar insists; his tone is captain-y again, but when he sees my quick glance to his injured side, he adds, with a slightly pleading tone, 'Please.' I can tell he wants to share his pleasure, wants me to know that mine is part of his.

Slightly against my better judgement, I get one knee on the med-bed, on his uninjured side, and as soon as I've got some stability, Toar sweeps me up, one-armed, and plunks me on his chest, my legs straddling both of his sides. My cock is directly in front of his eager mouth, and from the look on Toar's face, I get the feeling he'll swallow my aching cock right then and there—but instead, his long tongue comes out and gives a careful flick to my tip.

'You are the most beautiful creature I have ever seen, now and forever more,' Toar says to me, looking up with blue eyes all dark and powerful. 'I want you. I want all of you, with me for always. Give me all and everything, my Baron—I hunger for you.'

With that, his broad tongue spreads wide, and he pushes me forward, so that his tongue begins to snake its way dow ... oh, damn ... oh ... down my length—and when he reaches my base, so that I'm fully laid out atop that incredibly long tongue of his, he rolls the sides together and ....

... I was wrong before, this is the fucking hottest thing I've seen—no, no they're equal, different but just as powerful—Toar is using his tongue like I used my fist on him, and the explosion of sensation is so intense I need to bite my lip to stop this from ending too quickly. I want to enjoy all of this—I'm now fucking his handsome face, an expression of absolute bliss on it, the apex of each of my thrusts reaching deep into his mouth, causing satisfied grunts to escape both of us. Any concerns I had about his teeth are gone from my thoughts—his tongue encircles me almost entirely, protecting me from them, and it …

My God! He starts to hum a softer tone of that deep bellow of his, and the vibrations along the length of his tongue and my cock are mind-blowing. I give a short howl of ecstasy—it's almost too much for me—but his arm holds me fast against him, his claws carefully pressed into my thigh—I'm not going anywhere until he's sure I'm brought to the very pinnacle of rapture with him, and pushed over the edge.

Toar's other hand, I see from the corner of my eye, reaches over to start stroking himself anew—his previous orgasm has not satiated his raging cock— and the slick from his previous spending—the aroma of which, when combined with Toar's musky, spicy scent, is so fucking intoxicating that it's making me drunk with lust—provides him ample lubrication, and he's soon pounding away on himself—and I'm wondering if I'm going to get to watch another of his copious eruptions—fucking fertile indeed!

Between his humming and the licking of his tongue, plus my previously hiked level of arousal, I'm not going to last long—I've already hunched myself, fucking his tongue, fucking his mouth—and he's groaning in pleasure as much as I am— he can taste my pre-cum, it's driving his fist to fly up and down his length, his pace matching the one he's using on me …

'Toar …' I warn, and that's when his tongue goes even further, slipping under my balls, pulling all of me all the way into his mouth, and then closing his jaws over me so that the real firm suckling starts.

I cum immediately, hard, the intensity of this sensation ripping both my orgasm from my body and my own terrific growl as I fill Toar's eager mouth full of my seed. He fucking spurts again from this treat—grunting as his second orgasm (lucky bastard) gushes all over his belly, chest, and part of me—I feel his hot cum hit my back and butt and that just makes my own orgasm all the better. Toar follows through on his word—he drinks down every last drop I give him, suckling, guzzling, a look of absolute satisfaction on his face. He hasn't taken his eyes off me the entire time.

He keeps me hoisted on his chest, letting me catch my breath, but doesn't release my cock immediately; it's only after I squawk and squirm from a too sensitive tickle that he finally lets me go, a grin on his face and his bright eyes happy and content.

I leaned down and kiss him deeply, tasting myself on him, and he kisses me back eagerly.

'We're doing that again,' I pant.

'You're Eternal-blessed right we are,' he grins, sneaking another kiss to me afterwards.

He helps me dismount the med-bed, and once I'm on my feet, I begin to look for those cleaning supplies Toar mentioned—a stack of thick, fluffy cloths which might just be an Oarthecan towel, a few sachets of water, and a small jar that's labelled as 'sanitizer'. I hand Toar one of the fluffy towels and take one for myself; normally I'm all into helping my partner get presentable again, but I'm covered in Toar, and he's painted himself too, so it's best I tend to myself first before helping him finish up.

'You're doing okay?' I ask, casting a look down at his injury—the blankets have moved, and I can see the results of recently formed skin covering a once lethally large hole—the regenerated flesh is not quite the same shade of slate as its surroundings, and it's got a slightly puffy look to it, but it looks like it's survived our play well enough.

'I feel amazing!' Toar announces, carefully towelling his torso and groin clean—there's a lot to mop up. 'You're fantastic, you are!'

Seeing his blue eyes sparkle with the sincerity of these words tugs harder on my heart then I did on his tail, and while I admit I might be looking at him with a pair of love-goggles, Toar's glowing with a happiness that I've not seen on him before. There's a relaxed, contented look about him, not just a physical relief but an emotional one, like a tension in him has been snapped and he's able to just be happy.

'I think we bring out the best in each other,' I reply, thinking on this, and there's a surge of affection for him that catches me off guard. 'But I have to ask—that thing you did with your tongue there—how ... I mean I've never had that before—where'd you learn that?' I ask, grabbing another towel, having spent the first one I've used.

'A proper sire never shares his secrets,' Toar deflects, but then grins happily. 'Glad you enjoyed it though—watching you shoot down my throat was just absolutely *raur*—you're so damn handsome when you're in the throes of it—pushed me over, that did, watching you, tasting you, drinking you—looking up along your big chest and tummy, all covered in fur—you're very sexy, Rowland—I'm a lucky man!'

I chuckle happily at his praise, then lean over for another kiss. 'Same, big guy. Same. Seeing you cum twice like that ... talk about *raur*, and all. Looks like you're still primed to go, though.' I say, enviously, looking down at his still firm cock.

'Heh heh, that's normal—the Allure does that to us, when we're with our barons. Always ready to please and all. It'll go down though—want a little cuddle time with you instead, if you're up for it?' he asks, giving a hopeful look, scooting over so that there's a spot between the edge of the bed and his uninjured side.

I accept his invitation, carefully crawling into the bed, lying along his side, my head resting on his shoulder and one hand stroking his ear. His arm idly strokes my back and butt, and he places kisses on my head and draws me closer, pressing us together. As we pet, stroke and cuddle quietly, I find myself reflecting on what we've just shared, and why I enjoyed it so much: it wasn't just the physical act itself—which was loads of fun, literally—it was seeing how much Toar enjoyed our encounter, how much it meant for him that he was sharing it with me. How he gave himself over to me, how he wanted as much of me as he could have, as much as I wanted to offer—and I wanted to give him everything.

I'm not sure how much of this was due to my Allure, but after this time with Toar, I have to believe it can't be that much. It was the spark, but we are the fire, is the best way for me to describe how I think of it. Toar's made it clear it's me he wants—all and everything, as he said, and I want all that he is too—his powerful, intoxicating body, his noble and brave heart, and most of all, the incredible depth of his kind but fierce soul. This is what I had wanted for our first time together—not the med-bay, which wasn't too bothersome, but I'd prefer that hadn't been a necessity—but a chance to share each other, to really experience each other, and that's what we had. It was honest, it was real, and I want us to keep sharing. I think we both want that.

I just have to figure out how to give him that, is all.

CHAPTER 30

Toar

I am happy.

I know that sentence seems simple, trivial when attempting to describe how I'm feeling, but when you've not had a chance to say it for fifteen years, not had a chance to actually be it, then well—those three words have a fundamental honesty to them that can't be touched.

He—my Rowland—is curled against me, and I just can't describe the joy, sharing this moment with him. The physical part of our denning was great, obviously—he's a thoughtful, talented lover—and he tugged my tail, which isn't considered proper for a baron to do (since barons don't have tails of their own, it's considered to be degrading to the sire—even if it drives some drones like me absolutely bonkers).

Just to have Rowland touch me all over so thoroughly, tenderly but also with unmistakable want, put to rest those worries I've had about being too different from him—he played me like a master, giving it his all, but still being careful of my limits. Then he filled me, too, plunging deep in my mouth and drenching (but by no means satiating) my thirst for him, the taste of which was more satisfying than *arenlan*-blossom nectar, a reward I will remember and savour for the rest of my days. A proper denning, if there ever was one.

Proper isn't the right word, when I think of it. Significant sounds at once too formal and too marginal, and meaningful is just plain rubbish. *Raur* is close— emphatically wonderful, special beyond basic words, the absolute best of the best—a celebration. Our denning was pure *raur*, my heart was filled as much as my balls were emptied, which is a true sign that a denning's become more than just about the moment, and shines a light towards the future. There was real emotion from us both; I could see it in those charming forest eyes of his, hear it in his growls and grunts of pleasure and approval, feel it as he explored me and savoured me, and now, as he's close against me, cuddling like we're the oldest of bond-mates.

I ... I think I may be in love with Rowland, but that does seem foolish—it's too soon, and love takes time to grow. We've had an adventure together, exciting and terrifying, and intense situations like that obviously lead to intense feelings, let alone his Allure entering the mix. I'm well old enough, and experienced enough, to know that true love is nurtured; it doesn't just spring to life in a matter of hours ... does it? At my age? When I check my heart ... I ... I *do* love him, and there's this blurry memory I may have told him that, back when I was hurt ... but I think it's best that I get a better handle on my feelings before I repeat such a profound statement, even ... even if at this very moment, it is truly how I feel.

Because I know this moment can't last—he's departing, in a matter of hours, back to the CAPS. I wonder if I will howl for him after he's gone, like our poor embercoat does—though when I think about it, that's not going to be the case.

Rowland said he'd come back, and I believe him—man said he'd rescue his family, and killed fifty Pryok'tel doing just that—so if he says he's coming back, he is.

When is another matter, but we've shared something so important that it'll give me the strength I need to endure his absence until then. This moment is real, the future is only a dream—and whatever it holds, be it a misery or a miracle, I'll be all right, for him as much as me. Well, I'll try to be—let's be honest now, I suppose.

Some time has passed, not sure how much, and we both appear to be reflecting on our shared experience, both of us contented, both of us just enjoying each other's company. But no clock sleeps for a man, and there're some things that need to be said, while there's still a chance.

'I've heard that we weren't able to get back all of your family,' I start, and immediately kiss the top of his head, and squeeze him close. 'I'm so sorry, Rowland. It's terrible, that. I know how important they are, and that we couldn't save them all is a tragedy.'

He sighs, deeply, and kisses my shoulder. 'I think we did everything we could have done, Toar, if I'm being pragmatic—which I'm struggling to be—but from what I was told and then later verified, it looks like Bryce and Ivan both died during the initial attack—there was never a chance to save them. Bethany and Corculhoran were the only two we could have rescued, and that's what we did. As for Mia …'

'The Pryok'tel agent, the one I killed,' I acknowledge, quietly. 'I … I can't apologise for her death, Rowland—I believe I did the right thing there, all things considered. But when I see it from your point of view, I wish there'd been another way to end that situation. Those are my honest feelings, and I wanted you to know them, and that it's okay if you don't share them and are upset with me.'

It's a moment before he responds, but I don't feel any tension in his body, as he lies beside me—not sure I can say the same though. 'Mia was the person I loved, Toar—and she never existed. You stopped Secundus Vay'auh-ta, a Pryok'tel deep-cover agent who sacrificed my friends to complete her mission, murdered a stormcoat to prove a point, and threatened to kill me to secure an advantage for her people. I don't know yet how I feel about her being dead, but I know I have no ill feelings towards you about it. We're good, Toar.'

'I'm glad for that,' I answer, relieved. 'Your two other friends though—Vethany and Corculhoran—they'll be all right?'

'Yeah—Cor just needs to be monitored while he comes out of hypno-stasis—Harculcorians have sensitive metabolisms, but nothing the CAPS-F hasn't handled a million times before. Betts will be trickier, but I've seen worse get completely better—she'll be up in a few days, once we get her home, bawling me out for fucking this whole thing up.'

'I think she'll just be happy to know that you're okay, Rowland. I would if I was her.'

He's quiet again, contemplative, far away in his mind right now—I feel that distance, even though I'm cuddling with him as close as two people can be. Well, almost as close, but I'm not allowed to do that kind of truly deep connection that would actually bring us closer still. One day, I promise us.

'…and you didn't fuck this whole thing up, either, in my opinion. It was the Pryok'tel—they did all of this.' I'm trying to be helpful, but I worry I'm just making it worse.

'Shit happens, I know,' he answers, unconvincingly. 'And it's not like my line of work isn't without dangers; we all knew that, while we were doing it. Been lucky once too often I guess. I've just got a lot of self-reflecting before I can swallow what's happened, and not have it rip me up. I'll get there one day, Toar, don't worry.'

'You don't have to—you can be mad or sad about it for as long as you need to be. Just ... don't let it eat you, is all. You're worth more than that.'

He chuckles, ruefully. 'Have to disagree with ...'

'No,' I say, firmly, and gently put my finger under his chin, lifting it slightly in an invitation to look up into my eyes. 'You are worth it. I know you think about yourself as a "two-bit shit"—which, by the way, was as painful for me to hear as it was getting shot, I'll have you know—and that's entirely untrue. I'd not feel the way I do about you if it was. And that's not the Allure talking, Rowland, it's all me.'

He looks at me sadly, shaking his head. 'Toar, you don't know all the things I've done. I'm not one of the good guys. I'm ... I'm rotten, through and through. The only thing that's honest-to-goodness about me is that I'm a criminal.'

'I don't know all the things you've done, but I do know some things,' I say, ardently, kissing the tip of his nose, then gazing deeply into his eyes. 'I know that you woke up, wearing all the same clothes as you've got on right now, all by yourself with nothing but your brain and that magic hand of yours, with a bunch of people you'd never met before in a place you'd never been before, and faced finding out your family was likely all dead and you'd been the only survivor. That would have broken many people, Rowland—less than that would have.

'But not you. Not you and that giant, unrelenting heart you've got in your chest and that blazing star you call a brain. The ones that helped you, only twelve hours later, figure out a way to cross three light years, take on a full squadron of heavily-armed enemies, defeat them to the last one—including, from what I've been told, splitting a Primus down the middle, which I've never done—and rescue everyone you could possibly save. You're not a two-bit-shit. You're a hero. I am in awe of you.'

Rowland appears astonished by my words, and he swallows hard before saying, 'Holy shit Toar, that's ... that's one of the kindest things I've ever been told ... I had help though, remember.'

'Yes, a little. That's true. And I happen to know the fellow who helped you, rather well, mind, and he's not the type to fancy criminals. Even if ...' I stop, unsure if I want to proceed, but Rowland has to know, if there's to be anything genuine about our future together, '... even if he is one, himself.'

Rowland cocks his head, silently looking at me, and his quiet scrutiny causes the shame I keep locked down most of the time to find its way free. I look away, but he's got to hear this—just need a moment more to get myself as brave as he is ...

'You don't have to tell me anything, Toar.' He must be seeing me squirm, and he's showing mercy.

'Baron, you are kind, but if I am to be ... as you suggested ... your Halesire, then you need to know why I'm Toar Grithrawrscion, and not Toarculler Cralrensire, like I once was. It's important that ... that if you want me to bear your title, then you've got to have all the facts, first. It would be wrong for me to hide this from you.'

Rowland keeps his gaze on me, but it's kindly, if a little uncertain. After a moment, he places his hand, the one that's been so lovingly caressing my ear, gently against the side of my face, using his thumb to stroke my jaw. This gentle touch settles me, and when I'm able to return my eyes to him fully, he speaks.

'If it's important to tell me, then I'll listen.' The authority behind his words reminds me that he too is a captain, a leader and a warrior. 'But I'm no-one to judge, Toar, let alone a man like you. You know, a man who heard a cry for help from someone who posed incredible—*real*—danger to him, and knowing that, still helped anyway. A man who risked Under oblivion, just to undo a mistake he'd had no part in making, because it was the right thing to do. Who somehow—and we're going to talk about this later—found a way to escape an impossible trap and come to the rescue of the guy who trapped him. If there's anyone who's earned a chance to be listened to, it's you—but I'm not going to judge you. Fair?'

I nod, once, and he continues. 'Okay, then—why are you Toar Grithrawrscion, and how can we get you to think of yourself as Toar Halesire?'

I give a short chortle, mostly from nerves but I do admire his insistence.

'We've touched on it, a while back, just when we were looking at the war chest in *Blue Boy*. You asked if I was military, and ... I was. I was captain of the *Drethor's Glaive*, one of our war frigates, about fifteen years ago. I was a good captain—known for getting the job done, sensibly, and most importantly, safely. Not that I avoided risks or stayed out of trouble—if there was a fight to be had, I was in there—claws and full teeth—or full guns and maxed shields, whatever the case—but I was always smart about my fighting—kept my crew alive first and foremost, and never went into battle for glory's sake.'

'Sounds about right so far,' Rowland replies, resting on my shoulder again, playing with my ear.

'Well, seems my reputation for capability with minimum casualties caught the attention of a certain young man. A baron, no less. The Baron Thursk. Now, you need to understand, that barons are very important in Oarthecan culture ...'

'I've got an inkling,' he confirms, and I smile. Eternal I hope he keeps this good mood up when he finds out what happened to poor Baron Thursk.

333

'... and so when they want something, well, us drones are more than happy to provide it, if we can. Problem here was that Baron Thursk wanted something that's not usually at the top of a baron's list of things to do with himself. He wanted to be a Star Ranger.'

'That's rare, I take it?'

'Unique, more like it. I mean, barons aren't weakly, by any means, but because we've got so few of them, and because they've got the giant responsibility of keeping our species going, it's almost unheard of that they join us drones in battle—only the worst fighting would ever see a baron take the field. Here, though, with us having got our borders mostly secured, there was no real reason for Baron Thursk to join the OSSN. Except that he wanted to.'

'To play as a soldier, or for real?' Rowland asks.

'For real-real. Said he was tired of seeing his kinsfolk getting killed while he was kept safe. Said that if he was going to have sons, he wanted to make sure that he understood what it meant to have them go off fighting. Said that 'fair's fair', and such, and well ... he had a point, I suppose. That and Baron Thursk was young, twenty years old, at the time—just an adult, under our law, but not yet old enough to want to start his family. That doesn't usually happen until a baron reaches about thirty- or fortyish.

'Until then, because of the lifetime commitment they make to their families, in the gap between first becoming an adult and then becoming a father, barons have a lot of leeway with what they do with themselves. Most use that gap to build their baronies ahead of time, others pursue their dreams that would otherwise be hindered from looking after those baronies, and all the sires, clansmen and kids that are to join.'

'Baron Thursk had different ideas, it seems.'

'Indeed,' I reply. I choose not to let Rowland know that he, as a baron himself, would only say 'Thursk'—they're equals, after all—and instead return to my admission of my crime. 'And since I was considered a capable—and safe— captain, well ... I was more than pleased to have Baron Thursk, First Cadet, join my crew.'

'That must have been ... challenging,' Rowland observes.

'Not nearly as bad as I'd thought it would be. He was very capable: smart, dedicated, eager and easy to get along with. Beautiful, of course. Suncoat baron, straw-blond hair, rich umber eyes and even darker skin, and a pout so cute it could snap a mountain in two. Charming, complimentary, and insistent. Hard to resist, to say the least. That he wanted to be a Star Ranger—a pilot for our single-man close-range attack vessels—well, that was unnerving, for certain.

'But he showed proficiency—a good Ranger—not outstanding, but as good as many who sit in the cockpit. Served with me two years and earned himself a promotion to left-lieutenant—well and truly qualified to pilot his own starclaw, in battle, if it came to it. Later on, I'd find out his proficiency assessments had been slightly exaggerated, though. Turns out that if you're a baron, your qualifications officer might go easier on you—you know, so as not to ruffle you the wrong way.'

'Oh shit,' Rowland remarks, looking up at me. I nod—he can see how this story ends—but it still needs to be said out loud, just so there's no doubt.

'One day, the *Glaive* was escorting three transports from Oartheca to our outpost on Marden—a small moon orbiting the planet farthest from our sun. The transports contained supplies, medicine, equipment, and most importantly, a crew of ninety, to relieve the outpost garrison.

'And, well, during the tail-end of one of our Under-drive recharge cycles— we got ambushed by a Pryok'tel deathwing. They immediately went for the *Glaive*, and deployed their scarab fighters to take out the transports. So … I took the *Glaive* against the deathwing, and deployed our first wing of Star Rangers to keep the transports safe. If you've not guessed, the Baron Thursk, left-lieutenant, was on roster that day. Third from the top. Not that his position mattered, in the end—had to deploy the entire roster—all available pilots to their vessels.

'Could see it was going to be an ugly fight—had to buy time for the transports' Under-drives to spool enough for an emergency dive, and that meant giving everything we had, until the end. Deathwing knew it, and they sent all they had at us, and all their scarabs at the transports—targeting the troop carrier first. That could not happen—the death of ninety men—no OSSN officer would allow that, baron or not—it was our job to see them safely to the outpost.

I pause for a moment, thinking back to that day. 'I thought about holding him back, I did, our poor Baron Thursk. Could have used him at tactical, I reasoned. But Baron Thursk had already accused me of coddling him, limiting his starclaw time to just routine, safe patrols—and he was right, I'd been doing just that. So … so there wasn't an excuse I could fall back on, not that day— every pilot was needed. Sending Baron Thursk was the right thing to do, and unquestionably so, if he'd been a drone.'

I sigh, not wanting to continue, but I'm nearly at the awful end. 'The fighting was fierce, bloody—but we got our transports to dive, and they escaped to the emergency point. I damaged that deathwing something wicked, and I'd have finished it off if it hadn't spooled its drive and fled. We took out seventy percent of their scarabs too. And made it to the outpost, few hours later. All in all, a battle fought by the book, from start to finish—with as few as possible casualties on our end. Just like I'd always done.'

'And Baron Thursk?'

'Died in the opening fight with the scarabs,' I reply, darkly, bitterly, angry at myself, still. 'Got too eager and ended up being caught in a rookie trap—"follow my tail, I'm weak and hurt"—only to be taken out when his more skilled opponent flipped the scarab and opened full guns, close range. My fault, really, holding the Baron Thursk back as I did; if I'd given him a chance before that day, we'd have seen he wasn't quite ready. More drills, more tactics reviews, more combat simulations. More experience, is the thrust of it.'

'But as you said, he was qualified, and you needed all hands.'

'We did, I thought, at the time. My crew did not, after the fact, when the smoke cleared. Nor did the Assembly of Barons, when I provided my report. "One Star Ranger does not a victory make" was how it was explained to me. And they're right.'

'Ah, Toar,' Rowland commiserates. He lifts his head, wanting to kiss me, but I must turn this one down.

'I was the captain, Rowland. I should have known Baron Thursk was not ready; I should have handled his qualifications myself, instead of just carrying on as though he were just one of the other pilots on board. Should have sent him on more patrols—should have *taken* him on patrol, with me, to see his abilities for myself. Had I done that, there'd be no way he'd have been in a starclaw that day. But I didn't. I was negligent. It was *my* fault he died that day. I put one of our dear barons directly in the path of a scarab, and his death is forever on my hands.'

Rowland shakes his head for a good moment, wanting to argue with me based on his expression. Instead, he bites that back and only asks, 'So they stripped you of your rank?'

'Yes, but not just that. I was relieved of duty, essentially on the spot, after the OSS got word of what happened. First Officer himself placed me in the brig, much to the delight of the crew, apparently. Was charged as an accessory to the death of a baron; pretty much the worst crime in Oartheca other than the murder of a baron—which there's been no record of, even before the Pryok'tel invaded. Since it happened on board, it was a full court-martial too—with the death penalty on the table.

'Escaped that, obviously—but only barely. Trial was a nightmare, Dad had to pull every string he had to get me an Advocate—none of the ones I'd asked would even acknowledge I'd asked them. Managed to be cleared of the accessory charge, but only under the provision I plead guilty to a dereliction of duty charge and a charge of negligence leading to the death of a baron, both of which carry a life-sentence under normal circumstances. Dad managed to swing me getting a house-arrest with him though, on his word as a High Baron, so I at least avoided prison.

'But Dad couldn't stop the clan-kick that was mandated, by law, from the negligence charge—any Oarth who by action or inaction allows a baron to come to harm is to be barred from his baron, now and forever more. Since I was one of Cralren's sires, that meant he had to ban me from his house—hence why I lost his baronsname, and my kids took my sire dad's name—Culler —instead of mine. Still don't feel right calling my boys Grathculler, Harsculler and Rethculler, but that's part of the punishment. Dad also removed his name from mine, to show I was no longer a son of his … that's why I'm just Toar now, instead of Toarculler—still slip up though, but these days it's only in my head, rather than aloud. My baron Dad—Grithrawr—saw to it that the law only applied to Cralren's title, and not to his—and so I returned to being Grithrawrscion.

'All this happened fifteen years ago—ancient history from some perspectives, but it's still with me today, obviously—but I've not allowed it to ruin me. That's why I'm telling you this tale of poor old Toar—it's to show you that just because you've done something terrible in your past, Rowland, it doesn't mean that you can't turn it all around and come back from it. Since committing my crime, I've made a recovery, slowly finding my way back—I got work on the *Lurcaster's Claw*, only eight years later, and from there, I've put in my time to rebuild my standing—two of my sons are speaking with me now, and I'm no longer under house arrest when I get time off work. People are seeing me as being a valuable member of society again—well, those that know me, at least. Some of the angrier ones still use my name as a curse-word, but even that'll change, in time.'

Now I lower my head, and make to kiss him, which he accepts.

'And if an old worn-out coat like myself can turn his life around from that, then I know that if you wanted to, my Baron, all those parts about yourself—the ones that make you feel like you're a bad person, the ones that lie to you and tell you that you're not worth anything—you can defeat them all. Kick their arses just like you kicked the Pryok'tel's. It's hard work, sometimes painful, but it's worth it, knowing that you're stronger than your past, better than your mistakes. You've already won me over, and in case you've not noticed, I'm rather on the stubborn side.'

Rowland contemplates my words, and although his expression remains calm, I feel the tension in his body—his muscles flex, his fingers have stopped stroking my ear, and he's no longer relaxing into me, more like he's charging up for an explosion. I'm about to ask him to share his feelings, but he blurts out angrily and fast:

'First, you're not old, and you're not worn out. Second, I said I wouldn't judge you and I won't, but I gotta say how you were treated is pure *bullshit*! If you were a CAPS-N captain you'd have got a commendation for saving the transports, but to hear that you've basically been banned from your family instead is so *fucking unfair*—you were doing your job, and they *fucking tear your dad and sons away from you* because one man who made a choice to fight died doing his duty? I ...'

He exhales, sharply at first, but then slows his breathing on the inhale—doing this twice before continuing. 'I think this is one of those "cultural sensitivity" topics they warned me about in the Academy. How it's not a good idea to apply human standards to other societies. I'm going to try and keep that in mind, Toar, but I need to tell you that I don't think what happened to you was correct—at-*fucking*-all! Baron Thursk chose to fight, chose to accept the risk, and that was his right. He died protecting those transports, following *legit* orders his captain gave him, same as his peers. You didn't do anything wrong. From my human perspective, at least.'

'Some Oarth feel the same way you do, Rowland. My dad, my baron brother. A few of my former crew. Myself, when I remember to be kind. Baron Thursk wanted to be a starclaw pilot, and there's risk in that. He accepted that risk, and his sacrifice was not in vain—he did his part to protect Oartheca, which is a goal noble for all of us. He was and still is celebrated as a hero, so his life was not wasted by any means. But that's not the main part of this story, again—it's to tell you there's a way back, even from the worst of the worst.'

'I see that,' Rowland nods, 'and if there's anything I can say to make you feel better about the fucking bullshit you've had to endure, it's that I'm taking what you've said to heart. I'm done with the crime, Toar, I'm done with it. I don't know what it will take to fix my mistakes, or what I will do with myself, but it won't involve being a piece of shit anymore, that much is for sure. But I gotta ask you this, just for my own understanding—why were you so badly punished? I just don't understand the benefit of this "Assembly of Barons" ruining your life because Baron Thursk lived up to his obligations, and died defending his people.'

I nod, understanding his question. 'When a baron dies, Rowland, it's not just him that dies. It's all his sons, yet to be born. Oartheca is in trouble—our numbers are too low, and it's possible ... it's possible we won't recover. It's never been officially stated, but even the dullest drone can understand that there might not be enough barons left to repopulate us. The loss of even one baron threatens all of Oartheca.'

'Good thing we found two replacements then,' Rowland mutters, darkly, but then immediately looks mortified. I just kiss him—although he is a baron himself, he's not yet had a chance to understand just how significant they are to us—he's new to our culture after all. He's also angry on my behalf, which although misplaced, makes me adore him even more, I selfishly admit.

'It is a good thing we found two,' I reply. 'Plus our embercoat friend. That's a miracle, that is, Rowland. You'll be celebrated as a hero.'

'And you!' Rowland adds, his brows crashing together in anger.

I smile. 'We'll see. Certainly won't hurt. I'm even daring to dream it might be enough for people to overlook my past, if they can't come to forgive me for it. And none of that would have been possible without you.'

I kiss him again, this time on his forehead, and keep my lips there as I speak lovingly to him. 'So you keep that in mind the next time you dare risk calling my Baron a "two-bit shit"; I'll not have you slandered so ... I might get all angry,' I tease, pulling him close, tickling his sides carefully with my claws, lowering my lips from his head, down his neck, to nibble at where it connects to his shoulder. 'Might have to punish them that speak such ills.'

He chuckles and gently swats my claws from his side, then lifts my head so that he can kiss me properly. 'It's not a punishment if I enjoy it, Toar. But I get what you're saying—I'll work on turning this around for myself. If I'm to be your baron, I'd like you to be proud of me.'

'I am already,' I affirm, and pet his backside, as I feel his body relax again. 'But in that regard, about me being a Halesire ... that's the grandest honour you've bestowed on me, but ... I'm not sure if you understood exactly what it would mean, for us both, you know, beyond the name. I think your term 'husvand' comes close, in the legal bonding sense. I'd become a part of your house, and give you all my current and future assets—marginal as they are, mind—and in exchange, you'd become responsible for me, giving me a home and hearth, provisions and the like. Though I think very highly of you Rowland, obviously, I'm not sure ... if you ... if we ... are quite ready for that.'

He's quiet again, thinking, before he responds, 'Well, considering we've known each other, what, a day? A bit more? I see your point. Maybe ... jumped the gun there, I guess—not that the idea of one day being with you like that isn't appealing—but yeah, think we might need to get to know each other more before taking such a significant step. *That* sounds appealing—getting to know you more, I mean.'

I nod and immediately kiss him. 'It does, it does indeed. Sounds like an adventure I can't wait to start, whenever you're ready to.'

'In the meantime,' Rowland continues, 'if you wanted to, you know, think about yourself as a Halesire—in your head or something, whenever you needed to—like if you were feeling down or ... depressed, and needed a reminder that somewhere, someone in this universe owes you their life and thinks the world of you ... I'd be okay with that. Kinda sounds...nice, actually.'

'May I, really?' I ask, beaming with hope. 'Truly?'

He grins that beatific grin. 'Of course! Of all the Oarth in the universe, Toar, it's yours to use, whenever you need to.'

I kiss him, vigorously, fully, utterly. My heart is singing with relief, and I remember Derresion's words, 'a gift, a gift, a gift.'

'You are sweet to me,' I whisper, a bit maudlin, a bit soppy, my heart getting the better of me. 'I've been worried you'd not want me to have your title ... it does matter so much to me, and ... and I can't wait for the day when—uh, if—you decide you're ready to offer it, formally. I'll accept right away—right away.'

He laughs softly. 'Once you get to know me, too.'

I nod, but only to please him. I stood before his Allure, and survived, changed but unscathed by it. I already know him.

'Meant to say,' I mention, thinking of that very topic. 'That was clever using your Allure to save me—Dr. Yoz says he's never heard of an Allure saving a dead man. Thank you for your fast thinking.' I stroke his fuzzy rear again. Love the feel of that, by the way—its just a light dusting of hairs, fine and soft, but they feel as rich to me as the fullest of Oarth coats.

'The Allure didn't save you, Toar,' Rowland remarks, his fingers returning to fondling my ear, which if he keeps up for too much longer will send me into a contented slumber. 'You saved you. Your strength, your drive—the Allure was just the fuel, you were the engine.'

This touches me deeply, and I squeeze him tenderly. Didn't even cross my mind to think of myself like that—but he does, my Rowland. He sees the strength in me, that others cannot and I've forgotten. Oh, my poor heart—so full right now but will starve for him all too soon.

'What was it like, the Allure? Like with you and Cralren?' Rowland asks, carefully.

I take a good long moment before replying. 'This between us, only?' I check. Rowland's eyebrows rise, but he nods.

'Okay then—promising you won't share this—it was nothing like Cralren's Allure. His is like a loving whisper, an encouraging suggestion, a tempting promise. Yours? Like it's the only sound in the universe—powerful, deafening. Undeniable, irrefusable. Like the voice of the Eternal Oarth Himself, but that's being a bit blasphemous. It's, well ...'

I stop, recalling the overwhelming, utterly uncontrollable feelings that I will never forget from having been under Rowland's Allure.

'I'm sorry, Rowland—I'm just don't have the big, fancy words to do justice to things,' I start, trying to form the right words, but failing, so I kiss him tenderly instead, whispering, 'It was terrifying, but elating at the same time-like I was standing at the edge of the space, seeing what was beyond. Inspiring, unsurpassed in beauty, but ... entirely dangerous, wholly consuming. I ... I'm no poet ... might not be doing this justice.'

He looks at me apprehensively. 'No, no—that's a pretty powerful description, Toar. Kinda scary, though.'

'Yes, but only looking back—I felt no fear during. Don't worry, Baron, I was fine.'

'I could see that you weren't really in your right mind when it was happening—you looked like you were in pain?'

'I was, but it was ... I dunno ... I could tell I'd been badly hurt, it was ... a drag on me, that kept getting stronger, towards the end there. I wasn't afraid, even though I sort of knew where that dragging was taking me. I just wanted to get to you—even when I fell, the only thing that hurt was that I couldn't make my body do what you needed.'

'But you did, Toar—I don't think anyone else could've. You're unstoppable, you know.'

'Well, came too close to proving that wrong, but glad that's not the case. Plus, it looks like I'm pretty much none-the-worse for wear,' I say, but follow his sceptical eyes down where they're looking at my hurt side. 'Well, from the Allure part at least.'

'Captain Derrar told me that my embercoat friend isn't as fortunate though,' Rowland says, sadly. 'What's wrong with him?'

'Oh, he's just a little rattled, is all. We'll see him through it,' I reply, perhaps too brightly, because Rowland looks over his nose at me.

'Don't sugar-coat,' he says, sternly.

I'm at once confused and deeply touched by his term of affection for me—though I don't understand what he's asking me to not do, I've not been called 'sugarcoat' in ... well ... since Cralren, I suppose. Didn't realize we're already at the stage where we're using pet names—this is going very fast but it's quite thrilling!

'Don't "what" sw ... sweet Rowley?' I reply, stumbling over my own pet name for him, the one I know I thought up on my own, but don't remember when. I only hesitate because I think it's too soon and I'm not sure about using it. Still feel that way about him though.

He tilts his head, a puzzled look on his face, and then smiles after having figured that puzzle out. 'Don't downplay what's wrong with my embercoat friend—I might be able to help if I understand what's wrong.'

'Oh, uh ... well, Dr. Yoz says his brain's been hurt and he's gone crazy as a result. Says there's some damage that's been done to his nerves and such, like his nose and his hormones.' I interrupt myself, seeing Rowland's worried expression catch like a wildfire, and add quickly. 'It's not your fault—no one thinks that, and there's nothing wrong with me either. Dr. Pokey says I had enough of the sniffer-blocker left in me that it blunted the edge of your Allure, so to speak; I'm perfectly fine in my head.'

Rowland nods a couple of times, but that worried look lingers. 'I'll talk to our doctors, the CAPS-F—they might have some neurological specialist or something that can help. Don't know if they'll listen to me but generally, in cases like this—where a CAPS citizen has caused a problem with a non-CAPS species, they try and undo that damage, best as possible. Keeps everyone happy.'

'I'm sure that would be appreciated—whatever help we find him will benefit all of Oartheca, after all. I only wish we could find out where he came from.'

'I was able to get manifests for all the Oarth on the vulture,' Rowland indicates. 'I've turned those files over to you, and with some research, I'm sure you could trace down where he came from.'

I kiss Rowland's forehead. 'I was hoping that'd be the case—you've no idea the great service you've done for us, Rowland—I don't know how we'll ever be able to thank you properly, but whatever we do, it just won't be enough. We are all in your debt.'

He lifts his head up to kiss me under my jaw. 'Least I can do, after what you've done for me,' he says. 'Have to say though, given his current condition, I'm kinda still worried for you Toar, you know ... how we're exposing you to my Allure, even with the sniffer-blockers.'

'I've got a theory about that, actually,' I reply thoughtfully, and at Rowland's curious expression, I explain. 'See, I reckon that what happened with the embercoat—and probably what happened the first time a drone met a human man, was that there was no protection at all. The Allure hit full force, and well, blew that poor soul's mind. But you and I are different—we had some protection and used a lot of caution ... but still had a bit of contact, you know, a small amount at a time. I got a chance to get used to you, here and there, so that it wasn't as overwhelming as it might have been.'

'Sort of like an inoculation, or tolerance-building?' Rowland muses. 'That's ... that's actually a pretty sound theory, Toar. Maybe when that first contact happened, the results were so severe that they put the decree in place, to prevent it happening again—but also preventing the chance of a resistance forming. So what we've been doing ...'

'We should keep doing,' I assert. He gives me a look, so I add innocently, 'For science, you understand.'

He laughs and then kisses me. 'Of course,' he says, his voice now all low with a seductive rumble. 'And with any good theory, the way to prove it is with experimentation,' he explains, and his hand begins to wander over my hip, slowly towards my cock, and at just this simple touch, I can already feel myself hardening in anticipation.

'Yes, of course. That seems like the proper thing to do here,' I concur heartily, my hand lightly gripping his buttock, my claws carefully tickling his sensitive skin.

The next hour or so is a slow, tender, wonderfully romantic denning—the urgency from our first encounter has all been spent, so our affection for each other has a chance to grow and be savoured. There are many kisses, many caresses, many sweet words exchanged between us. He's noticed his pet name 'sugarcoat' causes me to go all weak-kneed, which delights him, so he whispers it in my ear while his hands explore my body, and I rain kisses, licks and tickles upon him, growling 'my sweet Rowley', which causes him to kiss me right away, each time I say it. I want so much to do more with him, the things my injury won't let me risk, but this denning is all about just being together, and it's just as enjoyable as anything we could share. Well ... almost, I'm sure.

As we slowly drive ourselves higher and higher into ecstasy, it's when he kisses my cock, taking the first of it into his mouth, suckling and licking, that I'm undone with only a handful of short bobs of his head. He greedily swallows my third offering—still copious enough that he guzzles a good amount of my still plentiful seed before letting some splash across his face and chest. Seeing my semen mark him like this, seeing how much he wants to be marked, as he rubs it through the pelt on his broad torso, down his wonderful tummy, and over his own swollen cock, thrills me to my core, but it is when he moves on top of me, to reciprocate his own marking of me, that he has me panting with anticipation. He's quick to bring himself to a powerful eruption, coating my chest, neck and face, my long tongue licking and catching what it can, before he offers his cock to my hungry mouth, letting me suck those last, delicious drops of his.

I do love this man, as I watch him over me, looking up his muscled length, into his beautiful, upturned face, his eyes shut in rapture. One day, I'll be able to tell him this in full, and that day I will be his sire, and he will be my Baron, in name, in heart, in body and in soul. It is the truest of truths.

*****

We get Derrar's warning that our time was nearing its end, and, well, so it has. We've had more than enough time to tidy and get decent before then, and Rowland's returned to that awful Pryok'tel spacesuit he's forced to wear—I wish I had known that he'd been left with only that, I'd have demanded he be given one of ours instead—as scratchy and awful as they are, they at least don't make you look like a soulless cannibal. He's even managed to return my captain's hat, which I'd forgotten about and had left in *Orlin's Hope*. As I don it, he kisses me, telling me how handsome I am, and, as we both know that this kiss will be our last for a while, it is deep, lasting, and memorable—it will need to sustain us, until we can share it again, one day.

On that topic, Rowland provides me numerous assurances of his return—which he estimates to be in three to four months' time, provided he sorts out his problems with the CAPS, which he assures me the return of the veil will go a long way towards accomplishing. Earth, his home planet, is at least four weeks away from Oartheca, and he says he's got some affairs to sort out before he can return to me.

In the meantime, I've promised him I will find a way for us to meet, safely and legally—he may not be able to come to Oartheca, but I will find a way to be with him regardless. I've put a lot in to my Dad's barony over the years, more than enough that I could be spared a nice, comfortable little ship that Rowland and I could travel the stars with, just the two of us, if that's all that we're able to manage, the idea of which is something that brings much hope to my heart. I'll also work to find a way to better manage his Allure—there's got to be a way around it, so that we can be together safely. I will find it, if there is one—and I just happen to know fourteen million minds that would likely love to help solve that puzzle.

But then Derrar signals that our time is now fully over, and Rowland and I have to say our goodbyes. I'm proud of myself that I don't openly blubber here—though I am bawling on the inside. I won't burden Rowland with weepy old Toar who needs looking after—I'm to be his sire, so I will need to be strong for him, after all. Besides, I will see him again, in three or so months. That's no time at all, not when I waited fifteen years to find him.

My sweet Rowley departs—Great Oarth spare my heart—with one last look at me, a cheerful smile but a deep sadness in his eyes, and gives me a salute, which I return, first having kissed the tips of my fingers to do so. The docking bay hatch closes behind him, and it's only when I'm sure it's shut properly, and he can't hear me, that a muffled sob escapes me, and I'm forced to tend to my too-watery eyes.

And though I am miserable, understandably so, I still have enough common sense to suggest to Captain Derrar to run a proper cycle of the quarantine chamber, with me inside—though I still cannot smell, I'm more than certain the air is thick with both Rowland's and my own scents, and I don't want the possibility of his lingering Allure escaping into the *Grolthon's Spear*. It's an eight-hour cycle, which is fine—Derrar assures me Rowland's transportation won't arrive until mid-day tomorrow, so I'll have time to see him depart back to his home.

So as the quarantine cycle runs, disinfecting the room and all within, I get myself a good sleep in—I'm tired not only from my injuries, but from our delicious denning—I've not pulled off a triple score in years, mind—so my sleep is deep and restful, and full of good, peaceful dreams, a reflection of the state of my mind in general.

It's in those dreams that I find one of pure happiness—all my family, together, at my side. My handsome boys—Harstoar, Rethtoar and even sullen

Grathtoar, all together with me. My two dads, Cullergrath—proud of me again, and my baron father, Grithrawr, holding his hand, like they used to when I was a boy. My brother Grithrawr, as well as all my brothers, including the ones that are no longer with us in the waking world, as well as nephews, uncles and cousins, gathered around me, their faces lit with joy.

And my Rowland, my brave and brilliant baron, standing by my side—my pride, because he is that beautiful, not just in body but in mind, heart and soul. They all call my name now, telling me they love me, cheering in unison one sentence that undoes all the pain I've felt over the long, lonely years:

Toarculler Halesire, welcome home.

CHAPTER 31
Rowland

Somehow, I manage to sleep.
Usually, the night before a big day, I'm wired, my mind racing as I plot—the recursive layers of contingency-planning, as Vay'auh-ta rightly observed. Tonight though, as I lie on the slab in my quarters aboard the vulture, I find that after my visit with Toar (and a long visit to the sonic showers) I'm pleasantly exhausted and content in both body and mind—the combination of which is enough to send me into a deep, restful slumber.

It seems though that my time with Toar is getting an extension, at least in my dreams. I don't know if it's an unknown biochemical side-effect of getting together with him, or just because what we shared had so much meaning for me, but tonight while my dreams are just as vivid as they've been of late, they're now much more … entertaining. Highly detailed, unusually creative, and wonderfully pornographic, my subconscious spills forth every carnal act it has in its library, casting Toar as the lead in a series of acrobatic vignettes that offer a sneak-peak at everything we're one day going to be able to accomplish together.

The intensity of my dreams has a surprising physical conclusion—when I wake the next morning, bedding soaked, the evidence that Toar managed to even the score between us is irrefutable. I've not had a wet dream since I was a teenager, and I wouldn't think it was possible after having been so thoroughly spent during my visit with Toar, but nonetheless, I'm having to ask *Blue Boy* how the Pryok'tel go about doing laundry. Not that I mind—the opposite in fact—it's just unusual how strong my dreams were. Perhaps it was something I ate before bed.

The consequence of such a thorough rest is that I'm now running late—the *CAPS-N Assiniboine* is scheduled to arrive shortly after 13h00, and it's already 10h00—and there're things I want to get done before I depart the vulture. The first is locating a portable data storage device, which is easy to find—the Pryok'tel's efficiency spills over to their technology, and locating a drive capable of storing a transfer of *Blue Boy's* current platform, including an integration of the Seraph and the copy of my purple gremlin, is a simple task. I'm not going to leave him behind; it's likely the OSS will purge the vulture's systems and instal their own, and the idea of losing *Blue Boy* to cyber-oblivion just doesn't sit well with me—not after all he's done for us—he was a part of the battle for the vulture as much as anyone.

The next part is a triple-check of everything else I'm taking back to the CAPS—primarily, Betts and Cor. I've had *Blue Boy* continuously monitoring their stasis-chambers, and they're both completely fine, but I'm fretting over them—the faster they're out of those contraptions, and on their feet, the happier I'll be. It's the one good thing about my impending return to the CAPS; they'll both get transferred to the med-bay and their recovery can start immediately. Ivan and Bryce are also secured, and part of my plans is a way to ensure the CAPS lets me put them to rest with dignity.

I've also checked the automated transport, ensuring all its contents are accounted for, and that its veil remains intact. The Pryok'tel extracted the transport's cargo, but that's easily remedied—their inventory system happily points out where everything was stored, and I make sure it's all carefully put back, just so. The veil was thoroughly scanned and detailed, but from what records I can find, there wasn't a qualified crewmember on board who could remove it— the decision was to take it back to a specialist facility on a Pryok'tel-controlled world, rather than risk extracting the veil and damaging it. I of course purge all of these records and details, even going so far as to corrupt the bits used to store them—I'm not sure of the CAPS relationship with the Oarth but I'm fairly sure they'll appreciate my efforts to keep the veil solely in CAPS hands.

The second-last part is a meeting with Captain Derrar, who's coming over to the vulture to formally 'see me off, safely home'—his words. I'm not sure the CAPS-N views my transfer quite so generously—I'd use words closer to 'the apprehension of a wanted criminal'. But I appreciate his kindness towards me, especially after risking so much to allow Toar and me a chance to be together one last time before I'm turned over. I've told Toar the truth—if all goes according to plan, I'll be seeing him again in three or four months' time—it's just that plan involves the equivalent of pigs learning how to open their own Under dive portals. I'm not betting that my return will be in that time frame, but I'm not giving up hope either.

After another sonic shower, a hot cup of *stól*, and a mighty breakfast—I'm starving it turns out, go figure—I meet up with Derrar in a conference room on the vulture's Deck C. He's in his full spacesuit, and I'm in my borrowed Pryok'tel gear, but I don't wear the radiation visor, much to his delight. He's still got that slightly stunned expression when we meet, but soon he's happily chatting with me, much like our time together over the touchpads, with the two of us sitting at a conference table, him inviting me to sit at the head of the table, while he takes the chair to my left.

Most of what Derrar is saying is a plethora of thanks for rescuing the embercoat, the two barons and the remainder of the Oarth in stasis—sadly he lets me know they've not yet been able to identify the stormcoat fellow Vay'auh-ta killed, but he's hopeful some genetic testing can identify a close relative on Oartheca. Regardless, Derrar assures me that the stormcoat will come to rest on his home-world's soil, which is a small but still comforting thought. The alternative was to become a meal, after all.

'How is Toar doing, by the way?' I ask, once Derrar's had a chance to ensure I've received the absolute best in Oarth gratitude.

He smiles mysteriously. 'He's all but fit and in fighting form, Baron Hale. Hard man to put down, harder still to keep down.'

It takes everything in me not to laugh at the double entendre, and I'm not sure if Derrar is aware he made one, or if he did so deliberately. One of my eyebrows twitches, and there's a small upwards turn of Derrar's lips—just a whisper, though.

'Had a visit with him this morning,' he continues, and reaches down to his side, bringing up a small portable storage container, its lid closed. 'He's got together a parting gift for you, and I thought it was such a good idea, that I've added some other tokens, just for you to remember us by.'

He presents his gift to me with a happy smile, and after thanking him properly, I can tell he wants me to open it. But when my eyes fall upon the first item stowed within, I find my breath stolen from me.

It's Toar's captain's hat.

Carefully, I remove it from a small pile of items it's resting on, and turn it— it's definitely the one I found in *Orlin's Hope* and returned to Toar last night, but its dark brim has been polished, the creases from having been scrunched have all been smoothed out, and the embroidered *Lurcaster's Claw* emblem's been given a thorough once-over so that it's bright and clear. His hat—the one that, as soon as he puts it on, causes his back to straighten and his chest to swell, making him the very picture of a captain, now mine to remember him by.

His thoughtfulness almost overwhelms me, but I manage to say, 'This is a treasure. Thank you for seeing it safely to me.'

Derrar nods. 'A pleasure, Baron.'

I reverently place the hat on the table, then remove my next gift: a good-sized pot of condensed *stôl*, which over the past two days I've figured out the exact right ratio of hot water to mix with in order to get the perfect brew; Toar's right, it has grown on me, but I still enjoy it with their *dulian* sweeties, a large bag of which is the next gift I bring out. It's inside a suncoat-sized mug made from a dark black ceramic, the emblem of the *Grolthon's Spear* engraved proudly on it. These earn Derrar a big smile and a touch to his hand; they're from him, I suspect, and his suddenly self-conscious look confirms this. These too are carefully set aside, as I retrieve my next gift.

It's a portfolio cover, made from a firm, stiff paper, and when I open it— well, if I thought Toar's captain's hat was sweet, this … this causes me to swallow and blink my eyes, holding back emotion. Inside is a hand-drawn portrait of me and Toar, together, drawn with such care and detail that it's like it's been taken with a camera. I've got a cheery, light-hearted expression, and Toar's got his handsome crooked grin—we're looking out together towards the viewer, our heads close like we're taking a holiday picture to send to family and friends. It's done in graphite on an off-white paper, and the detail … the artistry … it's just superb, but it's only when I see the artist's signature—Toar Halesire (with a small disclaimer indicating 'pending') that I suddenly realize I am holding the most valuable thing I own.

'This …' I start, but then pause, biting back emotion so that I don't upset Derrar with a display. 'I will never forget this. I have to thank Toar for this, personally—could you arrange that, if possible?'

'Your last gift,' Derrar indicates, gesturing towards the box.

I carefully stow our portrait in its protective portfolio, and set it down near my other gifts, before I take out the last item. It's an Oarthecan touchpad, identical to the one I've been using for the past few days, except new, like it's just come out of its packaging.

'You can use that to speak with Toar while you're here,' Derrar explains, 'and then take it with you back home. Range won't reach us, once you leave the system, but Toar and I loaded it up with some reading material—some of our history, our laws and customs, and a collection of our stories and legends, which is the best way to learn about us Oarth, in the long run. My favourite is *"Theongrawl, Champion of the Eternal Woods, and Tenerthrane, Baron of the Blackened Skies"*, an epic adventure with lots of sword-fighting, magic and a bit of mushy stuff—not too much though. Based on real-life events, or so the legend goes.'

I chuckle—I've got a feeling that story involves a handsome, brave woodcoat finding true love with a dastardly but beautiful baron. He doesn't stop trying, our good Captain Derrar, you have to give him that.

'Thank you, Derrar, there's got to be a way to show you how much all this means to me—care to risk a hug?' I offer, and he's halfway to his feet before he finishes his resounding 'Yes!'

I stand to give him a good, firm embrace, hugging around his middle section—which he returns but only after a few heartbeats; the first couple are sort of with him stunned in my arms, but he's quick enough to recover, respectfully placing his arms around my shoulders to squeeze me back firmly. He lingers, much like Gren did, but only for a moment, and again, like Gren, his eyes are filled with stars when we part.

'Oh, and it contains a copy of an official letter of recognition from the OSS Central Command, countersigned by our Assembly of Barons,' Derrar adds, almost absent-mindedly. 'For the folks in charge at your CAPS. Lots of fancy words, but the heart of it affirms that we're all in your debt for rescuing our barons and for bringing our embercoat back to us, and how this is another step towards the eventual union of our two peoples, etcetera, etcetera … basically, well done Baron Hale!'

That *is* a useful gift, I think to myself—nothing goes further towards repairing a bad reputation than the thanks of an entire people. All of my gifts are treasures, but this last one may save my ass.

I give Derrar another hug, which he returns wholeheartedly and immediately this time, and I pour my best thanks on him, not stopping until I see that bashful look of his again. I think I hear him mumble 'you *are* very cuddly' but he's very quiet if he does.

Parting again, he offers me a low bow, and tells me, 'I'll stay on the vulture to ensure you get a proper send-off while you have your chat with Toar. I do hope we get the chance to see you again, Baron Hale—hopefully by then our best minds will have found a way to work with your Allure—it would be the smallest way we could repay all you've done for us.'

'After all you guys have done for me, I consider us more than even, Captain. Take care of yourself, and I do hope we get the chance to meet again.'

He bows once more before turning to leave the room, and I settle in, powering the touchpad and establishing a connection, while simultaneously downloading its entire contents into my biocomp, just in case the CAPS confiscate the device. There's quite a lot of data, nothing I can't comfortably store, and I notice that some encrypted files have been included, but before I get a chance to take a look at those, Toar connects.

'Hello, sweet Rowley,' he rumbles happily at me.

'Hello, Sugarcoat,' I reply. 'Sleep well?'

'Beautifully.' He does look refreshed from our time together—there's a cheeriness to him, though I think I see a faint shadow in his eyes as he regards me. 'And yourself?'

'Vividly,' I remark, raising an eyebrow. 'You paid me a visit last night, in my dreams.'

He grins that lopsided grin of his. 'Hope I was on my best behaviour.'

'You were, in a manner of speaking,' I answer, winking.

He laughs and gives me a full grin. 'Well, we do den up rather nicely, it would seem. Not that I'm surprised.'

'Got your gifts,' I continue. 'Gotta say Toar, you know the way to a man's heart. Very impressed. That portrait you made is going to hang on the walls of my next ship, whenever I get around to finding one. You never told me you were so talented!'

He looks embarrassed, and one of his hands goes behind his neck, scratching himself. 'It's just a little doodle,' he says, humbly, 'but I'm glad you like it.'

'I love it,' I state, firmly. 'And between that and your captain's hat, I'll have all the motivation I'll need to make that four months shorter. I also can't wait to read some of those stories you sent—which is your favourite?'

He smiles. '*Drancral's Endeavour.* It's something I try to live by, his lessons and all. Pretty sure you'll like it, too—don't want to give too much away, but I will say it's a hopeful tale; makes you think and feel and all.'

'Well, I'm fairly sure I'll have some time on my hands in the next few months to give it a good read—it'll take me a while to go home and come back—all stuck on a vessel, too.'

'The sooner you're back, the better, though don't worry if you need to take some extra time while you're on Earth—I'll still be here, happy to look forward to seeing you.'

'About that,' I start, not really sure how to proceed with something that's been nagging in my brain. 'While I'm away ... I know that we're, I don't know ... sort of starting a relationship here, I want you to know that I'd be happiest if you kept being an Oarth ... you know, when it comes to denning.'

He cocks his head. 'Not too sure what you mean, Rowley.'

It's my turn to put my hand behind my head and scratch. 'See, I mentioned that while I was in a relationship, I just preferred one-on-one—but that's just my preference, and I don't want you to have to follow that—it's not the Oarthecan way and I don't want you to starve for company while I'm away.'

He furrows his brow and gives me an uncertain look. 'Are you sure? I understood that exclusivity was your preference, and am more than happy to provide that—I was thinking that's how we'd be, actually. You don't need to worry about me starving—had quite a fill, last night, after all.'

'Yeah, that's … sweet of you, Toar, but I can't help feeling I'm imposing. I guess that I'm more bothered by the idea of denying you, an Oarth, your social norms, just so that I, a human, can have my norms met. Seems unfair.'

'Well, you're the baron—whatever you say is fair, in my books.'

I shake my head. 'I don't agree with that part at all Toar; you and I are always going to be equals—we make decisions about us together.'

He frowns slightly. 'That seems … unusual,' he replies, unimpressed.

'It'll be an adjustment for both of us, I guess. But it's the best way—willing to meet me in the middle?'

He ponders for a moment. 'Well, sure, I suppose—but just because you say I can den, doesn't mean I'll do so. If I do, just know it's you I'd rather be with, and part of you will be there too, anyway. As for yourself, you're free to explore anyone you choose—that part of you being a baron I absolutely insist upon.'

'Okay good because Derrar's brought a sniffer-patch, and he wants to test it out with me,' I reply, faking relief.

I catch the flattening of Toar's ears against his skull and the fast baring of his teeth. 'I knew that scraggy-coated flea-pincher was bark …' he starts, but then sees my mischievous expression. 'Oh, you're teasing.' But when I don't answer immediately, his poor face collapses, and he asks worriedly, 'Right?'

'I am,' I say, with a small smile. 'Maybe you need to check how absolute your absolutely is.'

'Fair enough,' he grumbles, but not terribly hard. 'But—and this is just an example, not what will happen—would you mind if I had a turn with him? He's had to go to some great lengths on my behalf, and I'd like to make sure we've got only good feelings between us as a result. If there's a need to, that is.'

I surprise myself with how easy my answer is—I really do get that Oarth sex is more than just about getting your rocks off, it's that social fix-all, and that's what Toar's asking for. Toar's jealousy also makes sense for me—and I'd be lying to say it didn't give me a sense of satisfaction—but I also understand sex between a sire and a baron is viewed differently than sex between Oarth like Toar and Derrar are—the act of me taking on Derrar would be seen as more significant, making more of a statement, I believe, than if it were just the two of them. This is a big step for me—and I'm kinda proud that it turns out I'm perfectly comfortable with it—but only because he's Oarth, I think; if Toar were a human it'd be different, that much I'm willing to acknowledge.

'Sure! But again, this is not me giving you permission—it's just me saying that I'm cool with it. It's what would make me feel most comfortable, knowing that you were being yourself instead of trying to please me, when the thing that would please me most is if you were to be yourself. Does that make sense?'

'It does, and I understand. Just remember that my preference will always be you, regardless of whom I'm with, or not with. And when you get back, I'm going to be all yours—however you want me.'

'Good,' I breathe, relieved to have resolved this awkward topic, and surprised at how comfortable I am with it, in the end. It's a bit new to me, being in a relationship like this—but then again, Toar—all Oarth in fact—are new to me, so best to adapt, I say. 'That's settled then. Now, there's one last favour I'm going to need from you, and well—it's not quite as bad as skip-diving, but … there's risk.'

'Anything,' Toar says, immediately, sitting up in his med-bay, looking ready for orders.

'My plan is to return within four months—maybe shorter, probably later … but if you don't hear from me after seven months … something may have gone wrong.'

'I'll come get you,' Toar asserts. 'You've mentioned that you have some law-trouble, but that won't stop me. If I don't hear from you, there's not a wall in the universe that will hide you from me. I'll find you. I'll make sure you're okay.'

'Knew I could count on you. Don't get in trouble on my behalf though, last thing I …'

'Not a wall in this universe,' he repeats, and looks down his nose at me. The captain is speaking.

I nod. 'I'll transmit periodic updates—there'll be a delay before they reach you—but yeah, if you hear nothing from me in seven months, I'd appreciate the assist, Toar.'

'You'll have it.'

I smile, and then he and I, the business part to this session over, settle into more casual conversation—the mushy stuff, as Derrar mentioned—and I discover—Toar loves, even though he tries not to let on. Words of assurance, words of thanks, how much we'll miss each other of course, plans on what we'll do together when next we meet—a slew of compliments and sweet nothings, too. There's an undertone of optimism from us both, but also practicality—there are always challenges with couples, ours just manifest on a galactic scale, when it comes to my Allure, the decree, and how to work around both of those topics. There's got to be a way, and Toar's confidence in seeing us together regardless of what gets in our way is empowering.

Too soon though, our time's come to say good-bye—12h30 blinks on my display, and I receive a text comm from Derrar to let me know he's waiting at the starboard docking hatch, when I'm ready.

'Well, Sugarcoat, this is where I'll say farewell, for now,' I say, sounding intentionally cheerful. 'I hate long goodbyes, so just remember, three to four months from now, we get to say hello again.'

'Will do, my most sweet, my most beautiful Rowley. You'll take care of yourself for me, right?'

'I will. Get yourself healed Toar—I'll have missed you a lot by the next time we see each other, and I'll want to make sure we can get reacquainted properly.'

'Top of my list of things to do,' he grins. He then kisses his fingertips and salutes me. 'Fair and safe journey, Baron Hale—the Great and Eternal Oarth keep you safe. Peace to you, and all your kin.'

'And you too, my good Toar—see you soon.' I salute him, kiss my fingers, then end the touchpad's connection.

It takes me a couple of minutes, just sitting by myself, thinking, before I'm able to get on with the rest of what this day has in store. Oh well, at least it's not Pryok'tel this time.

*****

I'm gathered with Captain Derrar and two of his officers at the docking hatch, awaiting the arrival of the away-team from the *CAPS-N Assiniboine*. I'm dressed in the all-black Pryok'tel villain-suit, and for safety reasons, I've enabled the helmet's silver radiation shield. Derrar's disappointed expression is reflected right back at him as he speaks to me.

They're sending over two shuttles—a personnel shuttle for me, plus a cargo carrier for Betts, Cor and the automated transport. Captain Derrar assures me that I'll be the only human male in the room—though he's asked that at least one of the *Assiniboine* crew is a human, just to make me feel comfortable. There's no issue from an Oarth's perspective for human women—Derrar says he gets on well with them, finding women certainly becoming from an aesthetic perspective, but not 'enticing' the way he would find a male—if he'd ever seen one without his visor down, which he's not, of course.

On me, I've got my gifts stowed safely in the storage unit Derrar originally provided, as well as my backup of *Blue Boy*—Derrar confirms that once they get this vulture back to Oartheca, they'll dissect it to learn everything they can about it—he's particularly interested in their Under-drive, which has a different configuration from those the Oarth currently use, and he wants to understand the differences.

I've had a chance to go through some of the files I've transferred over from the touchpad; some are pictures of Toar, selfies he took in his med-bed. I have my biocomp preview them, displaying a thumbnail-sized version in the bottom corner of my vision.

The first is of Toar in a natural pose, with his crooked smile and a twinkle in his eye. Another is a silly face, him pulling one side of his mouth down and lolling his tongue out while he squints, and the last is a kissy-face, eyes closed and brows raised, lips puckered right at the screen—that one makes me laugh. There's six more, but I'm finding I'm listening to Derrar, and so I'll dig these others out when there's a chance. His kind chatting is making me feel better; I'm not sure Derrar knows exactly how much shit I'm about to get into, but from my body-language alone, I'm sure he understands that this is not a happy reunion.

I take a few steadying breaths as the alerts for the automated docking procedures begin, and when the lights of the hatch switch colour to indicate a seal's been formed, I straighten my back, chest out, hands clasped behind me, just like my CAPS-N training instilled in me all those years ago. If I'm going to persuade them that I'm no longer a criminal, might as well get a head start portraying that.

Derrar receives the official request for the *Assiniboine* crew to come aboard, and he provides it, the docking bay hatch sliding open to reveal three of them. My human liaison takes the lead—a commander from the insignia on her dark red uniform, her surname 'Dhawan' clearly displayed on her chest, in gold. That's the colour scheme for the CAPS-N—the opposite of my ship colours, but only by coincidence—my blues and silvers versus their scarlets and golds.

The commander is followed by two crewmembers—a burly Brolocon lieutenant, his muscled frame likely there to ensure I don't put up a fuss, but his dorsal tentacles are relaxed and folded against his back, to appear non-threatening. A Jylrelanrian sub-lieutenant, her uniform marking her as a medical officer, completes the trio. They all have an air of courteous professionalism about them though—pleasant smiles, easy mannerisms—no visible weapons, which is a surprise.

'Captain Derrar, I'm Commander Priyanka Dhawan, First Officer of the *CAPS-N Assiniboine*,' the commander greets diplomatically, standing at attention with her fellow officers joining her. 'On behalf of our captain, Lo-shar Pekrom, and our crew, please allow me first to say what a pleasure it is to meet you, and to have you welcome us to Oarthecan space.'

'Pleasure's ours, Commander,' Derrar beams. He'd be a good den-mate for Toar—I hope they do get a chance to meet up—actually, that'd be kinda … interesting to watch, if I'm honest. Don't know if I'm quite ready for that level of flexibility inside of a relationship, but I'm full of surprises, lately. 'Always happy to host the good people of the CAPS. Thank you for responding so quickly to our request. I'm sure Baron Hale is eager to get home.'

Commander Dhawan's eyebrow lifts just a fraction at my new title. Blink and you'd have missed it. She turns to address me.

'Captain Hale?' she asks, and I remember that I've got my rad-shield enabled, so she can't verify my identity visually. I turn to face Derrar, who quickly figures out the problem—he signals his two Oarth crewmen to turn around in place, facing away from me, and after a quick, conspiratorial smile, he does the same. Now in line with the decree, I drop the shield, and Dhawan nods her head when she recognizes me.

'I trust you're doing well? Oarthecan hospitality is well-known—I'm certain that's been the case for you, sir,' she says, as I re-enable the shield.

'It is and has been,' I reply, tersely. There's something off about all of this— I'm generally paranoid in the presence of the CAPS-N, and so, this … easiness? All of my instincts are telling me this is too good to be true—can't seem to catch a fucking break, even at the end. 'Though I think I've imposed on my Oarth friends long enough. Best we get on with this, Commander.'

'Immediately, sir,' the Commander responds, and I swear to God she stops

353

herself from saluting me. 'We're ready to depart when you've finished your farewells.'

It then dawns on me the reason for their behaviour, and I feel stupid for not having figured it out faster, 'Don't hurt the pretty human man in front of the Oarth'. It's the only explanation that makes sense—the CAPS is always about putting forward the right image, and while I'm *fairly* certain I'm not going to be subjected to a beating as soon as the Oarth's backs are turned, I also know that the kid gloves are going to come off the moment I'm out of their sight. Might as well enjoy it while it lasts.

I turn to address Derrar, giving a short bow, putting my hand over my heart and splaying my fingers. 'Peace to you and all your kin, Captain Derrar.'

Derrar returns my gesture in kind, but his bow is much lower. 'Great and Eternal Oarth keep you safe, Baron Hale.'

'I'm ready, Commander,' I advise, and she nods once, signalling her comrades to proceed with whatever plans they have for me. The Brolocon lieutenant steps forward, extending his hand behind him, indicating the path to the docked CAPS-N shuttle. 'This way, sir,' he indicates, his deep voice respectful but irrefusable.

As the two CAPS-N lieutenants escort me towards what might be the last few moments of freedom I'll be experiencing for a while, I give one last look behind me, catching Derrar's attention, and 'accidentally' release the rad-shield from my helmet, giving him and his two Oarth officers one final glance of me before I depart. The two officers become googly-eyed, one of them gasping quietly, but Derrar just grins and gives me a fast wink—and then returns to his conversation with Commander Dhawan.

As my escorts lead me along the connection bridge, I can see the interior of the CAPS-N shuttle rapidly approaching, and yes, I experience a moment of apprehension, part of my mind whirling to find a last-minute way out of all of this. But I silence it—I've promised Toar I'm going to start on the right path, and I'm going to trust that the first step is taking responsibility for my actions, both recent and historical. That'll probably mean some prison time, or fines—likely both. I know the CAPS-N are likely not going to turn me over to the Alconalc, like the Pryok'tel planned for me—Alconalc is an independent system, one of the nine I'm wanted by, and their relationship with the CAPS is best described as 'icy'—so at least that's going for me.

The lieutenant is leading the way, and I'm noticing our medic is already running a scan of me, her wrist mounted hologram display projecting some data, while she slowly waves the tip of her index finger back and forth in my direction—I suspect she's got a cybernetic medical scanner and is using it to give me a once-over. She doesn't appear bothered by what she's seeing, so that's a good sign at least.

We step inside the CAPS-N shuttle—and, I hate to admit, I find myself glad to see the familiar design and layout. I was, after all, a CAPS-N graduate, and spent at least four solid years living, eating, sleeping and training in surroundings just like these, and so there's some nostalgia here that I decide to enjoy. *Blue Boy* was an excellent shuttle, technically and operationally, but as I discovered, he'd been designed by the Pryok'tel—efficiency without comfort—and so it's nice to have an environment that incorporates a degree of comfort with its need for performance. Not quite as cosy as an Oarthecan ship, but still, it's a happy middle ground.

'If you'll have a seat, sir, Commander Dhawan will join us shortly, and we'll be on our way,' the Brolocon lieutenant offers, indicating one of the shuttle's passenger seats, set a few paces behind the two-person helm. His dorsal tentacles are kept still against his back—they don't even quiver when he speaks, meaning—normally—he has no hostile intentions towards me; then again, he could just have great self-control. Not wanting to find out if that's the case, I do as I'm asked, and take my seat while Commander Dhawan concludes her business with the Oarth.

'You can store your things here, sir,' our medic invites, indicating a nearby alcove, but when I involuntarily grip my gifts closer to me, she immediately follows up kindly, 'Or keep them with you, if you'd prefer—just that we're about to depart, and you know, regulations.'

My first instinct is to say, 'Fuck your regs,' but … new chapter, and all. Small steps, Row, small steps.

'Here,' I say, extending the storage container towards the medic, who carefully accepts it, stowing it neatly in the alcove, making her motions obvious to show the container is treated respectfully, and it's still in my line of sight.

Commander Dhawan joins us shortly after, sparing me only a nod of her head as she takes her position at the helm beside the Brolocon, who appears to double as a pilot in addition to my parole officer. Our medic is in the seat beside me— when I glance at her, she returns a smile, her purple eyes, solid and without visible pupils, communicate friendliness and good intentions.

A short series of departure protocols is exchanged between the two helm pilots, and moments later the shuttle powers and we detach from the vulture's docking port. As we begin to move away, I get one last look at my captured vulture, soon if not already a part of the OSS fleet—and feel the first pangs of loss. I remember that what I'm doing needs to happen: I still have the final obligations as captain of the *Luck of the Draw*, and I will live up to those obligations.

Our flight stabilizes and I can see us approaching the *CAPS-N Assiniboine*— she's a mid-sized cruiser, sleek, agile and not to be fucked with—not a war vessel, but she'd have no problem taking on her equivalent from any other navy—it would take at least three vultures to make her break a sweat. Again, that nostalgia sets in upon seeing the cruiser, but it is mixed with apprehension—I've spent the last decade or so making sure I never crossed paths with a CAPS-N vessel, and now it seems that all my efforts have led me directly into the heart of one.

'You don't look comfortable, Captain,' Commander Dhawan remarks, breaking my thoughts.

I frown slightly. 'I'm fine, Commander.'

She tilts her head towards the rear of the shuttle. 'Just mentioning it sir, because that Pryok'tel monstrosity you're wearing would look better in the recycler. If you're interested, there's a spare suit available, back in our utility area—just in the locker. You're welcome to it, sir.'

Something about her tone and her expression—it's inviting, casual, even friendly. There's no deception in her voice, it's like she is asking me to indulge her here—to play along, almost. Where's she going with this?

I stand, and Dhawan nods in approval, before swivelling back to the helm. Our medical officer looks away, trying to suppress a smile or something—and now I see one of the Brolocon's dorsal tentacles quiver ever so slightly: anticipation.

Fine. They want to play a game with me? Fine. I'm 'good' Rowland now—I get along. I follow orders. I respect the chain of command. Fucking ... fine. I turn and with as much dignity as I can, I head back to the utility area, a small, enclosed space that triples as a galley, lavatory or rest area, depending on what parameters you enter for its configuration.

Its current configuration is for a rest area, and so there the locker is, as promised, as is indeed the aforementioned spacesuit inside. Rather, it's a top-of-the-line, nanotech-forged, multi-environmental, cross-purpose utility outfit, complete with reinforced energy shielding, onboard supplementary computer systems, inbuilt kinetic stabilisers and my fucking surname printed right on the chest, in gold, 'HALE'.

What the hell is going on? Between Dhawan's ham-fisted excuse to get me back here, plus the reaction of her crew, I'm somewhere between annoyed, concerned but—as my eyes slide over the impressive and *exceptionally* expensive piece of hardware before me—intrigued, which is just adding to my annoyance. *Fucking typical CAPS head-games* is my first reaction—when Vay'auh-ta stated that nothing was ever straightforward with me, guess where I learned to hone that trait? The CAPS are the galaxy's biggest con-artists and, knowing that, I should've known there'd be some last-minute bullshit from them. Had a lot on my mind, I guess, but nonetheless, here that bullshit hangs, just waiting for me to try it on. Might as well—it does have my name on it, after all.

It fits me like a glove—at a half million credits, it damn well ought to—with the suit automatically updating its nanotech mesh so that it's snug against my frame, sealing me in as it completes its configuration, enabling the system to power on. My biocomp thrums alive as I integrate seamlessly with the suit's system, displaying a series of connection protocols that verify my own identity: Rowland William Hale II, Captain, T-47917190-C. I've not seen that series of digits after my name in years—it's my old CAPS personnel identification number, the one I ditched when I left the navy—but I was Midshipman Hale then, not Captain. Suit doesn't seem to know that though, because when this verification completes, it automatically updates its rank-display parameters, giving me a solid red left-shoulder epaulette, and a five-pointed golden star pip on my collar and each cuff. The official insignia for a senior officer, rank of captain in the CAPS-N.

Suit looks good on me; I mean, I try and generate some hate here, seeing myself in the scarlet and gold that I swore to myself I would never wear again, but as the system completes its auto-configuration procedure, that intrigued part of me builds momentum, nearly—but not quite—overriding my concern and confusion. Best to get this game going, then, if that's what's needed, and so I step out and back into the main shuttle area, only to see the three CAPS-N officers, standing to attention.

'Captain on deck,' Commander Dhawan orders, and they all salute me. *They salute me.* I … I salute them back. What else am I supposed to do?

'At ease,' the auto-pilot part of me says, but I am stunned to absolute silence with Dhawan's next words:

'Welcome back, Captain Hale. Congratulations on the success of your mission.'

~ End of Book One ~

To be continued in:

Barons of Oartheca
Book Two of the Oarthecan Star Saga

Made in the USA
Monee, IL
13 May 2022